TEMPTRESS

She took his hand again and slipped it down into her bosom. Rippled it across her breasts. She had worn very light clothing, and he began to be aware of this for the first time. It made him tremble a little.

When she drew down her bodice and the garments beneath it, he asked whether she had gone mad. Without a word, she pulled down his head and moved her body so that her breasts could rub against his cheeks. And after that, reason left them both . . .

~~CHILDREN~~
OF
KAYWANA

Edgar Mittelhölzer

A Bantam Book / published by arrangement with
Hutton & Lay of Colorado, Inc.

PRINTING HISTORY
John Day edition published 1952
Bantam edition / June 1976

This book may not be reproduced in whole or in part, by
mimeograph or any other means, without permission.
For information address: John Day Company, Inc., 200
Madison Avenue, New York, N.Y. 10016

Copyright 1952 by Edgar Mittelhölzer.

Bantam Books are published by Bantam Books, Inc. Its
trademark, consisting of the words "Bantam Books" and the
portrayal of a bantam, is registered in the United States
Patent Office and in other countries. Marca Registrada.

*This low-priced Bantam Book
has been completely reset in a type face
designed for easy reading, and was printed
from new plates. It contains the complete
text of the original hard-cover edition.*
NOT ONE WORD HAS BEEN OMITTED.

CHILDREN OF KAYWANA

*A Bantam Book / published by arrangement with
Thomas Y. Crowell Company, Inc.*

PRINTING HISTORY
John Day edition published 1952
Bantam edition / June 1976

ISBN 0-553-02775-1

PRINTED IN THE UNITED STATES OF AMERICA

Foreword

So little is known about the history of British Guiana—even in that colony itself and its British neighbour colonies in the West Indies—that I have felt compelled to add occasional footnotes to this work —more so than is usual in a work of fiction—and to include (at the end of the book) a list of the persons who actually lived and of the events that actually occurred. Without these footnotes and this list the reader would be at a loss to know what is fact and what is fiction, though I have no doubt that many will probably read this tale simply as a tale, not caring two hoots about the historical background. So much the better for them if they can, but, at the same time, I have to think of the others who might be interested in the historical angle.

In the instance of the Berbice insurrection—according to James Rodway in his *History of British Guiana,* "probably the most disastrous slave revolt that ever occurred in any colony"—I have stuck as closely to historical fact as I possibly could, as, indeed, I have done in respect to every other factual event. I should like to explain, however, that Amelia George's first name is not on record. I have searched everywhere, in Georgetown as well as the British Museum, without being able to trace it. Rodway refers to her simply as "Miss George," and Dalton as "a young lady." "Amelia" is therefore my own invention. The portrait I have painted of her, too, is purely imaginary, as nothing can be discovered about what sort of person she was.

The ultimate fate of several of the survivors of the Peereboom incident can only be conjectured at, as the records, again, are very hazy. The Zubli family, we must assume, perished, as did the parents of Amelia George. We know that Predicant Ramring and his family were spared to join the Governor and his party

shortly after the massacre. Jan Charbon and Mittelholzer wandered around in the bush for a fortnight
before Jan was captured. Mittelholzer, according to
Jan's account, was attacked, but resisted, cutting off
the hand of One of his assailants with a sabre; he, too,
must have succeeded in reaching the governor and his
party in safety. There is a sabre in the possessiy may—
family which is said to be the very one usssesy
cestor in this encounter; I have seen it myself in the
home of my uncle, the late Major John Vincent Mittelholzer.

Readers may wonder at the difference in spelling
between my own name and that of my forebears. Briefly, here is the reason: At nineteen, when I began to
learn German, I discovered that the plural of *Holz* was
Hölzer. Assuming that, due to anglicizing influences,
my immediate forebears had been careless in dropping
the Umlaut. I decided to "restore" it. Recently, however, as a result of the researches of a German journal-
ist acquaintance, Dr. H. G. Alexander, it was revealed
to me that the Mittelholzers of Switzerland (from which
country my eighteenth-century ancestor came) did not,
and do not, spell their name with an Umlaut; hence my
"restoration" was, though grammatically correct, erroneous in respect to strict nomenclature. As it would
create some confusion at this stage to drop the Umlaut
in my name, I have decided to let it stand but to omit
it when referring to earlier members of my family.

E.M.

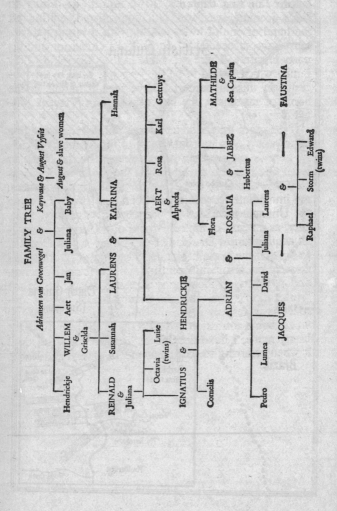

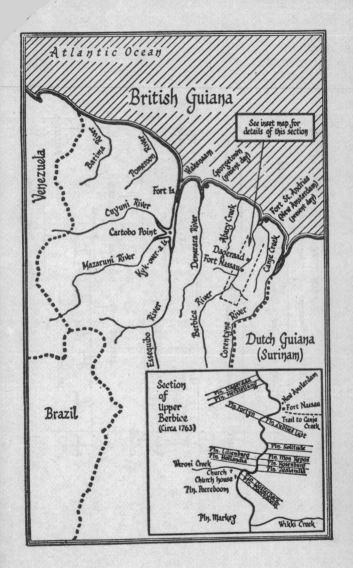

Atlantic Ocean

British Guiana

See inset map for details of this section

Venezuela

Barima River

Pomeroon River

Waikerraam

Georgetown (present day)

Fort St. Andries (New Amsterdam) (present day)

Cuyuni River

Fort Is.

Cartobo Point

Mazaruni River

Kyk-over-al Is.

Demerara River

Abucy Creek

Canje Creek

Dageraad Fort Nassau

Berbice River

Corentyne River

Essequibo River

Dutch Guiana (Surinam)

Brazil

Section of Upper Berbice (Circa 1763)

Pln. Dageraad
Pln. Herstelling
New Amsterdam
Fort Nassau
Pln. Fortyn
Trail to Canje Creek
Pln. Lilienburg
Pln. Ashley Last
Pln. Solitude
Pln. Lilienburg
Pln. Hollandia
Pln. Mon Repos
Pln. Rosenburg
Pln. Zealandia
Weroni Creek
Church †
Church house †
Pln. Peereboom
Pln. Hollerdam
Pln. Markey
Wikki Creek

CHILDREN
OF
KAYWANA

1 A Jet of Fire

I

SHE knew that August Vyfuis was following her but made no attempt to evade him. August, a nephew of one of the leading traders, had arrived with the last ship from Middelburg, and was twenty-three.

It was about an hour past noon when he followed her into the jungle. The sky did not have a cloud, but no sunshine penetrated the tangled foliage overhead. The air stood still amid the tree-trunks and the vines and the fallen palms; you could feel it like a humid cobweb around you. A brown twilight pervaded everything, and the silence pressed down, warm and damp and alive; now and then it seemed to lick your cheek.

Their feet made no sound, for the ground was covered with thick layers of moist leaves—decades, perhaps a century, of fallen leaves. A yielding, spongy carpet.

Kaywana halted near some wild pines and pretended to be interested in the spider webs. Deep in the center of each cluster of spiked leaves a hairy black spider had spun a white web. She could make out the fangs of one of them—two bluish-black legs, too, tipped with crimson.

August came up to where she stood and held her arm, and she looked at him and told him: "Loose my arm." But he continued to hold it. He had blue eyes and yellow-brown hair. His eyes were bright, and she could feel him trembling. He said that he had to have her. He glanced about with urgency, then looked at her again—at the nakedness of her. She wore only a lap-cloth. Her breasts were spiked, with golden tips.

"Loose my arm."

"No. I must have you—today. Now."

"My people won't like it."

"They won't mind. You're a half-breed. Your

1

...ther is English—an English sailor. You aren't pure Indian, so it won't matter."

"But who says I want you?"

"I'll take you by force. I must have you."

She began to smile. She had bluish-green eyes. "You're burning up," she said. "I can see it."

"Yes, burning up," he said. "From my uncle's cottage I've watched you day after day. I've seen you go to the river for water early in the morning—and sometimes in the afternoon. You laughed with the other girls, and whenever you laughed your breasts trembled—and I trembled too. I must have you. I don't care if I have to die after for it. I don't care if your *piaiman*[1] hears and tries to kill me. So long as I have you."

"The *piaiman* won't kill you for that. I'm not pure Indian. You said so only a minute ago. You're speaking wild."

"I'm speaking wild."

"You're strong. I like the way you hold me. I believe you when you say you would do anything to have me—even die. I like men to be so. To be strong —and to speak wild. I don't like them weak. The others want me, but they can't even look at me in my eyes straight. They beg and plead. I don't like men to beg and plead. They must hold me and take me and show they have more strength than I have."

"You're an odd girl, Kaywana. Different from the other Indian girls. And you speak our language simply and well. You're clever. You're everything better and different." He pulled her to him.

She said to wait, and took him into an alcove where there were dry palm fronds. She said it was a secret spot known only to herself.

On many other days they came here. He told her about Holland and about the sea and the ship in which he had come. "I have an uncle who came out here since 1604—nearly eight years ago. He's on the Pomeroon River—at the trading post there."

[1]Sorcerer or medicine-man. Pronounced pee-ay-man.

She said that she knew nothing about the othe. parts of the coast, so he told her about the settlements on the Pomeroon and the Essequibo. Since 1581 Dutch vessels had sailed along the coast and started trading posts and depots at various points. The Dutchmen, he told her, had set up one post at the mouth of the Pomeroon and another in the Abary Creek at an Indian village called Nibie. They had become very friendly with the Indians. "As friendly as we are with you here on the Corentyne."

"What are the things they trade?"

"My people give them axes and knives and trinkets, and they give us cotton and hammocks and pita hemp, and anatta and letter-wood and tobacco."

"We've taught them to plant properly," he went on, after a silence. "Just as we teach your Indians here to plant tobacco in rows. When you plant that way you get more—and the leaves are better."

He told her about the raid by the Spaniards in 1596. "Their ships came from Trinidad and St. Thomé on the Orinoco. They wiped out the Pomeroon and Essequibo settlements. All our people on the Pomeroon were killed, but some of those on the Essequibo escaped and went higher up the river to an island called Kyk-over-al. Some went to the Pomeroon, too, after the Spaniards had left."

"I've heard of Kyk-over-al."

"Yes, it's well known. It lies in the river. They call it Kyk-over-al—see over all—because it commands a view of all the three great rivers—the Essequibo, the Cuyuni and the Mazaruni. The Portuguese discovered it a long time ago and built a fort there. The ruins are still there, my uncle says. The arms of Portugal are carved over the arched entrance."

"Your people have Indians with them there, I have heard."

"Yes. They've cultivated the banks of the river opposite the island. They have small plantations at a spot called Cartabo Point. It's a neck of land. It separates the mouth of the Cuyuni from the mouth of the Mazaruni. A ship goes to Kyk-over-al every year from Holland, and the captain remains and acts as a sort of commandeur of the settlement until the next ship arrives, when his place is taken by the new captain, and he goes back to Holland. A company has been formed now—it's called the West India Company. Merchants in Holland control it, and they've made a rule that no private trading can be done anywhere along this coast without special permission from the Company's directors."

He smiled and said: "I've told you a lot about myself and my people, but you've told me nothing about yourself."

"You know about my father already. He was a sailor. He came ashore here years ago when an English ship came into the river. The captain was a man called Sir Raleigh."

"Sir Walter Raleigh. I've heard of him. He came here in 1595 with Keymis. He was on his way to the Orinoco. My uncle has told me about it."

"Well, my father was one of his sailors. He came ashore and came into the jungle with my mother. Perhaps they lay near this same spot."

"Who knows?"

"The ship stayed for eight days, my mother says. He was a short man with red hair, and he could laugh loud. He had eyes the same color as mine."

"You mean, you have eyes like his—but perhaps you purposely meant to say it the other way about. You're conceited. What does your name mean, by the way? I was to have asked you."

"It means old water. Kay—old. Wana—water."

A lizard made a dry rustling as it wriggled from one twig to another, moving over the dry fronds on which they lay. They watched the twig, silent, and after a moment saw it appear again, black and shiny. It seemed to be planning its next move; selecting another twig; calculating the number of intervening fronds. A suspension of time linked it with them and with the silence around them and with time traveling over the earth; time gone and time to come. Its head flicked round and it vanished.

"When months pass I will have a child, and I will name it August if it is a boy."

"Your *piaiman*—that fellow Wakkatai—what wi
he have to say?"

"He will be offended, but I don't care. I'm half
English sailor. His magic can't hurt me. I'm not
afraid. I fear no one."

"Yes, you have spirit. From the first day I saw
you I knew you were an unusual person. A jet of
fire."

She smiled. "I like that. A jet of fire."

One day the jungle quivered.

"What was that?"

"It sounded like a cannon," he said.

"A cannon?"

The jungle quivered again. The sound had come
from the river.

"Yes, it's a cannon. The settlement is being bombarded." His voice sounded harsh and breathless;
breathless with hatred. "The dogs," he said. "The dogs.
They have come."

"What dogs? Whose cannon is it?"

"Who else but those Spanish cutthroats from
Trinidad or the Orinoco! Whose cannon could it be
but theirs! And there's a truce on—the truce of 1609.
The twelve-year truce. They've violated it. I knew it
would happen. I told my uncle it would!"

She stared at him, puzzled; troubled.

He put on his clothes in a hurry and said that he
must go. "I've got to go now, Kaywana. Now. I can't
wait."

He squeezed her arm briefly and hurried off.

She moved after him—but slowly, not trying to
overtake him.

The jungle quivered again. She could feel the
sound deep in the earth—beneath the thick, moist layers of leaves under her feet. It gave her a feeling of in-
security. She distrusted the earth; for the first time in
her life she felt that the ground on which she walked
might betray her.

When she was nearing the edge of the jungle, a
whine came from above, and the trees crackled violently. This time the thud sounded near. It wriggled up out

of the earth into the soles of her feet. She cried out and cowered down near some wild pines. Not many yards away the branch of an *awara* palm crashed down with other leaves and pieces of creeper.

Voices and a commotion of noise came from the riverbank where the settlement stood. Two of her people approached, running into the jungle. Then three more. One of them was Patooka, her step-father. He told her: "Run! Run, Kaywana! Spanish ship in the river. Cannonball coming!"

He did not wait for her but went on deeper into the jungle.

Others came. Mothers with their babies and the older children. They went past, running and chattering. Lonaibo, one of her half-brothers, stopped and called to her to come with them, but she remained where she was, crouching by the wild pines.

Wakkatai hurried past, with his blowpipe and his *eumaraca*,[1] chanting a magic song and waving the *eumaraca* to keep off evil spirits and danger. He scowled and made a spitting sound at her. She gave him a look of defiance. And all the while the cannon boomed on the river. She could hear musket fire, too. August and his uncle and the other Dutchmen must be replying. They were in danger. She could feel it. That was why she remained here. If August were in danger she must be in danger, too. She must stay here and risk having one of the cannonballs fall upon her. To run far into the jungle with the others would be disloyal. She was different from them. August had said so himself. Different and unusual. She must be brave and risk the cannonballs. To run would be cowardly.

The boom of the cannon soon stopped. Only the musket fire she could hear after a while. And shouts. Voices of white men.

She crept out into the open, crawled slowly forward on her belly until she could see down the slope into the clearing near the river bank. Men were coming ashore. Four boats were alongside.

[1] A charm made out of a scooped-out calabash, with pebbles inside and feathers decorating it. Only a *piaiman* may handle it.

The Dutchmen were firing from their *troolie*[1] houses, but you could see that they were lost. They were outnumbered.

For over an hour she watched. Then she saw smoke begin to ascend from the *troolie* houses. The musket-fire had ceased. Only shouts came now. Strange white men swarmed all over the settlement. She heard a thump-thump. It was the storehouse. The strange white men were breaking down the door of the storehouse. The Spaniards from Trinidad. August must be dead. Yes, his uncle's cottage was on fire.

She felt a resigned numbness. Whatever had to happen had to happen. This was how he had been meant to die. Nothing could have stopped it.

She could hear the crackle of the flames. And inside her, the child that was his must have heard them, too, unborn though it was. It throbbed in her belly. It must be hearing the flames that were burning up its father. She hoped it would be a boy, and hoped he would have blue eyes and yellow-brown hair.

The flames crackled on. The *troolie* roof of August's uncle's cottage disappeared in a swirl of smoke.

II

About a month later a ship arrived from the Essequibo. It took the Indians aboard, and four days later they were at Kyk-over-al.

The Dutchmen put them ashore at Cartabo Point where there was a small settlement of Arawaks. The Arawaks received them with friendship, and, before many days, had recognized Wakkatai as a *piaiman* of great magical powers; the size and splendor of his *eumaraca* impressed them deeply, and what convinced them finally was that when, one afternoon, he called upon the rain to fall, the rain, within less than an hour, began to fall: it fell heavily, accompanied by thunder and lightning, and broke a drought which had lasted more than three months.

[1]The *troolie* palm. The fronds were used as roofing material.

In an abandoned *benab,* one morning in December, Kaywana gave birth to her child. No one assisted her. When the pains set in she left her hammock and went out to where the old *benab* stood. It was what she wished for—a boy. Seeing him in the grey light of dawn, she gave a tired moan of content and told herself that though the Spaniards had killed August he had, through her body, triumphed in the end. This was he again—a new August, and with some of her own blood added. And hadn't he called her a jet of fire? She was sure this new August would be a great man.

When he was three years old she met Adriansen van Groenwegel. In 1616—the year before Raleigh came to look for Eldorado. Adriansen came from Zeeland with three ships. He was a private trader, and meant to settle at Kyk-over-al. So she had heard.

She saw him on the deck of the largest ship—a tall young man of about thirty-five with yellow-brown hair—something like August's. There was fire in his eyes. He had strength—like the strength of August. He was the kind of man, she felt certain, who would not plead with a woman. He would hold her and take her, as August had done in the Corentyne jungle.

Standing in the morning sunshine, she felt what August had called her—a jet of fire.

Coming ashore at Cartabo Point, Adriansen saw her son in the water splashing about, and stopped. "What's that? A naked white child!"

"He's mine," Kaywana told him, before anyone else could reply.

He looked at her in surprise. "Yours? Who are you?"

"Kaywana."

"She's a half-breed," Mynheer Roosen explained.

"We had her brought here with some Indians from the Corentyne two or three years ago," Mynheer de Vries added. "A pretty thing, but very aloof. The young men are always fighting over her, but she ignores them."

Adriansen regarded her. His grey eyes remained

level and calm, but she knew that he was aware of her attractiveness.

"What did you say your name was?" he asked her.

"Kaywana," she told him. "It means 'old water.' " She was in no way shy or afraid.

He gave a grunt and smiled—still very calm; a trifle contemptuous, too.

"You look strong," she said. "Like August Vyfuis on the Corentyne."

"Any who may August Vyfuis be?"

"The nephew of one of our leading traders," Mynheer Roosen explained. "They were wiped out on the Corentyne, poor fellows. Those Spanish curs from Trinidad made a surprise raid on them in default of the truce."

"August was burnt up in his uncle's cottage," Kaywana said. "We found bones in the ruins afterwards. But they went down fighting. They were brave men."

Adriansen glanced at Mynheer Roosen. "She speaks our language very fluently."

"Yes, she's unusually intelligent."

"The most quick-witted of the whole lot," said Mynheer Jung.

"Her father was an English sailor, I understand," said Mynheer Meertens. "Explains quite a lot, I should say," he added, with a note of sarcasm.

Mynheer de Vries chuckled: "Jan de Vooge and Hendrik Plett—see them there blushing and fidgeting? —they once fought over her."

Everybody guffawed.

Adriansen smiled. He said casually: "She seems worth fighting over," and began to move on.

Kaywana watched them get into the boat. They were going across to Kyk-over-al to the Commandeur's house—a large wooden house of three stories, with a slated roof. She thought: Yes, that is the kind of man I like. Strong, cool and with fire in his eyes. He would not plead with me for my body.

The Commandeur received him politely but stiffly.

"May I inquire, sir," he said, "whether you come

here in the interests of the West India Company? Or am I to understand that this is purely a private venture of your own?"

"Purely a private venture of my own, sir," Adriansen replied. "I'm in no way connected with the West India Company—though the Company, needless to mention, has granted me permission to trade anywhere within the area of its influence."

"You have, no doubt, in your possession the documents signed by the Company granting you this permission?"

"I have."

The Commandeur stroked his beard. He had a tough, weathered face. He was the captain of the last ship that had come out to do the Company's trade. After a brief silence, he said: "I take it your intention is to settle here indefinitely?"

"That is my intention, sir." A slightly crafty gleam came into his eyes as he added: "And I fancy this island and the neighboring territory will suit me admirably as a base for my trading negotiations."

"I have no doubt." Suddenly glancing up: "Mynheer van Groenwegel, I suppose you are not unaware that a great many tales have circulated in these parts concerning you and your activities as a trader?"

"Tales?"

"Yes. Not very savory ones, either." The Commandeur spoke with deliberation. "About certain secret dealings you were supposed to have had from time to time with the Spaniards in Trinidad and on the Orinoco."

Adriansen clicked his tongue. "Deplorable, sir. Deplorable. I trust you did not put any credence in these scurrilous—eh—tales!"

The Commandeur shrugged, his face with a look of wooden dignity.

Adriansen, also very dignified but obviously laughing within, said, after a pause: "Yes, I do hope you didn't believe such slander, sir. And by the way, may I remark that you appear to have established very friendly relations with the Indians. Very wise, indeed.

You're to be complimented for such a policy. Any other would be disastrous."

"Thanks for your compliments, Mynheer van Groenwegel. And if I may make a remark in my turn, shall I say that you speak not like a newcomer but like a trader of many years' experience in these parts."

Adriansen smiled. "I speak like a man of common sense, sir. I think it's obvious that without the cooperation of the natives in any land newly discovered the pioneer would be at a great disadvantage. The Spaniards have learnt that lesson far better than we have."

The Commandeur fidgeted.

Adriansen cleared his throat and said: "It is my intention—with your sanction, of course, Mynheer—to visit the Indian village at Cartabo this evening. I've already inspected the area casually, but this evening I should like to distribute one or two trifling presents. A matter of policy. Establishing contact and so on. I trust you have no objection?"

"None whatever."

That evening he went through the village with a hum and a rush, his bulging canvas bag slung over his back, his virile frame in an agitation of ceaseless motion. His swift smile and his darting gray eyes held them in a trance.

"Your name, my woman? Ah! But what a pretty baby! Yours?"

"Yes, mine. My name Tanawaya."

"Make your choice, Tanawaya. Free gifts for everyone. A necklace, a brooch, a bracelet, a ring. Whatever you will. It's yours for the taking."

"I take a bracelet."

"Good. A bracelet. Here you are, Tanawaya—and the best of wishes to you. And to the baby! Yes, we mustn't forget the baby. Now, who's this? Is this your brother? Your name? Wonomo? What will you have, Wonomo? A tin whistle, a good sharp knife, a mirror, a jug? Make your choice. Oh, you want a knife. I thought so. Knives are popular, I see. . . . You there! Come. Don't be shy. Come and make your choice. Your name?"

"Patook."

"Patook. What do you wish, Patook? Tin whistle, jug, mirror, knife, pretty spy-glass, tin-plate! Everything is free today. Today is gift day. Free gifts from Adriansen van Groenwegel."

Patook gave a sheepish smile and asked for a tin whistle, then shook his head and said a knife.

"A knife. Very well. A knife it is. But see and don't cut yourself. You seem rather young to have a knife. . . . Now, who's this? What's your name? I always like to know names. It may be useful later."

"Manaima."

"Manaima. A name of charm. And what will you have, Manaima? Ah! I could have guessed. You want a mirror. A mirror it is, then. And you—ho! I met you this morning. Your name is Kaywana. Old Water. See what a memory I have for names? What will you have, Old Water? Mirror, too? Or ring, bracelet, necklace, jug——"

"I want nothing. Nothing that you have in your bag."

"So? Then with what else can I oblige you, Kaywana?"

"I want you yourself," she said.

"Me?" He stared at her and flushed slowly, a sly mischief coming into his eyes. He laughed. "We'll see by and by. I'm a hard man, you know—not as easy as you may think. But we'll see by and by. I'm very busy now." His eyes crackled over her, virile like lightning. He patted her arm briefly and moved on to the next *benab*. "Your name, madam?"

"Lataka my name."

"Very beautiful. Make your choice. . . . And you?"

"Wakkatai. Me *piaiman.*"

"*Piaiman?* What's that?"

"It means trickster!" called Kaywana, approaching. "He fools people he can work magic."

Wakkatai snatched up a hatchet and rushed at her, but Adriansen moved quickly after him and caught his arm. "Now, what's this? What's the trouble? Don't be so impetuous, Wakkatai."

Kaywana laughed. She had made no attempt to retreat. "He can't hit me. He can only rush at me and threaten me. I know him well. He can only puff himself up and talk of his magic and what he can do, but he has no more courage than a chigoe."

"One day," growled Wakkatai, "you insult me too often, Kaywana. One day you come to a bad end. I see it in the water, I see it in the air, I see it everywhere. Hear what I tell you this day. You will die bad."

She stuck out her tongue at him.

"Come, you mustn't quarrel," said Adriansen. He patted Wakkatai's shoulder. "She's a wicked girl, Wakkatai. She has no right to tease you. I must give you something special if you're a *piaiman*. Big magician, eh? Yes, yes. A magician is an important man. Come on, make your choice. Two knives? Two mirrors? Two rings? And some beads? You must have double gifts. In recognition of your importance."

Wakkatai's anger subsided. "I take two mirrors, white man," he said. He spoke with an air of dignity and condescension.

Adriansen handed him two mirrors, then made an elaborate fumbling in his bag and selected a ring. "Here is a ring, too, Wakkatai. It's a special ring. Solid gold"—it was brass—"a ring worthy to be worn by a great man. Take it as a special gift from me."

Wakkatai was flattered. He smiled a lot and examined the ring in the fading light. He nodded and said: "Thank you, Mynheer. I treasure it. I keep it safe in my best calabash." He threw a glance at Kaywana which said: "See? The white man knows my true importance. Go on. Sneer at me now."

But Kaywana walked away, her head at a contemptuous angle.

III

Many weeks passed before Adriansen took her. Many months. By then his ships had sailed with a large cargo of cotton and tobacco and anatta, and he had had himself built a high two-storied house with a slated roof, like the roof of the Commander's house on Kyk-over-al. He had it built on the west bank of the river where he had started a plantation.

One morning he rowed himself across to Cartabo and made his way into the Indian village.

"Good morning, Tanawaya."

"Good morning, Mynheer Adriansen."

"Ah! Wonomo. Good morning. That's a fine hammock you're doing there. You must let me see it when you've finished it."

"Yes, Mynheer."

"And how are you, Lataka? How is the baby today?"

Kaywana appeared from around a *benab,* a *mataipee*[1] in her hand.

"Kaywana. Good morning. It's you I've come to see."

She approached, the *mataipee* dripping a white trail of cassava juice along the ground. "You've come to see me?"

"Yes. I want someone to cook and take care of my home for me—and I thought of you. Would you like to come and be my cook and housekeeper?"

She did not answer at once. She gave him an appraising look. At length, she said: "Yes, I'll come, but I shall have to bring my son."

"Naturally. I'd thought of that. You may bring him. I'm fond of children." He made a gesture of his hand toward her *benab.* "Go at once and get your things together. I'll row you across myself. I'm waiting."

"You don't ask me. You command."

He nodded. "I always command—when I think I should."

Later that day he was in his bedroom when, without knocking, she entered. His bedroom was one of two on the west, and from the windows you could see

---

[1] A receptacle made of finely plaited straw, used by the Indians for crushing the juice of the bitter cassava.

the sunset sky over the distant green of the tobacco plantation. The air this afternoon was mild and water-vaporish, and the trade wind could be heard humming around the building, cool and evening-chilled with the scent of the jungle in it. The tobacco plants kept rustling with a far-off, mysterious peace.

After they had talked casually for a few minutes, he said: "I'm a hard man, Kaywana. I've told you that before, but I think it best to emphasize it again. I'm not easy. Some days you're going to find me very brusque and impatient."

He sat by the window with a huge leather-bound book. The sun made a halo around his yellow-brown hair. He was frowning in a thoughtful manner, his gaze on the windowsill, his fingers drumming lightly on the book.

"The meal you cooked today was good," he said suddenly, looking at her. "You have a capable air. Intelligent. I feel you're going to manage this household with success." He assumed a cunning expression. "My judgment of human beings is always accurate. I know that we two are going to get on splendidly together. But I must repeat it. I'm a hard man. It's just as well for you to be forewarned."

She waited.

"You may go now," he said.

She did not go.

He gave her an uncertain look. "Go and prepare dinner."

"I want to ask you something first."

"Well?"

"Is it I myself you like having here with you—or just the things I can do for you?"

"Ah, I see." He fidgeted; began to smile but checked the smile. "Yes, I do like you, Kaywana. You yourself."

She watched him, and he stared back at her as though deep inside him he were calculating something. He stirred and put down the book.

"Come here. Come closer," he said.

She approached and he stretched out and gripped her arm. "You're an odd young woman."

"August held my arm—and he said I was odd. He was I was unusual—different."

"He did? He made love to you—on the Corentyne?"

"Yes, but it lasted only a short time. We were in the jungle and we heard the cannon on the river. Then he left me. He said: 'I've got to go now, Kaywana. Now. I can't wait.' And that was all. He left me and went, and I never saw him again. Only his bones."

"H'm."

She stared at him and he stared back. His eyes never once wavered. Hers did—for a second.

"He called me a jet of fire."

"He did?"

"Yes."

"He was right."

He moved in the chair, and his grip on her arm tightened. He pressed his face against her belly and began to caress her breasts—with urgency, his face in a glow of blood and his limbs in a tremor. He took her desperately, the sunshine scarlet on their struggles.

IV

Some days there would be a gale on the Essequibo. High wind with slanting rain rushing over the bush and the choppy water. It would go swooping up the Mazaruni, and when she looked across at Kyk-over-al she would see it like a frayed monster sleeping mysteriously in the river, hazed but unheedful of the pelting moisture.

On other days the brown, muddy water flashed in a dazzle of morning sunshine. The trade wind hummed around the building, and small white clouds drifted in a blue sky.

On some of these days she never saw him at all. He would go off on expeditions with the Indians far into the bush, or down river toward the sea. He never confided in her.

One day, during one of his absences, she went across to Cartabo with August to see her people. When she was about to leave, Wakkatai followed her to where her *corial*[1] was moored and said: "Whenever your man is gone off on his secret journeys you come over to us. He's clever, that Adriansen. He knows how to fool you and make use of you."

"I like him so."

He sniffed. "You're a slut—like your mother. You desert Indians for white men. When he throws you aside no Indian will have you. This is the second white man you have lain with. You're double dirt now."

"I'm content to be so."

He glanced about as though to make sure they were not being overheard. "Perhaps," he said, in a low voice, "if you get your man to make me big gifts and you let me lie with you for one night every week for four weeks, I might cleanse you and make you fit to marry." He moved a pace closer. "What do you say to that?"

"This," she said. She spat on him.

He looked as though he would attack her. He growled and his fingers began to curl inward. But he did not move. He said: "You spit on me, Kaywana. Me *piaiman*. *Maconaima* watches all. One day you will be sorry for this. *Maconaima* will see that vengeance comes upon you."

She got into the *corial* and paddled off, August, too, paddling, for though only four, he was an expert.

Hate in his eyes, Wakkatai called after her: "One day you will be sorry you insulted me, Kaywana! Spit on me—me *piaiman,* master of many secrets! One day you will die bad! I curse you!"

Meanwhile, the traders were talking about Adriansen. "At first," said Mynheer de Vries, "I was inclined to think very highly of him. But now I know him for what he is. A cheap philandering adventurer."

"I don't agree," said Mynheer Roosen. "The man is ambitious. I admire his spirit. He has a genius for trade, too—and he's shrewd in other ways. Have you noticed how popular he's made himself with the In-

[1] Canoe. Pronounced kree-all.

ⅅⅼⅰⅰans? You hear me, I believe he's going to get far in this country."

Mynheer Meertens stroked his beard. "There are ugly rumors about that he uses the Indians to do trade with the Spaniards on the Orinoco and in Trinidad. Those cutthroats who have murdered so many of our countrymen."

"That's an old tale. Don't believe every whisper that reaches your ear, Meertens. When a man begins to prosper in this world, his jealous enemies at once attempt to besmirch his name. Van Groenwegel is sound, you hear me! We want more men of his type in this colony—men of spirit and ability, fearless and ready to exploit every opportunity that presents itself."

"I must agree with that," nodded Mynheer Jung. "I admire the man myself. I'm certain he's going to prove useful to this colony and to the progress of things generally."

"He certainly ought to prove useful to the birth-rate," said Mynheer de Vries. "That half-breed girl, Kaywana, who keeps house for him, is pregnant with his child."

"Come, de Vries!" frowned Mynheer Roosen. "Such a remark is unworthy of you. How many of us here can claim to be innocent of intimate relations with the Indians?"

"At least, we value our respectability enough not to flaunt these women openly as this fellow is doing."

"Respectability! Hypocrisy and lack of courage, that's what it is. Face the truth. Van Groenwegel has the courage we lack, that's why he can flout convention and live in open concubinage. We should very well like to do the same ourselves, but we're afraid of the censure it would bring down upon us. We're afraid of the wrath of the Almighty. Van Groenwegel is the sort of man who fears neither God nor man—and that's why he'll get far as a pioneer. That's why he'll be remembered when we are forgotten."

Lightning flickered in the south-east, and the air was warm. No wind blew. A five-day-old moon hovered ruddily in the west, and under its light the river lay in a shimmer of fine ripples. She could hear the hollow whisper of the river, awesome in the dead night silence.

Adriansen kept pacing, the lamplight emphasizing the reddish tan of his face. Now and then he would stop at a window and stare toward Cartabo Point. August was already asleep, for it was late. She sat near to him in bed, giving suck to the new child, a girl.

"Adriansen."

"Yes?"

"You haven't kissed me for two days."

He grunted. "A pity that fellow on the Corentyne taught you how to kiss. You're better than a European at it now."

"You haven't lain with me in bed for nearly a week."

"No?"

"You don't care for me that way any more?"

"Go to bed. Go to bed. I've told you I'm busy these days. When there is work to be done you can't expect me to be mooning over you. You ought to have learnt that by now."

On Cartabo Point a light winked white and died. After a moment, at the far northern end of Kyk-over-al, another light glowed.

He whistled softly. "So that's it. Good."

The light went out. Then glowed again. Went out and stayed out. He waited for a minute, then snapped his fingers. "I'm going out, Kaywana. You'd better go to bed. I'll be back just after dawn."

"Kiss me before you go."

"Oh, nonsense!" He was at the door already, but he came back, bent and kissed her, patted her head. "Satisfied? Sleep well. I hope Hendrickje won't squall too much and keep you awake."

He was gone in a rush. She listened to his foot-treads thudding downstairs. The foot-treads of a powerful man.

A minute later she got up and went to the window and watched him in the skiff moving dimly over the water—a lone dot heading for the northern end of the island. The light glowed again on Cartabo. Again on Kyk-over-al. What could it all be about? He did such odd things. No wonder the other white men called him a man of mystery. A queer, sly, scheming man—but good and strong. She loved and respected him.

She watched until the boat merged with the jagged silhouette of the island. Wind came in a veil, faint and warm, then the air was still again, the river in fine ripples under the setting moon. Lightning flickered in the southeast. A thing of alarm with crooked forks far away over the jungle. But no thunder came. Not even a distant rumble. Only the whisper of the river you could hear, monotonous and mysterious.

V

One day, a few years later, Adriansen called the Company's traders together at his house to discuss plans for building a fort.

"Next year, gentlemen," he told them, his eyes moving from face to face, "the truce between our country and Spain comes to an end. Since this truce came into effect eleven years ago our little settlements and outposts have not fared so badly, as I'm sure you'll admit. Good trade has been done and is still being done. In spite of the grievous lack of labor, our plantations are in a flourishing condition. Our relations with the Indians daily improve . . ."

"Especially yours," muttered Mynheer de Vries. "What with two bastards to your credit and a third on the way."

". . . Indeed, I may truthfully say that we have nothing of which we can seriously complain. But we must not allow ourselves to grow complacent, gentlemen. There is a circumstance to which few of us have given much thought." He paused and looked around. He was very sure of himself. This was the third time he had paused. He did it for effect, and also to give him an interval in which to study their faces.

"Next year, gentlemen, the truce with Spain— the twelve years' truce—expires."

"Well? And what of that?"

"We thank you for the information," mumble
Mynheer de Vries.

Adriansen bowed. "I appreciate your gratitude,
Mynheer de Vries. It gives me heart to continue." He
looked from one to the other of them and smiled—a
trifle superciliously. "Next year, gentlemen, in the
year of our Lord 1621, the truce with Spain terminates
—and so does our safety."

"What's that?"

"Our safety?"

"What do you mean?"

Adriansen smiled again. "You see how easy it is to
lull ourselves into a state of false security? You see how
easy it is to forget the disastrous raids of the past? It's
because the early pioneers were too complacent that
the Spaniards from Trinidad and St. Thomé inflicted
upon them such heavy defeats. Yet despite this fact,
you here, gentlemen, have come to feel that this state
of peace and prosperity will continue for ever——"

"And why should it be disrupted, pray?"

"You ask why, Mynheer de Vries? It's astounding. Surely it should occur to you that from the instant
this truce expires we shall be in danger from the
Spanish in St. Thomé and Trinidad! Have you forgotten
1596, Mynheer? If I am not mistaken, your esteemed
father and uncle were among those slaughtered on the
Pomeroon. I'm certain you weren't too young to appreciate the horror of that massacre."

Mynheer de Vries frowned and fidgeted. He said
nothing.

"My reason for convening this meeting, gentlemen, is to impress on you the need for defensive preparations. Our only hope of survival is to fortify this island and other advantageous points on the river, and
even along the coast if possible——"

"From the way you speak, sir," interrupted Mynheer Meertens "one would imagine that the Spaniards
in Trinidad had conferred with you in secret concerning their intention to attack us next year."

"That's an improper remark," snapped Mynheer
Roosen. "A downright improper remark."

"Thank you, Mynheer Roosen," Adriansen

smiled, "but I can afford to ignore the implication. To continue, gentlemen. After next year, as I was saying, we must be prepared for a renewal of these Spanish raids. Only eight years ago you had the grim example of the Corentyne settlement which was attacked in defect of the truce and wiped out. If we wish to avoid suffering a similar fate we shall have to look to our own defenses. I have already discussed a plan of defense work with the Commandeur, a plan which, I am glad to say, he is not disinclined to have put into effect, subject to the approval of the Directors, naturally. It is this plan I want to discuss with you now, for without your cooperation and backing the Directors may be inclined, in their usual manner, to treat the matter lightly and to deem the Commandeur and myself alarmists."

"I stood at the dining-room door and listened," Kaywana said, when the meeting was over and the Company's traders had gone. "You spoke magnificently, Adriansen. You handled them well."

Adriansen patted her head.

"One day you'll be Commandeur, Mynheer," said August, who was nearly seven now and blue-eyed like his father. Unlike his mother, who still went nude, he wore clothes. So did Hendrickje and the last baby which had turned out to be a boy.

Adriansen gave August a sly look. "Nothing to yearn for too earnestly in that, my boy," he told him. "The responsibilities of a commandeur are more burdensome than you may imagine. However, one day we'll see. We never know." He gave him a playful clout and laughed, as though at some private joke. "Anyway, come. Enough dreaming ahead. Bring your book let me hear you say your lesson. You, too, must one day make a man of yourself, and you can only do that if you know how to read and write. A hard world with hard circumstances to overcome—and it takes hard men to conquer it and keep it down."

VI

There was the day when he came in at about noon and told her: "Tonight we're in for a little relaxation. We're going across to Cartabo."

She frowned and asked him what he meant, and he said: "You look alarmed. The life over there doesn't appeal to you any more, eh?" He bent and kissed Hendrickje. "Hendrickje, your mother has lost her taste for Indian life. She is a westerner in thought and outlook these days. Yes, a European." Hendrickje climbed on to his shoulder.

Kaywana, serious-faced asked: "What are we going to Cartabo for tonight?"

"Wakkatai has invited me to be present at a *piwarri*[1] festival in honor of his eldest daughter's coming of age."

A troubled look passed over Kaywana's face. "You can go. I am not," she said. "And if you'll take my advice you won't go, either."

"What are your objections?"

"Wakkatai is a bad man. I've told you that more than once. And there's no such custom as this. A daughter, no matter if she is the eldest, is not held of such account that a *piwarri* festival must be held in honor of her coming of age. Wakkatai is clever. He is holding this festival in your honor, but for reasons of his own he cannot tell you so outright. He hates you. Haven't you learned that yet?"

"All the more reason why we should attend his festival this evening. It's the people who don't like you whom you must indulge and flatter." He laughed and bit Hendrickje's ear playfully. "Those are the people, Kaywana, you must be most pleasant toward—the people who bear you a grudge and scheme against you."

"I don't agree," she said. "I like the people who

[1]*Piwarri* is an intoxicating drink made from fermented cassava juice.

treat me well and feel good toward me. Those who hate me I hate in return."

"Ah. You won't get on in the world with that philosophy, Old Water. No. Life is not so simple as all that."

"I've heard many whispers in the village. I hear Wakkatai only shows you a pleasant face because he knows you have great influence in this settlement. Secretly he envies you your power. He talks against you among the other Indians."

"Yes, I've heard those whispers myself. There's little I don't hear. For instance, I heard you once spat on Wakkatai. He made you some proposal and you spat on him—and he cursed you. Some two or three years ago that occurred, if I'm not mistaken."

"Where did you hear that?"

He shrugged. "Many ears listen on my behalf. But that doesn't matter. About this evening—no excuses. We're all going over to Cartabo. We can't afford to offend Wakkatai. He and his magic command a great deal of respect from the rest of the tribe, and at all costs I must keep popular with them. Their friendship matters very much to me, I can assure you."

She smiled. "You don't need to assure me. I know. You and your perpetual schemes. One day you'll get into trouble over them. Never trust Indians, Adriansen."

"Old Water, your voice has a frightened note."

She was silent—after giving him a quick glance—then nodded slowly and said: "Yes. I'm losing my fire."

"Nonsense! Nothing of the kind. You're still a jet of fire. And not one bit less attractive." He came over and fondled her. He was genuinely affectionate and sympathetic, and she felt mollified, though within her a deep sadness remained. Age was upon her. No matter how kind he tried to be, she knew that she was less attractive now. It was the Indian in her. Indian women faded quickly. After twenty-two men no longer looked at them with desire.

That night at the *piwarri* festival she was in a glum, aloof mood. She sat in a hammock in her mother's *benab*. The sound of the drums and the twang-twang of the *tarimbas*[1] left her unmoved. At twelve and thirteen—at fourteen and fifteen—her blood would have boiled. But not tonight. Tonight she was twenty-four—nearly an old woman. The yells of the young men as they dashed round the blazing fires, the cracking of the *macquaries*[2] as they slashed at each other, the sour, heady smell of the ripe *piwarri* as they dipped it up with calabashes from the big earthenware bowls and quaffed it—all this failed to rouse any throb of response within her. Yes, the years were taking the fire from her.

Adriansen squatted with Wakkatai and some of the older men inside the circle of yelling, tumbling young men. The older men shouted and encouraged the revelers to greater activity.

"You're tame! You're soft!" they shouted.

"In our time we did much better!"

"Flog! Flog!"

"Jump higher! Higher!"

One of the old men suddenly sprang up and began to stamp and yell. He snatched a *macquari* from one of the younger men and slashed right and left. The young men screamed at him and slashed back. He ducked and laughed and dodged, dipped up a calabash of *piwarri*, swept his hand round, sending the sour-smelling liquid in a spray of brown drops through the air.

Wakkatai and the older men shouted approval.

"Makkowa still has some blood!"

"Makkowa is young tonight!"

Adriansen laughed and clapped loudly.

Wakkatai rattled his *eumaraca*—a new, special one which he had dedicated to *Maconaima,* the great Father who watched over the rivers and the jungles. Wakkatai was gaudy with toucan feathers and beads and anklets of palm seeds and fish teeth. He had made Adriansen sit next to him, and you could see how pleased and important he felt tonight.

[1] A *tarimba* is a rude kind of harp.
[2] Whips plaited from fibers obtained from the *aeta* palm.

Adriansen kept smiling all the while, sipping his bowl of *piwarri*—Wakkatai had given him an earthenware bowl instead of a calabash, as a mark of honor to a distinguished guest. Adriansen sipped as though he had been accustomed to drinking *piwarri* since boyhood; if he felt any disgust because of his knowledge that the *piwarri* had been fermented with the aid of human saliva he did not show it. Kaywana watched his strong, cunning face. It looked more cunning and scheming tonight in the flickering light of the fires. She wondered what could be going on in his head now. All these past four or five years she had lived with him and she still did not know him. He was still a mystery to her—as much a mystery as he must be to the traders and everybody else. He treated her well, it was true, and he was a good father to the children—even to August who was not his own. He was teaching August to read and write and work figures. He was good and generous in many ways, but in other ways he made her sad and rebellious. He would not share his secrets with her. He would not discuss his schemes with her. For all she knew, he might even have other women on the sly—though that did not trouble her, for he was a man and entitled to have how many wives he wished. What troubled her chiefly was these trips he made up or down river. His going off for days into the bush or to the coast. Every time he went off she wondered whether she would see him again, whether he might not be drowned or get killed in some fashion. Living with him had its sad and anxious moments, though she had to admit that the bright moments, when they came along, did compensate for a lot. If only she could have remained young and not have faded away like this. It made her ashamed before him sometimes to think that her charms were going and that what she had to offer him now was not as good as what the younger girls in the village had.

In the hammock near by the baby began to splutter and wriggle. She got up and took it in her arms, sank down again and began to suckle it. And while it tugged greedily she looked outside again at the wild scene.

The drums thumped on and the *tarimbas* twanged

with weird magic. The young men yelled, and the *macquaries* cracked and snaked through the air. The backs of the young men were livid and bleeding, but still they yelled and jumped about, still slashed tirelessly at each other. And the older men shouted and clapped.

In the east the moon was glowing—a cool ball that sent shifty feelers of blue-green light through the foliage of the trees into the gloom of the *benab* here.

VII

August came into the house one morning in a tremor of excitement. He wanted to know about the ships in the river. "Whose ships are those, Mynheer? They have a strange look. Are they Spanish?"

"No, they're ours," said Adriansen. "They're from Africa. Now that the truce with Spain is at an end, the Netherlands Government has granted a charter to the West India Company. Those ships have brought slaves from the Guinea Coast."

"Slaves? What sort of people are they, Mynheer? Like the Indians?"

"No. They are black people."

"Black people! I never knew there were black people."

"Would you like to see them at close quarters?"

"Yes, Mynheer, I should. I've never seen a black man."

"Very well. We'll all go."

The skiff held them with ease. While Adriansen plied the oar, August watched over the two-year-old Willem to see that he did not scramble overboard and swim back to shore, for that was his favorite trick when he was being taken anywhere in the boat. He could swim like a tadpole. Kaywana sat cuddling the new baby, another boy, born two months ago and called Aert.

That was not the only day they saw the black men. There were many other days when they stood and watched them sweating in the fields. Black bodies with muscles that rippled. Close-cropped kinky-haired heads—heads bent with the apathy of enslavement. The sun beat on them, and sometimes rain came and dribbled on their tough shapes. Men of Africa, thick-lipped and thick-skulled. They looked oft-times like beasts out there, toiling in the noon. But when you looked closer you were startled, for you could glimpse the flame of humanity like magnificent lightning in their blood-shot eyes.

It was not long after this that Mynheer Meertens asked Mynheer de Vries whether he had heard the news.

"What news?"

"The Company has obtained the right to appoint its own Commandeur."

"Is that a fact? I did hear some rumor——"

"It is a fact. But you haven't heard the cream of the thing yet. They offered the post to van Groenwegel and he has refused."

"Refused!"

"Astounding, but it appears to be true," said Mynheer Meertens. "I heard it from Roosen, and he and Roosen, as you know, are as close as two thieves."

Mynheer de Vries looked puzzled. "But I thought the fellow would have jumped at the offer."

Mynheer Meertens shrugged. "I would have thought so, too, but there you are. Van Groenwegel will always remain a mystery, de Vries." He grunted and added: "You may be certain, of course, that some sound reason lies behind his refusal."

"Yes, I don't doubt that. A sound reason that involves the furtherance of his cunning schemes. A deep rogue that, Meertens."

When Kaywana asked him whether the rumor were true, Adriansen smiled: "You heard that, did you? Well, as I think I remember once having said, a commandeur's work can prove burdensome." He winked at August. "Didn't I once tell you that, August?"

August smiled uncertainly. "But, Mynheer, if you were Commandeur you would be like a king—the highest man on this settlement."

"That is so, my boy, but the life of the highest

man may often be dull and—how shall I put it? Not so convenient for the business of accumulating wealth. As Commandeur, I shall have been compelled to live in the big house over there. And there would have been the tedious business of administration to see after. Most important of all, the Commandeur cannot be disappearing for days at a time without disclosing his reasons for doing so, can he?"

In the following year, 1623, the new Commandeur, Mynheer Jacob Canijn, officially appointed by the new chartered Company, arrived and took up residence at Kyk-over-al. His ship was greeted with a salvo of guns fired from the new forts, and on the day after his arrival an Indian delivered at his house a case of wine. The label on it read: "To Mynheer Commandeur Jacob Canijn, with humble respects from Aert Adriansen van Groenwegel."

VIII

One morning there were white clouds in the sky so that the sun looked weak and cowed and sent down only a dim yellowish light. The river was gray and choppy. The waves did not glitter as they might have done if the sun had been shining from a clear sky.

Adriansen was over at Cartabo at Mynheer Roosen's store-house.

In the next room August was doing his lessons, and in the room here with Kaywana, Hendrickje and Willem and Aert rolled palm-seeds on the floor and made so much noise that Kaywana could not even hear the sough of the river outside.

The house quivered; and Kaywana put down the mat she was plaiting, her face going pale.

The children looked up from their game. Willem and Aert moved toward the windows, Hendrickje following them leisurely.

"The forts are firing," said Hendrickje. "Mother, did you hear?"

Willem said: "It must be the biggest cannon."

The house quivered again. Kaywana stared out at the river.

August came in from the next room. "Mother, did you hear that? They must be doing cannon practice at the forts." Then he noticed how she stared out of the window and how pale she was. "Is anything wrong, Mother? You looked frightened."

"It isn't the forts, August," she said.

"Not the forts? Then who is doing the firing? A ship?"

"Yes, it's a ship. The sound came from downriver."

"But there are forts downriver."

"It isn't the forts."

They looked at her curiously and were silent.

From Kyk-over-al came the sound of voices—shouts and a commotion; a mumbling and a vague clattering.

The house quivered.

"It must be a Spanish ship," and August.

"Look! Father is coming."

Kaywana got up and went downstairs, the children crowding after her in a chatter of excitement. August said: "I hope Mynheer agrees to take me over to Kyk-over-al. I'm eleven. I can fire a musket."

"I, too," said Willem, who was six. "I know how to load a musket. I've seen father doing it. Once father let me apply the ignition."

Adriansen said: "Kaywana, take the children and get aback to the storehouse—the big storehouse. Immediately. Take enough food and water for the whole day."

"Are you going back to the island, Adriansen?"

"Yes, I'm going to the fort. I'll be needed. Now, hurry."

"Are they Spanish ships, Mynheer?" asked August.

His stepfather nodded. Another time he might have patted the boy's head. Now his manner was crisp and cold. "Yes, they are. We're being attacked."

"Can't I come with you, Mynheer?"

"No. Go with your mother to the big storehouse.

Help her with the other children." As he turned to go
aboard the skiff again Kaywana said: "Adriansen,
squeeze my arm before you go."

"Do what?"

"Squeeze my arm." She regarded him with a shifty
distraction. "Squeeze my arm and say: 'I'm going, Kaywana. I've got to go, but I'm coming back later in the
day.' "

He laughed. "Very well. I'm going, Kaywana. I've
got to go, but I'm coming back later in the day. And
you may be sure I'll be back," he added, pressing her
arm.

"Keep in the storehouse," he called as he pushed
off. "Don't leave there until I come for you myself or
send for you. Is that clear?"

"Yes, I'll do that, Adriansen. I'll do that." She
ran to the edge of the bank, and stooping, scooped
up some water in her hand and sprinkled it on him.
"This is for good fortune! The water spirits will be
with you!"

All that morning the boom-boom throbbed through
the air, muffled by the trees and the walls of the storehouse. Now and then they would hear a whine and then
a crash among the tobacco plants over in the northeast. Once a crash sounded about a hundred yards from
the storehouse. There was a thud. Hendrickje whimpered and huddled close to Kaywana, but Willem said:
"I'm going to dig that one up when the battle is over.
I know exactly where it fell."

"Father must have fired that one," said Aert.

"Don't be foolish," said August. "Mynheer won't
fire this way. The Spaniards must have fired that one."

Kaywana ignored them. She was plaiting a mat, her
fingers working mechanically, her thoughts out on the
river. Perhaps he was dead by now, she told herself
once—smashed to pulp by one of the cannonballs.
Or it might be that a musket ball had hit him. He was
lying dead, and they were setting fire to the fort and
preparing to smash down the doors of the storehouses.
They were swarming over the island, killing and burning.

Boom. Boom.

Shortly after noon the booming stopped. They could hear the pop-pop of muskets. Vague shouts came wavering through the air. The sky had cleared up and the sun shone brightly now.

Something big had happened yonder on the river. They could hear faint cheers—cries, musket fire. Uncertain and distant. A ghost noise.

"Let me go and see what's happened, Mother," said August excitedly. "I'll go as far as the big tree over there——"

"No. You'll do nothing of the kind. Mynheer would be angry with me. There may be danger."

Aert pointed and cried: "Smoke. Fire!"

They looked and saw black smoke over the trees.

"They're burning our house!" Hendrickje sobbed. "Mother, look! I'm sure it's our house."

Kaywana had stopped plaiting the mat. She stared and wondered. It might not be so, but if it had been fated to happen that way, then no one could have stopped it. She remembered the smoke that had enveloped the *troolie* roofs of the cottages on the Corentyne.

Willem, who had climbed up a ladder into the loft, shouted down: "I can see better from up here! I see people coming. It must be the Spaniards. No, they're Indians."

August went up and confirmed this. "Some Indians are coming this way. They're coming in a hurry. I believe something serious has happened."

Kaywana's heart went cold. It looked as though it would be like the Corentyne. It was the same way the Indians had fled. That time they had fled into the jungle. Now they were fleeing into the plantations.

August shouted down: "One of them is Wakkatai. I can make him out clearly. Makka and Wikki-Wikki, two of his daughters, are with him."

"I see Wonomo. And Lataka," said Willem.

Kaywana went to the door and looked out, waiting.

Musket fire broke out in the distance—over the east and in the north. She heard a low wail of voices.

A panting Indian came toward them. It was

Teekai—an Indian who had often come to Adriansen at the house. He was carrying a musket and a sack. He would have gone past, but when Kaywana hailed him he approached.

"What's happened, Teekai? Who won the fight?" She spoke in the Indian tongue, and he replied: "Can't tell you, Kaywana, but I hear some Spaniards are coming this way, so perhaps the Spaniards won."

"Where did you get this musket from?"

"Mynheer de Hooft gave me. I've got powder and shot in this sack." He brushed the perspiration from his face. "How you came to be in here? Where is Mynheer Adriansen?"

"He's at Kyk-over-al. Stay with us here, Teekai. How did Mynheer de Hooft come to give you this musket? Take care you stole it!"

"Stole it? No. I traded it with him for letter-wood I brought down from upstream last week. I can fire a musket. Yesterday I killed three big agoutis and a young tapir." He spoke in a voice of pride.

They heard voices and saw Wakkatai and two of his daughters going past. They did not look toward the storehouse and Kaywana muttered: "Let him go. Don't call him here."

She made Teekai come inside, and then closed and barred the door again. From the loft August shouted: "Mother, I can see one of them! It's a Spaniard. He's armed with a saber. He's coming from the northeast. He's passing under the big *courida* tree near the small storehouse."

"I can see another," cried Aert. "Under the *cookerit* palm where we caught the monkey last week." He was spying through a hole in the door.

"Let's all go up in the loft," said Kaywana, and Teekai lifted Aert in his arms and took him up the ladder while Kaywana brought the musket, and Hendrickje the sack with the powder and shot, though she held it as though afraid it would go off and blow her to pieces.

From the two windows of the loft they looked out and saw the two figures August and Aert had talked about. The one that Aert had seen from the door downstairs proved to be only one of the negro slaves who crouched under a *cookerit* palm, evidently very scared. The other August had seen was a stranger and certainly looked as though he might be a Spaniard. He walked with a slight limp and carried what looked like a sword. Then he disappeared from view behind a clump of shrubs.

They heard musket fire again in the east, but it soon died away.

Willem cried: "Look! Look! Another Spaniard. Shoot him, Teekai! Shoot him with your gun!"

"That's no Spaniard," said August. "It's a soldier from the fort. He's got a gun, too."

As it happened, the soldier's destination was the storehouse. He approached and shouted up: "Kaywana! Are you all right there? Mynheer van Groenwegel has sent me to tell you you and the children can return home, but you must let me escort you, for there are a few stragglers astray in the bush and around the plantation here."

"Then we've won the battle?"

"Yes, we've won."

A few minutes later, as they moved along the track, he told them that the Spaniards had been beaten off with ease. "We sank one of their ships—a small vessel—and some of the survivors swam ashore. They're wandering about in the bush, but we're rounding them up and killing them."

"And Mynheer van Groenwegel is safe, you say? He wasn't wounded?"

"No, he's safe. He was never in any danger, so far as I know."

"Didn't he fire a cannon?" Willem asked.

The soldier smiled and shook his head. "No, we have two gunners on the island fort and one each on the two *brandwagts* lower along the river."

Willem was disappointed. "I thought he was firing a cannon," he said. "Didn't he fire a musket and kill any of the Spaniards?"

"No, there was no need. The one big galleon didn't even come within range of our cannon. It turned and made off when it saw we were strongly fortified. It was only the smaller ship that didn't escape. It came too close and we holed her below the water-line and then put out from shore in canoes and threw firebrands aboard her. Before you knew it she was on fire."

"We saw the smoke. We thought it was our house."

Both Willem and August were thoroughly disap-pointed at the course events had taken. Later that day, when they were at home and Adriansen came in, August said: "Mynheer, I thought you would have taken part in the battle and killed a few hundred of them."

"You're a bloodthirsty young fellow," said Adri-ansen, slapping him on the back. "There's nothing romantic in war and bloodshed, my boy. It's ugly, dirty work. Whenever you can avoid it, always avoid physical force." His eyes twinkled with subtle guile. "Brute force should always be a last resort, August. If you can get a thing by clever scheming, get it that way. It's more comfortable." He guffawed and winked, and Kaywana frowned and said: "I don't like that teaching, Adriansen. He might take you seriously and grow into a wicked man."

"What is wickedness, Old Water? Who can define wickedness? Bah! There's no wickedness in this world, August, lad. Willem! Yes, you listen to me, too. There's no such thing as wickedness. A thing is wrong because we make it so in our thoughts. Everything in this world is right. It just depends upon how you twist it about in your mind and view it. The most upright and honest man can seem a rogue if you want to make him so and believe him to be so."

IX

"Yes, Meertens—a rogue. A deep, unscrupulous rogue."

Thus spoke Mynheer de Vries of Adriansen, a few years later. He was discussing with Mynheer Meer-tens a scheme that Adriansen had just had approved by the Directors of the West India Company.

"Only he knows the real object behind this move, Meertens." He wagged his finger. "And it's going to bring trouble. It's going to disturb our relations with the Indians. Already I hear that fellow, Wakkatai, is grumbling and secretly poisoning the minds of the tribe against us. Really, it baffles me what hold van Groenwegel could have over the Directors that they should sanction every hare-brained scheme he chooses to put before them. Why, he might as well be Commandeur, the influence he exerts over them!"

Mynheer Meertens nodded. "I agree. It's most upsetting. Van Groenwegel seems to think he's the only original brain in existence. Thirty Indians to go to Barbados to assist the English settlers there to till the soil and plant! In the first place, what have we to do with the English in Barbados? Why should we send Indians to assist them in their ventures? It's a preposterous scheme."

"Trouble will come of it. These Indians may seem docile on the surface, but, for my part, I don't trust them more than I see them."

Kaywana, too, was disturbed about it. One morning in the village, Patooka, her stepfather, told her: "Warn the Mynheer, Kaywana. Trouble is coming for him. Wakkatai is very displeased. He tells the people not to listen to the Mynheer—that the Mynheer wants to send them across the seas into slavery. Wakkatai is advising the thirty whom the Mynheer has chosen to go to change their minds, but they laugh at Wakkatai and say Wakkatai is a fool, that the Mynheer has greater magic and that the Mynheer has promised them good food and living in Barbados and that they trust him and feel certain he will not let the English enslave them. And Wakkatai is even more enraged that they should heed the Mynheer and not him. Wakkatai is so enraged he is working magic day and night against the Mynheer. He calls upon all the spirits of the bush and the water and the air to do harm to the Mynheer. Tell the Mynheer to be careful how he walks. Evil lurks in waiting for him."

When Kaywana told Adriansen what her stepfather had said, Adriansen did not laugh. He stroked his chin and nodded slowly. "Yes, I've heard about Wak-katai and his campaign against me. Patooka is right. I'm going to have to keep an eye on Wakkatai. He's getting dangerous. He's vindictive." He glanced at her. "I heard something else, too. He hasn't forgotten how you insulted him some years ago—that time when you spat on him. He's swearing that your time is draw-ing near, and he's calling upon the spirits to strike you down as you walk. You must be careful when you go to Cartabo."

He began to pace.

The house was quiet, for the children were out boating, and the last baby, a girl whom they had named Juliana, was asleep. Juliana was two months old. She was fifteen months younger than Jan, the boy who had been born a few weeks after the Spanish raid.

Adriansen's foot-treads made a solemn dum-dum on the floor. A dark sound, Kaywana told herself, a sound she always associated with his going away up-river, or down-river to the coast, on one of his expedi-tions, because it was always early in the morning that he left, and his foot-treads would sound heavy and ominous in the silence of the house as he moved about getting his bundles and haversacks ready.

"But, Adriansen, why have you got to send these thirty Indians to the island in the West Indies? What benefit will you get from their going? Won't you tell me about the plan?"

He smiled. "The benefit is not strictly a material one," he said. "It's a gesture—a generous gesture toward the English settlers. The shortsighted dullards of this settlement may not be able to see it as I do, but in years to come they will thank me for extending a friendly hand to settlers in neighboring colonies."

"But these Indians, won't the English make them slaves?"

"They won't. They have promised me faithfully to treat them well and give them good food and quarters. They won't be flogged, and they will be paid in coin or the equivalent of coin in provisions. And their sojourn will not exceed five years unless they themselves de-sire to stay longer."

"I see," she said, feeling within her a glow of wonder at his having bothered to explain. It was almost unbelievable. He had always been so reserved and secretive and reluctant to discuss with her anything concerning his projects and expeditions.

He went on pacing, and she stared at the floor, pensive.

Suddenly they heard voices outside—the children's voices. She got up and went to the window and saw the children coming ashore. They had just brought the *corial* alongside and were getting out. . . . She stiffened.

"Adriansen."

"Yes?"

"Look out of the window. They're lifting Hendrickje."

He came and looked out, and exclaimed at what he saw. He hurried out, and she followed him.

August and Willem were pale and scared. August told them: "We heard something go 'phfff!' in the bush, and the next minute Hendrickje put her hand to her neck and said that something had bitten her. See! There's a tiny reddish-blue spot on her neck. She went limp and began to breathe queerly. I'm sure it wasn't an insect, Mynheer. Somebody blew a poisoned dart at her from the bush."

Kaywana bent down over Hendrickje and examined her neck. She nodded and said: "Yes, it's a poisoned dart." Her face was rigid and calm; her eyes had a glassy look of hate. "It's scorpion poison—not *curari.*"

Adriansen grunted. "Friend Wakkatai must be credited with this. I suppose this is part of his campaign of magic directed against us. Very well. We shall see." He carried Hendrickje into the house and they put her to bed. She had a temperature.

"My children," said Kaywana, "have done him nothing—yet he tries to be revenged on me through them. He will pay for this. He will pay double, too."

"You'll do nothing in the matter. Leave it to me."

"Leave it to you! You! I know what you will do. You will go to him and make him a fine present. You will speak to him with soft words so that he will show you a pleasant face and promise to speak well of you to the others. You will try to pacify him. But I—when I hate, I hate. I offer no peace when I hate."

The following day Hendrickje was better. The fever had gone, though Kaywana made her remain in bed.

Adriansen came in during the afternoon and said: "All is peace again. I have had a long chat with Wakkatai, and we have been able to come to a very pleasant understanding, so I don't think we need fear any more scorpion-poisoned darts."

Willem asked: "Father, did he show you the blowpipe he used?"

Adriansen laughed. "No, I didn't think of asking him to show me."

August said: "If I were you, Mynheer, I should have put a musket shot into him. He's a bad fellow."

"Shoot him, eh? And turn the whole tribe against me? Turn the whole lot of them into howling wolves ready to strip the settlement bare? Where would be the wisdom in that, my boy?" His eyes narrowed with a deep cunning. "No, August, when you get to my age you'll learn that there are occasions when we must use force because it's impossible to do anything else—as on the occasion when we were attacked by those two Spanish ships. Then we had to use force or we should have gone down. But on occasions like this, when we're up against the Wakkatais of this world, force is not the weapon to employ, my boy. The weapon is subtlety. Guile, flattery, gifts—these can be far more effective than muskets and powder and shot. You bear that in mind. It will help you later on."

Kaywana sat silent, her face emotionless. She was suckling Juliana.

Outside, you could hear the river—the hushed sough of the river. In the west, the tobacco and balsam plants rustled in a soft land breeze. And the cotton trees. It sounded like rain coming over the jungle, but the sky was clear—blue with small puffs of white. White clouds drifting toward the southwest in the trade wind. The trade wind which, tomorrow, would help the ship on its voyage to Barbados—the ship that would take the thirty Indians to the English settlers in the little island three hundred and eighty miles north.

On the day after the ship sailed, in this year 1627, Wikki-Wikki, the third daughter of Wakkatai—she was twelve and eligible for marriage—was walking along a track on the mainland that led to a field of balsam. She was gathering herbs for her father, and her eyes kept sweeping the low line of shrubs and ferns that grew on either side of the track.

Once, as she stooped to pluck up two sprigs of dragon's blood, she heard a soft sound amid the clumps of bush at her back. Phfff! She felt a tiny stinging pain in her shoulder, and rose unsteadily. She could feel her heart fluttering. A breathlessness overtook her. There was a stiffening in her limbs. Then she collapsed, twitched and lay still.

That afternoon, late, they found her body. Wakkatai and four others who had set out on a search. They found her dead and stiff, and when Wakkatai examined her he said: "An enemy did this. An enemy has killed my daughter. See! It's *curari*." He looked up at the others. "The enemy who has done this is Kaywana. The spirits poisoned her daughter with the venom of the scorpion, and now she has killed my daughter with the poison from the trees." He was silent a moment, then slowly and solemnly he rose. "I shall do nothing. *Maconaima* who sees all and who guides the waters in the rivers will take his revenge—and it will be a terrible revenge." He raised his arm toward the setting sun. "Hear me this day, *Maconaima!* I curse Kaywana and call upon all the evil of the trees and the water and the air to conspire for revenge. This day I call upon all the spirits of darkness to work harm upon Kaywana!"

When Adriansen heard of Wikki-Wikki's death he said to Kaywana: "The rumor is that you had something to do with it. What have you to say?"

She met his eyes without flinching. "It is true. I did it, Adriansen. I hate him, and I did it to be revenged on him for what he did to Hendrickje—and

for every child of mine that he harms again I shall
kill one of his. He himself I shall kill if he drives me to
it."

"I never thought you could be so vindictive. You're
a murderer, Kaywana—in the eyes of Christians you're
a murderer."

"I care nothing for your Christianity. I only know
that when anyone loves me I give my love in return,
and give it freely—and when anyone hates me I hate
in return. If anyone hurts me I hurt them in return. I
don't give them fine presents and say sweet things to
them."

The children watched them, listening in an awed
silence, sensing that something big was in their presence—something strong and of the earth.

"Very well, Kaywana, we think differently. What
has happened has happened and can't be recalled. I
can't make you think as I do. If you care to live according to the laws of the beasts, then you must do so
and suffer as the beasts do." He turned and left the
room.

August approached his mother at once and said in
a lowered voice: "You're right, Mother. You're right.
Mynheer is a great man in many ways, but he's too
soft sometimes. I'm glad you killed Wikki-Wikki. I,
too hate Wakkatai for what he did to Hendrickje. You
were right to get your revenge on him. I, too, shall be
a murderer if anyone tries to hurt me."

X

This same year, 1627, Abraham van Peere, a trader
from Vlissingen, came to Guiana. He was entertained
for a week by Adriansen and took a great liking to
August.

One day toward the end of his stay, when they
were dining, he looked at August and said: "August,
lad, you have the eyes of a poet and an adventurer. I
believe a glimpse of Europe would give you poise.
How would you like to take a trip to Holland in my
ship?"

"Mynheer, nothing would give me greater pleasure."

Kaywana looked doubtful. "How far away is Holland, Mynheer?"

"Thousands of miles. Several weeks' travel."

"He's my eldest son—and the sea is uncertain. Years ago, when I came on a ship from the Corentyne, I was ill all the way. I thought the ship would have gone down, it rocked so much."

Van Peere laughed. "You think your August will go to bottom, eh? No, you needn't be fearful about that. Our ships are all seaworthy. I'll bring him back safely, I promise you."

"In fact," he went on, "I may tell you this in confidence. The West India Company has granted me a charter to colonize the territory along the banks of the River Berbice in the east. When I return, in a few months' time, I'm bringing a party of men and youngsters—forty elderly men and twenty young men, to be precise—and I could employ your August as an assistant secretary. Yesterday I happened to see his handwriting, and I assure you I've seldom seen handwriting more beautiful. He's a lad of great promise, and I need promising lads."

So it was agreed that August should go.

Before he sailed, Adriansen took him into his room and said to him: "I rather like you, young man. You have much of your mother's fire. You're developing fast, and now that you're going into a big country you'll take much bigger steps forward. But let me give you a word of warning. Remember what happened the other day? Remember Wikki-Wikki? You sided with your mother on that occasion. You felt that she was right in killing that poor girl. In the Indian way, it was probably right. But you're three-quarters white— three-quarters European—and in future you're going to live in accordance with the codes and laws of the Christian world. You can't apply Indian law to your dealings with men in the life you're going to lead. I've tried to educate you the European way, August, and if you want to live with Europeans and make a man of yourself, then you must behave and think as Europeans do. Do you understand?"

"Yes, Mynheer," said August—but Adriansen detected the gleam of resentment in the boy's eyes, and the defiant set of his lips. He looked as his mother had looked that day when Adriansen had taken her to task for killing Wikki-Wikki.

After he had sailed, Kaywana fell into a spell of sadness that lasted for nearly a week. She hardly spoke, and attended to her household duties in a mechanical, preoccupied manner. She looked old and defeated, and one night she said to Adriansen: "I feel I won't ever see him again. I shouldn't have parted with him. Now that he has gone it's as if my last bit of girlhood has gone with him. I have nothing now to remind me of what I was on the Corentyne. His father was a good man—a good, simple man. Strong and simple like an Indian. I believe he would have made me more happy than you have made me, Adriansen."

Adriansen laughed. "You mean, he had no guile, eh? I knew that long ago, from what you've told me. If he had had my qualities he might have been alive today, for he would have remained with you in the jungle instead of running off like a gallant fool to make a hopeless defense against the Spaniards."

She stiffened in anger. "Don't say that. He was brave. He was a man. A fighter. He fought and died. I wouldn't have respected him if he had stayed with me in the jungle. That would have been a coward's act. Almost as bad as making gifts to a man who has hurt your own child."

The air was still and warm, and the river kept up its hushed soughing against the bank, amidst the roots of the mangrove and the *courida* and the wild cacao. Far away in the south, over the jungle, lightning flashed in swift, crooked forks, but they could hear no thunder. Only, all the while, the river whispering. Monotonously, with vague menace.

XI

One night, a few months later, it was warm, too, and still, and there was lightning in the south. The river, as always, kept whispering. Now and then thunder would come in a deep muttering that died away nearly in the same moment that it came into being. But most of the time there would be simply that flicker-flicker far away in the south, over the jungle, silent but vivid and ugly.

Perhaps it was the lightning that had awakened her, thought Kaywana. There it went again. Two swift sheets of white fire.

She lay on her back and listened for a long while, but no thunder came. She could only hear the river, hushed and hollow. She frowned. Was it only the river, though? Or could she hear another sound?

Beside her, in the large bed, Adriansen was asleep. He snored in long deep rasps of breath. Dimly she could make out the shape of his powerful body. Then in sudden clarity as the lightning flashed. She sighed and turned over.

After a moment, she sat up and stared around into the darkness. She looked out of the window and saw the river. It looked indigo-gray in the starlight. There was a glow in the east—a bluish glow. A waning half-moon was rising. Lightning flashed again. A jagged fork this time.

She noticed something. Lights at Cartabo. Reddish, flickering lights in the Indian village. Fires alight at midnight. It was most unusual. There was no festival on; no *piwarri*, no celebration. And the Indians always retired shortly after sundown. All fires were put out before they went into their *benabs*.

She got out of bed and crossed over to the window. She could hear voices—a wavering clamor barely audible above the river noise.

"Adriansen."

He did not wake, though his snoring stopped. She had to go back to the bed and shake his shoulder before he awakened.

"What's it? Why aren't you in bed?"

"Something is wrong at Cartabo. Look. Fires."

"Fires? What fires?" He was irritable and sleepy.

"Look and see for yourself."

He looked. "Yes, that's odd," he murmured.

She fanned herself with her hand. "I couldn't sleep. The night is so close. Shall I light the lamp?"

"Yes. No, on second thoughts, you'd better not. I think I see a *corial* coming. It must be Teekai."

"That Teekai, eh? One day they'll find out he's your spy, and he'll die quietly."

"That day hasn't come yet, anyway. He's a very useful fellow. Keeps me posted regularly with all the gossip of the village. A good man."

She accompanied him downstairs and they let in Teekai by the kitchen entrance. He was thin nowadays and had developed a stoop. He had his musket with him, and the sack with his powder and shot; he never went anywhere without his musket and ammunition.

"Bad trouble coming, Mynheer," he told Adriansen. "Everything is upset tonight. The Indians are planning to kill out all the white men."

"But what's the trouble? What's happened?"

Teekai told them that Bissooki, the son of Macawana, had come back from Barbados as a stowaway aboard a ship called the *Emma de Voors* which had come in late that afternoon. Bissooki had been one of the thirty who had gone to Barbados. When darkness had fallen, Bissooki had escaped from the ship and swum ashore. The village had already retired but Bissooki had roused everybody. He looked meager and worn out, and there were long marks on his back. He had told them that the white Englishmen in Barbados had beaten him with a hide whip. All the other twenty-nine Indians whom Mynheer had sent over some time ago were being beaten, too, by the Englishmen. The Englishmen had made slaves of them all, and the Indians were suffering greatly. This news had enraged the village. There would be no sleep tonight, Teekai said. Wakkatai was talking in an angry voice. He was calling the white men usurpers and tyrants and saying that Mynheer van Groenwegel was the biggest usurper and tyrant of all. He had fooled the Indians. He had used them for his own ends and for the benefit of his fellow white men. The people were agreeing with Wakkatai and shouting for Mynheer van Groenwegel's life.

"Very well, Teekai. Thank you. I'll go over to them and see what I can do to quiet them down."

"No, Mynheer. No. Don't go. They will kill you."

"He's right, Adriansen. You shouldn't go."

Adriansen was thoughtful for a moment, then said: "Very well, Teekai. You can go back. I'll go to the fort and see the Commandeur. Tomorrow I'll choose a special gift for you. You've done me a great service tonight."

"I saw this trouble coming," said Kaywana, after Teekai had left. "I knew the English couldn't be trusted. My instinct told me so. I think the best thing you can do now is to call out the soldiers and march into the village."

"Nothing of the sort. We must never threaten them with violence except as a last resort. These Indians are good people. It's always a mistake to show them force."

She laughed contemptuously. "Adriansen, you're a fool in many ways that you don't know. I cannot read and write, but I know human beings. They only respect you when you show them that you're strong."

"There are other ways of being strong than the way of guns, Kaywana," he smiled as he got into his clothes.

"The way of cunning, eh?"

She stood at the bedroom window and watched him get into the skiff and push off, thinking: He and I are no more one. There is nothing between us these days except when we lie in bed. He thinks I am hard and bad, and I think him a fool for his soft ways of dealing with people. He's a queer man—a big man, but a man whose inside will always be hidden from me. So different from my August who was simple and frank in everything. August had no deep secrets and plans. August was not cunning and full of flattery. But I must not grumble. It had to happen like this.

And I'm getting old; more reason why I should take things as they are.

She went back to the bed and lay down, staring up into the darkness of the rafters. Lightning still flashed in the south. She heard thunder—low, faint, a portentous mumbling over the mysterious distant jungle. The jungle through which snakes and strange wild creatures moved. The rain must be hurling itself down in savage drops through the trees, and the lightning must be slicing giant *mora* trees in half, or splitting them down the middle. The thunder must be one continuous clatter of noise. In the Corentyne jungle, one day, a storm had broken when August and herself were in their secret spot making love. He had wanted to dress and let them go back to the settlement, but she had told him to stay, that it would be more dangerous to move through the jungle while the storm was on. They had lain where they were, and a huge *cookerit* palm had been cloven in two by the lightning and had fallen with a terrible crash amid the vines and undergrowth.

She sat up, telling herself that she must not think of those days. They were gone—gone like her son August. Gone like her youth.

She shifted restlessly, got out of bed and went to the window. There was a big fire at Cartabo. It looked like one of the storehouses on the plantation. They had set fire to one of the storehouses.

She saw a group of long dark forms moving on the water. *Corials.* She heard shouting. It came from the *corials.* They were going, she thought, to raid the west-bank plantations. . . . The thought sagged in her. No, it was toward the house here they were coming. They were coming here to kill Adriansen and herself and the children. Wakkatai must be leading them. He had long wanted to be revenged on her, and tonight he had seen his chance. The people were so incensed by the news from Barbados that he had had no difficulty in persuading them to come across to do injury to Adriansen and herself. . . . She could hear in her fancy what they were shouting: "Death to van Groenwegel and his wife and children!" . . .

She went into the next room. Hate writhed like a reptile in her chest. "Hendrickje! Jan! Juliana! Wake up! Willem! Aert! Wake up, children!" There was no panic in her voice. It might have been morning and she was calling them down to eat, reproving them for having slept late.

There was a slow stirring in the two big beds.

She went back into the room she and Adriansen shared with the last child, a boy ten weeks old. She took him up from his cot and hugged him to her breast, stood in the middle of the room looking out at the river through the square of the window. After a moment, she returned into the children's room. "Wake up! Wake up! All of you!"

"Is anything wrong, Mother?" asked Hendrickje. She sat up and yawned. The moon had risen, red and pathetic over the bush on the opposite bank. It shone on Hendrickje's sleepy face—on her long golden hair. She was twelve, and already well developed; her spiked breasts stood out erect under her white silk nightgown. Soon she will be like me, thought Kaywana, as I was on the Corentyne. A jet of fire.

Willem woke, too, but not Aert. Aert was a heavy sleeper. You had to slap him before he would wake. Willem slapped him and he woke. He and Willem were in nightshirts, long white nightshirts. The moon shone on them, too, both sturdy boys, Willem ten, Aert nine. They were gray-eyed like their father, Willem with brown hair, Aert with black hair . . . Willem has my spirit, thought Kaywana, but Aert is more like his father. Willem will hate and fight, but Aert will flatter and make peace. . . .

"There's a fire at Cartabo," said Willem. "Look, Aert."

"It looks like a small storehouse," said Aert.

Kaywana put down the baby. "I'm going downstairs to lock the back door. Willem!"

Aert exclaimed: *"Corials* are coming! Plenty of them!"

"Willem, go into the western room and open the arms cupboard. Take out all the four muskets in there and the ammunition. Let Aert help you. The key for the cupboard is on your father's desk."

"What are we going to do," Mother?"

"You see those *corials* coming? They're coming for us. They're coming to try to kill us, my sons. Wakkatai is leading them. But we will do some killing before they get into this house. Now, hurry. I'm going downstairs to lock and bar the doors."

"A fight!" chortled Willem. "Good. I can shoot. Father taught me."

"Where is Father?" asked Hendrickje. "Isn't he at home?"

"No, he is at Kyk-over-al."

Her mother hurried out, and Hendrickje ran into the next room after Willem and Aert. She was frightened. Willem, whining with excitement, had already dashed off toward the western bedroom, Aert, silent, moving after him. On the bed with the baby, Juliana and Jan were still asleep.

Outside, the *corials* were drawing alongside the bank. The reddish moonlight gave the river a soft, idyllic look. The jungle on the opposite bank stood out black and clear against the glowing sky.

Over at Kyk-over-al Adriansen was saying: "Gentlemen let us resort to firearms only if the situation becomes utterly impossible. These people can be won over by soft words. Let us try words first."

"That's nonsense," snapped Mynheer de Vries. "These savages won't be quelled by flattery. They're in an ugly mood. A firm hand must be taken with them."

"Fire upon them by all means," agreed Mynheer Meertens. "Teach them a lesson."

The Commandeur raised his hand. "Quiet, please, gentlemen. I think Mynheer van Groenwegel is perfectly right. We must not use firearms unless we have to. We'll try reason first and see what effect it has upon them."

A grumbling broke out.

"We could have expected that. Everything van Groenwegel says in this settlement is law."

"Soft words. What can soft words do against that howling mass of fiends?"

"This is the end of the colony. And all through Groenwegel's lunatic project. It was a foregone conclusion that the English would have turned those Indians into slaves. See what the Directors will have to say to this!"

"Look! They're setting fire to the small storehouse."

"Very well, gentlemen!" called the Commandeur. "We must be moving. I know you're not trained soldiers, but please try to be as orderly as you can. And remember that you're taking orders from me."

So, with the Captain of the fort and his men, they left the house and embarked for Cartabo. Landed, they made their way along the track that led toward the Indian village. They moved in a quick trot, in double file, the Commandeur at the head with the Captain, and behind him Adriansen with a lieutenant.

On the left of them, over the trees, the glow that marked the burning storehouse grew brighter.

"We have to give that up as lost, I'm afraid," muttered Adriansen to the lieutenant. "We must try to save the larger one. It's likely they're moving toward that one now."

They were just in time. The Indians were piling faggots against the walls of the storehouse—the large storehouse which contained most of the cargo brought by the last ship from Holland.

"Stop there! Stop!" cried Adriansen, advancing ahead of the column. He carried no musket; he had handed his musket to the lieutenant. He raised his arm commandingly.

"Look! Van Groenwegel!"

"Kill him!"

"Van Groenwegel, traitor to Indians!"

A stone was hurled at him. Two *awara* seeds hit him in the chest. He did not retreat. "Palm seeds. Think of it. What children!" He laughed and shouted: "Stop there, I tell you, people! Put down those faggots. Don't dare light that fire."

They hesitated, but still howled at him. They

pelted him. A stone struck him in the chest. But he stood where he was, his arm raised.

"Kill him! Kill van Groenwegel!"

"Kill all white men!"

"They make Indians slaves!"

"Shoot the savages down," cried Mynheer de Vries.

The Commandeur looked around and frowned. "Remember! I'm giving the orders, de Vries. And I insist on being obeyed."

The howls went on. The stones came one after the other.

But Adriansen stood firm.

"Mind you! I warn you. Don't dare to light those faggots. Put them aside. Take them away and go home. Behave yourselves like good people and go back to your *benabs,* and tomorrow I promise you presents in abundance. But light those faggots and you'll be sorry!"

A sulky murmuring and jabbering broke out. Several of them dropped the faggots. One or two of them began to kick away those piled against the wall of the storehouse. Some began to edge away toward the bush.

"That's beginning to look better. I see that my friends the Indians are men and women of good sense. I knew I could depend upon them."

"You traitor, van Groenwegel. You traitor to Indians!"

"You sent Indians to Barbados and made them slaves!"

"Oh, no! You're wrong. I'm your friend. I have always been your friend. But for me you might have been made slaves as the black men from Africa. It was I who interceded for you. It is not my fault that the English in Barbados have made your countrymen slaves. It is their treachery—and you may be sure I shall take immediate steps to have your relatives and friends brought back. The English have broken faith with me if what Bissooki says is true. I'm very angry with the English. But put your faith in your old friend van Groenwegel, and everything will be made right."

The stones and palm seeds had stopped coming.

The Indians were listening—mumbling doubtfully but listening.

"And remember! Tomorrow there will be gifts for everyone. My countrymen here are armed with mus- kets—guns and powder and shot. But I told them—I said to them: 'No. Oh, no. My Indians are good peo- ple. They will go home if I tell them to. You will not have to fire upon them.' And see, I was right. I knew I could depend upon my Indians. . . ."

As he talked they began to move away and slink off up the track—by twos and threes—silent and doc- ile, like reproved children.

"Yes. Good people, my Indians. Go back and sleep and await your fine gifts tomorrow. Van Groen- wegel is pleased with his people. . . ."

When they had all gone and the Commandeur was congratulating Adriansen on his success, a man sud- denly appeared from out of the bush. The Captain ex- claimed in alarm, but Adriansen said: 'It's Teekai. Teekai is a good fellow. It was he who warned me.' He asked to be excused and drew aside with Teekai. "What's the matter now, Teekai?"

"Mynheer, you must hurry. Trouble is happening over at your house. Wakkatai and plenty of them have gone over there and are trying to kill your woman and her children. They think you are there in the house, too."

While some broke down the back door, some pelted the house with stones and clods of earth. They howled and pelted.

Willem and Aert were eager to fire upon them from the bedroom window, but their mother told them: "No. Hold your fire for when they try to come up- stairs here. They'll soon have the back door down, and then they'll rush up the stairs. It's then you must fire upon them, sons."

She spoke calmly, and they felt confidence in her and in themselves. Even Hendrickje had stopped whimpering. In the children's room Hendrickje sat in one of the two big beds with Juliana and Jan and the baby. In the adjoining room Kaywana and Willem

and Aert were preparing for the attack. The door
that gave on to the corridor stood wide open, but before
it they had placed a heavy table. This door commanded
a full view of the stairway. On the table rested four
muskets. They were loaded and ready for action.

Kaywana and the boys stood waiting; listening
to the thuds downstairs on the back door and waiting.
Willem and Aert were excited and moved restlessly
about.

When a loud rending crash came downstairs, however, Willem stiffened and Aert's face grew serious.
They peered anxiously down the well of the stairway.
Aert murmured: "They've broken in." Willem whispered: "You're right."

Kaywana said: "Get ready, boys. Don't fire until
I tell you, though. As soon as you fire I'll take the guns
and reload them." She turned as footsteps sounded
behind her. "Juliana! Jan! Get back into the next room
with your sister. Go!"

"Mother, I'm afraid," Jan said.

"I'm afraid, Mother," Juliana said.

"Go back. Go back!" There was a quaver of panic
in her voice now. "My babies. My poor babies. They'll
kill you. Get back to your sister!"

"Mother! Mother! They're coming up!" cried Aert.

Kaywana turned. "Yes. Fire! Fire, Aert! Fire,
Willem!"

The house thundered, and the table shook under
the flashing muskets.

Jan and Juliana shrieked and ran back into the
next room.

Yells and a confusion of noise sounded on the
staircase. One of the Indians had been hit. He kept rolling down the stairs.

Kaywana was reloading the two muskets the
boys had fired. Willem and Aert were trembling. Aert
whimpered now and then. He had hurt his finger.

"Fire again! Aert, fire! Fire, Willem!"

The powder kegs and sacks with the shot were on
Adriansen's desk. Kaywana loaded one musket and
was loading the second when Willem—Willem had
taken hold of the third still-loaded musket on the ta-

ble—fired, and again the table shook and a roar of sound clamored through the house. But Willem had fired too high. The shot prattled along the corridor— along the floor and the walls.

Kaywana hurried to the table with the two loaded muskets. But three of the invaders had reached the top of the stairway. They rushed the table.

Willem and Aert gasped and ran. Kaywana dashed down the two loaded muskets and picked up the one that Willem had dropped. It still smoked. She hurled it at the first figure rushing at her and the fellow halted, struck across the face. The two others collided with him and there was a confused scrambling. Aert took advantage of this confusion to grab a musket. With it he ran toward the desk, jumped on to the desk, using the musket as he might a pole in pole jump. Willem, who had been about to run into the next room, paused and followed Aert's example. The musket he seized was one of the two newly loaded by his mother just before the table was rushed. Kaywana saw him and shrieked: "Careful, Willem! It's loaded. Don't try to strike them with it. It may explode."

Willem, trembling, darted into the corner where the desk stood and got up on to it. He and Aert stood there in their long white nightshirts panting, the muskets shaking in their grasp.

Kaywana rushed to the door of the next room and tried to shut it after her as she passed through, but the three had recovered by now and were upon her. Then four more came in. One of these was Wakkatai. He shouted: "Leave her to me! Leave Kaywana to me!"

"Aert," quavered Willem, "we must fire. They're going to kill Mother."

Aert was too scared to reply.

Two more came in. They saw the boys.

Aert raised his musket halfway—it was heavy for him—pointed it at them and applied the ignition. There was a roar and flash and both the invaders collapsed, coughing and grunting. Another appeared at the door, then turned and ran. Willem muttered in a stammer: "Good! Load again. The powder and shot are here on the desk." He trembled and kept looking from the door that opened into the corridor to the door that gave into the next room.

In the next room Kaywana was fighting savagely. Once the moonlight struck full on her face, and her eyes glinted with a terrible hate. She struck back at Wakkatai with clenched hands, jumped on to the bed and aimed a kick at his face which landed home. But Wakkatai recovered and pulled her down, began to beat her head with a stone. He spat on her. "This is your day, Kaywana," he panted. "This is your hour."

"Mother, help me! Please! Quick, Mother!"

That was Hendrickje. They had stripped her of her nightgown and were scrambling over her. They had thrown the baby through the window. It lay on the ground outside, a smashed lump. Jan had crawled under the bed, but they pulled him out, battered in his head with a large stone. Now it was Juliana's turn, for she, too, had crawled under the bed.

There was a cool, blue-green patch of moonlight on the bed sheet. The bed sheet was ruffled, and here and there you could see a spot of blood—and in one place a big jagged patch where Jan's head had been battered in.

In the next room Willem's musket banged. Willem had pulled up the table, and Aert had helped him to tilt it over on to its side. With the desk at their backs and the table in front of them like a rampart, they crouched, their muskets resting on the edge of the table. Their bodies shook. Their hair was tousled, their eyes bright and scared. But there was defiance in them both. They had recovered from the first shock of terror. They kept darting their gazes from the outer door to the inner.

Once two figures approached the outer door and Willem's musket exploded, and the figures turned and ran back downstairs yelling. The shot passed over their heads, for Willem's hand trembled too much, and the musket kicked when he applied the ignition. Aert loaded the musket as Willem passed it back, but before he had completed this operation they saw the inner door swing open and two figures come tumbling into the room. Aert squealed and dropped the musket, snatching up his own which was still unfired. Willem began to load hastily. Willem said: "Don't fire, Aert. It's Mother and Wakkatai. You might hit Mother."

Willem and Aert, their muskets pivoting around indecisively on the table edge, watched the struggle between their mother and Wakkatai. Kaywana bled from her nose and from her mouth. The moonlight kept flashing on and off her face. Wakkatai was trying to rape her, but finding himself too weak. She was too furious an animal for him. He grappled with her in vain. She threw him off, pounded his face with her fists, snarled and spat blood and spittle into his face.

"Watch the door," warned Willem. "They might try to come in again from downstairs."

Aert nodded and gulped. He was very white.

Kaywana and Wakkatai broke apart, Wakkatai rolling toward the wall. Kaywana sprang up and rushed to snatch a musket lying on the floor near the bedpost. Wakkatai scrambled up and dived at her.

There was a bang. It was Willem's musket. The butt kicked back and Willem staggered, whimpering and holding his chin as the musket fell from his grasp. Aert coughed from the fumes that hazed the air about them.

Wakkatai had crumpled up and was making gargling sounds, blood oozing from his ears and mouth. He tried to rise but collapsed again. Kaywana brought down the musket she had snatched up and it landed with a crunching thump on his back and neck. He grunted and lay still. She continued to belabor him.

Two figures leapt out of the next room and brought her down. They began to pummel her head with a stone.

Aert trained his musket shakily. Willem clutched his arm and said: "Don't, Aert. Don't fire. You'll hit Mother."

"But they're killing her with that stone. They're killing her."

"Fire, then. Fire!"

The musket flashed and thundered.

One of their mother's attackers staggered off, clutching his face.

A voice shouted up from downstairs: "Who is doing that firing? Kaywana! What are you up to?"

Willem threw down the musket he was loading and made a rush for the outer door. "Father! Quick! Come up here. They're killing Mother. They're fighting us." He broke into sobs.

Aert saw three figures appear at the inner door and applied the ignition to the musket he had just loaded. Following the roar one man fell doubled up, a hand pressed to his stomach. The two others dashed to the window and jumped through with yells.

His father and two soldiers came in, followed by Willem. Adriansen was carrying a lantern. Willem sobbed: "Look, Father! Look! They've killed Mother."

Aert darted from behind the table. "Wakkatai! We got him, Father. I killed him. No, it was Willem. Willem fired on him—and Mother finished him off." He began to blubber uncontrollably.

One of the soldiers was examining Kaywana. "She's dead," he said.

"It's those others who killed her," blubbered Aert. "They came in from the next room. Wakkatai didn't kill her. Mother beat him—and Willem killed him."

"I put a shot in him," said Willem. "The beast. I'm glad. Glad."

The moonlight shone in upon their nightshirts. In the southeast and south lightning flashed, but no thunder came. The river kept whispering all the while, hushed and monotonous.

‖ The Family

I

THE Indians, this morning, were saying that today he would die. They were grieved. "Our good Commandeur," they said, "will not see the sun go down today. The spirits of the river are calling him."

The surgeon of the fort felt, too, that he would not last out the day. "We'd better send and tell his son to come at once," said the surgeon.

So a message was sent to Willem and his family on their plantation up the Mazaruni, telling them that Commandeur Adriansen van Groenwegel was dying.

When Willem and Griselda and their two sons and daughter arrived, they found that Adriansen was still aware of the scene around him. White-haired, his face wrinkled and cracked like old leather, in this his eighty-third year, he lay on the wide bed, the fire gone from his grey eyes. His breathing, though weak and labored, was regular, and there was still enough energy in him for him to turn his head slightly and look at them.

A soft moan came from him as he looked at Willem—Willem who at forty-six stood by the bed, brown-bearded and dignified, stocky and serious of face, a man of many voyages and many experiences. Beside him, his wife had an ineffectual air—nervous and uneasy, dabbing frequently at her Germanic blue eyes or putting up her hand to touch her yellow hair which, before leaving home, she had plaited and piled rather hastily on her head.

The three children stood stiffly at the foot of the bed. They had an awed air, for this was the first time they had found themselves in the presence of a dying human.

Reinald, at eighteen, was tall and physically not unlike what the dying man had been fifty years ago. But the curve of his mouth was weak, and his blue eyes were the dreamy, nervous eyes of his mother and his maternal grandfather who had been an artist-musician in Hamburg. It was in Hamburg that Willem had met and married Griselda.

Laurens, at fourteen, had something of his father's strong, stocky solidity, and his eyes were gray. Alert, too—like Susannah's. Susannah was sixteen; she stood between her brothers, pale and uneasy like her mother whom she resembled in everything except her hair, which was a fiery red. "My Great-uncle Friedrich had red hair," Griselda had said. "It must be he whom she has taken after."

Adriansen was saying something. Willem bent quickly.

"I remember you, Willem . . . that night . . . terrible night, son. In your nightshirt . . . your mother . . . the Indians . . . the muskets. . . ."

Willem nodded and made a deep sound. He remembered. Remembered so clearly it might have happened yesterday.

Griselda began to squeeze her fingers and rub her palms together. She dabbed hastily at her eyes.

Laurens' gaze had strayed out of the window. He saw the river, choppy and shimmering in the bright mid-morning sunshine—the river his grandmother, Kaywana, had heard whispering in hushed monotony on many a night when she lay alone in the big four-poster in a room in the old house on the mainland.

A soft land breeze came in. It smelt of the jungle, chilly and with a suggestion of old leaves in it. A suggestion of wild flowers, too—perhaps the large purplish ones on the mainland that bloomed on the tangled vines which covered the patch of earth under which the bones of Kaywana and her children lay: Hendrickje and Juliana and Jan and the baby.

Adriansen was speaking again. Willem bent his head.

This time, however, the words were only a blurred mumble and not intelligible. The old man's eyes had a hazed look, and after a while a slight quiver went through the long, slim frame.

An hour later the guns of the fort began to boom.

"He was a good man," Griselda sobbed. "He was like a father to me. My own father could not have treated me more affectionately. He was a fine, upright man. And the Indians loved him. This colony will never have another like him."

Willem ignored her. He had just finished writing two letters, one to Aert at the Pomeroon fort—Aert was Captain of the troops there—and one to August in Berbice; August was the manager of one of the van Peere plantations near Fort Nassau, fifty-five miles up the Berbice River.

Willem sat for nearly half an hour staring out of the window into the fading afternoon. He stared across the river at the mainland, a somber expression on his face. He kept pulling pensively at his well-trimmed brown beard.

The old house was still standing on the west bank of the river, though only the Indian caretaker and his wife and child lived in it now. It had been repaired several times during the past thirty-odd years, but in this year, 1664, it did not look any different, especially viewed from the island here. The clearing in which it stood seemed more bushy and weed-grown, and there were high shrubs and ferns at the water's edge. No shrubs and ferns had been there that night when the *corials* had drawn up and those naked figures had sprung ashore and swarmed toward the house . . . . And that vine he could make out running up the southern wall, that had not been there on the night when he and Aert and Hendrickje had stood at the window watching the fire at Cartabo. It was a hardy vine. Aert, he recalled, had planted it—eleven years after the Event. He had planted it to celebrate his twentieth birthday, the romantic fool!

"I'm tired of being an overseer on this plantation of Father's," he had said. "The Indians say that this vine should grow from the seed and bloom within three months. If three months pass and it hasn't bloomed I'll go to sea with you in November."

"And if it blooms before three months?"

"In that case, I'll ask Father to let me go to Hol-

land and train for the Army. With Father's influence
I'm sure I can get a commission."

Ten weeks after planting the seed the vine had
bloomed, so Aert had gone to Holland to train for the
Army. Sometimes Willem wondered what would have
happened to him if the vine had taken longer than three
months to bloom. Aert might not have been such a
success as a seaman. He was too imaginative and un-
practical. The Pomeroon fort was the right place for
him. As Captain of the troops there he had all the
time he wanted to read and dream and collect rare
insects and make notes on them.

The sea suited me, though, Willem told himself,
because I am something like what Mother must have
been—a person of action. According to what Father
told Aert and me, she was so bold she stopped him
the first day he arrived in the colony and said she
wanted him. That's one thing I'll miss the old man for:
his tales of the old days. He certainly lived, by God!
And he got things done: all these settlers he induced
the Directors of the West India Company to permit
to come into the colony. Dutchmen from Tobago,
and these Jews from Brazil who have planted themselves in the Pomeroon and on the Barima. And the
negro slaves from Africa, and all the sugar and indigo
we're producing now. Yes, the old man has done
some good for this place. And all in seven years. If
he had been Commandeur before 1657, when he did
agree to accept the post, things might have been better
even. The colony will miss him——

"Willem."

"Yes?"

"Did Father ever tell you about the thirty Indians
who caused the trouble that time long ago? Were they
brought back from Barbados?"

"Yes—after a lot of troublesome negotiations with
the English."

She sighed. "He was a great man, Willem. The
Indians are very grieved. I hear they are going to hold
a funeral festival tonight. Heavens! But those children
are still over on the mainland. They said they were
going across to see the old house."

"And what of it?"

"It's time they returned. You're so sharp with me nowadays, Willem. I can't say a word but you have to fly at me."

He snorted and rose. "You're too emotional, Griselda. Hysterical. I can't tolerate that sort of thing. And Susannah is copying you. Even Reinald shows signs of it at times." He paced about the room, frowning heavily. "What you seem to forget is that we have a name to uphold. We can't be soft. Father always impressed upon us that this is a hard world, and it calls for hard men if it's to be mastered. Since we were married and came to live in this colony our years have been spent in smooth and sheltered security. We've lacked nothing. The plantation we own, thanks to Father's position in the colony, is well supplied with slaves and couldn't be in a more flourishing condition. Life is easy for us—too easy, I think sometimes, Griselda. Our children have grown up in pampered comfort. They know nothing of the dangers and alarms of my early boyhood——"

"Oh, please don't talk about that again, Willem. I can't stand hearing tales of bloodshed."

"You must thank Providence you live in peaceful times."

"I am thankful. I've never denied that we live a comfortable life."

"So comfortable that you're encouraging our children to be soft, spineless weaklings. Pampered puppies. They have no blood—no steel in their marrow. Before I met you I had no genteel life. I tumbled all over the world, from port to port. I've seen men at their best and their worst."

"Willem, you've said these things so many times before——"

"And still it's had no beneficial effect on you." He shook his head in a distracted manner, stopped pacing and glared at her. "Let me tell you this, Griselda. Now that that old man, my father, is dead it falls to us, his successors, to see that his name goes on—and goes on with honor. And I'm not being merely heroic. I mean it."

"But why should we fuss over the family name? Does it matter as much as that? Why, Father was not even married to your mother, Willem. You're not legitimately entitled to the name——"

"I know that very well. You don't have to drum that into me. But that circumstance is a mere quibble. What's the law? Or what does the ecclesiastical side of things matter?" He hammered his fist into his palm. "It's blood that counts, Griselda. Blood. Men can say we're van Groenwegels with the bar sinister. Let them say it. Not a mortal can drain the blood of that old man from my veins—or the veins of my children. What was in my father is in me and in mine. Ha! And my mother! Who can take her blood from me? Who can rob me of the fire she put into me? My mother was a fighter. Do you know what it is to have a mother who can stand up with her sons and fight to the death? You think that a small thing, Griselda?" He was deeply moved. His head shook, and a low guttural sound came from him. "Two sons of ten and nine— against that horde of fiends. And she stood up and made us fight. Yes, that was no small thing."

Griselda watched him with a resigned air.

"I'm proud of my mother." He pulled at his beard. "I venerate her memory." He was silent, as though his spirit were in the past reliving the events of his early boyhood. He flashed her a look suddenly and said: "Our name must go on, Griselda. The name van Groenwegel must never be forgotten in this colony. It must go down the centuries with honor and glory. We come of tough stock. Fighter stock. There must be no softening up—no pampering. We must keep hard. We must stamp down the obstacles of this world."

"*Mein Gott!* How you do work yourself up, Willem! And yet you accuse me of being sentimental and emotional."

"I'll have my say. My two boys are all we have to see that the name does not perish. Aert at Pomeroon— a bachelor! Captain of the troops! A bookworm. A dreamer. An insect collector. A naturalist. What's he doing to help us carry on the name? Father offered him a plantation—just as he offered me. He refused it. He wasn't interested in property, he said. The management of a plantation would have been too boring for him. So he's a Captain of the troops. In Berbice there's August. He's not a van Groenwegel, it's true, but he adopted the name—and he's got Mother's blood in him. Fireblood. But what's he doing? Managing a plantation for the van Peere company. Stagnating there and debauching the black slave women—producing a host of mulatto bastards. If I'm not mistaken, Blair bought two of them in a deal last month. Young olive-skinned brats about twelve or thirteen——"

"Is it a fact, Willem? Those two little girls Set Blair bought are August's children?"

"Of course they are. I heard it on good authority. Katrina and Hannah, I think their names are." He snorted, but the fury left him at once. He stopped pacing, and his face looked composed. He shrugged and said: "Anyway, that's the situation—and we can't do anything about it. But our own children must not be pampered." He laughed and approached her, patted her head. "You're too soft, Griselda. That father of yours, eh?" He fondled her under the chin, and she smiled and began to stroke his wrist. "A painter and musician. You'd like one of our boys to take up painting, I suppose, wouldn't you? Eh? Wouldn't you?" He pulled playfully at her plaits.

"I can't see any of them being painters," she said. "Reinald has said already he wants to study medicine—and he's so brilliant at his studies. Mynheer Queseda is always complimenting him."

"Medicine is a good thing—an honorable profession. I'll certainly encourage him in such an undertaking if he's set on it. In another two or three years we'll see." He grunted good-humoredly.

On the mainland, Reinald, as it happened, was saying to the Indian caretaker: "When I'm a doctor I'm going to make a study of these herbs and shrubs that grow wild about here. I'm sure they must contain many valuable curative properties."

Laurens and Susannah had taken off their clothes and were swimming in the river.

"What's your name, by the way, my man?" asked Reinald.

"Teekai."

"I see. Have you been here a long time?"

"Years and years, Mynheer. Your grandfather put me here to keep the house good when they made him Commandeur and he went to live in the big house on the island over there. I knew your grandfather since your grandmother Kaywana lived in this house." He smiled, revealing two yellow teeth. He was thin and wrinkled.

"You knew Grandmother, then?"

"Yes, Mynheer Reinald. I came the night to warn her and the big *baas,* your grandfather, that trouble had started at Cartabo."

"Oh, it was you, was it? How interesting!" Reinald made clicking sounds with his tongue and flicked a fiber of silk cotton fastidiously from his coat. Fibers of silk cotton from a tree near by were drifting on the air. "I must make a note of that when I get home. Teekai, isn't that your name? H'm. Imagine living in such exciting times." He fell into a thoughtful silence.

In the river Susannah squealed: "Laurens. I'm certain a fish snapped at me. Do you think it could be a *perai?*"

"Nonsense! You must have imagined it," said Laurens. "The water here is too muddy and saltish. *Perai* only live in pure fresh water."

"Mother would die if she could see us bathing here."

"Mother is soft. Father is right. She tries to pamper us too much. I'm not going to be pampered. I've got to be tough. I'm going to sea like Father. As soon as I'm nineteen I'm off."

"But the sea is dangerous. You might get shipwrecked in a storm."

"Father was shipwrecked twice and he lived, didn't he?"

"You can go if you like. I'm going to marry and have a big house and ten children on a big plantation."

"You're a girl. That's what you ought to do."

They saw Reinald waving at them and heard him

call out: "It's getting late, Laurens! Susannah! Come in and get dressed and let's be going."

"Ten minutes more!" Laurens called back, diving.

Susannah swam in and clambered ashore.

Reinald frowned: "You have no modesty. Naked like this, with the caretaker and his family in the house there!"

"He's an old man. He won't mind," she giggled. "You behave like an old man yourself."

"I have a sense of propriety, if that's what you mean. Haven't you heard what Mynheer Queseda said? He said propriety is the essence of gentility, and gentility is the salt of civilization."

He got into the skiff and sat waiting in moody silence.

II

Early one morning, a few months later, Laurens and Susannah, who had gone boating downriver, came home with the news that England had declared war on Holland. Willem exclaimed loudly and demanded to know where they had heard it.

"We met the Blankenburgs," Laurens said. "They went down to Kyk-over-al yesterday to a slave sale."

"Heinz has a cold," said Susannah. "His nose was red."

"But this is serious—if it's true," Willem frowned. "War, eh?" He pulled at his beard. "Yes, there was rumor of it last week. Captain Haas of the *Middleburg* did drop a hint, I remember now."

"Any likelihood of our being attacked here, Father?"

"Not much—though you never know. These English are a queer lot."

"They're very belligerent," said Reinald. "I wouldn't be surprised if we were attacked. Suriname isn't so far off—or Barbados." He frowned and added: "Mynheer Queseda says he had an ancestor who fought in the battle of the Spanish Armada in 1588.

He was cast up on the coast of Holland. That's how the family name started."

"I wouldn't mind if they attacked us," said Susannah. "I'd fight. I can fire a musket. Remember the other day, Laurens, over at the Blairs?"

Willem gave her a hug. "You think you'd want to stand up to them, daughter?"

"Of course I would."

"I wonder." His face went troubled. "It would be good to know that a daughter of mine stood up and fought." He gave her a moody look. "Grandmother stood up and fought. But you—puh! You're your mother over again, Susannah. I doubt whether you've got the blood of your grandmother. You'd get hysterical at the first shot."

"I wouldn't. I'd fight."

"Get off. Get off. You'd run." He guffawed and pushed her from him.

Laurens agreed. "You're right, Father. She'd run at the first sound of the enemy. She and Mother would bolt like that horse the Bakkers have. You only have to hiss at it and it's gone like a breeze."

"Anyway," said Willem, "I'm laying in a good store of ammunition against eventualities. I think we have enough muskets already. Father stocked us with a good many from the fort during that scare of a raid from Venezuela when you were younger. It never came to anything, but Father let us keep the muskets."

"They're in those boxes in the Number Three Loft," said Laurens. "I had a peep at them one day."

"You had no right to go in there," frowned Griselda.

"Father, can I practice after lessons today?"

"Nothing of the kind!" said Griselda. "You are far too young to handle a musket alone. They are heavy things and dangerous."

"Aha," grunted Willem. "See how you try to soften them up, Griselda! Why shouldn't he handle a musket! He's entered his sixteenth year. Aert and I handled muskets when we were eight, nine, ten. Father encouraged us to use them—and they were far clumsier things in those days. We had no flintlocks then."

Griselda sighed. "Very well, Willem. If you think he should go in for musket practice, let him. I was only speaking for his good."

Willem laughed. "Ah! Mother is hurt." He moved over to her and gripped her shoulders, shook her playfully, winking over her head at Laurens. "Very well, Laurens, my boy, I'll come with you when your lessons are over. Don't dare touch any of those muskets until I give the word. Reinald, you, too, will come with us." He nudged Griselda. "That satisfy you now, Mother?"

Reinald frowned: "Father, I have to put in some extra work on my Latin, I'm afraid. I don't think it will be convenient for me."

"Latin! To the devil with Latin!" barked his father. "Our country is at war with England. Latin must come last."

"But do you think any invaders could hope to get past the fort at Kyk-over-al? Why is it necessary for us to indulge in musket practice?"

"I won't argue with you. I have spoken. After lessons this morning you will join Laurens and myself in musket practice in the fields."

"Father, may I come, too?" asked Susannah.

"Yes, come if you wish. By all means come, my girl."

Willem left the room, frowning and muttering to himself.

About three weeks later the letter came from the van Peeres' general superintendent telling them of the death of August. "He expired," said the general superintendent, "after an illness lasting four days. He contracted a very dangerous fever not uncommon in these parts. It was accompanied with black vomit, and he was delirious on the last two days.

"I was present at his death, and am grieved to say that it was most disturbing as there was raging at the time a violent thunderstorm. A few minutes before he breathed his last a mango tree not very far from the house—a tree imported from the Eastern countries and planted by our Mynheer van Peere himself—was cut in two by the lightning, and the few slaves in the room cried out and chanted a foreign dirge which I suspect must be African in origin, though there were several words of Dutch to be heard in between. They were frightened, and one of them muttered audibly that this storm was with a purpose. The spirits of the sky were angry with their master for his cruelty toward them (you will bear in mind that I repeat what I overheard). I fear that your relative was not a man of great kindliness. On the contrary, he treated his slaves with extreme cruelty, and was very much hated by them. However, for myself, I found him an excellent companion, and care nothing for slave gossip or slave sentiments. We shall mourn his loss, for he was popular among the planters and all Christians in this small colony. Whatever his failings, he was a man of great conviviality, and entertained his friends in lavish manner at all times. . . ."

"His style," commented Reinald, "is not without distinction."

"Who cares about style!" snapped Willem. "I think he gives a very good picture of the kind of man your Uncle August was. Yes, August, I fear, was always inclined to cruelty. Father hinted at it quite often. There was some occasion when Mother killed an Indian girl with a poisoned dart. Father called it murder, but Mother thought it perfectly just an act— and August agreed with her. He spoke up in the cause of murder."

"He was a barbarian," murmured Reinald, frowning. "Anyone who condones murder and violence is a barbarian. Violence is the cornerstone of barbarism, Mynheer Queseda says——"

"Bah! You and your Mynheer Queseda! You can only repeat what Mynheer Queseda says. You don't seem to have two original ideas in your head."

"Mynheer Queseda, nevertheless, considers me brilliant," said Reinald coldly. "At least, I pay some attention to my studies, which is more than Laurens and Susannah can say. Susannah's Greek is hopeless."

Willem shook with soft laughter. "What I know is that she's an attractive little witch, and in a woman that's what matters most. You don't need to be good at Greek to be a successful wife. Bakker's boy is pining himself into a stick over her. And that nephew of the Andersens, too. She won't die without a husband, that's one thing I'm sure of!"

"She lacks modesty," frowned Reinald. "She bathes naked in the little creek aback of the cotton fields. Perhaps that is her conception of being a lady, but it isn't mine."

"She goes there with her brother, so what does it matter? You're too stiff, boy. A gloomy prig. And at your age! Why don't you shake yourself and forget your dusty books sometimes?"

Reinald left the room, his brows heavily wrinkled.

Outside, the sunshine made dappled shadows on the ground under the sandbox trees, and there were sackies and kiskadees cheeping in the big saman tree near the outhouses. Far off, in the fields, a monotonous wailing chant could be heard—the chant of the negro slaves as they worked in the heat.

Laurens and Susannah were out on a ramble in the bush with the two Bakker boys and a Blair girl. They were setting traps for tapirs and agoutis. As this was Saturday afternoon, there were no lessons, though Mynheer Queseda had wanted Laurens to stay at home to complete a piece of Latin translation which Laurens had done very badly the day before. The Bakker and Blair children came to Willem's house for their tutoring, for it was at Willem's house that Mynheer Queseda resided. He had been with them for over eleven years; Willem, through his father's influence, had had him brought out from Amsterdam.

"I don't believe he's ever kissed a girl," Susannah said, with a giggle, as they moved along an Indian track that led through tall mora saplings. "Yesterday Laurens met him in the garden and asked him if he had a sweetheart in Amsterdam and he blushed and shook his head. He said he had no lady friends at all. His mother and sister are the only two females he is on intimate terms with."

"Laurens had pluck to ask him that," said Karl Bakker.

"He only did it because I dared him," said Susannah. "He's shy of girls himself. I know the one he's in love with, but I won't say."

Laurens growled: "You're talking foolishness."

"I know the girl, too," said Hendrik. "He wrote her name on the margin of his copybook yesterday when he thought I wasn't looking."

Laurens laughed. "You're off the track, Hendrik. The name I wrote yesterday on my copybook was Ariadne, the girl in the story about Theseus and the Minotaur."

"But there's a girl down-river called Ariadne Pieters."

"That's not the one," said Susannah. "If you guessed the whole day you wouldn't hit on it, Hendrik."

That evening, when they were alone, Laurens said to his sister: "You should never have said what you did about my being in love. Who told you I was in love with any girl?"

She smiled: "I have eyes in my head. I see things when you think I'm not seeing. It's one of those two slave girls the Blairs have. The ones who are supposed to be Uncle August's children. Isn't it one of them? Admit it, Laurens."

"Of course it isn't," he said, but his manner was such that she knew she was right.

"You needn't have any fear. I won't say a word. Which one is it, Laurens? Tell me. I'll keep it a secret. I promise."

"I don't know what you're talking about."

"But what's there to be shy about in that? They're only slaves. There's nothing in a man going to one of the slave women. Kurt Andersen goes to his father's slave women. So his sister says. She says she's seen him herself going into the women's quarters."

"Whenever," he said, "I go to a woman it'll be because I'm in love with her. I can't do it in cold blood as Kurt and some of the others I've heard about."

"That's because you're shy."

"It isn't that."

That evening he was in a thoughtful mood, hardly

saying a word. It was only when, at table, his father happened to bring up the subject of August's death that Laurens became alert and interested. He asked: "How old was he, Father?"

"About fifty-one, I should say," said Willem, after a frowning calculation. "I was six years old when he was eleven. About the time of the Spanish raid in '24 that would be."

"He never got married, did he?"

"No. But I understand his children are all over the colony there."

Susannah said: "Why don't you buy those two girls from the Blairs, Father? Hannah and Katrina. They're our half cousins, aren't they?"

Willem snorted. "Who told you that? I suppose you've been gossiping with her, Griselda. Tchah! You women and your tongues!"

Griselda shrugged. "I saw no harm in her being told, Willem. It's the truth, isn't it? You told me yourself."

"I know I did, but we don't want such tales broadcast over the country. It won't do the family name any good."

"You and this family name!"

He was on the point of exploding when Laurens asked: "Were their mothers pure negresses, Father?"

Willem gave him a look of surprise. "What! Their mothers! I don't know. I'm not interested in them. They're slaves. So far as I'm concerned, they have no connection with us whatever—and I hope that will be clearly understood by everyone in this house. Don't let me hear you ever referring to them as your half cousins."

Susannah said: "I'm sure Katrina's mother must have been a mulatto. Katrina is fair and has lovely wavy brown hair. She must be a quadroon. But Hannah looks as if she's half and half. Her hair is very curly, and she has an olive complexion."

Willem opened his eyes at her. "Well! And who asked you for descriptions of them, Susannah?"

Susannah giggled.

Laurens' gaze was lowered.

"Let this be the last time I hear them discussed in this house," said Willem. "They're not your equals. Remember they're slaves——" He broke off and coughed, for Mynheer Queseda was coming down the stairs. He was always late for meals.

In this abrupt manner the subject was dropped. Susannah, however, brought it up again on several occasions when she was alone with Laurens. One day, when she and her brother were at the Blairs, she even made an opportunity to speak to Hannah when Hannah was engaged in sweeping the portico. Susannah left the others in the dining room on the pretext of going into the garden to pick flowers for the vase on the sideboard. Mevrouw Blair had remarked casually that she wanted some limonia and ferns for the vase, and Susannah offered to go and gather some.

Hannah was not very pretty. She had inherited her black mother's broad features. But her eyes were blue-green—like Kaywana's—and she had a quick, bold smile.

"You're very busy, Hannah," said Susannah.

"Yes, missy," said Hannah, her manner in no way shy or subservient.

"Do you prefer being with Massa Blair, or did you like it better on the Berbice?"

"I like it better here, missy. Massa Blair treats me good, and Missy Blair, too."

"Do you remember your mother?"

"Yes."

"She was black, wasn't she?"

"Yes. She was black slave, like me."

"But you're not black. Your father was white —at least, three-quarters white and a quarter Indian. Like my father."

Hannah hung her head. "Yes, missy, my mother told me that once, but she said I'm same as any other black slave."

"Did you know who your father was?"

"Yes. He was Manager."

"Yes, but I mean his name," said Susannah impatiently. "No one ever told you his name?"

"Yes. His name was Massa August van Groenwegel."

"You know that, then. That happens to be my name, too—van Groenwegel. Did anyone tell you that we are half cousins?"

"I heard so."

"You and Katrina are half sisters, aren't you?"

"Yes."

"Her mother wasn't black, though. She was a mulatto, wasn't she?"

"Her mother was half black and half white."

"Yes, I thought so. I was right." Susannah regarded her critically, as she might have regarded a tapir or an agouti that one of the boys had trapped. "You're not so pretty, but you have a good figure. The black blood is plain for anyone to see. Your lips are thick and your nose is wide. Katrina is much better. She has good features—European features— and she's fair in complexion. She can almost be taken for pure white."

"Yes."

"Say 'Yes, missy' to me. Don't forget yourself. You are a slave. Both you and Katrina."

"Yes, missy," said Hannah, but there was resentment in her manner.

"Very well. Go on sweeping," said Susannah, and moved on down the steps out into the garden.

She and Laurens were spending the day with the Blairs—the two families were very intimate—and it was not until they were returning home that she had an opportunity to tell him of her encounter with Hannah.

He was dismayed. "But what made you speak to her? Why did you have to ask her all those questions?"

"Because I was curious. Laurens, I believe it's she you're in love with."

"You're a fool," he said, his face very red.

III

One noon, about a year later—in the year 1666, two years after Adriansen had been chanted and wailed into the care of the spirits of the earth and the jungle by his friends, the Indians—a rumor came up the Mazaruni.

The children were at lessons with Mynheer Queseda in the dining room.

Karl and Hendrik Bakker sat on one side of the table with Laurens and Dorothea Blair, and on the other side sat Reinald and Susannah and Woglinde and Hermina Blair. Mynheer Queseda was at the head of the table—Willem's place when they were dining.

In the middle of the Greek lesson Griselda came in and said: "Mynheer Queseda! Children! I'm sorry to interrupt, but a very serious rumor has just come from Kyk-over-al. It's said that the English from Barbados have invaded the colony."

Books were set aside with a rustle and thump.

"Where have they invaded?" asked Laurens.

"I knew they would have come from Barbados," said Karl Bakker.

"You never said Barbados, Karl," said Woglinde. "You said Suriname."

"I didn't."

Hendrik Bakker said: "I'm sure it isn't Barbados they've come from. It's Suriname. They must have come by the jungle over the Corentyne."

"An invasion is only possible by sea," ruled Reinald loftily. He asked his mother: "Mother, have you heard exactly what part of the coast they have landed on?"

"They say the Pomeroon settlements have been wiped out, but there are no details. Your father is at Kyk-over-al. When he comes back he'll tell us what the position is."

"Oh, they can't take Kyk-over-al. Kyk-over-al is too strong."

"Yes, Kyk-over-al is invincible."

"Let us hope so," said Griselda, in a very worried voice. "It would be terrible, terrible. It would mean the end of the colony."

"Don't get hysterical, Mother," said Laurens. "The rumor may be false."

"I can use a musket, anyway," Susannah said excitedly. "And Father is keen on having me fight. He likes to think I have Grandmother's spirit."

Reinald gave her a look of reproach. He disapproved of family sentiments being discussed before outsiders.

Willem, when he came in, two or three hours later, confirmed the rumor. "The Pomeroon settlements," he told them, "have been destroyed."

"What of Uncle Aert?"

"I have heard nothing of him, but I won't be surprised to learn that he has been killed. The fort there was badly garrisoned—and Aert was never intended to be a soldier. He was only good at collecting insects."

"Who is leading the raid?" Reinald asked.

"One Major John Scott. He's from Barbados, and he's got a large force of Caribs under his command."

Griselda asked anxiously: "Willem, do you think Kyk-over-al can withstand an attack?"

"Couldn't say. In Father's time it would have, you may be sure. They wouldn't have done anything against Kyk-over-al if the old man had been in command. But with this new fellow there I won't be too confident."

"Willem, do you say this—I mean, is it just family snobbery that makes you feel the fort isn't as strong now as it was in Father's time, or do you honestly think it's weak?"

He nudged her playfully. "Always taking me to task over this family pride, eh? No, it isn't snobbery. It's my personal opinion the fort won't be able to stand up to a determined assault. I may prove wrong, of course. I'm not God, and everything in war is uncertain."

"I believe your fears are unfounded, Father," Reinald said. "The fort is strong. I doubt whether this Major Scott would dare launch an attack. That island is in a most strategic position. This Englishman and his Caribs will probably go on to Berbice. I've just been discussing the situation with Mynheer Queseda, and he agrees with me."

Willem shrugged. "Your views and Mynheer Queseda's don't impress me. I'm going ahead and preparing for an attack." His eyes flashed round from one to the other of them. "We're defending. I hope you all understand that clearly. We're not running. No van Groenwegel must ever run from an enemy. We stay and fight."

"But what could we do against a horde of Caribs, Willem! How could we hope to defend this house against them!"

"We'll do it," he said, his voice purposeful. He made a growling sound, his brows lowered, his beard jutting forward aggressively.

The Bakker boys and the Blair girls had gone home, and Mynheer Queseda was upstairs in his room. Only the five of them were present in the dining room.

"If we have to go down," said Willem quietly, "we'll go down. If we have to perish we'll perish fighting. It must never be said afterwards that the van Groenwegels were among those who fled when the English came to Essequibo in the year 1666. We must be different. We must show we have something that everybody hasn't got."

Reinald shifted his feet about and said: "Yet, Father, I think prudence should come before this—this fanatical family pride of yours. Remember how we have been brought up. We're of gentle breeding. We haven't lived in the troublous times that you knew in your boyhood."

His father did not explode as he might have done on another occasion. He nodded and said, his manner as quiet as before: "That's a good argument, boy. I'm aware of what you say. I'm no unreasonable fool, Reinald. I have many faults. I'm hasty, moody,

and I daresay I'm not a quarter as learned as you
are. I'm just a rough seaman. But I can say this
again, I'm not a fool. I've tumbled all over the world,
and I've seen a great deal of people and life. I can
sum up a situation far better than you might imagine.
I know how soft you children are. You've had life
easy—too easy. But as I often tell your mother, I'm
determined that our family must keep hard. It isn't
too late. Perhaps this attack, if it does materialize,
will be a blessing for you. It may help to wake you
up to the harsh realities of this world. Stiffen you up.
Life isn't all books and friendly visiting between
planters and their families. There is ugliness that you
don't dream of. It will do you good to see some of
this ugliness. Balance your outlooks." He began to
hammer his fist slowly into the palm of his hand.
"No. We're not running. We're going to face up to
whatever physical dangers we encounter. Get that
firmly fixed into your soft heads. We're fighting. We're
van Groenwegels. Your grandmother was Kaywana.
Fire-blood. Fighter-blood."

He turned abruptly and began to walk toward
the stairs. Stopped as abruptly and looked around at
them. "None of you will leave the precincts of this
house without my permission—from this minute. Not
even over to the Bakkers or the Blairs. I want you
to be within a moment's call of the house."

IV

Two days later the news came from downriver. The
English had entered the Essequibo and were engaging
the fort at Kyk-over-al.

The Bakkers and Blairs had come to lessons as
usual. Karl Bakker said: "We're not making any
preparations like these. Father feels certain there
won't be any danger up here."

Woglinde Blair said: "Father, too, is sure Kyk-
over-al can keep them back. We're doing nothing
about it."

Mynheer Queseda, with a quick glance about

the room to make sure that Willem was not within
earshot, said in a conspiratorial voice: "My children,
there is no need for alarm. That English officer and
his rabble of Indians could not get past a well-forti-
fied place like the island downriver. Kyk-over-al is
strong. I am confident that they will be beaten back,
and with serious losses, too."

They could hear the boom of guns downriver.
The field slaves had come in and were out in the yard
jabbering in scared voices. Willem was instructing
them in the use of the musket. The big barn, like
the house, had been barricaded. Tables and heavy
furniture had been pushed before the windows. Powder kegs and sacks of shot lay ready in corners, and
muskets were in view everywhere.

Eventually, Mynheer Queseda wagged his head
and said: "Under present circumstances, children, I
fear we can do little work. We shall have to leave
off here for the day."

"I agree heartily, Mynheer," said Laurens, clos-
ing his Virgil with a snap. "Susannah, let's go down
to the river. We might hear some news from a passing
boat."

The Blairs accompanied them, the Bakker boys
overtaking them shortly after. The morning was inclined to be drizzly, but now and then the sun shone
through the huge shifty wads of clouds that kept
drifting from the east. *Corials* with Indians passed
frequently on the river, heading upstream: getting
away from Kyk-over-al. One *corial* told Laurens and
the others: "English guns big. Fort can't hold out
against them." Another said: "English can't pass fort,
but better to make safe and go higher up."

"Personally, I'm sure we're safe up here," said
Karl Bakker. "They can't do anything against the
fort."

"Father feels it's better to be prepared," Susannah told him, "and I think he's right. I don't see
why we should risk everything on the fort. Your people are making a mistake, Karl."

Shortly after noon Mynheer Bakker and Mynheer Blair called on Willem. The Bakker and Blair

plantations were lower down the river, the Bakkers on the same bank, the Blairs on the opposite.

Mynheer Blair said: "I don't think all this fuss is necessary, Willem. From the reports I've heard the fort is standing up well to the attack. They can't get past there easily."

"And even if they did get past," said Mynheer Bakker, "we couldn't hope to do anything against them. It would mean taking our families into the backlands—or higher up the river."

"Why? Haven't you muskets and an ample supply of ammunition?"

"Certainly. But we're not soldiers, Willem. How could we hold out against a horde of Caribs led by this Englishman?"

Willem's beard came out. "That's just the point, Set. I feel we *can* hold out. It's this taking our families into the backlands or upriver that I won't countenance. We won't run. We van Groenwegels stay and fight. That is my decision, and I don't care if I seem a heroic fool."

Mynheer Blair smiled: "We can admire your spirit, Willem, but we have to be practical. We have to put the safety of our families first. Are you going to depend upon these slaves to defend your house? They're trembling already as it is. What's going to happen if it did come to a point of fighting?"

"I'll shake them up," Willem said. "I'll make them fight. They're out in the fields now practicing with Laurens and my girl. They'll do it. I'll make them do it."

After Mynheers Blair and Bakker had departed, Griselda said to her husband: "We'll be the laughing stock of the colony if no attack comes. These grand preparations. I can't see the necessity, Willem. If Kyk-over-al falls we'd have to flee. We couldn't stay here. You know we couldn't."

"Do I?" He gave a short laugh and walked off. He went out on to the back veranda and began to pace slowly, listening to the reports of the muskets in the fields and the dull boom-boom downriver. Slight doubt attacked him. He asked himself if perhaps the others weren't right—Bakker and Blair and Griselda. Should he jeopardize the safety of his family like this? Those Caribs under Scott must be a ruthless pack of cutthroats. Not necessarily well trained, but effective. If the defense failed, the result wouldn't be pleasant. They would rape and murder without the slightest qualm. This was a big thing he was taking on. But, by God, hadn't his mother done a big thing when she put Aert and himself before that table with loaded muskets? She must have realized the hazards. It must have occurred to her that night that she could have fled from the house with them into the bush or into the plantation. But no. She had stayed and fought it out.

He clenched his hands. "I'll do it," he muttered. "It's a big thing, but I'll do it."

It suddenly occurred to him that the guns had ceased firing downriver. Reinald came out to him and said: "Father, the guns have stopped."

Willem nodded. "Take the *corial* and go down to the Bakkers. See if you can get some news."

Reinald was off at once, a look of concern on his face.

Griselda came out on to the veranda with a nervy flutter. "Willem, what's happened down at the fort? I don't hear the cannon any more."

"I'm not God," he snapped. Then he patted her shoulder and said soothingly: "Don't trouble yourself, my dear. I've sent off Reinald to see if he can get some news. Perhaps the attack has been beaten off."

"You think so? Oh, heavens, Willem, I do wish it's true. It would be terrible if the fort has fallen. It would mean the end of the colony."

"Don't get hysterical. Let's wait and hear the news before bemoaning the fate of the colony." He kept glancing anxiously toward the river. The sun had gone permanently behind a heavy bank of clouds and the afternoon was still and sultry.

They heard Laurens and Susannah coming. Susannah's voice was shrill and excited. Behind them, when they appeared in the compound, trailed some of the slaves who had been practicing with them in the fields.

Laurens' eyes were bright. "Father, what's happened? The cannon fire has ceased downriver."

Willem laughed. "You all come to me and ask the same thing. How should I know what's happened! I've sent Reinald to get some news."

"Can we go, too?"

He waved them off. "Go on. Go on. No further than the Bakkers, though."

It was nearly twilight before they returned.

"It's happened!" Laurens cried. Susannah shrilled: "Kyk-over-al! The English have captured Kyk-over-al!" Reinald nodded and confirmed it. "Yes, Father, it's true. It's authentic. The fort has fallen."

"The Bakkers are getting ready to go up the river," said Susannah. She seemed more excited than afraid. "Mervrouw Bakker has had all her jewelry buried, but she couldn't find the ring her mother gave her when she was fifteen. She was in tears because she says she valued it more than everything else put together. Her mother brought it from Middelburg years and years ago. It's a kind of heirloom."

"They're burying all their valuables in stone jars," Laurens said.

"The Blairs, too, are preparing to retreat up the river," said Reinald.

"Lieutenant Lepps," Susannah told them, "is wounded in the leg. He says Major Scott has begun to plunder the plantations downriver. By tomorrow morning he should be here. And, Mother, the Blankenburgs' baby is ill. It had fever all last night, Jan told us. He was at the Bakkers when we got there."

A silence came upon them.

Willem was staring out into the darkening sandbox trees. A cicada cheeped harshly, and other insects had begun their nighttime churring. The air was cool with vegetable scents and the vague leafy-dank smell of the black river.

Griselda and the children watched Willem.

Willem had a strong inclination to turn and smile reassuringly at them and say: "Don't upset yourselves. Get your things together. We'll go up the river like the Bakkers and the Blairs." It seemed such an obvious course. The commonsense thing to do. His back began to tingle, and he felt that he was cutting a ridiculous figure before them, standing here in silence while they waited for him to say something. But he would not turn. If he saw the alarm he suspected their faces held he would want to weaken.

In the outhouses the slaves were chattering excitedly. They must have heard, too, that the fort had fallen and that Scott and his Caribs were coming. The sound of their voices came clearly across the yard. It irritated Willem. He felt like going out and kicking them.

Griselda said tentatively, on the verge of tears: "Willem, dear, aren't we going to get ready to leave?"

He snapped round: "Get upstairs, Griselda. Get upstairs." Then, as always, he relented and patted her arm. "Keep calm. Don't upset yourself, my dear. The moment has come when we must keep cool heads. Sit down and compose yourself. Laurens, go and fetch your mother a glass of wine."

"No, thank you, Willem. I wish nothing. And I can't be composed. You shouldn't expect me to be composed after the news we have just received."

"Father, I think it would be prudent to get ready to leave," said Reinald. "We can't do anything against them."

Willem looked at the sandbox trees again. A deep calm came upon him. He felt big and confident and stable; unshakable. He felt like his mother. He tried to throw his mind back to that night when he was ten, and the blood began to move up through his chest as though it were a scarf reaching for his head. He felt suddenly dizzy with pride at the memory of the past. The scarf of blood swayed round and round his head. He turned and looked at Susannah.

"Susannah, what do you say, my girl? How do

you feel? Afraid? Or do you want to fight with your father?"

Susannah murmured: "I don't mind fighting, Father—if you think we can beat them."

He guffawed, and pulling her to him, gave her a hug. "Good. You're surprising me—yes, by God! I thought you had too much of your mother in you. But perhaps your grandmother will come out now that we're faced with this situation. And you, boy! Laurens, what do you say? Fighting it out with me, or you want to do the commonsense thing and run off upriver?"

Laurens grinned self-consciously. "No, Father, I'll fight with you, if you mean to fight. I don't want to run off anywhere."

"Good. Reinald! I suppose it's no use my asking your opinion. Mynheer Queseda has already made up your mind for you that it would be prudent to pack our things and go upriver."

Reinald avoided his father's gaze and said: "I should think not, sir. I'm not such a mean poltroon as you seem to fancy. I'll stay and do my duty by the rest of the family, since you have decided that we are to defend the house."

"Huh. Just as well you feel that way, because not one of you is leaving this house until I give the word—and I won't give the word until we're beaten. *If* they can beat us."

Reinald asked in alarm: "Father, what of Mynheer Queseda? Are you going to force him to remain?"

"He can go. I'll send a message to the Blairs and ask them to stop in on their way up and take him with them."

V

After Mynheer Queseda had left with the Blairs, Willem said: "Now we are alone. Now we're one family against the enemy, and we'll show the colony that we van Groenwegels are different. Different blood."

They were in the dining room, about to eat.

"When this is over, whatever happens, we'll be remembered as the only family who stood up and fought, who didn't run. That's no small thing, van Groenwegels. That's no petty thought. You don't know how much strength it calls for for me to agree to do this." He looked at Susannah quickly, almost furtively. She was serious and tense, a little frightened, but she had shed no tears. "I prefer to see you dead, Susannah, even if you have to die as my sister Hendrickje died. I prefer that than to know you were with those Blairs or those Bakkers cowering in security up the river."

They said nothing. Over the trees, in the north and east, they could see the glow of fires.

One or two of the slaves had deserted and gone into the backlands, but the majority were under control. The murmur of their voices could be heard in the compound and in the logies. Willem had spoken to them and warned them that if they deserted and went into the bush he would tell Major Scott and his Indians to go after them and kill them. He had treated them as though they were children; scared them with various kinds of threats.

After dinner he told his family the plan of strategy he had devised.

"I'm taking the women and children into the big barn with me. I'm going to bundle them under the loft where they'll be out of the way. About two-thirds of the men will fight with me in the big barn. The rest will help defend the house. Laurens will take charge of those who will man the barricades in the dining room and sitting room. The other lot, Reinald, you'll command. They'll fire from the bedroom windows. Some will load while others fire. Susannah, you will help to load. The barn will most likely be attacked first, as it's the obvious place any marauders would make for if they're after plundering the plantation. When they find they're up against stiff resistance they'll either retire and go higher up after the other places or they'll attack the house. That's where you, my sons, will have to prove what you're worth. And you, Susannah. Your mother is a negative quantity. I can't count on her for anything. But I'm looking to you children to hold out—to see the slaves don't panic and get cowed. I know it's a lot to ask of you. You're young, you're inexperienced, you've never been up against adversity. But I feel you will put up a good fight and show that you have metal in your souls. Remember your grandfather. Remember, above all, your gallant grandmother. . . ." He turned away, too moved to say anything more.

Toward dawn they could hear a wail of noise down-river, and the sky was lurid with fires. Susannah pointed and murmured: "Laurens, look. I'm sure that's the Bakkers' house."

"Yes, I know. It's the Bakkers' house."

Now and then they would hear their father's voice coming through the still dawn air. Willem was with the slaves in the big barn whose roof showed above the slaves' quarters near the saman trees in the northeastern section of the compound.

Upstairs, their mother uttered soft moans, and Reinald's slaves kept up a jabbering murmur. Most of the slaves were frightened, and whimpered often, but one or two were dependable fellows who even tried to keep up the spirits of the frightened ones.

Once a crashing sounded amid the bushes in the northwest, but it proved to be only two or three escaping slaves. Probably from neighboring planta-tions. They hurried across the compound, moving in a southerly direction; they were evidently trying to get as far upriver as they could.

Susannah said: "The Blairs and Bakkers didn't take all their slaves. Reinald said that when he went with Mynheer Queseda to see him into their boat they had only one field gang and a few household slaves in three other boats and two *corials*."

Laurens nodded. "I suppose they couldn't very well

take all. The others must be faring for themselves in the bush. I wonder if the Blairs took Hannah and Katrina upriver with them."

She gave him a sharp glance. "Laurens, which of the two are you in love with? Why won't you tell me?"

He was silent for a moment, then said: "I like them both. I don't know which I like better. But don't tell anyone, please."

"You know you can trust me." She clutched his wrist. "You think we'll get out of this alive?"

"I don't know, but we've got to do our best. I think I agree with Father. It's better to stay and fight than to let the dirty brutes burn our house and help themselves to our produce."

"Are you afraid?"

"A little," he nodded, "but I'm fighting. I'm going to kill a few of them before they get into this house."

"I hate the sight of blood, Laurens."

"I, too. I hate all killing—even birds. Remember the day Karl wanted us to kill that tapir we trapped? I believe I would have burst into tears if he hadn't spared it."

"You're softhearted," she smiled.

They heard musket fire.

A new glow appeared above the trees in the north. Susannah gave a gasp. "Oh, heavens, Laurens! The Blairs' house. It's on fire."

Upstairs, Reinald uttered nervous grunts. He told one of the slaves whose name was Bemma: "You had better get ready, Bemma. I hear firing, and if I'm not mistaken, I think that's the Blairs' residence on fire. They must be getting near." He hurried into the next room. "Mother! Mother! The Blairs' house is on fire. I think they're getting near."

Griselda moaned afresh. She wrung her hands. "My boy. Oh, what is this that Willem has brought me into? Reinald, please don't leave me. I'm feeling terrible. Please get me some water."

Footsteps thumped on the stairs and Laurens

entered. "Reinald, they're approaching on the river. Two boatloads. We can see them from the dining room. Get ready."

Reinald hurried out after him.

Shouts came and went downriver. And now and then musket fire broke out. Laurens said to Susannah: "They're probably potting at escaping slaves."

Birds were twittering awake in the trees: in the saman and sandbox trees. In the southwest, distantly, sounded the chatter of parrots.

They heard Willem's voice in the big barn.

Willem was in the loft. He was shouting down to his slaves: "Be quiet down there, you rascals! No whimpering or I'll use the whip on you! Bannah! Teekaba! You whip them every time they behave badly!"

"Yes, massa!"

Willem watched the two boatloads approaching. He could make out some weapons. He told himself: I don't see many muskets. I believe most of them are armed with cutlasses and hangers—perhaps a saber or two. However, it's dark, and I can't be sure. That firing downriver sounds none too pretty. . . . Wonder how they're getting on over at the house. I believe Susannah will keep up. I was wrong about her. She's got a good bit of her grandmother in her.

Beside him, Memba murmured: "They coming ashore, massa."

"I see them. Pass the word around to be ready to fire when I call out. Go on, Memba. And lash out if they whimper. Lash them hard."

Memba went off. He was a good fellow. Like Bannah and Teekaba, you could depend upon him.

Willem watched the two boats draw alongside the bank and their occupants step ashore. As he had thought, most of them seemed to be carrying hangers and cutlasses. It was evident that they were unaware of what awaited them in the barn. They must have had things easy on the other places. They were probably expecting no resistance here. Willem counted seventeen of them. In a group they began to move toward the barn.

"Fire!" called Willem. "Fire on them!" His voice shook with excitement, and a vivid picture of himself in a nightshirt arose in his fancy. It was as though the past had miraculously surged into being once again. He was ten, and his mother was directing operations.

The half-gloom below flashed. The barn thundered.

Three, four of the approaching figures stumbled and crumpled up. A confused yelling broke out.

Willem put aside his smoking musket and pulled up another, snapping at the slave behind him: "Hurry! Load!"

The barn thundered again. The acrid fumes drifted through the building, and one or two of the slaves could be heard coughing.

At the river's edge there was a wild splashing and shouting. One or two of the invaders, Willem saw, were getting into the boats again, but one or two flattened themselves down on the ground behind low shrubs lining the bank.

A moment later Willem saw three more boats appear. There was a bluish mist swirling in slow wreathing wisps over the water. The boats looked unreal; ghostly. He saw them change course. They were going to some point lower down where they would be out of range of musket fire from the barn. Willem fired into the mist and heard a yell. The mist cleared and he saw the occupants of one boat in a scrambling panic. The craft rocked. He had hit one of them in that boat, he was sure. He grunted with satisfaction.

The three boats went out of view behind the bushes.

One or two of those who had flattened themselves near the bank began to fire at the barn. They seemed to be using an old-fashioned type of musket, Willem thought. They probably couldn't aim well, either. He doubted whether they would even hit the barn, big as it was before them. All the same, he had miscalculated slightly. They did have muskets as well as cutlasses and hangers. He shouted down to Memba and Bannah and Teekaba to keep up the firing. "They're hiding among the bushes by the water's edge. Take aim and fire!"

The barn shook. The twilit interior down below looked hazed with the smoke of gunpowder.

Memba was shouting up at Willem, but the noise was too much. Willem could not make out a word. He called down: "Come up to me, Memba! I can't hear!" Memba came halfway up the ladder and called: "Massa, some of dem coming up from de other side. They bringing up a log to smash down de big door!" Willem called back: "Give it to them hot! I'm coming down."

Willem went down, and standing on top a pile of packing cases, looked through the small window at the rear of the building and saw what was happening. Invaders from the three boats were moving round to the front door of the barn. They were carrying a log.

Willem gave orders, and Memba and Bannah and Teekaba gasped.

"How we can do that, Massa?" said Bannah.

"Do as I say!" barked Willem, raising his whip threateningly.

So Memba and Bannah and Teekaba removed the bar from the front door and pulled the door wide open, the cool air billowing in.

"Now pile those cases along here. Quick! That's it!"

In less than three minutes they had erected a rampart of packing cases before the open doorway. Willem arranged the muskets for the men and told them: "Hold your fire. I'll tell you when to let loose at them."

Memba, up on the packing cases at the small window at the rear, was watching the enemy. The voices of the invaders could be heard now outside in the chilly air. The sun had begun to throw weak beams through the trees, beams bluish with mist from the river. The foliage of the trees was wet with dew, and now and then the rank smell of vegetation came

in with the cool drift of air, dispelling the smell of
the gunpowder.

Memba began to gesticulate, and Willem said:
"Get ready. Get ready." He peered between the packing cases where he had made his men leave spaces
for the barrels of the muskets. There were eight
apertures, each with a waiting musket.

The invaders came on with their log.

Willem heard a thin singing in his head. This,
he told himself, is a moment of fulfilment. Without
knowing it, I've been living for this moment since I
was in my teens.

He listened to the birds twittering. A campanero
clanged out its bell-like notes far upriver.

"Fire!" bellowed Willem. "Fire! Let them have
it!"

A haze of smoke rose with the deafening roar
from among the packing cases. The barn echoed. A
babel of yells drowned the bird sounds outside. The
invaders dropped the log and turned and ran—except two; these two writhed about and uttered hiccuping noises.

Willem trembled and chortled. "By God! By
God! That's it. Change muskets!"

The packing cases exploded again; shook and
clattered.

There was a wild rustling amidst the bushes
beyond the saman trees. And more yells. Willem
could hear them yelling on the river, too. He rushed
for the ladder and returned into the loft. He was
panting, but within he felt a deep, saturating satisfaction.

Two more boats, he saw, had rounded the bend
downriver. The mist looked like phantom spider-
webs in the reddish sunshine—though, to Willem,
it was just mist. A kiskadee was flapping its wings
and shrilling "Kisk-kisk-kiskadee!" and this caught
Willem's attention; it was in sympathy with the
crowing of triumph inside him. He uttered a brief
guffaw, and looked to see if he could make out the
bird. It stood on the branch of a *courida* tree that

overhung the water. Yes, he saw it; it looked a bit hazy because of the mist.

He switched his thoughts back to the two boats. New forces meant that the house would soon be coming in for an attack. He hoped the children were on the alert—and in good spirits. He had confidence in Laurens. Laurens was the youngest, but he had stern stuff in him. About Reinald he had grave doubts. Too much of his mother in Reinald. A bookish dreamer. His Uncle Aert. . . . Which reminded him. No news of Aert. Had an idea he must have gone under on the Pomeroon. . . . I am right about those two boats. It's the house they're after. They're going to land at the clearing beyond the *courida* tree.

Over at the house, Reinald was hurrying down to Laurens. He was trembling. He stammered: "Two boats are disembarking in the clearing near the big *courida* tree. I—I believe they mean to attack us here."

Laurens nodded, his eyes bright. He said quietly: "I'm ready for them. Go back upstairs."

Reinald hesitated. "You think it will be safe for Susannah to remain down here, Laurens? I—I mean, in case they should break in."

Susannah said: "Yes, I'm staying down here, Reinald. Go up and see after your slaves. You shouldn't have left them." She was pale. She squatted on the floor, hugging her knees, but she spoke in a steady voice.

Reinald turned and hurried away back upstairs.

His mother was moaning softly in bed. He went in to her and hissed: "Mother, we're going to do our best. Cheer up. I think Father has beaten off those who assaulted the big barn." He bent over her and patted her cheek, as his father might have done.

"This is the end, my boy. This is the end." She cried out as a volley sounded over at the barn. *"Mein Gott! Mein Gott!"*

Reinald hurried off, grunting nervously. He returned to his post at the window. The mist was very thin now—mere coils twisting about over the black water and amid the foliage of the trees.

The raiders were landing in the clearing near the *courida* tree. They began to approach the house, creeping round by the water-tanks[1] for cover.

"Massa, we should fire on them now."

"Do you think so, Bemma? Very well. Give the order. I fear my voice will not be very effective."

Bemma looked at him and grinned. He was not accustomed to giving orders.

"Did you hear what I said, Bemma? Give the order."

Bemma bent his head, still grinning. He mumbled something Reinald could not make out.

Reinald glanced outside with alarm, and in a cracked voice shouted: "Fire! Fire upon them, men!" He felt tears coming.

His slaves opened fire. Griselda shrieked. Reinald's teeth chattered. He thought of going in to his mother to soothe her, but changed his mind. He was in charge. It would be desertion, he supposed. He peered past the haze of gunpowder fumes that rose from his shaking musket and saw figures dashing past in the compound. One lay in the space between the two water tanks. Flat on his back and stirring slowly; trying to arch up his back but seeming to find the effort painful. He collapsed finally and lay still. Reinald thought: Could it have been my ball that struck him? He seems to be dead. Perhaps I've killed a man.

Downstairs, Laurens and Susannah stood behind a table barricade watching the scene outside. Laurens said: "I think we should hold our fire downstairs here until they get round by the logies. We're not in a good position to hit any of them."

"I think you're right," said his sister. "They're hiding behind the tanks."

There was a volley over at the barn. Yells and a patter of feet. Laurens swung round so abruptly that his elbow smashed into his sister's face. "Fire! Fire, slaves!"

The sitting room windows thundered. Three of

[1]Rainwater storage tanks.

the enemy fell, struggling, and four others dashed across the compound, making for the bushes in the west. Reinald, from upstairs, showered down another volley upon them. They could hear Willem shouting at his men in the barn.

"Reload! Reload!" cried Laurens. "Don't waste time." He bent quickly and muttered: "I'm sorry, Susannah. My elbow got you. I'm really sorry. Good! Is it loaded?" He grabbed the musket she held out. There was a red bump on the point of her left cheekbone.

"Massa, look! More boats coming up."

"Hold your fire. Wait and let them land up first and come this way. Massa Reinald will fire upon them. His positions upstairs command the clearing much better."

A spasmodic pop-pop-pop opened up from the bushes in the west, and a shot made a soft splitting noise against the ceiling.

Upstairs, there were only trifling barricades at the windows. Light tables and a few wooden screens. The heavier furniture had been used in the dining room and sitting room and in the barn. One of Reinald's slaves received a ball in his shoulder. He cowered back from the barricades, whimpering and clutching his shoulder, and the others near him left their posts and began to crowd round him. Reinald saw the blood and hastened up. He was on the point of blubbering.

"What's happened? Is he wounded? Who is it?"

"He bleeding, Massa."

"Oh, my God! Who is it? Is it a very bad wound?"

"It's Bakky, Massa. He bleeding bad in the shoulder."

Reinald glanced toward the river. He trembled and said: "You must get back to your posts, I'm afraid. I don't know what to say. We ought to do something for this fellow. One of you had better go downstairs and call Missy Susannah. This is a woman's job. I can't help him. The rest of you get back to the barricades! They're landing. More boats! Get

away from around Bakky. Don't you hear me?
Please," besought Reinald. "Please."

"Massa, he bleeding badly."

Reinald bent over the wounded slave, then
turned off with a shudder. He rushed to a window,
uttered a whine, raised his musket and fired blind
into the morning. Invaders were landing in the clearing by the *courida* tree. Some of them had muskets,
some cutlasses.

"For God's sake, get back to your posts. They're
coming toward the tanks. Fire on them before they
get behind. Quick! I beseech you! Quick!"

None of them made any move to obey.

"Massa, plenty of dem coming. We can't hold
out."

"We should run into de bush, Massa. Only
way."

"We—we can't run. We must hold out. Look
there! Why aren't you reloading?" He broke into a
hacking sob. "My God! My God! You people won't
obey me. You must obey me, please," he besought
them. "Please go back to your places."

Over at the barn, Willem was watching the
bedroom windows anxiously. Why doesn't Reinald
open fire on them? he kept asking himself. Minutes
are valuable, by God! Doesn't the boy realize that?
Now is the moment to open up on them. Why wait
until they begin to cross toward the tanks? The
young muddle-headed fool!

He saw a few smudges of smoke in the bushes
over to the west. Some of the enemy were there.
They were firing at the house. Seemed to be aiming
at the bedroom windows.

Willem sent a round across the yard into the
bushes. No obvious effect. No yells or threshing
about in the lower shrubs.

The dining room windows thundered and hazed.
Laurens. Good boy. But he was not in a good position downstairs. Something must have gone wrong
upstairs with Reinald's lot. Knew he couldn't depend
on Reinald. Soft. Foppish dreamer. His uncle and his
mother . . .

Over at the house, Griselda walked up and down wringing her hands.

Reinald went downstairs to Laurens, and Laurens stared at him and said: "Why haven't you opened fire on them, Reinald? What's happening to you? My God! You're crying. What's the matter?"

"They won't obey me, Laurens. They won't obey me. Bakky is wounded, and the rest of them are frightened. They won't fire. They're shirking. They won't go to the windows." His voice broke. His body shook with sobs. "I don't know what to do. I've coaxed until I'm tired. But they won't heed me. I spoke to them as kindly as I could——"

"That's your mistake. Never speak kindly to slaves, or try to persuade them to do anything. How many times hasn't Father told you that!" Laurens glanced at Susannah. She was afraid, her hands tightly clenched, but her mouth was set with determination despite her fear. "Susannah, have an eye on them for me. See they go on firing. I'm going upstairs. I won't be long. Make them fire. Take my whip and lash them if they won't obey. It's the only way to treat them." His voice quavered from excitement.

Susannah said: "I'll see they go on firing." She spoke in a whisper. He barely heard her. He hesitated, staring at her. She smiled and said: "Go on, Laurens. I'll lash them if they stop firing."

He turned and rushed upstairs, Reinald following him, still blubbering. When they were passing through their mother's room, Griselda tried to clutch Laurens. "Laurens! Oh, Laurens, my boy. Stay with me. Don't leave me. Please!" Laurens, however, did not glance at her. He rushed past into the next room. He took one look at the slaves crouching around the wounded Bakky and shouted: "Get up! Up! Up! Every one of you. You skulkers! You shirkers! Back to your posts!"

"Massa Laurens, we can't hold out. Too much of dem coming."

"Bakky bleeding bad, Massa."

"Get back to the windows and fire upon them!"

He grabbed a musket and presented it at them. "I'll fire upon you if you refuse to obey me! Do you hear me?"

They recoiled, whining and whimpering. Like wild beasts.

"Get on. Take up your positions again and start firing as Massa Reinald directs you or I'll kill you. I mean it. I'll kill you, you black cowardly clumps of filth!" He trembled. He had an insane look.

They began to edge off toward the windows.

"Get back! Go on. Get back!" The musket in his hands exploded, and one of the slaves reeled, uttering hacking sounds, a ball in his throat.

In the next room, Griselda shrieked.

Reinald grasped his brother's arm. "Laurens! Laurens! He's hit. He's bleeding. You've killed him."

"I don't care!" cried Laurens. "I meant to kill him. I'll kill every man who doesn't do his part. Up with that musket!" He turned suddenly. He was sweating. His head moved in jerks. "Reinald, go downstairs and help Susannah to keep order. Quick! I've got to stay here with these foul brutes."

Reinald turned and darted off. Almost at once there was a volley downstairs, proving that Susannah already had the slaves in hand.

Laurens went round the room kicking and clouting savagely, his breath coming in gasps. The slaves whined but kept their places and fired. The loaders whined, too, but kept reloading as the muskets were passed back to them.

"Look! Over there in the bushes. Fire that way!"

Downstairs, the firing was steady and regular.

Willem, too, had opened fire from the barn, aiming at those taking cover behind the water tanks and the slaves' quarters.

In the dining room and the sitting room Susannah had no trouble. Her slaves kept on firing. Kept reloading. The back of the house was quiet.

Soon all firing on the part of the enemy ceased. Willem bawled down to his men to hold their fire. He told Memba: "Keep a sharp eye out down there. I believe they're going to try on new tactics. They may make a rush."

"We ready for dem, Massa!"

Good man, Memba. Willem felt a glow inside. It was good to know you had someone you could put confidence in. Memba stood out from the others. Bannah and Teekaba, too. Good fellows.

Over at the house, Laurens called to his slaves: "Stop firing! They've held off. Hold your fire. You there! I didn't tell you not to reload. Get them loaded and ready." He was hoarse.

Downstairs they were still firing. Reinald came upstairs. "You're not firing any more, Laurens? They're still there hiding in the bushes."

"I know, but they've stopped firing, so we must hold off, too, for the time being. We can't waste ammunition. How do we know they haven't crept away to some other spot?" He chortled hysterically. "We're winning. We're too much for them. How's Susannah downstairs? Is she all right?"

"Yes, she's keeping them in order." He shuddered. "But look at that fellow, Laurens. He's dead. I think his name is Bamwah. He was in the Field Seven gang. Oh, this is horrible."

"Get back downstairs. It was only an accident. I didn't mean to kill him. The musket went off before I knew it." He was on the point of tears. He moved agitatedly to a window. "I wonder what they're doing. I believe they want to creep up round the back of the house. Reinald, go down and have a look from the kitchen windows."

Reinald went down and looked, but there was nothing doing. There was a wide clearing, and beyond it the small barn and some fruit trees, and then the indigo fields. Returning into the sitting room, Reinald told Susannah to stop the slaves firing. "Laurens says we had better hold off for the time being. They've stopped firing from the bushes."

"Stop firing, men!" she called.

Reinald started and exclaimed. The slaves shouted.

"Look! Over at de barn, missy!"

From the vicinity of the water tanks the enemy had made a dash toward the rear of the barn and had piled bramble and dried leaves against the wall. Willem had opened fire on them, but they returned to the cover of the tanks without suffering any casualties.

"They're trying to set the barn on fire," said Susannah.

In the barn, Willem muttered: "I can see what this prank is going to lead up to. A few more trips like that one and they'll have piled a considerable lot of inflammable stuff against that rear wall. Then they'll light it and we'll have the choice of being roasted or coming out and being hacked to pieces. Very well. I'll have to settle this now."

He went down and gave instructions to Memba and Bannah. "Teekaba, you remain here and watch the door. Don't stop watching, mind, for they may rush us at any moment. Memba and Bannah, get the axes and come with me."

In a few minutes Memba and Bannah with their axes had slashed open eight wide gaps in the woodwork of the rear wall.

"Good," Willem told them. "Now, Bannah, you bring up your squad with their muskets and post a man at each of these openings. Let them have it at point-blank range when they come back with their brambles. They're behind the logies at the moment."

The raiders, however, had seen what awaited them, and no further attempts were made to bring bramble. Willem took advantage of the lull to eat. He saw that the men ate, too, but made Memba and Bannah arrange the meals so that one group at a time was fed, those not eating continuing to keep watch. Bannah shared out the cassava bread and salted meat.

Over at the house, too, they were eating. Laurens was in high spirits now. He said: "They know they're beaten. We've turned out to be too much for them. They're short of muskets. They must have expected to come to grips with us and slash at us with cutlasses and sabers." He stood at the window as he spoke, his eyes darting from his sister's face to the yard.

"Father was right," said Susannah. "If we had gone up the river like the others our house would have been burnt down and we'd have lost all our produce in the barns. We'll show them we're not afraid, the beasts!"

Laurens stretched out and gripped her wrist. "You're brave. I really didn't think you'd have stood up like this. Father must be right about our blood. You can't keep blood down."

Upstairs, Griselda moaned in exhaustion on her bed, and Reinald, in the next room, paced agitatedly, glancing out of the window every now and then. He had made them clean up the mess of blood on the floor and take the corpse down into the kitchen. His face was drawn and worried, and twitched nervously. Once or twice he muttered to himself.

Downstairs, one of the slaves rushed in and told Laurens and his sister: "Massa! Missy! Quick. Do something. They piling up brambles and sticks against de kitchen at de back. They going to set fire."

Laurens hurried into the kitchen. He looked out and saw the brambles.

"We ought to have kept watch behind here. Anyway, the clearing is wide. If they make another attempt to come with more brambles we'll pepper them. Nemwa, tell six men with muskets to come, and bring loaders, too. Aha. I can see them dodging about in the indigo fields. They're gathering more brambles and stuff."

Susannah came in. She recoiled at sight of the corpse. It lay on the floor covered with a rough canvas sheet. "Is this the one you killed, Laurens?" He nodded and told her to get back to the sitting-room.

"Massa, look! They going to make another rush."

Laurens told the men to get ready. They had come in after Susannah and were already in position at the windows.

The enemy seemed to suspect an ambush, however, for nothing happened. The one or two figures with bundles of faggots lurking among the shrubs beyond the small barn made no attempt to approach.

"They know we're waiting for them," murmured Susannah.

Shouts and reports came from the sitting room.

"Go and see what's wrong, Susannah."

Susannah hurried back to the sitting room. She nearly collided with one of the slaves. "Missy! They rushing the house from the front." She heard Reinald shouting: "Fire! Fire!" in a frantic voice. The firing was spasmodic, however, and the slaves showed signs of fear.

About ten Indians were in the rush. They were trying to storm the house in a determined attack at two windows. The slaves at the two windows ran off shrieking, dashing down their muskets. Reinald, at one window, fired in a panic. The heavy table was being pushed away. Laurens and three of the men from the kitchen arrived. Laurens stood up and fired point-blank at two of the invaders whose heads and shoulders appeared at the barricades. There was a spatter of blood and yells and a thump and scramble. At the other window the heavy cupboard was giving the enemy some trouble. One of the defending slaves inserted his musket in the slowly widening crevice and fired. Another spatter of blood resulted and another confusion of yells and thumps. But one of the invaders succeeded in hurling himself in through another window. Laurens snatched up a loaded musket from one of the slaves seated on the floor, but before he could use it one of his men brought down a chair with a powerful crunch on the invader's head. A short brown fellow with tattoo markings on his shoulder and neck. As Laurens bent over the silently sprawled body he had a whiff of aniseed—a smell that remained in his memory for years after.

Susannah aimed and fired at another invader who was trying to push past the table barricade, but the shot gashed a hole in the table top without touching the attacker. The Indian, however, scared, turned and sprang out of the window into the yard.

Laurens climbed on top the big cupboard that had been nearly pushed aside by the enemy. He used his musket butt with good effect. Twice he brought it down on the skulls of the would-be invaders who tried to wriggle past into the room.

The attack failed, and the survivors retreated back across the yard and took cover beyond the slaves' logies and the water tanks.

An attempt was made to fire the brambles at the back, but Nemwa, who had been left to keep watch in the kitchen, put out the flames with buckets of water. Laurens gripped Nemwa's arm excitedly and congratulated him. Laurens trembled, and his laughter was nervous and boyish. His eyes shone with an unnatural brightness.

There were no more attempts. The day advanced. Rain fell shortly before noon, then the sky cleared and the sun shone weakly from behind a thin layer of clouds. The air felt steamy and warm. On the river, boatloads of the raiders kept passing, going upriver most of them, though occasionally one would pass headed downriver and laden to capacity with plundered goods, or plundered slaves.

"I heard Father saying the other day that the Andersens hadn't yet paid the Company for their slaves," said Laurens. "A good many other people haven't settled up yet for theirs. The Company will be ruined after this."

"The Bakkers have settled for about half theirs, and the Blairs only a third. They were hoping that after this year's sugar crop they would have been able to settle up for another third. Dorothea herself told me that, and she helps her father keep the books, so she should know."

"Yet they've run off and left their property. I'm sure they had as many firearms as we have—though it's true Father laid in a lot of extra ammunition. They could have held out if they'd had the guts."

About midafternoon they heard thudding sounds over at the small barn. The raiders were breaking down the back door. The front entrance was exposed to fire from the kitchen.

Laurens became furious. "We ought to do something about this. That barn contains cotton and anatta and hemp. We can't let them help themselves to it as they please."

"But what can we do?" said Reinald. "We have no means of getting at them."

"If I thought I could depend upon these slaves, I'd lead a rush on them and chop them up. We have a big supply of hatchets and axes and cutlasses in the house here."

"That would be suicide," said Susannah. "We'd lose."

They had to watch the raiders break open the barn and plunder it. After its contents had been removed it was set on fire. Shortly after the enemy set fire to the slaves' logies, too. Willem and his men downed about eight of them as they scurried about round the tanks and logies with their faggots and torches. By evening the small barn and the slaves' quarters had almost ceased to smoke. Wooden structures, they were burnt right down to the ground.

That night was an anxious one of watching, but no attacks materialized. Susannah insisted on taking her turn to watch, though Laurens wanted her to go upstairs and spend the night in bed. She slept in the sitting room on the floor, with only a cushion for her head.

Over at the barn Willem did not sleep at all, for he anticipated an attack at any moment, reasoning that the enemy would be tempted by the open front entrance. When dawn came, however, the inactivity had remained unbroken. The river lay black and sluggish, wisps of bluish mist hovering above it. Not a boat went past either way for hours, and by midmorning Willem decided that it was time to make an attempt to establish contact with the house. He and three of them went across, while Memba remained at the barn in charge of the rest. They got over without incident, and Willem listened to the excited tales of Laurens and Susannah. He was moved. He said: "I wasn't mistaken, my children. We've brought you up soft, but what's underneath your gentility had to come up in a crisis." He blinked rapidly and turned off.

Reinald kept his head bent, fumbling with the front of his coat. He had a harrowed, cowed look. He seemed very conscious that his father's words applied only to his sister and brother—not to him.

VI

Eight days later they heard cannon fire downriver, and in the late afternoon an Indian *corial* gave them the news that Dutch ships were attacking the English soldiers Major Scott had left at Kyk-over-al. Willem was puzzled. He said: "But what Dutch ships can these be? And why has Scott left so quickly? I don't believe it. It's probably a pirate vessel. I won't be surprised if we're in for another raid."

So they got ready for another attack.

Griselda, who had recovered from her hysterics, began to suffer a relapse, and Willem told her: "This time, if you shriek out as you did last week, I'm going to have you bound and gagged. I won't be surprised if it wasn't your behavior that contributed to the panic Reinald's men got into that first day. You've got to brace yourself, Griselda. Look at Susannah. Kept her nerve all through."

No attack, however, came. During the night the cannon fire ceased, and the following morning a boat came up with the news that Kyk-over-al was in Dutch hands again. Commander Mathys Bergenaar of Fort Nassau, in Berbice, had been attacked by an English privateer who had been routed with heavy losses, so Bergenaar, hearing of what had happened in Essequibo, had set out with a force, and last night they had recaptured the fort and wiped out the English soldiers left behind by Scott.

It was a tent-boat that brought the news; a tent-boat under the command of a sea captain whose

ship had been forced to take refuge in a creek when
Scott had arrived the week before. In the boat were
also the secretary and bookkeeper of Kyk-over-al,
who had escaped over to the mainland an hour before
Scott's ships opened fire on the fort.

"Commandeur Bergenaar," said the secretary,
"has sent us up here to get an estimate of the damage
done. You're the first family we've met."

This was Willem's big moment. "If you want
to find the other families," he said, "you'll have to
go much higher up. You'll probably find them living
with the Indians or camped out somewhere in the
jungle. We, sir, are the only family who stayed and
defended. We've lost a small barn and some produce, as well as the slaves' logies, but our house is
still intact—and our big barn where most of our sugar and tobacco and indigo are kept. We stayed and
fought. Note that, please, Mynheer Secretary. No
enemy will put a van Groenwegel to flight."

After the party had left—Willem entertained
them to lunch and brought out six bottles of his best
wine—the house was not big enough to echo Willem's
self-satisfied chuckles. He paced up and down, first
on the back veranda, then in the sitting room, then
upstairs in the corridor, his hands in his pockets.
He had had too much wine. They had all had too
much wine. Laurens fell asleep on a sofa in the
sitting room, and Susannah giggled a great deal until
she, too, fell asleep in a large armchair.

Griselda wept as well as giggled, but Reinald
became gloomy and began to wonder whether Mynheer Queseda was safe. He suggested to Willem that
they should send two slaves in a boat upriver to see
about the old man, but Willem waved him off. "Forget Queseda, boy. Forget him. Refugees don't interest
me. No, by God! I have nothing to do with those
people upriver. No blood in them. I respect only
men with blood."

Two days later the refugee families began to return
to their ruined plantations. Willem said: "Let them
come. I don't grudge them shelter. They can share

all I have. No man can accuse me of inhospitality. My food stocks are theirs until they can make other arrangements."

Three families set up camp in Willem's compound: the Bakkers, the Blairs and the Blankenburgs. Willem insisted on the women and children sleeping and eating in the house. The sitting room was converted into a dormitory and the dining room into a general refectory. Willem ruled that Laurens and Reinald and Mynheer Queseda and himself should sleep and eat in the tents. "This is an occasion when we men must rough things," he said. "No confounded softness! The era of gentility has passed, and I can't say I'm so sorry, either." He glanced at Reinald and added: "This will help to make you understand that life isn't all books and philosophy." He guffawed and walked off with a self-satisfied strutting gait.

Susannah shared her room with her good friends, Dorothea and Woglinde Blair. The big four-poster held them not too uncomfortably.

It was on their first night together, before falling asleep, that Susannah asked them: "What of Hannah and Katrina? Did you take them up the river with you, or were they captured by Major Scott's men?"

"We took them with us," Woglinde said. "We took our household slaves with us. It's only the field slaves we had to leave. Every one of them has been stolen and taken away."

"Yes, I hear hundreds of slaves[1] have been taken away," said Susannah sympathetically, though her thoughts dwelled on Hannah and Katrina. It was a relief to hear that they were safe. Only that afternoon Laurens had asked her whether she had seen anything of them. The slaves were all over the place —those that had not been captured—and up to now they were uncounted and unsorted; some slept under trees, some slept in hastily erected *troolie* huts. Willem had decided to let his own use the barn for the present, though he had warned them that if they

[1] Scott took away 70,000 lbs. of sugar and 1,000 slaves.

helped themselves to what did not belong to them there would be severe punishments for the culprits. He threatened boiling water and tar and feathers.

Dorothea told her after a brief silence: "Father thinks we'll have to go away to St. Eustatius in the West Indies. We have an uncle there."

"I'll miss you terribly," said Susannah. "Will he sell out his slaves? I mean the few household slaves you took up the river with you?"

"Naturally. He'll have to. He's still indebted to the Company."

The following day Susannah told Laurens what she had learnt, and Laurens frowned. "Do you think there's any way of persuading Father to buy Hannah and Katrina when the Blairs are ready to sell out?"

Susannah said: "Perhaps if we spoke to him and convinced him that it was a matter of family pride that we should have them with us. After all, they have Grandmother's blood in them—and you know what Grandmother means to him." She smiled. "What would you like to do? You want to make them your mistresses?"

He nodded. "I did think that when I was older I could have them as household slaves—and keep them as mistresses."

"I'm going to help you."

"You don't think me immoral, do you?"

"Of course not. Why should it be immoral for you to have two mistresses if you want them? I'm going to tell you a secret, Laurens. I have my eye on Karl Bakker. He's in love with me. I believe he'll make me a good husband. And his people have a lot of jewelry."

Two days later news came from the Pomeroon that Captain Aert van Groenwegel had died of wounds received in the encounter with Major Scott and his Indians. The only surviving officer, a lieutenant, told Willem: "We were outnumbered, but he decided to remain and fight. They bombarded us for a whole morning, and three of our men were killed and seven wounded. Then shortly after noon the Captain saw that the position was hopeless, so we spiked our guns and retreated into the bush up the river. The drummer and the sergeant died the same afternoon. They had been severely wounded in the chest and head. The Captain died the following morning of a severe wound in the groin. We couldn't stop the bleeding. We had to trudge for miles in swamp and thick bush, and the Captain insisted on taking his books and his collections of insects. We packed them into haversacks, and they made our burden doubly heavy. But he would not hear of them being discarded. He died clutching two haversacks of books to his bosom as though they were beloved creatures to whom he was greatly attached. You cannot imagine how deeply he loved his books and insects. . . ."

I can imagine it, thought Willem. The soft fool. Reinald will be Aert over again. A misty-brained bookworm. Anyway, there's Laurens. I have hope for that boy. I must build him up. I must consolidate him. He won't let me down. He'll take our name far, and take it with honor and power. I'll keep on drumming that into them. Honor and power. Fire-blood. I'll make them see that it was no mere chance that we stood up and fought Scott's Indians. It was no haphazard circumstance. It was one thing for me to have ruled that they should stay and fight. It was one thing for me to have compelled them to remain and put up a defense. But the way Laurens and Susannah handled that situation over at the house when the enemy rushed the windows was not a matter I could control. It was something with which they were born that came out that day. . . .

"I don't care what people say of me," he muttered. "I know they talk about me and sneer behind my back. They call me a crank. They think me a fool over-inflated with family pride. They consider me a bore because I keep stressing the importance of blood. Very well. But this raid has shown them what blood can do. It proves the difference between strength and weakness. My house is still standing, and my slaves are intact—save the one Laurens killed. Even the deserters have turned up."

He tugged at his beard and grunted deeply.

"Let them talk. The years will prove that my pride was not in vain. The decades will show whether my faith in our blood was justified."

III Laurens

I

SOME days there would be a gale on the Essequibo. High wind with slanting rain rushing over the bush and the choppy water. It would go swooping up the Mazaruni, and when Laurens looked across at Kyk-over-al he would see it like a frayed monster sleeping mysteriously in the river, hazed but unheedful of the pelting moisture.

On other days the brown muddy water flashed in a dazzle of morning sunshine. The trade-wind hummed around the building, and small white clouds drifted in a blue sky.

Grandmother, thought Laurens, must have seen it often like this. Perhaps she used to stand at this very window looking out, as I am doing now, and feeling lonely. On the days when Grandfather was away. He used to go up the river or to the coast on secret expeditions with the Indians. They used to say he dealt with the Spaniards in Trinidad and on the Orinoco, but I don't believe that. I'm sure he wouldn't have been so mean. Though he was a queer old fellow. Father always talked of him as being a man of mystery. And he himself once told us what a wily fellow he was and how he used to baffle the Company traders and get them envious because of his influence with the Directors and his power over the Indians.

That west room used to be his—his alone. Grandmother never slept in there, and the children were kept out of it. The arms cupboard was in there. It was in there Father and Uncle Aert went to get the four muskets that night the Indians attacked them. I like watching the sunshine on the trees from in there. In those days tobacco was grown on this plantation, but now it's all sugarcane and cotton. I wonder if Grandfather ever thought that one day Father would have revived this plantation and put me here to manage it. Sometimes I think I can feel Grandfather's presence in this house—and Grandmother's. It was in the next room they raped and murdered Aunt Hendrickje. I get odd feelings in this place. It's so lonely. I feel like an exile. If Susannah hadn't advised me so strongly to fall in with Father's plans I wouldn't have agreed to come and live here and manage this plantation. I'd do anything Susannah advises. Her advice generally makes for good in the long run.

I think the experience will benefit me. After all, I've got to carry on the planting tradition and keep the family name going in the colony. Father is never weary of impressing that on me. He's right. We certainly seem to have something in us that other families haven't got. I mustn't let the family down. I must learn to be a good manager.

This plantation should be worth a great deal in time to come, especially as it's just opposite Kykover-al, the seat of government. I suppose that must have struck Father, too. He must have been thinking of the contacts I'll make: the government officials and the people who matter in the colony. This family pride is on his brain. Susannah says it's a mania. He can think of nothing but our blood: our fireblood, as he calls it. Our stand up the Mazaruni against Scott's Caribs has made him trebly pompous and obsessed with the importance of the family. He can hardly utter a sentence nowadays without making some reference to that affair. A little ridiculous, of course, but, still, he does have some excuse for being proud.

I won't let him down. This house is going to be my family seat—if I can ever persuade any girl to marry me. Somehow, I can't see myself offering marriage to a girl. Women awe me in a strange way. I'll have to get over that, though, for I can't go on living here for ever with only servants for companions. This house is not so bad now that it has been thoroughly overhauled and repaired, but it's lonely. Though tomorrow Hannah and Katrina will be here. That's an event to look forward to. I can't imagine why I should have taken such a strong fancy to those two girls. They're both very attractive, it's true. I like their breasts—and Katrina's hair. And Hannah has a most roguish way of glancing at you. But I've seen other girls equally as attractive. Woglinde Blair was lovely. At one time I thought I was in love with her—when I was fourteen. I used to write her love letters which I never let anyone see and always burnt as soon as I'd finished writing. I don't believe even Susannah knows I used to be in love with Woglinde. But when Hannah and Katrina were purchased and came to live with the Blairs I found that I suddenly changed about Woglinde and could only think about the two girls. I tell myself sometimes that it must be the color in them; I must have an instinctive partiality for colored women. I wonder, too, if it couldn't be because I know they are related to me by blood yet are, so to speak, forbidden territory. Perhaps it's simply a degenerate streak in me. . . .

The trouble with me is that I'm shy of women. I'm shy of intimate relations with people, on the whole. How I'm going to make these two girls my mistresses I don't know. I'm getting a little nervous already when I think about that. It's true they're only slaves and they ought to feel honored if I made overtures to them, but I'm not sure of myself. My being attracted to them, if anything, makes it harder. However, I mustn't worry about that yet. When they're here will be time enough. Susannah sent a message yesterday to say that Karl will bring them when he comes to Kyk-over-al. Karl has to interview the captain of the *Baerland* about the passages he's booked for Suriname. . . .

I'm going to miss Susannah when she goes. She has been a good sister to me. She has helped me in a great many things. She is clever—pleasure-loving and perhaps a little too unsentimental, but she's shrewd. She knows how to handle people. Karl is lucky to have got her for a wife—or, better, I should say he's lucky that she decided he was to be the lucky man. He's a good, quiet fellow; a bit dull, but Susannah's brilliance makes up for that. If Susannah hadn't made up her mind that he would prove a good financial proposition as a husband there would have been no wedding. It's she who maneuvered the whole thing. All those notes and messages she used to get me to take to him on the sly. Oh, Susannah is clever. She's going to make a man of Karl. This going away to Suriname is wholly her idea, and she has got what she wanted. Persuaded Karl's father to sell out the share he held in that plantation his brother runs in Cayenne so that Karl and herself can use the money resulting from the sale to go to Suriname and settle on a small plantation of their own. She handled that affair with genius. Flattered the old man and wheedled the old mother. She feels sure that the prospects in Suriname are rosy—especially since Suriname became a Dutch colony a few years ago, after the Peace of Breda. She is probably right, too, for I hear the other families who went over there are doing well. The Blairs should have gone to St. Eustatius, but they went to Suriname instead. So did the Andersens and the de Vries and a good many of those ruined Pomeroon people.

If nothing else, Susannah will be at home in Suriname with her old friends. I don't believe she's too happy up the Mazaruni with Karl's people. Of late she has been hinting that Karl's mother tries to interfere in matters that shouldn't be her concern. Susannah is not the kind of girl to put up with that.

I'm certainly going to miss her a lot. She's the only person with whom I can discuss anything in a straightforward, sensible manner. Father is too moody and ready to flare up, and there's this family obsession of his that warps his views. And Mother is unable to be logical about anything; she's too emotional to be logical. And Reinald is abroad at Louvain University engaged in his medical studies, though, in any event, he would have been nobody for me to talk with seriously; he was too engrossed in his books and his Mynheer Queseda and their philosophical bosh. I'm glad that Queseda monkey isn't here any more. That was what Father called him. Gone back to Holland. That's the place for him. Not in a country like this, just coming to life. I never could tolerate him.

Yes, Susannah is the only one I can confide in. She's sensible and quick; quick to see a point and sympathetic; her advice is always sound. I have admired her, too, ever since that time of the raid. She showed such courage—yet we were both afraid. I can remember how I gripped her wrist and she told me my fingers were cold. And that moment when I saw the Indians crossing the yard and gave the order to fire. I turned and smashed my elbow into her face. She didn't make a fuss, and it was a hard blow. . . . I can see events in a much better perspective now that I'm five years older. That poor slave I killed upstairs in the bedroom. . . .

That same afternoon Susannah paid him a surprise visit. Mynheer Blankenburg had come to Kyk-over-al on business, and she had taken the opportunity to accompany him down. "I'm going to spend the night with you here," she said, "and Karl will take me back tomorrow when he comes to see Captain Stoltz."

She had grown plumper—childbearing had done that to her—but her gay, alert manner was the same. Her giggle, too.

"Only this morning I was thinking of you," he said. "I'd just come in after inspecting the work in the western fields, and I stood at one of the windows in Grandmother's old room and looked at the sunshine on the river and at Kyk-over-al——"

"It was Grandfather's room, too. They shared it. I remember Grandfather himself telling us that. That Sunday, don't you remember? Over at the Commandeur's house when we didn't like the Indian soup."

They went upstairs into Kaywana's room.

"I'm going to feel lost without you," he said, as he seated himself by the window and lit his pipe. She sat on the big bed: a new one that Willem had had installed after the house had been repaired.

"I realize that," she smiled. "Poor fellow. You sound sixteen when you say that."

I know, he thought. I feel myself that mentally

I haven't grown up very much since I was sixteen. It's this shyness that I can't get rid of. Uncle Aert was like that when he was my age, if what Father says is true. Uncle Aert never mixed with women.

"Anyway, you've got to learn to take care of yourself," she said. "You can't have me all your life to advise you."

"I do realize that," he nodded. "It's very lonely here."

"I know."

A soft breeze came in—a land breeze.

"This house makes me dream and introspect. I keep thinking about the past and of the stories Father and Grandfather have told us about the happenings of those days. This morning I looked out on the river and wondered about Grandmother, how she must have been lonely, too, when Grandfather went off on his expeditions. And I thought about you and your going away and my being here as the manager of this plantation."

"I hope you'll get friendly with the Blankenburgs. Frieda and Rosa and Wilhelmina are not bad girls. I like them." She gave him a sudden earnest look. "You must marry, Laurens. Father is depending upon you to carry on the name. I doubt whether Reinald will get married."

"I doubt it myself. I'll get married eventually. Would you like me to marry one of the Blankenburg girls?"

She shrugged. "I only suggested them because they're very sensible girls. Rosa, especially, is a fine creature. They would make good wives. But you must choose for yourself. Don't do as I have done," she laughed. "I married for convenience, not for love. You won't be happy unless your heart is with the woman. I know you so well, Laurens."

"You don't think I should marry just for the sake of carrying on the family name, then?"

"Certainly not. Fall in love first. Your happiness comes before any such considerations as family survival. Not that you mustn't try to see that the name goes on. I do get a little throb of pride when I re-

member that I'm a van Groenwegel, but the idea
can be overdone. Father overdoes it shamefully. You
mustn't make the same mistake or you'll ruin your
life. By the way, I hear you drink a lot of wine
nowadays."

He grinned: "What else is there for me to do in
this place?"

"Don't let it get a hold on you."

"It won't. I don't think I'll ever be a drunkard.
I'm not made that way. It's only this loneliness."

"Tomorrow you won't be lonely."

"Yes, I was thinking that this morning. You're
sending down Hannah and Katrina with Karl, your
note said."

"Yes, Karl will bring them."

"But, Susannah, you're sure it won't cause any
inconvenience in your home? I mean, I shouldn't
like to know———"

"Don't be foolish. They're mine now. I can do
what I want with them. I've given Karl's father two
of my best kitchen slaves in exchange for them. If
there's any inconvenience it will be mine."

"And you think you can spare them?"

"Certainly. I'm arranging it that I can spare
them." She frowned and told him: "You're too self-
effacing, Laurens. You should try to rid yourself of
that trait. You let people see too much that you're
conscious of their doing you a favor. Even with the
slaves you're inclined to be like this."

He thought: Yes, I've pondered on that myself.
In many ways I'm too soft. I don't like hurting people's feelings. I must be really roused before I can
be brutal.

"What you must remember is that I've done
this for you because I'm very fond of you and want
to see you happy. I knew you had set your heart on
having Katrina and Hannah, and I was determined
that if I had to shift the whole colony I'd get them
for you. It isn't by accident they are among the Bakkers' slaves. I never mentioned it to you, but it was
I who secretly urged Karl to get his father to purchase
them from the Blairs when the Blairs sold out and

went away. I knew it would have been hopeless tackling Father about it. Father would never have agreed to buy them. I did hint to him once, soon after the raid, that it would be a good thing to acquire them, but he pounced upon me at once and said that he would never tolerate them near him. He said he much preferred to know that Hannah and Katrina were in the hands of strangers."

She giggled. "I remember that day well. He said that if he bought them their eyes would compel him to treat them as equals—and, of course, it would have been too much of a strain on his pride to recognize slaves as his equals."

"But why should their eyes have compelled him to treat them as equals?"

"They both have Grandmother's blue-green eyes."

"Oh, I see." He looked at her in a trance of quiet admiration. "You're clever at arranging these things. You have no idea how I'm looking forward to having them here with me."

"You're blushing." She laughed, came over impulsively and kissed him. "You're still so naïve, Laurens. But before you begin to praise me for being clever, you'd better wait and see how Father is going to react when he hears that you have them here as your mistresses. I'm not so certain he will be pleased."

He pulled agitatedly at his pipe. "You mustn't imagine I'm going to announce it everywhere that that's what I intend to do. Only you are supposed to know I'm keeping them here as my mistresses. To everybody else they'll be my household slaves like any of the others about the house."

"I see your point, but Father won't be so innocent. He'll suspect what's up and come down here to investigate."

He looked at her in dismay. "What do you think he'll do?"

She shrugged. "He's so unpredictable. He may object strenuously to your having them here in any capacity whatever, and he may shrug the whole thing off and forget it."

He looked troubled. He thought: I had feared this. I hate to have Father here questioning me. It always unnerves me. The last time he came on one of his visits of inspection, as he calls them, he took me to task about the grass in the clearing behind the slaves' logies. I'd never noticed that the grass had grown so high. Nothing escapes his probing gaze.

"Don't let it upset you," she laughed. "Father can be handled if you know how to go about it."

"That's just it. I don't."

"Study him. Flatter his vanity," she said carelessly.

"I was never good at flattering people."

"It isn't hard to flatter Father. You've only got to say nice things about the past history of the family. Refer to Grandmother's bravery in fighting Wakkatai —or Grandfather's speech to the Indians on the night of the uprising. He'd do anything for you if you harked back to one of those events." She rose. "Let's go exploring around the plantation. Tell me about crops and show me your vegetable patches. I'm trying to learn as much as I can about planting so as to be of help to Karl in Suriname."

II

On the following afternoon, when he stood on the long plank at the water's edge and watched the boat drawing away with Karl and Susannah, he thought: This is the moment I've lived in my fancy every hour since I got that note from Susannah two days ago: the moment when I'd wave good-bye to Karl and then go up into the house to talk to Hannah and Katrina and tell them what arrangements I have made for them. I hadn't envisaged Susannah in the boat with Karl—that's the one detail that's not as I had imagined it.

Susannah waved and called: "Happy nights!"

He blushed and nearly slipped off the plank into the water. He waved back and waited until the boat had rounded the point and vanished beyond the mangrove and *courida* before making a move. His fingertips were cold, and he could feel the tenseness in him. He told himself: This is nonsense. I must remember that I'm master here. They are only slaves. I'm doing them an honor treating them like this.

He found them in the dining room where he had told them to wait. They were squatting on the floor near the sideboard, but stood up as he came in. Katrina wore a pink smock, Hannah a blue one. New smocks. Susannah must have seen to it that they came with a new outfit. Trust her to have thought of such a detail. Their bundles were on the floor.

They both had lovely breasts. You could see the points prominent under the smocks. He cleared his throat, frowned and said: "I want you to come upstairs, Katrina—and Hannah." He spoke without looking at them, in a stiff voice; the voice of master to slave. "I'd like to show you your room. I have decided that you will sleep upstairs in the northeastern room. Please follow me."

They followed him upstairs.

"This will be your room," he told them, as they entered the northeastern room. "And I'd like to let you know that I want you to confine your duties to —to the rooms. I don't want you to be mixing too freely with the other household slaves." He looked out of the window and said: "There's a special reason why I have brought you here, but that can be discussed some other time. You'll do light tasks about the house—and attend on me personally." He gave Katrina a quick glance. Her hair looked very beautiful. "I hope you both understand what I mean?"

Katrina inclined her head and murmured: "Yes, Massa." But Hannah gave him a bold glance and smiled. "Yes, Massa," she said. "We understand."

He hesitated, thinking: I ought to speak plainly so as to leave them in no doubt. . . . No, there's no hurry. That should be done delicately. Later on. Tonight perhaps. . . .

He said: "This is the room in which your grandmother died." He caught himself quickly and amended: "I—I mean, the next room. This is where my Aunt Hendrickje was raped and murdered. Your father, my Uncle August, used to sleep in here. So Father says."

They stared at him with interest and surprise. Hannah began to smile, but Katrina kept a glum, subservient expression.

There was a silence. They could hear the river whispering. It was a fine day, with white clouds in the sky, and the trade wind was blowing—not a chilly land breeze. Out in the river there were several ships at anchor. The Company ships were the largest.

"It's a fine view from here. I think you'll prefer this room to the west room. And—and there's a connecting door with my room. I sleep in the next room. That's where Grandfather and Grandmother slept."

He felt like a fool. "You have your bundles?" He glanced toward the bundles on the floor, then smiled and said: "I see you have new smocks. I suppose Missy Susannah had them made for you?"

"Yes, Massa," Hannah smiled.

"I hope you'll like being here."

He hesitated, cleared his throat and then left the room.

He was no sooner gone when they began to whisper. Hannah said: "I think he like us. He bring us here to sleep with him. Remember I tell you I think his reason?" Katrina, however, frowned and replied: "I not think dat his reason. Massa Laurens not man like dat. He don't trouble women. I hear so."

"I can see from how he talk and look at us dat he bring us here for dat. I think he like me. You see how he turn red when I look at him and smile?"

Katrina shrugged. "Time show what happen," she said. "But I feel he only bring us here for servants because we fair more than other slaves, and he got big name, so he prefer fair-skin slaves in his house."

"I hear Commandeur Rol sometimes come over here to see him, and he go over to see Commandeur

Rol. He big man, Massa Laurens. Like his father and his grandfather. They all big people."

Katrina looked round the room. "This nice room. He say this where our father used to sleep. Hannah, suppose we see his jumbie in de night?"

"Jumbie not true. I never see no jumbie."

"Jumbie true. Mabella see plenty jumbie in her logie. Remember she tell us so? I believe in jumbie."

Hannah sniggered. "Massa Laurens sleep in next room. If we see jumbie tonight we can run in to him."

"You talk stupid."

"Not stupid. I believe Massa like me." She patted her breasts. "I got good fat up here. I sure he come in and call me one night soon."

"You like too much man. I not want no man all my life. Semwa ask me plenty times to sleep wid him, but I tell him I not want no man. Banwak ask me, too, but I say no. I want keep same as I born all my life. When baby come it make work more hard. Do work and mind baby not easy. I not want no baby."

"I like my man sometimes," said Hannah. "I sleep wid Hoobakka and Jemma four, five times. Hoobakka not so good, but Jemma do it nice. If we didn't have to come here to live I woulda let Jemma sleep wid me plenty more nights. I like Jemma."

"Go on sleeping wid men. When you get baby your own trouble. Take care baby and work not good for me. If you want dat you can go on."

"I like baby. If baby come I glad. I not care if I have to work and look after baby, too."

Katrina gave a sour smile. "Perhaps Massa Laurens give you baby."

Hannah hugged herself ecstatically. "So much better if it happen so. I prefer have white baby. You stupid, Katrina. If you taste man once you want more every night."

"Not me. Only way I have man is if Massa put me to breed, den I can't say no, because I slave-girl. But me myself, I not want no man."

"Not even if Massa Laurens himself want you?"

"Dat different. If Massa want me I must glad take him, because he'll treat me good and not give me plenty work—and he big massa. All other slaves got to treat me wid respect if Massa make me his woman."

"He never take you, though. He take me when he ready. I know so. I see it in his face how he look at me."

Katrina shrugged with indifference.

At dinner that evening Laurens drank three glasses of wine instead of two as was customary. He told himself: I don't suppose it will matter, though, for wine seldom gives me courage for anything. It simply makes me lethargic and sleepy. No, wine won't do it. It's I myself who must take matters in hand and be a man.

Later, in his room, he sat by a window and smoked, listening to the whisperings and movements of the two girls in the next room. He was in darkness, but the girls had a lamp burning. He could see the light over the wall. There was latticework at the top of the wall that divided the two rooms.

I wonder what they're talking about in whispers like that. I have an idea they must suspect what my intentions are. Hannah looked at me very significantly when she was handing me the wine at table. I think she has more fire in her than Katrina. Katrina seems quiet. But she's fair-skinned, and her hair is really beautiful. She has good hips, too. They're both very tempting. I can't say I like one better than the other. I want both.

He frowned out at the dark river. There was moonlight, but it was too pale to make much difference. The crescent was only two nights old, and it was low in the west. He could see two reddish lights in the Commandeur's residence. He knew them. They were the two decorative lanterns in the big drawing room. There were red, green and blue glass sections in those lanterns. As a boy they had fascinated him. Grandfather once held him up to look at them at close quarters. . . .

I wonder whether I should call one of them in now and tell her I want her to sleep with me to-night. Say Hannah. Hannah seems as though she might be more ready to go to bed with me. And yet —well, she's got such bold eyes; they discomfit me. She looks at me sometimes as if I were her equal. The whole thing is distinctly awkward. What am I going to say to her? "Sleep with me in here tonight. I want you to be my mistress." But that would be so crude. I couldn't bring myself to say that. No, I wasn't made that way. If only I could think of some delicate method of telling them. . . .

The light in the next room went out. He shifted in the chair, staring at the latticework. It was too early for him to sleep. He had better do some reading. He must have the lamp lit.

He was about to call: "Hannah!" but arrested the breath, made a throaty sound and called instead: "Katrina!"

"Yes, Massa!"

The connecting door opened after a brief de-lay, and he heard Katrina enter. He did not turn his head. She came within range of his vision, and stood a few feet away, waiting. She said: "Yes, Massa?" in a low voice. Was he mistaken, or was there a slightly expectant note in her voice? It must be his imagination. He could make her out dimly in the reflection of the pale moonlight that came in at the southern windows. She seemed to be wearing a different smock. Her sleeping-smock, of course. How stupid of him!

"I want the lamp on the desk lit, please, Ka-trina." The "please" came out before he could stop himself. "I've decided to do some reading before turning in." He tried to speak casually, but knew that his voice sounded self-conscious.

When she had lit the lamp he saw that the smock she was wearing was threadbare. He could see her body through it in places. He took a swift breath and said: "Katrina, is everything—are you two girls comfortable in the room there?"

"Yes, Massa."

"You—you don't need anything?"

"No, Massa."

"I see." As she was moving off he said: "How old are you? Are you the elder or—or the younger?"

"Hannah younger, Massa. I twenty and Hannah nineteen years. Our old Massa van Peere tell us our age before Massa Blair buy us. We not know our age until Massa van Peere tell us."

"You were about thirteen when Massa Blair purchased you, I think?"

"Yes, Massa."

His fingertips were cold and his mouth dryish. The desire to call her closer to him and to stretch out and fondle her breasts made a burning in his head. He nodded, however, and said: "That's all, Katrina. You can go back to bed."

Two weeks passed and he had still not found the courage to call one of them in to his room at night. During the day he treated them aloofly, especially in the presence of the other slaves, but in the evening at dinner he would relax and address a few personal remarks to them, asking after their comfort or how they were eating. Hannah would always give the replies. Katrina retained a deferential silence, her gaze lowered. She seemed afraid to smile—unlike Hannah who not only smiled but often laughed, her eyes sparkling at him so that he would turn away his face and pretend not be aware of any familiarity. Something in him objected to familiarity with his inferiors. One day he had been on the point of gripping Katrina's arm as she went past but at the very last moment had desisted, the feeling rising up in him that it would be undignified. No, he simply couldn't do it.

"It's my upbringing," he muttered to himself one morning. "I can't help it."

At times he felt a sense of elation at his superiority, his being better than they. He felt glad that he had not broken the layer of reserve that still existed between him and them. Let them know that he was their master—Massa Laurens van Groenwegel. He would condescend to make them his mis-tresses at his leisure, at whatever time he chose. There was no hurry. He was no weak libertine who could not glance at an attractive female but must pounce on her and go to bed with her. No, he was strong. He could resist such temptations.

Inevitably, however, it would come upon him that this was only a defensive make-believe attitude. Only a desperate attempt to excuse his lack of cour-age—his bashfulness. His whole body was writhing with desire for them, but he couldn't shake off his diffidence. Let him be honest. He was soft. He was not a man. He would be like Uncle Aert. It must be heredity. He would go through life a bachelor, afraid to approach women; always blushing and avoiding their glances. He would take up insect-col-lecting.

He pressed his hands to his face, that day in his room, and sobbed, though only dry sounds came from him—no tears. He fought back the tears.

The two girls, meanwhile, discussed him and specu-lated about how long he would take to overcome his shyness. Katrina was no longer in doubt now about his intentions. She said one day to Hannah: "I believe you talk right, Hannah. He bring us here to make us his women. He burning up for us, but he not yet able to make himself ask us. I know it for certain today. He look at me when I come in de dining room, and his eyes get bright, and he call me when I go up to him. He raise his hand, then he tremble and look away and tell me to bring him a jug of water. He wanted to hold me but he too shy." She gave a slow smile, her manner thoughtful—a little tender, too.

Hannah said: "I like him. One day he will lose his shyness and ask one of us. I don't believe he ever had to do wid a girl before. He better ask me so I can teach him. If he ask you it will be bad for him," she giggled. "You never sleep wid a man and he never sleep wid a girl. It will be trouble for you both. Ma-bella tell me so. She say when she sleep de first time wid a man he was no good because he never had any before her, so when I take my first man I take one who I know sleep wid plenty others before. Parkab de first man I sleep wid—and he do it good."

Katrina smiled sourly. "You can think only about man. I not think about no man. I do my work. I not want no man."

"You're a queer girl. Every girl like man. I believe you only say dat to fool people. One day you must see a good strong man and want him."

"Sssh! Massa coming upstairs."

They fell silent and went on with their work, Katrina cleaning the lamp and Hannah sweeping. They heard Laurens go into the west room; heard him getting his riding kit from the cupboard. When he had gone downstairs again, Katrina said quietly: "He's a nice man. He should marry and get children. I would like to take care of his children."

Hannah gave her a surprised look. "You would like to take care of his children! De children he have wid his wife! But why?"

"Because I like him. If I like a person I like to do things for them!"

"Just do things for dem and get nothing from dem?" Hannah looked puzzled. "You is a really queer girl, Katrina. If I do anything for somebody I like to get something for it. My work is different. I must do dat because I slave, but if I do something for somebody dat they not force me to do as a slave, den I must get something in exchange. If I sleep wid a man and he treat me good I do anything for him, and if I have babies of my own I take care of dem good—but I not take care of no other woman's babies."

"I not so," said Katrina. "I like doing things for people if I like dem, and I don't want nothing for doing it."

"And you like Massa so much you can take care of his children if he have any when he marry?"

"Yes."

III

Susannah and Karl spent the night with him prior to their embarking on the *Baerland*. They occupied the west room with Set, their sixteen-months'-old son, and in the afternoon Susannah went for a walk with Laurens into the plantation so that they could be alone together to have a chat. One of the first things she asked him was: "How are you getting on with Hannah and Katrina?"

He turned away his face and answered: "Oh, very well. Splendidly."

She gave him a keen look. "Which did you have first?"

"Katrina. I—the truth is I haven't had either of them yet. Later on. There's no hurry, is there?"

She smiled and squeezed his arm affectionately. "Poor fellow. Never mind. You'll pick up courage soon. Why not get thoroughly drunk one night after dinner? Wouldn't that help?"

"The last time you were here you warned me against wine," he laughed. "No. Wine only gets me befuddled. It never helps to give me courage for anything. And I think I'd lose some of my self-respect if I had to resort to such a method of going about things. If I can't bring myself to approach them when I'm sober, then I'm not a man."

"Your morals are very high. I like you for it. You wouldn't be you if you didn't feel that way."

The young canes loomed on either side of them as they moved along the dam. The slim, long leaves rustled softly in the breeze, making shifty shadows on the ground. The sunshine was mild, for the sun was low in the west. Now and then an insect would make a sharp chit-chit! among the canes, and the sound, if anything, would heighten the deep peace in the scene around them.

"You'll probably have a visit from Father some time next week. Commandeur Rol has invited him to spend a few days at the Residence. There's going to be some banquet, I understand, in honor of that fellow van Berkel, the factor of the Berbice colony."

"Yes, I'm asked, too. Adrian van Berkel is due here next week. It's a big occasion. Rol was telling me about it two or three weeks ago. He came over to see me shortly before that surprise visit of yours a fortnight ago. It will be van Berkel's first visit to Essequibo. You've heard of the disputes he and Rol have been having over poaching on each other's territory?"

"I did hear something, but I wasn't interested."

"It appears that van Berkel has been persistently doing trade with the Indians on The Demerara River, and, of course, Rol feels that the Demerara is his territory and that van Berkel has no right there. Anyway, the upshot of the matter is that van Berkel has decided to come and discuss the matter in a friendly spirit so that they can fix a definite boundary between the two colonies."

She laughed. "I told you I wasn't interested and still you explained. Thanks, all the same. To go back to Father—when he comes down here he may make a fuss if he finds that you've installed these two girls in the northeastern room. I think it would be advisable to have them live in the logies during the few days he's down in these parts."

"You're right—and yet. . . . Personally, I'd prefer to have it out with him and be done. Let him know right away that I intend to keep them here in the house as my mistresses. I don't like the idea of concealing it from him and being always in a state of suspense wondering when he'll discover what's going on."

"If you feel so, face it out," she smiled. "You have courage, Laurens, dear. You'll get over your diffidence in time. Don't be depressed."

This is what I like Susannah for, he told himself. Sometimes I tell myself it's a pity she's my sister. She would have been the perfect wife for me.

He told her: "I never feel diffident when I'm with you. You're the one person I can be at ease with."

The following day at a window in the northeastern room, he watched the ship moving down the river, and as it vanished, at last, round the bend, only the tip of the mast showing above the bush, he had to bite his lip hard. Moisture had gathered in his eyes.

He was on the point of moving back into his own room when the door opened and Katrina came in. She hesitated in the doorway, her face surprised and shy, but he told her: "You can come in, Katrina. I was only looking at the ship Missy Susannah has gone away in."

The very next instant he regretted saying this. He remembered what Susannah had told him that morning two weeks ago. "You let people see too much that you're conscious of their doing you a favor. Even with the slaves you're inclined to be like this." This is an example of what she meant, he told himself, as he went into his own room. Why did I have to make an explanation to her for my presence in the room? I'm her master, am I not? I have a right to go into any room in this house at any time.

He clenched his hands. Anger began to spiral up inside him. He had a good mind to go back inside there and tell Katrina that he was master here. "Look here, I'm your master, do you understand? I'll come into this room whenever I want to." But that would be foolish—undignified. All the same, he ought to do something about his self-respect. . . .

He moved toward the connecting door, hesitated, then went into the next room again.

Katrina turned with a soft exclamation.

He felt the blood coming to his face. He said quickly: "Katrina, I'd like—please come in and sweep my room."

"Sweep de room, Massa? Massa, Hannah sweep it already."

"I want it swept again. I don't consider it—I'm not satisfied that it was properly swept out." He tried to make his voice as stiff and commanding as he could, but kept his gaze out of the window as he spoke.

Katrina said: "I will do it again for you, then, Massa," and turned to leave the room.

"Wait," he said. His head wanted to tremble. He felt an inclination to swallow.

She paused.

"There's something I have to say to you."

"Yes, Massa?"

He felt his fingertips getting cold. He gulped and said: "I want you to come to my room this evening— tonight—after dinner. As soon as I have come up- stairs after dinner."

"To your room, Massa?"

"Yes—after dinner." He strode out and left her, trying not to show any haste. There was a hollowness within him, and the top of his head felt numb. In his room he halted and clasped his hands together.

Well, I did it. That's the first big step I've got over.

Nevertheless, he felt an uneasy triumph. He felt shame and excitement and anticipation. A bewildering medley.

Later, when he was riding through the fields, he nearly slipped off the mule from the vivid fantasies that hurried through his imagination. But as he righted him- self he muttered: "I feel more like a man now. And I'll prove tonight that I'm a man."

At the house, meanwhile, Hannah was staring at Ka- trina. "I not believe it," she said. This was the fourth time she had said this. "How he can ask you? You never look at him, and I always smiling at him and giving him my eye. I not believe it. You sure he say you must go to his room after dinner? Take care he have something for you to do for him and you mistaking what he mean?"

"No, I not mistake him. He say: 'I want you to come to my room dis evening—tonight—after din- ner. As soon as I have come upstairs after dinner.' Dose de very words he say to me. What else he could want me in his room for after dinner?"

"He's a funny man. You never give him de eye, and he still call you, and I give him de eye so much and he won't call me."

"All men don't like girls who give dem de eye and smile at dem. Some men like quiet girls who don't try to go after dem."

Hannah fell silent and looked subdued.

They were seated on the big bed in their room. Katrina was regarding her face in a jagged piece of mirror rescued years ago from the ruins of the Bakkers' house. She touched her hair, turning her head this way and that.

"And you never sleep wid a man before," said Hannah. "If it was me he call I would have teach him to do it. He would have like me, because I would have known how to make it sweet for him." There was disappointment in her voice—and a little anger. "All right, if he want you, let him have you. When he learn how you not want men and can't do it good he will quickly put you aside—and den if he call me in I tell him I feel sick bad and can't sleep wid him."

"You! You never tell him dat. You will go in quick if he call you any time. But perhaps he will never call you," said Katrina. "Your skin dark. Mine fair like his. Perhaps that is why he call me in and not you.

Hannah said nothing, but a troubled look came to her face.

"My hair long and smooth and glossy like his hair," said Katrina. "Your hair curl up and short and black. It must be dat's why he not want to call you in."

"But I slave same as you. And our father same father. And my body same good as yours." Hannah's eyes gleamed. "I not care. Plenty other man here. I can take other man if he not want me."

Katrina grunted. "Perhaps dat's why he not want you, too. I hear white massa like girls better when they not sleep wid no other man. He must be hear you sleep wid plenty other men before."

"But dat stupid. Girl who never sleep wid man before not as nice as girl who sleep wid plenty man."

"White massa think different."

IV

That evening only Katrina attended him at dinner. Hannah remained upstairs in a sulk. Katrina took pains to dress her hair carefully, and she wore a clean smock. There was no difference, however, in her manner toward him. She was still deferential and serious-faced, still shy and careful in her speech.

He did not say very much at dinner. He seemed tense and anxious, and Katrina told herself that it must be the shyness in him. Once he said: "I like your hair done that way, Katrina," but kept his gaze on the sideboard when he spoke. She replied: "Yes, Massa," in a murmur.

She could sense that he was puzzled about Hannah's absence. He kept glancing expectantly toward the stairway. At length he asked: "What has happened to Hannah this evening? Why hasn't she come down to serve at table?"

"She not well, Massa. So she say."

"What's the matter with her?"

Katrina began to fumble with the front of her smock. "I don't know, Massa."

He divined that it was an untruth. Hannah was well. She had remained upstairs for some other reason. He thought: I wonder whether she has fallen into a sulk. Can it be that Katrina has told her I've asked her to come to my room and she's jealous? But she's a slave. What right has she to neglect her duties because of a mere huff? If I was certain it was that I'd command Katrina to go upstairs this instant and call her down. The impudence! Hannah is forgetting herself.

He could not bring himself, however, to pursue the matter any further. He was too nervous with anticipation. He tried to assure himself the circumstance was too trivial to be bothered about.

Seated in his room, after dinner, he glanced up at the latticework and saw that there was light in the next room. Hannah was probably lying in bed or sitting by the window sulking. Sulking while Katrina was downstairs clearing the table.

He heard movement, and on impulse called: "Hannah!"

"Yes, Massa?"

He heard the thump of her bare feet on the floor.

She came in and stood before him. She was in her daytime smock.

"Why weren't you downstairs to help Katrina serve at table?"

"Massa, I not feel well."

In the reflection of the light from the next room he began to make out the details of her features. He could see the surly pout of her mouth.

"What is the matter with you?"

She made no reply.

"I'm speaking to you. Answer me."

"Massa, I not feel well."

"I have heard you. Is it fever? It's your duty to inform me if you're not well, so that I may have the surgeon come over and examine you. Tell me what is the matter."

His tone seemed to surprise her. She shifted her feet about and said: "Massa, nothing matter wid me. I well."

"Then why didn't you come downstairs to attend me at table?" He rose.

She was silent.

"Speak up."

"Massa, I didn't feel like coming down."

"You didn't feel like coming down!" His self-confidence came back in a rush. She might have been one of the field slaves he was taking to task for negligence. If he had had his whip he would have raised it preparatory to lashing her. "And since when has it come into your head that you can act as you feel? Are you your own mistress?"

She kept her head bent.

"If this happens again I'll flog you."

She said nothing.

"Go back to your room—and please know your place in future."

He felt a burning of resentment as he watched her return into her room. Pride made a hard lump inside him. He experienced a sense of aloofness and superiority, and it increased his resentment against her.

He stood glaring at the dark wall. He would make

her know her place. She was no companion of his, by God! He was a van Groenwegel. His grandfather had been Commandeur of the colony. He was a friend of the present Commandeur.

It was this mood that influenced events that night. A few minutes later, when Katrina came in—she had put on her bedtime smock—he told her curtly: "Light the lamp." And after she had done so he snapped: "That is all. Get back to your room. There's nothing more I need."

She hesitated an instant, then, without a word, went out, her bare slave's feet thumping softly on the floor.

He sat for a long time glaring round the room. I'll not have a slave forget herself with me. Something in me objects. I'll have to master this infatuation of mine. A slave must be a slave—male or female. They must be taught to remain inferior. I soon won't be respected by any of them if I made free with these two. Tomorrow I'm going to order them to get out of the house and take a logie. That's their place. The whole project was wrong: a stupid, absurd blunder of mine. I should never have brought them into the house.

The following morning this mood had passed. He told himself: I ought to have controlled myself and not acted so hastily. In a way, I was justified in not having had anything to do with Katrina when she came in. It would have been humiliating for me to have been intimate with her after Hannah's show of insubordination. But I lashed myself into too great a fury. I made myself look ridiculous. No doubt, Katrina must have thought it was shyness again that stopped me from having her in bed with me. She must have thought that at the last moment I failed in courage.

He felt stronger, though, for what had happened the previous night. He felt that he had acted like a man. The thought of them in the next room did not bother him so much this morning. He assured himself that the next time it would be easier to tell Katrina. He would find it less awkward to order her to come in to him.

That day there was a high wind, with fierce slanting rain. It broke out at about midmorning when he was aback in the fields. At the house the two girls stood at the windows of the west room looking out for him.

Hannah said: "De tracks muddy when rain fall like dis. I hope de mule won't slip and make him fall."

Katrina nodded, her face anxious and thoughtful. "He will come back safe. He can ride good."

"If he fall down and get killed, Massa Willem will send for us. I not like Massa Willem. I hear he not treat slaves good."

Katrina made no comment. Suddenly she said: "I going down to de kitchen."

"What for?"

Katrina made no reply. She left the room. Hannah followed her down, asking: "What you going down to do, Katrina?"

Katrina gave a sour smile and replied: "Dat not to do wid you."

In the kitchen they found Janwak and Beffy busy preparing the midday meal for their master. Two pots were bubbling on the fireplace.

Katrina set about to light another fire, and Janwak asked her: "What you want in here, Katrina?" Janwak was Beffy's man. He was tall and thin.

"Dat not to do wid you," said Katrina.

Hannah laughed. "What get into your head so sudden, Katrina? What you want to cook now? You not cook."

Without a word, Katrina filled a kettle with water. She put it over the new fire she had lit, and then seated herself on a wooden mortar. A wooden mortar in which boiled plantains were pounded. Janwak and Beffy began to make jokes about her, but Katrina ignored them.

Hannah sniggered: "Katrina must be working *obeah*. She going to boil herbs and chicken beak."

Katrina kept a glum silence. After a while she got up and went to the door. She opened it a few inches to peep out at the rushing wind and rain and the bending trees. Water gurgled in swift, pocked rivulets all over the compound and in the clearing beyond the compound. The track that led to the fields was a roaring stream. The ditches had overflowed.

"It's Massa she looking out for," laughed Hannah. "Katrina, you getting your head turn over Massa? Because he ask you to go to his room last night to light de lamp? Massa not want you. You making yourself fool." She turned to Janwak and Beffy. "Yesterday Katrina come and tell me Massa want her to go to his room after dinner, and she think he call her to sleep wid him. When she go in to him last night Massa tell her to light de lamp and go back to her room." She gave a shriek of laughter, her body shaking so lusciously that Janwak's eyes gleamed.

Katrina ignored her, still watching the track anxiously.

Beffy called: "Katrina, your water boiling!"

"Let it boil!" Katrina called back.

Laurens, on mule back, appeared on the track, the water swirling about the mule's hoofs and seeming as though it would sweep the animal away. So thought Katrina, her hand clutching the front of her smock. But the mule came through safely and approached the house across the clearing.

When Laurens was dismounting at the foot of the kitchen stairs, and two slaves, who had run up, were taking charge of the mule, Katrina opened the kitchen door wide in spite of the rain that came in. She went out on the landing as her master came up the four steps, and Laurens looked at her in surprise and exclaimed: "Katrina! What are you coming out in the rain for? Where are you going to?"

"Massa, I have some water boiling for you. You must come quick in de bathroom and let me soak your feet in hot water, or you take cold."

"Take cold? No, no. I don't take cold easily," he smiled, asking himself in wonder: What can have happened to her? Why this solicitude on my behalf? He said quickly: "What I can do with is a good hot cup of coffee, Katrina. Prepare it and bring it up for me."

"Yes, Massa. I do dat now."

"You can take off my boots. They're full of water."

She obeyed, and he hurried upstairs, leaving a trail of water on the floor and on the stairs.

A little later Katrina brought him the coffee. She found him in dry clothes, seated in the most comfortable chair, near the desk. He gave her a curious look and smiled: "Katrina, what made you think of boiling water for me?"

Her gaze lowered, she replied: "I know you was out in de rain, Massa, so I boil water for you to put your feet in so you not take cold."

"That was very good of you. Very thoughtful." He took the coffee from her and placed the mug and cup on the desk. As she began to move toward the door he said: "I wish I could get every one of the others to be so considerate of my welfare. Katrina!"

"Yes, Massa?" She paused and turned round. The rain had wet the front of her smock, and he could see the tips of her breasts shaped clear and prominent under the calico. He rose and said: "I wish I could —I wish I knew how to express what I mean." He stopped speaking, very red-faced. He cast furtive glances about the room, frowning in his discomfiture.

She hesitated, then turned off and began to move again toward the door. He took three quick steps after her and gripped her arms, standing behind her, his body in a tremor. He felt her stiffen. She turned her head a trifle.

"Can you—will you—I want you to come in here tonight after dinner."

She said nothing.

"Will you come?"

"Yes, Massa." She was breathing quickly.

The scent of the coffee came across to them from the desk. Outside, the wind howled and the rain swished fiercely against the window-panes. He could see nothing of Kyk-over-al. Only a white pall of thick rain.

"As soon as dinner is over," he said, breathing quickly himself. He could smell her hair—the dryishness of it. He relaxed his grip on her arms. "Go now," he said. But when she moved off he reached out and gripped her again. This time he turned her so that she faced him.

She kept her head bent, and when he tried to fondle her breasts she drew her arms across and murmured: "No, Massa," pulling away slightly from him. He persisted, trembling, and slipped his hand down inside her smock. She did not resist any longer. He saw her throat move as though she had swallowed. Her eyes were bright.

"You must stay with me—now." He left her and hurriedly locked the doors: the one that opened into the corridor and the one that connected with the next room.

When they were in the big bed they could smell the coffee fumes coming across from the desk: Adriansen's old desk on which Willem and Aert had climbed that night long ago, the muskets shaking in their grasp.

The wind and the rain made a savage noise outside.

In the next room Hannah was listening to them. She had come upstairs to see why Katrina had not returned downstairs. She had tried the door and found it locked. Now she stood still and listened to them: the sounds they made that were audible above the noise of the weather: murmurings and the lisp of the bedclothes, a creak of the bed. She could not believe it was happening. In the morning now. The two of them in there. And Katrina who had always said she didn't want any man. The lying bitch!

I give him so much eye. I smile at him—and she not even want to look at him. She always wid her face serious. How dis happen so? . . . But I not care. Let him have her. I can get other man. Plenty man here I can have if I want.

She smelt the coffee. She glanced up at the latticework. Curiosity burned within her as though it were a candle flame just come alight. She pulled up a chair and climbed on to it, then climbed up on to the top of the cupboard and looked through the latticework.

Look at them on the bed. Like two white people.

Both their bodies are white. . . . My body dark. But I not care. I can get other man. Janwak want me. I can take him on the sly when Beffy gone for firewood. . . .

She climbed down. The chair slipped when she put her foot on it. She clutched at the cupboard. It broke her fall, but she hurt her elbow.

In the next room they seemed not even to have heard the noise made by her falling. She heard the whine of their breath in rapture. Or was it the wind? She hated them both. Hated them.

She began to sob. She beat her head on the floor. She looked at the windows. Rain blurred the glass, and the wind outside sounded male and evil.

V

Many mornings on awakening I've told myself that the night before did not happen, that only the day is real. Night has always appeared to me a fantasy state: the darkness, and the stars and moonlight and the insects cheeping. But day, with its white sunshine and the landscape green and brown and people actively engaged in this or that task—the day is very real. This evening it appears the opposite. This evening seems more real than today. I can't believe that today happened. That rain and wind, and she and I in here and the coffee on the desk. Whenever I smell coffee in the future I shall remember today. The darkness now and the stars in the sky and the river look as though they can be believed in, but today seemed to have passed in a haze. She said she likes me—liked me since the day when I wanted to hold her arm in the dining-room, but, instead, asked her to get me a jug of water. I would never have guessed that. A strange girl. . . . And Hannah. Hannah is jealous. She gave me some sulky looks at dinner, and she didn't smile as she generally does. But it doesn't matter. It's Katrina I want.

He slapped his cheek. Yes, this is real. In a few minutes she will be coming to sleep with me. By God, I feel good. I can sing. I can dance and sing.

He heard footsteps. She was coming upstairs. He saw light glow up at the latticework.

Later, when she had come in, he asked her in a whisper: "What did Hannah have to say? Did she seem angry?"

"She angry and surprised. She say I deceive her, because I behave as if I not want man. She disappointed you not ask her instead of me."

"I thought so. I could tell from the way she looked at me when I was dining."

Today in bed they had talked very little. Tonight they talked a lot. She asked him: "Why you choose me and not her? Because my skin fair and hers dark?" He replied: "No. I never thought of that. In fact, I like color. To me she is——" He broke off, thinking: I'd better not tell her that. I was going to say: "To me she is just as attractive as you. I am enamored of you both," but she might feel jealous. I can't risk that.

She insisted, however. She asked: "What you want to say? Tell me. You like me better than her, that's why you choose me?"

He decided to be frank. "No, I like you both the same. You both excite me. I don't want to hurt your feelings, Katrina, but I must be honest. I'm not in love with you—neither of you. I only want your bodies. From the moment I saw you some years ago, when the Blairs bought you, I wanted you. I like colored women. The Indians attract me the same. I'm not fond of white girls, though I suppose I will have to marry one some day in order to carry on the family name."

"You not hurt my feelings," she said. "I don't care if you not love me. I like you plenty, and I do anything for you. I will take care of your children for you when you marry. Let me do that for you and I glad. I want nothing more."

"You wouldn't be jealous?"

"No. So long as I can stay here and be slave for you I not care. You can have Hannah tomorrow night if you want. Even tonight. I not mind."

"That doesn't seem natural to me. Look at Hannah. She is jealous because I've selected you first. She's sulking. I can understand that. It's human."

"Dat is how I am," she said. "I not care about people loving me. If I like a person I do things for dem. I give dem all I can give dem, but I not want nothing from dem."

"You must be a rare kind of person, Katrina."

Her attitude, he discovered a few days later, was genuine.

Hannah, instead of keeping up her sulks, began to do what she could to attract him. She smiled at him often, and one morning when he returned from his inspection round the plantation he found a bouquet of flowers in a vase on the cupboard in his room, and Hannah told him at lunch: "Massa, I pick some flowers for you. I put dem in your room."

"Was it you who put those flowers on the cupboard? Thank you, Hannah. It was very good of you."

At table, she hastened to forestall Katrina in serving him, and Katrina seemed indifferent to competition. Katrina behaved exactly as she had done before she had begun to sleep with him. She had the same quiet, respectful manner and spoke in the same tone of voice. She never attempted to be familiar in any way.

On the fifth day after the rain he was coming down the stairs and Hannah was going up, and in passing each other Hannah purposely brushed close against him. It excited him—as she had intended—and he stopped and held her arm. She gave him her bold look, and when he smiled and awkwardly began to fondle her she did not draw away or try to shield her breasts as Katrina had done the day of the rain. She came closer and rubbed her hand along his neck. He uttered a soft gasp and told her to come into his room with him.

Later that day, when Hannah told Katrina what had happened and that he had asked her to come to him that night, Katrina was only mildly surprised. "I glad he ask you. Go in and make him happy."

Hannah frowned. She had a cheated look. "But you not angry?"

Katrina smiled sourly. "What I must angry for? I like him. I not tell you dat before? When he want me again I go to him. If he want you always he can take you. I not mind."

"But you queer girl! You queer too bad, Katrina."

For the rest of that afternoon Hannah could do nothing but exclaim and say how queer Katrina was.

That night she made herself so pleasing to him that Laurens told her: "I don't think I could do without you after this, Hannah. You're so alive—and warm. I should have known it, though. From the way you used to smile at me. And you didn't give as much trouble as Katrina. It's almost as though you've been with a man before. Do you swear you've never had another man before me?"

"I swear it." She looked at him straight in the eyes.

Throughout the next day he kept living over what had happened the night before between himself and Hannah. His nights with Katrina seemed dull and pale by contrast.

In the afternoon his father arrived. Except for one or two strands of grey in his beard, Willem looked hardly any older. His eyes darted about with the same fire as they had done when he was forty-eight. His brows lowered abruptly in the same moody way and his cheeks seemed ready to puff out in a snort at the slightest provocation. He had gained around the waist, but this only added to his stocky solidity—not to his age.

As they moved toward the house he kept looking critically about as though on the alert to pounce upon some defect: some instance of neglect.

"I have the whole clearing weeded at least once a fortnight," Laurens told him. "Weeds grow so quickly."

Willem grunted. "I suppose they do." He jerked his thumb toward the bush in the northeast. "I'm thinking of getting that tangle of stuff cut down. Your grandmother's grave is somewhere under that mass of vines and creepers. I don't believe in messy sentiment, but I think it's only proper that Mother's grave should be preserved. It's been shamefully neglected."

"Is there any cross or slab that marks the place?"

"There's a stone slab. Must be mossy and half-buried by now, but it can be found if we cut away the bushes."

"I'll see about it as soon as I can."

"No frantic hurry," his father frowned. "The field work must come first." When they were passing through the dining room on their way upstairs he gave Katrina a stare but did not show any recognition. Halfway up the stairs he asked: "Who is that fair-skinned female? I don't remember seeing her the last time I was here?"

"She's Katrina."

"Katrina? Who's Katrina?"

"One of the two girls who used to be with the Blairs. The Bakkers bought them over when the Blairs sold out after the raid. Susannah happened to acquire them before she sailed, and she passed them over to me." He spoke without stammering, his tone confident and his eyes steady.

Willem frowned, as though still not aware of whom he was talking about. "What two girls? What two girls do you mean?" He started. "You're not referring to those bastards of your Uncle August?"

"Yes, I mean those. Katrina and Hannah. They're here now. They're my personal slaves."

"Indeed!" They had entered the southeastern room. "Your personal slaves! And why did you have to pick on them in particular?"

"I've just told you, Father, that Susannah gave them to me. She made me a present of them."

Willem's frown deepened. What was the matter with the boy? There was hostility in his manner. He looked defiant. Guilty. Very odd.

"I gather that perfectly well. But what I mean is, why did she have to pick on these two girls in particular? I quite appreciate that you might have a preference for mulatto slaves in the house, but why did Susannah not choose another pair? Why *these* two?"

"Father, I may as well tell you. They're my mistresses. They live with me in the house here—in the next room. I happened to have taken a fancy to them since I first saw them some years ago."

Willem spluttered. "Your mistresses! Oh, indeed!

Your mistresses!" There was an instant of silence, then Willem broke into a low guffaw. "So you've begun to meddle with women, eh? Oh, so that's it! Mistresses. And two of them. Not even one but two." He seemed too dismayed and amused to be annoyed. Abruptly, however, he frowned again. "If you want to get married, why don't you go about it in the right way? It's true the colony is badly lacking in women since those ruined families left for Suriname after the raid, but Blankenburg's two daughters are pretty marriageable. Rosa and Frieda. Seventeen and sixteen. The other one is only eleven. And there's the de Graaf girl, though she's no beauty. Don't you want to get married? You're twenty-one. I see no reason why you shouldn't."

Laurens thought: I can see this is going to be most awkward if he persists in talking about marriage. He didn't get married until he'd seen a great deal of the world. Why does he expect me to be content to settle down here and get married before I've traveled a bit?

"I'm thinking about it," he said aloud. "Some time, soon. By the way, do you think I should cross over before the Berbice Factor arrives, or should I wait until the ceremony is over?"

Willem guffawed again. "A crude manner of changing the subject, boy. No, you must be over during the morning to be present at the ceremony of welcome. Look here, see and don't let these two girls forget themselves. Keep them in their places. I don't object to you having your fling. It will do you good. But let them know that you're master here. No familiarity." He chuckled. "At least, not outside of bed."

"I keep them in their place, no fear."

Willem must have referred to the subject at least half a dozen times during the hour he spent in the house before embarking again to cross over to the Commandeur's residence. He laughed and said: "It'll do me good to watch your mother's face when I tell her of this. By the way, does Rol know about it?"

"Yes, he was here two days ago on his way to the creek. He wanted me to join him. He was hunting *lab-*

ba. He admired Hannah a lot and asked me if I didn't want to sell her, so I had to explain the position."

Willem shook. "Oh, well! No harm in it. And I'll admit, the one I saw down there was not bad to look at. You have taste, boy. Like your father, by St. Peter! I had some pretty succulent lumps myself when I was your age. Used to attract them like mice to cheese."

Laurens was relieved when he left. . . . I'm never comfortable when he's in this place. Anyway, it's good to know he didn't make a fuss about the girls. Susannah was right. You simply can't predict how he'll react to any given set of circumstances.

Dusk was gathering outside. The insects were beginning to churr, and the air tingled with the chill of evening. From over the water came the grating of anchor chains. A ship had arrived, a small trading vessel. He watched it and recalled what he had thought earlier that afternoon. . . . Do I want to travel? No, I don't think so. What I really want to do is to marry and settle down. I like this place: the river and the island and the peacefulness of everything, especially when dusk sets in. At heart, I am not an adventurer. I used to think so when I was younger, but now I know myself better. I like being at home. I'd like to have children and watch them grow up and talk and laugh and know they're mine.

That night in bed, Hannah made him recall this thought. She said: "I would like to have a baby by you. Perhaps two, three. I always like having babies. I tell Katrina so plenty times, but she say she not like have baby, because baby bring too much work. But I must have some. I take care of dem good when I get dem."

He said: "Yes, I should like to have children, too —but I don't want slave children."

"You can keep dem in de house and treat dem good, Massa."

"Don't address me as Massa. I've told you not to. When you're in bed with me you must forget you're a slave. You're bad at adjusting yourself to a situation, Hannah. Katrina is much better in that respect."

"You want me to leave, den, and go and call her to come in to you?"

He laughed and told her not to be foolish. On and off, afterwards, he kept thinking about children. It would be awkward if these girls began to have children. He couldn't imagine children of his as slaves. Two daughters of his walking around the house in smocks and addressing him as Massa. That would be unnatural. He wouldn't be able to stand it. His own flesh and blood with the status of a menial?

He was still thinking about it when he stood at the landing place with his father and Commandeur Hendrik Rol the following morning at Kyk-over-al. He was so silent and pensive that once Rol glanced at him and laughed. "Laurens, boy, you don't look happy—but I shouldn't be surprised, should I?" He winked significantly, glanced at Willem and said: "Sir, your son has courage. When I was his age I could only tackle them one at a time."

Willem quivered. "His father, Rol! Blood will out! I've been known to sleep with three at one time. Oh, yes —in Alexandria. No less than three: two Arabs and a Nubian." Willem went into details, and Hendrik Rol listened eagerly and made the air vibrate with his laughter.

Rol was a man of about thirty-four, bearded like Willem, and extremely jovial. He had no affectations because of his position, and, at all times, addressed Willem with the respect due to his senior in years and in planting and trading experience. Once he had said to Laurens: "What have I got to be puffed up about, Laurens! It's just a title I have—nothing else. You private planters are far above me in actual wealth. My salary is thirty guilders[1] a month, with rations— and look what I've got to do to earn it. I'm Governor, I'm Captain of the troops, I'm storekeeper and I'm Indian trader. Every few weeks I'm off into the interior on some expedition. When I'm back there's no peace for me. Always some dispute to settle or some matter to write the Directors about. I can't see that I have anything to get swelled up over in this title of mine."

The tent-boat with Factor van Berkel and his

[1] $12, at the rate of exchange then in existence (in sterling, about 50s).

party was in sight downriver, and while they waited
Hendrik Rol talked trade and planting with Willem,
Laurens listening but seldom saying anything.

In another group, nearby, the Secretary and
two or three Government officials and traders also
waited and chatted. Near the entrance of the fort a double line of soldiers stood at ease with muskets, for Rol
had decided to do things in style and provide a guard
of honor for the visitor. He himself was in full-dress
uniform, and as he talked he kept patting his
sheathed sword which made a clink-clink against his
leg, the scabbard glittering in the bright sunshine.

When the party came ashore and the muskets
thundered out in salute, Laurens felt a shiver of memory
tingle through him. The sound took him back five or
six years to that day of the raid. He remembered the
aniseed smell of the felled Carib. . . . I'm too imaginative, he told himself.

It was a whole-day function. Van Berkel wanted
to retire with Rol to discuss business, but Rol insisted
that they must forget everything of a serious nature
for the next two or three days, and so they sat down
in the big drawing room in the Commandeur's residence within the fort and indulged in conversation and
gin and wine. Willem had provided a large jar of wine.
He and another planter, Mynheer de Graaf, were the
only two who had supplied wine and provisions. But
de Graaf went a step further than Willem. He had not
been able to be present at the function, but in the late
afternoon a messenger arrived inviting the whole party
to the de Graaf Plantation house for a banquet—a
banquet arranged for the following day, for the de
Graaf plantation was an hour's journey from the fort.

Laurens was in a fidget of alarm lest his father
should suggest his sleeping the night at the Residence,
for it was planned to set out by *corial* early the following morning. As it happened, however, dinner was a
very merry affair, and so much wine and gin was drunk
that Rol said: "I doubt whether any of us will be in a
fit condition to travel early in the morning. We'll have
to leave at about ten o'clock."

Laurens interposed quickly: "That suits me

splendidly. There's a new field I must see after tomorrow morning. By ten o'clock I should have finished my inspection."

He did not return to the mainland until after eleven o'clock, and the slave who rowed took his time, for he was heavy with sleep. Laurens looked up at the stars. The stars swayed about, some merging into others. He thought: I'm drunk. I shouldn't have let Hendrik persuade me to take that gin. It doesn't mix well with the wine.

He found Hannah in his room, waiting for him. "I keep looking out for you at de window but you wouldn't come. I sleepy. I nearly fall off de chair wid sleep."

"Wish you had," he said. "Would have taught you a lesson. Too damned hot."

"You drunk. You not know what you talking."

"I'm not drunk. Who said I was drunk? Remember whom you're speaking to, you damned slave! You're too familiar."

"Massa, I didn't mean no harm."

"Don't call me Massa in my bedroom. I've told you that before. How many times must I tell you the same thing. Get out! Back into your room!"

"I sorry. Let me stay. I behave good."

"Get out. Get out, I say!"

She went.

He looked around the room, swaying on his feet. The lamp was burning on the desk. He shook his head sharply, thinking: This is not like me. I shouldn't have behaved like that. Hell! That gin. . . .

He went to the connecting door, hesitated, told himself: I'll call her in again and tell her I'm sorry. No, I mustn't do that. Remember what Susannah said. Mustn't make them feel I'm inferior. Let them know I'm master. I apologize too much to people. But I must have a woman tonight. I'm in the mood for a woman. He pushed the door in.

"Katrina! Come here!" he called. "Come and sleep with me!"

So Katrina slept with him that night. They heard muffled sobs in the next room. "She's got more fire than you, Katrina. But I like you. You have a sweetness in your nature she hasn't got. You're kind and thoughtful, and I can see you want to give me all you have it in your power to give. That's good. I appreciate it, but I'm also fond of people who can express themselves—people who can resist, talk back at me. Hannah is like that. She has fire. Fire-blood. But she annoys me sometimes. She's too forward. She gets me resentful. I often wonder about her, too. She says she's never slept with a man before me, but she behaves in bed as if—well, you can see she knows what she is about. She maddens me—makes me feel I can kill for her. But still she insists she's never been with another man. Is that true, Katrina?"

"Yes, dat true," said Katrina, without hesitation.

"By St. Peter! Then she must be a born genius!" He laughed. "Born genius. She moves like a greased snake. Yet . . . yet I like you, Katrina. Soft. Sweet-natured. Anyway, you're both slaves. . . . Both slaves. . . ."

His voice trailed off. He fell asleep, breathing heavily.

Katrina bent over him and kissed his forehead and his hair and then his lips. There was moonlight on his face. A waning half-moon had risen over Kyk-over-al. The same half-moon Kaywana had seen. In this same room. Katrina watched his face and smiled, and whispered to herself.

During the next two or three months it was Hannah with whom he slept. He and Hannah developed a fierce, unreasoning passion for each other. He told her one night: "I'd go mad and kill myself if anything should happen to you." She said: "I, too. I kill myself if I not have you. You must never send me from you. I remain with you forever and have children. You must give me six, seven babies. Dat de only way I happy."

This side of the affair continued to disturb him. I want to have children, he assured himself. I should like to see a creature of my own and to know that I was responsible for its existence. I think nothing can be bigger than that. It is an experience I'm longing to have.

I'd feel I've achieved something worth while. But a slave child. . . ."

Hannah, too, was obsessed with the idea of having a child. She said to Katrina one day: "Soon I will have a baby, and then plenty more will come after dat one. Six, seven—ten. I will mind dem all myself, and he will treat dem good. He say he will give dem everything they want——"

"And what about his other children wid his wife?" Katrina interrupted. "What will happen to dem? He will take care of yours and de other ones his wife give him?"

Hannah uttered an impatient exclamation. "He not marry! He keep me for his woman all his life. He tell me so. He say he can't have no other but me, because I give him all he want. He say he would die for me." Her voice was so impassioned that it sounded a little cracked. "I would die for him, too. I do anything for him."

Katrina said quietly: "I like him plenty, too. I not care if he not want me. Nobody can stop me from liking him."

"You stupid!" Hannah snapped, jealous and resentful. "You like him and he not like you! You foolish. Weeks now he not look at you. Weeks now he not touch you—not even your arm—and still you say you like him. You stupid girl! If you not stop liking him I tell him to put you out de house. I tell him to send you to Massa Willem. He do anything I tell him."

Katrina was in no way upset. She said: "I never stop liking him. You can say all you want. You can't stop me doing dat. He himself can't stop me, no matter how big Massa he is. No matter where he send me, I still go on liking him all de time."

Hannah glared at her. She called her obscene names. She was so incensed and disturbed that she decided that she could not wait until night to talk to Laurens about it. She waited in the dining room, and when he came in from his inspection around the plantation she said to him: "Massa, I want to tell you something. I can come upstairs now?"

The urgency of her tone impressed him. "Very well. Come."

When he heard what it was he laughed and told her: "That's absurd. Send her away because she likes me? Do you think that would be fair?"

Hannah looked sulky. "She not got right to like you. Only I got right to like you. I not like her stay here. I want her to go away."

"Oh, indeed! *You* want her to go away! And are you in a position to say what you want done and what you don't want done? I thought I was master here."

"All right, you master. Me slave. I not come in to you tonight!"

He slapped her face. She sobbed and cringed away —then turned and struck back: hit him with her clenched hand on his cheek.

"You filthy slave-bitch!" He grabbed her by the shoulders and hurled her from him with all his strength. She landed on the floor with a heavy thump, crying out. He kicked her and told her to get up.

"Up! Get out! You've forgotten yourself. A dirty slut of a slave to dare hit me! I'm a van Groenwegel, damn you!" He kicked her again—in her face. She put her up hands to shield herself, but her lips and chin were bleeding.

"Massa, I sorry," she wailed. "I not mean to hit you."

The fury in him passed. He stooped and murmured: "I'm sorry. I didn't intend to hurt you." He lifted the hem of her smock and dabbed at the blood on her chin and lips. He looked up and saw Katrina at the door. "Katrina! Go down and get some water and a clean rag. Quickly."

"Yes, Massa," said Katrina, and hurried off.

Hannah did not stop sobbing. She made all the fuss she could. Even after he had lifted her on to the bed she continued to moan and shake. "You not like me no more, or you not treat me like dis."

He told her not to be foolish. "You made me lose my temper. I'm master here. I'm getting tired of telling you that. I won't have a slave take up an attitude of defiance toward me—not even you."

Some note in his voice must have made her realize that further hysterics would avail nothing. She stopped sobbing. "I sorry I speak to you as I speak," she murmured. "I not speak that way again. I behave good."

"What's happened to Katrina, I wonder? I sent her for some water and some clean rags."

"She hate me. She not bring up none."

"Katrina couldn't hate anyone. You're talking nonsense." He left the room and went downstairs, prepared to scold Katrina. He found her seated at the foot of the stairs, a bowl of water and a piece of cloth beside her. Her head was pillowed on her knees, and he saw that she had been sick on the floor.

"Katrina, what is the matter?"

"I walk too fast, Massa. Soon as I reach de stairs my head spin around and I feel bad."

He lifted her upstairs and put her to bed. Hannah came in and looked on in dismay. "What wrong wid her?"

"She's not well. She must be sickening for some disease," he said, a look of concern on his face. "I'm going to send a message to the surgeon to come at once."

Later that day the surgeon told Laurens with a smile: "It's no disease. She's going to have a child."

After he had gone Laurens sat by a window in his room and looked out at the weak sunshine. It was a cloudy afternoon, but the clouds were not gray; they were white and broken up and stretched in an unmoving wad over the sky. The air felt steamy, and there was a general oppressiveness.

It must be the weather, he told himself, that makes me feel like this—and yet I'm not certain. I can sense a glowing inside me. It's as though there were a ghost in me that laughs but laughs so that I can only feel a trembling in my chest. This is foolish. I'm letting my fancy run away with me. I suppose some things we feel can't be defined at all.

For the fourth time within half an hour he rose and went into the next room and looked at Katrina and smiled: "Are you sure you don't want anything, Katrina?" For the fourth time she smiled back: "No, Massa. I not want nothing. I feel good now."

"You mustn't go downstairs again for the day. You must rest."

"Yes, Massa."

He stood looking at her, a foolish wonder on his face. "I can't believe it yet," he murmured.

She hung her head. She was sitting up in bed, two pillows at her back. She looked like a lady—a white lady at ease in the morning. I've seen Mother like this, he thought.

"So you're going to have a child. Mine and yours. No, I can't believe it. It seems . . . I'm being foolish, Katrina."

VI

That night he did not sleep with Hannah. He slept alone. The next day he went across to the fort to the surgeon. He asked questions, and when he returned home told Katrina: "The surgeon says I can sleep with you—up to the sixth or seventh month."

Hannah took it badly. She cursed Katrina. "Let him sleep with you. What I care? I believe you work *obeah* on him. You're a bad *obeah* girl. You throw gray powder on him."

Katrina said: "I not care what you say. I have his child in me. You can't take it from me. And you! You sleep wid him weeks and weeks and still you not have any child. You barren. You like Dakkana who Massa Bakker had. She sleep wid man after man, but she not get no baby."

"I not like Dakkana!" Hannah broke into sobs. She threw herself down on the floor and beat her head on the boards. "I not barren. You wish me bad, but I show you you wrong. I have baby, too—soon."

Katrina sniffed. "Before you come here you not sleep wid Jemma and Parkab and Hoobakka? Why you not swell wid baby since den? And now you come here, Massa sleep wid you weeks and weeks, and still you not swell. Massa sleep wid me four nights, and den one more night, and now I get baby for him. You not good. All you can do is to take man, but you can't have baby."

Hannah sat very still. Her breath came in jerks.

"You better not let Massa know you sleep wid other man before him, or he might put you out. When he ask me I say you not sleep wid no man before him."

Outside, no wind blew. The sun shone down from a hot, cloudless sky. They could hear the river whispering against the bank in the breezeless silence. A dull hammering came from Kyk-over-al. The soldiers must be erecting some new shed.

Hannah rose slowly and left the room.

That night, as soon as Laurens had gone upstairs after dinner, Hannah went up. She entered his room and said: "Massa, I can ask you something quick before Katrina come up?"

"Very well. Speak on."

She stared about in the darkness in a distracted manner, then took a pace toward him and clutched his sleeve. "Massa, you let me sleep wid you one week more—just one week more? I get baby if you let me sleep wid you one more week, Massa."

"What gives you reason to think so? Why should one more week make a difference?"

"I drink bush-water every morning, Massa. Dat make me get baby."

"Bush-water? Don't be absurd. Katrina didn't have to drink bush-water, and she's pregnant. But why are you upsetting yourself like this, Hannah? I haven't told you I'll never sleep with you again, have I?"

"I know, Massa—but please. I beg you. Let me sleep wid you for seven nights from tonight and I sure have baby. De moon just right now—and I drink bush-water. Please, Massa."

He hesitated, moved, then said: "I'm afraid my spirit is not with you at the moment. I want to have Katrina with me tonight—and for a good many more nights to come. She's bearing my child. I feel toward her. . . . I can't express what I feel, but—but I want her with me."

She tried to argue, but he cut her short and told her to get out.

Yes, my spirit is not with Hannah now, he told himself. Katrina has taken on a preciousness in my fancy. She has my child in her. I feel she is someone I must protect and be very tender toward. She seems very big and real to me now—and close to me; part of my flesh.

Later, when she came in and lit the lamp in her usual silent fashion and then smiled at him and sat on the bed, he knew as he watched her that he had begun to love her. . . . I know it, he thought. It's cool and real. He told her, and she said it was the same with her. She, too, loved him.

When he had put out the lamp and they were in bed he said: "Tonight I have come upon a great thing."

"What you mean?"

He said nothing.

"What you mean?" she asked again.

"A great thing, Katrina. I mean not to lose it."

They lay together breathing quietly.

"I'm going to marry you, Katrina."

"Marry me?"

"Yes."

"But what you saying? How can you marry me? I only a slave!"

"I don't care. Tonight I'm seeing things differently. Tonight I can see you as a human being. It doesn't matter how you speak—or that you wear a smock. You've broken down my pride. I see you now as a woman. You have my child in you, and you're good. You have a good nature. You're kind and sympathetic, and under your glum look there is sweetness."

She said nothing. After a moment he heard a sniffle.

He stroked her hair. "There's no need to cry."

"But I spoil your life if you marry me. I can't make you a wife. If you marry white girl I stay wid you and take care of your children. Do dat and you make me happy. But if you marry me I get sad and feel sorry for you."

"You won't be sad. You'll be happy—because I'll be happy."

She was silent.

"Tomorrow I shall write to Father and tell him what I intend to do. And I shall go over and see Hendrik Rol and arrange for him to marry us."

Like the day, the night was exceptionally hot. It was a long time before they fell asleep.

No breeze blew. Once he woke and heard the river's hushed sounds. He thought: the river sounds secretive and ominous, as though a terrible event were about to happen. I wonder if Grandmother thought so, too, that night when she woke up and heard it. Grandfather said it was a still night, and lightning was flashing in the south over the jungle.

He turned his head and looked out of one of the southern windows. . . . I don't see lightning, but the air is still—and hot.

He fell asleep again, but woke before dawn. Beside him, Katrina sighed and tossed in her sleep. He looked out and saw Kyk-over-al, a dark, long shadow in the river. The sky in the east looked muddy-gray. The jungle on the opposite bank stood out against it jet black.

I don't think I can sleep any more. Too much is in my thoughts this morning. Today is the beginning of a new phase. The sunshine won't look the same to me as it did yesterday.

He watched Katrina. . . . My father's grandchild is inside her. A new van Groenwegel. . . . People with fire-blood, the van Groenwegels. The people who stayed and fought when Scott and his Caribs came. . . . What is Father going to say when I tell him I have decided to marry a slave? Hendrik Rol will understand. He is broad in his outlook. He has tact—and vision. Yes, vision. Look how successfully he handled that business with van Berkel. The Abary Creek is now the boundary between the Berbice colony and our colony. Hendrik maneuvered that well, and now the disputes are over. He's a man who can see far. He isn't cramped like Father. However, it doesn't matter what Father thinks. I am a man for myself, and I'll hold my own against all opposition. I'm no more a diffident, yielding boy. Father can't handle me as he likes. I'll stand up to him. I'll make him realize that he is only too right about our blood. He himself has said that we have fire in us. He has emphasized it so often. Very well. I'll show him that it's true. I'll give him a taste of the fire in me.

The river kept on whispering. The east did not look so muddy now. A touch of yellow was evident. He sat up and hugged his knees. Far away a jungle bird cried harshly. The bird the Indians called the *carra-carra*. He heard a gurgling swish on the river, and told himself that it must be a *corial* passing.

He glanced at Katrina and smiled. . . . Such a fine body she has. Is there any mark on her body that can make anyone who didn't know think she is a slave? None. She is human like any white planter's daughter. Frieda and Rosa Blankenburg are no better than she. . . . She looks soft and beautiful asleep in this gray light. I can feel her spirit in me, quiet and shadowed, peaceful, like this dawn.

He heard the bird again. "Carra-carra-carra-carra!" . . . The sky was getting dull red and brown. He heard a gurgling swish on the river. . . . Was it a *corial?* He craned his head. . . . He got out of bed and went to the window in a spirit of idle curiosity.

No, it's not a *corial*. It seems . . . Someone is swimming out from the bank. From the bank here. I can make out the head and an arm. But at this hour! Strange.

As he looked he saw the gray water, daubed with red reflected from the sky, pattern itself with ripples. After a moment, however, the ripples began to fade, and suddenly the water smoothed itself out and recovered its glassy calm. He could see the reflected shape of a long blue-black cloud. He kept on looking, and then it came upon him that the swimmer was not there. The swimmer had gone down. Silently and undramatically. Gone down without a cry or a struggle. . . . Can I have imagined it?

He stood frowning out at the scene. The insects had not ceased their nighttime churring. It was peaceful, and there seemed an intelligence in everything: a silent awareness. An invisible overwhelming cloud seemed to hang above the river. He was too imaginative.

When he was moving back to the bed a thought came to him. He halted and glanced at the latticework at the top of the wall. He crossed to the connecting door and pushed it in, looked around the room the two girls used. The big bed, he saw, was empty. Hannah was not in it.

"Hannah!"

He hurried across the room to the other door. It was ajar. He went out into the corridor and called from the top of the stairs.

"Hannah! Are you downstairs?"

No answer. The shadows of the house seemed to well up at him from out of the dark stairway. A gray fear moved in him.

He went halfway down the stairs, calling.

Outside, far away still, the *carra-carra* bird uttered its harsh cry. And after he had listened a moment another sound came to him through the quiet dawn air. The hacking yap of a raccoon.

VII

"So far as I am concerned," said Willem, "what has happened is no tragedy. An event may be described as tragic when it involves a person or group of persons of consequence." He pointed out of the window. "The body that lies under that mound of earth is the body of a slave—a creature of barter. Nothing either of you may say will convince me that such a being can be looked upon as someone to be reckoned with or considered as important in my scheme of living. No. It is fruitless to continue this discussion. For me there can be no argument. You may call it a tragedy, Laurens, that this girl drowned herself, and claim that it was because she was human like any of us and could feel as you and I can feel. You may claim, too, that her sister is a person of character, despite her speech and the smock she wears, and that she is good enough a human to make you a wife. But it will not alter my way of thinking. You, Rol, may legalize the bond between them. I can't say you nay. But what I could do is to disinherit him—sever him from the family, forget that I ever sired him, forget that he is a van Groenwegel. This is what I could do." His voice became gruff with emotion.

"I won't do it, though. Blood means too much to me. Our blood." He was looking out of the window, looking across the river at the house on the mainland. Dusk was gathering. He put his hand to his beard. "You'll never know what stirs in me, Rol, when I gaze across at that house. You couldn't know."

Laurens and Hendrik Rol watched his solid form at the window, silhouetted against the slate-gray and yellow clouds in the west. From below in the courtyard came the slow tramp of booted feet. The soldiers were changing guard.

Hendrik Rol said: "Sir, I'm aware that you hold strong views on this question of your blood, but if you may permit me to say so, we in this small colony should not put too much importance on matters of blood and lineage. We are still pioneers. We are not established yet. When I came out here in '70—barely two years ago—I found this colony practically desolated. You know yourself how low this place fell after Scott's raid. And even now, much as I've tried to do to restore some measure of prosperity, we're still far from being on our feet. Why, besides your plantation opposite this island and the one up the Mazaruni, how many others are there worthy of going by the name? Five, six—let's call it six private plantations really well laid out and flourishing. We have no social life here that counts. It's true in your homes you live magnificently in your own way—what with your deer and fowl and duck and turkey and pigeons, not to mention your gin and *mum* and wine and brandy." He smiled good-humoredly. "I admit you live well. But look how scattered you are. What social activities do you indulge in more than an occasional *labba* hunt? How many women have we in the colony who might make eligible wives for our respectable men? Not more than two dozen—if so many.

Well, why the fuss over family ties and blood! This girl Laurens wants to marry is a slave, but she's three-quarters white, reckoning her father as pure white—which he was not; he was a quarter Indian, like yourself. But what does it matter? Who is going to question the pedigree of Laurens' children? Look here, sir, we're at war again—and this time with France as well as England. We don't know what moment some raiding force won't enter this river and wipe us all out—though, personally, I doubt whether any privateer, filibuster or buccaneer will deem it worth his while bothering about us. Nevertheless, there's always the chance—and then what? Where will your blood or your family pride count? Mynheer van Groenwegel, I honestly cannot support you in this objection. I respect you very much, but in this instance I must stand by your son. In my humble view, sir, every man has the right to choose what woman he wishes to make his wife, and if Laurens feels that this girl Katrina will prove a fitting life-mate for him, then I say let him marry her. Not only will I legalize the marriage but I shall drink to his happiness and prosperity in all sincerity as a good friend of his."

It was a long while before Willem spoke. They could hear the churlish screech of a *creketteh* hawk by the water's edge; it was hunting prey and trying to avoid the hostile swoops of other birds.

Willem said quietly: "Very well, Rol. Since you have decided, I can do nothing. Providence has ruled it so. He must marry her. I shall do nothing. I shall lift no finger against him—because he's my son. There's my blood in him—and the blood of his grandfather and his grandmother. Kaywana. But I'm a disappointed man. The bitterness of this day will never fade. I shall never be converted to the belief that our family has not been tainted. I shall never be reconciled to this slave-blood which Laurens has seen fit to introduce into our family. Never, Rol. Never."

IV Hendrickje

I

RAIN was falling heavily when Hendrickje was born. Hendrik Rol came through it. He stood beside the bed, water dripping from his clothes, and said: "See that forehead! She's got character, Laurens. She's going to be a remarkable woman." He insisted they should name her after him. Her eyes were blue when she was born, but, eventually, turned gray-green.

When she was a year old Reinald returned from Europe with a wife, and this event caused such an explosion of joy in Willem that Willem sent down and invited Laurens and Katrina to the banquet of welcome. Griselda, less of a somersaulter in her sentiments, objected to having Katrina sit at table with them, but Willem told her: "I have decided that she shall sit with us. That's enough. You and a cyclone together won't alter my resolve. She's a slave. Very well. I haven't forgotten, nor have I forgiven Laurens for marrying her, but by God, he's my son, and she's my daughter-in-law—twist it whichever way you will. I can't hate them. I can't keep up this hostility any longer. And don't forget she's got my mother's blood in her. Kaywana was her grandmother. We can't overlook that."

"But, Willem! What sort of man are you! You swore you would never have them cross the threshold of this house. You swore you would never allow their names to be mentioned on this plantation."

Willem patted her shoulder and guffawed, his huge form in a quiver of mirth. "That was how I felt yesterday. This is today. Today we have Doctor Reinald with us—and his wife. His Juliana. And have you noticed it? She's pregnant. Do you know what's in her belly? Ho, ho! Don't blush, Griselda. I'm a seaman. Crude. No modesty. Do you know what she's carrying in her belly? It's a son. A new van Groenwegel, by St. Peter! That's no light matter. That puts a different complexion on things." He looked defiant of

161

a sudden. "And in any case, I have a right to change my views if I wish, haven't I? Come, come, Griselda! I won't be criticized. There's too much in my heart to-day for me to quibble over light sentiments." He strutted about the room, his weighty form making the boards creak. "Today I have no room for ill feeling. Reinald, eh? That bookish devil and his Mynheer Queseda. Who would have dreamt that he would have taken a wife! Ho, ho! Today I'm at peace with the universe. Today every man is my friend, planter or slave." His eyes were moist.

Juliana was a large-boned Flemish girl, and she did not disappoint Willem; she gave birth to a son whom they called Ignatius, after her father. But seventeen months later, the twins, Octavia and Luise, took her life and brought gray hairs to Reinald's head. Reinald never recovered from the shock; he did not practice for four months after, and at one time they thought that he had gone out of his mind. Within a year he had assumed a senile stoop and a general air of defeat. His voice became a definite whine. At thirty-one he was a dreamy, pensive old man who wagged his head and moaned to himself in gloomy retrospection.

When Hendrickje was a little over three years old —Aert, her brother, had been born in the meantime —Hendrik Rol died on the 31st of March 1676, and Laurens said: "There goes my best friend." Laurens thought: Why of all people Hendrik? Why should Fate be so haphazard? A useful man like Hendrik. A jovial, big-hearted human being. Look what he's done for this place. He's rebuilt this colony. He's brought out more slaves, he's established plantations for the Company, he's set up trading posts in the interior. He was as popular with the Indians as Grandfather in his time. The Indians loved him, swore by him. Everybody loved him. Yet, of all people, Fate must slash him down.

Four days following the death of Rol a ship belonging to the Company arrived with supplies from Zeeland and eighty-six slaves from the Cape Verde Islands. The Captain, Jacob Harz, took command of the colony. He soon, however, became involved in disputes with the Indians. He was a poor governor and unpopular with everyone. Laurens said of him: "He's only a crude sailor. He has no tact whatever. A poor substitute for Hendrik." Willem agreed with him. "Yes, Harz is incompetent. He'll never do as Commandeur. I don't give him more than a year here."

Willem nowadays came often to see Laurens and Katrina. He had grown used to Katrina, and one day he even tweaked her chin as he used to do to Susannah.

Susannah wrote often. She was producing baby after baby. She told Laurens in a letter, after the birth of her fourth child, that her weight was a hundred and eighty pounds. "Karl says he prefers me so, but, of course, Karl would like me anyhow. I've made him what he is, and he knows it. We own two plantations now, and there's only one other family that can equal us in wealth." Toward the end of the letter she said: "Give your beloved Katrina a kiss for me, and tell her I hope she'll have as many children as I'm going to have. When you write again, tell me how she is progressing in her speech. I'm glad that she can write now. I wish you success in your educational program for her. Every day I tell myself how glad I am that you married her. You're such a fine, dear man, Laurens. I'm certain you'll make a perfect lady out of her before long." In a postscript she said: "Ignore Mother. Mother can be expected to keep up her prejudice. She's empty and weak. I've despised her ever since that day of the raid when she behaved like such a coward. I knew Father would have forgiven you in the long run and become friendly with you and Katrina. He may be snobbish and absurd over family pride, but he has a great heart."

In July 1678, when Jacob Harz was dismissed and Abraham Beekman sent out to take his place, Hendrickje had already begun to puzzle them. She asked her father one day: "Father, why is it Uncle Reinald groans when he's alone in his study?"

Laurens laughed: "That happens to be his way."

"And why doesn't it happen to be your way, too? And Grandfather's?"

"Because Grandfather and I see the world differently, I suppose." He added uncomfortably: "We can't all see things alike."

She looked thoughtful. "I said so to myself, too. I see them differently. Very differently."

"I can't understand a child of her age saying what she say," Katrina frowned. Laurens held up his finger.

"What she *say?*"

"What she says, I meant. Sometimes I think she has a bad jumbie in her, Laurens."

"I've told you before, there are no such things as spirits or jumbies and *kanaimas*. Only ignorant people believe in nonsense like that."

"No, Laurens. I cannot agree. Spirits live in the bush and in dark rooms. Long ago, Mabella used to see them in her logie."

"Now, just you forget what Mabella used to see. These are new times. You're my wife now. You're one of the family. Don't go harking back to the old days. You must forget you were ever a slave. Remember you are Mevrouw van Groenwegel. We have a name to keep up, Katrina."

She smiled. "Sometimes you make me think of your father, Laurens. The way you speak nowadays. This family, eh? You make it a big thing."

He nodded. "Yes, you're right. It's queer how much influence Father seems to have on me. I hadn't realized it until recently. Many times I catch myself viewing things in exactly the way he does. It's blood, Katrina. Father is right there. Blood does matter. Not that I shall ever be a fanatic like Father. Yet I do feel that we van Groenwegels have good reason to be proud of our name, and I'm certainly going to see that the children grow up feeling so."

Both Willem and Laurens became close friends of Abraham Beekman and visited him often. Beekman went across to Laurens, and sometimes joined Willem and his planter friends up the Mazaruni in *labba* or tapir hunts.

Beekman proved himself to be possessed of excellent judgment and ability as Commandeur. He was given Letters of Patent by the new company which was formed in 1674 (the old company had failed and gone into liquidation, the creditors receiving 30 per cent of their claims and the shareholders 15 per cent in the form of shares in the new company), and according to these Letters, Beekman's powers consisted of "full command not only on the water but also on land, and consequently over the people, fortifications and their preservation, and also over the trade and navigation, which authority every person in the service of the Company, being on land as well as on the ships and boats, shall be bound to recognize and obey in all that he shall order or command. . . . But in matters concerning Justice, the Commandeur shall be bound to assume as his Councillors the Sergeant of the garrison and the Captains of vessels who may be there at the time, and he shall not administer Justice but with the aforesaid Council. . . ."

That was how, in 1678, the first Court of Policy and Justice began.

"Yes," said Willem, "we're advancing. Essequibo is taking shape as a colony. More than ever now we, the van Groenwegels, must stand together as a family and keep our name on the pinnacle. There must be no backsliding. Forward all the time. From big things to bigger things!"

"What big things, Grandfather?" Hendrickje asked him.

"Oh, you! You're too precocious." He snatched her up and seated her on his shoulder. He strutted around, booming: "Big things! We're a big family. We have fighter-blood in us. We never run. No! The van Groenwegels never run!"

Hendrickje began to chant: "The van Groenwegels never run! The van Groenwegels never run!"

Griselda sighed. "Susannah was right. It's a mania." She was mending a coat for Reinald.

It was Beekman who suggested that the Secretary, Mynheer Heytmeyer, should devote a few hours every day to tutoring the children. He had been in the colony since Hendrik Rol's time and was already well acquainted with the family. "He's a highly educated fellow," said Beekman to Willem and Laurens. "He can sketch and play the harpsichord as well as read Latin and Greek. I don't see why you should go to the expense and trouble of getting a man from Holland when we have Heytmeyer here. And he'll be glad for the little extra you give him, poor fellow. These Directors pay us such confoundedly miserly salaries. I don't know how they expect us to put any heart into anything we do for them. A man must have a real love for this kind of work to be Secretary or Commandeur in this colony."

The children became very fond of Mynheer Heytmeyer. Laurens thought: If the Queseda monkey had been like Heytmeyer I might have paid more attention to my Latin and Greek. This fellow is human. He takes them out of doors and teaches them about Nature and sketches and plays on his harpsichord. That's the kind of tutor I should have had. . . .

Reinald's Ignatius and Luise and Octavia took up permanent residence at the Essequibo house, for Mynheer Heytmeyer would have found it impossible to make trips up the Mazaruni every day. Laurens had three bedrooms and a back veranda added, and the dining room and sitting room were considerably enlarged. Willem had a tent-boat built and the two households mingled often. Only Griselda refused to visit Laurens' house, holding to her prejudice against Katrina.

Ignatius, from an early age, began to reveal a talent for sketching, and Mynheer Heytmeyer encouraged him. "I believe he will get far," he told Willem one day when they were all at the Mazaruni house. It was a special occasion: a banquet to celebrate Willem's sixty-fifth birthday and Hendrickje's tenth, for the two birthdays came close together, Willem's on the 2nd of February and Hendrickje's on the 5th.

"It's his German great-grandfather," Willem nodded. "Nothing to wonder at. He's got it from Griselda's father. That cobweb-brained old fellow with his etching needles and his copper plates and canvases and his violins. That man lived in the clouds nine-tenths of his time. He talked nothing but art and music and philosophy morning and night. There's only one sensible statement he made in all my memory, and he made that the day he was talking to me when we announced that we were betrothed. Remember, pet? He told me: 'My dear young man, you must not think I'm wilfully attempting to oppose you, but I fear I should tell you that my daughter is not temperamentally suited to marry a seaman. I intend it as no insult, but I think it would be wise to ponder well before taking this grave step. I cannot foresee any happiness in such a union as you contemplate.' Wise words, by heaven! But like a fool, I wouldn't listen—and that's why I'm saddled today with this misery. Eh? Not so, Griselda Liebchen?" He broke into gruff, baying laughter.

Griselda sighed from habit, and smiled weakly. Nowadays her one interest in life was Reinald. She gave all her affection to Reinald, who received it with a heavily sentimental appreciation, whining in gratitude at her fussy attentions. . . . "You are everything I have, Mother," he would say, wagging his head. "The world for me is a sounding vessel—a clattering cymbal. Dross. Once there were golden threads that bound me to the earth—but Atropos has clipped them."

Hendrickje, a frequent witness to these scenes, once commented: "I can see it. Grandfather is right. Uncle Reinald is a lost man."

"Don't be disrespectful," said Laurens, frowning at her.

"But it's true, Father. Uncle Reinald isn't alive. He won't bring any glory and honor on the family. That's why he's a lost man."

She's beginning to disturb me, Laurens thought. Her mind is outstripping her body in growth. It isn't natural that she should voice such sentiments. She's far too young to have such ideas. And Grandfather and Grandmother loom as exaggeratedly grandiose figures in her imagination. That shouldn't be. It's Father's fault for filling them up with those tales of the old days. Children oughtn't to be told such tales. Father has the children firmly in his grasp. To them he's a grand and magnificent hero.

Aert always wanted to hear of Willem's adventures at sea, and Willem would tell them of cyclones or typhoons, and fights in Marseilles and Alexandria and Rotterdam, and strange animals in Africa and the Orient, and sea monsters in the Pacific. But eventually he would end up with Kaywana's fight with Wakkatai or the Spanish raid of 1624 or Scott and his Caribs.

"But why did you open the door of the barn, Grandfather?" Aert asked, wide-eyed. "Weren't you afraid they would have rushed in and killed you?"

"Good question! That's the kind of questions I like you to ask. Now, listen. Remember what I told you about Grandmother Kaywana—your *great*-grandmother? Remember I told you how Grandmother Kaywana made us open the bedroom door and push the table up across it? Great-uncle Aert and myself——"

"Yes, you and Great-uncle Aert were in that room Mother and Father have," Hendrickje interrupted quickly. "The southeastern room with the desk that's falling to pieces."

"That's right! That's it! That was the room!" Willem nodded, almost dancing in his seat with pleasure. "You remember, eh? Good." He patted her back briskly. Aert intervened: "And you and Great-uncle Aert put the four muskets on the table, and you fired on the Indians when Great-grandmother shouted: 'Fire! Fire!' "

"That's it! That's it!" Willem shook. His eyes gleamed and his beard trembled. "Good fellow. You haven't forgotten. Splendid. Well, now I was telling you. Grandmother Kaywana put the table before the door, because that door commanded a perfect view of the stairway, and if things had gone according to plan and Great-uncle Aert and I could have handled muskets like men we'd have mown them down as they came up the stairs. That was why we had the door open——"

"And Great-grandmother Kaywana fought like a tiger, didn't she, Grandfather?" Hendrickje interrupted. "Like a tiger. When Wakkatai tried to kill her. She fought like a tiger."

"She did! She did!" Willem chortled. His face grew red. He struck his fist against his palm. "Like a tiger. Whack, whack! Let him have it, by God! And we just stood there waiting for a chance to fire. But I was telling you. It was that ruse of Grandmother Kaywana's about the table before the open door that gave me the idea when I was in the barn years and years later. Yes. I made the slaves open the big door of the barn. They thought I'd gone mad, but I shouted at them. I kicked and thumped them. Forced them to obey me. If the door had remained closed the enemy could have smashed it down, because we wouldn't have been able to bring our fire to bear on them from the windows without exposing ourselves, and, in any case, the windows were widely spaced and not in good positions for firing down at the door. But with the door open and that rampart of packing cases before it we were able to concentrate our fire upon them. We could mow them down at point-blank range if they attempted to rush us. Yes, it was Great-grandmother who gave me the idea. . . ."

II

When Hendrickje was fifteen she and Reinald's Ignatius had become close friends. Ignatius admired her and thought her clever—far more clever than his own sisters, Octavia and Luise. Hendrickje, on her side, liked him only because, as she once frankly told him, "you're good-looking and the only boy near my age in these parts."

There came a day when she startled him.

They were squatting on a fallen palm frond in the small clearing where the oblong stone slab that marked Kaywana's grave lay. She told him that she had made up her mind to marry him when they were five or six years older, and he exclaimed: "You must be mad! We're only good friends, Hendrickje—not lovers. And we're cousins."

"That makes no difference," she said, serious and calm.

"You say things as if you were a grown-up person."

She smiled. "I observe people and I think. I'm not so clever as you all seem to imagine. Why I've made up my mind that we must marry is because of the family. I believe what Grandfather says. We have fire-blood in us, and we must see that our name goes down the decades and the centuries with honor and power. That's why the two of us must marry and keep the blood together."

"Keep the blood together? What do you mean?"

She stared through the bush at Kyk-over-al, her freckled face thoughtful. She had tiny brown freckles not only on her face but also on her throat. Like Katrina, she was handsome in face and figure, and she was tall—five feet five. Her hair was brown and dead straight—"European in color but Indian in texture," as Willem had commented one day.

"Hendrickje, what do you mean?"

"To keep the blood together, I said. Don't you know what that means? I mean, I don't want to marry outside of the family. You remember what Grandfather said once about Grandmother? He said she's soft— she has no blood. No fire-blood. He said that that was why Uncle Reinald had turned out so dreamy and old-man-like. Uncle Reinald has no fire-blood. He's soft— a lost man.'

"You mustn't say that. He's my father."

"That doesn't matter. It's true, isn't it?"

"But Grandfather was only making fun when he said that."

She smiled enigmatically. "His voice sounded as if he was making fun. He even hugged Grandmother when he said it. But I know that he meant it. It's because she's soft that Uncle Reinald is soft. She brought weak blood into the family. That mustn't happen again. You must marry a girl with fighter-blood. A girl like me. Then we'll have hard children to carry on the tradition. We have to keep hard. We have to go through the centuries with power and honor."

"You're just repeating what Grandfather says. Uncle Laurens once said that it's wrong to take what Grandfather says too seriously. He said that what we should aim at is to be good people—generous and big and ready to help anyone in trouble."

She nodded. "I've heard him say that. I agree

with that, too. But we have the family name to consider. We mustn't let the name down. We are children of Kaywana. We must be fighters."

"I don't like fighting. I want to paint. And, in any case, we're cousins. I couldn't marry you."

"Cousins can marry. I asked Mynheer Heytmeyer, and he said it was all right for cousins to marry." She glanced at him. "You wouldn't like me to be your wife, Ignatius?"

"Of course," he said. "I like you a lot or I wouldn't be always talking to you like this. But I've always looked on you as a sister. It would be queer marrying you."

"I don't see why it should be. I like you a lot, too, and the best marriages are those which come about because the two people like each other. Do you notice how fond Mother and Father are of each other? They are always hugging and kissing and saying something in a whisper."

After a silence he frowned and said: "You're clever, Hendrickje. But do you think Father and Uncle Laurens would want us to marry? And Grandfather? They mightn't like it."

"I've thought of that, too," she nodded. There was a certain calculation in her manner as she gazed across at the island. Around them rose the scent of dried leaves and rank herbs—leaves that had fallen and dried and rotted during the past decades. Leaves on which rain had been dripping since the time of Kaywana and Adriansen. But the shrubs were new—of the past year or two, or less. By next year they would be dead and others would have sprung up. The leaves remained, however, piling thicker and thicker, the new dead ones pressing down the old dead ones. . . . "That's a problem, I admit, but it can be overcome. I know of a way, but I won't tell you about it now."

"Why?"

She shook her head. "The time hasn't come yet. You must keep this to yourself. This must be our secret. To let others know what we're planning would be bad strategy."

"I won't tell. Everything we say when we're here is secret. Let's talk of painting now."

"If you like—but, if you don't mind my saying it, Ignatius, I think you give too much of yourself to sketching and painting. Painting is only a pastime."

"A pastime? But what of all the great painters? They did it seriously, didn't they? Why couldn't I?"

"They had to suffer—and many of them were only recognized long after their deaths. Don't you remember what Mynheer Heytmeyer was telling us last week about the hardships they had to undergo? They were poor men. We have to be rich. Like Aunt Susannah in Suriname. She's rich—one of the richest over there."

He said in a doubtful voice: "All the same, I like painting pictures. One day perhaps I'll paint you in the nude—and I'll call it 'Venus reclining.'"

She laughed. "Yes, I'd like that. It would be odd letting you see me naked—but I'd like it. I wouldn't let you touch me, though—unless we were already married. You might lose respect for me. I couldn't have that."

"Why should I want to touch you?"

Her face took on a sly look. "Don't you know how people have children?"

"Oh, you mean that! I see what you mean now. No, I wouldn't want to do that. I'm not so immoral."

"There's nothing immoral in it, but it would be immodest—and you would think little of me. It would lower my dignity in your sight."

Laurens was getting definitely worried about Hendrickje. He said to Katrina one day, about a year later: "There's something about her that disturbs me, Katrina. I can't define it exactly. She has a calculating manner that doesn't seem to me becoming in a girl of her years. She's a schemer. It's true her aunt was a little like that, but Susannah was not so deliberate. Susannah was warm and feminine and generous in spite of her materialistic outlook. In fact, at Hendrickje's age, Susannah was irresponsible and frivolous. She liked to tease and indulge in mischievous pranks with the Bakker boys and the Blairs and myself. But Hendrickje is so mature in her ideas. And I don't approve of this friendship with Ignatius. It seems harmless up to now, but you never know what it may develop into."

"You wouldn't like her to marry Ignatius?"

"Most certainly not. He's her cousin. Inbreeding is bad for a family. I heard Reinald discussing that with Mother only last Sunday when we were up there. Apart from that, Ignatius will never make a man of himself. He's only interested in painting."

"But painting is a fine thing, Laurens. I wish I could paint."

He tugged at his beard. Nowadays he wore a beard —a trimmed brown beard like Willem's—and he had cultivated the same mannerism of tugging at it when in contemplative mood. He was getting big and stocky, too, like Willem. "I know painting is a fine thing," he said, "but it's an occupation for one's idle moments. Ignatius wants to put it first and make it his career in life. I've heard him say that more than once."

"But if they love each other, Laurens, what then?"

"Love? There are other considerations. Practical considerations." He spoke without self-confidence, however, and thought: I'm afraid I'm getting narrow-minded. We're prospering too much. A complacency is settling on me. I don't look at the world with the same breadth of spirit I did when I was twenty-one. It's this family consciousness that Father has infused into us. Even I am beginning to believe in it and champion it. Half my concern over Hendrickje originates from this anxiety about the honor and glory of the van Groenwegels and our survival. I'm taking it to heart—like Father. It's blighting my soul. I must fight it.

"I think Hendrickje is a good girl," said Katrina. Nowadays she was not so passive. Nowadays she expressed herself. She had shaken off the slave outlook. Her accent was not cultured, but she spoke correctly, and she could write. Laurens had made her write to Susannah so that Susannah could see for herself how well he had succeeded in educating her.

"Hendrickje," said Katrina, "is not like either of us. She has gone back to one of the others. She has taken after one of her old people. Kaywana."

" 'Ancestors' is the word you want. Yes, perhaps she has taken after one of them. I hope not Kaywana, though. Kaywana was a cold-blooded creature, if we can believe what Grandfather used to tell us of her. She murdered an Indian girl. Grandfather was a hard man, too, and I've noticed some hard traits in Hendrickje. She moves by her head always. Her heart plays very little part."

III

Once again there was fear and tension in Essequibo.

Lying on their stomachs near Kaywana's grave, Hendrickje and Ignatius gazed through an opening in the bush and watched Kyk-over-al. Ignatius had deep-blue eyes and light brown hair, and was slim and inclined to be tall, like his father. On his face, at the moment, was an anxious, pained expression.

"I don't really understand what it's about," he said. "What caused it? Why have we declared war against France?"

"That's simple," said Hendrickje. "The King of France has been persecuting our people in his country —the people of the reformed religion. We had to put a stop to that, so William of Orange has declared war against them, and being King of England, too, William has brought in England on our side. That's why we have to be on our guard now against French raiders."

"And suppose the French raided us, what do you think would happen? You think we'd be able to beat them off?"

"That's a question I can't answer. War is a very uncertain thing. But I know we'd fight—fight to the last. We, the van Groenwegels—we would fight. We would never run. The van Groenwegels never run."

"Of course not. In '66 Father and Uncle Laurens and Grandfather beat Major Scott and his Indians from Barbados."

"Yes. Thanks to Father and Grandfather and Aunt Susannah. Uncle Reinald was a coward. He sobbed and couldn't handle the slaves in the bedrooms. It was Father who had to rush upstairs and thump them about. Grandfather told me that."

"I don't like the way you speak of Father, Hendrickje."

"We must always face the truth, Ignatius. No matter how unpleasant it might be sometimes."

"But it hurts me when you speak of Father slightingly. How can you say you like me and still do things to hurt me?"

She laughed. "I can like you and still hurt you. If we want to be rich and a power in the land we must be hard. It would be no use my liking you and then being soft and avoiding what is the truth. We can't win out that way. We must both be hard. If I feel there is a defect in you I must tell you about it—and you must do the same to me. Never hesitate to point out my faults."

"But you have no faults. You're clever—and you're beautiful. There isn't a thing I could say against you."

"I'm glad your worship of me is so complete, but it's dangerous to imagine that I'm perfect. None of us is perfect. If you think and observe you'll see that everybody, no matter how good they may seem, has a fault somewhere—a weakness. Look at Father and Mother. They are the most perfect people I can think of—and yet I know their faults. Father is good and generous, but he shifts about in his decisions. One moment he's thinking that the family pride is all that matters, and then another time he sneers at it and says it's absurd and that Grandfather is filling us up with narrow, bigoted ideas. That's weak. A strong man is one who holds to one idea or policy and sticks to it."

"And where will such a policy get him?"

"To the top. To the pinnacles, as Grandfather says. He'll be a power. He'll be able to sway people. Control their destinies." She was sitting up now, and her eyes were bright. She kept twining her fingers together. "It's the only way. You must be firm and steady in your outlook, and you must be hard and face the truth."

"I don't want to be hard. I don't want to cause people pain. I like painting and drawing and making things of beauty to please people."

"I like that, too—but as a sideline. So long as it doesn't get in the way of my attaining to power I won't mind." She looked at him. "You must try to remember, Ignatius, that the main thing is the family. Everything should be secondary to the family—even our personal feelings."

He shook his head. "I can't see it that way. To me the most important thing is being happy painting pictures. I prefer to leave the family to take care of itself."

She stroked his hair. "Yes, I've realized that. But it doesn't matter. I will see after the family. You paint and draw. We'll have to be like Aunt Susannah. Aunt Susannah manages her husband, Uncle Karl. She made him what he is. But for her he would still have been up the Mazaruni struggling along. Now they are both rich people—one of the richest families in Suriname. We're going to be like that—but we'll go to Berbice. Berbice is going to be a flourishing colony. I listen to Grandfather and Commandeur Beekman and Father when they get talking, and I can see it. Essequibo won't last. But Berbice will go far."

"You mean, when we're married you want us to go and live in Berbice by ourselves?"

"Yes, I'm going to get Father to purchase us a plantation there. He knows influential people who can arrange it with the van Peeres. We'll live in Berbice and start a branch of the family there. We must establish ourselves everywhere. Aert can remain here and carry on, but the two of us will go to Berbice. And perhaps when we have children we can send one of our sons to Suriname to start another branch of the family there. We must spread and become powerful, Ignatius."

He said quietly: "Sometimes you frighten me, Hendrickje. Sometimes I can't believe you're only two years older than I."

After a silence she said: "Of course there's the present. Those Frenchmen. If they raid us here it would put my plans out badly."

"But I heard the French hardly have any navy to speak of."

"That's so, but there are many privateers in Cayenne. They settled there three years ago—in '86, and Commandeur Beekman thinks they might get active again."

"Kyk-over-al is strong, though. There are forty men there now."

"In 1666 everybody thought Kyk-over-al too strong even to be attacked."

A few months later a ship arrived with news. Suriname had been bombarded by a corsair called du Casse. Laurens came over from Kyk-over-al, where he had been on a visit to Commandeur Beekman, and told them about it.

"Du Casse and his ships arrived off Paramaribo on the sixth of this month.[1] He had nine vessels and they bombarded the fort for three days, but were beaten off. One vessel went aground and our men captured it with all aboard. There were a hundred and eighty-four men on it. But Captain Meist thinks that du Casse is making for Berbice."

"For Berbice!" exclaimed Hendrickje.

"Why the amazement?" her father asked.

"Nothing," she said quietly. Only Ignatius knew why she was dismayed.

"I doubt whether Commandeur de Feer in Berbice can stand up to an attack. This is going to be the end of Berbice, I'm afraid."

Katrina looked troubled. Later that day, when she was in the southeastern room with Laurens, she said: "What will happen if they attack us here, Laurens? Do you think we could beat them off as Suriname did?"

"Yes, we're strong. We can stand up to them. Beekman isn't worried about that. What's worrying him is the Pomeroon. As you know, he doesn't get along

[1] 6th of May 1689.

very well with Commandeur de Jonge of Pomeroon, and he thinks Pomeroon may be attacked. If it is it will go under, for the fort isn't strong. That will mean that de Jonge will retreat up here and Beekman will be burdened with him. He's a most overbearing fellow, de Jonge. I myself could never tolerate him when he used to be in these parts."

"I could never understand what the trouble with de Jonge was about."

"He was on a visit in Holland, and it appears he spoke to the Directors of the Company and persuaded them to let him reestablish the Pomeroon. The Directors fell in with his plan and appointed him Commandeur of Pomeroon. That was in April 1686—three years ago. De Jonge came back, and Beekman gave him one or two soldiers, two cannon and some slaves, and de Jonge went off to Pomeroon and got things going. De Jonge feels that the lower reaches of the rivers are more fertile than the upper. Beekman feels the opposite."

"And do you think Beekman is right?"

He shrugged. "Personally, I wouldn't like to give a definite opinion. De Jonge may be right, in a way, but Beekman's ideas for developing the interior are good. We have so much rich territory unexploited up here. Why should we concentrate on the coast alone? And yet, on the other hand, the coast has the advantage of being nearer to the sea and thus being more convenient for shipping away our produce. But I believe in Beekman. Beekman has done a lot for this colony since he came, and he could have done more if the Directors hadn't been so mean. His ideas are too advanced for the Company. Look what he suggested the other day. He told them he would like permission to build another fort on Flag Island further down the river, and he actually started building it. But what! The Directors sent out and said that they could not agree to support two forts. It would be too expensive. And Beekman wanted to open the colony to settlers of all nations and to start regular trade with the Indians on the Orinoco—but the Directors sat on that, too. Then, of course, Beekman feels slighted that the Directors should have fallen in with de Jonge's project to reestablish the Pomeroon. Beekman feels that if even they did agree with de Jonge that the Pomeroon should be reopened, they should have appointed him, Beekman, Commandeur of Pomeroon as well. That was how it was in Grandfather's time. Grandfather governed both colonies. Another thing is that de Jonge, in the past three years, has been making a mess of the project to resettle the Pomeroon. His expenditure exceeds his revenue by far, and Beekman has more than once advised the Directors to abandon the settlements there. De Jonge is furious because Beekman dared to try to influence the Directors against him. The last time he came here he abused Beekman. I was present myself. And what increases the friction is that when settlers come out from Holland they have to come here to Kykover-al first, we being the more important trading center—and Beekman takes advantage of this to persuade them to remain in Essequibo and not go on to the Pomeroon. Many settlers de Jonge has looked out for have never turned up. Beekman enticed them to remain here. You can just visualize now what's going to happen if de Jonge is forced to come up here as a refugee. Beekman will have to put him up at the fort, and life won't be easy for either of them on the island there."

By a remarkable coincidence, de Jonge arrived that very afternoon. Aert brought them the news. He came in and said: "Father, a boat has just arrived from Pomeroon. Commandeur de Jonge has come with some other people. The French have raided the Pomeroon."

"And only this morning your mother and I were discussing the possibility of such a thing. I must go over at once and hear the facts."

When he returned, Laurens told them: "It's true. But it wasn't du Casse who attacked them. It was some other fellow—a French pirate. They don't seem to know his name."

"But do you mean, Father," said Hendrickje, "that de Jonge has left the plantations behind to be plundered? He didn't fight?"

"What else could he do? The fort up there was

no good. It was expected that if he was attacked he would have to retreat. Beekman is extremely unhappy about it. And de Jonge, as usual, is in a surly mood. You should have heard him swearing. He even swore at Predicant Heynens!" [1]

The next day Willem was down in the tent-boat.

"There must be no panic, van Groenwegels," he told them. "If any pirates come this way we know what to do. We stand up and fight—as we fought in '66."

They were gathered in the sitting room, and Willem, a shortish, bull-like, aggressive figure, gray-bearded and flashing-eyed, jerked his head around as he looked from one to the other of them.

"Did you all hear me? We fight!" A sudden mischievous twinkle came into his eyes. "Now, who is with me? Hendrickje baby pet! Are you with your grandfather? Do you fight with grandfather?"

"To the death, Grandfather," Hendrickje smiled. But despite the smile, they could see that she was solemnly in earnest. She stood near a deal table, tall and slim and freckled, calm and with poise, her gaze steady.

"I'll fight to the last breath," she said. "The van Groenwegels never run."

Willem barked an oath. He strode up to her and hugged her. "See that! Laurens! Did you hear your daughter? Her great-grandmother's blood. Strong in her. Fire-blood, by God! This is Kaywana speaking."

"I will fight, too, Grandfather," said Aert. Aert who was olive and black-haired and brown-eyed at fifteen.

Willem nodded and waved his arms about. "I know you'll fight, my boy. You don't have to mention it. Can't stop the blood from showing. What's in you must come out." He began to strut up and down, patting them and grunting and chuckling. "You my little Gertruyt! You'll fight, too. I can see it in your eyes.

---

[1] Beekman inveigled the Directors into sending him out in 1688. He was the first Predicant to come to the colony.

Fire. Fire in your eyes! And you, Karl! And you, Rosa! Fighters—every one of you!"

He guffawed loudly and shook his fist at an unseen enemy. "Let them come. We're ready for them. What's our motto? Tell me our motto!"

"The van Groenwegels never run," chanted Hendrickje and Aert and Rosa in a solemn chorus.

"That's it. That's it." There was moisture in Willem's eyes.

Laurens shifted uncomfortably.

Katrina smiled quietly. She was seated in a big armchair, looking very composed.

By a window that looked out on the cane fields, Ignatius leaned, fumbling with the front of his coat. He glanced from his grandfather to Hendrickje in an irresolute manner, perplexed and troubled.

His sisters, the twins, Octavia and Luise, sat on the floor not far from him, writing Greek characters in copy books for Mynheer Heytmeyer. They did not seem to be interested in Willem.

Later that day Laurens thought: I notice that Father didn't give any attention to Reinald's children. It isn't the first time, either. I've seen instances of it before. He secretly despises Reinald. He considers Mother and Reinald weak links in the family chain, and he must feel that Ignatius and the twins are going to be soft, too. Sometimes I'm a little sorry for Ignatius. He seems to live in a dream state of his own. His painting absorbs him. It puzzles me why Hendrickje should have become so attached to him. They're so completely different from each other—such distinct opposites. Or perhaps that's the reason. He is weak; she is strong. Her attitude toward him always impresses me as being that of a protector. More and more that girl disturbs me. Hendrik Rol predicted right. She's no ordinary child.

IV

A few days later more news came. Berbice had been attacked. Du Casse and his corsairs had plundered several plantations, and Commandeur de Feer had been compelled to call a truce. Beekman told Laurens: "The situation looks grave, van Groenwegel. De Feer has promised this cutthroat Frenchman a ransom of twenty thousand guilders. He's given him a draft on the Patroons, though I understand that the Governor of Suriname has taken a hand in the matter. They hold a hundred and eighty-four of du Casse's men in Suriname. The sum will probably be reduced."[1]

Laurens nodded. "Father is preparing for an attack. He's brought down muskets and powder and shot. I have it stored away in readiness."

Beekman chuckled. "That hot-headed old father of yours. He really believes he can stand up to them, does he?"

"Father is a fanatic where the family pride is involved. It's absurd, but sometimes I'm inclined to agree with him. We fought in 1666 and won, and I don't see why we shouldn't do it again. Of course, conditions are different now. If raiders came here my house over there would be exposed to cannon fire."

Beekman regarded him. "But you'd still fight?"

"Oh, most assuredly," Laurens said. He stiffened automatically. "If we all have to go down, Beekman. If we all have to perish. We never run. It's our motto."

"I know. The van Groenwegels never run." Beekman smiled. "You're a remarkable family. I've always thought so. Fighter-blood, your father calls it. Fireblood. Anyway, I wish you luck. Personally, I feel confident my men can hold out against anything. They won't get past this island as easily as they might think."

"By the way, how is your friend, de Jonge, faring?"

"He's down with a slight fever. Just as arrogant and intolerable as ever." He looked thoughtful. "I have a feeling, van Groenwegel, that I won't be here as Commandeur much longer. I'll tell you this in confidence. I've heard on good authority that de Jonge has written several poisonous letters to the Directors against

[1] Du Casse eventually got 6,000 guilders and a few hogsheads of sugar.

me. He's told them about that plantation of mine up the river, and, of course, as you know, strictly speaking, it's a breach of the Articled Letter issued when the new company was formed in '74. Oh, he's been telling them a host of tales about me. He's accused me of extravagance—a deadly sin in the eyes of the Directors. And this question of Indian slaves. It appears that one or two rogues have been taking hold of Indians up the river and conveying them to Berbice as slaves. It's a thing I can't stop. I do my best, but I am not God. That's another of my sins—negligence in not guarding the monopoly the Company holds in the African slave trade. But I'm getting indifferent. I've done my best, and I get nothing but curses for my trouble. And for a salary of sixty guilders a month! It isn't worth it!"

"Hendrik Rol got thirty when he first came, poor fellow—though later they did raise it to fifty."

Laurens returned home in a pensive, gloomy mood.

No attack came, however. The year passed without event, and the fear and tension died down. Early in the next year death came to Griselda. It was a heart attack, Reinald pronounced. He wagged his head and told Laurens: "I knew it would happen one day. I warned her. This is the last thread—the last golden thread Atropos has cut. Now the world is a barren place for me. An empty, barren desert."

Neither Laurens nor Willem made any comment. Willem was quiet and solemn-faced. He hardly spoke, not even when people sympathized. Hendrickje said of him, the day after the burial, when she and Ignatius were in a *corial* on the little creek at the back of the plantation: "The shock of it affected him more than anything else. His grief won't last long. You must respect a person before you can grieve over their death, and he didn't respect her."

Ignatius said nothing. He wielded the paddle automatically, his dark-blue eyes on the black water.

"Uncle Reinald will feel it hardest. He and Grandmother were so attached. I won't be surprised if he goes off suddenly, too."

"Sometimes I wonder if you have a heart, Hendrickje."

"If I hadn't one I'd have stopped being friendly with you a long time ago, Ignatius."

He said nothing.

"It's only because I have a genuine affection for you that I go on being close to you. We have nothing in common."

"I thought it was because you wanted to marry me to keep the blood together that you still hold to me."

"That's true. But apart from that, I've come to feel very tender toward you. I couldn't do without you now." She glanced at him. "Could you do without me?"

"No," he said.

After a silence she said: "You're so young, Ignatius. I feel at times I'm doing wrong in talking to you about love and marriage. And you're so sensitive. That day when Grandfather came—the day when we thought we were going to be attacked—I kept watching your face. You were standing by the window. You wouldn't have known it, but I felt sorry for you then. Grandfather never noticed you. He asked us all if we would fight with him—but he didn't ask you."

"I know. He thinks me soft—like Father."

"He's not wrong. You are soft. Painting and sketching. Uncle Reinald, in his day, was the same—only with him it was Greek and Latin and that tutor whom Father once called a monkey—Mynheer Queseda. Those were Uncle Reinald's obsessions. He lost himself in books—and now you're losing yourself in painting pictures." She stretched forward and stroked the back of his head. "But you mustn't mind. I'll look after you all your life. I'll see that you're happy and have all the painting you want."

He said nothing.

"Often I'm afraid of hurting you irrevocably with my candor. Whenever I hurt you even slightly I feel hurt myself. I find myself wanting to cry. I have to fight hard to stop myself from crying, because that would be soft—and at all costs I must eschew softness.

I have to be hard for us both. Hard so that I can see us through to the top. Hard so that I can bring up our children hard and make them conscious of our blood and the power in us." Her voice trembled, and her gray-green eyes were very bright and wide.

Later that year another death occurred in the family. Laurens' Karl. Karl and Gertruyt fell ill with dysentery, and Karl died. He was four years old and the youngest. Willem was depressed for weeks. "I had hopes for that little fellow," he said. "He had something in him. He would have been a credit to us, I'm sure."

After the burial Katrina said to Laurens: "I don't believe in any Christian God, Laurens. That Predicant and his Bible talk—I don't like him. He tells us about God's love and God's wrath, but he can't explain why God should want to kill off our little Karl who has harmed no one. If He is a God of love, why should He want to kill off Karl?"

"Religion is a hoax, Katrina," said Laurens. "Don't trouble about it. Life is a blind scheme—no one will convince me it isn't. But the best policy is not to think about it at all. Let's live and do our best to be generous and considerate of others. Let the Predicants take care of their God and their churches."

Hendrickje, who overheard what they had said, told Ignatius later: "I believe as Father does. God is nonsense. Life is blind. We simply live from day to day, and we have children, and the children grow up and have more children, and perhaps an old person dies or perhaps a young person or a child. Grandmother died a few months ago—and now it's Karl."

"And he was such a beautiful fellow. I wanted to do a sketch of him, but somehow I always put it off."

"He would have carried on the name. Why couldn't Gertruyt have died instead!"

"How can you say that, Hendrickje! Poor Gertruyt! She's so sweet and friendly. I couldn't imagine her dead."

"But she might have died, too. It's merely her luck that she recovered and Karl's bad luck that he went

under. It's sheer chance. People get born and die anyhow. Look what happens when a war or a raid comes
on. Soldiers and people get killed off whether they're
good or bad. If there were a God who really guided
life and cared what happened to the good people, He
wouldn't allow things to go on haphazardly. He would
arrange it so that the evil people got wiped out and
the good people lived on to an old age in happiness.
And look what happened a week or two ago! The Directors have dismissed Commandeur Beekman.[1] A good
man like that who was doing so much for the colony
—and just because de Jonge has told tales against him
he's dismissed. Why did God allow that to happen?
I'll never bother about religion. I agree with Father.
It's a hoax, and I'll teach our children to have nothing
to do with it."

He nodded. "I agree with that. It does seem silly.
I think the Greeks were much more sensible. They
loved art and conversation and kept their mythology
in its place. They didn't let it influence their lives as
Christians try to make their Bible stories influence
theirs."

V

The day after her twenty-first birthday Hendrickje said
to her father: "I want to tell you something very important, Father. Can we go upstairs?"

"Certainly, my girl." Laurens smiled. "I suppose
there is no objection to your mother being present, is
there?"

"None at all," she said. She had a stately bearing
at twenty-one, and was taller than her father: five feet
eight.

Laurens found that nowadays he could not look
her straight in the eyes without wanting to turn aside
his gaze. There's power in her, he told himself. A
strange force that awes me. Sometimes I marvel that
it's I who have produced her. Hendrik was right. She

[1]Beekman received his dismissal on 30th October 1690.

has character. She exudes something magnificent. She's got beyond us.

Willem thought so, too. Willem told her one day: "You should have been a man, Hendrickje. Yes, by God! You're the personification of old Adriansen and Kaywana. But man or woman, I believe you're going to do big things for us. You have the right spirit."

To her younger brother and sisters and her cousins she was a heroine. They consulted her about everything. Her ruling in any argument was final. Even the one or two children of the other planters with whom they were friendly, and the Predicant's children, looked up to her as a superior person. They asked her advice, and when she scolded them or cautioned them they took it for granted that she was right and qualified to speak.

Katrina was sitting in the large armchair by one of the southern windows when Hendrickje and Laurens came in. She did not show surprise. She was mending clothes, and merely glanced up and smiled slightly.

Laurens seated himself by an eastern window and lit his pipe, and Hendrickje leaned casually against the bedpost, at complete ease, tall and elegant in her long dress. She might have been a seasoned woman of the world who had arrived from France or Holland with the last ship. . . . It must be her poise that makes her seem so awesome, Laurens told himself, beginning to puff at his pipe. I wonder what it is she wants to talk to me about. Aert perhaps. Father was telling me last week that she suggested that Aert should go up the Mazaruni and learn about the plantation there because one day he would have to take charge. I wonder if it's that she wants to discuss. Father takes her too seriously. He's getting her conceited. . . .

"Is it what you were talking to Grandfather about a few days ago you want to bring up now?"

"You mean about Aert going up to get familiar with the plantation? Yes, that's one of the things I wanted to discuss with you," she nodded. She moved away from the bed and crossed the room to a southern window where she could view them both without having to turn her head.

She has a sense of drama, thought Laurens, and she carries off her airs well. The way she walked across the room was good. I've never been to Europe, but it must be like that these actresses walk across the stage. And she's biding her time to talk. She won't blurt it out as she might have done a few years ago. I'm proud of her, I must admit—yet she does disturb me. Her aloofness annoys me, too.

"Don't you think it a good plan, Father? Grandfather won't live for ever—and Uncle Reinald knows absolutely nothing about planting. He does little medical work nowadays, and hardly meets anybody. He's out of touch with everything. Just reads all day in his study. The plantation up there would be in chaos if Grandfather died suddenly."

"Grandfather won't die suddenly," he smiled. "He's a tough soldier. He'll live to Great-grandfather's age, you hear what I say."

"He was complaining of dizziness in his head a few days ago. Those were the symtoms Mynheer de Graaf experienced shortly before he died. He was three years younger than Grandfather and seemed perfectly fit."

"But Aert is an effcient overseer on this plantation. And in any case, don't you think it would be fitting that Ignatius should take over when Grandfather dies? That is really his home."

"I was expecting you to say that." Her tone was even, unflustered. It made him nervous. "That brings us to another matter I wanted to discuss with you. Ignatius has no planting ability. He paints, and that is about all he can do well. He will never make a good manager for the Mazaruni plantation. Grandfather agrees with me——"

"Is there anything he doesn't agree with you on?"

"As a rule, we see very much alike." She was examining her nails—idly and with an affected insouciance. "Ignatius' temperament won't allow him to be a successful planter. He's the sort of person who must have a wife to take care of him and manage him, and that's why I told him—since I was fifteen—that one day I would marry him."

It was very dull of me not to have suspected that it was this she wanted to talk to me about. . . . Laurens took his pipe from his mouth.

Katrina stopped sewing and looked at Hendrickje.

"You want to marry him, Hendrickje?" said Katrina. She glanced at her husband. "Laurens, I told you she was serious, didn't I? You said it would fizzle out, that they were like brother and sister now. But I could see what you could not."

"Since you were fifteen you told him this, Hendrickje?"

"Since I was fifteen, Father. He was thirteen."

Laurens was silent.

"I knew this was coming," said Katrina.

"But it's not going to happen," said Laurens. His beard came out aggressively—like Willem's when Willem was going to say something forceful. "Not that boy. No, Hendrickje. I won't hear of it."

"What are your objections?"

"I don't believe in inbreeding—and he won't make you a proper husband. He's a dreamer. He won't make a man of himself." He felt a little foolish, realizing that he was speaking without thought—repeating ideas that had played about in his thoughts off and on during the past few years. "There are other young men," he went on in a loud voice, avoiding her gaze. "Jan Roosen and Hendrik Blankenburg. I've heard they are both very much attracted to you."

"But what if I'm not attracted to them?"

"Nonsense! What are you trying to tell me? That you're attracted to that artistic young stripling?"

"It happens that I am."

"But how—but I don't understand that. Your outlook is so entirely different. It's absurd."

"I know. I know just how weak he is. I'm not blindly in love with him. I love him despite his defects."

"And is he in love with you?"

"Yes."

He uttered a snort. "It strikes me that you must have done the proposing. You're a most unusual girl. I can't fathom you. Often I don't feel you're a daughter of mine. When I speak to you sometimes I feel I'm speaking to a strange woman who happened to enter the house by accident."

"Everybody thinks me strange and precocious. I can't help how I was made. Father, there is another matter I want to bring up in relation to my marrying Ignatius. I've spoken to Grandfather about it already, though I asked him not to mention it to you. I'd like to go to Berbice and settle there on a plantation of my own, and Grandfather thinks that he'll be able to purchase one near Fort Nassau."

"A plantation in Berbice! What's this now?"

"Hendrickje, my child, you want to leave us?"

"Yes, Mother. I want to start a branch of the family in Berbice. The prospects are good there, despite the raid a few years ago. Our family can only become powerful if we spread. In time, I shall send a son of mine to Suriname, and perhaps one to Cayenne. I'm determined that we must be the most powerful and influential family along the whole Wild Coast. We can do it. We have it in us to do it."

"But, Hendrickje baby, I don't understand. You speak so—so big. So big and wise. How do you come to have such plans? You a girl—who taught you such things, baby?"

Hendrickje smiled. "No one taught me, Mother. I think, and I observe. I have some vision, and I can plan far ahead."

Laurens, frowning out at the river, thought: This is a critical moment. If I don't assert myself now and let her see that my will is as strong as hers she won't respect me. She'll forever after hold me in contempt. She's subversive. She has got too big for herself. She wants to elect herself a sort of family matriarch, and overturn our way of life. She must be curbed.

Katrina asked: "Hendrickje, have you told Grandfather about your wanting to marry Ignatius?"

"I have."

"And what does he think?"

"He doesn't like Ignatius as a husband for me, but when I told him that I'm aware how weak Ignatius is and that my idea in marrying him is to keep the blood intact and to carry on the name in Berbice, he said that he could agree with me. He has confidence in me and feels I'll make a good manager for any plantation—and for any husband."

Laurens flashed her a look. "Young woman, you're too calculating. You're too cold. Cold and ruthless. Even for a man it would be bad—but for a woman!" He rose in his agitation. "I can hardly credit that you are my flesh and blood. Sometimes I get the feeling that I've produced a monster."

"I have no doubt that is the impression many people have—that I'm a monster, that I'm cold and without sentiment. In a way, they may be right, too, but I can't help how I was fashioned, can I?"

Katrina stared at her.

Laurens paced for a while, then resumed his seat.

"You haven't given me a definite reply, Father."

"Haven't I? Well, I'll give it to you now. I refuse to hear of your marrying your cousin, and I consider your going to Berbice preposterous. I disapprove of both schemes—definitely."

He found that he could not look in her direction as he spoke. Resentment rose up in him. In this instant he hated her. He felt distracted and frustrated. Her serenity infuriated him.

As he refilled his pipe he told himself that perhaps time had not passed. Perhaps he was still twenty-one and alone in this room. In the next room Hannah and Katrina were whispering about him and telling each other that he was too shy to call one of them in to sleep with him. . . . Over at Kyk-over-al Hendrik Rol is chatting with the Captain of the troops or the Secretary. They're discussing van Berkel's coming visit to decide that the Abary Creek should mark the boundary between the Essequibo-Demerary territory and Berbice. . . . Yes, I'm not forty-three. There isn't a pair of cold gray-green eyes staring at me and making me feel like a boy of six or a frightened puppy. It's my imagination. . . ."

"Is that absolutely final, Father?"

"Absolutely final," he said, feeling like a coward as he said it; feeling afraid of her eyes watching him.

He felt the inclination to turn his head quickly and say: "I didn't mean that. I'll consider it, my girl. I'll think it over. Your grandfather and I will talk it over." He ought to say that, but he could not. A hard rock of pride checked him. She might have been Hannah— Hannah attempting to be familiar with him. Hannah a mere slave smiling and speaking to him as though she thought herself his equal. . . .

She deems herself my superior in intelligence— and will. I can sense it. She thinks she only has to fix her gaze on me and I'll wilt and agree to her proposals. But I'm her sire. I'm her creator, by God! When she respects me and learns that I can be as determined and resolute as she, then perhaps I shall come to terms with her. I won't tolerate this chilly, superior attitude of hers. Some instinct tells me I must resist her—even against reason. Though it may seem narrow and bigoted, I must hold to what I feel in the matter and refuse to shift. It's the only way to make her humble. It's the only way to curb this monstrous conceit of hers. . . .

"Father, I hope you won't say afterwards that I didn't discuss it with you and ask your permission."

"What do you mean?"

"I mean, I've given you a fair chance to think it over. I had hoped that, at least, you would be willing to consider it."

"What you mean, Hendrickje," he said, "is that you think us so much beneath you in intelligence and breadth of outlook that you merely have to broach a subject when it goes without saying we'll fall down before you and concur, and say how clever you are. You're too inflated with yourself."

"Why indulge in a criticism of my character? That's evading the issue. The matter under discussion is my proposed marriage to Ignatius and my plan to settle in Berbice——"

"Get out of here! Get out!" He rose and pointed at the door. "Get out before I throw you out!"

"Laurens!"

Hendrickje smiled.

"Don't smile like that! Stop it! I'll kill you, you imperious little reptile! Out of here! Out!"

She began to move across the room—calmly, with ease and elegance.

He could not stand it. He rushed at her and slapped her face, grasped her by the shoulder and shook her.

"Father! Are you mad?"

Abruptly the fury left him. He returned to his chair by the window.

Hendrickje stared after him with incredulity.

"He struck me, Mother. Did you see?"

Katrina, who had risen, told her to leave the room. In a soft, frightened voice, her face pale.

"I thought he wouldn't like the idea," said Willem, the following day. "As I told you, my girl, I don't, either. But you don't strike me as being a fool. I do believe you'll handle that boy fittingly if you two get together on the Berbice."

Willem was very wrinkled these days. The brown had gone from his beard and from the hair on his head. He was getting old in spirit, too; the fire was leaving him.

"Grandfather, what I want to know is this: Will you still proceed with the deal? Will you still continue negotiations to purchase the plantation you told me of in Berbice?"

"I could. I could. See no reason why I shouldn't. Property is property. It would be no harm acquiring a plantation over there." He gave her a doubtful glance. "What's in your head, my girl? How do you propose to alter your father's decision? He's stubborn. I didn't want him to marry your mother, but he held out. He surprised me, Laurens. Deep. Appears mild on the surface, but he possesses subtle undercurrents."

"He puzzled me yesterday. He did a thing I should never have expected of him. He attacked me—struck me across my face and shook me."

Willem grunted. "You must have roused him. I remember that day of the raid in '66. He went mad. He shot one of our slaves—in this very room."

"You've told me about it. Grandfather, can I depend upon you, then? You'll go through with the deal? You'll get this plantation?"

"Certainly. It's as good as ours already. Just a matter of writing Angelica at Fort Nassau. I'll do it today."

VI

Far up the little creek that ran aback of the plantation on the Essequibo there was a small clearing where Hendrickje and Ignatius had often sat and picnicked. It was lonely here, and the only sounds were the crackling of lizards amid the vines and undergrowth of the jungle and the sucking gurgle of the black water against the bank. Bamboos and *cookerit* and *awara* and *manicole* palms made a gloom in the clearing. It was cool.

"Today," Hendrickje told him, "I have something important to talk to you about. Perhaps," she went on, "you've forgotten, but years ago when I first told you about our getting married you asked what would happen if Father refused to consent, and I think I replied that I knew of a way of overcoming that problem. Do you remember?"

"I can't say I do."

"Ignatius, dear, don't look so depressed. There's nothing to be worried about."

"I feel distracted. Last night I hardly slept."

"Why?"

"I asked Father about our getting married, as you suggested, but he wouldn't hear of it. He quoted Latin at me. Virgil. He even forgot what I was talking about. I had to keep reminding him. Oh, it's terrible."

"What were his objections?"

"Inbreeding. He said something vaguely about it's not being good."

"I see."

"You speak in such a matter-of-fact tone. I wish I could. You don't know how desperately I want you, Hendrickje. I'd die for you. With me, it's not just a matter of keeping the blood together. I really want to marry you. I want you for yourself. I want you because I love you—not because I love the family name."

"That bitter note again. Poor boy." She rested her head in his lap, put up her hand and stroked his cheek, her eyes affectionate. "I understand how you feel, dear, but if you lose your head, if you let sentiment get the better of your reason, we'll be defeated. My manner only seems hard, but under it I'm just as anxious as you, just as desperately eager to be together with you. It's because I want us to win out that I have to assume a cold and matter-of-fact manner. Kiss me."

He did it as though it were the last thing he would do in his life. She held his hand and slipped it down into her bosom, but he withdrew it, gasping: "I've told you I can't touch you there. I couldn't stand it, Hendrickje. It would mean trouble."

"Now it wouldn't be trouble."

"What do you mean?"

"It's what I wanted to talk to you about. Today must be different from the other days we've come here."

"Different?"

She said nothing. She took his hand again and slipped it down into her bosom. Rippled it across her breasts. She had worn very light clothing, and he began to be aware of this for the first time; it made him tremble a little. When she drew down her bodice and the garments beneath it, he asked her whether she had gone mad. Without a word, she pulled down his head and moved her body so that her breasts could rub against his cheeks. And after that, reason left them both.

Later, when their breathing had quietened down, she murmured: "You mustn't look so troubled, my darling. This is how I wanted it to happen."

"I feel like a beast. But you made me do it. You know it's wrong. It's what I've always wanted to avoid."

"I, too. But today I wanted it to happen. And tomorrow it will happen again. We'll come here again tomorrow—and the day after and the day after. Don't you see what my plan is now, Ignatius?"

"Your plan?"

"My plan. I thought of this since I was fifteen and you thirteen. I knew they might try to prevent us from marrying. But if I get pregnant it may change their views. They couldn't let me have a child by you and not let us get married."

"You mean, this—this is deliberate?"

"That's what I mean. Don't look so distressed and astounded, Ignatius." She drew his head down again. "Don't you see, dear? It's the only way to force their hands. I didn't like doing it like this, but Father has suddenly grown like a rock toward me. He hasn't spoken to me for nearly a week—since that day he struck me. A stubbornness and resentfulness have come into his manner. He fears me, and seems to hate himself for being afraid. He's going through a battle with himself, and in a way I'm sorry for him. At heart, he's not as hard as he wants people to think he is. Nor am I as hard as people think me. It's only when I know I must be hard and firm that I'm so. You don't find me hard, do you? Tell me."

"Not when we're here alone—but many other times, Hendrickje, I feel afraid of you. You're cold and —and like a man. Your eyes stare and flash."

She said nothing.

They heard the water sucking at the bank. The scent of dead leaves rose dank around them, mingled with the delicate perfume of wild flowers—and with the perfume of her body. There were tiny brown freckles on her throat and breasts, and on her shoulders and arms.

"I'm afraid, Hendrickje. Something tells me this won't bring us any good. You should never have let me do it."

"You mustn't worry. I'll protect you from them all. You must always have faith in me." She stroked his hair. She made murmuring, fond sounds, and he shut his eyes, and his face lost its pained, anxious look. A quiet came upon him.

Day after day they came here, and gradually he lost his sense of guilt. During the first week he was very worried. He told her: "I believe Aert and Rosa suspect. They look at us very oddly now." She smiled and replied: "I would have known if they suspected. Why they look at us as they do is because they sense that something is afoot between Father and myself. They've observed that he doesn't say anything to me now, and they've guessed it must be because he disapproves of our getting married. You mustn't be afraid, Ignatius. So long as I'm with you they can't do us any harm. They'll never separate us. Father is furious because he knows my will is as strong as his—perhaps stronger. It stings his pride, and he resents it. But we'll win. It's a pity Father has taken this stand, because I like him. I respect him, even though he struck me last week— or, who knows, perhaps because he did; I believe most women, though they won't admit it, have a deep respect for men who knock them about. Anyway, I mean to fight him to the last. He will have to give in."

"My conscience troubles me at night. I feel like a criminal. Taking your pure, fine body like this. It isn't right. It's immoral. We're sinning—sinning against your beauty and your nobility."

"You idealize me too much, darling. I'm like any other woman so far as my body goes. What are beauty and nobility? When we're here together I care nothing about such things. I like being with you physically, and you like it. We both revel in it—and it's natural and right that we should. Nature made us this way, so why should we form foolish ideas about immorality? Let's squeeze every ounce of pleasure out of it while we're young and can enjoy it. Immorality was invented by religious and frustrated people whose one aim was to make life as difficult and bitter as possible. To such people all pleasure is sin—the utter fools!" She sniffed. "They don't realize that such an outlook is as good as condemning oneself to a sour old age of barren memories."

After the third week she had driven the fear out of him—and the guilt. He even suggested that he should bring his canvas and easel and his paints and brushes and do a picture of her in the nude.

"That would be nice," she said, "but suppose th

see the picture when we take it home. Luise is always hunting about among your canvases. We don't want them to discover what we come here for and ruin our plans. When we're married will be time enough for that."

"You're so warm, Hendrickje. Who would think you could be so chilly and rational at other times! I worship you more and more every day. When I paint you I'm going to call the picture 'My Goddess'. You're the best goddess that ever existed." He hid his face in her hair. "I feel wild and despairful when I think that one day you'll get old and die like everybody else. If only I could stop it. If only I could hold back time and keep you like this—keep us both like this—with the little freckles on your face and on your throat and your breasts. Oh, Hendrickje, why is today going to fade? Why must it? Can't we remain here always and not have to think about eating and other people? I love you so much I can hold you and melt away with you into the earth here or turn to water or leaves."

When nearly a month had passed she told him: "Grandfather gave me some good news this morning when he came down. Of course, in confidence. He's bought the plantation in Berbice—in my name. The deal has been completed. He got a letter from Angelica, the van Peere agent at Fort Nassau who sees after the sale of private estates."

But he was not interested. He shrugged and said: "I don't care about plantations, Hendrickje. These days I'm living in a fairyland. Everything is blue and green, or soft violets and reds, and you're the colors and the lines and the whole composition. When I breathe I smell your hair, when I walk it's as if I can feel your spirit trembling under my feet, when I'm asleep you're all around me in the darkness and I can see your freckles when I'm falling off into a doze. Yesterday when I was painting I felt you in the paint and in my brush as if—as if your smile and the color in had fused together and I was using them. My weak and tender for a minute and I had to ing and look outside at the river. I felt I could have run upstairs and called you and not cared whether the others heard or what they said."

One night Katrina said: "Laurens, you shouldn't treat Hendrickje as you do. You haven't said a word to her since that day in here. She's our child. Our first. You don't love her any more?"

"I don't care to discuss Hendrickje, Katrina. My mood is too dangerous." It was late, and they were in bed.

"I know. But please, for my sake. It's hurting me. I don't like to see you sitting alone staring over at the island. It makes me remember the days when I was a slave and used to be sorry for you when you were so shy to ask us to come in to you. Many days I would cry in secret when Hannah was downstairs in the kitchen and you were away in the fields."

He said nothing.

She stroked his beard. "You're just the same to me now. I still love you as much. You must treat her well again, Laurens—for my sake. Talk to her. She is our first—the one we were so happy over because she was coming. Remember how hard it was raining when she was born? And remember that day when you first lay with me in bed? It rained heavily that day, too—and the coffee was on the desk that used to be there. A pity we had to throw away that desk, but it was so rotten. Are you listening, Laurens?"

"Yes."

"Laurens, I believe you know what is happening."

She felt the heaviness of him move beside her.

"You know, don't you?"

He said nothing.

Outside, the insects kept up their cheeping and churring. There was moonlight, and the river shimmered whitely, whispering against the bank.

"About Hendrickje—you know, don't you, Laurens?"

"I'm not such a fool as she imagines me to be, Katrina."

"I could see it in your face that you knew. It's

been going on for weeks now. They go up that little creek aback of the plantation."

He grunted.

"Laurens."

"Yes?"

"I don't like you silent like this. It frightens me. It makes me think something bad will happen."

"Don't be foolish."

"How did you discover?"

"I suspected that these daily excursions had an object—and one day I sent an Indian after them to find out and report."

"To spy on them? But that was not fair."

"Why should I have scruples if she has none?"

"I'm sorry you did that. I love her, Laurens. She's a fine child—and he, too. Such a soft, good boy. I think you should treat them well. Let them marry. They're in love, Laurens. Like us—since that day with the rain and the wind. It hurts me that you should feel badly toward them."

"Don't you realize what she's trying to do? She's trying to force my hand. She knows that if she becomes pregnant I'll have to agree to her marrying him. That's what hurts me, Katrina. The calculating, scheming, deliberate way she goes about things. She has adopted an air of defiance toward me, and my pride can't stand it. I won't have a child of mine take up such a stand against me."

"No, you mustn't look at it so. You felt the same about your father when you knew that he was against your marrying me. You said you would fight him to the end if he tried to stop you. You said you would show him you have the same fire that he has. Now how can you blame her if she says the same thing? She has fire, too—your fire. You put it into her. She your own flesh and blood. You should be proud that she show the same fight as you show when you her age. She good, fine girl, our baby. I proud of her." Her speech always suffered when she was deeply moved.

They heard a loud knocking downstairs.

"Someone is knocking at the kitchen door."

"At this hour?" He got out of bed. "Who can it be, I wonder?"

"Laurens, wait for me. I'll come with you. Don't leave me in the dark. I feel somehow there is a jumbie in this room tonight."

"Don't be foolish. Stay where you are."

The knocking sounded again.

In the next room—the northeastern room—where Hendrickje slept with Octavia and Luise, her cousins, there was a stirring. Presently the three of them came in, looking like ghosts as the bright moonlight struck in on their long white nightgowns.

Katrina lit the lamp on the deal table beside the bed—the table which had replaced Adriansen's old desk.

A moment later Rosa and Gertruyt came in, too.

"I wonder if it could be a message from Grandfather," said Rosa. "Perhaps Uncle Reinald has taken ill."

"Or Grandfather himself," hazarded Gertruyt.

"Those giddy feelings he's always getting."

Luise called at the door: "Aert! Ignatius! Aren't you awake?"

"What are you waking them for?" said Hendrickje.

They heard Laurens' footsteps on the stairs. He came up and told them: "It's Grandfather. He's had a stroke. Uncle Reinald has sent a message."

"I said it was Grandfather," murmured Gertruyt.

"Laurens, I told you I heard the death-bird before dinner."

"I'll have to go up there now," Laurens frowned. "The slave is waiting in the *corial*."

"Uncle Reinald must be in a state," Rosa murmured.

"Father, may I come with you?" asked Hendrickje. "No."

Hendrickje followed the others into the northeastern room, and Katrina said quietly to her husband: "Laurens, let her go with you. She is so attached to her grandfather. He will be glad to see her."

"He's not conscious. I don't want her to come with me."

After he had gone the girls came into the south-eastern room again. Hendrickje seated herself in the big armchair near the southern windows, but Octavia and Luise sat on the bed with Katrina. Rosa and Gertruyt posted themselves at one of the eastern windows, gazing out at the river, Rosa exclaiming over the moonlight.

Octavia and Luise, at seventeen, were big-hipped like their Flemish mother, and inclined to plumpness. Octavia was slightly shorter than Luise, and though there was a close resemblance between them it was not very difficult to distinguish one from the other, especially as Luise had a brown mole on her throat.

"It's just what Hendrickje said," Rosa told Gertruyt. "Hendrickje said he might die suddenly. That's why she said it would be good for Aert to go up and learn about the plantation."

"Father never likes to listen to what Hendrickje says," said Gertruyt. "Hendrickje is clever. Whatever she says always comes true."

Rosa, at seventeen, was not as tall as Hendrickje, but she was well shaped and well developed; handsome in face, green-eyed and with red hair like Susannah's. Gertruyt was thin and plain at fifteen. She had a long, oval face, was flat-chested and spindly-legged.

"Those boys sleep so heavily," Octavia said, staring at the wall in the direction of the northwestern room: one of the three rooms Laurens had had added to the house.

Katrina told Luise to close the door. Laurens had left it ajar when he went out. "I believe a bad spirit entered this room tonight," said Katrina. "Uncle Laurens says they don't exist, but he's wrong. I'm sure there are spirits. And I heard the death-bird cry in the bush before dinner."

They could hear the river, for the night was very still.

Hendrickje rose and moved across the room to the door.

"Hendrickje, are you going downstairs?"

"Yes, Mother. I'm going down for some water."

"There's a jug on the table here."

"I know—but I'm going down for some."

After she had gone Katrina shook her head. "That girl is so strong-willed. You can't advise her about anything."

"Hendrickje is clever, Aunt Katrina."

Rosa exclaimed: "A *corial* is coming!"

A minute later Gertruyt said: "It's gone past. It didn't stop here."

"It must have been an Indian," said Katrina.

Wind came in at the windows in a low humming, smelling of the bush and of the river. Far away they heard the yap-yap of a raccoon.

"Aunt Katrina, do you think we should wake Aert and Ignatius?" Octavia asked, and Katrina answered: "No, let them sleep. We may hear nothing until morning."

Luise yawned. "I feel as if I can go back to sleep."

Rosa and Gertruyt came over to the bed. Rosa said: "Mother, suppose Grandfather dies tomorrow, won't Aert have to go up to manage the plantation, as Hendrickje said he would have to?"

"My child, I don't know. Only your father can decide that. But I should think it would have to be so. Your Uncle Reinald is like an old man. He dreams all day. He can't manage the plantation. The slaves don't respect him."

"You see?" said Rosa, glancing at Gertruyt. "I knew that. Hendrickje is right. Aert will have to go up there and manage the place. He should have gone a long time ago. If Father had listened to Hendrickje——"

"Quiet!" Katrina put up her hand.

"What is it, Mother?"

They listened. From downstairs came a sound as of someone sobbing.

"It must be Hendrickje," said Luise.

Katrina got out of bed. "Let's go downstairs. Come. Come with me, children. I never like going down there alone at night."

They found Hendrickje at a dining room window. She was not sobbing. She was being sick. Katrina held her forehead.

"My baby, you're sick. Why didn't you tell me?"

"It's nothing serious, Mother."

"Children, go upstairs again. Please. I will stay down here with Hendrickje."

The other girls went upstairs.

Hendrickje was being sick again out of the window. As Katrina held her forehead, Katrina thought: I remember that first day for me when Laurens sent me down to get water and a rag for Hannah's face. That day he kicked Hannah. I was sick at the bottom of the stairs.

"This the first time it has happened, my baby?"

Hendrickje shook her head.

"Since when did it begin?"

"Three or four days ago."

Kyk-over-al looked like a black reptile sleeping out on the shimmering water. There was moonlight.

"I think I'll go upstairs now," said Hendrickje.

"Hendrickje baby, you should have told me. Your father knows. I asked him tonight. I knew, too."

"You knew? And Father?"

"He sent an Indian to spy on you. But me—I just guessed. And when I saw you dressing one day I knew for certain. Your breasts are fuller—and the tips are dark. It was so with me, too. I sat at the foot of the stairs there and was sick. He found me there when he came down, and he lifted me upstairs."

"An Indian to spy on us. That was mean of Father." She turned toward the window again, but nothing came up. She was about to move away when she saw the *corial* on the river.

"I think there's a boat coming here."

From the top of the stairs Rosa called: "Mother! A *corial* is coming! It's coming here!"

"Can we come downstairs, Aunt Katrina?"

"Yes! Come down! All of you, my children!"

Hendrickje seated herself at the dining table, saying that she was not well enough to come with them to the kitchen door. Katrina went with the other girls to receive the slave. The slave told them that he had passed Massa Laurens and the other slave on their way up. Massa Reinald had sent him off shortly after the other slave had left. Massa Willem was dead.

VII

They buried him in the clearing with Kaywana. Every planter and plantation manager in the colony came to the funeral. The whole de Graaf family was there, and the Blankenburgs and the Roosens and the Pletts and the widow of Abraham Beekman. Predicant Heynens performed the service, and Commandeur Samuel Beekman gave an oration at the graveside.

There were three lines of *corials* and skiffs along the bank. And eight tent-boats.

It was a drizzly afternoon, and the Predicant had a cold. He kept his hat on all through the ceremony. His nose looked very red.

Hendrickje and Aert stood at the head of Kaywana's grave, and Ignatius, a very pained and anxious expression on his face, kept behind them with his father who wagged his head and made soft moaning sounds at intervals. There was moisture on Reinald's cheek, but it was only a drop of water that had fallen from the *paraipee* palm whose fronds hung twenty or thirty feet above them. Reinald had a faraway, resigned air and hardly seemed conscious of other human presence around him.

When everything was quiet and everybody had gone and moonlight was white on the river, Laurens said to Aert in the dining room: "You must get your things ready to go up the Mazaruni tomorrow morning, Aert."

Aert, olive-complexioned, black-haired like an Indian, with finely cut European features, nodded and said: "Very well, Father. I've already started to pack."

Laurens went into the sitting room where Ignatius was sitting with his sisters and Gertruyt. He said to

Ignatius: "My boy, you must get your things ready. You have to go up the Mazaruni tomorrow morning to assist your cousin on the plantation."

"Assist him, Uncle Laurens? Assist Aert up there?"

"Yes."

"But, Uncle Laurens, I've never done any over-seeing."

"You'll learn. Aert will teach you. You can ride a mule. That's all that's necessary for the time being." Laurens squeezed his arm. "Don't be too dismayed, my boy. You'll get accustomed to it."

"Yes, Uncle Laurens."

Later, in the pantry, Ignatius said to Hendrickje: "Have you heard, Hendrickje? I have to go up the Mazaruni."

"Yes, I heard him speaking to you. You must go. It will be good experience for you, dear. It's time you learnt something about planting and handling slaves."

"But, Hendrickje, I'm a painter! You've said yourself that I wouldn't have to bother about planting——"

"That's when we're on our own. We're not on our own yet." She smiled and stroked his hair. "Don't look so upset, Ignatius."

"But I won't be seeing you any more. What am I going to do without you, Hendrickje? You speak so carelessly—as though it doesn't matter."

"You'll still see me. I'll come up there every other day. At times I might even spend a week with you all up there. Don't trouble."

"But I won't be able to paint!"

"You can't have everything," she said patiently. "Your painting will have to wait. You'll have to put it aside for a while. Be reasonable." She looked at him with sudden intensity. They were in the dark, but the moonlight shone in on them through some jalousies. "Ignatius, you must try to be more manly now. Remember Grandfather is dead. My one big friend and ally is gone. I have to face everything for us both alone. I have to depend upon myself now to get Father on our side—myself alone. You must try to do your best to help me, not to be a burden. I'm strong and I can fight, but, still, it's good to know I have some-

body behind me sometimes. I have my frightened moments. I'm human. You mustn't think me a superhuman creature who can move the world." She spoke
agitatedly, breathing quickly and glancing round into
the dining room. She kissed him and said: "Go upstairs
now and get your things packed, there's a good darling. Day after tomorrow I'll come and see you—and
I'll have something important to tell you. Go."

"Something important? What's that?"

"No. Go. Upstairs. I'll tell you when I come up the
river to see you."

All that morning Hendrickje remained in bed. At the
midday meal Laurens asked Katrina: "Why doesn't
Hendrickje come down to eat?"

"She's not feeling very well today, Laurens. I told
her to keep to bed."

"Is it fever—or a cold?"

"Fever," she murmured, avoiding his gaze.

He thought: I know what it is. It is no fever. She
is pregnant. Just as she planned it. A clever girl. My
clever daughter. By contrast, I am a fool. I don't count
any more. But I'm being foolish. This attitude is the
wrong one. I've lost my reason these past two or three
months. And it was a mean act, my sending that
Indian into the jungle up the creek to spy on them.
By God, but there's my pride! I won't allow a mere
creature born only the other day to treat me like an
inferior. I suppose she doesn't intend to be disrespectful, but, all the same, her airs infuriate me. I can sense
that she would like to call off the feud between us, but
no doubt her pride won't allow it. In a way, the whole
thing is absurd, but I will not give in. Until she comes
to me and makes the first move to be friendly I shall
hold out. She must know that my pride counts, too—
and I'm her elder. Her parent.

After the meal, however, when he went upstairs,
the desire came strong upon him to go into the next
room and speak to her. He thought: She's going to have
a child—my grandchild. Another van Groenwegel.
That touches me. I feel as I did that day I lifted
Katrina and brought her into the room here. I ought to

go into the next room now and ask her how she is feeling. Let her know that I'm moved to know that she's going to have my grandchild. Tell her that we have both been behaving like stubborn fools. Like father like daughter. Laugh it off. . . .

He rose and moved toward the connecting door, then paused and shook his head.

No, it would be too painful, too humiliating—undignified. I can't do it. She must come to me. She must be humble. I mustn't give in to sentiment. She wants to make out she is hard. Very well. I am hard, too. She must know that I am a van Groenwegel—as much as she is; as stubborn and as unrelenting.

He stood where he was, feeling suddenly foolish. He was aware of a smallness in him. But he would not go in to her. He walked back to the chair by the window, sank down and began to fill his pipe.

He felt a certain satisfaction that he had not yielded, but the sense of smallness would not be shaken off. He thought: This is not like me—or it ought not to be like me. I've always prided myself on being liberal, generous. This is what I should have expected of Mother. Mother was small, narrow, prejudiced. To the day of her death she never recognized Katrina as an equal.

He heard footsteps, and turned his head and saw Hendrickje come in. She crossed the room without a glance at him and went to the table by the bed, poured herself out some water. As he regarded her, tenderness began to move in him. . . . Taller than I am. Look at her. And graceful. There isn't another in the colony like her. . . .

"Hendrickje."

She put down the cup and turned at once. "Yes, Father?" Her eyes returned his gaze, gray-green and surprised. Expectant.

It took a great deal of effort to keep looking. The desire to avert his gaze was urgent. In a moment his head would tremble.

"You're not feeling well, your mother said."

"No, not very."

"You're going to have a child, I understand?"

"Did Mother tell you that?"

"Not directly. I guessed, more or less. Come and sit here." He tapped the arm of his chair.

She came and sat on the arm of his chair, and he rested his elbow on her leg and patted her knee. The nearness of her was terrible—and the feel of her. His pride, stubborn as it was, could not hold out against her. He knew now that she was above him. He had produced a human who had surpassed him.

"I hope you'll feel better," he said. "Don't exert yourself too much."

"I've had nausea all morning."

He nodded slightly. "It was like that with your mother." He steeled himself and said: "I'm sorry I lost my temper that day two or three months ago. I should not have struck you."

He felt her hand on his head. She was stroking his hair.

"I found some documents up yonder," he said, trying to make his voice matter-of-fact. "I see Grandfather purchased a plantation in Berbice in your name."

"Yes. He told me of it a few weeks ago."

He grunted. "Things seem destined to go the way you want them. I won't fight Providence." After a pause he said: "You have a right to be conceited, girl. You're big. Your airs annoy me, but—but you carry them well." He stopped speaking, feeling foolish and confused.

She uttered an affectionate sound and pulled his head against her, began to rub her hand along his cheek and his beard and kiss the top of his head. After that everything cleared up. She might have been four or eight years old and sitting on his knee for him to tell a story of the old days. He put his arm around her waist, and she put her arm around his shoulders and they began to talk as though there had been nothing between them these past two or three months. He said: "You feel confident you can make this venture of yours a success? What's going to happen in Berbice? I mean, about the plantation. Are you going to run it yourself?"

"Of course. I can ride well. I'll superintend things. I know Ignatius will never be able to carry out a manager's duties efficiently. He's soft, Father—weak and dreamy. He's taken after Uncle Reinald. He'll be good only for painting pictures. But, poor fellow, I like to see him happy with his brushes and canvas. I'll do the donkey work while he paints. I like managing affairs and people, Father. I'll enjoy doing it. I'm not going into this venture with my eyes closed. I've thought it over carefully. I know where the dangers lie, and I know what difficulties I'll be called upon to face, but I feel I'm capable of facing them—and overcoming them."

He smiled. "You'll win. I'm proud of you. I've always been proud of you. And proud of myself that I've produced such a specimen." He went on quickly: "What I don't quite understand is your wanting to marry this cousin of yours. It still seems to me inconsistent of you. You've always preached your grandfather's doctrines about keeping the family hard. Do you think it likely that Ignatius will give you the kind of children you want? Isn't it likely that you will produce weak-livered sons and daughters?"

"I've thought of that," she said, her face taking on a troubled look. "That side of things has never been out of my mind. But I'm a woman, and if I marry another man I can't retain my name, and I'm determined to remain a van Groenwegel—in nature and in name." Her body stiffened and grew erect. Her hand on his shoulder began to clench, and out of the corner of his eye he could watch the slow, regular rise and fall of her full breasts—fuller and more imposing now that she was pregnant. He could sense the power in her: the terrible massiveness. She might have been fifty instead of twenty-one.

"The family, Father. The family, for me, will always come before everything else. I know it's a risk marrying Ignatius. I know there are good chances that we may produce a few weaklings here and there. But I keep trying to convince myself that there will be enough strong ones like me—and yourself and Grandfather and Greatgrandfather and Kaywana—to see us through, to take the name down with honor and power, to keep up our motto. I have faith in myself. My spirit is strong, and my body is strong. I'm going to prove a good breeder. I'm hoping to have no less than ten children—twelve, if possible. More. And among these a few must be like me.

"I have great plans—great dreams for the future. I know I'm human. I know that we're all of us mere twigs that Destiny keeps shifting around, stamping upon or causing to sprout and bloom. Everything is a haphazard game. But in spite of that I feel strong. I feel strong enough to fight even Destiny—and win. Get my own way. Bring all my dreams into actuality. I'm going to do it. We're going to be the most powerful family along this Wild Coast. We'll be masters in every sphere of activity."

V The Way to Power

I

On the 9th of March 1709 Laurens wrote a letter to Hendrickje. It began with references to the safe receipt of her last letter and a few commonplaces relating to the health of the family, then went on to say: "I have been in no mood for letter writing these past few months, Hendrickje, and even now my pen is heavy and reluctant. I write this only because I know you must consider it strange that no word has come from any of us since the recent misfortunes that have befallen our colony and our own family in particular. This letter, I fear, is a duty the performance of which calls for some effort of will on my part, for at the moment there are many urgent matters concerning the welfare of our plantations to occupy my wits at full pressure, added to which, as I said before, my health is not very good.

"The news of Ferry's raid and of the more recent raid, last month, should probably have reached you by now. Briefly, this is what occurred: On the 18th of October, the watchman of the Brandwagt at the mouth of the Essequibo observed three strange vessels entering the river, and came up to the fort in a fast *corial* to give the alarm. Commandeur van der Heyden Resen, who, as you may have heard, was appointed provisionally by the late Commandeur Samuel Beekman, immediately sent messengers to warn the planters. I was in the fields when the message came, for it was about eleven in the morning. When I returned to the house I made instant preparations for an attack, barricading the windows and telling your mother that we would on no account flee into the bush or go up-river as the other planters and their families were doing. Your mother, as I had anticipated, took this decision with composure and resignation, while Gertruyt and Octavia responded with a show of courage and a

determination to fight to the end if we were called upon to do so.

"As it happened, however, no attack came. Captain Antoine Ferry, the leader of the raiders, sent a
boat of truce to the fort after having plundered many
of the plantations lower down, and Commandeur
Resen agreed to open peace discussions. Eventually, on
the 25th, the terms of capitulation were signed and
Ferry left the colony with slaves, goods and cash to
the value of 50,000 guilders (112 slaves reckoned at
300 guilders each, meat, sugar, tobacco, sundry other
provisions and a thousand pieces of eight). One third
of this sum we private planters were compelled to bear.
The Company stood the rest.

"But the most tragic part of this event, for us,
was the fate that befell your sister Rosa and her husband and their three children—also Antony de
Wiecjk, your brother-in-law, Gertruyt's husband.
When the raiders began to plunder downriver, Rosa,
arguing that she was a van Groenwegel and could not
flee, refused to leave her home, and this in spite of a
message brought in that her husband had been shot
in the fields. She created quite a scene—she called her
parents-in-law cowards—and despite all entreaties and
her pregnant condition, fired upon the raiders from the
kitchen, but was soon brought down by a shot. She
and her five-year-old son perished in the flames that
destroyed the house.

"Luise, who had been spending the day with
them, managed to escape with the two little girls,
Frieda and Katrina, but on the path, on the way to
the house here, they were attacked, and though your
brother-in-law, Antony, who had gone to meet them,
put up a gallant fight, Frieda was shot in the foot and
later died of blood poisoning. Little Katrina was shot
through the head and must have died instantaneous-
ly. Antony developed pneumonia and died six days
later, but Luise, who also became very ill through ex-
posure—it rained heavily—recovered.

"Last month, February, the colony suffered another
raid by two French privateers whose names we still

do not know. These were very wanton cutthroats and
burnt and destroyed for the sheer pleasure of doing so.
The Commandeur sent some of the Indians after them,
but with little effect, though I did hear some tale that
in a surprise attack the Indians actually succeeded in
carrying off the French colors. These desperadoes,
unlike Ferry and his lot, were in no mood to make
peace. They plundered and burnt all the Company's
plantations and most of the private ones, eventually
taking away about five hundred hogsheads of sugar
and a great number of slaves.

"Again, both here and up the Mazaruni, we stayed
and barricaded our houses against attack. But there
was no battle to speak of. When we opened fire on
the raiders from the windows they ran off. Cutlasses
and sabres seem to have been their only weapons.
Most of our cane fields, both here and up the Mazaruni, were set on fire and destroyed. Our sugar mill
here, too, was burnt down, but Aert's up the Mazaruni
is still standing. He led an attack against the raiders
when they were on the point of setting fire to it and
drove them off. The big barn, too, was saved in the
same manner. Aert, as you will gather, displayed great
bravery.

"At the moment, there are only two sugar mills
standing in the colony. Everywhere nothing but devastation meets the gaze—burnt out sugar mills, burnt
out barns and slaves' logies and plantation residences.
I fear that once again, as in '66, Essequibo is faced
with ruin, though the Commandeur seems confident
that we shall be able to make a quick recovery. For
ourselves, I admit, the situation is not as hopeless in
outlook as it had appeared at a glance a few weeks
ago. Though there are a number of problems to be
tackled and overcome, I have good reason to believe
that, with hard work and persistence, we shall recover
within two or three years—always provided, of course,
that we suffer no more raids.

"Concerning more intimate matters, it may interest you to know that your Aunt Susannah's husband, your Uncle Karl, died in June last, but that she

herself is in the very best of health. Your widowed cousin, Octavia, is about to embark on her second marriage. Next week the ceremony has been planned to take place, and the groom is Hendrik de Fruizt. Naturally, in view of the recent tragedies, there will be no merrymaking. Your Uncle Reinald fell out of his study window three weeks ago, but, miraculously, sustained no injuries to speak of. Though his mind is entirely gone, he still keeps perfect health physically. Aert's wife gave birth to a daughter a fortnight ago, and this time it was not a stillborn child. They have decided to call this girl Mathilde after Alpheda's mother. The two other children, Flora and Jabez, are doing very well. Jabez is a promising boy.

"To refer to something you said in your last letter. You stated that though a bitter and frustrated woman, your spirit and will are still strong and far from being shattered. You seemed to imagine that I was in doubt about this, but you are wrong, I never doubted it, Hendrickje. But what I said, and what I say again, is that I consider your treatment of that poor young man your husband to be disgraceful and inexcusable. It puzzles me how you could have dared to write and describe the events you have done—and to me your father. I fear I could never bring myself to feel any tenderness toward you again. The love I once had for you and the pride I felt in you are completely dead. That is why corresponding with you has come to mean to me nothing but a mere duty.

"But for our recent misfortunes, I think I can claim to be a fairly happy and contented man. Your mother and I mean as much to each other as we did when we were twenty-odd and passionate, though, naturally, with a more serene depth than we were capable of at that time. If there is any undercurrent of sadness beneath our happiness it is you, Hendrickje, and your letters describing your life these past fourteen or fifteen years in Berbice that have brought us this alloy of gloom. But I still wish you well, and hope that one day you may find peace for your ambitious soul. Your mother and I are the only ones here who

are aware of the vicious deeds you have committed.
We would not dare to reveal the contents of your letters to the others. . . ."

II

Cornelis—Hendrickje had named him after one of the
Berbice Patroons, Cornelis van Peere—had been born
at the old place in Essequibo, and when she and
Ignatius arrived in Berbice, he was only two months
old. He had blue eyes like his father's, and pale yellow
hair. His grandparents had been very proud of him. His
Great-aunt Susannah had sent him a gift of five hundred guilders.

The plantation was on the same bank as that of
Fort Nassau, and only a few hundred yards further
upriver. The residence was a brick place of four bedrooms, a dining room and sitting room in one, with a
dividing screen, and a large portico shady with fern-
creepers and honeysuckle. There was no veranda. The
furniture was heavy and solid but comfortable. One
large armchair had the initials of the former owner
carved on the back within a heart. The bedrooms were
cool and well lighted. The kitchen was spacious, with
a large fireplace for cooking.

"I think we'll be happy here, Hendrickje," Ignatius smiled, as they stood on the portico that first evening looking out on the river. The river was about two
hundred yards wide at this point. It ran past not twenty yards from the bottom of the three stone steps that
led down from the portico.

The jungle on the opposite bank looked dense
and wet and full of unknown dangers from which they
would be safe in this house.

"I think so myself," said Hendrickje. "The sur-
roundings are lovely, if primitive, but it's up to us to
improve the place and give it a civilized air. We're
master and mistress here. And soon there will be the
cries of our children and the sound of their footsteps.
That thought overwhelms me." She spoke as though
addressing herself. She squeezed his elbow in an ab-

sentminded way, gazing past him at the sluggish water with the dusk coming down upon it. The insects had begun their nighttime chorus—a more shrill and intense chorus than on the Essequibo, it seemed. The air smelt wet and leafy-rank with the jungle and dead leaves. Over the trees, the sky was pink and mauve.

They heard the squeak of a pet monkey over at the fort. The wooden palisades loomed dullish gray above the low *awara* palms that intervened in the northwest. They could see the roofs of the buildings, too—the Commandeur's residence and the barracks in which the soldiers lived, and the various officials like the Orphan-master and the Surveyor and the Commandeur's Secretary. The people who mattered.

"I must remember that jar of wine," she murmured. "I'm sending a jar of wine for the Commandeur. We have to cultivate the officials at the fort as much as possible. They're going to prove useful to us in time to come when we begin to expand."

The very next day the planning began. "First of all," she said, "we have to get the carpenters from the Company plantation upriver. The kitchen and pantry need some repairs. Then I've got to see about the slaves. I'm going to pick out the best fellows and see if I can train them into leaders for the weaker ones. I must have a few upon whom I can depend absolutely. I'll give these chosen ones special quarters and special rations. I'll flatter them and keep them keen and eager to lord it over the slack and the idle. I'm going to do things systematically, Ignatius. I want this plantation run without a single hitch. Everything must go like a machine." She looked at him suddenly. "And understand this. Now and then you've got to assist me in writing up the records. You have a good handwriting, and I want the books neatly and accurately kept."

"I'll help you in whatever I can, Hendrickje, dear. It's only the field work that bores me so much. Those months up the Mazaruni were terrible. I came near to committing suicide one day. The rain and the mud and the slaves giving trouble. I'm not suited to that sort of life."

She laughed shortly. "Yet you'll be content to see me going out in the rain while you remain at home, snug and safe, and paint pictures!"

"But you said you *wanted* to do that sort of work. I know it's a man's work, but you said——"

"I know what I said—and I meant it. Don't upset yourself. I'll do the overseeing. Mud and rain won't intimidate me. Anyway, the experience up the Mazaruni was very good for you. I'm not sorry you went up there for those few months with Aert. We never can tell what may happen in the future. Your knowledge may yet come in useful."

She gave him a swift glance, and it was this glance that put the first dark tentacle of fear around his heart. "My knowledge may yet come in useful? What do you mean, dear? I'm afraid I don't understand."

She shrugged. "Never mind. Don't trouble your poor head, my darling. I think I hear Cornelis fretting. It must be time for him to have some nourishment."

He stood at the bedroom door watching her suckle the child. "I'd thought of doing a Madonna study of you, Hendrickje. But I'm doubtful now if you would make a good model. Your face isn't soft enough in expression when you hold that child to your breast. You don't look as a mother should."

He came over to where she sat and began to stroke Cornelis' head. "Spendid little fellow, isn't he?"

"There's something I've just thought of, Ignatius. Go downstairs and see whether those stone jars have been brought in. I told Rabonne to have them removed from the steps."

"What stone jars?"

"The ones I told you we were going to store our valuables in if the necessity arose. Go down and see if Rabonne brought them in."

III

Within a few months everything was running as she had planned. The Commandeur and the officials had called to see them, and she and Ignatius had returned their calls. She had selected her gang leaders and special favorites among the slaves, and the system of bullying was working. Every morning she rode around to inspect the work. The repairs to the kitchen and pantry were satisfactorily carried out. She superintended the white carpenters from the Company plantation upriver, told them exactly what she wanted done and stayed to see that it was done, criticized them when she thought criticism necessary, flattered them occasionally.

Many times Cornelis would fret and squall upstairs and she would not be at hand to feed him, and Ignatius would have to leave his easel to go and look for her. She would exclaim in annoyance and hurry back to the house, muttering: "This breast-feeding is a nuisance. I must see if I can't wean him off to goat's milk."

"Goat's milk, Hendrickje! How could we give a little infant like that goat's milk!"

"It's been done already. It can be diluted with water. I have no time to be always rushing in to give him my breast. If I can get him to take goat's milk you could mix his feed and give it to him while I'm busy outside."

"That doesn't seem natural to me. You his mother and don't want to give him your milk! Surely you ought to put him before everything else."

"How can I put him before everything else! What would happen to the plantation and the work about the place! I have no one to assist me. You stay in the house here painting all day. I can't divide myself into six people, can I?"

"But, my dear, it's your own plan. You said it would work——"

"Don't argue! Don't whine! You're getting every day like your father up the Mazaruni. You do nothing but whine."

He sighed and went out.

One day when he told her that her temper was becoming frayed, she replied: "And who is to be blamed for that! If you would make some attempt to help me my temper mightn't be half as bad as it is."

"That's unreasonable," he told her. "You're going back on your word. You particularly promised me that you wouldn't interfere, when it comes to my work, or allow anything to disturb me. I can't paint and do housework and take care of the baby. I must put all my energy into my pictures if they are to be of any value——"

"That's just it. Of what value are they?"

"The Commandeur himself said that in Europe I may be able to fetch a good price for them."

"In Europe. We're in Berbice—in the wilds. Pictures are worth nothing here. What I'll have to do in future is to limit you to certain hours. You can't paint all day. You must give me some help, Ignatius. I have a great deal of energy, but I'm human. I'll break down if I continue at this rate."

"You're cruel, Hendrickje."

"All life is cruel. All life is brutal. One day you'll discover that. Soft methods take men nowhere."

Many nights when he attempted to make love to her she would push him off impatiently, saying that she was tired and did not want to be annoyed. There were other nights, however—especially those nights following days when things had gone smoothly in the fields—when she would be passionate and eager and even remorseful. "I don't mean to be cruel, darling. You mustn't take me seriously when I speak sharply. I have so many matters to think of and to attend to that sometimes I can't help being irritable."

Then came the day when her milk dried up and they had to resort to goat's milk. Cornelis' stomach rejected the goat's milk for the first few days; he suffered from diarrhoea. But suddenly these disorders ceased and he became weaned to the new diet.

"This means, then," said Hendrickje, "that you'll have to regulate your painting to suit his feeding hours. From tomorrow you'll mix his feed and give it to him. Two parts water to one part milk."

He submitted to this ruling, but there were several days when Cornelis either went without a feed or had his feed an hour or more late. His loud squalling would sometimes penetrate the creative mist of his father's awareness and Ignatius would put down his palette and brushes and hurry off with a worried face and clucking sounds to mix the feed.

Cornelis must have been on goat's-milk diet six weeks when Hendrickje discovered that she was pregnant again. She took it casually, saying: "I suspected it would happen before long. Let's hope it will be another son. If I could control it I'd have nothing but sons. Sons to carry on our name."

"I don't care what it turns out to be," said Ignatius. "What I'm worried about is your riding that mule in this condition."

"Don't trouble yourself," she assured him. "I'll ride the mule and bring my son safely into the world. I'm strong. I'm a born breeder. Can't you look at me and see it, Ignatius?" She slapped her stomach and her hips. "I'm physically invincible. My will and the strong constitution I was born with will overcome anything. Even nausea and riding on mule back. The nausea I felt two or three mornings ago has gone. I've mastered it. It doesn't trouble me now."

Regarding her, he told himself that she did seem invincible. She was a great woman—though now and then she frightened him. There were moments when she seemed a monster. Yet, curiously, he loved her all the more for her cruelty. At times he would have been glad if she had struck him, if she had snatched up her hide whip and slashed him across his back as she did to the slaves. When she snapped at him or ordered him around he pretended to be aggrieved, but, in actuality, he was secretly thrilled. He felt a cringing, fearful, aching pleasure.

Some nights in bed when she spurned him irritably he would feel as great a thrill as though she had yielded. He would curl himself away from her in the big bed they shared and feel hurt and aggrieved and puny—but would know that he was purposely forcing himself to feel this way because it gave him a secret bliss.

IV

She rode the mule in her pregnant state without ill effects, though when her condition had become advanced, Rabonne, one of her leader-bullies, who worshipped her, said to her: "Missy, not think it good for you to go on riding on mule any more. Better wait till after baby come."

"How am I to get about, then?"

"Missy, I can make lift-up chair for you, and four of us can take you round de fields every morning."

"You mean, a chair with poles or handles? Like the palanquins they use in the Orient, eh?" She gave him a smile. "You are clever, Rabonne. Good man. And will you see after this chair for me? Can you make it?"

"Yes, missy," he said. He was a shortish, thickly-built fellow with huge muscles. "Two-three days and I have it ready for you."

Before the week was out she was being borne into the fields on a crude but comfortable chairlike contrivance. Rabonne had so made it that two slaves could lift her with ease, one in front and one behind, and travel at a brisk pace. During the first four mornings, Rabonne himself insisted on being a bearer, taking the front position. His duties, however, were such that he eventually had to give place to another. The Field Four gang was giving some trouble and his presence was required to bully them into order. He carried a hide whip. There were two others like him—Henwah and Pardoom, both burly, tough fellows who reveled in their authority and venerated their mistress, and were, therefore, allowed to carry whips.

When Hendrickje became confined to bed with the new baby—another boy—it was Rabonne and Henwah and Pardoom who ran the plantation, Rabonne coming up to his mistress's room every day at noon to make a detailed report concerning the work in the fields and all that had taken place during the morning half. In the evening, Pardoom came up to report. This went on until Hendrickje was in a condition to be up and about again.

The new son had dark hair and gray eyes, and Ignatius thought that he resembled Reinald, but Hendrickje told him he was talking nonsense.

"I can't see any resemblance," she said. "And if later on he does grow to resemble Uncle Reinald, let's pray it will be a purely physical resemblance. I'd thrash the life out of him if he showed any signs of mooning about the place with books under his arms. Every son of mine must be hardy. I want my sons to swim and boat and mix with the soldiers at the fort. They may be a crude lot over there, but crudeness has its virtues sometimes. Art and literature are apt to produce effeminacy. Your painting is responsible for half your softness. The other half, of course, is heredity; you can't help that."

She began to complain again about the inconvenience of suckling the child. She tried goat's milk on Adrian—that was the name she decided he must have —but it made the child so ill that she was compelled to resume breast-feeding.

Meanwhile, Cornelis, who was beginning to make intelligent sounds and could toddle around, depended solely upon his father for everything. He was a mild, quietish fellow, and, of late, seldom indulged in prolonged bouts of crying. He had come to learn that, yells or no yells, it made no difference; no one came to soothe him.

"It's just as well," remarked Hendrickje, "we neither of us have the time to fuss over them. Neglect will make them independent and self-reliant."

"If you say so, my dear, it must be so," Ignatius nodded, "but sometimes my conscience troubles me. I do feel we ought to pay them more attention than we do. All young children should be given some affection —especially from their mother."

"Why don't you mother them, then? I'm virtually the man in this place. It's I who have to go out and brave the elements."

"You really shouldn't say that, Hendrickje. I do my best to feed Cornelis and do what I can about the house——"

"Don't whine! Don't whine! Nowadays you cringe and whine at the slightest provocation. I'm beginning to feel you like me to scold you. I believe you must find some quaint pleasure in my bullying you. Come here! Don't go outside."

He moved over to a window, gazing at the river with a troubled, hurt expression. His whole attitude was one of self-pity and self-abasement. She watched him, a look of curiosity and perplexity on her face.

"I'm discovering many things about you, Ignatius. And many things about human nature I hadn't thought possible. In a way it's edifying."

"What do you mean?"

"Never mind. We won't follow up the subject."

About a week later she wrote telling her father: "He has a twist in his nature. He seems to enjoy being bullied, and, so far as I am concerned, he may continue to abase himself as much as he wants. My love for him is dwindling every day into a kind of pity and mild contempt. The more I have to do with him the less I can bring myself to respect him. However, it doesn't matter. I have enough to absorb my attention—what with running this plantation and keeping the slaves in order. Let Ignatius make himself into a cringing drone. So long as I can use him in the capacity of a husband to give me children I shall be satisfied. . . ."

The plantation prospered. The Commandeur told her one day: "Mevrouw, I wish we could have secured your services as General Superintendent of our Company plantations. For a woman, you are remarkable."

She laughed and returned: "Since I was an infant, Mynheer Commandeur, it was predicted that I would be a remarkable woman." And later, to Ignatius: "I'm becoming quite a figure in the colony. They respect me. I can hold my own with any of these managers when it comes to handling slaves and sweating them. And this is only the beginning. I tell you, we're on the way to power, Ignatius. Power." She tapped her clenched hand slowly on the windowsill. "The one pity is that Grandfather isn't alive to witness this. I had far more in common with him than with Father. Father is sound in his way, but he's inclined to be weak at times. He hasn't a stable philosophy. He calls it being liberal and generous—but it's simply weakness. To get to the heights in this world one must have a hard, firm, ruthless policy. Look at the system I've created among the slaves. You see how successfully it's working! I encourage them to tell tales on each other, and I give the talebearers extra rations and reduced tasks as a reward, and the malefactors get less rations and more work as well as punishment. My three lieutenants, Rabonne and Pardoom and Henwah, look upon me as a great queen or empress. I can see it in their eyes how they venerate me. And why? Because I've lifted them into a stratum of dignity by giving them whips and investing them with the authority to mete out punishment. I've flattered their vanity, and they would die rather than betray me. Are you listening, Ignatius, or have you fallen asleep?"

"I'm paying attention." He was sitting by the cot patting Adrian to sleep.

She smiled, and the contempt in her expression gradually faded. Tenderness came into her eyes. Her mouth softened. She crossed over to him, held his head and pressed it against her, stroking his cheek and his hair. He remained passive, his face with a strained, sensitive look.

Outside, the black water kept sucking at the bank, making a low, sensuous sound. Not a whispering as on the Essequibo. Lights had begun to gleam in the fort buildings—in the upper story of the Commandeur's residence. And in the ships lying at anchor in the stream. A voice came through the dusk, loud and disturbing, then a laugh raucous and with a lecherous note. There was the smell of woodsmoke in the air. The slaves were cooking their evening meals in the compound. Once or twice shouts of laughter came from that way, too.

Soon she was pregnant again, and as on the previous occasion, she rode the mule about the plantation without fear. She said to Rabonne: "I'll be needing that chair of yours again in three or four months."

"It in de storehouse, missy. Soon as you ready I bring it for you."

The chair, however, was never used again. One morning, during heavy rain, she fell from the mule and had to be taken home, and when the surgeon from the fort came and examined her he said: "I'm afraid you're going to lose the child, Mevrouw. You should never have ridden that mule."

"I rode it during my previous pregnancy and I kept the child, didn't I? This is only an accident. I was crossing a drain." She spoke with petulance. The surgeon did not argue.

She lost the child and was ill for a few days. Ignatius wept and thought she was going to die. She was so ill that she could hardly concentrate when Rabonne and Henwah came upstairs to give her their reports. Ignatius did no painting. His time was too occupied taking care of her and of the two children. He proved capable, and one morning even asserted himself to the extent of refusing to permit Rabonne to come upstairs to deliver his report.

"Your mistress is not well enough this morning to hear your report," he told Rabonne. "Get out of the house."

Rabonne did not move. He said surlily: "Massa, yesterday Missy tell me no matter how sick she is I must come up and report."

"*I* am telling you you cannot go upstairs. She is in no condition to see anyone. She must have rest and quiet."

Rabonne glowered at the floor.

"Get out of the house."

"Missy vexed wid me if I not go upstairs, Massa."

"Are you daring to disobey me?"

"I get orders from Missy. I must obey, Massa."

"Get out—or I'll thrash you for impudence."

Rabonne hesitated, then turned and went.

Not ten minutes later, when Ignatius went upstairs, Hendrickje asked in a weak voice: "What time is it? Rabonne should have come to me to report? Have you seen anything of him?"

He related what had happened, and she said: "You've acted foolishly. Send out and tell him to come to me at once."

"Hendrickje, you're not well enough to see him."

"Do as I say. Send one of the kitchen slaves to call him."

He left the room, and a few minutes later Rabonne passed him on the stairs and gave him a deliberately mocking glance.

Ignatius went to his room, muttering: "This is my lot. I must bear it and not grumble. It's she who ordered it, therefore it must be so. The very slaves treat me as dirt. I must suffer and say nothing."

He stood beside his easel, rubbing his hand along his forearm and breathing deeply, his head bowed. Suddenly he pressed his hands to his face in an ecstasy of self-abasement, trembling and weak with a delicious, aching, aggrieved joy.

When she was well and active again he found that most of his time was still taken up with care of the two children. He did not grumble aloud, however; he resigned himself to the situation, extracting a secret pleasure from the fact that she was robbing him of the hours he should have devoted to his art. "She ought to be doing this," he assured himself in a mutter; he had developed the habit of muttering aloud to himself. "She is their mother, but she forces me to do a mother's tasks. Very well. I must be prepared to suffer under her tyranny. It's my fate."

One night, when they were making love, he abruptly began to kiss her feet and make whimpering sounds, and she said in a puzzled voice: "What's the matter with you? Did I tell you that kissing my feet excites me?" He went on doing it, as though obsessed, until the realization came upon her that it was causing him pleasure—a strange, subservient, toady pleasure. She smiled, a slow understanding seeping through her.

She went out of her way, the following day, to find fault with him; scolded him at the slightest pretext, snapped at him at every opportunity. When he turned away and pretended to be hurt she would look after him without his knowing, and smile quietly to herself and nod.

In her periodic letter to her father she said: "Life with Ignatius becomes daily more interesting. I have no doubt now that he is developing into a pervert. This self-abasement is not natural. Two days ago I purposely picked a quarrel with him and got into a temper —at least, I pretended I was in a temper. I slashed him across his back with my whip, and he howled and cringed away and implored me not to strike him again. But he couldn't fool me. I know he enjoyed it. And, for some reason, I rather enjoyed it myself. I believe I was born with a streak of cruelty. I wonder if it could be Grandfather August I've got it from. Wasn't he supposed to have been very cruel? Anyway, the arrangement seems to me perfect. If he enjoys cruelty inflicted and I enjoy inflicting cruelty, then we ought both to be content. . . ."

V

When Adrian was about nine months old Rabonne one morning said to his mistress: "I still have de lift-up chair in de storehouse for you, missy. Soon as near time you must tell me."

"I'll let you know when I'm ready, Rabonne," she smiled.

For the rest of that morning she was pensive and inclined to be ill tempered, slashing at the field slaves for the most trivial misdemeanors.

At noon she said to Ignatius: "I want you to go across to the fort and ask the surgeon if he would be so good as to come and see me. I want to consult him on a certain matter."

"Are you unwell, Hendrickje?"

"No, but I want medical advice. Has it struck you that it's time I should have been pregnant again?"

"You mean, you're afraid you'll be unable to have another child?"

"Don't be a fool. I never said so, did I?"

"I wonder if that fall you had some months ago when you lost the child didn't cause some internal injury."

"That's what I want to find out," she said quietly. A tenseness came into her manner. She sat for a long while silent and thoughtful.

"You'd be very disappointed if you didn't have any more children?"

Without a word, she rose and went upstairs.

He gazed after her, and a shudder went through him. A shudder of fear mingled with delight.

The surgeon could not tell her anything definite. "It's not unlikely that the fall may have caused some displacement of your organs, Mevrouw," he said, "but one can never be certain in such matters, and I fear I am not sufficiently advanced in my knowledge of that branch of medicine to give you any reliable opinion. Only time will prove whether the fall did harm you in the manner you think."

For days after she was in a brooding mood. Often a gleam of alarm would appear in her eyes. At night she made love to him with a frantic passion; almost with panic. She began to take more interest in Cornelis and Adrian, giving him help in feeding them or bathing them. One day he came into the room and found her standing by the cots gazing at them as they slept, an earnest, pondering look on her face. She scowled on becoming aware of his presence, and pretended to be occupied with folding up petticoats. During this period she seldom struck him with her whip or picked quarrels, nor did she talk about the plantation nor of the day's work, as was her habit. Rabonne, too, noticed the difference in her manner, and grinned ingratiatingly one morning: "Missy, anything wrong? You look quiet and sad, missy."

"I'm thoughtful, Rabonne, that's all." She uttered an uncomfortable laugh. "There comes a time when we must all grow sober and thoughtful."

The months moved on, but still no sign of pregnancy appeared. One day she said furiously: "I won't give up. It's only a temporary irregularity. I refuse to believe that that fall has rendered me barren for the rest of my life."

One night she got out of bed, snatched up her whip and flogged Ignatius. "It's you," she snarled. "You've become weak! Effete! It's this effeminacy you've developed. This cringing pleasure you take in my hurting you. It's not natural. It's a perversion!"

She flung the whip down and sank into a chair, sobbing harshly.

The following day she took Rabonne aside near the storehouse and said: "Rabonne, there's a matter I want so speak to you about. It's a little delicate, but I think I've got past the stage of delicacy. Do you know of any African drugs or potions that can give aid in making women conceive?" She flicked her whip about selfconsciously and went on hurriedly: "I may as well be frank with you and tell you that I suspect that the fall I got from the mule some months ago has prevented me from having another child. That's why I've decided to ask you this. The surgeon at the fort doesn't seem able to help me."

At first he stared at her in wonder; then his face took on an understanding look. He nodded slowly and said: "I can find out, missy. Gansibah should know. He know *obeah*. I see him burn feathers and gray powder."

"I won't have anything to do with that. I have no confidence in black magic. What I want to know is if he can tell you of any herbs or roots that I can boil and drink to help me. You Africans have a lot of secret knowledge. I'm sure one of you ought to know."

He promised to do his best to help her, and three days later told her that Gansibah was preparing a potion. It was a bush preparation. "He say you must drink it two nights before full moon, missy, and you sure to get baby."

"Why two nights before full moon? Why not on any night? I think I told you, Rabonne, that I won't have anything to do with black magic."

"Dis not magic, missy. When de moon full it draw out what inside you. Dat's why you must drink it when de moon nearly full. Full moon help draw out de baby from your inside."

She consented reluctantly to follow the instructions, and though the concoction looked and tasted disgusting, she swallowed it on the two nights before full moon. When she discovered that it acted on her as an aphrodisiac, her spirits rose. She told Ignatius: "I believe this will do it. I feel different inside already. These Africans know more about these things than European doctors."

Ignatius shook his head doubtfully. "I still don't like your using these strange medicines, Hendrickje. I don't trust these slaves. I believe many of them hate you. You don't treat them particularly well. How do you know that this fellow Gansibah isn't trying to poison you?"

"I have confidence in Rabonne," she parried. "In any case, I can't resign myself to this condition. I must have more children, Ignatius. Before we were married I planned on having at least ten. I told Father that, and I know I'm capable of it. I'm strong." She stood up and threw out her bosom. "Look at me! Don't you see what a fine specimen I am! I'm made for breeding. It would be senseless, cruel waste if a mere fall should prevent me from conceiving again. I won't give up. I'm determined to overcome this incapacity. I must and will have more children. By sheer will I'll conceive again."

The weeks, however, and then the months, moved on, and still there was no sign of pregnancy. Again she tried the concoction Rabonne secured for her from Gansibah, but it had no effect.

Ignatius said: "Hendrickje, my dear, we'll have to content ourselves with our two boys, and I think we'll have reason to be proud of them. They're strong and handsome. I'm sure they'll be like you when they grow up. You mustn't upset yourself in this way."

For this she slashed him across his face with her whip, cutting his forehead and the tip of his left ear. As he cringed away, moaning with pain, she snarled at him: "Don't dare to console me! I haven't given up.

I'll never give up. Never! Nothing will defeat me!" The next moment she was sobbing and asking him to forgive her. "I didn't mean to hit you on your face, my darling. I'm not in my right senses. I'm going to kill myself, Ignatius. I can't go on living like this. It's intolerable. It's humiliating. Why should this happen to me of all people! It isn't just. I was made to have children. Every inch of me was fashioned for it—and now because of this trifling accident I'm robbed of the capacity to breed. If I don't have another child I shall hate life. I shall hate people. I shall hate the earth and everything on it. I shall be a terror to every creature with which I come into contact!"

She spoke with such passion that he gazed at her with fear. "I can't understand why you should take it like this, Hendrickje," he said. "You still have so much to interest you in life. The plantation and Cornelis and Adrian."

"I don't expect you to understand. You have no fire in you. You have no ambitions. You're an ineffectual drone. The more I see of you the more I despise you, the more I hate you and feel like kicking you and stamping you out of existence." He tried to cringe away from her in another shuddering ecstasy of humility, but fear dominated him. He simply stood still, on the alert for another attack from her.

A few days later she told Laurens in a letter: "I can see that it's the will of Destiny to thwart me in my plan to have children, but believe me, Father, I shall never be defeated. I'll still have my way in the long run. I'll live to see my grandchildren multiply in this colony, and through them I'll fulfil my dreams. Through them I'll bring into actuality the large and powerful family I've planned. I'm not afraid of Destiny. I defy Destiny. I believe that with enough strength of will a man or woman can bring under subjection all the forces of life. . . .

"At the moment I'm going through an extremely hysterical phase, but it will pass. Already I can feel a cold, hard calm descending upon me. Already I can sense a deeper strength coming into being. . . ."

VI

Despite resignation to her sterility, deep within her she never entirely gave up hope. When Cornelis was slightly over four years old she experienced certain symptoms that gave her reason to believe that she had conceived again. For a fortnight she lived in a tense bubble of hope. Then the bubble burst and another cold, savage period of bitterness and frustration followed. The field slaves whimpered under her lashes, and Ignatius drew more and more into the solitude of himself, fearing her now with the primeval fear of a weaker animal, worshipping her now in a perverted rapture of selflessness, sometimes hating her in a spurt of self-assertiveness.

The two boys were fond of him because he took notice of them and petted them in their mother's absence in the fields. One day he smiled at them: "You're my little friends, aren't you? We're together against her and her tyranny. We must keep together."

On an occasion after she had struck him with her whip and stamped out of the house Cornelis came to him and stroked his cheek and said: "You mustn't cry, Father. I'm sorry. Mother is very cruel."

"Yes, Mother is very cruel, my boy. But we mustn't mind. This is our lot. She is cruel to us all, but we must bear with it. Come and let me teach you to draw. It will be our secret. You mustn't tell her of it or she will be annoyed."

"No, I won't tell her. She's cruel. I don't like Mother."

Inevitably the day came when she discovered the alliance that was springing up between him and the boys. She came upon Cornelis with a piece of charcoal drawing warped elliptical figures on the wall. She snatched the charcoal from him and snapped: "None of that! You're spoiling the walls. Ignatius! Did you give this child charcoal? Haven't I told you not to leave your drawing things lying about where the children can get at them?"

"He must have found it by accident, my dear. I really have no idea how he————"

"Don't bother to make excuses. Get the wall cleaned." She flung the piece of charcoal through the window, and Cornelis began to sob.

"Mother, that was my best charcoal! My very best! And now you've thrown it away! You're cruel!"

Ignatius, busy rubbing off the marks Cornelis had made on the wall, did not notice the gleam that came into the eyes of his wife. It was not until she said in an icy voice: "Ignatius, have you been in the habit of giving this child charcoal?" that he started round with the realization of danger and stammered: "What's that, Hendrickje? What did you ask?"

"You heard. I'm asking if you're in the habit of giving this child charcoal to draw with. He's just mentioned that the piece I've thrown away was his best piece."

"I don't ever—I have never given any to him at any time."

He was too obviously alarmed; she knew he was lying.

"That's enough. Now I know that you have been giving him charcoal. Sit down. I want to speak to you. Sit by the window over there."

"But, Hendrickje, my dear————"

"Sit down!"

He seated himself hesitantly in the big armchair by the window.

On the floor Adrian, with a collection of pebbles and palm seeds, looked on, wondering and expectant. There was a smudge of green paint on his dark-brown curls, the result of an absentminded caress his father had given him a short while before.

"Perhaps you've forgotten what I told you some time ago, Ignatius. It might be a case of bad memory." She leaned casually against the bedpost as she spoke: "Might, I repeat. If I thought that you had deliberately decided to go counter to my ruling, the consequences for you would be serious."

"Your ruling?"

"My ruling. You needn't pretend you don't know

what I mean. You are perfectly aware that I disapprove of these two boys having anything to do with art. I'm certain you haven't forgotten what I said on that subject some time ago. You've defied me. I'm convinced of it now. You did this on purpose, didn't you?"

"But, my dear, I don't know what you're talking about. I've told you I had no idea Cornelis had taken up that charcoal——"

"Quiet! And stop wriggling about in that chair. If you imagine I'm going to be so kind as to oblige you with the pleasure of a flogging, let me disappoint you at once. This time it will be something much worse. This time it will be punishment with genuine pain. Pain that will strike home at your very soul." She moistened her lips. "This is an important occasion, Ignatius. It has just come to me in a flash what has been happening when my back is turned."

"Hendrickje, I swear it. I never did anything consciously that you didn't want me to. If I did, it was without knowing that I'd done wrong." He sat erect in the chair watching her, a troubled, wary look on his face.

As though he had not spoken, she said: "Ignatius, I've just begun to see the significance of certain scraps of talk I've heard these two children indulging in from time to time. You've been filling them up with your own effeminate ideas and poisoning them against me. You've been doing your best to win them over to your side. Probably trading on the fact that they've seen me often flogging you. You tell them I'm a cruel woman, don't you?"

"No. No, no. I've never told them that."

"You have. I'm certain of it. My intuition, apart from the evidence, tells me that you have. I'll have to mete out a severe lesson to you, Ignatius. What I'm about to do will seem heartless—unusually brutal. It's going to hurt you to the core, but it must be done. Stand up." She spoke softly, with a sensuous coaxing tenderness. She grasped his arm as he stood up. He was trembling.

"Hendrickje, I don't understand. What are you going to do?"

She smiled. "To think of it, Ignatius. Does it seem possible that only five years ago we used to go up that creak on the Essequibo to make love—and make love so passionately? We've both changed a great deal since then, haven't we?"

He turned away his gaze in a troubled, fearful way.

"In a way, I foresaw this, though. I don't regret marrying you, because I see now that a masculine man, a man with real self-respect, a man who was domineering and hard as a man should be, would never have suited me. Perhaps it was a deep, blind instinct that made me choose you. But that's irrelevant. Come with me."

She urged him forward and took him into the next room—the room he used as his studio. She paused just inside and stood looking around with a casually interested air.

"It's in here you bring them to tell them about your work and let them know what a horrible creature their mother is. Do you deny it?"

"Hendrickje, you misjudge me. I don't tell them anything against you. You know I wouldn't do that."

"No, I don't know you wouldn't do that. I believe you have done it. And what I'm going to do will teach you very effectively that it's wrong to try to encourage these two boys to be weak and effeminate like yourself. This punishment I'm about to inflict will teach you that never, never again must you ever let them have any charcoal or drawing materials or tell them anything about drawing. You said it was only an accident that Cornelis happened to have that piece in his possession. Well, in future you will have to see that accidents like that do not occur."

As she spoke she kept looking slowly round the room. "Some very interesting canvases you have in here, Ignatius. That one there you spent a long time on, didn't you? More than a year, if I'm not mistaken. The Adoration of the Lamb. Isn't that the one for which you used Cornelis as an infant model?" She smiled at him and it was almost a friendly, sympathetic smile.

He suspected what she was about to do only when she had moved casually and unhurriedly across the room to the easel and had taken up his palette knife. He darted after her with a croaking cry. He gripped her arm. "Hendrickje! What are you planning to do?" His lips had turned a grayish purple. "Why are you looking at that canvas? Don't touch it! If—if you touch it I'll kill you!"

She was unmoved. She stood gazing up at the big canvas; his Adoration scene. It was about twelve feet by five and the most striking of all the works that hung on the walls in the room.

With a sudden urgent motion he placed himself between her person and the picture and took up a defensive attitude.

"You won't dare touch it, Hendrickje. I mean it. I'll kill you. Do you know how much work I've put into this? How much of myself?"

She continued to smile and regard the work, ignoring him. Toying with the palette knife.

Cornelis and Adrian had followed them in, and stood near the door watching them. Cornelis' cheeks were still damp with tears. His hands were black with the charcoal he had been using on the wall.

"Stop bobbing about in front of me, Ignatius."

He stood where he was. "I tell you, I won't have you touch that work, Hendrickje. I'm in earnest. Don't try to damage it. You can do anything to me myself. Flog me, hurt me as much as you wish. But don't trouble my work. That's all I have in life to give me happiness. It's all I live for. I'm in great earnest. I shall kill you if you attempt to ruin this canvas."

Without warning—and to her utter dismay—he snatched the palette knife out of her hand and retreated a pace so that he stood directly beneath the canvas, his head almost touching its frame. He was like an animal waiting to be attacked, his eyes wild and his head trembling.

She stretched out her hand. "Give that knife back to me."

"I refuse."

"Give it back to me."

"I say I refuse."

She turned off and picked up a stool to throw at him, but he was so tensed and alert that he anticipated this move and rushed at her and grabbed her arms, letting the palette knife clatter to the floor.

The two boys retreated out of the room, startled, as their parents began to struggle for the possession of the stool. Hendrickje was strong, but in his desperation the masculine strength natural to Ignatius came to the fore and the next instant he had hurled her to the floor. It was as though more than his life depended upon his triumphing—something beyond mere physical safety.

As she tried to get to her feet he struck her in the face, kicked her and sent her down again. Before she could recover he snatched up the stool, which had gone skidding toward the wall, and brought it down on her head. The blow stunned her temporarily. Her forehead began to ooze a slow red trickle. But even this did not dismay him. He caught her by her shoulders and dragged her toward the door, dragged her right through into the next room. He rushed back into the studio and slammed and bolted the door, scuttled across to the other door—the one that opened on to the corridor—and locked and bolted this, too. He made a moaning sound and stood with his hands pressed to his face. He sobbed, his whole frame swaying from side to side.

"This is going too far. My work. Not my work. This would kill me. I couldn't stand by and see this done. No, Hendrickje. This is really too much. Oh, not my work. No, no!"

He was still muttering to himself when the heavy thuds sounded at the door that gave on to the corridor. He whined like a beast which knows that it is doomed. He began to pace about, throwing quick glances at the door.

"Hendrickje, stop that! Stop that! Don't let them break the door down. If you let any of those black brutes come in here I'm going to kill. I mean it."

When the door cracked and splintered and suddenly burst inward as the bolt and lock were wrenched away, he was crouching in a corner with the palette knife ready to pounce. He rushed straight at Rabonne as Rabonne came in. Rabonne grappled with him, and then Pardoom held him from behind and they brought him down, twisting the palette knife out of his grasp. He struggled with a desperate, whining fury.

Hendrickje stood in the doorway looking on, erect and dignified despite her disarray and the blood on her bodice and skirt. Her face might have been made of marble it was so rigid and impassive.

After they had pinned his hands behind his back, she said: "Stand him up so that he can face that picture—the large one."

He was blubbering now, his eyes bulging like a maniac's. He could not utter two words coherently.

Cornelis and Adrian had appeared at the door. They looked on with wide eyes—eyes naïve with wonder and baffled curiosity. Adrian had two purple *aeta*-palm seeds clutched in one hand. They fell with a prattle on the floor, and his lips parted when he saw his mother raise the axe she had taken earlier from Pardoom and chop at the big picture of the Adoration. The canvas split and tore in loud rasps of sound, and their father struggled and gibbered in the grasp of the two powerful black men.

VII

"It's over three months since that occurred," she told her father in a letter, "and the shock of it hasn't worn off yet. He's still in a daze, still in a trance of bitterness. I can sense hate in his manner now. He seems to derive little pleasure these days from self-abasement. He still cringes, but there is a difference. Yes, he fears and hates me now. The lesson has been effective. He will never dare to defy me again, for he knows I would not hesitate to ruin every canvas in his studio. . . .

"In your last letter you described my methods as being incredibly inhuman. Perhaps they are, but they achieve results, Father. The world respects only those

who can show results. The man or woman who says
that this might have been so if so and so had been so
is only smiled at, and rightly, too, for everybody feels
that he or she could achieve wonders if circumstances
were favorable. The strong man or woman creates circumstances, compels circumstances to be favorable. To
do this one must be brutal, one must be ruthless. A
soft policy never brought anything worth while into
being. Every living thing has been brought into being
through friction and struggle; one has only to look
around one to observe this. . . .

"Cornelis and Adrian live in dread of me now—
which is a good thing. The less love and pampering
they get from me the more metal will harden in their
souls as they grow up. Remember how Grandfather
always abhorred pampering. I agree with him. No pet-
ting. No sentimental cuddling. . . .

"The main thing is to keep them all cowed—husband, children and slaves. Only in this way can I be
complete master of the situation. Only in this way will
I have a free hand to do as I please without inter-
ference."

VIII

Between the ages of six and eight Cornelis and Adrian
heard the stories of Kaywana and Adriansen and the
raid of 1666. Hendrickje told them these stories in the
stern spirit of lessons that must be learnt and not forgotten. She would say: "That will do. Put away your
books. Now, Cornelis, stand still there and tell me
about Kaywana and the Indians. That night of the raid
—how did Great-great-grandmother Kaywana set about
to defend herself against the attack?"

Cornelis, eyes lowered, would begin a faltering
account of what happened. His mother might interrupt: "No, there were four muskets—not three." Or:
"No, the ammunition was on the desk in the corner,
not on the table."

Once she clouted Adrian because he could not
remember what action Willem took when the raiders

attempted to burn the barn. "I told you that the last time we discussed the raid. He ordered the slaves to break away the wall in eight places, and a man was put at each opening with a musket, because in this way if the Indians had attempted to rush up with more faggots and brambles they would have been shot down at point-blank range. Get that into your head. I'm going to ask you again tomorrow."

She gave them frequent lectures for the purpose of instilling into them a consciousness of the importance of the family.

"The family is what matters. The family must come before all other considerations. You must keep repeating to yourselves: 'I come from a great family. I must never let down the family name. I'm proud that I'm a van Groenwegel. The van Groenwegels never run.' Adrian!"

Adrian started. He had been staring out of the window. A hawk was perched on the swaying frond of a tall *paraipee* palm, screeching as other birds swooped down and past.

"Yes, Mother! I'm listening!"

"What is the motto of our family?"

"The motto of our family?"

"Yes."

"The van Groenwegels never run, Mother."

"Yes. And pay attention when I'm speaking to you. This is no time to be staring out of the window. Cornelis!"

"Yes, Mother?"

"What is our family motto?"

"The van Groenwegels never run, Mother."

"Good. Keep that fixed in your mind. Suppose the new war that has broken out in Europe comes here. Suppose ships came up the river and began to bombard the fort and soldiers landed and attacked this house, what would you do?"

"We'd stay and fight," said Cornelis and Adrian in a parrotlike monotone, Cornelis adding: "As Grandfather Willem did in 1666." Adrian, as though catching himself, said quickly: "As Grandfather Willem and Grandfather Laurens did in 1666."

"Good. And I hope that that of all things will stick in your memories. We never run. I don't want you to say it like parrots and not realize what it signifies. We never run. Whenever we the van Groenwegels are attacked we fight. We fight to the last breath. We defend our property to the end—as Greatgrandfather Willem did in 1666, as Great-great-grandmother Kaywana did in 1628. Remember that always."

In the next room Ignatius, before his easel, smiled and wagged his head. "So futile," he muttered. "As though telling them that will alter the course of Destiny. In many ways, Hendrickje is a simpleton. A great woman, but a simpleton. She doesn't really know human nature, or she wouldn't drill those children as she does. Life is going to laugh at her one day."

Since news of the new war against France had reached the colony she had begun to train the slaves in the use of the musket. There were over twenty muskets in the storeroom that adjoined the pantry, some of which she had had sent from the Essequibo and some of which she had obtained through the Company in Berbice. Rabonne and Henwah and Pardoom each commanded a squad of men, and musket practice took place twice a week under Hendrickje's supervision. Those who showed up well received extra rations.

Ignatius had now adopted an attitude of furtive reticence toward the two boys. His studio was strictly out of bounds for them. He spoke to them only when their mother was present, and even then only in a very guarded manner. His status in the home was virtually that of a prisoner. Before Hendrickje left for the fields at about nine she locked him in his studio in order to make sure that the boys did not go in to him in her absence. At noon, on her return, she opened the doors. It was a recognized routine now, and, incidentally, by no means effectual, for many mornings Ignatius would hear a chortling at the keyhole, and one of the boys would call through: "Father! We can see you drawing!" And from the other keyhole: "I, too, Father! I can see you. You're painting in the lady's hair!"

Ignatius would laugh softly, glance round and

wag his brush in mock admonition. Sometimes when the boys got no response from him they would call across at each other: "Cornelis! Can you see the little angels up in the top corner?"

"No, Father's head is in the way. But I can see the naked lady with the long hair and the wreath in her hand! Can you see that?"

"Yes, I see the lady, but not the wreath. Can you see the yellow cloud over the tree?"

Ignatius would smile, and his body would shake with mirth and affection, but the fear in him would prevent him from turning to hiss even a word to them. He lived in perpetual dread of a recurrence of the event four or five years ago. There were still occasions now when he would weep in the seclusion of his studio at the memory of his Adoration.

Intimate relations between husband and wife had become now a mere duty—a duty, for him not always devoid of revulsion. He told her one night: "There is no more beauty in this for me, Hendrickje. I feel like a hired man." He said it in a spirit of disgust and not in a bout of self-abasement. Unlike himself, she had no sensitiveness where making love was concerned, no aesthetic considerations. Her approach was purely animal and sensual. "I don't care how you feel," she had replied. "So long as you give me physical satisfaction. You may be sure I'm not going to let any quarrels we have during the day prevent me from having what I want when I want it." She had added as a threat: "The Captain of the troops at the fort would sleep with me if I merely beckoned to him." He had murmured back: "I shouldn't object. You've killed all the affection I had for you. I'm past the stage where I can be hurt by anything you say or do. I live now only for my art. All I care about is to see that I do nothing to give you cause to damage the things I create."

"I like the way you bare your miserable soul. So you wouldn't mind if I were unfaithful. In that case, I must see the Captain tomorrow."

She never attempted to be unfaithful, however. Her pride would not have allowed her to be. It was a matter of an obsession with her that everyone in the

colony should respect her—from the Commandeur and
his officials to the Company managers and the private
plantation people. One night, after a banquet at
Mynheer de Veerman's house, in celebration of his
election to the Governing Council[1]—he had just been
appointed manager of one of the Company plantations—the Captain of the troops attempted to be familiar with her on the back veranda where he had
followed her. She slapped him and told him: "Please
remember in whose presence you are, Captain!"

"No harm meant, Mevrouw. I've been told that
your husband is a rather incapable fellow. And being
a handsome woman——"

"Captain, you're drunk. Had it been otherwise I
should have reported this to the Commandeur."

The next day he had written her a letter apologiz-
ing. She had replied immediately forgiving him and
asking him to come and dine. For while she was determined to command full respect from the officials at
the fort, she was equally determined not to lose any of
her popularity with them.

IX

Cornelis and Adrian were both good swimmers,
though Cornelis was a coward and afraid to venture
too far out for fear of *perai*, the vicious swordfish
that abounded in the river.

"*Perai* won't harm you if you splash about and
make a noise," his mother told him. One day she made
him swim into midstream and back despite his fears.
When he scrambled ashore he was pale and shaky,
and she gave him a look of contempt and struck him
across his legs with her whip.

One day when he was ten she said to him: "I can
note a tendency in you to be soft, and I'm going to
thrash it out of you. Rabonne says you refused to row
yesterday when he told you to. You shipped the oar

[1]The Governing Council was composed of the Commandeur and the
six Company managers.

and said you were tired. A healthy boy like you tired after a few minutes' rowing!"

"Mother, we were going against tide."

"And what of it? Don't you want to develop the muscles of a man?"

He was silent, hanging his head and smoothing down his clothes.

"That's another thing. You're always concerned about your clothes. Your clothes and your person. Your clothes must never be disarranged, and your hair must always be brushed and combed. I don't like it, Cornelis. It's a sign of effeminacy." For an instant a thoughtful look settled on her face, then she turned off and crossed over to the dressing table. She stood surveying the toilet articles with a contemplative air.

The following day when he went to brush his hair, he found that the toilet things had vanished. He uttered an exclamation of dismay, then, in the mirror, saw his mother. She was standing at the door regarding him.

"Mother, I—I was going to comb my hair, but I don't see any of the things."

"No, I've put them away," she said quietly.

"Put them away?"

"Yes."

"Oh. But—mustn't I tidy myself today?"

She did not reply at once, then started and said: "Yes. Yes, of course." She came over to the dressing table and unlocked a drawer. "The comb and brush are in here. I put them away because I had intended to have the room cobwebbed today."

He gave her a suspicious, wary look, but her face was blank. When she left the room he felt uneasy, but went about his toilet as usual. After combing and brushing his hair, he looked at himself in the mirror, tilting his head this way and that. He smoothed his clothes down fastidiously and smiled at himself, standing back a pace and turning his head so that he could view his face at half profile. He touched his eyebrows delicately.

By now he had completely forgotten his mother. He became so absorbed in examining himself that he did not observe in the mirror that the door had opened silently and slowly. He patted his shoulder, smiled at his reflection, took up the brush and set to work again on his pale yellow locks. Bright sunlight shone in at the window to his left. He adjusted the mirror and moved into the sunlight, watching his hair gleam.

The door opened wider and his mother came in. He started round.

She was smiling.

"I didn't—you came in so suddenly, Mother."

"I startled you, didn't I?"

"Yes, Mother."

From the next room came sounds indicating that Ignatius was getting ready to work. A paintbrush fell to the floor with a sharp clatter.

"Why were you startled, Cornelis?"

"Nothing, Mother. I was just startled."

"I came in too suddenly?"

"Yes, Mother."

"Are you sure you didn't feel you were doing something you ought not to be doing?"

"No, Mother. I was only combing and brushing my hair."

She looked about her slowly. In the next room a stool was shifted.

"You were not by any chance preening yourself, Cornelis?"

"Preening myself?"

"Yes."

He said nothing.

"Preening yourself. Admiring yourself in the mirror as though you thought yourself a pretty little girl. Your complexion is lovely, isn't it?"

He began to squeeze his hands together.

"It's a pity," she said, "it didn't occur to me to keep an eye on you two boys when you make your toilet." She glanced out of the window. "Is Adrian still bathing in the river?"

"Yes, Mother, I think he is."

They could hear splashes. And shouts. Two slave boys were with Adrian. They swam about and pelted each other. Adrian was a normal, healthy boy. He liked the open air, and was never in a hurry to leave the river. He was not afraid of *perai*. He played games with the slave boys. It was only in the house that he grew shy and quiet—and fearful.

Hendrickje considered Cornelis. She had an air of appraisal, as though she were noting every detail of his person and his mood and trying to form an estimate of his worth. At length she said: "Cornelis, are you afraid of me?"

"No, Mother."

She began to pace about. "I know you are. Both of you. All three of you. You fear me. Every time I appear you grow silent and look guilty." She laughed: "I've written telling your grandfather Laurens about it, and he replied saying that he expected it, that the three of you have his pity. He doesn't spare me in his letters—and I don't spare giving him the details about our life here. It satisfies my soul to let him know what a bitter home we have and what a bitter, calculating woman his eldest daughter has grown into. I believe that deep down in me I hate Father. He has a streak of softness, and I hate softness in people. I know it hurts him to read in my letters how I treat you three, but I want to hurt him. I want to hurt all soft and weak things. Only the strong and the hard deserve to populate this earth. The weak should be crushed out." She stopped pacing and looked at him, and he trembled.

"You are soft, Cornelis."

"Yes, Mother," he whispered.

"You admit it?"

He said nothing, on the point of tears.

"Look up. Look up at me."

He glanced at her—and glanced away.

"See it! Fear. Your own mother, and you're afraid of me. Terrified of me as if I were a horrible monster from the bush. I merely have to lift my hand and you wilt and cower. Like your father in there. It's so plain to see that you've taken after him—the weaker side. Your Grandfather Reinald. Your Great-grandmother Griselda. Let me tell you this, Cornelis, I'm not going to tolerate weaklings for sons. If you can't fight against this effeminacy I see coming out in you, if you can't crush it out of your system, life is going to be terrible for you. I shall hound you down, nag at you, thump you about, flog you into pulp until you either change or you break—and if you break, then I have no use for you. I'll get rid of you—in some fashion. I won't tolerate weaklings. Your father has his uses, that's why he's still here. I would have done away with him long ago if I didn't need him as a husband—and need him to write up the records and to make himself useful in other ways about the house. To me, your father has come to mean nothing more than a special kind of slave whom I employ to satisfy my physical desires at night and to do odd jobs. That may sound ugly, but there are many ugly things in this life, and we must face them. The truth. Let's look at the truth as it is. That has always been my philosophy. But what I want to tell you in particular is this. Don't you ever let me come into this room and find you admiring yourself in the mirror or being fastidious about your person. Are you listening to me?"

"Yes, Mother."

"Only a woman is supposed to preen herself and admire her face in the mirror. You are a man. You must be rough and unconcerned about personal appearances. Are you paying attention to me?"

"Yes, Mother."

She caught him by his coat-front. She shook him and rumpled his clothes, ripped down one of his pockets. She tumbled his hair into confusion, and releasing him, said: "Now you look as a boy ought to look. Unkempt. You'll remain like this for the rest of the day. After meals you will refrain from washing your hands. Do you understand?"

"Yes, Mother."

Ignatius, in the next room, listened and smiled. He had cultivated a secret cynicism, an introspective calm and indifference, a sniggering callousness. Safe and at ease in his studio, he sneered and muttered. Self-abasement gave him no ecstasy now.

X

Life for Cornelis became a precarious affair of minor terrors and alarms and revulsions. One day Henwah took him out in the *corial,* and when they were nearing the shore Henwah suddenly shouted, leaned sideways and overturned the small craft. Cornelis shrieked and swam ashore in a trembling fright. His mother, watching from a bedroom window, smiled and nodded approval. Some minutes later she told Henwah: "That was well maneuvered, Henwah. Next time let it happen when you're further out in the stream."

There was the day, too, when his mother sent him to the toolshed for a shovel. As he pushed in the door he set off a booby trap and brought down a deluge of soft mud and filth upon his person. His mother laughed and told him: "A most unfortunate accident. Now you can walk around the compound and let it dry a little then it would be no harm if you took a dip in the river. Swim a little distance out and return."

She saw to it that he remained in the compound for over an hour, filthy and blubbering. Saw to it, too, that he swam out into the stream despite his terror of *perai.*

Another day she had Henwah chain his feet to the two heavy stones which the slaves had to drag around the compound as a punishment. Cornelis was made to walk around the compound three times as a punishment for having spent too much time washing his face after the morning meal. When the ordeal was over, he whimpered so much in the bedroom adjoining the studio that Ignatius shook off his fear and went in and comforted him.

Hendrickje had gone off to the fields. Adrian unlocked the studio door. Cornelis was very grateful. "I won't tell her you came in to me, Father," he said. "I wish you could speak to me sometimes. I'd keep it a secret. Adrian, you won't tell her, will you?"

Adrian, standing by with a solemn face, shook his head. "I won't tell her a word," he said. "I hate her. I hate her terribly. One day I'll ram a stone down her throat and choke her to death."

"She's not human, my boys. She's a monster. But this won't continue forever. One day it must end. In the meantime, we must hold together and endure it." He started, rushed to the door, opened it and peered out into the corridor. But there was no one there. Once she had been in the habit of sending up a slave to listen at the doors.

"I'm mistaken," he said, "I thought I'd heard a sound."

He cautioned them to be careful not to mention his coming in to see, them. "Lock me in again, Adrian, and hang the keys on the peg from where you took them." He patted their heads and smiled. "My poor boys. Never mind. Now and then we'll have little chats together as we've had this morning. But secrecy must be our watchword. I think you're old enough to be trusted."

That was how the alliance between the three of them was reestablished—and this time the secret was well kept. Every morning after Hendrickje had left for the fields one of the boys would unlock the door of the studio and the morning's "conference" would begin. "Our little daily conference," their father simperingly called it. "This proves," he said to them one morning, "that tyranny and brutality can be defeated. Your mother thinks that 'hard' methods can conquer the world. By 'hard' she means cruel, heartless. But despite her attempt to segregate you from me, despite her ruthless and despicable methods of crushing the humanity out of you and infusing fear and brutality into your innocent souls, we have found a way of communing, and communing in safety."

"We'll fool her every day," said Adrian. "She doesn't like me to read except at lesson times, but I read just the same. I go over to the fort, and one of the soldiers lets me read a book he has."

"Good. Good. Your mother is an imbecile in many ways, my boy. She doesn't know human nature. She imagines she does, but she's blind and ignorant. Her egotism has grown into a mountain that obscures her view of the finer qualities in men. What of you, Cornelis, my boy? Have you a soldier friend at the fort, too?"

"Yes, Father. His name is François."

"François?"

"Yes. François Tirol. He's a Frenchman."

"I didn't know there were Frenchmen among the military over there."

"He's the only one. He's very nice. He can read poetry beautifully, and—and he sometimes lets me brush my hair."

"Poor lad! To think of it! He sometimes lets you brush your hair! You aren't even permitted to do that in your home. If this isn't downright wicked madness!"

In spite of their elaborate precautions against discovery, there were anxious moments. One morning they heard footsteps on the stairs. The boys scampered into the next room and locked the door, pretending to become engaged in a game with pebbles and palm seeds on the floor—a game they had played three or four years ago but which still held some interest for them occasionally.

It turned out to be Pardoom. His mistress had sent him for her medicine box. A slave had hurt his foot—hacked a piece out of his ankle with a cutlass. Pardoom explained this to them when they, in very self-conscious voices, asked him why he had come to the house.

"We can never be too careful, my boys," their father said when they returned into the studio. "Are you certain you didn't let him see the keys? Did you hide them carefully?"

"Yes," said Cornelis. "I hid them under the bed as soon as I locked the door. There wasn't time to hang them up on the peg."

These meetings benefited them, brought cheer and good fellowship into their lives. They discussed each other's sufferings.

"Remember how she made me walk up and down the stairs two hundred and seventy times! At one time I thought I was going to faint. And just because I told Pardoom he was a fool. Pardoom wanted me to use the big oar and he the small one, and I said no, and I called him a fool, and he complained to her. . . ."

"She made me kneel down for an hour and a half on those sharp pebbles near the old toolshed. Look at my knees—bruised and cut up. A few nailheads were with the pebbles, and because I picked them out she purposely put them back and made me kneel on them. I hate her," said Adrian. "I hate her terribly. When I grow up I'm going to choke her to death with my bare hands. Just wait. Just wait and see."

"No, my boy. Don't entertain such feelings against her. That would harm you more than help you. Hate and fear are the emotions that have the most damaging effect on the soul. Leave her to run her course. Submit to her and try not to hate. Instead, pity her. She deserves pity, my sons. She's an unfortunate woman. Didn't you hear what she told me yesterday? She admitted that she is bitter and frustrated. Simply stand by and wait, and watch her travel down the road to destruction. Let that be your revenge. Indifference, passivity. It hurts her that I have drawn into myself and treat her as I do—with aloofness, with silent contempt." A purring chuckle escaped him, and his eyes glittered with the hate that could not be concealed. "Within her she knows that I laugh at her in secret. That adds to her bitterness a hundredfold. Adds to her frustration." He patted their heads, moistening his lips with a simpering, gloating contentment.

XI

Their secret meetings continued for nearly a year. Then Hendrickje awoke one morning and was sick. "Such a thing," she said, "hasn't happened to me since I was pregnant with the child I lost."

"Your body must be undergoing a change," Ignatius said.

She gave him a quick glance, as though detecting a subtle note of mockery in his voice. She smiled. At thirty-three she had lost none of her freshness. Her beauty had simply hardened; her lips were thinner and her eyes more penetrating in their stare. Her figure and shape remained perfect; her carriage erect, graceful, her movements well coordinated.

On four successive mornings she was sick.

"This is looking very odd, Ignatius. I don't know what to think, but—but, well, it's not usual for me to be sick like this."

"Not usual, I agree," Ignatius nodded.

"You must go to the fort and ask the surgeon to come."

"Do you think he will be able to tell so soon?"

"Tell what?"

"What is the matter," he said, his face blank of expression.

She gave him a hard stare, grunted and said: "There's no harm seeing him now. These spells of nausea must mean something. Some—some change must have occurred in me."

"Indigestion, perhaps."

She laughed. Her manner contained a nervous excitement; almost a buoyancy. Her eyes seemed a trifle softer.

That morning she did not ride the mule. She made Rabonne get out the chair—the "lift-up chair," as Rabonne called it. "I don't feel very well this morning, Rabonne," she said, trying to make her voice as casual as she could. "A temporary disorder."

The surgeon, when he came, told her that she would have to wait. Perhaps in six weeks he would be able to let her know what was wrong. "It could be pregnancy, Mevrouw, but I would not like to be definite."

In his studio Ignatius told the boys: "Your mother thinks she's going to have another child. I'm afraid the Fates have, indeed, selected her as a target for a dastardly game." He sniggered.

"It will be funny," said Cornelis, sniggering too, "to see her swell up." He added with a sniff: "I don't think I'd want to go near to her. She would repulse me."

"Repulse you? Why?"

"I can't stand ugly sights, Father. I like nice, soft,

beautiful things." He stroked his hair and rubbed his hand along his neck. "That's why I like François. He's so clean and soft and refined. And he has a lovely voice. You should hear him reading poetry. Oh, it's wonderful!" He hugged himself.

His father shrugged. "Anyway, my boy, I don't think there will be any need for you to avoid her. In two or three weeks' time she'll discover, as she did some years ago, that it was a false alarm—then God help the poor field slaves! And ourselves! She'll be like a wild beast in her frustrated fury."

"I feel like poisoning her," said Adrian.

This time, however, it was no false alarm. She was pregnant. One morning she said to Ignatius, in a voice shaky with excitement: "It's true, Ignatius. It seems like a miracle, but it's true." She paced about the room, naked, cupping her breasts and examining them. "See! They're fuller, and the nipples have got darker. A sure sign."

She came to a halt and looked out at the river. A sluggish mist was drifting in wisps over the surface of the black water. The morning air felt chilly and water-vaporish but exhilarating, fresh and leafy. She uttered a whine of ecstasy.

"I feel great, Ignatius. This is a revolution. This means that my dreams may still come true. I'm only thirty-three. I still have ten or twelve years of child-bearing before me."

Her exuberance, that morning, was so great that she did not lock him into his studio. She said: "This morning you can all do as you please. There's too much in me, Ignatius. I can hardly contain myself. I feel as though I'm going to explode from joy." Her eyes softened. She approached him suddenly and kissed him.

He did not respond. His face remained impassive.

She recoiled. "I don't matter to you now." She stared at him, a look of dismay on her face. A slow remorse seemed to stir within her. "I suppose I've brought it on myself," she said quietly, "so I mustn't grumble. I can't expect you to share my joys now-adays."

XII

During the weeks and months that followed, as her body filled out, her attitude toward them underwent a complete change. She softened and tried to win their affection. She bought new clothes for Cornelis, taking him to the Company storehouse to select the materials himself. She allowed Adrian to read outside of lesson time, and wrote to Essequibo to ask that some of her old books be sent as she would like Adrian to have them.

"I feel," she told her father in a letter, "that something new and important has entered me. I feel almost superstitious. I can't believe this miracle yet. A spirit of generosity has taken hold of me which I find it hard to control. It makes me want to be easy with the slaves, and I often have to be stern with my-self, for, of course, with them there must be no soften-ing up. That would be a fatal mistake. The punish-ments must go on as before. I still make them walk around the compound dragging those two heavy stones. I still flog them myself, though not so often, for I want to do nothing that might cause me to lose this child. And the other tortures like the broken glass and the hot stone and the ants' nests, all these continue; other planters favor them, too, so you needn't imagine I'm the only brutal one in these parts. However, I'm telling you about this new spirit that has come over me. I do my best now to be kind to Ignatius and the boys, but I fear my efforts meet with little response. They are cold toward me—cold and suspicious. In-deed, Adrian frequently gives me openly baleful glances. I can sense he hates me with a hate I wouldn't have thought possible in him at his age. But I admit that I have given them all reason to hate me. I don't mind. I'm hard, Father. I can take anything that comes to me. All I want in life is to get what I have planned to get. Love and tenderness can go. I'm prepared to live without them. So long as I have my children as planned, so long as I have them established in the country and the most powerful family, all else can go. . . ."

But though she wrote this, the actuality was different.

One morning before setting out for the fields she paused at the studio door and regarded her husband at work. Suddenly she moved toward him and put her arms about him.

"Ignatius, please, my dear. Give me a little affection. Please."

He went on painting, his only response being a slightly surprised look.

She stepped back and gazed at him with a numbed inarticulation. It was a long time before she was able to say: "Ignatius, surely you must be a little pleased that I'm going to have this child. Aren't you?"

"No."

"Doesn't it affect you at all?"

"It does," he said.

"Well?"

"It saddens me and depresses me."

"Why?"

He gave a vague smile but made no reply.

After another silence she said: "You don't think that at a time like this I'd need some tenderness from you?"

"No, I wouldn't have thought so."

Another silence.

"Ignatius, do you really hate me?"

"It takes," he told her, "strong people to hate, and I confess I haven't that strength."

"You don't love me any more? Not—not even a trifle?"

"Not even a trifle."

She went back to her room and sobbed. That morning she did not go into the fields. She sent a message to Rabonne and told him to see after things for her and come at noon with a report.

It was from that day—she was nearly seven months in pregnancy—that a tension came alive in the house.

One morning, when she was away in the fields, Adrian said to his father: "Something feels wrong these last few days, Father. It's as if at any instant the walls of the house might cave in upon us."

His father nodded. "You've felt it, too, have you, my boy? Yes, it is as though a spell has been cast on us and at any moment some unspeakable horror will break and overwhelm us."

There would be lengthy silences between them sometimes, and while their father painted the two of them would gaze out at the river or at the bush, or at the ships in the stream opposite the fort.

"Father, Dirk says he believes in God. I told him you don't!"

"It's not bad if he does, my boy. Ofttimes I do wish I had something to believe in—even if it were a myth like God. There's a great deal of consolation in believing in something."

"I believe in beauty," said Cornelis. "François says that's what he believes in—beauty and truth and nature. Oh, François is lovely. He has beautiful hair and blue eyes—like the sky."

A *corial* with Indians was going past on the river. Two women were paddling; they could hear the bump-bump of the paddles against the sides of the craft.

A few shouted orders came from the fort. The guard was being changed. They heard the tramp of boots and the clink of swords and sabers. Far away over the jungle in the west there arose a soughing noise, but it was not rain. Only the wind. In a few seconds it had died away.

The sun shone with a glaring intensity, but the morning was not very hot. Rain had fallen heavily during the night, and in the shade here they could feel the water-vaporish coolness of the trees, as though the trees were puffing waves of moisture at them out of the mystery of their depths.

"Father, would you like to go back to Essequibo to live?"

"It's a matter of indifference to me, my boy."

"Don't you write to them as Mother does?"

"I have written your aunts once or twice. When your mother and I first came here. But that was over ten years ago. These days I have no heart for letter writing. And, in any case, I shouldn't like having to discuss the kind of life we lead here. Your mother does the letter writing. She writes to your Grandfather Laurens, and, from what I can gather, she enjoys telling him of the many pleasant incidents that occur in our home."

"Does Grandfather Laurens believe, as Mother does, that the family must be powerful?" asked Adrian.

"No," said his father. "Your Grandfather Laurens is a balanced man. You would have liked him. It was your Great-grandfather Willem who began this power campaign. But even he was not the fanatic that your mother is. He was human despite his obsession. He had a sense of humor your mother lacks, and that excused in great measure his heroics and his bombast. He never took much notice of me, but I was fond of him."

"I don't believe in power and glory," Adrian frowned. "I'm not going to teach my children anything like that."

"Nor I," Cornelis nodded. "I'm going to teach my children about beauty and poetry and lovely things. If I can bring myself to have any children," he added in a thoughtful, slightly troubled manner.

Ignatius nodded pensively.

They heard the wind again. Far away in the jungle.

Hendrickje was taking the boys with their lessons after the midday meal when she complained of not feeling well.

"I think that will do for the day," she said. "I don't feel up to continuing." She was pale, and her eyes lacked her usual fire. She looked tired and foiled.

As the boys were leaving the room she said: "Could one of you stay with me in here in case I need to send across to the surgeon?" She spoke tentatively, without self-confidence. "Cornelis, would you stay with me?"

"I wanted to go over to the fort to François, Mother."

"What of you, Adrian?"

"I was thinking of going to the van Doorns, Mother. Claas and his sister are digging a duck pond. I promised to help them."

"In that case, Cornelis, you'll have to remain."

"Very well, Mother."

He sat by the window, but after a while she told him: "Pull your chair up and sit by me here."

He obeyed, drawing nearer to the bed. He sat, silent and uncomfortable, his head bent, as though in punishment.

After a long interval he heard her take a sharp breath. He frowned slightly, but other than that made no response.

"Cornelis."

"Yes, Mother?"

"I've just had a pain."

"Yes."

"Didn't you hear me gasp?"

"Yes, Mother."

"And it never occurred to you to ask what was the matter?"

He was silent.

"Cornelis."

"Yes, Mother?"

"It wouldn't matter to you if I died, would it?"

He said nothing.

"Cornelis, I spoke."

"I heard you, Mother. I—I don't know."

"You don't know what?"

He made no reply.

"I understand. You wouldn't mind. Neither you nor your brother would mind—nor your father."

A few minutes later another spasm of pain attacked her.

"Mother, must I go and call the surgeon?"

"Not yet. Not yet. I don't think it's anything serious. I'm only seven months pregnant. These are false pains. They'll pass."

But the pains did not pass. They grew in frequency and in sharpness. She clenched her hands and moved her head from side to side in a distracted manner. "It mustn't be. It mustn't be. It's not time. I'm not going to lose it. I won't."

Cornelis fidgeted.

"Get me some water."

He got her the water, glad and relieved to be able to leave the chair for a few moments.

She muttered to herself, staring at the roof: "If only I knew what to do. What to appeal to. Whom. God? Bah! I don't believe in God. Only fools do. For me the truth. I won't submit to delusion. . . . Yet it may live. At seven months. . . . It may. Cornelis, go and call the surgeon."

"Very well, Mother."

He sprang up, and was at the door when she called him back.

"You're glad to be rid of me, aren't you?" she scowled.

He stared at her and gulped.

"Aren't you? Answer me!"

"No, Mother," he murmured.

"You can't deceive me. You hate me. It's plain on your face. Little rat! Be off! Go and call the surgeon!"

He had hardly left the house when Ignatius entered the room. "What is the matter, Hendrickje? Do you think your time has come?"

She nodded, her eyes shut.

He regarded her, his face impassive.

Abruptly she opened her eyes. "Ignatius, do you think it will live? It may. Sometimes they do at seven months. What do you think?"

"I couldn't say."

"Reassure me. Please. Say it will live and be strong. Please. I'm desperate, Ignatius. Give me a little affection. I . . ."

It was another pain.

After she had recovered from the spasm she said: "You don't care, I suppose. You must wish it would die. Do you?"

He smiled slightly and turned away, began to move toward the door.

"Do you, Ignatius?"

He paused. "For its own sake, yes, Hendrickje," he said, a look of great pain passing over his face. He went out.

Later that day—dusk was gathering—the child was born. It was a blue lump, and the surgeon pummeled it about and did all he knew to give it life. But no cry came from it. It was a girl.

XIII

On the fourth day after the delivery they thought she was going to die, too. A temperature set in. Traces of the afterbirth, the surgeon confessed, had been left behind. He was not a capable fellow, and admitted the poverty of his medical knowledge.

Rabonne, undaunted and unchallenged, went up to her room every day at noon to report. He was soft-voiced and sympathetic, and one day she smiled and touched his wrist and said: "Thank you for your good wishes, Rabonne. You're the only one who has expressed the genuine hope that I may recover. Thank you." She was greatly moved, and shut her eyes tight after he had left the room.

Ignatius attended upon her in a spirit of rigid duty. He made the boys come into the room every morning and every evening to inquire of her how she was feeling. They, too, acted as though impelled by a spirit of rigid duty.

On the sixth day, when the temperature had passed and it was certain that she had overcome the threatened infection, she told them: "Don't bother to come in and inquire after me, boys." She spoke in a hurt voice, almost with a note of self-pity. To Ignatius she said: "I know now that I assessed your character badly, Ignatius. I never dreamt that you could have kept up such a cold face toward me indefinitely—and under such circumstances."

He made no comment, his face stony.

A few weeks later she began to make love to him again at night. She told him: "I'll conceive again. You needn't gloat over my disappointment. Nothing will ever break my spirit, Ignatius. Not you and your passive cynicism combined with a thousand disappointments will smash my will. I'll never admit defeat."

One night, a month or two later, when he refused to respond to her overtures, she threatened to make the boys suffer. "I've been letting you three have a pretty easy time of late, but I can start again to flay your souls. I won't hesitate to make those boys pay for your sins. I know how you dote over them—and I'm not blind to the confederation which has sprung up between you three."

After that he never refused her, and events began to repeat themselves. Within four months she was pregnant again. Her spirits rose. She paced about the room admiring her naked body, reveling in her invincibility and in her physical consitution.

"I'll never be beaten. You doubt me, Ignatius? But you'll see I'm right. This time there won't be a hitch. The last time I must have done too much. This time I'm going to rest every day after meals. You'll have to take the boys with their lessons. You'll go downstairs into the dining room and take them. I'm feeling grand again. I'm a fighter. Blood must out. Circumstances won't defeat the van Groenwegels—not the ones with fire! I defy the world! The sky!"

Now and then, however, her flow of dramatics would abruptly ebb and a look of fear would settle on her face. She would stare before her as though listening to some warning music in the distance.

One night she woke him and told him that she had had a terrible dream. She was trembling. She behaved like a girl. "I'm afraid, Ignatius. I'm afraid. Comfort me. Please. Don't be so cold." She pressed her face against him and sobbed. "Nothing will happen to my baby this time. Tell me nothing will happen to it. Please, my darling. Say it once."

"No, nothing will happen to your baby," he said, but said it as though it were a recitation he had learnt. Close against him, she watched the moonlight on the river. They could hear the water sucking at the bank. The water in the little creek on the Essequibo often made similar sounds in the quiet of the afternoon. The little creek up which the two of them used to go secretly to make love. The moonlight looked silver-chilly. Fireflies flashed in white bright blobs amid the low hanging foliage of the trees on the opposite bank. The whoof-whoof of a baboon sounded very remotely upriver. They did not hear it again.

Another night it was not a dream. She woke him and said that she had felt the child throb in her and wondered whether she had hurt it, for she had awakened and found herself in an awkward position. When he told her sleepily that it was very unlikely that she had hurt it she snapped: "I know you don't care what happens. It could die in me and I with it, and it would be a matter of indifference to you!" Then violent sobbing.

She rested every day after eating, but when her pregnancy was about six months old she got restless and could not keep in bed. She would walk up and down in the room, a harrowed look on her face. One day he came in and found her naked, examining herself, anxious-faced. She insisted on his putting his ear against her to listen for the baby's heart. When he told her that he could hear it beating, a look of great relief came to her face, and she dressed and sighed and lay down.

Approaching seven months, she began to suffer from insomnia. Some nights she hardly slept as much as two hours. She was in a frenzy of anxiety, wondering whether she would have another miscarriage. She had the surgeon over every week to examine her and to ask his opinion. But it was always the same. He would smile and shake his head and tell her that he could not express any definite opinion. "What happened last time may not happen again, Mevrouw. We can only wait and see."

"She's a tortured woman," Ignatius told the boys in his studio. "I don't believe she's perfectly sane. It isn't normal that any woman should behave like this over a child she is expecting."

"It's this family idea, Father," Adrian frowned. "Didn't you hear what she said once? She's determined that we must spread. That's why she wants to have a lot of children. She wants one of us to go to Suriname and one of us to Cayenne to start branches of the family there. Isn't that stupid?"

"Most certainly it is, my boy. I'm glad you think so. Power and glory are illusions. It's being content with a few things of value that matters in this life. A good companion—a kind, soft woman; a good wife and mother—and cogenial occupation; doing what you want to do and like doing. You don't need more than that to be happy."

"I agree with that," Adrian nodded. "No power and glory for me when I grow up. I'm going to get away on a ship and go to sea. I think I'd like the sea. Great-grandfather Willem was a seaman. I'm going to travel round the world as he did."

"If that will satisfy your soul, by all means, my boy." He grunted ominously. "I have a strong feeling, however, that your mother's ideas won't coincide with yours. What you'll have to do is to fight her." He glanced toward the door and lowered his voice. "Fight her, Adrian. Fight her with determination. Don't be weak as I have been. Stand up to her. Defy her and show her that you won't be bullied. You have a stronger spirit than I have, my boy. I can see it in your eyes. You can defeat her if you wish."

He glanced round quickly. Footsteps had sounded on the stairs.

But it was only Cornelis. He said that he had just come from the fort where François had been reading him poetry. His father smiled: "Is that what you want to be when you grow up? A poet?"

Before he could answer, Adrian pointed out of the window and exclaimed: "Look! Look what Henwah is going to do! Make that poor old fellow walk around the compound with those heavy stones. And he's not well. He had fever yesterday."

"Henwah only obeys orders, my boy."

They stood in silence, watching the old slave slowly dragging the stones around the compound, the chains that secured them to his ankles clanking depressingly. Once he stumbled and collapsed, and Henwah slashed at him with his whip and pulled him up with a jerk. "Get going! Get going!" Henwah shouted. "More delay longer time you stay!"

"I sometimes feel like that," Ignatius murmured. "As though two heavy stones were shackled to my ankles."

"I have actually had them shackled to my ankles," said Cornelis.

"Yes, I remember," growled Adrian. "That's one of the things I'm going to make her pay for when I grow up."

The following week labor pains set in. Hendrickje behaved as though demented. But, though premature, the child was not stillborn. It lived, and though weak, seemed as though it would survive. Furthermore, it was a boy. Hendrickje was hysterical with joy and triumph.

"You see what I told you, Ignatius! I must win! Nothing can stop me! It's the will. My will can do anything!"

She could hardly lie still. Every few minutes she would shift and raise herself on one elbow to look at the tiny red face of the baby which was all of it that was visible, for the surgeon had had it wrapped up in warm woolen cloth because of its prematurity.

Three days after its birth, Ignatius was taking the boys with their lessons in the dining room—they were doing Virgil—when they heard her scream. Ignatius lowered the book.

Adrian grinned: "Perhaps the baby said something in Latin and it frightened her."

"Ignatius! Ignatius! Come quickly. Come!"

They all went upstairs.

She was sitting up in bed, her face pale, her eyes wide and distracted. She was squeezing her hands together.

"Ignatius, go and get the surgeon. Adrian, run off. Don't stand there staring at me. Go! Quickly!"

None of them moved. Ignatius asked: "What's the matter, Hendrickje? Are you ill?"

"Look. Look and see. Go and call the surgeon. Don't stare! Don't stare! Call the surgeon!" She began to tear at her nightgown.

Cornelis moved off nervously. Adrian stood firm, an aggressive look on his face.

Ignatius took a pace toward the bed and looked at the baby. Its face was blue, and its eyes stared rigidly from the slit-like openings. He touched its cheek, and said quietly: "This child is dead, Hendrickje. There's no necessity to send for the surgeon."

She struck him in the face.

"Get off! Go! If you won't go I'll get up and go myself." She made an attempt to get out of bed, but he grappled with her and pushed her back.

"Don't be a fool. You can't move about in this condition. One of the boys will go for the surgeon. Adrian, go and call the surgeon."

"Yes, Father."

After the surgeon had come and gone, she lay on her back beside the dead lump that had once been a living child and gazed blankly at the rafters. For more than an hour she lay like this, without uttering a sound. Ignatius remained in the room with her. The boys had wanted to remain, too, out of morbid curiosity, but he had made them go out.

Evening had come down before she stirred. She said: "Are you still in here?"

"Yes. In case you needed anything."

"I had decided to call him Willem—after Grandfather."

Ignatius made no comment.

"Perhaps he had my strength. Grandfather's strength. Kaywana's fire. We'll never know now."

"No."

"What?"

He was silent.

"A lump. Cold and dead. What's the matter with me that I can't bring a healthy child into the world? I brought two. Why not more?"

They heard shouts and the tramp of feet over at the fort. The guard was being changed. The night-time wheeze of insects was rising.

"Another smashed dream. It's like a game. I'm being played around with. The Fates are having fun at my expense."

"I'm glad you've begun to realize that, Hendrickje."

She half-raised herself on to her elbow. "You'll pay for that remark."

The room was very dark. They could barely make out each other.

After a silence he heard a soft thud. It was the corpse of the baby. She had pushed it off the bed on to the floor. He half-rose and then sat down again. She was laughing softly to herself. Malevolently.

One morning, about two weeks later, when she had gone off to the fields, the boys and himself were in the studio discussing her and the grim silence that had come upon her.

"She looks mad to me," said Adrian. "Do you notice the way she keeps glancing at Father? As if she's thinking out some scheme against him."

"I've noticed it," Cornelis nodded, stroking his hair and fondling his neck. "I get a little frightened myself sometimes."

"I think I have passed that stage now," said his father. "I'm simply resigned to whatever happens."

"Then do you think something is going to happen, Father?"

His father shrugged. "Your mother is an uncertain person, Adrian. It's hard to predict. But should she attempt anything drastic again I've already decided what I shall do."

"What will you do, Father?"

Ignatius shook his head and went on painting.

Cornelis, after a while, looked outside and ex-

claimed: "She's come back from the fields already—
and it's not even eleven o'clock!"

Nowadays, they did not have to hurry out of the
studio in fear, for it was no secret that they gathered in
the studio to talk. So they remained and watched her
get out of the chair and move toward the house. She
moved with grace and dignity, her face coldly beautiful in the bright slanting morning sunshine.

Cornelis murmured: "She does walk beautifully.
Don't you think so, Father?"

"Certainly, my boy. She has poise."

They heard her footsteps downstairs. Then on the
stairway. There were other footsteps, too.

They looked at each other. Adrian said: "She's
bringing up those three fellows with her."

Cornelis nodded, going pale. "It sounds so. Rabonne and Pardoom and Henwah."

Ignatius stood with his brush poised above his palette, gazing toward the door. "Perhaps she's going to
have some heavy piece of furniture moved in the next
room," he said quietly.

"Yes, it must be that," murmured Cornelis.

"Father, did I tell you about the toucan Claas
caught?"

"I think you did mention something about it, my
boy."

"I told him I'm sure you would like to paint a picture of it. The feathers are of all colors."

"Is it a toucan or a macaw? I think that is what
I've heard it called," said Cornelis, squeezing his wrist
slowly. "A macaw."

"A macaw?"

"Yes," whispered Cornelis.

The footsteps paused outside the studio. The door
opened, and they saw Hendrickje appear in the company of the three big black fellows, Henwah, Rabonne and Pardoom. Her leader-bullies. In an even,
clipped voice she said: "Ignatius, stand aside from that
easel. Boys, stand by the windows."

Cornelis began to move toward the door that gave
into the next room, but she stopped him. "Don't leave

the room, Cornelis. Stand by the window there. Ignatius, that applies to you, too."

Ignatius obeyed. He had just noticed that Pardoom carried an axe.

Adrian uttered a growling noise as he moved over to a window with Cornelis. Rabonne's gaze strayed in his direction, bearing a threat.

Hendrickje took the axe from Pardoom and set to work. Without a word; with clean, precise movements.

The three black men stood aside in stolid, waiting postures, like guards in the event of trouble.

One canvas after another she hacked down. She perspired, for there were many canvases to destroy, but she went on.

Cornelis sobbed softly.

Adrian was pale, but he did not cry. Once, when the axe ripped through the reds and greens of a flower study he himself had asked his father to paint when he was three years younger, a glint came into his eyes and his hands clenched.

Ignatius stood gazing out at the river, his palette resting on the windowsill. His brush, wet with paint, he held poised in his right hand, as though waiting patiently to be allowed to continue work.

The canvas on the easel depicted the head of a slave boy—a boy of about Adrian's age, thirteen. His name was Jeremy, and he and Adrian had often disported themselves together in the river. It was Adrian's idea that Jeremy should come up to the studio to pose for his father. The portrait was complete. Ignatius had been putting the finishing touches to the background when the studio was invaded. It was the last thing Hendrickje hacked down. Adrian turned away his face. Suddenly, unable to control himself, he broke out: "Mother, you're a beast! A terrible black, dirty beast! I hate you! I hate you like the worst thing in the world!"

She was almost breathless from exertion. She handed the axe back to Pardoom and said gaspingly: "Seize Massa Adrian, Rabonne!"

As Rabonne moved toward him Adrian rushed for the door that gave into the other room. He was through in a second.

"After him, Rabonne!"

Henwah cut him off as he was darting through the door of the next room into the corridor, Rabonne close behind him. He struggled and struck out fiercely at the two men. "Don't touch me, you black brutes! Don't touch me!" Henwah held him with ease and pinned his arms behind him. His mother appeared. She slapped him twice across his face—with all her strength. He glared back at her in defiance. He blubbered.

"Wait until I grow up! I'm going to make you pay for this! You beast! You black, stinking beast! I hate you! Hate you!"

"Henwah, take him to the toolshed and lock him in."

"I don't care. I'm going to kill you when I grow up. Kill you! I'm going to make you suffer. Wait! Just wait!"

In the studio, Ignatius was sitting on the stool. Cornelis, after Adrian had been taken away, came in and went up to his father. "I'm sorry, Father," he said. "I'm terribly sorry."

"Your pity is misplaced," smiled his father. "Weaklings should be spurned. For me you ought to feel only contempt."

XIV

It was four days after this event that Hendrickje received the letter from her father dated the 9th of March 1709. She smiled at the last part of it. She read over certain sentences.

". . . I fear I could never bring myself to feel any tenderness toward you again. The love I once had for you and the pride I felt in you are completely dead. That is why corresponding with you has come to mean to me nothing but a mere duty. . . . If there is any undercurrent of sadness beneath our happiness it is you, Hendrickje, and your letters describing your life these past fourteen or fifteen years in Berbice that have brought us this alloy of gloom. . . ."

Two days later she replied, saying: "Your letter was full of interesting meat. Vague rumors of the raids you spoke of did reach us here, but up to now I had heard no details, and, to be truthful, I made no effort to inquire. I have had too much to occupy my thoughts these past few months. In October when you were being raided I was just about two months pregnant with my last child. It was born alive, but died a few days later.

"In your letter, you refer to my bitterness and frustration. What I was when I wrote that about myself, Father, cannot compare with what I am now. Since the death of that last child I have been a Fury. I hate the world now with a hate that I'm sure has never existed before. I hate everything: men and dumb things alike. Bitterness! You'll never in your most desperate nightmares experience such bitterness as simmers in me today. Six days ago I hacked every canvas in Ignatius's studio to pieces—in great measure to relieve my feelings, and, in small measure, to punish him for a remark he made after the child died. A trifling remark, but it stung me, and I vowed I'd make him pay for it.

"You say that corresponding with me has become for you a mere duty. I smile, for I'm sure that after this letter you'll probably never write me another as long as you live. What I have to say won't raise your opinion of me. Not that I care. Your opinion never mattered, nor the opinion of anyone. However, let me say what I have to say. As I mentioned before, I hacked to pieces every canvas in my husband's studio. That occurred six days ago. On the night of the occurrence he vanished. I woke the following morning to find that he was not in the room with me. As I may have mentioned before, we have always slept together in one bed. In the morning there was no sign of him, and he has been missing ever since. Not that there can be any doubt what his fate must have been. At noon on the same day Rabonne, one of my head slaves, discovered our *corial* drifting on the river a little way upstream. Furthermore, the two stones with the chains which we kept in the compound for punishing the slaves were missing, and it seems fairly obvious what must have happened. Up to now we have found no trace of his body, but this river is very deep, and with stones chained to his ankles there is little hope that he will ever be found.

"I can see now that he must have premeditated this deed a long time before. He has done it out of sheer spite, to be revenged on me. He knew that henceforth I should be a tortured woman—tortured because I should never marry again; there are no more eligible van Groenwegel males for me to marry—and he knew that my pride would never allow me to be sexually intimate with a man unless he were my husband in the legal sense. Yes, he knew that robbed of physical relations with a man I should be a bitter, wretched creature in my starvation. But what he didn't know was that his revenge would convert me into an absolutely inhuman fiend, a being without tenderness or regard for any living creature, child, slave or acquaintance.

"I was glad to read of Rosa's behavior. She's a true van Groenwegel. She has lived up to our traditions. She died well, and you have no cause to be sorrowful. If I ever do have grandchildren—I can be certain of nothing now, in the face of the calamities I have suffered—but if I ever do have grandchildren I shall drill that into them, that above everything else they must live to uphold our traditions. Yes, even now I will not admit defeat. Even now I will not give up my ambitions. I have these two boys, and I shall make them, mold them, into what I want them to be—or break them. I will never surrender. . . ."

VI   Oedipus

I

WE'RE both going to come to bad ends, but hers will be worse than mine. . . .

"Adrian! Pay attention to what's being done here."

He said nothing.

"Baccam! Dig up that sucker and plant it again so that Massa Adrian may see how you did it."

"Yes, missy."

"Adrian!"

"Yes?"

"Yes what? Is that how you address me?"

She slashed at his legs with her whip. He sat on the mule, his dark eyes dull with the hate in him.

"Yes what, Adrian?"

"Just yes. I don't have to say 'yes, Mother' to you. I told you yesterday I'll never address you as Mother again, and I meant it."

She doesn't know how I keep burning to strike her, to drag her off that mule and stamp on her. Beat her, pound her face into a pulp, tear her limbs apart. . . .

"You think you can defy me openly, do you?"

"I mean to defy you. Every day, every day!"

Let her stare at me. That won't cow me. I'm not Father. She could frighten Father, and she can frighten Cornelis. But I'm not afraid of her, and she knows I'm not. . . . She's smiling now. That's always the sign that she has backed down. One day it will be more than a smile. I'm going to make her whimper and beg for mercy. This can't go on every day. She has a strong will, and my will is just as strong. I mean to fight her, as Father said I should do. I'm only waiting until I get a few more years older, then I'm going to harrow her soul. I'm going to hurt her and hurt her. Only yesterday I was looking at that black hairy spider in the wild pine clump. I hate it. It made me shudder. But even that doesn't make me shudder and hate as much as she does. I feel a dry, bitter taste at the back of my mouth

273

whenever I think of her. She wants me to go up the Canje Creek to manage that new plantation she purchased last year. That's why I have to go through this training in the fields with her. But I don't mind. I want to learn about planting. I told Father that when I grew up I'd run away to sea, but now I know I'll never do that. That day when she smashed up his pictures I swore that the rest of my life must be spent in nothing but hating her and doing what I could to make her suffer. Let me become manager of that plantation up the Canje. I'm going to take pleasure in disregarding her wishes. I'm going to plan to do everything to thwart and disappoint her. If I marry and have children I'm going to teach them the things I know she wouldn't like me to teach them. Power and glory? I'm going to teach them to be dissolute and weak. I'm going to teach them how to bring down the family name—disgrace it, make it the most despised name in the colony. I shall pay her back for what she did to Father. Four more years and I'll be twenty. I'm almost as tall as she already. . . .

When they got home he went to the room he and his brother shared. Cornelis was reclining in bed reading a book François Tirol had lent him. He put it down at once, his face taking on a worried look.

"Adrian, something terrible has happened." He spoke in a lowered voice. "Can we take a stroll in the compound and have a chat?"

"Yes, come on."

Look how he limps, poor fellow. Through that fall he suffered last year when she made him climb to the top of the big wild cacao tree. Because she knew he was afraid to climb she forced him, threatened to lock him in the toolshed for a fortnight. So he did it and fell and hurt his foot—injured the tendon in the left heel. All that I'm going to make her pay for. . . .

"What's the trouble? What's this terrible thing?"

"Adrian, Henwah saw us."

"Henwah? Saw what? Saw whom?"

"François and me. He saw François kiss me."

Adrian gave him a blank look. "François? How could François kiss you? Why should he kiss you?"

Cornelis blushed. "I'm going to tell you a secret, Adrian, dear."

"Don't call me 'Adrian, dear.' I've told you before I don't like it. I'm not a girl."

"You're so good to me, Adrian. I always feel I must call you something affectionate."

"Very well. But go on. You were telling me about François."

"Adrian, I'll tell you a secret. I know I can trust you. You're so sweet and good to me. Adrian, François and I are in love."

"In love!" Adrian gave him another blank look. "But you're men. How can you be in love with each other?"

"You wouldn't understand," Cornelis said quietly, hanging his head. "Our love is a rare kind of love—a pure, sweet, clean love."

Adrian shook his head. "I certainly don't understand it. I don't see how you can feel like that. If he were a girl, of course."

"Women are gross. I'll never love a woman. Look at Mother! Is she a person anyone could love!"

"All women aren't like her. She's a brute. There are others who are good and kind. Like Claas van Doorn's mother. And Mevrouw de Vervuyt. And Mevrouw Heyn. They're not pretty, like Mother, but they're soft and kind."

"Adrian, Henwah saw us kissing. We were boating, and we went in by that little alcove near the creek mouth, and we didn't notice that a *corial* was behind us. Henwah was in it. He came round the bend suddenly and saw us kissing."

"Kissing like two lovers!"

"But we are lovers, Adrian, dear. Please don't think ill of us, please. It would grieve me dreadfully. It's a clean, pure love."

"I can't see it that way. It seems to me most unnatural."

"It isn't. Oh, but, Adrian, tell me. I'm so worried. Do you think Henwah will tell Mother?"

"Is it that you're afraid of?"

"Yes. If he did she might want to stop me seeing

François, and I think I'd die, Adrian. I'd die." Tears began to gather in his eyes.

Adrian stared at him, puzzled, thinking: This is most odd. I couldn't see myself· being friendly with another man in this way. It would be revolting. I wonder if he could be losing his wits. It wouldn't be surprising. Mother gives him such a hellish time. Poor fellow. . . .

"Adrian, you think Henwah will tell her?"

"He might. He's such a disgusting spy. Always telling tales on us. Not that I care what he tells her about me. I defy her. I'm not afraid of the toolshed. She can lock me in there a month, it won't get me down."

"You're brave. I wish I could be brave like you." He glanced timidly toward the house. "If she should stop me from seeing François, life would be empty."

"It would be your fault if you let her stop you. She couldn't stop me from seeing my friends. How I hate her, Cornelis! How I hate her!"

"You shouldn't hate, Adrian. It isn't good. Remember what Father used to tell us. He said hate damages the soul. He said we should be sorry for her."

"Father only said that, but he hated her, too. Hated her bitterly. He told me to fight her, and I mean to do it. When I grow up I'm going to make her sorry she brought me into the world. I'm going to be cruel to her, make her suffer tortures."

"She's our mother, Adrian. You shouldn't say that."

"She's no mother to me. She's a beast. Sometimes I feel as if I'll go mad if I don't spring on her and choke her. I believe I'm mad already. Claas van Doorn thinks as you do—that I shouldn't feel this way about her, but I can't help it. When I remember what she did to Father, how she made Father drown himself—and all she's done to both of us—I tell you, I'm going to be revenged on her. One day I'm going to torture her to death. One day I'm going to stand by and watch her die in a slow fire. And I'll chop her up piece by piece. I'm going to be a murderer." He began to stammer incoherently. He made choking sounds, trembling.

After a moment he told himself: I'm sure now I'm not sane. She's made me into a mad beast like her. All I want to do is to kill—hurt and kill. If only I'd been a van Doorn instead of a van Groenwegel. Claas and Karena are so happy with their parents. I envy them. They laugh and talk with their father and mother. They don't have to hate like me. They don't have to defy their mother and wish her dead, or want to strike her down and stamp on her. . . . Father was right. Hate is damaging my soul—damaging and damning my soul. But I can't help it. I can't help it. . . .

II

At meal time she gave no sign that Henwah had told her anything, but it would be just like her to leave Cornelis in a suspense of dread for days, to lull him into the belief that she knew nothing—then suddenly pounce upon him.

Three days later she had still given no sign. Then letters arrived from Essequibo, and the news contained in them put the subject of François well into the background.

It was Adrian who brought the letters from the fort. There was one for him, for he corresponded with his cousin, Jabez, Aert's son, who was a year and a half his junior. The other one, which was for his mother, was not addressed, as usual, in his grandfather's handwriting; it was an unfamiliar handwriting, and Adrian examined it curiously, thinking: I wonder whom this could be from. Why hasn't Grandfather Laurens written to her this time? Something must be wrong. I won't be surprised if he's decided not to write to her any more. She was boasting the other day how he said in a letter that she has the heart of a reptile. . . .

When he opened his letter from Jabez, however, he knew the real reason. Jabez told him: "First, I have very sad news for you. Grandfather Laurens died yesterday. He had been ill for several weeks, and we were more or less expecting it. The surgeon from the fort said that his kidneys and liver were bad. We're going to miss him very much, because he was such a nice, pleasant old fellow; he was sixty-two, born in 1650, exactly the middle of the last century. I wonder if I shall live to such an old age, but Great-grandfather Willem lived to a much greater age. He was over seventy when he died, and I believe, from what Father has told us, that Great-great-grandfather Adriansen lived to eighty-three or eighty-four; I will never live to that age, I'm certain. I'm going on for fifteen now, and if I lived to eighty-four that would be 1782. Can you imagine living to 1782? When we think that this is only 1712, 1782 seems like a million years off.

"Father is writing to your mother. He says the last time he wrote to her was when you were about two years old. He hasn't written since then; the work here keeps him so busy. Father thinks my handwriting the best he has ever seen, though Samuel de Haart, my good friend, can write almost as well. I'm sorry your mother won't consider your coming here to spend a few months with us. We have such good times trapping birds and tapirs. Sometimes Flora and Mathilde come with us. Samuel likes Flora, but he won't admit it. We tease him about it and sometimes he gets into a temper, because he has a bad temper when he's roused. He kills ducks and fowls for his aunt when she wants to roast a duck or fowl, and Mother says he has a cruel streak, but that's silly; his uncle and aunt are both very kind people. Why should Mother think he's cruel because he likes cutting the throats of ducks and chickens? Ducks and chickens were made to have their throats cut when you're going to eat them, though, I admit, I can never bring myself to do it. I don't like seeing blood. And I can't believe what you said in your last letter that your mother is so cruel to you all and that it was she who caused Uncle Ignatius's death. How could you have said that, Adrian? I'm sure Grandfather Laurens would have mentioned it, because he always corresponded with her, and he never once said anything about her cruelty—not to Father or any of us. We used to hear him talking about her, and he only spoke of how your plantation was getting on, and he said that she had bought another plantation up the Canje last year and that you would manage it when you get older. But he never said that she was cruel. Father was very puzzled when I told him, and Mother, too. They say you must be spinning tales. . . ."

At this point Cornelis, who was reading the letter with him, interrupted. "Adrian! Mother is going to be furious when she reads this. She has particularly told you that you must never mention anything about her in your letters to Jabez. How could you have told Jabez that she's cruel and that it's she who caused Father's death?"

"Because it's the truth!"

"Don't shout like that. She's in her room."

"I don't care! I'm not afraid of her! I'm not afraid of her!"

"Sssh! Quiet, Adrian!"

"I won't be quiet. I'm not a worm."

The door opened and their mother came in. "Haven't you finished reading the letter you received from Jabez, Adrian?"

"Yes, I have—nearly."

"Then bring it to me the instant you've finished."

"I'm not letting you see it."

She stretched out her hand. "Hand it over. At once."

"You're not having it. Get out of the room, you stinking bitch!"

Cornelis gasped.

Their mother turned and went out.

"Adrian! You told her to get out! You called her a bitch!"

"That's the way to speak to her."

"I believe she's gone downstairs to call Rabonne and the others."

"Let her go. She can't break me. She'll never break me."

He began to walk up and down.

They heard their mother's footsteps approaching along the corridor. Unhurried. They watched her appear at the door. She had her whip. She advanced into the room and made a slash at Adrian. Adrian dodged and sprang at her. He struck her in her face with his clenched hands, and a tiny trickle of blood ran from her nose. He snatched the whip from her, muttering obscenities—obscenities he had heard the soldiers using. She caught him by the collar and sent him hurtling from her. He fell with a heavy thud and skidded a foot or two. His mother advanced upon him as he was rising and grasped him again by his collar, yanked him up. But he struck out and caught her a blow in the face that made her nose bleed more profusely.

Cornelis whimpered.

Adrian struggled and tore at her. His white lace collar was off, and his coat ripped down. His mother's hair had fallen in two loose plaits behind her back.

One of the kitchen slaves appeared at the door.

Hendrickje's will and strength told. She forced him to the floor and held him down despite his furious struggles. But he went on struggling, pinned down though he was.

Pardoom appeared at the door. "Missy, stand away, let me hold him."

"Get out, Pardoom! Get out! I'm handling this alone. Today it's one thing or the other. Either I am mistress here or he is master. We'll see which it is."

Adrian's struggles ceased abruptly. His mother crouched over him, her mouth and chin bloody, her hair in a brown, shifty mass about her shoulders. But she relaxed too soon. Without warning, Adrian heaved himself up, and, freeing himself at one wrench, smashed his fists into her face. The attack took her by complete surprise. She tried to rise, but before she could do so his fist landed in her left eye and she stumbled and fell. He was upon her like a wild beast. He seemed to lose all sense of fair play and judgment. He grasped her hair and tugged at it, blubbering and calling her a bitch, a bitch, a bitch! He pummeled her head, pummeled her face, kicked her throat, her temple, her ear.

"Bitch! Bitch! I'm going to kill you! Kill you!"

Pardoom moved forward into the room, his face

anxious. Rabonne came in after him. "Missy, let me hold him for you," Rabonne said. But Pardoom put out a barring arm, murmuring: "No. She say not to interfere, Rabonne."

"He beating her," Rabonne murmured back.

The doorway was crowded with black faces. Henwah, who had arrived late, was pushing through the lot of them with snappish growls of rebuke.

Hendrickje rallied and succeeded in hurling Adrian off. Her left eye was half-closed and getting blue-black. Her hair kept threatening to tumble forward and obscure her vision. Her throat was bruised where Adrian's shoe had landed. Her bodice was torn down.

Before Adrian could recover she snatched up her whip and rose. As he was rushing at her she slashed at him and caught him across his face, a red weal springing up on his right cheek. He staggered, and she slashed at him again. He came at her with a blubbering whine, but she retreated and slashed and slashed.

He staggered back under the fury of the attack, his hands pressed to his face. She moved forward, slashing; panting and putting all her strength behind the lashes.

The faces of the slaves at the door were rigid.

Cornelis had hidden his face behind his hands.

Hendrickje never stopped until Adrian stumbled against a chair and collapsed near it. Then she stood, whip raised and ready, dominant, dignified despite the blood and her disarray. She prodded him with her foot to make sure that he was not shamming, then turned off. She flicked her whip and snapped: "Make way there! Make way there!"

The slaves fell back to make way for her to pass.

III

But she had not broken him.

Not yet, he told himself, as he sat on a box in the toolshed where she had had him locked up. She's had me put in here because she wants me to feel she won that struggle upstairs. But she hasn't won. This tool-shed can't hold me. Watch and see what's going to happen in a minute.

There were several implements lying around: axes, hatchets, hammers and mallets, hangers, cutlasses. He took up an axe and in less than a minute had hacked away two boards from the door.

Henwah came running up and called: "Massa Adrian! You gone mad! Stop dat! What you smashing up de door for!"

Adrian ignored him. In another minute another board went. He threw the axe aside and passed through the aperture into the open. Henwah and Pardoom—Pardoom had just come up—made a rush at him, and he slipped back into the shed, snatched up a cutlass and emerged again.

"Come near to me now," he told Henwah and Pardoom. "See if I don't slice your black heads off!"

"Massa, put down dat cutlass. You only making more trouble for yourself. Why you must behave so bad?"

Adrian began to walk toward the house.

"Massa Adrian, drop dat cutlass!" Rabonne had come up.

The three men moved after him—cautiously. Rabonne spoke in a voice of entreaty. "Massa, where you going? You can't go in de house wid dat cutlass. De missy not well. You hurt her. She in bed. Come, Massa Adrian. Put down de cutlass and behave yourself."

Adrian turned his head and growled: "I'm warning you. If you approach too near to me I'm going to hack you to pieces."

The three men followed him into the house. The kitchen slaves joined them, and they all moved after him up the stairs.

They must imagine I'm going to attack her. I will —if she comes to me with her imperiousness. I'll cut her to pieces. Both she and I are destined for bad ends. I can see it every day. . . .

When he entered the room he and Cornelis shared Cornelis gasped: "Adrian! You broke out of the tool-shed!"

"I did. And I'm keeping this cutlass in here, and anyone who comes in to interfere with me is going to get murdered."

No one came in. Rabonne and the others, after hesitating at the top of the stairs, decided to go down again, Pardoom muttering: "He gone into his own room. I don't think he go in to trouble Missy."

His mother took no action, did not attempt to have him locked up again. She kept to her room for days, permitting only Rabonne to go in to her to make his report, and had her meals sent up. Many times the two boys heard her pacing slowly about the room.

She's a beaten woman, Adrian told himself. She knows I've got too big for her. She knows she could never hope to control me after what's happened. She must see that I'm only sixteen by age but otherwise I'm a man. The van Groenwegels have fire-blood in them. She has said so often. Well, I have fire in me, and it's going to be used against her. All those tales of the old days she used to fill us up with. Violence. Nothing but violence. Great-great-grandmother Kaywana and Wakkatai. And the raid of 1666. And Aunt Rosa three years ago. Yes, Aunt Rosa is the latest family heroine. Violence, violence. She's brought us up on violence. She mustn't be surprised now if she gets violence directed toward her. . . .

One morning—it was two days after the incident in the bedroom—he got out his riding kit, and Cornelis asked him where he was going.

"Into the fields," he said. "I'm going to see after the work—and keep the slaves in order."

"Adrian! You're only sixteen. How could you go out into the fields alone! They won't obey you."

"They're going to. I'm going to make them."

He did. He took a four-thonged whip and a loaded musket. His voice had already changed, and when he shouted at them they knew that he was their master. Rabonne and Pardoom and Henwah gave him astonished stares, then smiled sheepishly and carried out his orders.

When Rabonne reported to Hendrickje at noon,

Hendrickje smiled. Her left eye was still blue-black. "So he went into the fields, did he? And how did he get on?"

"He get on good, missy."

She looked thoughtful, then said: "Let him carry on. Tell the others to cooperate as much as possible."

"You letting him take charge, missy?"

"Yes. And why not?"

"But he only a boy, missy!"

"Not now. Not within this past week. He's a man, Rabonne. And a van Groenwegel. I hope you'll bear that in mind when addressing him. He must have absolute respect from you and from the others."

"Yes, missy."

Before he left he asked: "Missy, we never going to see you in de fields again?"

She smiled. "Occasionally I'll come and have a glance round, Rabonne."

It was Jeremy, one of the slave boys who had swum and frolicked with him in their younger days, who stopped Adrian as he was crossing over to the fort and said: "Massa, I glad for you."

"Glad for me? What do you mean?"

"I mean, I glad you make big massa now."

Adrian frowned. "I'm afraid I don't understand."

"You not big manager since yesterday? You go out in fields alone on mule."

"Oh, you mean that. Well, why not? I've got to be in charge some time. I see no reason why it shouldn't be now."

"I hear Missy glad. So I hear Rabonne saying."

Adrian gave him a sharp glance. "Missy is glad? You heard Rabonne saying that? When?"

"Dis morning he say it. And he say it yesterday, too. He say Missy tell him dat in future you manager, and we must respect you and work for you good, and we must obey you."

"She said that, did she?"

"Yes, Massa. I glad for you, Massa Adrian."

Adrian smiled uncomfortably. "Thanks, Jeremy.

It's a surprise to me. I didn't know she had said that about me."

That was April. By June a close understanding had sprung up between him and his mother. He told himself: Six weeks ago I wouldn't have believed this possible. She's a clever woman. She knew it was hopeless resisting me, so instead she has given me authority. Nowadays she talks to me and discusses the plantation business as though she considered me a man of twenty-five. She doesn't try to flatter me, because she knows it wouldn't be effective. She knows that that method might antagonize me, so she treats me with a kind of formal respect, and now and then drops a comment to make me know in a subtle way that her formal airs are only for effect and that at any time I felt like being outright friendly she would be willing to let the past be forgotten. . . . Somehow I can't resist her wiles. I'm beginning to feel a sort of friendliness and devotion toward her. My hate seems to have melted away during the past few weeks. It's still there; the slightest thing can rouse it up in full fury. I mustn't deceive myself; I can't ever forgive her for what she did to Father. But, still, something has happened to me since that day when Jeremy told me that she had spoken well of me to Rabonne. She's winning me over to her side in spite of myself, in spite of my desperate vows to be revenged on her. I try to lash myself into a fury and hate her as I did a few weeks ago, but I can't. It seems like a waste of energy trying to hate her, and as if to go on trying would be silly and boyish. I feel as though I've got past that stage; got past what I was six weeks ago. Now I ought to think differently, look at everything anew and be less impetuous. Even toward Cornelis I'm beginning to feel contemptuous—especially since he's told me what he did about that French fellow. In love with each other! It disgusts me. And he's so effeminate. Always preening himself. He even talks like a girl and walks with a girlish swing. I can't imagine what has happened to him. I can see now why Mother despises him. She must know of his relations with Tirol. Henwah must have told her what he saw on the river that day. She ignores him, and she's right. I feel I ought to do the same. I've told her I want a room to myself. Can't go on living in the same room with that girlish fop. . . . Yes, I'm looking at things differently now. And Mother, I've discovered, is not such a bad person, after all. I'm finding much in her that I wasn't aware of before; much that I couldn't appreciate before. She has some admirable qualities. She has dignity. She's hard, but it's a healthy hardness; she has strength. That counts in the long run. Strength. . . . And she's handsome. Sometimes she gives me a look that makes me feel that if I weren't her son she might try to make love to me. And I feel that way about her, too, many times. She doesn't look thirty-nine. She might be no more than twenty-five. I haven't seen a woman in this colony who can equal her for beauty. . . . Strange that I should be thinking of her like this now. Is it possible I could have changed so much in these few weeks? . . .

One day she stopped him in the portico and said with a slight smile: "Commandeur de Waterman has invited me to dinner tomorrow night, but I told him I couldn't very well go without the master of the house. Would you like to take me?"

He avoided her gaze and mumbled: "Certainly— if you like."

So they went together, and Mynheer de Feer smiled: "He's as tall as you, Mevrouw. You haven't a boy any more."

"He's my manager, Mynheer."

On the way home, on the path, she made him take her arm. It was nearly eleven o'clock, and there was moonlight. She said quietly: "I'm getting very proud of you."

He said nothing, uncomfortable—especially at the closeness of her body. It gave him queer, shivery feelings. She might have been a strange woman. . . . In a way, he thought, she is a strange woman. The touch of her in an intimate way is foreign to me. I have no memories of her ever having held me in an affectionate manner. I have memories only of blows. . . .

"Do you still hate me so much?"

He shook his head. "Not now."

After a silence she said: "Do you know what I just felt? That you're a strange young man I'm about to be very friendly with."

"That's odd."

"Why?"

"I was thinking the same about you."

"I'm afraid the blame rests entirely on me. I've never shown you any affection—not even as an infant."

"I know."

They could hear the river sucking at the bank. She said: "Let's stop for a moment and look at the river."

They stood in the moonlight near some plumbagoes and looked at the water with the stars and the moon reflected in it. Fireflies flashed on the other bank among the low-hanging foliage of wild cacao and young *mora*.

Behind them the plumbagoes looked like pale ghost coins. Around them, intensifying the silence of the night instead of disturbing it, the insects churred in high-pitched monotony. The water kept sucking at the bank. Sillip-sillip, it went.

He felt her hand tighten on his wrist, and sensed her breathing. She was dressed in style, the neck of her dress low so that he could see the freckles on her throat and on her bosom.

"Would you like us to be friends?" she murmured.

He could feel the blood creeping up into his cheeks. His heart did not seem to be beating any more. It had traveled far off into the night.

She said: "Why don't you answer?"

He nodded and mumbled: "Yes."

"Let's go inside now."

He had his own room, and before undressing he stood at the window a long time looking out at the moonlight. His face was warm, and he had to keep massaging his wrist. He could not think at all. Every thought that tried to settle in his mind darted off like a scarlet spark.

IV

Early in July, during the thunderstorm period, Cornelis came into his room after the midday meal and said: "Adrian, dear, you keep avoiding me so much now. Is anything the matter?"

"If you can't stop using those endearments to me, don't address me. I hate to hear them. I'm not your François."

"Adrian, why must you speak so roughly to me? It isn't like you. You seem quite changed these past few weeks."

"I have changed. I thought that would have been obvious to a fly."

Cornelis glanced timidly toward the door and lowered his voice. "You seem to get on very well with Mother nowadays—ever since that terrible tussle in my room. You don't hate her any more?"

"I don't want to be questioned."

His brother gazed at him in a troubled, perplexed manner. "Yes, you're a changed person. You've got so cold toward me—almost as cold as she is. You say hardly anything to me. You don't love me any more, Adrian?"

"Oh, get out! You make me sick, Cornelis! Can't you be a man?"

Cornelis looked hurt. "That isn't like you, Adrian, dear. You used to be so sympathetic—so kind and brotherly. Like Father. But of a sudden you've become a different person. If you turn against me, too, I'd have no one but—but François to care for me." There were tears in his eyes.

Adrian said nothing.

"I think I see what's happening," said Cornelis. "It's Mother. She's taken you over. You're speaking like her. Saying the things she used to say to Father and to us. You're getting hard and cold like her. Oh, Adrian! Why did you have to change like this!"

"Get out! Get out, I say! You're making me angry now. I don't want to hear a word more. Get out!"

Cornelis uttered an aggrieved, girlish sound and went out.

I don't like treating him like this, Adrian told himself, but he gets on my nerves—and I'm in such a turmoil with myself these days. Sometimes I feel I'll go out of my mind. But I mustn't think. I'm trying to train myself not to think. It's bad for me. It's damaging me. . . .

He had the room next to his mother's; the room that used to be his father's studio. He could hear his mother moving about in her own room, and in his mind he saw her, tall and graceful. Her hair must be hanging in two loose plaits down her back. She must be preparing to rest.

He began to walk aimlessly around the room.

Next month I'm seventeen. On my last birthday I remember how I told myself I wished I were twenty so that I could hurt her with all my strength—with the strength of a man. I hated her so much then. Now . . . no, but I can't understand why I should feel like this. Something must be the matter with my mind. It isn't natural. But, of course, nothing has been natural in this house. We haven't grown up like other children. She is not to me as Claas van Doorn's mother is to him.

In the southeast a rumble of thunder vibrated. The air was still, and the sun shone down with a spiteful intensity.

He fanned himself with his hand, letting his gaze move out of the window at which he had stopped in his pacing. . . . The compound, the water tanks, the slaves' logies; beyond the indigo fields, the cane fields—his eyes took them in and roved round toward the edge of the upriver jungle. Beyond this jungle there were more fields—fields of another plantation. Then more jungle. More fields . . . more residences, water tanks, slaves' logies. . . .

Suppose I had been a slave and not a Dutch master. . . .

Lightning over the indigo fields. He heard it click.

About a second later came a softer, nearer click, and he knew that the connecting door had opened. He turned and looked, and it was as he had thought a few minutes ago. The two loose plaits hung down behind her.

She smiled and said: "You keep walking up and down."

"It's the heat," he mumbled. "A storm seems to be coming."

She moved over to a window—not the same one at which he had paused. She looked shapely and elegant in the housegown she wore; it was of silk and glimmered dully with a look of affluence. She might have been a queen.

God, I wonder if it couldn't be my hatred for her that makes me feel like this. I do hate her still now and then. I feel a kind of grudge against her—a resentful feeling, as though I should rush at her and strangle her or beat her. Yet I know that before I could do that I'd be wanting to . . .

He would not complete the thought, but the rest of the thought moved like thin flames through his brain.

"It's coming over from the southeast." She glanced at him and smiled: "Put on your nightshirt. It will be cooler."

"I'd intended to. In a few minutes."

She moved back toward her room, paused at the connecting door and looked back at him. "Something is on your mind," she said.

"No, no."

He looked outside again, pretending to be interested in the thunderclouds piling in the southeast. He heard her utter a soft sound, and detected a tender note in it.

Why doesn't she go back into her room? Why is she staring at me and trying to see into me? I know that that is what she's doing. Trying to discover how I'm feeling about her. I can kill her for not going back into her room. She has no right to do this. She ought to know it upsets me. It's that old hardness of hers—that lack of sympathy. She doesn't care about other people's feelings. One day I'm going to throttle her. . . .

Yet the instant he heard the door shut he was sorry that she had not stayed. If only she had come to him here at the window and asked him what was the matter.

She could have said: "What's the matter, Adrian? Has anything happened to put you in a mood?" In a soft, half-breathless voice like the voice she had used that night when they stood in the moonlight and looked at the river.

I'll never forget that night. I can hear the water making a sucking sound. I can see the fireflies on the opposite bank. And the plumbagoes were behind us. She was pressed close against me.

He started. The thunder was getting louder. That last peal was like a hundred cannon going off at once.

Rabonne was collecting some agouti hides which had been drying in the sun. The sun had gone. A gloom was settling rapidly over everything. The clouds looked slate-gray and ominous above the fields.

Rabonne is not such a bad fellow—nor Pardoom and Henwah. Now that I've come to know them better I even admire them. They're efficient and loyal. I can't imagine why I couldn't see that before. Or is it that I'm biased in favor of everything and everyone that she is in favor of! I wish I could confide in somebody. If Father were alive I might have been able to tell him about it. He would have understood, I think. I wonder, though. He was so afraid of her. And he hated her under his fear. He never let slip an opportunity to speak against her. It's he who helped me to hate her so much. . . . I'll go mad if I remain in this room thinking about things like this. I'd better go for a walk along the Company path. I'll go and see Claas and Karena.

He moved toward the door that gave into the corridor, then hesitated. He heard her footsteps in the next room. She seemed to have got out of bed. She suddenly appeared and said in surprise: "You're not going out, Adrian?" There was a breathlessness in her manner that puzzled him.

"I wanted to go for a walk—perhaps to the van Doorns. It's so hot in the house here."

She came close to him and held his arm. "Don't go. The thunderstorm will overtake you." She spoke quietly. There was a tenseness in her manner that reminded him of the night in the moonlight.

"I don't care about the storm. A wetting won't harm me."

"The lightning will be dangerous. Why must you go? Couldn't you stay and talk to me?"

He said nothing.

"Come into my room."

"No, Mother. No. I think I'll go out."

"You called me 'Mother.' Call me Hendrickje." Her grip on his arm tightened. "You'll feel better if you come in and talk to me. There's something on your mind."

He allowed her to lead him in. He began to tell himself that he should defy her and tell her that *he* had decided to go out for a walk, and *she* would not stop him. No matter what *she* said, he was going. She must remember that she had no authority over him now. His will was as strong as hers. Stronger. He would kill her if she tried to resist him, hold her and strangle her. . . . But he sat down on the edge of the bed without any attempt at argument. He saw the sudden brassy glare of the lightning outside. The thunder tumbled down upon them, making the very foundations of the house vibrate.

"And you wanted to go out in that. Adrian, I want us to be friends—real friends. Not as we are now, casual and polite. I'm lonely. I want someone to talk to and to be affectionate to, and someone to be affectionate to me." She spoke in an impulsive burst and with agitation. Her face was troubled and human. She sat beside him and put her arm about him. "I'm not really a dragon. I've tried to fool myself that I am, but I'm just a woman—a human being. I have my soft side. You must believe me, dear. Please. Try to forget what's happened between us in the past. I've been a brute—to all of you. But I'm not a brute all through. If I were only given the chance—if life would only be kinder to me, I could be very tender. And I like people being tender toward me. Adrian, what's the matter? You're trembling, dear." She began to stroke his hair.

He rose and said: "I think I should go out. I want some fresh air. It's—it's really hot in the house."

"No, please. The rain will soon be down. Sit and talk to me. Please, Adrian. Don't go out. Sit and tell me about yourself—what you've been thinking. Tell me anything——"

"I can't stay. You don't understand. I can't explain. I must go."

"Is it something I've said?"

"No, no." He turned and looked at her. "I wish I could tell you, but—but—heavens! No, I can't. I'm ashamed. It would be terrible to tell you that. You wouldn't understand."

She held his arm, a faint gleam in her eyes. "I think I do understand. I'm much older than you. Sit down."

He sat down beside her again, his eyes with a dazed look. He was trembling again. She drew close to him, put her arms about him and pulled his head against hers, and he remained quiescent.

"You mustn't be upset, dear," she said. "I'm glad you feel this way about me. It gives me hope again for myself. I'd begun to fear I'd never get anyone to care for me. I'm not really a fiend, Adrian. Circumstances have contributed immensely to my hardness. I've been thwarted so often in my ambitions, and I'm not a good loser——"

They both winced at the startling crack-crack and boom. She got up and hurried over to the windows and drew down the blinds. Rain came down in coarse, dense drops. He shut the two southern windows, and she shut the three eastern ones. The damp chill from the rain struck through the room. The roof seemed as though it would cave in under the spiteful drops.

The diversion restored some of his self-possession.

"One or two of the logies are leaking," he said. "I was looking at them yesterday. We'll have to see after them."

"Yes, Henwah did mention it," she said. "We'll have to get some shingles and materials from the Company store, and Hebban can get to work next week. Take off your shoes and make yourself comfortable. Let's have a nice long talk."

He took off his shoes and they squatted on the bed, hugging their knees and talking. She asked him about Jabez. "Did you write him recently?"

"Yes, about a fortnight ago." He felt at ease now, though he knew that the tenseness was still beside him like a ghost waiting to envelop him. His inside felt cool like the rain and pleasantly aching. I feel good, he told himself. I thought it would be awkward being alone with her in here. So long as she sits near me without touching me, like this, it will be all right. I wish I could remain here and talk for ever and ever.

"He seems to be growing into a fine fellow."

"Yes. He says he's going out in the fields now with Uncle Aert. Grandmother has gone to live with them up the Mazaruni."

"Your uncle mentioned that in his last letter to me. They're selling the Essequibo plantation and extending the one up the Mazaruni."

"I'm sorry Grandfather Laurens had to die off. It's strange. Why couldn't Grandfather Reinald have died instead? He's older, and he's of no use to himself nor to anybody, and yet he still hangs on to life."

"That's the way of life. Everything is blind and haphazard. That's why I have no faith in religious practices. No one who thinks and observes what goes on around us can believe in such a myth as God or in the teachings of the Church. Life is brutal, Adrian. The stronger survive, the weaker get crushed. It isn't pleasant to think of, but it's the truth, and one must not avoid the truth. Deluding ourselves with soothing myths won't help us to solve the mysteries of this existence—and the problems that persistently assail us."

"I believe that, too. There isn't any God. People are simply born anyhow, like the animals, and if they can fight their way through the world they get on. If they can't, they get beaten and die."

"Listen to the thunder and lightning going on over us. It's only Nature. If it were being controlled by some God up in the sky who could hear us speaking now and be offended we'd have been struck down already."

"That's true. Mother, about the family—do you

still think as you did before? I mean, that we must be powerful and spread?"

She said quietly: "Yes, I haven't given up. I won't ever give up that ambition. My plans get frustrated and smashed with every move I make, but I haven't given up."

"I think I'll help you in whatever way I can."

"You will?" She touched his knee impulsively.

He looked away and said in a mumble: "I'd do anything for you."

"Thank you." Her voice sounded a little husky. "Just at present," she went on, after a silence, "it isn't power or the family I'm concerned about. It's having someone close to me—someone to whom I can say things to, so that I can feel I'm a woman. I'm starved for affection, Adrian. I can be just as warm as I can be cold and hard. That night when we stood in the moonlight I began to hope desperately that we could be good friends—in spite of what has happened between us. I wanted to hug you and tell you I was sorry we were strangers and ask your forgiveness for being a brute and for not being the mother I should have been. I've felt very humble these past few weeks—humble and ashamed. Since that night I've gone down very much in my own esteem. Before then I was a callous, conceited girl. I've only now begun to grow up. I'm seeing myself much more clearly, and the revelation frightens me. That's why I need a companion with whom I can discuss myself intimately and frankly—a companion I can be soft with and get some softness from in return. You don't know how much happiness you're giving me by sitting here with me. You're trembling again. You're pale, Adrian."

"I think I'd better go now."

"No, stay."

"I can't—I must——"

"Don't think of me as a strange woman."

"But you are a strange woman! You make me feel—you make me want to do what I shouldn't. I can't explain—don't touch me! Don't touch me, please! It isn't natural. I can't stand it. Let me go."

She held his wrist and said: "Don't be foolish.

You're so wild and uncontrollable. It must be the fire-blood—and the way I've brutalized you. Well, think of me as a strange woman, then. Since we can't sit and talk like two good friends, then do what you must. Do anything, but don't leave me. Call me Hendrickje. It will make it easier for you." She glided her hand along his cheek, smiling at him as though he were really a stranger—a man with whom she had only just become intimate and to whom she had taken a fancy. She sidled up against him and let the softness of her shoulder rest on his arm. He drew away the arm, muttering: "I can't believe this. No, I can't believe this." He seemed in a stupor.

She buried her face in his lap. It was as though she had begun to fight an unseen presence. He could hear her breathing in agitation. She seemed afraid to raise her head for fear of seeing the phantom adversary —as though seeing it might weaken her defense.

When he made an attempt to get off the bed she resisted him, curled one of her arms around his waist and pressed her face harder into his lap. "Don't leave me, Adrian. Don't go. I can't believe it, too, but I can't help myself." She said something else, but it was muffled and unintelligible. She was in a trembling fever, and there was something of the spirit of the rain in her quick breathing and soft grunts. The rain had thinned. It swished in uneven hissing bursts against the windows, and the thunder and lightning came at longer intervals, the lightning in brassy silence.

She raised her head and looked up at his face. Strands of her hair made a fuzzy network round her temples and forehead, and the tiny brown freckles stood out against her pink, smooth cheeks. She might have been twenty-one instead of nearly forty. She smiled and murmured: "I think I'm feeling shyer than you are, Adrian. Look at me. Don't frown so. Look at me. Look in my eyes."

But he kept looking straight before him, his lips set together tight.

"Look in my eyes."

He kept on staring before him.

"This is wicked of me, but in a way you've

brought it on yourself. I would have been content to sit
and talk in innocence with you—like two good companions. But you will remind me that I'm a woman and
still young and warm. It's your masculinity—you have
an animal masculinity. You make me forget that there
is blood between us and that this is something that
should seem unnatural. You will treat me as a stranger,
and when you do I want to respond. I can't help it. I
don't believe in repressing myself. I know my weaknesses and I indulge them. If you behave toward me as
a son toward a mother I'll be only too pleased and content to let it rest at that, and I'll welcome your companionship. But I can be your mistress with equal willingness. Don't blush. It's the truth, my dear. We can't
help how it sounds. It is the truth. Let's see it in a
balanced way——"

"I can't see anything in a balanced way when I'm
with you. I feel sometimes like killing myself so as to be
rid of the whole problem." He made another attempt to
get off the bed, but she stayed him again, holding his
wrist and twisting herself into a new position so that she
could rest her head in his lap and look up at him. There
was a reckless determination in her manner, a feverish
intensity, as though this were some game she was engaged in: a serious, earnest game with a stake that was
high. In changing her position her gown had come
open, exposing her bosom, and automatically her hand
moved to adjust it, but at the last moment she seemed
to change her mind. She let it stay as it was.

"You're making yourself believe it's a problem,"
she said. "Nothing should be a problem, my boy. It's
only your attitude toward it that makes it seem so difficult and insoluble. Would you like me to solve it for
you? Have you enough confidence in me, Adrian?"

"You couldn't help. You couldn't do anything for
me."

"Look at me."

"I'm afraid to. Don't ask me to."

"Look at me."

"No."

They listened to the rain. It was falling softly now.

"You're afraid to look at me?"

"Yes."

"Please don't be afraid. Look at me."

"No."

"Look at me."

There was too much insistent demand in her tone now. The power in her told. He looked down into her gray-green eyes staring up at him. And he saw how she was lying with her gown open. It was too much. His restraint went. She did not stop him. She let him kiss and fondle her, responding with as much warmth and unrestraint. Abruptly, however, she gripped his exploring hand and hugged him to her, saying: "I think you must go now. This is so good of you, Adrian. I don't deserve it. You make me feel wicked and small." She sounded sincere; sounded deeply moved: the way her eyes narrowed and the way she moved her hand over his back and shoulder proved this beyond doubt. If she were an evil person the evil in her was, in this moment, at its lowest ebb, Adrian felt. . . . She couldn't be evil. She's a queen. The most perfect creature. I'd die for her. . . .

He behaved as though she had not spoken. He persisted, kissing and fondling her in a trance of passion. She resisted very gently, saying; "You must go now. Go for a walk in the rain. It hasn't stopped yet. It will do you good. You'll be refreshed, and then when you come back we can have another long chat. Please. Go now. Believe in me and I'll see you don't have any difficulties. Adrian, please. You really must go."

"I can't go now. You know I can't. Why do you want to send me away? You're making it harder for me."

"Will you believe in me? Will you trust me?"

"Don't ask me that. I'd believe in you if you were the worst thing in the world. You know I can't do without you now. You're purposely saying this to show me you're invincible and—and powerful."

"I'm not. You mustn't misunderstand me. But you must leave me now, Adrian. Please. Do as I ask. Go for a walk—go anywhere, and when you come back we'll both be calm and we can have a long talk together. Don't spoil everything. There's a good boy——"

"Don't call me a boy! Don't call me a boy! I'm not a boy. You'll make me want to hate you again if you say that." He pressed his head against her in a groaning tremor of passion, but she would not respond. She pleaded with him to go. There was a touch of distraction in her manner now. She said: "I'm just as eager for you to stay as you are, Adrian. It takes a lot for me to send you away. It takes strength. Don't think I can't feel as passionately as you can. But I want you to go. Show me you have as much strength as I have, dear. Please. You'll respect me and I'll respect you if we restrain ourselves for the present. But it will leave a bad taste if we give in rashly now. You must believe in me, Adrian. I know more of these things than you."

As at the outset, the power of her character told. He relaxed.

"Perhaps you're right," he said. "This does seem rash. I don't believe I'm sane. Hell, but I want you more than—more than . . ."

He broke off and looked at her and looked away.

"I understand exactly how you feel. I feel the same about you. At this very moment. You can't know how desperate I am, Adrian—how utterly agonized—and starved." He heard her breath whistle softly. "But I'm keeping myself in hand. I'm almost dizzy, Adrian, from curbing myself. There's lightning in me. You couldn't feel madder than I. But I can master myself. This is where we can both prove we have character. We're van Groenwegels—the strong ones. The hard ones. Go for a walk, and when you come back we'll sit quietly on the portico and have a chat."

When he was at the door she smiled and called: "Come. Come back and shake my hand."

He retraced his steps, and saw that there were tears in her eyes. She was still smiling—a fixed smile of tenderness and admiration. She gave her head a slight nod as she squeezed his hand.

She sat and watched him go out, then got up and went to the window and saw him moving across the compound. The rain was a mere wispy drizzle, though the lightning still flashed sharply and the thunder boomed heavily.

He looked back and saw her at the window. He waved, and she waved back.

V

When he returned from his walk she was waiting for him in the portico, fully dressed and carefully groomed, and they sat and talked about the plantation and about Essequibo. Twilight found them still in conversation. There was mauve in the west, the sky without a cloud, though the air was oppressive, and perhaps before midnight there would be another thunderstorm. Once, during a short silence, when they were looking at the jungle on the opposite bank, he thought: This is like something I've planned, only much better. I feel that coolness inside me. I know it's a coolness that won't last, but I like fooling myself that it will, and that she and I are now above anything physical.

"In future," he said aloud, abruptly, "I think I'll call you Hendrickje."

She nodded. "Please. You must."

I wonder whether she would prefer not to hark back to earlier today. She can be so inscrutable at times. I can't always tell what's going on inside her. Heavens! She has such poise! Just watch her now. I think I can worship her always.

"Hendrickje."

"Yes?"

"What are you thinking about?"

She shrugged.

"We've said not a word about what happened today."

"Do you want to say something about it?" she smiled.

"I was wondering," he said.

"What's going to happen eventually, you mean?"

He nodded.

She said: "You could come to my room tonight."

"Tonight?"

"Would you like to?"

He hesitated, trying to pierce her mystery. "Would you like me to? I think that's more important."

"What you feel is equally important."

They were silent for a long while. The insects were churring shrilly, and the dampness rose from the earth and from the trees into the still air. The river never ceased to suck at the bank.

"You puzzle me a little."

"There's nothing to be puzzled at, Adrian." She looked at him. "Don't let my silence put you off. Would you like to come to my room tonight?"

"You speak as though you're challenging me."

She smiled, leaned toward him and kissed him. Kissed him on his lips. "Does that convince you now that I'm in earnest?"

"Then I will come."

Long before bedtime, however, he had made up his mind that he would not go. He lay in bed and gazed up into the darkness of the roof, feeling unusually at peace. He said to himself: I mustn't take her at her word. To go in to her would be in bad taste. Perhaps it was that she wanted to imply by her reticence before she made the suggestion. She was saying to me in effect: "I would like nothing better than to have you with me in bed, but it will be in bad taste for us to go so far in our intimacy. Though if you think it over and still decide to come to me I'll submit." She told me what she wanted to without words and without rebuffing me and making me feel a foolish, ignorant, impetuous boy. I respect her for doing it like this. She is wise. Wise and perfect in every way.

The following morning she asked him nothing, and he gave her no explanation. He found that he was perfectly at ease with her.

Cornelis gave them odd, troubled glances, his manner vaguely suspicious. They ignored his presence.

During the weeks that followed a softness came into her manner. It was obvious even in her attitude toward the slaves. Formerly she always made it a point to be present at floggings; now she avoided these occasions. She increased the house slaves' rations, and seldom shouted at them. Instead of using her whip on them for misdemeanors she merely threatened them with a cut in rations.

Every day she and Adrian had long chats in the portico, or in his or her room. They discussed the prospects of the plantation and their hopes for the one up the Canje. When letters arrived from Essequibo they read them together, lying on their stomachs in bed or sitting close together at the dining table.

In one of these letters Aert told them: "We have changed our plans about the Essequibo plantation. We intend to retain it, after all, and abandon the Mazaruni one. We're doing this on the advice of Laurens de Heere who has some excellent theories on the future of this colony—theories which, I'm convinced, won't remain theories always, because it has been hinted that de Heere may succeed van der Heyden Resen as Commandeur. Resen is petty. I believe the trouble is that, while efficient and energetic, he doesn't know human nature and doesn't get on well with his fellow officials. He and Gelskerke, the Secretary—a fine fellow and a regular visitor at our home—are always at loggerheads. However, let me tell you something of de Heere's theories. De Heere feels that the coastal soil is far more fertile than our interior soil here. The coastal soil consists of oozy black mud and is often inundated by the sea at high tide, but it is rich soil and only requires proper drainage. De Heere feels that it would be possible to obtain as many as four successive crops of equal tonnage from the coastal soil, whereas, as you know, up here with every crop we show a marked decrease in tonnage. Our fourth crop recently has amounted to hardly more than a thousand pounds per acre, as compared with a first crop of three thousand to the acre. In brief, then, de Heere is predicting a gradual migration toward the coast, and advises that we should abandon the Mazaruni plantation and hold on to the lower plantation on the Essequibo. Indeed, he thinks that even the Essequibo plantation we shall soon have to dispose of in order to go still nearer to the coast, as the land around the fort area is becoming rapidly exhausted. . . ."

Jabez, in the course of his letter, said: "The de Haarts have bought the plantation next to ours on the Essequibo, so Samuel and I will still see a lot of each other in future. I'm beginning to believe what Mother said about him. He has a cruel streak. Last week he caught eleven of those wriggly, shiny black lizards that you see in the sand sometimes, and he killed every one by putting a noose around its neck with a piece of grass and then holding it over a fire and watching it sizzle and die. I told him he should never have done such a thing, that it was unnecessarily brutal. We had an argument over it, but he laughed at me finally and said I'm jelly-hearted; he said there's nothing wrong in killing wild creatures. I disagreed. I said I saw no harm in killing wild creatures that you can use as food, but harmless creatures that you can't eat should be left alone. . . ."

"I used to think so about you—that you have a cruel streak."

"Now you don't think so?"

He shook his head. "I know you haven't," he said. "It's only circumstances that have made you appear cruel."

She smiled. "You must be careful you don't exaggerate my nobility. I am cruel, Adrian. I have a streak of brutality in me. I was born with it. You mustn't harbor false ideas about me. That would be almost as bad as hating me as you once did."

That was the first disturbing note. It sounded in September, more than two months after the incident during the thunderstorm. But it was slight. It did not upset him as much as the incident a week later when Cornelis said to him: "She's a terrible woman, Adrian, dear. She couldn't win you over by opposing you, so she has sold herself to you by guile and soft words and glances."

He caught Cornelis by the collar and shook him. Threw him to the floor. "You dirty beast! Fancy saying that of her! I could kill you. You don't know what you're saying. Can't you look at her and see she's a changed woman! She's noble and upright and strong. A goddess. She's genuine. If she wasn't genuine I'd have discovered her long ago. Our friendship is a pure and beautiful one. The kind of friendship you could never know. You and your dirty Frenchman over at the fort!"

"He's not dirty! I won't have you say that!" Cornelius rose, his girlish frame in a spasm of rage. "François has been the only person to show me any affection—except Father, and even he could only be sparing because of the kind of life we've lived under her. She's been no mother to me. She's never once kissed me, never once put her arm around me. Do you think I could feel tenderness for her! And now you call François dirty because he loves me as she has never done. She's the dirty one! She has seduced you! I know she has! Your own mother! You make love together at night——"

"That's a disgusting lie! Take it back or I'll kill you!"

Hendrickje came in to them. "Adrian, you should know better than to take notice of this piece of trash. Shove him out of the room, dear, and let him go. Please. For my sake."

After he had put Cornelis out and slammed the door, she came over to him and gave him a hug and stroked his hair, murmuring: "Don't let what he said upset you, my darling. And in effect he spoke no untruth. I have seduced you. Nothing actually physical has taken place between us, but in my imagination I've been to bed with you every night since that day of the thunderstorm." Her eyes narrowed with desire as she regarded him. She kept stroking his cheek and his hair, and made a soft passionate sound, biting her lip in a tortured way.

"You mustn't get annoyed and furious when he drops remarks like that, Adrian. What does it matter what others say? It's what we feel about each other and how we behave toward each other that counts. So long as we respect each other and love in the way we do, you should have nothing to get into a temper about. Don't idealize our love too much. That would be a mistake. Remember my old adage. Face the truth, no matter how ugly it may be, or how much pain it may give. Don't let's have illusions about ourselves. We're mother and son, but we're in love like two animals. We want to be in bed. That's what will give us the greatest satisfaction. But because of the blood between us we feel it would be distasteful to be physically intimate, so we deny ourselves this ultimate satisfaction and content ourselves, instead, with a deep, close companionship, and, as a result, we not only retain our self-respect and respect each other but in the very fact that we deny ourselves we feel that we are doing something strong—something even superhuman—and this gives us an ecstasy few people know. That's all, darling. That's the situation between us summed up in as frank and accurate a manner as it can be. Don't build anything more on it, Adrian. Don't fly into a temper when anyone taunts you or accuses you of being physically intimate with me. Simply smile it off and say to yourself: 'I can't deny that, because it's virtually true. In effect, she is my mistress.' "

On another occasion—an evening in early October when they were sitting in the portico—she said to him: "Our chief difficulty is one of faith, Adrian. Having faith in each other and having faith in ourselves. If I didn't feel as deeply as I do about you it wouldn't matter, but being sincere—perhaps more sincere than I was with your father in our early days—I keep dreading that I may do or say something to shake your faith in me. I often find myself lacking faith in myself—in my ability to hold you. And I can sense that you must have the same problems, for despite your strength of character you're immature——"

"I'm not! You mustn't say that, Hendrickje. I hate to hear you imply that I'm still a boy. I read a lot, and I think a lot. That book you got for me the other day—Spinoza's *Ethics*—I've studied it through and through, and there are others I've read that have given me a thorough understanding of human nature and higher thought——"

"No book could ever teach you about human nature, darling. You must live before you can know human nature thoroughly, and what you mean by higher thought is merely ordinary thought made mystifying and complicated. Philosophers are vain people—people with an inflated opinion of their mental powers. That is why they try to baffle the layman and make him feel they are so much higher in thought——"

"Hendrickje, you're a cynic! I don't like that. You shouldn't scoff at things like that. According to what I've heard you saying from time to time, there is no nobility at all in human nature."

"There isn't, Adrian. Nobility, like God, is an idea that we have invented in order to delude ourselves that we are immensely better than the beasts."

"We *are* better than the beasts. Immensely better——"

"Don't let us discuss it any more, dear. We'll soon be quarrelling." She patted his wrist. "This is what I dread. Saying something that might cause friction and upset your ideas about me and make you lose faith in me." Her voice became husky. She gripped his arm. "Adrian, it would be a major tragedy for me if this friendship of ours were to come to grief. You wouldn't guess how important it has become to me. Don't let us argue. Don't think ill of me because I'm cynical sometimes. I can't help it. You know what I have suffered during the past ten or fifteen years. Try to be understanding and forgive me when I seem ironic toward the things you hold sacred. Please. Please, my darling."

VI

The 10th of November dawned with light mists on the river. The sky was cloudless, except low in the east where the pink and purple clouds that generally appeared as though on purpose to greet the sun still loomed like remote cupolas over the jungle.

After Adrian had left for the fields Hendrickje sat down to write up the records.

"*November 7th*. Hebban, the carpenter, fell ill. The fort surgeon summoned. He thinks it is black water fever. The surgeon is most incompetent. *Note:* We must have a surgeon for the Canje plantation.

"Work on Field 6 and Field 11 continued today. Balsam patches inspected; all in flourishing state, despite dryness of weather. Provision fields 7 and 9 reaped. Biweekly rum ration served to slaves. Double rations to No. 2 Gang for the work they put in on cotton fields. Men on punishment—three. Petty theft and laziness. . . ."

She wrote from notes made by Adrian on slips of paper.

Presently she put aside the record book and began to make her toilet. She sat before the mirror in the sunlight that came in at the eastern windows, and regarded her reflection. Her cheeks were smooth, and there was no surplus flesh under her chin. About a month ago she had discovered a single gray hair in her head—the first. She smiled and told herself that she might have been twenty-five to judge by her appearance. No one who did not know her could have guessed that she was nearly forty and had two tall sons eighteen and seventeen.

She was nearly dressed when she heard hurried footsteps on the stairs. It sounded like Cornelis, and she tilted her head with a puzzled air. It was not often that Cornelis moved with such speed. She turned as he came bursting into the room.

"Well, what's happened?" she asked coldly.

"Mother! I'm just from the fort!" He was blowing as though from running. "They've just received a message that French ships have entered the river—ships of Jacques Cassard!"

"What's that?"

"Yes, Mother. They've landed on Plantation Hooft. The Commandeur says I must tell you to get ready to go upriver or flee into the bush. He says the house here will be in danger when the French open the attack on the fort."

She stood up.

"Mother, must I tell the slaves to begin to pack our valuables in the jars? The jars you have in the pantry?"

"You'll tell the slaves nothing. Go to your room."

"But, Mother——"

"Go to your room. This instant!"

She finished her toilet hastily and went downstairs. She sent off a message to the fields by one of the kitchen slaves. "Be sure you deliver the message to the *baas* himself. There'll be ten lashes for you and short rations if you don't. And hurry!"

Within half an hour Adrian was back. The horns were cooing in the fields; the horns that would have sounded at noon to call the slaves in for the midday meal. Adrian was puzzled. "What's the matter, Hendrickje? Why such an urgent call? I thought you must have fallen ill, but when the message said I must order the gangs in——"

She interrupted and told him the news.

"French ships! But how is it the news has only just got to the fort if they have already made a landing on Plantation Hooft? Take care, there's some mistake. I'd better go over to the fort and find out for certain. Perhaps Cornelis misconstrued——"

"I doubt he has. At the back of my mind I've been expecting this. Anyway, go over to the fort and speak to the Commandeur. Hurry, Adrian."

He was back in less than twenty minutes. He told her: "Yes, they've landed on Plantation Hooft. The Redoubt Samson[1] was not garrisoned, that's why they came up without any alarm being given before. Commandeur de Waterman says they're advancing along the bank toward the fort." He was a trifle breathless from running. "What are we going to do, Hendrickje?"

"That's what I want you to tell me, Adrian."

He gave her a look of surprise. "I don't understand." Suddenly: "Oh, I see what you mean. The family motto."

"Exactly."

He shrugged. "Well, let's remain—if you think you can brave the danger. They're going to bomb the fort."

[1] Guard-house midway between Fort Nassau and the mouth of the river.

"I'm willing to brave the danger. But are you? Be honest, Adrian."

"Most certainly! Why should you ask that? You don't think I'd run off and leave you here alone, do you?"

"No, I didn't think you would do that." She hesitated, then said quietly: "Adrian, tell me this. Do you feel you ought to remain and fight because of our family traditions—because we're van Groenwegels and don't run from danger?"

He shook his head. "I don't care one jot about our family traditions. I'll stay because you want me to stay."

"I see."

"It's no use my pretending, Hendrickje," he said. "This family pride you've always tried to instill into us is nothing to me. I think it foolish and small—unworthy. Why should we consider ourselves better than other people? It's not right. I haven't forgotten what we all had to suffer at your hands because of your obsessions. You yourself mean a lot to me. I'd do anything for you—bring down the stars if I could—but I'll never forgive you for what you did to Father— and Cornelis. And when I remember that it was because of this fanatic ambition of yours to uphold our name and achieve power for the family I detest the idea of family superiority more than ever."

"You speak sensibly. It hurts—but it's the truth." She turned away, blinking rapidly. He moved after her and put his arms about her. "Don't let it hurt too much," he said. "You know I don't like hurting you."

She nodded, and seemed to steel herself. "Come, let's get busy," she said. "Go and get Rabonne and the others here as quickly as you can. There are the muskets to see after—and the barricades. We mustn't waste time."

"I'll go now and get them."

About an hour later the house was in a ferment. In the middle of their preparations a soldier arrived from the fort. He wanted to know why they had not left yet. "The bombardment may begin at any moment, Mevrouw. The enemy is throwing up earthworks in readiness to lay siege to the fort. The Commandeur has sent me to inquire why you and your people are still here."

Hendrickje told him: "We are defending. Go and tell the Commandeur that. Tell him we in this house are van Groenwegels, and it's our tradition that we never run from an enemy. That's why we're not leaving."

"But, Mevrouw, do you realize the danger? The French have mortars. They are going to hurl explosive bombs at us. Some of the bombs will fall around the house here."

"Very well. That doesn't intimidate us. You go and give the Commandeur my message. Tell him we're van Groenwegels and we never run. Tell him that if we have to die, then we'll die. We are not afraid."

"I shall deliver your message, Mevrouw."

Cornelis, to the surprise of them both, was in no way upset about their decision to remain and fight. He said: "I think it's the best thing to do. We have the muskets and the ammunition. Why should we run?"

Adrian and his mother exchanged glances.

Cornelis, his gaze averted, said: "François was telling me what these bombs are like. He says they are hollow, spherical things with gunpowder inside and a combustible substance that burns down to the powder and sets it off after it has been ejected from the mortar."

Adrian and Hendrickje were silent. Later, when they were alone, Adrian commented: "It doesn't seem like him. I don't feel easy about it."

"What do you mean?"

"Well, is it natural that he should take the situation so calmly? He's always been so girlish and hysterical over the slightest danger, and now that we're faced with this supreme danger he behaves as though he's a general in command, smiling and complacent and brave."

She smiled. "Perhaps it's blood, my boy. We never know. Even he, weak as he is, may still feel the surge of pride that is part of his hereditary background. Blood will always out, Adrian."

"I can't see it that way. I have an instinct in these things, and I feel there's more in it than we can see on the surface. He can be deep, Cornelis. Very deep."

"Don't be imaginative, dear. There's work to be done. Come."

He grunted. "In many ways you can be surprisingly insensitive, Hendrickje. Especially for a woman. You're a strange mixture."

She laughed. There was the old brittle note in it. "Don't let's stop to analyze each other now, Adrian. We're at war. Come, let us see about the barricades in the dining room."

As they worked they could hear a jabber of voices out in the compound where the slaves were gathered in frightened groups discussing the situation. Some of the women whimpered. One wailed: "Frenchman coming to take us all away. We going to punish. We going to punish." Another squatted on the ground, her two small children hugged close; she kept moaning and wagging her head. An old man slapped his white woolly head distractedly with the palms of his hands.

Hendrickje moved upstairs and downstairs in a fever of activity, her eyes bright and hard. She issued orders in a clipped, curt voice. The softness of the past few months had left her, and Adrian thought: You can see this is an occasion she has lived in her imagination time and time again. She is an obsessed being. She must feel she is fulfilling herself. The belligerent ideas Great-grandfather Willem put into her head are flamingly alive today. The fire-blood of Great-great-grandmother Kaywana is blazing magnificently. Perhaps she thinks she is Kaywana reincarnated. Poor thing. I do hope she won't meet the same end. If she got killed I'd have to die with her.

Once, when they happened to be alone in the corridor, he told her: "This is not the fort. This is our home. And these fellows are only slaves. They're not soldiers. You can't treat them as if they were trained military men. You've lost your sense of balance, Hendrickje. Why don't you go to your room and rest?

There's nothing more you can do. The barricades are in place now, and Rabonne and Pardoom and Henwah have the muskets and ammunition in readiness, and the men seem keen up to now, so what's the purpose in your marching up and down the house snapping at them?"

She nodded and smiled. "I think you're right. But I couldn't help it, Adrian. I've lived this occasion so many times in my dreams. A few years ago I envied them in the Essequibo when they were attacked by Ferry and his lot. By God! But it would have been good to have stood by Rosa's side and fired out upon the demons———"

"Aunt Rosa was shot dead before she had got started."

"Adrian, I can't help it. The fighter-blood is strong in me. There is nothing that elates me more than the prospect of a battle. I should have been born a man. Nature made a gross mistake."

He hugged her and laughed. "Yes, I agree. You ought to have been a man." Musket fire came in a spasmodic pop-pop-pop from the fort. He felt her body tense against his own.

"Let's go up into your room," she said. "We'll be able to see better from there."

The house vibrated as a cannon boomed over at the fort.

The slave women, locked in the logies, set up a wailing.

"Those cowardly black sluts!"

"You can't expect them to be like you, Hendrickje." They were in his room. He pointed. "It's beyond those bushes the enemy is building his earthworks." They saw a bluish-white puff of smoke rising above the fort buildings. A boom shook the house again.

When a kitchen slave came up and informed them that it was time to eat, Hendrickje did not want to go downstairs. "Send up something for me," she told the girl curtly. "I can't be bothered to come down."

Adrian said: "Jarra, your mistress and I will be down at once. Bring up nothing."

"Yes, Massa."

The afternoon was quiet. When dusk was coming down, Hendrickje said: "That's odd. What could have happened? What are they waiting for?"

The night was quiet, too, and it was not until about eight the following morning that Rabonne, who had been scouting in the vicinity of the fort, came in and told them: "A soldier tell me they trying to settle de matter without fighting, Massa. De French send a messenger wid a flag and say if de Commandeur wish they can hold parley, but de French say Commandeur de Waterman must strike his flag and surrender first, and de soldier say de Commandeur say he not surrendering. He just send off de messenger to tell de French dat he will defend de fort to de last."

"I should think so!" Hendrickje exclaimed. "The impudence! Why should they imagine the fort would give in without a fight!"

Adrian chuckled. "Everybody isn't as bloodthirsty as you, Hendrickje. I suppose they thought it would be a good plan to offer peace first and so save bloodshed."

"A weak policy! We can only get what we want by fighting for it." Even as she was speaking spasmodic musket fire broke out beyond the bushes, and the house throbbed to the boom of a cannon in the fort. Then from beyond the bushes came a roar and then a loud explosion within the palisades of the fort.

All that morning and afternoon the boom-boom went on. Shortly before noon a bomb lobbed over the fort and crashed down not far from the small water tank. They saw it on the ground sending up a white column of smoke, then it exploded and they heard the ping of the fragments against the cast-iron water tank. during the afternoon another fell in the compound, and this one smashed several windows in the dining room.

Adrian said: "I think we ought to get those women and children out of the logies and send them upriver."

"Why?" asked his mother.

"The logies are only wooden. It isn't fair to have them locked up like cattle in them."

His mother shook her head. "It's too late to think of that. They will have to remain."

"That's a heartless attitude to adopt."

"They must take their chance, Adrian. The fact that we are in a brick building does not mean we are not in danger. At any instant one of those bombs can crash in upon us. If we can take a chance, why can't they?"

He gave in. "I suppose there is some sense in that. I don't think it's fair, all the same, to have them herded together in four logies and locked in. At least the doors should be unlocked."

"And in a trice they'll be out and bolting off into the bush."

Instances of friction between them were frequent. Sometimes he held out bitterly and had his way; sometimes he gave in. Once he told her: "I can see you as you really are now—an icy monster!"

She rapped back: "I'm content to be so. I was born a monster."

There were moments, however, when they softened.

"I don't mean to be churlish, darling, but my nerves are on edge. I'm eager to see what will happen —if they'll launch an attack on us here. Do you think they will, Adrian?"

"We just have to wait," he said, stroking her hair.

"They keep bombarding the fort. Why don't they make a rush?"

He chuckled. "Make a rush and get mown down by the musketeers behind the palisades? You think they're fools?"

"You don't feel afraid, do you, dear?"

He shook his head. "As long as I'm with you I feel perfectly safe. They couldn't kill you. You're immortal."

"It's nice hearing you say that. I do wish I were in a position to protect you. Look! That one fell among the provision patches!"

"I saw it. Hendrickje, I'm getting suspicious of Cornelis."

"Suspicious of him?"

"Yes. He keeps looking out toward the fort in a most peculiar way. It isn't usual. It's as if he were expecting something—or someone."

"What are you trying to say?"

"I'm not certain myself. I suppose it's my imagination—yet, somehow, I'm not satisfied that his behavior is normal."

"The subject of Cornelis doesn't interest me in the slightest, Adrian. He might not exist so far as I am concerned."

"That's how I feel, too—though now and then I do find myself a little sorry for him. Indirectly you are to be blamed for much of his effeminacy. It's the way you brutalized him that made him turn to the Frenchman for affection."

"You may be right, but please don't let us go into that now." After a silence, however, she went on: "His effeminacy was born in him. It's the weak strain in our family. Grandfather always told me about it. He said that his brother Aert was soft—a dreamer and a bookworm. And Grandmother Griselda's father was much the same: the weak, dreamy, artistic type. That's where the weak vein comes from." She spoke seriously. "But thank heaven for you. You belong to the hard side —you and I." He felt her hand moving slowly along his arm and shoulder, not in the usual sensuous way but with a tense suppressed agitation. He could feel the vitality of her as though it were a palpable, tingling thing.

"That's why I haven't given up hope," she said. "You have a lot of me in you, Adrian. You're even precocious as I was precocious—old in mind before your time. If we both work together we can achieve big conquests. In time you'll see with me and my ambitions for the family. Power matters, my boy. It makes a difference whether you're simply an underdog or whether you tower over the heads of your fellow men and can control them at a gesture of your hand."

He gasped and ducked away from the window, dragging her with him, as a bomb thudded in the compound hissing and smoking. It roared, and the house shook. There was the tinkle of glass downstairs.

"Let's go down and find out if they suffered any casualties in the dining room," she said. When they were hurrying along the corridor, they happened to glance into the room Cornelis occupied. The door was wide open, and they saw him. He was standing by a window, gazing intently outside.

Adrian muttered: "See what I was telling you? That's what he has been doing since yesterday. As if he's on the lookout for something or somebody."

"He's watching the fort as we do ourselves. What's strange in that?"

He shrugged but did not argue the point.

They discovered that two men had received cuts from flying glass, neither very seriously, though.

All that night the bombardment continued. The house rocked as though in a perpetual earthquake. Sleep was almost out of the question.

Shortly after midnight, when Adrian was on his way upstairs, he happened to glance toward the sideboard which was barricading one of the dining room windows. He saw a figure, uncertain and shadowy, standing as though on watch. He went down again and approached the sideboard. There was a gasp. "Who is that? Oh, it's you, Adrian! You startled me."

"What are you doing here?"

"I couldn't sleep. I can't sleep in this noise, Adrian, dear. Oh, it's dreadful! I think I'll go off my head if it doesn't stop."

"Why have you come downstairs? If you couldn't sleep, you could have got into bed, at least, couldn't you?"

"I'm going up in a little while. I—I was tired of the room. I was up there all day."

"It's unsafe to stand by the window."

"Yes, Adrian. I'm going upstairs in a few minutes."

As Adrian went upstairs he thought: More and more I don't like his behavior. He's up to some trick, though what it could be baffles me.

His mother was dozing in a chair when he entered the room. She looked unreal in the reddish crepuscle that pervaded the room. Everything in the room looked unreal—and sinister—in the reflected glow from outside. The big four-poster registered most clearly the flashes that heightened the general glow. The tester's billowing whiteness turned red and dimmed off and on.

He heard the heavy breathing of his mother: a sound that contrasted strangely with the background boom of the guns and the roar of exploding bombs. He sank down into a chair and was soon dozing, too. Almost at once, however, he was wide awake again. He heard Cornelis shouting.

"Adrian! Mother!"

Cornelis came bursting in. "Mother! A bomb has struck one of the logies! I believe some of the women and children have been killed!"

Henwah and Pardoom accompanied Adrian and Hendrickje out across the compound to the damaged logie. It was not as serious as it had seemed. They found that part of the roof and a few boards had been shattered, but none of the occupants had been hurt. They were in a screaming, sobbing terror nevertheless, and Adrian said: "We must let them out and find other quarters for them, Hendrickje—the storehouse or the carpenter's shed. They're in misery in there, poor people. Henwah, go and open the storehouse."

"Do nothing of the sort, Henwah. Adrian, are you mad? The storehouse would be in a fine condition if we put them in there! And the carpenter's shed, for that matter."

When they had returned into the house she said to him: "It's no use trying to be generous in the matter. Softness doesn't always pay."

"Always! Never, according to your way of looking at things. You should have had a son like that fellow in Essequibo—Samuel de Haart."

"Jabez's good friend?"

"Yes."

She laughed shortly. "The boy who kills lizards by dangling them over a fire. Well, what's a lizard! Others are coming into the world every minute. Like men. You can wipe out as many as you like, others keep being born to replace the losses." She clutched his arm. "What's that? Did you see?"

"See what?" They were standing at the window.

"Over there." She pointed. "Someone darted from behind the large water tank and ran toward the provision patches."

"I didn't notice."

"I'm sure of it."

"I wonder. . . . Wait a moment. I'm going downstairs."

"Don't go out into the compound, Adrian."

"I'm only going down into the dining room."

On the stairs, he encountered his brother coming up.

"Cornelis! Have you been out?"

"Been out, Adrian?"

"Yes. Have you been out in the compound?"

"No, Adrian! No, no! Why should you think I have!"

"Come upstairs with me into Mother's room."

"Adrian, I didn't go out. I swear it. You must believe me."

"Come with me. Come on." He tugged his brother's arm roughly, and, despite his protests, took him into their mother's room.

"What's this, Adrian? What have you brought him in here for?"

"He's up to some queer business. Earlier tonight I caught him at the window where we've put the sideboard. He was on the lookout for something or somebody we don't know about."

"No, Adrian, no! I swear it! I was watching the battle. I haven't been out of the house. You *must* believe me!"

"What necessity is there for you to swear so vehemently?" said his mother. "That's always a sign of guilt. Adrian, release him. Let him go. Go back to your room, Cornelis—and see you remain there for the rest of the night."

"I haven't been out, Mother. I'm speaking the truth. I was watching the battle. Nothing more."

Hendrickje flashed him a look as he was going. "Did anyone come to the window down there and speak to you?"

"No, Mother! No, no. I swear. No one came to me."

She waved him off. "Get out. Get to your room."

After he had gone she said: "I agree with you. His manner seems peculiar. Don't say anything to him again. We'll keep an eye on him in future. Tell Rabonne and the others."

VII

Shortly before dawn Henwah went out scouting and, on his return, told them that the enemy had almost completely surrounded the fort. "They plenty, Massa. They plenty. De fort can't hold out long. And some o' dem gone off on de plantations and raiding de storehouses. I meet two slaves from Plantation Hooft, and they tell me so. Berbice finish, Missy."

His mistress nodded. "The van Groenwegels aren't finished yet, though, Henwah. They'll realize that when they attempt to attack us here."

Adrian smiled. "Do you think we could hold them off indefinitely, Hendrickje? With mortars and bombs against us?"

"We shall!"

"This isn't 1666. Great-grandfather Willem didn't have to cope with bombs. It might have been a different ending to that story if he had."

"Bombs or no bombs, Adrian, we're standing up to them. If we have to go down then we go down. Very well, Henwah. Go and have something to eat. You're a brave fellow to have ventured out."

"Yes, Missy," smiled Henwah, content on his face; he seemed to have been waiting for the compliment.

After he had gone, Hendrickje said: "Those three men have blood. Pity they are not van Groenwegels. I can depend upon them—more than I can depend upon you and your brother."

"Me?"

"Yes, you. You're too casual. You hold our blood in contempt, Adrian. You would let us down if I didn't stand behind you."

He laughed. "Most certainly I would. I've told you already I care not a jot about the family. I hate the idea—and you yourself are responsible for that. Deep down in me I still hate you for what you did to Father. Deep down in me I want to see you disappointed in your ambitions. It would be a fitting punishment for your sins."

For a moment they stared balefully at each other. It was his gaze that faltered first. He turned off, thinking: Inside me the old hate is still there. Those early years can't be wiped out.

The house jolted. There were shouts downstairs.

"I think it's the kitchen."

They hurried downstairs. They heard Pardoom saying: "Messab and Herruff was inside dere. Come wid me, Rabonne. Help me move away de bricks."

"Pardoom, don't venture in there until the smoke and dust clear!"

Adrian looked out of the window and saw a hole in the kitchen roof.

Pardoom and Rabonne had already gone into the kitchen. Presently Rabonne emerged coughing and gasping, a limp figure in his grasp; a figure dripping blood. Then Pardoom emerged bearing another figure.

On examination, they found that Herruff was dead, his head smashed in. Messab was alive, his legs and chin badly bruised, a cut on his wrist.

All that night the bombardment continued, and throughout the next day, the thirteenth, but no more bombs fell in their vicinity until shortly after seven o'clock in the evening when the darkness near one of the logies suddenly spurted red and roared, and there was the sound of splintering wood and the shrieks of the women and children.

This time there were three fatal casualties, a woman and a boy of about eleven and a two-year-old baby. Two women and a child received leg and face wounds, and Adrian dressed the wounds and had them brought into the house.

"The survivors must be put in the carpenter's shed," he told Pardoom.

Hendrickje raised no objections, but her lips tightened.

A little later, when they were eating, Adrian remarked to her: "Some of the men are beginning to lose heart. That bomb on the logie frightened them a lot."

His mother murmured: "I've observed that."

He glanced at her. "I believe you're afraid, too."

She said nothing, continuing to eat. They were upstairs.

He stretched out and patted her arm. "It shows that you're still a woman, after all. I so like to see you behaving like a human being, Hendrickje. Why can't you be human always?"

They started up. It was a bomb in the provision patches.

"Why can't they do something besides bombard?" she said, as they resumed their seats.

"It's getting on my nerves, too," admitted Adrian.

"Since the eleventh. Tomorrow will be the fourteenth."

"You should try to get some sleep tonight," he said. "Last night you hardly slept. You look older now, Hendrickje."

"Older?" She glanced at him sharply, almost with alarm.

"Yes, you look older. You look your true age. It's the strain of things. This bombardment. I myself feel ten years older." He got up and went to the window. Looked outside.

"Beyond the trees over there they're throwing up fresh earthworks. The fort must be completely surrounded now. Surrender is only a matter of time."

"Don't say that! Don't say that! Never talk defeat!"

"The truth, Hendrickje. Remember your old saying."

She began to walk up and down. Once she paused by the cupboard and pressed her hands to her face. He went up to her and patted her and fondled her—in silence. She began to sob, but by an effort controlled herself.

He watched her with admiration, his face pink with the reflection of the glow outside. He thought: She has a will—a terrible will. One can't help being impressed when one watches her. She's no ordinary person. She has strength. She, at least, of us van Groenwegels can afford to feel conceited about herself. She's an exceptional human. . . .

It must have been about two o'clock when the alarm came.

Henwah told them: "Massa Cornelis jump through de window downstairs and gone off, Missy!"

"Gone off where?" asked Adrian.

"Weren't you keeping a watch on him?"

"Yes, Missy. We was watching him. He come downstairs before midnight and he stand by de window near de sideboard looking out. He not move from dere. But just sudden he force himself past de sideboard and jump outside before we can stop him. We didn't expect him to do dat."

"Which way did he go?"

"He go toward de fort way, Massa. Rabonne gone after him."

"Rabonne has gone after him?"

"Yes, Missy."

"But it's dangerous venturing out that way now. They have earthworks beyond the bushes over there. What could Cornelis want to go that way for? Did you see anyone come up under the window, Henwah?"

"I wasn't looking out at de moment, Missy."

"It's that Frenchman, Hendrickje. I'm sure of it."

"But how could Tirol come here? He would have had to pass through the enemy lines. The fort is completely encircled."

"He could have got here by *corial*. The river side of the fort is not invested."

They waited, their gazes on the provision patches. The guns boomed monotonously. They saw an *awara* palm shattered in the vicinity of the fort, saw its fronds in spattered silhouette against the glow. Then there was only the trunk jutting up ugly and frayed.

After a long while Adrian exclaimed and pointed. "I saw something move near the water tank!"

"Missy, let me go out and take a look around."

"No, Henwah. We can't risk both of you out there."

"Look! I believe it's Rabonne!"

Footsteps drummed on the stairs and Pardoom appeared at the bedroom door. "Massa, Rabonne coming back, but I believe he hurt. I must go out and give him help?"

"Go, Pardoom," said Adrian. "Hurry."

"How do you know he is hurt, Pardoom?" Hendrickje asked anxiously.

"He limping, Missy. He near de large water tank."

"My God! Poor fellow. Henwah, go with Pardoom. Quickly!"

They all went downstairs. Hendrickje and Adrian watched the two men move swiftly across the compound toward the large water tank. In the glow of the battle a dim humped figure was barely visible on the ground near the tank. Hendrickje was breathing quickly, her hand on Adrian's shoulder, her body rigid. Adrian thought: I think if Rabonne had not been a slave she would have allowed him to make love to her. I have noticed her eyes gleaming on many an occasion when she was speaking to him.

Presently they saw Henwah and Pardoom returning. They were carrying something. Hendrickje shouted: "Bring him through the front door! Come round by the portico!"

"Yes, Missy! Coming!"

"Poor fellow. Poor Rabonne. He should never have gone after that piece of trash. He was a fool to have bothered about Cornelis."

"He went after my brother—the trash you produced."

She ignored him.

"I hate you, Hendrickje! Hate you!"

She said nothing. She might not have heard. She helped him to drag away the barricade from the front door.

Rabonne was in a low state. He was bleeding from

a wound in his chest, and seemed injured in his left leg, too.

"Didn't you have a *corial* to follow them, Rabonne?" Adrian asked him, and the man shook his head feebly. "No, Massa. They not go by *corial*. They join Frenchmen over that way." He pointed. His arm collapsed.

"Don't question him, Adrian. He isn't well. Pardoom, go and get some water and lint and bandages."

Adrian, ignoring his mother, said: "I don't understand, Rabonne. They've joined the Frenchmen? What do you mean?"

"Yes, Massa. They join Frenchmen. He and soldier-man Tirol. I see dem together and hear dem talk. They gone over to enemy's side." His voice was very weak. He was evidently in great pain. His breath came in uneven gasps. He asked for some water, but before Pardoom could bring the water Rabonne had coughed and sagged limply over on to his face.

"Missy, he dead," said Henwah.

Hendrickje bathed Rabonne's face with water. She ripped open his overalls, felt for his heart, put her ear to his chest. Henwah was right. He was dead.

Hendrickje went upstairs sobbing.

Adrian thought: What baffles me is what he said before he died. Cornelis and François have gone over to the side of the enemy! He must have been mistaken. And yet, isn't François a Frenchman? Is it so unlikely that he might have come to the decision to betray his fellow Dutch soldiers and go over to his countrymen's side—especially as the fort is surrounded and the situation seems so hopeless for the defenders? But why did he have to involve Cornelis in his desertion? Why couldn't he have left Cornelis alone? I wonder if Cornelis knew that François had intended to desert. Perhaps he did know. Perhaps François took him into his confidence since the day the alarm came. Cornelis was over at the fort with François when the news reached the Commandeur. Or perhaps it was two nights ago that François came here and communicated to Cornelis what he intended to do. Poor Cornelis. He must have been overjoyed at the prospect of getting away from this house. He was only tolerated here. I wonder if he and François mean to go away with these privateers. Perhaps that is their plan. . . .

He went into his mother's room and said: "You're sobbing for Rabonne—a slave—and for your own son you don't even enquire. I'm ashamed of you, Hendrickje."

He left the room again and returned downstairs. He was crossing the dining room when the roar came. The house seemed to tilt over. A fog of fumes and dust came billowing down the stairs. He heard a muffled scream.

Without a thought to danger, he went leaping up the stairs. Halfway up he stumbled and fell and rolled down three or four treaders, coughing and gasping. The stairs were strewn with bricks and mortar. He heard Henwah and Pardoom shouting up at him, heard their footsteps and the footsteps of the other men. He got up and tried to continue upstairs through the dense fog of dust. He called his mother's name as he went. Presently he collided with the wall in the corridor. Then he heard her voice and came into collision with the softness of her.

"Hendrickje, are you hurt?"

"No. It wasn't in my room. It fell in your."

"Let's go downstairs."

"No, no. Come into my room."

"Missy! Massa! You all right?"

Adrian felt a groping hand on his chest. He grabbed it. "Yes, Pardoom, we're safe. Bring up a lamp."

There was a confusion of voices on the stairs. Thuds and coughs.

Adrian found himself in his mother's room. He saw the tester glowing and dimming. A thin cloud of dust swirled about in the room. He lit two candles that stood in brass holders on the table beside the bed.

"I thought you had been hit, Hendrickje. I thought you had been killed."

"Adrian, you're dusty."

"You, too. My God, but suppose you had been killed, Hendrickje!"

They heard bricks and dust and mortar coming down in the next room.

"We must get out of this house, Hendrickje."

"No. Never! Don't say that, Adrian. Don't say that!"

Pardoom arrived with a lamp. Adrian told him not to bother. "Take it away. I forgot there were candles in here." His voice shook. Footsteps came. Henwah asked: "Missy, you not hurt?"

"No, Henwah. Thanks for asking."

He and Pardoom and the others went.

"Hendrickje, we have to leave this house. The next bomb mightn't be so kind to us. We can't stay. It's foolhardy. We can't fight against bombs."

"We're remaining. Adrian, you mustn't mention such a thing to me. Don't speak of running. We don't run. We're van Groenwegels. Haven't I driven that into you time and time again? How can you suggest that we should flee!"

"You're a fool. If you don't agree to leave I'll go alone. We can't stay here for the sake of a foolish tradition. Why can't you rid yourself of that absurd nonsense!"

She struck him in the face. "Don't dare to say that again! It's not nonsense, Adrian!"

"I do say it. Nothing but vain, crass stupidity! You'll leave this house now! We'll all leave. It's dangerous to remain. Common sense should tell you that."

"I don't care what common sense says. I remain. Go, if you wish. Go and leave me. I'm a van Groenwegel, by God! I'm no poltroon. No bomb will frighten me from my home. I'll stay here and die. You go. Take all the slaves with you and go. I give you permission to take my lieutenants, too, if you wish. Take them all! Pardoom and Henwah! Go! Get out of the house!"

"Very well. The decision is yours. We remain." He spoke quietly, gripped her arm and told her to sit down and compose herself. She sat down and sobbed.

"If only they would stop bombarding! I feel distracted, Adrian. Distracted. I didn't anticipate this. I thought they would have attacked with muskets—as in '66. I didn't reckon with bombs."

"Never mind. Don't let us think of it, Hendrickje. Look, there's dust in your ears." He gave a jerky laugh, soft and affectionate.

A bomb exploded outside.

"It seems like one of the logies," she said.

"I believe they've changed their direction of fire. Why should the bombs be dropping here so frequently now?"

"Let's go downstairs. It will be safer in the sitting room."

"Hendrickje."

"Yes?"

"I wonder."

"What do you wonder?"

"I believe François has revealed the weak spots in the fort, and they're concentrating on them. There are one or two weak spots. Dirk has told me of them more than once when we discussed a possible attack on the fort. It's that, Hendrickje. That traitor François! He's deserted to the enemy, and he's told them, and now they're centering all their fire on the vulnerable points."

"And that is the filthy rogue a son of mine has run off with! And you expect me to be sorry for him! Let's go downstairs. Come on."

Downstairs they found the men in groups discussing the situation. Many of them were in a funk. Henwah and Pardoom were shouting at them, telling them to get back to their places, threatening to have them flogged if they did not obey.

In the midst of the shouting a bomb landed in the compound, and bricks and mortar fell in a prattling shower in the already damaged kitchen. Also upstairs in Adrian's room.

"Missy, we can't stay in here no longer. House soon smash up."

"We must go in bush and hide, Missy."

"Plenty danger now, Massa. Massa Adrian, let us go in bush. Please, Massa! No use stay here longer."

Adrian's only response was to smile vaguely.

Henwah and Pardoom began to use their whips. And Hendrickje shouted.

The men moved back to their places at the barricades, but they grumbled. One of them said audibly: "Missy never treat us good. Why we should stay in house and fight for her?"

Adrian glanced quickly at his mother to note her reaction to this remark. She remained unmoved. She had a strange, barbaric beauty, he thought, watching her as she stood in the middle of the room, dusty and unkempt, her hair in a shifty mass about her shoulders and fuzzy around her temples and forehead. She looks real and solid in this dawn light. But at this moment I feel nothing tender for her. I'm merely glad that she's suffering discomfiture at the hands of these fellows. I won't move a finger to support her. I hope they will continue to be unruly. I hope they insist on leaving the house and going into the bush. I want to see her foiled, humiliated. . . .

She said to him: "Adrian, go upstairs and bring my whip. Quickly! I'm going to show these brutes whether I'll tolerate any insolence."

He went off, smiling to himself. On his way down he heard the portico collapse with a rumble as a bomb exploded in its vicinity. The house rocked. By the time he reached the dining room many of the slaves were already through the windows and scampering across the compound. His mother shouted in vain. Pardoom and Henwah slashed, and bawled themselves hoarse, but to no avail. The stampede had begun, and there was no stopping it. Within a few minutes only three of the slaves remained in the house besides Pardoom and Henwah. Discarded muskets lay at all angles on the floor.

"Get the barricades back into place!" shouted Hendrickje. "We aren't beaten yet."

She herself helped to push the furniture back into place before the windows, her face pale and determined. Dust fell from her skirt and bodice in desultory dribbles. When some sort of order had been restored she said that she was going upstairs, but Adrian tried to stop her.

"You know it's dangerous up there. At any moment a bomb can land on the roof and smash down into the bedroom."

She shrugged off his hand. "I'll chance the bombs. Don't try to stop me."

He saw that it was useless to argue with her, so accompanied her up. She lay down on the bed and gazed up at the tester. The steady pink light of dawn coated the tester's billowing whiteness.

Outside, the boom-boom continued.

Adrian lay down beside her, telling himself: I wonder what it would be like to see those rafters cave in and splinter and to have this whole room explode about us. At any instant it can happen, but I won't be afraid. If it is destined to happen nothing can stop it. I think Father became a fatalist before he died. . . .

Whoo-oom!

Another one in the compound.

"Hendrickje, are you afraid?" He touched her wrist.

She made a sound in the negative.

"It's nothing to be ashamed about. I am—a little."

"Wait—quiet. What's that?"

"What's what?"

"Listen!"

They listened.

"It's coming from the fort."

"It sounds like a drum."

He sat up. "I wonder if it could be the chamade."

"The what?"

"The chamade. Dirk has told me of it. He says that when a beleagured fort decides to surrender the Commandeur gets the Drummer to beat the drum. It's called a chamade, and it means that the Commandeur is ready to call a truce and discuss terms with the enemy."

She said nothing.

"It's a drum," he said. "It's the chamade."

"The cannon in the fort has stopped firing for some time now."

After a while he murmured: "See that? The French guns have stopped."

The dull thump of the drum alone came now. It sounded lonely and portentous and sad.

It might be speaking to us, thought Adrian, telling

us that this is the beginning of a new phase for us. I wonder what's going on in Hendrickje's thoughts. I wonder if she knows now that we're beaten and that she will have to behave from today like one of the vanquished. . . .

"Missy! Massa!" It was Pardoom.

"Yes, Pardoom?"

"Massa, de guns stop yonder."

"Yes, so I've observed."

"Massa, I can go out and hear what happen?"

Hendrickje sat up. "No, Pardoom. It will be dangerous. Wait until later. They may launch an attack against us. We haven't surrendered yet."

After the man had gone Adrian smiled: "Hendrickje, do you still insist in thinking that we can hold out here?"

She said nothing.

"Surely you must know that we are beaten."

"I know nothing of the sort!" she snapped. "What I know is that we are van Groenwegels, and we never surrender." She got off the bed and began to pace about with firm, precise steps.

He smiled and thought: She is certainly not normal. Her mind is warped. Now I know it without doubt.

"You'll fight without me," he told her. "You and your heroes downstairs. I'm not ready to die for the family traditions."

"Do you mean that, Adrian? You would walk out of this house and leave me?"

"I do mean that. You seem surprised, but I'm serious. I spit on the family traditions. I'm glad to see them in the dust."

VIII

The test did not come until some time after two o'clock that day. A soldier came from the fort and told them: "The colony has capitulated, and the Commandeur requests that you gather your valuables together, including slaves and all other effects of any worth. The French officers will call at any moment to take tally, and the Commandeur requests that you will give them all help and not obstruct them in any way."

He delivered this message to Hendrickje at the kitchen door, and Hendrickje told him: "You may go back and tell the Commandeur, my man, that French officers will cross this threshold at their peril. You can tell him, further, that nothing belonging to us will be surrendered without a bitter, bloody struggle. Tell him that van Groenwegels live in this house, and it is our tradition that we stay and defend our property to the last. Go and tell him that."

"But, Mevrouw———"

He was silenced by Adrian, who called: "Just a moment, my man!" and came toward them across the rubble on the kitchen floor. He said to the soldier: "You won't deliver any such message to the Commandeur. You'll tell him that we thank him for his message and would like to inform him that his instructions will be carried out and that we shall cooperate in every way possible. Tell him that the master of the house gave you that message. Go!"

The man looked from him to his mother.

Hendrickje turned. She called to Pardoom and Henwah, and they came at once. "Seize Massa Adrian and have him securely bound. Take him upstairs into the southeastern bedroom."

Adrian laughed.

Pardoom and Henwah made no move to obey.

"Pardoom! Henwah! Did you hear me speak?"

Pardoom muttered something inaudible, burrowing a shallow hole in the dust with his big toe. Henwah said: "Missy, you can't expect us to do dat. He Massa here. You always tell us obey him."

Pardoom nodded agreement.

"Do I understand that you are refusing to obey me?"

They were silent. Pardoom was still making holes in the dust with his big toe.

Adrian stood leaning against the doorpost, his arms folded.

The soldier gazed from one to the other of them.

Adrian turned his head slightly of a sudden and jerked his thumb in the direction of the dining room. "Pardoom! Henwah! Get back inside. When I want you I'll call you."

The two men went in.

Hendrickje followed them but said nothing to them. She went straight through the dining room and up the dusty, brick-strewn stairs.

Adrian smiled at the soldier and asked: "What are the terms of capitulation?"

"They haven't been settled yet, Mynheer."

"Who is the commanding officer of the French ruffians? Have you heard? Is it Cassard himself?"

"No. Cassard himself has not come. The force is under one Baron de Mouans. He and some of his officers are over at the fort now conferring with Commandeur de Waterman and the Governing Council."

"By the way, have you heard anything of my elder brother, Mynheer Cornelis van Groenwegel?"

"Isn't he at home here with you, Mynheer?"

"No. He disappeared from the house early this morning."

A look of enlightenment came to the man's face. "Then it was he who fired upon one of our scouts! François Tirol deserted us, Mynheer. He went over to the enemy and gave away our weak points, and one of our scouts reported that he was in the company of a civilian whom he could not recognize in the dark. They both had pistols, and the civilian fired upon Jan, but fortunately missed."

"And you've heard nothing more of him?"

"No, Mynheer. Nothing more."

"Very well. Thank you. Go and deliver my message to the Commandeur."

He watched the man go, then went upstairs, taking his time. He opened the door of his mother's room and saw her. She stood by the window staring out. She did not turn to look at him. He thought: This is my moment of gloating. How happy I am to see her beaten. This is some of the revenge I have always wished for. Cruel, hateful bitch! Yet look at her! Like a goddess. So full of regal dignity. So aloof and beautiful. She'll never forgive me for what I've done this day, but what do I care about her forgiveness? I hold the whip now. I'm master. She doesn't dare treat me like a boy now. Pardoom and Henwah made her see in very clear fashion how she stands in relation to me. Good fellows. Her own lieutenants letting her down and supporting me. Yes, Hendrickje, this is a moment of triumph for me. Father is avenged in some measure. And Cornelis, poor fellow. . . .

A few weeks later he wrote to Jabez and told him: "She and I are mere acquaintances now. The deep companionship I spoke of in my previous letters is no more. She is too bitter against me for having let down the family, for having surrendered our goods without a struggle. I admit we had to pay heavily, for Baron de Mouans and his rogues were a greedy lot. The terms of capitulation were harsh. The demands of this Frenchman and his men were so heavy that Commandeur de Waterman and the Council at first refused to meet them. But Baron de Mouans threatened to burn every plantation down and destroy the whole colony. The final upshot was that it was agreed to pay the Frenchman half the amount demanded—300,000 guilders. But the difficulty was how was this sum to be paid, for, as you must know, there is very little actual cash in the colony, sugar being our standard of exchange most of the time. Eventually, de Mouans agreed to take all the Company sugar together with some slaves, stores and a barque, all of which amounted to 118,024 guilders in value. For the balance of the sum they have accepted a bill of exchange drawn by the Commandeur and the Council on the van Peeres in Holland to the order of Baron de Mouans. But this wasn't the end of the affair, for de Mouans considered this 300,000 guilders merely a ransom on the Company plantations and the fort. For the estates and goods of us private planters he demanded 10,000 guilders in cash, this as prize money to be distributed among the officers and men of the squadron. Naturally, 10,000 guilders in cash could not be found, so we had to collect all the plate and jewelry we had in our

possession and hand it over, the value of this coming
up to about 6,000 guilders. The balance we had to pay
in sugar and slaves. We of ourselves have lost a quarter
of all the slaves we possessed before the attack (including the casualties we suffered during the bombardment)....

"At the moment we are preparing to leave for the
Canje plantation which, as I have mentioned in a previous letter, is in a very poor state of cultivation. However, we still have Henwah and Pardoom and one or
two good workers, and with the few on the Canje, it is
likely we shall soon be on the way to recovery again.
It is on my urging that we have decided on this move.
My argument is that we are too near the fort and I
can see no sense in remaining here to be in danger
again if future attacks should be launched against the
colony. Our other plantation is on the upper reaches of
the Canje and should be fairly safe from pillaging invaders.... She is hurt but resigned to the change, and
now and then I feel remorseful when I watch her face.
I want to console her, but I control myself, for I see
now that I must never be soft toward her again. I
must be firm and hard if I am to have my own way.
I have my infatuation well in hand....

"One day you must arrange to come and visit us
on the Canje. I wish I could come and see you all in
Essequibo, but the situation here being what it is, I can
never hope to be able to leave the colony. I must never
give her the slightest opportunity to gain the upper hand
over the slaves. I must always be on the spot to handle
affairs. Already I can see that the future will bring more
friction and a continual battle of wits, but I mean to
be the one who will triumph....

"We have seen or heard nothing of Cornelis or
François Tirol since Cornelis disappeared. This is the
one aspect of the affair that grieves me deeply, but I
try to console myself with the thought that the poor
fellow is happier where he is now. As for Hendrickje,
she is only upset because of the bad light it casts on
the family name! Think of a van Groenwegel being
party to such an act! A van Groenwegel in the company of a traitor and deserter! People have dropped ugly

remarks, and that adds to her bitterness. But how glad I am to see her suffer. In future one of the things I shall work for is to destroy the memory of the old days and the deeds of our ancestors. I could never describe the terrible hate that boils up in me whenever I think of what Father and Cornelis and I had to go through at Mother's hands because of this family superiority mania. I shall live to wipe it away, to poison the minds of my children against it. . . ."

VII Rosaria

I

CASSARD had not troubled Essequibo, and the plantations there were in a fair state of prosperity. The epidemic[1] which broke out in 1716 took off Gertruyt and Luise, though it helped to make Commandeur van der Heyden Resen decide to build his new Colony House —the Huis Naby (the house near by), as he called it —at Cartabo, for Kyk-over-al had become overcrowded and conditions on the island, generally, were definitely contributive to the spread of the epidemic. Katrina and Aert also fell ill but recovered.

"Mother and myself are made of tough material," Aert wrote. "No plague can take us off easily. It's extremely sad, all the same, about poor Gertruyt and Luise. Luise had practically made up her mind, at long last, to marry. The bridegroom was to have been Set Roost from down-river. . . . Uncle Reinald was seventy last May, and is still very much alive, despite his vacant demeanor and his perpetual soliloquizing. One day last week we heard him shouting and rushed into the study to find him standing before the bookshelves waving his arms about and crying frantically: 'Get back to your posts! They're coming toward the tanks! Fire on them before they get behind! Quick! I beseech you! Quick!' Then of a sudden he ceased his gesticulations and smiled in his dreamy fashion and wagged his head and turned off. . . ."

Reinald lived to see his eightieth birthday. He refused to die. He could recognize no one, and hobbled around the house as though he were the only occupant, but ate and smoked like a normal, healthy man of sixty. He reminisced aloud in his armchair, and, sometimes, did a little reading, for his sight remained perfect.

"I believe he will live to a greater age than old Adriansen," Jabez told Adrian in a letter. "Everybody

[1] Probably typhus, though the records do not specify.

336

else dies, but he goes on. Uncle Hendrik, Aunt Octavia's husband, who died last year, was only forty-three, and if Grandmother Katrina had lived just seventeen more days she would have been seventy-five. Even Commandeur de Heere, who succeeded van der Heyden Resen, seems as though he won't last much longer, for he has cancer and suffers a great deal of pain. All the elderly people are dying off one after the other, but old Great-uncle Reinald survives year upon year like a sandbox tree, though, of course, he hasn't the sturdy look of a sandbox. Perhaps I should liken him to one of those slim-trunked palms that grow to such a height and are supposed to live for over a hundred years. . . ."

As it happened, this was the last letter Jabez was to write to Adrian, for it was not more than three weeks after dispatching it that a big event took place. An event vital in the history of the family.

At twenty-eight Jabez was still an unmarried man, like his good friend, Samuel de Haart. He was of medium height, with a round, cheerful face like his mother's, and dark, sleek hair like Aert's. At the time of the occurrence he was betrothed to Antonia de Fruizt, a niece of Hendrik de Fruizt, Octavia's second husband, now deceased, but as Samuel had remarked: "Jabez isn't in love with Antonia. He's marrying her because his father insists that he must carry on the family name. Jabez and myself were born to be bachelors. Polygamy is our specialty."

Jabez and Samuel were notorious. There was hardly a young female slave on the two plantations with whom they had not been intimate.

It was Rosaria, a half-breed slave—half Carib, half Spanish—who caused the trouble. She had come from the Orinoco with five other slaves, for by a proclamation nine years before (in 1717) each planter was allowed to have six Indian slaves who might be got by purchase or barter from the Orinoco. Rosaria belonged to the de Haarts, and she was an unusually alluring girl.

Jabez was on his way one afternoon to the de Haart home (the two plantations adjoined each other). He moved along the track that led through the coffee fields, his pace leisurely and his round, pink face composed and content, for the day's work was over and he and Samuel would smoke a pipe and discuss the tiger[1] hunt they had planned for the following week (tigers had been worrying the livestock on the de Haarts' plantation).

Abruptly, however, his face lost its composure.

Coming toward him was the half-breed girl, Rosaria. He had seen her about the house at the de Haarts', but this was the first time he had encountered her in the open. She had arrived only two or three weeks ago, and he wondered whether Samuel had tackled her yet. She looked extremely promising, and the calico smock she wore hardly concealed the points and curves beneath. She had a lovely olive complexion. It was not often you saw that type of complexion among the slaves. The slaves of negro-white admixtures had a different kind of olive—a muddy olive. But this girl had pink mixed with her duskiness. He decided to test her out.

This, as it happened, was not difficult, for as they were getting near to each other he saw her smile, her black eyes beginning to twinkle with a wanton invitation.

"Are you going to our house, Rosaria?"

She nodded and made a creamy sound. "Yes. I take the letter and this the bottle of wine to your father, the Señor van Groenwegel. The Señor de Haart, he send it." She spoke a mixture of Spanish and Dutch, but he found it easy to understand. He liked it, and thought it extremely quaint.

"Yes, I heard your Massa when he promised to send my father a sample of the new wine he's brewed." He smiled and fondled her under the chin. "Are you in a hurry to deliver it, Rosaria? Sit down with me for a while in the shade here and let's talk. Tell me about life on the Orinoco."

She accompanied him to a secluded spot some distance from the track. The coffee trees made a cool shelter from the sharp four o'clock sun. He asked her

[1]Called a tiger locally, but actually a species of tiger-cat.

whether Samuel had had anything to do with her, and she said no. "I not like de Señor Samuel. He too cruel. He beat the slaves in the fields with iron on the ends of his whip. He very bad." She uttered her creamy sound, moistened her lower lip and murmured: "But you, I like you the plenty much, yes. You look like one man I know on the *llanos*. He make me the much-big sweet when he hold me."

Her quaintness fascinated him, excited him more than he had ever known himself to be. Some minutes later she put up no resistance when he attempted to pull off her smock. She merely chuckled with a husky-mellow, exotic sound. Her long black hair smelt of cinnamon. It was obvious that this was nothing new to her.

They spent a long time together, and she was like a wriggling snake of charm that had lured him into a magic valley. He kept breathing in her cinnamon fragrance. It eclipsed the smell of the earth under them; the smell of the dry leaves and the leafy chill in the air when twilight began to close around them.

When, eventually, he parted with her, taking the letter and bottle of wine to deliver them himself to his father, he felt as though he had emerged from an enchantment. The ground seemed violet and blue and mauve, the coffee trees a dazzle of emerald green in the reflected orange and pink in the western sky. And there was the scent of cinnamon on his hands and on his clothes.

By secret contrivances they succeeded in meeting again and again under the coffee trees, meeting always in the day time, morning or afternoon, when Rosaria could slip away during an idle hour. Sometimes it was only for a few brief minutes, for she had to be careful that her absence was not remarked. "The Señor Samuel, he give me the funny eye one time, two time," she told him once. "I have to make my way the very careful."

"Don't be afraid. The Señor Samuel doesn't know we meet. We're good friends. He would have given himself away by now if he had suspected. But are you sure he has never attempted to take you into the store-house, Rosaria? An attractive creature like you? I can't understand Samuel being blind to your charms."

She shook her head. "He never take me. He look at me that way the many time, but me? No, no. I give him back the bad look and move off quick, quick, quick."

Jabez, despite his experience with slave women, was a naïve fellow. He believed her. It never occurred to him that she could be a snake in mentality as well as in bodily motions. Every night she met Samuel in the de Haart storehouse, and she surrendered herself to him with such eagerness and delight that Samuel gave himself the credit for having won her affections by sheer masculine technique and not by authority as her slave master. She so enchanted him, too, that, like Jabez, he would never have dreamt that she could give herself with equal willingness to another man, especially as she had particularly begged him not to tell anyone that she met him in the storehouse. "I not like everybody know I make sweet with you. The other slaves, they treat me not so good if they know. They turn jealous and give me the bad time without you know."

Inevitably, however, Jabez and Samuel shocked each other.

One day, after the love meetings had been going on for nearly a month, Samuel happened to let fall a hint to Jabez while he and Jabez sat smoking their after-lunch pipes on the back veranda of the van Groen-wegel home. After seeing after the midday meals for the field slaves, Samuel generally dropped in at the van Groenwegel home.

The two of them had been talking, as they not infrequently did, of their amorous experiences, when Samuel smiled his sly, thin-lipped smile and said: "I may tell you, however, that there's one I never speak about. She's sacrosanct. Believe me, Jabez, I think I'd commit murder for her."

"Is there anything you wouldn't commit murder for?"

"No, but I mean it. She's something exceptional. I can't explain it. And she never makes a fuss, that's the best part of it. I have her every night in the storehouse, and she's always there waiting for me. She's never failed me once."

Jabez smiled. "Mine is like that—the present one. Luscious thing. I can honestly say I haven't come across any like her before. Her hair smells like a Persian garden."

"That's an odd coincidence. Mine has a distinctive smell about her hair, too. A sort of cinnamon smell."

Jabez started. "A cinnamon smell! I don't believe it!"

Samuel guffawed. "You don't? It's true, though. I can't imagine what she uses in her hair, but long after I leave her my hands and person retain that cinnamon smell."

Jabez continued to stare at him. At length he said slowly: "Has she got long black hair?"

"That's right. How did you guess? What's the matter? You're as pale as a jumbie."

Jabez smiled a sickly smile, and leaned back in his chair. "Samuel, I believe we've both been making thorough fools of ourselves."

"What are you driving at?"

"Does the girl you meet in your storehouse happen to be the half-breed one who arrived with that batch you people got from the Orinoco a month or two ago? The one called Rosaria?"

"That's right, Rosaria." Samuel went gray. "What are you trying to tell me now, Jabez?"

"Surely you've guessed. Rosaria is the girl I'm meeting, too. I've been having her in the coffee fields practically every day for the past three or four weeks."

There was a silence. In the sitting room Mathilde and Flora were laughing over some pleasantry. Outside, the river kept up its hollow murmur, and from Kyk-over-al came a dull sound that might have been the carpenters at work, or packing cases being moved from one storehouse to another. A tent-boat was moving slowly toward Cartabo, probably taking an official to the Huis Naby.

"What right have you to interfere with our slaves, Jabez?"

"That's foolish."

"It isn't. You're a miserable dog. I never thought you could have stooped to this, Jabez. You have no honor."

"Who are you to talk about honor?"

"You know very well that we have an unwritten law between us that we never trouble each other's slave women except by special permission."

"Yes, I know. And have you always observed that law? How many times haven't you poached on my preserves behind my back! You think Jalwa and Harmah and Betsy have never told me how you've waylaid them aback of our provision patches? I never said anything, because—well, you're a friend, and I have a sense of humor."

"But Rosaria is new. She has just come. At least, you could have waited until I got tired of her. You must have known I would have wanted her to myself for a while."

"She told me that you hadn't tackled her, and that she didn't like you." He fidgeted about in his chair. "Anyway, she's an attractive little bitch, Samuel. I couldn't resist her, and I'm certain if you had been in my place you would have been just as lacking in scruples."

Samuel rose. He was scowling. "You're a miserable dog, Jabez! That is all I have to say. From this day you can go to hell. I'll never set foot in this house again—and don't ever come near me."

"All over that half-breed slut! Samuel, I'm surprised at you!"

Samuel left without another word.

II

From that day they ceased to be friends. But this did not prevent Jabez from meeting Rosaria in the coffee fields. On the very day following the quarrel he met her. She was frightened and tearful, and there were red weals on her back and a blue-black mark on her temple. She told him: "The Señor Samuel, he know we come here to make sweet. He the very angry with me. He not tell me why, but I know it is because he find out we come here. Somehow he make the find out, and he beat me and beat me and give me the hard blow in the face. He call me one big dirty slut, yes."

Jabez consoled her. "The Señor Samuel is cruel. He has always been cruel. Since he was a boy. We had a quarrel yesterday."

"You tell him I meet you here, not so?"

He shrugged. "It came out in the course of conversation. I didn't tell him purposely. He happened to mention the cinnamon smell in your hair and that caused everything to come out."

She stared at him.

"I didn't think I would have seen you today. You're brave, Rosaria. You've still come to meet me in spite of the beating he gave you?"

She pouted. "Me? I not afraid one thing when I want to make sweet with the man. I walk in the danger the most bad to meet the man to make sweet. Yes, I say that true."

"You lied to me, though. You told me that the Señor Samuel had never troubled you and that you had never been with him in the storehouse."

"That's because I afraid you not want me if I tell you about the Señor Samuel. When I want the man I tell any lie, yes. That true." She made a mellow sound, twinkling at him with her large black eyes and fondling him. "That's how I make, Massa Jabez. Man all I take interest in, yes."

He laughed. "Yes, I think I understand your outlook."

So the meetings between them continued. Samuel made no attempt to stop them. He met Rosaria in the storehouse every night as before, but, unlike before, was brutal. He was familiar with her responses, and knew what gave her pleasure, and when, and purposely, at the precise moment, would deny her, so that some nights when he left her she cursed him in her frustration. She began to hate him with a cold, animal hate. But still she never failed to meet him.

"One night I kill him, sure, sure, yes," she told Jabez. "He the very bad man. He take me and he do things to me and make me get the very hot, and then he not want to give me what I want. That I never pardon, no! I kill him bad one night. Wait! Sure, sure I do it. I only meet him now because he massa."

"Are you sure that's the only reason? Or is it that you secretly like his teasing and always live in hope that he will satisfy you?"

"No. I hate him the most bad," she said, avoiding his gaze. Suddenly she smiled. "You. You give it to me good. I like you. When I come to you I forget him far away, yes."

Night after night she bore with Samuel, reveling in the perverted game of frustration, and hoping to outwit him and thereby extract a new ecstasy from her relation with him. One night, however, when she imagined that she had won and her whole being was on the brink of a tortured whine of pleasure, Samuel, with a technique perfected to a nicety, thwarted her.

She flamed up savagely, crying: "I kill you if you let go now. I kill you!" She fought to hold him, but his strength told. He uttered low, cold quarkings as he released her gradually and with a demonic callousness.

Suddenly she heaved herself up. Her jaws snapped shut to the accompaniment of the snarl that gurgled out of her. She bit a chunk of flesh clean out of his cheek.

Tearing herself from his embrace, she ran out of the storehouse, the sobbing howl of pain trailing after her in the dark.

That night Samuel did not sleep. He lay awake and planned. He hatched schemes of vengeance, trying to convince himself that it was Jabez who had put Rosaria up to doing this injury to him. He swore to himself that he would make Jabez pay for what had happened tonight. But for Jabez she would never have dared to show such fury—she a slave. It was Jabez who had put rebellion into her. Jabez must be poisoning her mind against him, the filthy cur! Meeting her every day in the coffee fields. Very well. He would give him something he would remember for a long time. He would teach him to interfere with other people's slaves.

Two days later, by a previous arrangement, Jabez and Rosaria met in the coffee fields. It was midmorning, and the sky alive with large masses of gray-white clouds that drifted southward, dimming the sunshine off and on. The coffee trees rustled in the wind, and the air was cool with leafy scents.

"I have exactly forty minutes, Rosaria. I'm in charge of two gangs in Fields Eight and Nine." He stopped speaking abruptly as he noticed the expression on her face. He frowned at her inquiringly, and after a moment asked: "What has happened now? Did he give you an extra big beating?"

When she told him what she had done to Samuel he exclaimed: "He must be like a tiger! He's extremely vain about his looks."

"He bad man," she said. "I make him suffer every time he trouble me and not give me the sweetness I want. Last night I not go to meet him, and this morning he not look at me or say nothing. He got big piece plaster on his cheek." She laughed creamily. "My teeth, they leave mark on his face for the always."

In the shade of the coffee trees it was pleasant. The foliage made a joyous sizzling above them, and the sunshine moved in small, shifty patches on their legs and feet. They saw no reason to anticipate danger.

Jabez told her: "I could live with you forever under these trees."

"I, too. You make sweet more sweet than any other the man I have."

"How many men have you had before, Rosaria?"

"I not count. One-two-three all about. Man is all I want, yes. That all I take the interest in."

"I've noticed that. Perhaps one of these days soon I'll talk to Mynheer de Haart and see if I can't arrange to buy you over."

"That the thing you say at this moment. The weeks go past and you get tired with me and take other girl, and I have to go about to look for the other man to give me the sweetness."

"No, I don't think I could put you aside now. You fascinate me too much. This scent of yours. Who could ever forget it! It isn't only cinnamon. There's something else mixed with it—something that is you and only you. You're the most singular woman I've ever met. I mean that."

"That talk, it is too far away for me," she smiled.

They were at the peak of their rapture when a crackle of dry leaves sounded on the ground. Before Jabez could turn his head he felt a jolt and a flash of pain. Lights sparked, and a dull singing rocked his brain. Then darkness.

Rosaria gasped, trying to scramble apart. She had a glimpse of Samuel's plastered face hovering above her. A dark blot whizzed at her. She heard a hum, saw a whirl of jewels in her head. Then blackness.

When Jabez came to, he was aware of a burning, insistent pain. He could not be certain what it was, but did not trouble. He rubbed his forehead, feeling the bump. There was a lazy weakness in his limbs. The coffee trees rustled on in the breeze and the sun dimmed as a cloud drifted by. Eventually, it was the insistent pain that drew his attention away from the idyllic quality of the day and brought his senses fully alive.

His hand groped toward the area of the pain. He uttered a snarling cry, tried to sit up, but went dizzy again. He saw his blood, saw and knew the calamitous thing that had happened to him.

Beside him Rosaria moaned and stirred.

"Rosaria."

She opened her eyes and sat up. "The Señor Samuel," she muttered. "He come and strike us, yes. I see him." Then full intelligence came. She looked down and saw the blood on him, saw what had been done to him. She screamed and clapped her hand to her face.

"*Dios! Dios mio!* Look! Look what he do to you! *Dios mio!*"

She sprang up, wringing her hands.

"Go and get help. I'm weak." He moaned and lapsed into a faint.

When the whole story of the events leading up to Samuel's fiendish deed broke upon the two households both families were horrified. Rosaria had not hesitated to talk, and Samuel, faced with the charge of his villainy, had no defense whatever. The wound on his cheek where Rosaria had bitten him stood as proof of the truth of the girl's story, in which she told of his behavior in the storehouse.

Samuel's uncle had him strung up by his wrists from the branch of a tree, and before all the slaves his uncle gave him twenty lashes. He was sent to sea, and his uncle told him that he must never set foot in his house again.

When Jabez recovered from the wounds that had rendered him a eunuch he told his parents that he did not want to remain in Essequibo. "I can't face anyone here again," he said. "I'll go to Berbice. Adrian has often expressed a wish to have me there."

III

Unlike the house near Fort Nassau, the Canje place was wooden. There were five large bedrooms, and, downstairs, besides the dining room and sitting room, a back and front veranda, the latter being added when Adrian and Hendrickje came to live here in 1713. The plantation was in a flourishing state—like all the other plantations on the upper Canje. Coffee, which had been introduced in 1721, was the chief product, though indigo was also grown, and sugarcanes.

At fifty-five, Hendrickje was still free of wrinkles. Even the tiny ones under her eyes had not deepened perceptibly. Only her hair had aged; there were several strands of gray—not enough to detract from the youthful smoothness of her face but enough to betray the fact that her beauty was in its final struggle with the years. Her figure had lost none of its shapeliness, and her carriage remained erect and imposing.

Adrian, at thirty, was a big, broad fellow, over six feet. His voice was deep and powerful. But despite his towering proportions and his frowning, defiant calm, there was about him a certain furtiveness, as though he were perpetually on the lookout for some danger known only to himself.

On the night of Jabez's arrival Adrian sat with his cousin until after midnight talking. "I'm glad you've come, Jabez. I wanted someone like you here—someone I can talk to and confide in. That woman is my greatest enemy, though you wouldn't imagine so if you saw us together. Remember this evening how she smiled at me? Don't trust that. We've been smiling at each other like that for the past fourteen or fifteen years, but behind our affability we hate and distrust each other like serpents of different varieties. We watch each other day and night."

"You did hint in your letters that there was some friction between you, but I didn't think it went as deep as this."

"You didn't?" Adrian smiled, glancing round toward the door. As though from fixed habit, he lowered his voice. "Since that day when I made her small before the soldier in our ruined house at Fort Nassau we have been like two reptiles waiting to pounce and destroy each other. I couldn't tell you everything in my letters, Jabez, but she's a bad woman. I never look upon her other than as an evil partner with whom I have been unavoidably saddled. Long, long ago I ceased to think of her as my mother. I live now solely to disappoint and frustrate her. That's why I'm not married yet. There's a girl called Jannetje van Hoost downstream I've thought of seriously. She loves me, and I know she would marry me if I asked her, but I won't do it because I want to balk that monster to the end. She wants me to marry and have children so as to carry on the family name, but I mean to wait until she's dead before I marry. The only women I have anything to do with occasionally are the slave women——"

He broke off, for Jabez had winced and was showing signs of discomfiture.

"Is anything the matter?"

"No, no. Nothing. Go on. I'm interested, Adrian."

"Only the slave women I have anything to do with. I don't like it, but I'm purposely producing as many bastards as I can because I know that that hurts her. I have about four or five olive-skinned children around the place already. Whenever she sees them it stabs her to the heart. Her pride in the family isn't normal like Uncle Aert's. I've told you that time and again but you didn't seem to believe me. Uncle Aert and the rest of you on the Essequibo have lived normal, healthy lives, but not we here in Berbice. She's a monster, Jabez. A monster. If you had had to go through what Cornelis and I and Father went through with her on the Berbice River, you would know what I mean. You in Essequibo couldn't understand it when I wrote telling you about her cruelty. Grandfather Laurens must have been ashamed to tell you, because she used to describe her doings in every letter, and it surprised me that none of you knew."

He glanced toward the door again. "We never heard of or saw Cornelis since he disappeared that night with the Frenchman, Tirol. He must have gone away with the privateers, and I don't blame him, Jabez. Poor fellow. He lived in misery in that house at Fort Nassau. He was like a hunted beast. Like myself—until I broke out and defied her." His eyes gleamed, and Jabez could see that he was abnormal. He leant forward in his chair, speaking in a lowered voice and throwing furtive glances toward the door.

"You people have never credited the tales I told you in my letters. But they were true. True, I tell you." His voice grew shrill. "She's not human, Jabez. She's a fiend. It was she who made Father commit suicide. She hacked all his works to pieces with an axe, and in the night he disappeared, and we found the *corial* drifting in the river. You people on the Essequibo never knew the horrors that we had to endure here—and all because of this family pride idea of hers. I hate her and live to defeat her, Jabez. I live to make her suffer in whatever way I can. I'll never leave her. I'll never go away from this place. I've vowed to make her pay, and pay bitterly, for what she did to Father and Cornelis and me, and I shall stay and see it through. I mean to persecute her in every way I can."

He grunted. "I must seem strange to you, Jabez. I'm as much a monster as she is. It's she who made me what I am. Fifteen years ago at Fort Nassau I used to fancy I was in love with her and I would have brought down the moon for her. I wanted to be in bed with her, and she wanted it, too. Many times we nearly committed the act like man and wife, but somehow we restrained ourselves. Yes, you stare. I knew you would stare. You grew up like any normal fellow. Your mother was a real mother to you. But mine was a fiend. We never had any affection from her. She never once fondled us. All we had from her were shouts and thumps and lectures about the family traditions and the tales of our ancestors. Power. The van Groenwegels never run. Power and glory. Empty, absurd doctrines of superiority. Uncle Aert never told you tales of the old days———"

"He did. Adriansen and Kaywana and the raid of 1666. We know all about those tales. But Father never hammered them into us as you say Aunt Hendrickje has done to you. I can't understand this, Adrian. You amaze me. I knew something was wrong, that you had had a hard boyhood, but to hear what you're telling me now—it's incredible."

Adrian grunted. "I know it's incredible. Even Claas van Doorn wanted to disbelieve, and he lived so near." He leaned forward again, speaking now in a husky murmur. "Do you know what's happened since we came to live on the Canje? She has taken up with a mulatto slave. He comes up to her room every other night after dinner. A fellow called Bangara. He's one of her few lieutenants—that's what she calls them. On the Berbice we had three. Rabonne, Henwah and Pardoom. Rabonne died the last night of the bombardment, and Henwah and Pardoom have come over to my side. They're still with us. I'll introduce you to them tomorrow. They obey me entirely. They have nothing to do with her. But this fellow Bangara and four others are her men. And Bangara is her lover. It's been going on for years now. When she first had him up in her room he was only nineteen. He's about twenty-six now. Tall, burly fellow, much like myself. You should hear them some nights together in the room there. They make noise, like two beasts——" He checked himself, for again Jabez had begun to show signs of discomfiture.

"Am I boring you with this talk, old fellow? Do you prefer to get into bed now?"

"No. No, no. Please go on," said Jabez hastily, stirring in his chair.

"I believe something is on your mind," said Adrian. "Something happened back in Essequibo you don't want to talk about. You can confide in me if you like. I won't say a word. I keep everything to myself these days. I live to myself entirely."

Jabez was silent.

"I thought it strange you didn't write to me before you came."

"I had meant to, but at the last moment I asked Father to do it for me. I asked him to tell you I wanted to come and spend some time here to see what the place is like."

"I got his letter safely and I was overjoyed. You're the very person I want here. From your letters I might have met you in the flesh since we were boys of twelve or thirteen. You were the only person I had to confide in. Except her, of course, during those few months before the bombardment when we were so close." A dark look passed over his face. He rubbed his hands along his thighs in a fevered manner. "I used to enjoy writing to you, Jabez. You must confide in me. We must keep close."

"One day I'll tell you everything," said Jabez.

"Then I'm right! Something has happened! A love affair?"

Jabez was silent, and Adrian said quickly: "Don't upset yourself. I'm a thoughtless fool. Keep it to yourself until you feel you can tell me. I wish I could have you here for good. I wish you never had to return to the Essequibo."

"Adrian, I was going to broach that before long. Do you think it would be possible for me to remain here always? I don't want to return to the Essequibo. I want to stay here for the rest of my life."

Adrian half rose from his chair. "Do you mean that? You want to stay here always? I knew something was wrong. Uncle Aert's letter was so brief and—good God! This is the best thing you ever suggested. Remain by all means. We have five rooms in this house, three more than we can use. The family who lived here formerly was a big one. French people. Most of the plantations along here are owned by French people." He stretched across and patted Jabez's knee eagerly. "By hell! This is good. We can form ourselves into a league against her. She's strong. But we can beat her if we get together. You'll fight with me?"

"Fight? But why fight? What have we got to fight for?"

"It's the only way to survive. She'll overpower us if we don't fight. She isn't human. She'll stamp on us and hold us down if we don't fight her and keep on fighting." He trembled. "You don't know what we're up against in that creature. She even works *obeah* nowadays. Hoobak is an *obeah* man. He's one of her lieutenants, and she believes in his *obeah*. At least, she pretends she does, because she lets him burn black candles in the house and boil poisonous vegetable concoctions in the kitchen. Bitter cassava and hog-tannia and rare herbs. It's a deadly poison. Every Sunday it happens."

"This thing is a deadly poison, you say?"

"Deadly. It turns your face blue, I've heard. That's why I have a special cook. I have my meals cooked outside in a little detached kitchen shed. I'll show it to you tomorrow. I have my own favorite slaves, and she has her own. We're divided into two separate camps. She and I don't live as mother and son. We're enemies. She'd poison me tomorrow if she got the chance."

"You're not serious!"

Adrian chortled, glancing swiftly toward the door and edging forward in his chair. "That's how we live.

You wouldn't have believed it if I had told you in a letter. No one outside this house would believe it. A she-devil, that's what she is, Jabez. Fight on my side and we'll defeat her. What do you say? You'll support me?"

"Yes. Yes, of course," mumbled Jabez, bewildered.

Adrian frowned. "You have to be careful. She's so clever—so deep. She's going to talk to you and try to poison your mind against me. I could see her angling to get you alone to herself today, that's why I kept by your side so assiduously. But you look out tomorrow. When I'm in the fields she's going to tackle you." Adrian gave his cousin a serious look, his manner one of grave portent. "You be on your guard. Don't let her overpower you with her wiles. Treat her as you would a dangerous snake. That's what she is—a snake. Venomous."

The following morning Jabez remembered Adrian's words, for his cousin had hardly left the house for the fields when there came a tap on the door of Jabez's room. Hendrickje came in, tall and imposing, a quiet smile on her freckled, handsome face.

"Your cousin has kept you so much to himself I haven't had an opportunity to exchange a word with you, my boy," she said. "Did you spend a pleasant night?"

"Yes, a perfect night, thank you, Aunt Hendrickje. Sit down, won't you?"

She did not remain long, and her manner was soft and charming. Unlike Adrian, there was nothing fanatically obsessed or abnormal in her behavior. She conducted herself exactly as he would have expected an aunt of his with whom he was just becoming acquainted to have done. Despite Adrian's warning, he could see no reason why he should be on his guard.

During the course of their conversation she only once mentioned Adrian's name, and made no attempt to touch on the subject of her relations with him. She discussed the plantation and the prospects for the near future. "Personally, I think neither coffee nor indigo will last very long in this country," she said. "Sugar will always dominate. What of the Essequibo? How are you faring there with your coffee?"

"Not very well, either, I'm afraid," he told her. He kept avoiding her gaze. "De Heere insisted that we should give it a trial and we have done so, but the trees don't seem to flourish as well as they should. I think it's the soil. The soil is unsuitable. The biggest trouble, though, is that the slaves don't like picking and preparing the berries. We have no little trouble persuading them to work when the berries are ripe."

"We experience much the same difficulties here," she nodded, "though where the slaves are concerned we've instituted such a system of punishments that they don't dare to try on any organized slacking when picking time comes around. We don't hesitate to have them tarred and feathered."

"Tarred and feathered! Literally?"

"Literally. You seem shocked." She wagged her head slightly, smiling. "We have to be severe, Jabez. It's the only way. The other planters do it, too. The stocks, also, are proving very effective. For serious offenses we have them put in the stocks for days, administering a daily dose of lashes. That always breaks their rebelliousness."

"In Essequibo we've begun to use the stocks, too," he told her.

"Tell me something of Essequibo. I hear you have a new Colony House at Cartabo, and your Council has been altered in constitution."

"Yes, the Huis Naby. It was built some time ago —about ten years ago. Between 1716 and 1717. Van der Heyden Resen had it put up. Kyk-over-al had got too crowded, and then the epidemic broke out."

"Gertruyt and Luise died of it, poor girls. I was terribly upset when your father wrote me. And Luise on the point of getting married."

"Father and Grandmother were ill, too, but they managed to get well." He shifted about in his chair, and a troubled light came into his eyes, as though suddenly he had remembered his incapacity.

Hendrickje watched him keenly, but in a subtle, unobtrusive manner.

"What of this new Council? Tell me about it."

"The new Court of Policy and Justice?" He shrugged. "There's not much to be told about it. About eight years ago they revised the constitution—in 1718. The new Council comprises the Commandeur and the Secretary and the Assistant Secretary as well as two managers of the Company plantations. It's by no means representative. The Company still continues to hold absolute sway in everything. We private planters have no voice in any matter."

"What happened exactly between Secretary Gelskerke and van der Heyden Resen? I heard there was some serious misunderstanding."

"Yes. That happened about the same time that the constitution was altered. Van der Heyden Resen was an energetic and capable fellow, but he knew nothing about handling people. And then there was this spy system the Directors have always encouraged. One official writing in reports against another. That's what really brought about the final quarrel. Gelskerke had sent in a series of reports concerning the state of the colony's finances and Resen's methods of running affairs. The upshot was that after this big quarrel Resen packed Gelskerke back to Holland. But Gelskerke put up such a strong case before the Directors that they sent him back as Secretary and dismissed Resen. That was in 1719. July. And then Laurens de Heere was appointed Commandeur."

"That's the man who advocates a gradual migration toward the coast. Your father has told me about him."

"Yes, de Heere has sound ideas for the advancement of the colony. He has even given permission for expeditions to go into the interior to prospect for precious metals. The Indians say there's gold—and perhaps silver—up the rivers."

It was not until toward the close of their conversation that she became personal. She smiled at him casually: "Well, what do you think of me? Am I the sort of person you had expected to see?"

He returned: "To be honest, I had thought of you as an older-looking person. You seem remarkably young, considering you're the mother of Adrian. How did you succeed in keeping so fresh, Aunt Hendrickje?"

"By living thoroughly," she twinkled. "The secret of youth is to live thoroughly—and by that I mean indulging your normal, natural inclinations. Not over-indulging, mind. Nothing ages more than frustrations, Jabez—especially sexual frustration. I've discovered that these past few years. What of Adrian, by the way? From his letters, do you find him the sort of person you had expected him to be?"

He smiled uncomfortably. "That's somewhat hard to say," he told her cautiously. "During the past few years our correspondence has been rather brief and sketchy. Planting is such an exacting occupation. One loses the inclination to write letters after a time."

"You're a very efficient overseer, I understand." She beamed on him. "I hope you intend to spend a long time with us here, my boy. By the way, you are betrothed, aren't you?"

He wiped his eyebrows with the back of his hand, avoiding her gaze. "No. No, Aunt Hendrickje," he said in a voice barely audible.

She waited for him to continue, but when he did not and his discomfiture increased, she said in a bantering manner: "I think I understand. A little lover's quarrel. Well, perhaps you may find someone in these parts to suit you, my boy—we never know." She rose and wagged her finger at him. "Don't forget you have to carry on our name, Jabez."

She went out, beaming and pleasant and feminine.

Jabez liked Hendrickje. During the weeks and months that followed he sided with neither camp, but secretly he sympathized with his aunt rather than with Adrian. He did not approve of her intimate relations with the burly mulatto, Bangara, who came up to her room every other night, but, on the other hand, he found Adrian tiresome in many respects. Adrian kept harping on the subject of the feud between his mother and himself, and never ceased in his efforts to persuade Jabez what a fiend Hendrickje was and how necessary it was to fight her.

Jabez accompanied Adrian into the fields every day to assist in overseeing and instructing, but Adrian made the work difficult. "You mustn't have anything to do with that gang. Those are her men. Bangara sees after them. And over there, those are her indigo patches. Let her own men look after them." When Jabez pointed out how much this system of boycotting and segregation complicated and hindered the work, Adrian frowned: "It can't be helped. I'll have nothing to do with her lot. I don't trust them, Jabez. They are snakes —every one of them."

"But, Adrian, your mother doesn't seem to want to oppose you as you want to oppose her. Even the slaves. I don't hear them speaking of any feud. Don't you think you're letting your imagination run away with you?"

Adrian grunted ominously. "There's much you don't see. She doesn't work in the open. She works in the dark. Don't be fooled by her bland airs. That's the devilishness in her tactics. She's so sweet and soft, so charming. You'd never dream that underneath she's a serpent waiting to strike. . . ."

Jabez, however, was not impressed, and that was why he refrained from confiding in Adrian. He kept the secret of his physical incapacity to himself. He suffered from shame and a sense of inferiority and would have welcomed someone with whom he could have discussed his misfortune in a sympathetic spirit. But neither his aunt nor his cousin, he reasoned, would have sufficed. Despite her soft charm, Hendrickje had a certain aloofness that awed him. Her gray-green eyes were too steady when they looked at him. Her poise and dignity and her calm chilled him. And she never went out of her way to be friendly toward him; she had a smile for him whenever she met him, and at table she was cordial—as cordial as she was to Adrian—but she never attempted to get closer to him.

Adrian was too much a fanatic to prove a good confidant. He would probably have wanted to treat the matter lightly; probably told him not to let it prey on his mind, and then proceeded to go off on another long tirade against his mother.

When the letter came for him from his father, however, it was Hendrickje he decided to consult. He was forced to make this move; the nature of the letter's contents called for an immediate consultation.

He told Adrian, on the morning after, that he was not feeling very well and would not accompany him into the fields as usual. Adrian, to his surprise, winked at him and returned: "I know. It's that letter you got yesterday from Uncle Aert. That love affair in Essequibo. He's made some reference to it and it has upset you. Never mind. You'll get over it. Never get despondent over a woman." He lowered his voice, glancing toward the door. "You take up with one or two of our slave women here. Beget a few bastards as I'm doing. It will hurt her. She hates to know that all the children I have up to now are illegitimate mulattoes. She wants white legitimate van Groenwegels to carry on the name. But she'll never see those from me. I won't have any legitimate white children until she's dead, and if you take my advice you'll do the same. Beget mulatto bastards. . . ."

It was a relief when he had left.

A little later Jabez said to his aunt: "I'm sorry to disturb you, Aunt Hendrickje, but I was wondering if you could spare me a few moments. I have a rather important matter I'd like to discuss with you."

"My dear boy, you're at liberty to discuss anything with me at any time. A pleasure, Jabez. Come into my room and make yourself at ease."

He was very awkward and confused, however, sitting opposite her, with the sunshine slanting in at the windows and the kiskadees and sackies cheeping in the mango trees outside.

"It's several months since I've been here with you, Aunt Hendrickje, and I had intended to speak to you about my staying on. I mentioned it to Adrian and he thought it a good idea that I should remain here always."

"Always?"

"Yes. I don't want to go back to the Essequibo."

She waited for him to go on.

"Certain occurrences there before I left would make it awkward for me to go back. Presently I'll attempt to explain, Aunt Hendrickje, but what I wanted to find out, in the meantime, was what you would say to my settling here with a—with a wife and child."

The only sign of dismay she betrayed was a slight lifting of her brows. Otherwise, her manner remained under perfect control. "My dear boy, I should be most delighted," she said. "Nothing would make me happier."

"Thank you." His gaze was still out on the mango trees. The birds were feasting on the ripe fruit. He could smell the fresh, sweet aroma of the pecked mangoes mingled with the general wet, dank scent of the earth and the vegetation. Rain had fallen the night before.

"I'm afraid I'll have to explain the situation," he said. He fell silent again, sitting there, a big-faced, stoutish, flabby-limbed figure.

"In Essequibo I had a somewhat unfortunate experience with a half-breed girl—a slave. She's Spanish and Carib, one of those we're allowed to procure from the Orinoco by the proclamation of 1717. She's named Rosaria, and in a letter I got from Father two or three days ago he says that she gave birth to a child a month or two ago and that the child resembles me so closely that there can be no doubt that I'm the father."

Hendrickje's features twitched a trifle. But this was the only evidence she gave of being impressed by what he had said. She waited, erect and calm. Inscrutable.

"Father is suggesting that I should marry this girl in order to make the child legitimate. It's a boy, and Father has acquired Rosaria from the de Haarts. He feels that it would be well for the boy to carry on our name, as I may never have any other children——"

"As you may never have any other children! Why, my boy? Aren't you fond of children, Jabez?"

"I am, but—I'm afraid—the fact is that I met with an accident before I came here." In a slow, stammering voice he related what had happened to him at the hands of Samuel. Hendrickje listened with an air of fascination. Her calm deserted her temporarily. She interrupted once.

"When you were a boy you used to speak of his cruelty in your letters, I remember. You once told Adrian how he burnt lizards over a fire."

"You remember that, do you? Yes, he was always cruel, but I never dreamt that one day he would bring it to me—me his best friend. That's what hurt me more than anything else, Aunt Hendrickje."

"I can well understand that, my boy. Jabez, you have no idea how much this grieves me. Grieves and upsets me." There was sincerity in her tone, and he felt mollified. "By all means you must let your father send the girl and the child here. You can be married quietly at Fort Nassau."

"You have no objections to her living in the house here?"

"None whatever! None!" Her voice rose in her insistence. "You must marry her and legitimatize the child. A son, my boy! A son! A male van Groenwegel! Your father is perfectly right. It's your duty to the family to marry her and bring up the child."

Relief came into his manner. "I'm glad you think so. I didn't know what to decide. Could you keep this to yourself until—well, until a little later, perhaps? Do you think it would be wise to tell Adrian?"

"You must, my boy. He would feel very insulted if you didn't. You have seen for yourself how touchy he is." She tapped his knee. "Don't let this upset you, Jabez. What happened wasn't your fault. Don't let it prey on your mind. You have a son. Let that help to build up your self-respect again."

He smiled. "I'm afraid nothing could succeed in giving me back my self-respect, Aunt Hendrickje. To the end of my life I shall feel myself a negative quantity. Nowadays I merely exist because I can't help existing. Many times I've contemplated ending my life."

She watched him, her eyes keen and calculating, as though a thousand different schemes were rushing through her mind at once. She had a vulturine look. Abruptly her eyes softened and she smiled and said:

"No, my boy, you mustn't take it that way. Be brave, Jabez. Never admit defeat. Remember you're a van Groenwegel. There's different blood in you. Fire-blood. Fighter-blood. Stiffen your back and defy Life. Face adversities and never surrender. Did your father tell you what the motto of our family is?"

He nodded weakly. "The van Groenwegels never run. Yes, I know. We're supposed to defend our own, aren't we? Never give in when attacked. But this is an enemy I can't fight, Aunt Hendrickje. Physical impotence. How can I resist a circumstance that remains always a flat, unrelenting fact? How will I ever begin to forget that I'm a useless cipher! A eunuch. A sexless nothing." He buried his face in the crook of his elbow and cried softly.

IV

Jabez went, by the trail, to Fort Nassau to meet the ship that brought Rosaria and the child whose name was Hubertus.

"They name him," said Rosaria, "after the seaman Massa, the Captain Hubertus Lodewiecjk—the nice, big, tall man who come to see your sister, Missy Mathilde. Oh, but he so nice, Jabez! He so tall and big! I wish bad he could ask me to make sweet with him, but he! He not look at me. He all for Missy Mathilde. His ship, it sail next week. He like my baby the too plenty. He say yes, we must call him Hubertus, so Massa Aert, he say yes, and we call him Hubertus. And look! See how he like you! Your same round face. Your eyes and your mouth. And your ears. Even the little mole you have on your shoulder—look, Jabez! See! He have that, too. Same shape and size. That what make we so sure. Nobody not doubt he yours after they see that mark. Just as if come inside my belly and put it dere, yes."

They were married by the Commandeur, and on their arrival at the Canje plantation Hendrickje and Adrian were on the veranda to welcome them and wish them good fortune.

There was no condescension in Hendrickje's manner as she kissed Rosaria. The girl might have been a social equal, Jannetje van Hoost or Amelie Fourie or any of the other planters' daughters or nieces along the Canje. "You're very welcome, my child," said Hendrickje. "I hope you'll be happy here with us." She glanced from the child to Jabez. "Good heavens! What a resemblance! There isn't a detail of him that isn't you, Jabez!"

Jabez avoided her gaze.

Rosaria showed Hendrickje the birthmark. "Even that he has. Ask Jabez show you the one he got on his shoulder. The very same!" As Hendrickje took the child from her, Rosaria smiled around and said: "Oh, but this place! I like it already, what I see of it. It is the most beautiful, yes." Her eyes traveled slowly round, black and large and cunning. "I shall be the very happy here—yes, I know."

She looked up at Adrian as he took her hand, and smiled: "You the Adrian, eh? But you so big and tall! *Dios mio!* You taller more than the Captain Lodewiecjk who they call my baby after."

"Who is Captain Lodewiecjk?" asked Adrian indulgently.

"He visit Missy Mathilde. He come from a ship. Big, tall man. But you taller more than him. Yes, I talk true." She ogled him, openly wanton, and he flushed uncomfortably.

Jabez asked for an excuse, frowning, and went downstairs to see after the slaves who were removing Rosaria's baggage from the mule.

When she and Rosaria were going upstairs, Hendrickje said: "I think you'll like your room. It's cool and spacious, and I have had a small bed made for Hubertus."

"You do that, Missy Hendrickje! But that so good of you!"

"I'm Aunt Hendrickje to you, Rosaria. I don't want you to look upon me with awe and dread. We must be good friends. You must confide in me, and I shall confide in you, and I'm sure we shall get on splendidly."

"I do that for the very certain. I so like you already, Aunt Hendrickje. You nice and tall, and you smile so kind. I very certain we get on nice, nice. I like all the tall people."

"You do?" As they entered the room Hendrickje glanced at her. "Adrian has taken after me in height and build. Do you like him?"

"But yes, Aunt Hendrickje, that I do!" She uttered a creamy sound. "Perhaps one night I make to creep in to his room soft, soft, and give him the little tickle, yes. Not so?" She broke into husky-mellow laughter, and Hendrickje laughed, too.

"One day I may arrange it for you, Rosaria, we never know. But tell me how you like your room."

"The room? Oh, but I like it plenty, plenty!" She patted the bed. "This for Jabez and me? This nice big bed?"

"Yes. And the small one here is for Hubertus."

Jabez came in, followed by two slaves with the baggage.

"Jabez, look! You see! How you like it, this big bed? One big bed for me—and you!"

V

Day after day Jabez watched Rosaria—not jealously but with a detached anxiety, his manner nervous and sensitive; it was as though he were awaiting an evitable cataclysm and it was the suspense, rather than the apprehended event itself, that proved harrowing to him. He retired deep into himself and kept to his room, avoiding even Adrian, much to Adrian's alarm.

"I believe she's trying to pull you over to her camp, Jabez. She's doing it subtly, but I'm not fooled. She's done it to some of my slaves before."

Jabez tried to assure him that such was not the case, but Adrian still looked doubtful.

Jabez took a great interest in the plantation work, but even this proved inadequate as a means of shutting out the awareness of his lack. There was ever present in the background of his mood a bitterness against his lot. He continued to be diffident and shifty-eyed, as though nervous lest he should reveal to the others the depths of his depreciation, as though fearful, too, of the pity he might discover in their gazes.

At table he would keep flicking his glance from Rosaria to Adrian. But Rosaria's face would be childlike and smiling. Innocuous. Adrian's face would be passive and unconcerned, or, as more often, frowning and furtive with the fanatic hate for his mother which forever smoldered within him.

Hendrickje, too, like Jabez, watched. She watched them all. She gave the impression that she was secretly enjoying herself. The delicate shadow-play of brewing drama seemed to entertain her.

One day Adrian said to Jabez on the back veranda: "There's some game afoot. Keep a sharp eye out. My personal theory is that she's going to make an attempt to get your child into her clutches so that she can train him up her way. Drum those old tales into his head and try to make him into a power-mad monster like herself. You watch out, Jabez!" He glanced swiftly into the sitting room. "Warn Rosaria, too. Tell her not to listen to her when she begins to preach her family pride philosophy. Fight her off, Jabez. Both of you. Never cease to fight her."

One morning, when Adrian and Jabez were in the fields, Hendrickje entered Adrian's room to find Rosaria sitting on the bed. Rosaria smiled and said: "This the first time I come in here. I like it outside there, the view through the window. The trees, they look so nice!"

"How long have you been in here?" asked Hendrickje.

"Me?" Rosaria seemed surprised. "Only two-three minutes."

"Is it because of the view you came in?"

Rosaria nodded. "But yes. That why I come in. Me? I like nothing more the better than to look at the trees. Not you, too, Aunt Hendrickje?"

Hendrickje grunted. "I came in to tidy up. Do you wish to help me?"

"That give me the most great pleasure."

"By the way, you had better not mention that I found you in here. I mean to Jabez. He might be apt to misunderstand."

"Jabez? I must not tell him I come in the room here?"

"No. I think it would be wise not to."

Rosaria stared at her, then laughed. "Ah! But yes. I see what you make to say. You think he believe I come in to make sweet with Adrian?"

"Precisely." Hendrickje asked: "Are you happy with Jabez?"

"Me? Happy? Plenty, plenty. I not look so?"

Hendrickje's face remained inscrutable. "That's very good. I only wondered. Are you fond of children?"

"Me? Children? Oh, but I love children! Why you ask?"

"Wouldn't you like to have more children?"

For a moment Rosaria's face became blank. She did not answer at once. Then she gave Hendrickje a quick glance and nodded. "Yes, I would like that. Funny you ask me that. I think about it the so many times."

"Do you?"

Hendrickje moved about the room with composure and unconcern. Of a sudden she said: "Poor Jabez. He tries to drown his self-pity in hard work and reading. A most fiendish misfortune to have befallen him. They sent Samuel de Haart to sea, didn't they?"

Rosaria nodded. Her exuberance had vanished. She seemed wary and suspicious. "Yes, they send him to sea," she murmured. She had seated herself on the edge of the bed again. Hendrickje came and sat beside her. Put an arm around her and smiled. "You're far more clever than most people would think, Rosaria. We must be friends."

Rosaria smiled uncertainly, her eyes shifty and keen.

"I think I know what you need, my child. Let's be frank. It's a man you need, Rosaria. Am I not right?"

The girl was silent.

"Am I not right?"

Rosaria looked up. "Yes, for sure that what I need." A gleam of trust came into her eyes. She said in a lowered voice: "Jabez no man to me. You know that, not so?"

"I know. He told me what happened in the Essequibo."

"If I not have man soon I go mad, Aunt Hendrickje."

Hendrickje nodded. "I was thinking so myself. If you choose to trust me I could arrange the matter for you." She gave the girl a significant stare. "You like my son, don't you?"

Rosaria hesitated, then nodded. "That I do. He tall and big. The minute I see him I feel to make sweet with him."

"I guessed that, too. You like tall men, don't you?"

"That I do. Tall men or men who broad and strong. Jabez, he was good before the Señor Samuel cut him up."

"Our tastes are remarkably alike, my dear. I like them tall myself—or broad and strong. Would you like me to plan it so that you could have Adrian?"

"But certain! You think you able to make him sleep with me? He look so full of the big frowns. He not notice me when I give him the eye. He little funny, I think."

"He *is* funny." Hendrickje touched her temple. "He suffers from a mania. He imagines I'm his personal enemy, and that I'm forever planning to do him harm. I think I know of a way to take advantage of his mental condition. We can entangle him to the benefit of us both. We must have a long chat, my girl. Sit still and listen to me carefully. You're intelligent in your way, and I feel sure you'll be able to handle this little scheme successfully."

The chat lasted for well over an hour, and Rosaria was an interested and enthusiastic listener. Many times she chortled creamily, and once she gripped Hendrickje's wrist and exclaimed: "Aunt Hendrickje, I never think you have so much the brain! That good! I sure that work good. I do it just as you say how, yes, I want the man bad, bad. I do anything to have the man. I go mad soon if I not have the man."

Toward the end of the conversation, however, she said in a serious voice: "I see what you mean, Aunt Hendrickje, but that, it would be very terrible, not so?"

"It would be," agreed Hendrickje, "but he would be out of his misery. He's not happy, Rosaria. It would be the kindest thing that could happen to him. We must be sensible. Practical and unsentimental. Why should we pause to consider the means? You'll discover, as you live longer, that only results count in this world. Men respect deeds accomplished, not deeds that might have been accomplished. It's so easy to say that we might have done this or we might have done that if this or that circumstance had been favorable. Any inept fool can say that, but it is in results that we prove whether we have the ability or not."

Later that day, when she was with Jabez in their room, Rosaria said: "Your aunt, she such a fine lady—so kind and good. We had the nice talk this morning."

Jabez grunted noncommittally, turning a leaf of the book he was reading.

"Yes, she the very nice. We talk so many little interesting things."

"What sort of interesting things?"

She shrugged. "Nothing the very particular. She talk. I talk. She say this, I say that. She say about you, how you work so hard, and how she so the sorry for you."

"Sorry for me? Why is she sorry for me?"

"Why? But you know why, not so? For what the Señor Samuel he do to you in Essequibo. How he cut up your little things so you no more the man."

She looked out of the window. "You should not work so hard, I think. You should rest the little more."

"Why do you think I overwork?"

"Your aunt, she so wise woman. She say how hard you working so as to hide what you feel inside. She so the sorry for you. She ask me not to tell you, but I say I will speak to you about it. You should take the rest more often. Sleep more. It help you to forget."

"You needn't trouble about me. I rest perfectly."

"You sleep good at night, Jabez? Good, sound sleep?"

His manner became suspicious. "Yes, I do. Why do you ask?"

"Oh, but you not vexed with me! Oh, Jabez!" She rushed across the room and began to caress him. "You mustn't be vexed with me. I say what I say for your good. Poor Jabez. I so sorry for you."

"I'm not vexed. Please don't imagine things. And if you don't mind, I should like to go on reading. I prefer to be left alone."

"No, Jabez, don't speak like that. Talk to me good. You make me feel you vexed with me. I so sorry for you."

"You have no need to be."

"You still love me, Jabez?"

He made no reply.

"Jabez, you still love me? Like how you say you love me when we make sweet in the coffee fields in Essequibo?"

He winced.

"You make love to me so sweet those days. Remember? You was really nice that time. So big and broad and strong. I like you plenty then. You make me so happy. Sometimes I wish bad you could make sweet to me again like you do those days. I want the man so much, Jabez. Some nights when you fall asleep I take the pillow and make pretend it is the man, yes."

"Please." There was anguish in his voice. "I want to read. I want to be alone, Rosaria. Please leave me. Aunt Hendrickje is on the back veranda with Hubertus. Go down and join her. Leave me to myself."

She would not move. She said in a soft voice: "But, Jabez, I love you still. True. Don't send me downstairs. Let me stay here with you."

The tears came to his eyes. He uttered a sobbing sound and hid his face in her skirt. He pulled her toward him and kissed her with an agitated desperation. Almost at once the frenzy died down and he released her and turned off, his hands pressed to his face. He slouched there, a gross, ineffectual figure.

She stared at him for a moment, then patted his head lightly and went out of the room, a smile of satisfaction on her face.

Two days after this incident Adrian was on the back veranda reading Spinoza's *Ethics*—a volume he delved into at odd moments—when Rosaria appeared and hesitated near his chair.

Adrian turned his head briefly and smiled in acknowledgement of her presence, then went on reading.

Upstairs, Jabez was in the northeastern room with Hubertus.

Rosaria said: "When you not in the fields you always with the books, Adrian. Same as Jabez. You like to do the reading, that not so? Yes?"

He looked up again, his manner surprised. "Yes, I do read a great deal. There's a lot to be learnt from books. Do you wish something to read? Oh, excuse me. I forgot you can't read or write."

She sighed. "Yes, poor me. You sorry for me, Adrian?"

He thought: Now, what does she want with me? I wonder if Hendrickje sent her. Is this some new trick to get me into her clutches? I had better be on my guard. I won't be surprised if Hendrickje has decided to use Rosaria against me now. She's so deep—so infernally cunning!

"Adrian, you sorry for me that I cannot read or write?"

"Yes."

"I should like someone to teach me one day."

"Yes, it would be useful to learn."

"You would not like that job? To teach me to read and write?"

He smiled slightly. "I'm very much afraid I couldn't promise you that, Rosaria. Perhaps, though. We never know," he added in a mutter. He could smell the cinnamon. He stroked his chin slowly. . . . She's a seductive creature, but dangerous. From the looks she has been giving me of late I can see she finds me attractive, in her wanton fashion. But I don't intend to become involved with her. Jabez is my good friend. I must do nothing to hurt him, poor fellow. Besides, I have to be careful to keep him on my side. The slightest slip and he may go over to Hendrickje's camp. I can't risk that.

Rosaria watched him. After a silence she said: "Yes, we never know. One day you try to teach me, when you not got nothing to do, not so?"

"Why couldn't Jabez teach you? Why don't you ask him?"

"Jabez, he behave the little funny to me. He not like me ask him too many the things. I believe he not like me."

"You're mistaken. I'm sure he's very fond of you."

They heard footsteps in the sitting room. The footsteps stopped.

Adrian half rose, then sank down again, tense.

They heard the footsteps receding.

Adrian grunted ominously. "You heard that?"

"It was your mother," hissed Rosaria.

"I know. No need to tell me. Spying on me. She's a snake, Rosaria."

Rosaria moved past him and stood against the veranda rail where she was closer to him. "Your mother," she said, in a conspiratorial voice, "she is the person I not like. She hate me. She talk to me the day before the yesterday, and she say: 'Rosaria,' she say, 'I hope you understand that you are the Jabez's wife. I have notice you the many times looking at my son Adrian in the very funny way. If you not careful and anything it should happen between you and Adrian I shall not tolerate any children of the mixed blood in this house. You will have to leave, Rosaria. I warn you the most solemn.' Yes, she say that to me, every word."

Adrian's eyes glittered. "She actually told you that, did she? She warned you that she would put you out if you had any children by me?"

"Yes, she tell me that, every word true. She say she want white van Groenwegel children. She not want no children with the Indian blood to carry on the family name."

"It's exactly what she would say, Rosaria. Exactly. She's a monster. An evil, desperate monster. You must be on your guard against her. She's going to do all in her power to win that child of yours over to her side. She's going to try to fill him up with her power ambitions and warp his mind." He shifted about in a fevered manner. "Hasn't Jabez told you about her? Hasn't Jabez told you of the way she brought up Cornelis and myself—and of how she treated our father?"

"He say something once, but he and I not hold the long talk."

So he told her about the past, in the same intense, obsessed manner in which he had told Jabez. She kept leaning forward to give him a generous view down her bosom, but her efforts were wasted. He glanced from her face to the sitting room door, squirming about in his chair, edging forward now and then to touch her wrist in order to emphasize some point. He ended up by telling her: "You stick by me. Keep on my side. I want all the help I can get to defeat her. And remember you have your son to think of. Don't let her get him, Rosaria. Don't let her take him from you and spoil his life." He was trembling slightly. "Come, what do you say? You'll be on my side? You'll fight with me, Rosaria?"

"But certain, yes," she nodded. "You and me, we must be the good friends. We fight together and beat her. Since she hate me and not want my children then I hate her, too. That only fair, yes, not so?"

"Good. Good. That's it. Hate her. Hate her with all your soul." He caught her hand and shook it, chortling excitedly. "By hell! I believe you'll make a good ally, Rosaria. You mustn't mind if I appear over-obsessed about this subject. I can't help myself. Nowadays I live for nothing but to defeat her—frustrate her in whatever way I can. Cause her as much pain and suffering as it's humanly possible for me to bring into her life. I mean to make her pay bitterly for what she did to Father and Cornelis and myself. . . ."

She listened to him patiently, and when he came to the end of his tirade, smiled and held his arm. "No

fear, Adrian. I your best friend from this the very minute. I not make you disappoint. I help you good."

VI

On a day not long after this incident Hendrickje met
Jabez coming down the stairs with Hubertus. She smile
"Taking him out for a walk, Jabez, my boy?"

"No, Aunt Hendrickje," he said. "I'm looking for
Rosaria. I think it's time for him to have his feed."

"She's on the back veranda."

"Is she there?" He looked undecided for an instant, then said: "Would you mind taking Hubertus to
her for me?"

"Certainly, my boy. But why? Have you and she
been quarreling?"

"No, no." He avoided her gaze, passing his hand
across his forehead in a tired manner. "No particular
reason, but—I have to go upstairs again. I have to
write a letter to Father."

As he was about to turn off he said: "Aunt Hendrickje, I think I'm going to send him back to the
Essequibo to Father. I'm writing to ask Father to make
arrangements to keep him there."

"Good heavens! But why? Send him back to his
grandfather—away from us? Away from his mother?"

"I think that the best plan," he murmured, very
uncomfortable. "For certain reasons which I don't care
to discuss at the moment I've decided on this course."

"It is a great shock to me, Jabez. A great shock.
I've become so fond of him. The dear little fellow."
She seemed genuinely dismayed, and suddenly said:
"You won't change your mind, Jabez? You won't re-
consider your decision?"

"No, Aunt Hendrickje." There was finality in his
tone.

A slightly baffled frown passed over her face.
Abruptly she smiled and said: "By the way, Jabez,
about the veranda—you may go out to Rosaria if you
wish. She is by herself now. I saw Adrian showing her
how to write, but he went out a short while ago."

"I don't—I never suggested——"

"I understand perfectly, my boy," she interrupted quickly, her manner sympathetic and motherly. She held his arm and said softly: "It's unfortunate. Very unfortunate. But you shouldn't let it upset you."

"Upset me? I'm afraid I don't know what you're talking about. Did you say Adrian was showing her how to write?"

"Yes, she asked him to show her—a few days ago. I suppose it's only natural, Jabez. She so needs his company, my boy. You grasp what I mean, don't you?"

"No, I—no, I don't quite know what you mean. At least, not what you want to imply. . . ." He broke off, completely confused and discomfited.

His aunt nodded. "Don't trouble to explain, my boy. I see everything clearly. In a way I suppose it was inevitable. It's nature, Jabez. She can't help it. You mustn't blame her. She's young and healthy and it is to be expected that she would need the company of a fit man. Be brave, my boy. Don't let adversity get you down."

He turned off with a choked sound and went upstairs.

The following day happened to be a Sunday. At about two o'clock it was very hot, though off and on a soft breeze came from the east.

A peaceful quiet pervaded the house. In the sitting room, on a small table, a black candle burned. It stood in a brass bowl containing clotted blood—the blood of a rooster. On another table, in the darkest corner of the room, the feathers of the bird had been arranged around an iron pot half filled with a greenish mess—a concoction that gave off a sweetish-rank aroma. On the floor, under the table, lay the head of the rooster. This was the work of Hoobak, one of Hendrickje's leader-bullies. Hoobak was an *obeah* man, and his mistress allowed him these liberties because it flattered his vanity and, incidentally, satisfied the wishes of Bangara, who was superstitious and believed that unless these rites were performed at least once a week the bush-gods would wreak evil on him for being sexually intimate with a white woman. Bangara was an Angola mulatto who had arrived with the batch of two hundred and fifty slaves imported through the cooperation of the West Indian Company after the Cassard raid in 1712.

Upstairs, in his room, Adrian, sitting by a window, dozed over a book. His pipe had gone out. Across the compound, outside, the slaves sat around their logies beating a tom-tom and wailing a monotonous African chant: a lulling, hypnotic sound in the hot mid-afternoon air.

When the door opened and Rosaria entered, Adrian's head came up with a jerk. Rosaria said: "I just come in to ask you to show me to write one-two letters like how you show me yesterday." She had in hand a quill and a piece of paper.

"You shouldn't have come in here," he frowned. "It's indiscreet."

She wore a pale green gown, and it was of transparent material. She came toward him, smiling. "You mean Jabez; what he think of me in here? I not forget that. I leave him in the room. He deep asleep. He give off the plenty snores. Like so." She uttered a few mimic snores, then made a succulent chuckling sound and leaned against the windowsill.

"Still I don't like it, Rosaria," Adrian said. "The veranda downstairs is the place for your lessons. If he found you in my room he might think you were in here for another purpose than that of writing."

"But I do come for the other purpose, Adrian." She laughed. "What for we must pretend now? We not agree to be the two good friends? I only bring this the paper and the quill for in case of anything it should go wrong, then we say I come in here to do the writing. It is so the very simple. Nothing to make the worry about."

"Simple? You call it simple? Do you forget you are his wife? I want no entanglements, Rosaria. And Jabez is a good fellow. I like him. I look upon him as a friend. We have been corresponding since we were eleven or twelve—the only human being I had to confide in when life was a burden, when *she* had us under her foot. Nothing would distress me more than to commit an act of disloyalty against Jabez."

"What you must talk about disloyal to Jabez?" She sat down in his lap. "That silly talk. I not understand it. Me? All I want is to make sweet with the man. I not know nothing else more than just that. Yes, I say that true, true."

He uttered a half-hearted growl and attempted to push her off, but she had anticipated this. She pressed closer to him and put her arm around his neck, deftly shrugging off the gown.

"Come, Adrian, you not make the disappoint now. Please. We alone here today in this room and everything is so quiet and nice. What wrong? You not like me? Give me the try. I do it good, good. True. I make sweet the way you like best. Any way you like. I know all the ways, yes."

He was so taken aback that he hardly seemed to know what to say. He shook his head in a harrowed manner, glancing past her toward the door. At length he said: "Rosaria, this will get us both into a most awkward situation. I don't like it. Already Jabez seems a little odd. He told me this morning that he's sending Hubertus back to Essequibo as soon as he can arrange for someone to take him. He has written to his father about it. It's a wise move, I admit. I told him so. He must realize that she is trying to get the little fellow into her evil clutches——"

"That not the reason. He send him away to Essequibo because he had the quarrel with me. I tell him I not feed no baby any more at my breast, and I tell him how Aunt Hendrickje she not too like have children in the house with the Indian blood. That what make him decide."

"You told him that? Poor fellow. He has such a brooding look. He hardly says much. No, Rosaria, you mustn't come in here again. You must go. Please. If he gets to hear of this he'll be terribly upset. It will deepen his despondency. He's very fond of you—and he's my good friend. A blunder like this might send him over to her camp, besides, and I can't afford to lose him. I must have as many on my side as it's humanly possible. We have to fight and fight that fiend——"

She cut him short by kissing him full on the mouth. She rubbed her hand along his neck. "I tell you Jabez, he deep asleep. He not find out. You can't make the disappoint now, Adrian. I sure he not hear about this. I keep it quiet from him. True, Adrian. True."

"But he's my good friend, Rosaria. It would be morally wrong." He tried to detach her limbs from around him, but she was like an active, persevering snake avid in motion in his lap. "It's a case of ethics, you must understand. It would be villainy. We should leave that sort of thing to her. It's what *she* would do, the depraved monster! She and her Bangara. Did you see the black candle burning downstairs? Now, please! You really mustn't persist like this. I'm going to get annoyed. I have scruples in such matters."

In voice and manner he betrayed the unbalanced fear and persecution mania from which he was suffering, but she was in too urgently erotic a mood to take notice of this. She said: "He not husband to me, Adrian. You know well he not give me the sweetness. He no good now since what the Señor Samuel do to him. Yes? You not know that?"

There was desperation in her manner. Her eyes glittered with an intense hunger. She moistened her lips feverishly and kept swallowing.

"I mean it, true, Adrian. I go mad soon if I not have the man. I can't live without the man every day, one after the other—no! I go mad—surely! I mean that the very true." Her voice became shriller. She was breathing fast. He could smell the cinnamon as she pressed herself to him and caressed his face and neck.

"I talk all that true. You know it. They make me marry him because no other the woman she will make the marriage with him—that why. And they want to make his son lawful—that why, too. I slave so I compel to make the marriage with him, yes." She breathed into his face, warm and damp and urgent, determined not to be foiled, determined to overcome the difficulties presented by his mental derangement.

"You see the position how it stand, Adrian? Yes? He not the husband to me, so what I must do when the night come and I want to make sweet? If I not have the husband soon I scream and tear my clothes. True. I scream and behave the most bad, bad. I go the worse mad." Her voice quavered sobbingly. "I mean it true, Adrian. I go the very mad. Every day you see me here I look calm, but I hot inside. I boil up, boil up, yes. I must have the husband or I go mad, mad, mad."

Automatically, all the while, he had kept on trying to push her from him—in a feeble, absentminded, mechanical way—but she clutched at him with a determined singleness of purpose.

"You mustn't push me away, Adrian. I beg you. Perhaps we not get one more the chance before many weeks go along passing. Take me quick while he asleep there now. He not know. Please! You not drive me off, Adrian. I scream if you send me away. I beg you hard. I make myself the slave for you. I keep on your side the always and fight your mother. I hate her with you and do the things to hurt her, yes. I mean it true. I fight and fight just as you want me to do."

Gradually the stimulus of her presence in his lap was taking effect on him, breaking down the defense of his mental indisposition. He said in a groaning murmur: "I don't like this, Rosaria. I don't like it. Go and lock the door quickly before she comes in and surprises us. No, don't bother. I'll do it myself. By hell! But this is madness! Madness! This is going to bring about complications. It's going to create an ugly situation. It was very cruel of you, Rosaria, to have precipitated this scene. I don't know what to say." He broke off and began to fondle her, trembling and gulping agitatedly. Then he pushed her from him and rushed over to the door and locked it.

Lying on the bed waiting for him to undress she hugged herself and rubbed her hands down her thighs, uttering moaning sounds of anticipation. That he was a worried, half-demented creature did not trouble her. It evoked no pity in her.

Twilight had begun to gather before she left the room. She said: "I try to come again soon—some time, some way." She looked at him with a squinting, dog-like worship. "You too nice, Adrian. I mean that true. Too surely." She held his head and kissed his hair. "I enjoy you the best more than any the other man I ever have, yes." She kissed him again. "I mean that true, true. Very true."

He made no response, staring past her head in a contemplative, anxious manner and shifting himself so that he could glance past her toward the door.

After she had gone he paced about the room, frowning and muttering.

"I feel unsafe. She's a delightful creature, but the ethics are wrong. Wrong. My poor friend Jabez. It's so unfortunate that she should be his wife. I believe she would make a good ally. . . . I must not spurn her. It might drive her over to *her* camp. . . ."

That same night, when Jabez had fallen asleep, Rosaria crept out of bed and went in to Adrian.

"Rosaria! How could you have risked such a thing! Suppose he wakes and discovers that you are not beside him. Go back at once."

"He asleep deep. I had to come again, Adrian. The fire it burn me inside. I know the risk it is big, but I go mad if I not have you."

"I feel unsafe. I don't know what to think." He caressed her tentatively, then pushed her from him. But she would not be pushed. It took her a long time to persuade him to let her stay, but she succeeded, and, after this, every night she came to his room.

Soon he took it for granted, her coming, and made no protest. She taught him perverted ways of love making, and he found himself gradually becoming very attached to her. Not that this solved the problem of his mania. If anything, it increased the anxiety in him, and the forever active fear that his mother was about to attack him and defeat him. He went about with a guilty, worried air, his outward calm deserting him. Often he would sit on the back veranda for hours muttering to himself, though at night when he was with her in bed his outlook would grow almost normal. Night became for him his time of greatest relief from the anxiety that plagued him during the day.

He avoided Jabez as much as possible, and so marked did this attitude become that one day Jabez smiled and asked him outright: "Is anything the matter, Adrian? You seem to have become so distant toward me of late."

Adrian became confused and told him: "No, nothing is the matter. I'm worried. Various matters. I wish I could discuss them with you, Jabez, but I can't. My mind is in a jumble. In a jumble."

Jabez gripped his arm in a friendly manner and said: "Don't let anything upset you. I know what your problems are. I have mine, too."

Adrian gave him a wondering stare.

Jabez said: "You're feeling guilty, Adrian—I understand. Don't feel that way any more. It isn't your fault, what has happened."

"But—what do you mean?"

"I mean I know about Rosaria. The first time she went to your room was a Sunday when she thought I was asleep. Every night since then she has been going to you. I'm not as foolish as she thinks I am. But I have nothing against either of you. It was inevitable that it should have happened this way. How could she have helped going to you when I'm no good!"

Adrian, pale, bewildered, stared at him. At length he nodded weakly and mumbled: "Thank you, Jabez. Thank you. You've relieved my troubles by half. I feel very foolish. I don't know what to say."

"Please tell her nothing. She seems to be under the impression that I'm unaware that she leaves our room every night, so let her continue under the delusion. Poor girl. She can't help it, Adrian. I know that now. It's like a pernicious drug with her."

Adrian gripped his arm, then turned off and left him. From that day he was much more relaxed, and relations between himself and Jabez improved considerably. He lost his guilty air, though often could not meet Jabez's gaze without betraying signs of discomfiture. Jabez went out of his way always to put him at ease.

Hendrickje knew what was happening. She and Rosaria held long chats every morning after Adrian and Jabez had gone into the fields. In the presence of the two men, however, they pretended to be stiff and cold with each other. Occasionally they staged tiffs at table for the benefit of Adrian.

One night Rosaria said to Adrian: "You see how she talk to me today because I make the mistake and use my spoon to put it in the dish? She hate me. I know it, yes. One day come soon when I make bad for her."

Adrian grunted. "She hates you because you won't side with her—because you won't cooperate with her in her villainy. If you fawned upon her and plotted against me you would be her greatest friend. She even hates your child now. She doesn't croon over it or pay it any attention as she did at first. I suppose it's the Indian blood in it. She despises both you and the child for the Indian blood in you."

He was sitting up in the bed. She told him to lie down again, but he might not have heard her. He said abruptly: "Rosaria, I've come to a big decision. A terrible decision, in a way, but there's no help for it. It's all part of the strategy——"

"I know, my Adrian, but you will tell me about it later on, not so? Lie down with me again and let us make sweet one more time, then we sleep. When we wake, you tell me about the terrible decision."

He did not heed her. He clutched her arm and told her to pay attention. "This will hurt Jabez, Rosaria, but it can't be avoided. It must be done. We must have children—you and I. It will harrow her soul to know that I'm producing another brood of children with colored blood. My mulatto brats cause her enough worry, but think if we were to raise a family of dusky-skinned, Indian looking children! I've been turning this scheme over in my mind for some time now—ever since that day when you told me on the back veranda that she dreads your becoming the mother of my children. And from her aggressive and contemptuous attitude toward you of late I can see that it will be a big blow to her if such a thing did come to pass. By hell! Rosaria, we'll do it. We'll have children together—children with Indian blood. A whole horde of bastard black-haired van Groenwegels. It will cut her to the depths of her black soul to watch them moving about the house."

The following morning Rosaria went off into creamy gurgles of laughter as she related to Hendrickje what had passed the night before.

"Aunt Hendrickje, he really funny in his head, yes! *Dios mio!* He talk and he talk and he talk! He even get out of the bed and walk around in the room and I think he never want to stop talking and lie down to make the second sweetness with me. I have to shut his mouth with the plenty kisses and give him the special tickle-tickle before he agree to lie down with me again. All he want to do is talk about how he hate you and how he want to harrow your soul——"

"Anyway, you say he's eager to have children with you?"

"Eager! You talk it so the soft! Aunt Hendrickje, he want that so the very bad I believe he kill me with the musket if I say no I not want to have any. Yes, he himself tell me he want to have the children—same as you say he do! You have the brain, Aunt Hendrickje. The plan, it all coming out same as you say it will work out. We have him good and nice. And he so sweet and big and strong. He give me the everything I want. I teach him the new ways, and he like them every one, yes. We have plenty sweet times, Aunt Hendrickje. This plan, it suit me good, good, good. . . ."

VII

Rosaria was nearly three months pregnant with Adrian's child when Jabez announced casually one morning that he had heard from his father and that arrangements were complete for sending Hubertus back to the Essequibo. The chief mate of a ship sailing from Fort Nassau in a few days was a good friend of Aert's and had volunteered to take charge of the child during the voyage.

Adrian offered to accompany them to the fort, and Jabez smiled and said: "Thank you, Adrian, I should be glad for your company."

So Adrian accompanied him, and the two of them arrived back late at night after a hard ride on the trail.

The following morning Hendrickje met Jabez coming along the corridor and noticed that there was an unusually tense and contemplative air about him. It was not until later in the day, however, that she smiled at him and commented: "My boy, this morning you passed me in the corridor as though entirely unaware of my presence. You don't seem yourself today. I hope nothing happened yesterday on your way to or from the fort to upset you unduly?"

He looked at her steadily, almost aggressively, and seemed on the point of saying something bitter. But his voice was controlled when he spoke. "No, nothing happened on the way to or from the fort to upset me. Adrian and I had a very uneventful journey."

"I see." She seemed puzzled, and evidently wanted to probe him. She kept up her pretense of kindly interest, and moved closer to him. Touched his arm affectionately. "I think something is the matter, all the same, my boy. I'm getting old, and I'm experienced. I see much that younger people don't."

"Do you?" There was no mistaking the sarcasm in his voice.

It did not daunt her, however. "I fancy," she said, "I know what your troubles are, my boy. But you must be a philosopher, Jabez. If life is to be tolerable for some of us we must be prepared to be resigned to our lot."

He said nothing, but the stare he gave her was glassy.

"Our world is so fashioned that we can't all be happy, Jabez. Those of us who have been victims of an unkind fate must brace ourselves with the smaller joys in life. Take me, for instance. I'm not a happy woman. Much has happened to embitter me. My husband disappointed me. He was a poor, effete, contemptible weakling. It may seem cruel to say it, but my husband lived off me like a parasite—lived off my womanly strength while he painted away his time. My elder son was a disappointment, too."

After a silence she continued: "Another bitter instance was when Adrian refused to defend our property that day when the fort surrendered. That, perhaps, was the most galling of all. Our family traditions are to me precious above everything else in the world. I feel profoundly about them. To the day of my death I shall be a true van Groenwegel—a fighter like our ancestors, Kaywana and Adriansen, and Grandfather Willem. Naturally, however, I realize that life has to go on, and I'm not downcast by my disappointments. I'm thankful for the smaller interests that have prospered. I have this plantation, and it is doing well. I have Bangara, and he means a lot to me. He satisfies my deep physical urges; I'm not ashamed to admit it, for I see no reason why one should be ashamed of natural urges; I'm not ashamed of eating. I always face the truth, Jabez.

"In your case, my boy, you have your son, and you have the work on the plantation which seems to interest you immensely. Why not let these things suffice! Why not build them up in your imagination and make them seem important and worth living for!" She sighed and added: "Unless, of course"—a subtle significance came into her tone—"unless you deem yourself so hopelessly placed in the scheme of living that nothing at all can satisfy you or give you even moderate peace. In that case, then, I agree, no one could blame you for committing any rash act, for I myself do not see any point in existing in total misery. Not that I'm suggesting for one moment that you should do anything foolish—why, Jabez!"

He had listened to her patiently, a slight smile on his face; now he scowled with such utter contempt and hate that she recoiled.

"Is anything the matter, my boy? Have I said anything to annoy you?"

Without a word he turned and walked away.

At about five that same day, when Jabez and Adrian were in the compound superintending the day's punishments, Hendrickje said to Rosaria: "I can't understand what could have happened to Jabez overnight. Do you think you can explain his attitude toward me today?"

"I not sure myself," said Rosaria, "but I feel it have something to do with the little Hubertus, his sending him to Essequibo. He hate you, Aunt Hendrickje. He turn now like Adrian. I see it in his eyes the many times when I talk to him. And he hate me, too."

Hendrickje looked thoughtful. They were in Rosaria's room.

A freakish shower was falling. The late afternoon sunshine shone brilliantly through the hissing drops, and the drops flashed orange and blue and green, especially those that dripped from the foliage of the trees.

The punishments went on just the same. Bangara and Dooley and Hoobak were the lashers today. Adrian, sheltering in the doorway of the toolshed, stood smoking a long-stemmed pipe and surveying the scene with a slightly pensive air.

Hendrickje frowned and murmured: "Didn't Jabez go out with Adrian to see after the punishments?"

"Yes, he go with Adrian. I see him go myself. He not there?"

"No, I don't see him. Only Adrian is by the toolshed."

"That funny," said Rosaria.

The rain abruptly thinned off and ceased. The trees glistened. Long shadows lay across the compound, and the air smelt of leaves and gurgling water seeping swiftly into the earth and into hidden drains.

"Perhaps he walk by himself and gone to look over the logies."

"Perhaps," said Hendrickje.

The sound of a tom-tom came dully from the vicinity of the logies. One of the slaves being flogged began to howl mournfully. High overhead, a flock of parrots was passing with a remote chatter. They could be seen vaguely green against the pink feathers of cloud that streaked the sky.

Adrian moved out into the compound and said something to Dooley, and Dooley lowered his whip and began to unbind the feet and hands of the offender.

Hendrickje sidled away from the window, in case Adrian should happen to glance up, for he would have thought it strange to see her in Rosaria's room. In his eyes, she and Rosaria were enemies.

It was Rosaria who heard the sound first. She said: "What's that?"

"What's what?" asked Hendrickje.

"You not hear something in the passage?"

Then Hendrickje heard it, too. A thump-thump, as of bare feet. Someone seemed to be gasping and whimpering in the corridor.

"Somebody crying," said Rosaria. She looked frightened.

Hendrickje cocked her head, listening.

The sound came again. Hendrickje was about to cross the door when the door was pushed in.

It was Jabez.

Rosaria exclaimed.

Jabez's clothes were damp, as though he had been walking in the rain. His face was pale and his eyes bleary. He did not seem to recognize them or even to be aware of their presence in the room. He moved toward the bed with a lumbering, mechanical gait. He was barefooted, his toes and ankles sticky with soft, wet mud. He breathed in audible gusts— a labored wheezing. His lips were parted, and there was a greenish stain around them. A long, thin string of saliva dangled from his chin.

He collapsed heavily on to the bed.

Rosaria rushed toward him excitably, but Hendrickje restrained her before she could touch him. "Leave him! Leave him!"

"He sick, Aunt Hendrickje! Look his face!"

"Very well, very well," snapped Hendrickje. "Control yourself. Can't you see what's happened? He's poisoned himself. It's the vegetable concoction Hoobak brews to kill off the evil spirits. Look at his eyes. The pupils are dilated—and traces of the stuff are on his lips."

"What we going to do, Aunt Hendrickje? Run go get the surgeon?"

"That would be useless. Remain where you are. Keep your head. Don't you see he's saved us a lot of trouble?"

"Oh, but it horrible, Aunt Hendrickje! It the very terrible!"

"Go to the window and call Adrian."

Rosaria obeyed, and Adrian looked up and frowned. "What do you want, Rosaria? What's the matter?"

"Something it happen, Adrian. Something bad! Come quick!"

Hendrickje did not leave the room. She had taken up a position by the bed, pretending to be gravely concerned over the condition of Jabez. That was how Adrian found her when he entered. He glanced from Rosaria to the bed in a bewildered manner. Rosaria stood behind his mother with a frightened look.

Hendrickje turned abruptly. "Adrian! Come and see. Come and see what has happened. Have a look and observe what you and this slut have driven your poor cousin to do."

"Are you addressing me?" Adrian snapped.

"I am. Come over here and see. Jabez has poisoned himself."

"Poisoned himself?" The aggressiveness vanished from his manner. He came toward the bed.

Jabez's face was getting blue. His tongue lolled out. His heavy body, stout and awkward, had begun to squirm slowly, and a thick, rasping sound came from deep in his throat. His muddy feet made gray smudges on the white sheet. Suddenly he tried to arch his back, his big, paunchy belly bulging forward grotesquely.

Rosaria, her hand pressed to her mouth, whimpered softly.

"Yes, he's poisoned himself," Hendrickje repeated. "Through you and this strumpet. I met him coming upstairs a few minutes ago and his last words were a curse on you and his wife."

Rosaria broke out: "She lie! She lie! Adrian, she say that because she want you to send me away from here. Jabez not say nothing like that. He say to me I must marry you, that he not blame you nor me for what it happen between us. That what he say, Adrian. Believe me. I not lie. I speak true. Your mother, she hate me bad, that why she say Jabez he curse you and me. She want me to go away from you."

Adrian nodded, glancing from the writhing man to Rosaria and his mother. "You needn't be afraid, Rosaria," he growled. "She can't harm you. You'll stay. She can't send you away. My God! But Jabez is dying. We should do something. I'd better go for the surgeon."

"No, Adrian. Don't go. It not the use now. He dying already. Stay with me, please. I the too afraid, Adrian."

"What did he take? How did this happen? I don't understand. He was outside with me. He said he was going to inspect the logies. Just before the rain came down he told me that."

Rosaria was clutching his arm. "I not know nothing, Adrian. Your mother, she know about poison. She say it something Hoobak he brew for the evil spirits."

Enlightenment came to his face. "By hell! That disgusting mess! They make it from bitter cassava and hog tannia and wild herbs. Where did he get it from? Who gave it to him?" He turned suspicious eyes on his mother, but Rosaria said quickly: "Perhaps he take up the pot Hoobak he always leave in the sitting room on Sunday. It must be that how he get it. Adrian, this thing it too horrible, yes. I too bad the frightened. *Dios mio!* Look what come from his mouth now!" She hid her face against him.

Hendrickje, impassive, stared at the dying man.

Through the open door a beam of sunlight came in from the corridor window.

In silence, the three of them watched Jabez. The sound of the tom-tom could still be heard. Bangara was shouting something to Hoobak in a mixture of Portuguese and an African dialect. Hoobak replied in the same patois, for Hoobak, too, had come from Angola. These sounds, however, made no impression on the senses of Adrian and Rosaria and Hendrickje. They listened to the labored wheezing grunts of Jabez.

The beam of sunshine faded. The twilight had deepened and insects had begun their nighttime churring before Jabez finally grew still. The bedsheet was smeared with a greenish frothing liquid that had issued from his mouth—and with the mud from his feet. In death, his face and hands appeared bluish-green and blotchy, and his eyes stared wide, the pupils dilated to the full circle of the irises.

Rosaria made a sobbing sound.

Before Hendrickje left the room she looked at the two of them, her tall, shapely form tense in the dusk. "I hope you're both satisfied now." She spoke quietly, her tone laden with venom. "You ought to be. You've got what you wanted."

"Get out of this room," said Adrian coldly. His manner subdued.

"I'll go," said his mother. "You can remain and console her. But before I go, let me tell you this, Adrian. If you insist on keeping this woman in this house after what has happened this evening I shall wipe you completely from my thoughts. I shall never again consider you as a relative of mine. You have brought me much bitterness in the past, Adrian, but I've tried to overlook it. I've tried to forgive you as much as a mother could. But if you keep this woman beside you I shall never forgive you. Never! Never as long as I live!"

Adrian uttered a low quavering sound; it seemed an epitome of all the hate and triumph of which he was capable.

"It will have to be so, then, Hendrickje," he said. "You can wipe me from your thoughts. You can cease to look upon me as a relative. I ceased to do that toward you fifteen years ago. You can do anything you like now, you despicable monster! This is my day! And

I'm glad it hurts you! Rosaria will remain here—and perhaps you may be interested to learn that she is already pregnant with my child."

"Pregnant with your child!" Hendrickje turned her gaze to Rosaria. Her gray-green eyes steady. Not by the flicker of an eyelash did she betray her true feelings.

Rosaria slunk behind Adrian, as though in fear, but, in reality, to conceal the twitching of her face. It seemed all she could do to prevent herself from bursting into a gurgle of creamy laughter.

Adrian nodded. "Yes, she's pregnant, and now Jabez has committed this terrible act I'm going to marry her. I've just this minute decided."

"Marry her, Adrian! This half-breed wretch! She's half Carib!"

"Wasn't Kaywana half Indian, too? Aha! I knew it would cut you to the marrow. I'm glad. This is my moment of victory, Hendrickje, and there will be many more such moments for me as time goes on. You thought you could defeat me. You didn't know how strong I was—and how clever! I have shown you now that I'm your better, Hendrickje. And I mean to live for nothing but to wound you. I'm going to harrow your soul. I'm going to fight you and live to see you die a more horrible death than this poor fellow here. It's you who urged him to do it. It's you. With your insidious methods—your soft tongue. It's you!"

Hendrickje left the room.

"Go!" shouted Adrian. "Go, you demon! Tomorrow Rosaria and I set out for Fort Nassau to be married! By hell! Legitimate van Groenwegels with Carib blood! It hurts you! I know it hurts! I want it to hurt you!"

Rosaria, shaking and sputtering, tried to disguise her mirth in a long wail. "Oh, Adrian, I feel so sorry. Only thing puzzle me is why he take off his shoes. Why he barefoot when he walk in the room? You can tell me that, Adrian? I so puzzle at that."

Adrian, unheeding, went to the door to shout up the corridor after his mother. He bellowed with laughter.

"Defeated! Defeated! Haw, haw, haw! Monster! Cur! Defeated! Haw, haw, haw, haw!"

"Oh, Adrian, I so puzzled. Jabez, why he barefooted. . . ."

"Haw, haw, haw! Snake! My day! You hear me! This is *my* day!"

VIII The Old Blood

I

"Is this man still ill?"

"Yes, Missy. He got fever."

"He has been ill for a long time."

"Yes, Missy."

"Haul him out, Bangara. Bring him along."

"What you going to do to him, Missy?"

"What I did to Pardoom a few weeks ago. Bring him along. Take him behind the wild pines."

Bangara still hesitated, a look of fear on his face —fear of the evil spirits. "Missy, what you going to do to him? Tell me."

Hendrickje did not reply. She gave Bangara a stare. At sixty-five she was still erect and shapely. If anything, the years had augmented her regal bearing. Her hair, too, gave her a certain majesty; the gray strands were in the majority now, and they had a glimmer like the glimmer of pewter.

Bangara's gaze fell under her stare.

On the floor of the logie the ill old slave moaned.

"The evil spirits cannot harm you for performing a useful act, Bangara. You yourself have said so before. Pardoom was of no use to us because he had grown feeble and diseased, so you disposed of him for me. This is a similar case. This man is about seventy-five. He came with me from the Essequibo. He's only a burden to us now, and we need this logie for the new arrivals tomorrow. Look at it! In a filthy condition!"

"He could get better, Missy—if we give him medicine."

"No. I've asked the surgeon. He says there's no hope at all for him. His age is against him." She smiled indulgently and patted Bangara's rump. "Trust me, Bangara. We'll burn a few candles tonight and boil some of Hoobak's death-broth as a precaution against the evil spirits."

Bangara seemed somewhat reassured.

"Bring him along."

The old man moaned. "Missy, na take me away. Na bury me, Missy. Me na dead yet. True, Missy. Wakky na dead yet. Two-three more days. Please."

"That's right, Bangara. Bring him along."

From near the smaller water tank Pedro saw. He ran off.

Lumea and Jacques and David were in the sitting room preparing their lessons for the following day. Pedro told them: "Come quickly. Grandma is going to bury a slave."

"Which one?" Lumea sprang up at once.

"It's Wakky," said David. "He's been ill for weeks. I told you Grandma would have him buried alive as she did to Pardoom."

Lumea chortled. "The next one she'll bury will be Father himself. I heard her saying last week that Father's no good to himself now and may as well be got rid of. All alone in his room talking to himself in his madness."

"Come quickly," Pedro told them. "Bangara is pulling him along to the same spot where she had Pardoom buried. Behind the wild pines."

"If she sees us she'll flog us," said Jacques. "We'd better not go."

"You can tell her you've finished your lessons. She won't say anything if you've finished your lessons."

"But I haven't finished my lessons."

"You can still tell her you have, can't you? What's a little lie?"

"Yes, Jacques. Come on," Lumea urged. "Dave. Let's go."

Jacques yielded, and they all went scampering across the compound in the direction of the wild pines. Pedro, however, made them stop near the water tank.

"We can watch from here and she won't know a thing," he said. "You lie behind the cask there, Jacques. Lumea, you stay here with me. Dave, you go under the tank. You're small. You can squeeze under."

Pedro always directed their exploits. He was the eldest and ten years old. He had dead-straight black hair, like his mother's, and black eyes, but he was fair-complexioned like his father. Only one of the six children had inherited any Indian duskiness, and even so it was slight. Laurens was the olive-skinned boy. He was the last child. He had a deformed right foot, and toddled around with a limp. The rest of them could easily have passed for pure white. Jacques and Lumea both had green eyes and light-brown hair. Lumea was the second and Jacques the third child. David, who had come fourth, had gray eyes and dark-brown hair. Juliana, the next, was an outright blonde, blue-eyed and golden-haired. Rosaria had given birth to them one after the other, every year, and there would have been others after them had Adrian's mania not developed into a morbid melancholia which kept him to himself day and night, a severe hermit in his room.

"Look! There's Bangara. He's bringing the spade to dig."

They heard the old slave wailing. "Missy, me na dead yet. Wakky na dead yet, Missy. Na bury Wakky yet. Please, Missy."

Lumea uttered a whinnying sound. "I'd give anything to see them throw him in. Remember how Pardoom crawled out again and Bangara had to hit him on the head with the spade?"

Bangara was digging, his mistress looking on. Once she frowned and gave the old man a kick, telling him to stop wailing.

"You'll be out of your misery, so what's the fuss about?"

"Missy, me na dead yet. Me get better soon. Give me till next week, Missy. Me get better. True, Missy."

"About two feet deeper, Bangara. And you'd better widen it more."

When Bangara had completed the job of digging, he and his mistress set about tumbling the old slave into the hole. He tried to crawl away into the pine clumps, so Bangara had to hit him over the head with his spade and drag him back by an ankle. Hendrickje caught the other ankle, and between them they sent him toppling over into the pit. Then Bangara muffled his desperate cries with a bucket of quicklime, and Hendrickje took up the spade and piled some dirt upon him.

Pedro and his brothers and sister uttered ecstatic crowing sounds. Pedro ran the risk of his grandmother seeing him by standing up to his full height so that he could see better.

Soon there were no more cries—only the sound of the dirt being dumped back into the hole and the clink of the spade as it struck a stone. The earth, as Hendrickje watched, heaved slowly in the grave. But not for long. Bangara worked quickly and efficiently and made a neat elongated mound.

"The next thing," said Hendrickje, "is to have that logie thoroughly cleaned out. Tell Dissak to take two or three others and have it done before darkness falls."

"Very well, Missy," Bangara mumbled, wiping his forehead. He looked at her, fear and veneration in his eyes.

II

Some nights Adrian would pace up and down in his room talking to himself. No longer did the children bother to climb on to the cupboard in their room to peer at him through the latticework at the top of the wall; they had grown too accustomed to his habits now. It was the same with their mother; they had grown tired of spying at her over the other wall when she and Bomba were in the big four-poster in the next room. Bomba was a big fellow like Bangara but pure negro; he satisfied his young mistress, and during the day was given only very light tasks about the house. The children were fond of him, chiefly because of the lewd tales he told them of jumbie-men and jumbie-women. Bomba had a rich imagination.

Pedro said to him one day: "I want to see Grandma when Bangara is with her. I've never seen them together. She always keeps that next room locked up. You don't think you can steal the key, Bomba?"

"No, Massa Pedro. That lady, she work with spirits. Bangara not like me. I never go near him or Missy Hendrickje since I begin to go in bed with your mother."

"Grandma is afraid you might have children with Mother," Lumea said.

"It's the family," nodded David. "Grandma doesn't want any bastards about the house. That's why she doesn't let those mulatto children Father had before we were born come into the house. Teekat is everything like Father, have you noticed? And Mabella has his nose and eyes."

Bomba nodded. He was squatting on the floor of their room, and they were gathered about him. Laurens and Juliana sat on one of the two big beds, but Pedro and Lumea and David sat on the floor. Jacques was perched on the small table on which stood the candlestick and the water jug and tumblers, his green eyes languid and droll-looking as he regarded the others. He had tiny brown freckles, like his grandmother's. He had been named after Jacques Vernsobre who owned Plantation Magdalenenburg up-creek.

It was nearly ten o'clock, and Hendrickje was in the fields overseeing the gangs. Since Adrian's eclipse, she had taken complete charge of the plantation. After the midday meal she took the children with their lessons. The children held her in great awe, but she saw to it that they did not hate her. She ruled them with sternness but observed a strict policy of justice; they were flogged only for deliberate offenses such as direct disobedience of an order or persistent neglect in the preparation of their lessons. She told them tales of the old days, but never thumped them about when they failed to recall some detail. She had other methods of stimulating their memories. One day, for instance, she asked David to tell her what happened when Antoine Ferry attacked Essequibo in 1708, and David replied: "That was the time when Great-aunt Gertruyt's husband, Antony de Wiecjk, died of pneumonia. He shot several of the raiders, and Great-grandfather Laurens came and found him half dead in the mud with Great-aunt Luise."

"Anything more?"

David frowned and shifted his feet about. "And," he said. "And . . ."

"And," prompted his grandmother.

"Antony had four pistols he used to walk around with——"

"Quiet! Lumea, can you help him out?"

"Yes, Grandma. The children died, too. One got shot through the head and the other got its foot shot off. And then . . ."

"Pedro! What are you whispering into her ear? I'm seeing you!"

"Seeing me whispering, Grandma?"

"Yes, seeing. I can't hear from this distance."

"Grandma, I was only picking an ant out of her ear."

"How considerate a brother you are! It's really astounding! Jacques, you seem to be having trouble with your nails. I've noticed you for some time digging very diligently at the windowsill. Can you tell me what was the outstanding event of the Ferry raid in 1708? I don't want any of the sordid details you've picked up through those old letters of mine I gave you all to read. Tell me what incident you consider the most vital—the most striking in that whole affair in 1708."

Jacques raised his eyes languidly and said: "Aunt Rosa refused to leave the house. She went into the kitchen and fired on the raiders until they got her. She was pregnant, but she still refused to run. She was a true van Groenwegel. She lived up to our traditions."

His grandmother flushed and smiled. She looked from one to the other of the rest of them. "Did you hear that? Jacques has told you. That was the outstanding incident of the Ferry raid. The heroism of your Great-aunt Rosa. She stayed and defended. She went down fighting. She died a heroine. Yes, Great-aunt Rosa has her place among our heroes and heroines, never forget that. We must venerate her memory to the same degree that we venerate the memory of Adriansen and Kaywana and your great-great-grandfather—old Willem. Also Great-uncle Aert in the Essequibo. What did Uncle Aert do in the following year when the second raid came? Tell us, Pedro. . . ."

Between Hendrickje and Rosaria relations, while not openly strained, were precarious. "Remember this,"

Hendrickje had told her one day soon after Bomba had begun to do bedroom service, "I'm now supreme mistress in this house, and if you have any kinky-headed children with that man I'm going to have them disposed of one by one in the quicklime pit aback of the storehouse. Is that perfectly clear?"

Rosaria gurgled creamily. "But, Mother, what you worry? You see me here? I not want no more the children. Six not enough? What I want more for? Bomba and me, we know what to do not to make the more children come. We have the little things we use."

"Very well. I hope the little things won't fail you, for I'm serious. I'm having no kinky-haired brats in this house."

"You leave that to me, Mother. I see we not make the more babies."

"But haven't you any pride? A coal-black fellow like Bomba? I don't know how you can tolerate him being intimate with you."

"Not mind his skin it black, Mother. He know to make the sweetness the very good." She went into details. "Yes, he can do that one, too. He teach me that one himself. I not know it before. He call it the jump-hop." She dissolved into husky gurgles.

Hendrickje laughed. "Rosaria," she said, "if such a personage as the Devil does exist I'm certain that it is he and no one but he who fashioned your soul."

"Yours, too, Mother, not yes? You so old and you still make sweet with the Bangara in your room."

Hendrickje grunted. "I dread to think what these children are going to be like when they grow up." Her manner became a trifle musing. Her slim white fingers drummed slowly on the table. Suddenly she shrugged and said: "Oh, well. Better dissolute animals than high-thinking dreamers. We've had too many soft-brained van Groenwegels in the past. It's kept down the fire. I want these children to have guts. I want them to live like men and women of iron. They must be ruthless and unscrupulous. They must have no foolish notions about pity and nobility——"

"Pity! They not know that word, Mother. They cruel bad, yes. Especial Pedro. That Pedro! *Dios mio!*

I believe he get it from my father who name Pedro, too. My father, he was cruel same, I used to hear. My mother say one day a man ask her something in the Dutch, and because she talk back in Dutch and my father he not understand, he hold her by her lip and drag her into the bush. And the things he do to her! He put sand in between her legs and he make ants bite her in that same place—the red ants what sting so hot. Yes, my Pedro, he get his cruel ways sure from my father. I name him right name, yes."

"You half-breed bitches always bring a lot of rottenness into a family."

"You, too, not yes, Mother? You not have the rottenness plenty, too? Perhaps he get some of his cruelty from you, too."

Ignoring the interruption, Hendrickje said: "However, I suppose a little cruelty is not a bad thing, especially when one has to handle slaves." She gazed at the table, as though addressing it. "Pedro should make a very proficient slave master when he gets older. A new spirit of rebelliousness seems to be coming alive among the slaves. It has to be watched and sternly treated. The Company planters are too soft with their people. They don't put enough sting into their punishments."

"They want somebody like you to teach them, not yes, Mother?"

"Precisely! It's people like me, Rosaria, who are successful in ruling. Hard, unmerciful tyrants." She struck the table with her fist. "The hard, cruel way is the only way. Life is brutal. I've said so often before, and I say it again. Only by brutality can we ever attain to the heights—to power!"

Hendrickje encouraged the children to be cruel. Many times the slaves came to her with complaints. Jakkara once told her: "Massa David come to my logie and throw salt on my woman and burn her eyes, Missy."

"Very well, Jakkara. I shall flog him as soon as he comes in. By the way, how did he come to perform this feat? What was your woman doing that she should have allowed Massa David to throw salt in her eyes?"

"Missy, she was sleeping on de bed and Massa David come in soft and drop salt over her face, and when she open her eyes de salt get in her eyes and burn her."

"That certainly was wrong of Massa David. What is your woman's name?"

"Dassiki, Missy."

"She's pregnant, isn't she?"

"Yes, Missy. She get baby soon."

"Excellent. That will mean extra rations for you both. Very well, Jakkara. I'll deal with Massa David as soon as he comes in."

Later, when David came in, his grandmother gave his ear a playful tweak. "So you've been throwing salt in Dassiki's eyes, I hear?"

"Grandma, she sucked her teeth at me this morning when I asked her to fetch me some water."

"She did, did she?"

"Yes, Grandma."

"And you threw salt in her eyes as a punishment?"

"Yes, Grandma."

"Very good. Never stand impertinence from a slave, my boy. Always let them know that you're a van Groenwegel. A superior person. They are your inferiors. Mere dirt!" She patted his head and went her way.

On another occasion Lumea and Pedro trapped two black centipedes in a bottle. With innocent expressions on their faces they approached Sakky who was pounding cassava in a mortar. Pedro suddenly brought the bottle from behind his back, opened it and shook out the centipedes down Sakky's bosom.

The woman sprang up, dashing down the pestle. She shrieked and tore at her clothes. She capered about in fierce pain as the venomous creatures sank their fangs into her flesh.

Pedro and Lumea danced about in delight.

"That will keep you warm for a few days, Sakky."

"You're sure to get fever from the bites."

"You won't have to work for the next day or two.

You should thank us. Go on. Say 'Thank you, Massa.' "

Later, Hendrickje twinkled at them: "So I understand you've been experimenting with centipedes on Sakky?"

Lumea giggled. Pedro smiled uncertainly.

"Rather cruel thing, don't you think?"

"She gave me rudeness yesterday, Grandma," said Pedro.

"That's a lie, Pedro. You know as well as I do that you did it out of sheer wanton cruelty." She stood frowning upon them, her manner faintly appraising. Then in a purring, good-natured voice she told them: "I don't mind your being cruel, children, but there is such a thing as being orderly in one's cruelty. You're growing up, Pedro. One day you'll have the responsibility of managing these slaves—and I want you to handle them like a man. Like a van Groenwegel. No softness. Be hard. Show no mercy. But—note this, my boy—never inflict pain for the sake of inflicting pain. No matter how much you may want to revel in seeing others squirm in pain, control yourself. Punish viciously—but punish only when punishment is merited. In this way you'll make them fear and respect you without hating you. The people who fear and respect you are your potential assassins, but add hatred to their fear and respect and you augment the potentiality a thousandfold."

She patted his head and moved on, going upstairs slowly and with conscious majesty.

III

Wednesday, every other week, was letter-writing day, for Hendrickje insisted that they must keep in touch with the Essequibo branch of the family. "We must never lose contact with them," she said. "It is only by holding together as one loyal group that we can be a powerful family. Our devotion to each other must not be merely warm; it must be perfervid. It must be unassailable. A van Groenwegel for a van Groenwegel."

Jacques, droll and casually innocent, posed the statement: "But, Grandma, Faustina is illegitimate. That sea captain was her father, and he never married her mother. You told us so yourself."

"That matters not! Her mother is a van Groenwegel—your Cousin Mathilde. So long as a drop of the blood of Kaywana and Adriansen runs in her veins she is entitled to be treated as one of the family. Furthermore, she goes by the name of van Groenwegel, and that settles the matter. In Suriname, too, we have your Great-grand-aunt Susannah and her family. It is true that the family name has been lost, but the blood is still there—and, most important of all, Susannah is one of our heroines, remember. Tell me something about her, David."

"She was in the raid of 1666. She and Great-grandfather Laurens repelled the attack on the house and kept the slaves under them from panicking. Great-grandfather Laurens accidentally struck her with his elbow in her eye, but she didn't cry. She went on loading the muskets."

"Good. In May next we are all going to write to her to congratulate her on her ninetieth birthday."

Jacques, however, had not finished. Digging at the windowsill, he said: "Grandma, what about Father's slave children who live in the logies outside? Are they to be treated, too, as members of the family?"

For an instant a dangerous gleam lingered in his grandmother's eyes. Then she smiled. "It's evidently your speciality, Jacques, to ask questions that are absurd. No! Your father's illegitimate slave children are outcasts. Your father brought them into the world with the deliberate intention of spiting me. They are kinky-headed mulattoes. Blood or no blood, no kinky-headed people will be admitted into our family pale. Understand that once and forever!"

It was through corresponding with the Essequibo folk that they learnt of Flora's coming to Berbice. Flora, Aert's daughter, was married to a Teuffer, and the Teuffer family had decided to leave Essequibo and settle in Berbice. "They lost heavily with their last coffee crop," Aert told Hendrickje in a letter, "and have concluded that the prospects for the future don't seem bright enough to merit their remaining in Essequibo."

The Teuffers were given a concession on the Berbice River, and they were no sooner settled when Hendrickje arranged for an exchange of visits. Flora took a great liking to Juliana, and even suggested adopting her as a playmate for her own two children, Sarah and Vincent. Hendrickje told her: "I shall consider it when she is a year or two older. I must have her well grounded in our traditions, Flora, before I let her out of my sight."

To the children Hendrickje said: "I want you to cultivate your cousins and their family on the Berbice. They live near the fort, and the people you will meet through them are people who will be of use to you in time to come. You must always take care to cultivate influential people. The fort officials and the Company planters are the people who matter. Play up to them. Get them on your side. Use them!"

It did not take Flora long, however, to discover about Bangara and Bomba and the general state of morals in the Canje household. Sarah and Vincent, on their return home from a visit to the Canje, shocked their parents by repeating one of Bomba's jumbie-man-jumbie-woman stories. They told, too, of what they had seen. "One night," Sarah said—she was five—"Lumea lifted us on top the cupboard, and we saw Bomba and Aunt Rosaria in bed. We could see them through the latticework. They were both naked, and when Vincent laughed, Aunt Rosaria looked up and saw us—and she laughed, too. She laughed and pointed up at us, and Bomba put out the candle on the table, but Aunt Rosaria said: 'Why did you put it out, Bomba? It's good for them to see. They must learn how to do the sweetness like us.' "

Sarah and Vincent never spent time again at the Canje house. Flora made polite excuses which did not deceive Hendrickje. But Hendrickje did not take offense. In a letter to Flora she said: "My dear, I suppose it was inevitable that you would come to hear of the scandalous doings of your late brother's wife. I have spoken to her until I am tired. She is too seasoned in vice to change. As a mother she is a failure, and I merely tolerate her presence here because I cannot do better. . . ."

Toward the end of the letter she said: "Little Juliana is such a dear creature. I dread the influence of the older ones upon her. In fact, I am seriously considering accepting your offer to have her there with you permanently. You must let me know what you feel in the matter—if you are still willing to take her. . . ."

Flora replied, making no reference whatever to Rosaria, but simply stating that she would be pleased to have Juliana at any time. Her letter, indeed, was significantly brief and to the point, and Hendrickje murmured to herself: "This requires prompt action. Flora's temperature is dropping."

When, however, she made the announcement that Juliana was to be sent to the Teuffers, Rosaria had something to say.

"No, Mother, I not like this plan. How you can send my little Juliana away from us? She my child. I want her to remain here."

"Since when have you become so loving a mother! Why didn't you make a fuss when Hubertus was sent to the Essequibo!"

"That long ago, and Hubertus he was a baby."

Hendrickje shrugged. "It can't be helped what you feel in the matter, Rosaria. It's for the good of the family that Juliana should be adopted by the Teuffer family. She'll provide a splendid link with the Berbice River people, and we need such a link."

Rosaria had always submitted to her mother-in-law's ruling, but on this occasion she held out. "I not care about no family," she said. "What I say is Juliana she my child, and I not part with her."

"Very well," said Hendrickje. "You can make your choice. Either Juliana goes—or Bomba."

Rosaria laughed. "Oh, that the trick you try on me, yes? No, Mother, that not work with me. I missy in this house same as you, and if I want to keep Bomba you not say one word to me. You can't send him away."

"You seem to be alarmingly ignorant of the law in such matters. Has it ever occurred to you that this plantation and all the slaves on it are my property? It's a pity you can't read or I should let you see the documents in order to convince you. I'm at liberty to sell one or all the slaves if I so desire, and I am informing you now that if I hear any more objections from you concerning my sending Juliana to the Teuffer family I shall send Bangara to Fort Nassau to arrange for the sale of Bomba."

Rosaria put her arm akimbo and blazed: "You go to hell! Do all you like. Sell Bomba if you want. I not care. I find other man quick time. Plenty other man take me if I only look at them. And white man, too. Jacques Fourie, he give me the eye plenty time. Jan de Groot. Hendrik de Fruizt. Raoul Laplace. All planter white men, they like me come and sleep with them if I only raise my finger. So what you talk about selling the Bomba! Sell him! But I keep my child here. If you send her away I go to Fort Nassau and make trouble for you."

Hendrickje remained unruffled. She smiled and said: "Very well, Rosaria," and turned and went upstairs. That very day she wrote Flora, saying: "It will be a relief to get Juliana out of this sordid house, and I am sure she will be happy in your midst. Her mother has raised no objection to her being adopted by you. On the contrary, she seems only too relieved to be rid of her. . . ."

Juliana, who had overheard the row, sobbed and said: "I don't like Mother. Grandma is much better. Grandma would have let me go to Aunt Flora, and I so wanted to go!"

Pedro soothed her. "Don't worry. Grandma will have her way. It doesn't matter what Mother says. Grandma always wins."

"I'm sorry I missed the fight," rued David (Lumea who had witnessed the quarrel in the absence of the boys, had, on their return, described a wild, desperate fight between Rosaria and Hendrickje). "Is the blood still on the dining room floor, Lumea?"

"No. Dissak and a few others came in and cleaned it up. Everything is in order again. I believe Mother is upstairs hatching a plan to kill Grandma. We're going to have some sport in this house before long."

"Where's Jacques, by the way?" asked Pedro, who did not believe a word of Lumea's story. "I haven't seen anything of him for the morning."

"I saw him in the bamboos hiding near the Siki Creek," said David. "Two slave girls were bathing there, and he was spying on them."

Hendrickje went ahead with her preparations to send Juliana to the Teuffers. Rosaria sulked. Two days after the quarrel she said to Juliana: "I your mother, yes. I tell you you not going nowhere. You listen to me. Your grandmother, she not make you. I make you in my belly, and I must say where you go and where you not go."

Juliana sucked her teeth and turned off.

Rosaria rushed at her and boxed her, and Juliana ran off sobbing.

The others consoled her. "Don't worry. Grandma always wins."

IV

That night there was no moon, and a cool steady breeze came from the east under a cloudless, starry sky.

Bangara went to his mistress's room twice a week, and this was one of his off nights. His logie was the one nearest to the large water tank. Both water tanks were locked every evening, the cocks being enclosed in box-like contraptions, and the keys were brought into the house. This was to prevent a waste of water, for during the night the slaves had been in the habit of drawing water for various trivial purposes. The keys were hung on a nail in the pantry.

Jacques, a light sleeper—he was a nervous boy— woke suddenly and stared around at the darkness. He and Pedro and David slept in one big bed. Lumea and Laurens and Juliana occupied another in the same room.

Jacques wondered what could have awakened him. He heard the insects outside, and he could see a few stars winking at the window. As he watched, a firefly flashed past brightly.

He had just decided that he must have been roused by a screech owl—owls sometimes flew past the window and awakened him; he heard one now in the distance—and was turning over to settle down again when he heard a faint thud and knew that it came from the next room; his mother's room. It was the door; the door had been shut. He heard the creak of the key in the lock. Perhaps Bomba had gone downstairs to get something for his mother, he told himself. Again he prepared to settle down.

Almost at once, however, a sharp crackling noise caused him to raise his head. It came from outside.

He waited, his ear cocked alertly.

He heard it again. Wrinkled his nose and sniffed.

Hopping over Pedro, he got out of bed and crossed swiftly and silently to a window. He looked out across the compound toward the logies where the household slaves slept, but there seemed nothing wrong. Then he craned his head far out and looked in the direction of the large water tank. . . . Wasn't that a glow? . . . Bangara's logie was the first one you came to after passing the large water tank.

He saw a flame shoot up above the tank. He turned from the window. "Pedro! Dave! Lumea! Wake up—quick! Wake up!"

From the next room his mother called: "Jacques! What wrong, boy? What you waking the others for?"

"There's a fire, Mother! It's Bangara's logie!"

"That stupid, boy! Go back to bed!" There seemed more anger and impatience than was necessary in her tone.

"Look out of your window, Mother! It's true!"

Pedro had awakened. "What's the matter? Is that you, Jacques?"

"Yes. Bangara's logie is on fire, Pedro. Wake up!"

"Fire! What!" Pedro was out of bed at a leap. He rushed to the window and looked out. "You're right!

It's Bangara's logie. Mother! Wake up! There's a fire outside!"

Lumea and the others were awake. All of them went dashing out into the corridor. Pedro hammered on the door of his grandmother's room.

"Grandma! Wake up! Fire!"

There was a stirring. Hendrickje called sleepily: "What's that? Who is shouting like that at this time of night?"

"Fire, Grandma! Bangara's logie is on fire!"

Outside, the slaves in the household logies were waking up. The compound flickered redly with the glow of the flames.

Bomba and Rosaria hastened down the corridor, Rosaria naked, Bomba with only trousers on and carrying a lighted candle that threatened to go out at any second. Downstairs there was a hammering on the kitchen door.

Pedro reached the pantry first and reached up to the nail where the keys for the water tanks were hung. Then he exclaimed: "Who has removed the keys? Where are the keys for the tanks?"

David opened the kitchen door. It was Dissak and Hoobak and Dooley.

"Where the keys, Massa? Where the keys?" Dissak asked excitedly, pushing past David into the pantry. Pedro bawled: "I can't find the keys!"

They saw Hendrickje coming, in nightgown, her two long loose plaits dangling behind her back like pewter snakes softly a-glimmer in the light of the two candles Lumea had lit on the dining table.

"Get out of the way, Pedro," she said to Pedro as she entered the pantry. "Dissak! Dooley! Hoobak! What are you doing in here? Why aren't you at the tanks?"

"We come for the keys, Missy. We want the keys."

"The keys aren't here, Grandma!"

Bomba and Rosaria appeared from the dining room. Bomba's candle was still alight. Hendrickje glanced toward the nail where the keys were always hung. "Where are the keys? Who has removed them?"

"I was first down, Grandma," said Pedro, "but they weren't there. Somebody had removed them before I came down."

Marrak came in crying: "Quick! The keys! Bangara inside the logie calling out for help. He burning up! Dissak, where the keys for the tanks?"

"What's that, Marrak? Is Bangara inside the logie?"

"Yes, Missy. He lock up inside. He can't come out."

"What do you mean? How could he be locked up inside?"

"Missy, the door lock up from outside—and de windows. Somebody do it on purpose. They pile up boxes and wood before the door and the windows and set the trash roof on fire. Brambles pile up all round the logie and burning. No chance go near to break open the door, Missy. Dis is spite work, Missy Hendrickje."

"Good God! But where are the keys? Where are the keys, I say?" She looked from one to the other of them. "Pedro! Are you sure you didn't touch them?"

"No, Grandma. I swear it. They weren't there when I looked."

"Someone in this house must have taken them from that nail. Who was it? Speak up!" She fixed her gaze on Rosaria. "Rosaria! Do you know anything of this? Did you come down here at any time tonight?"

Rosaria gave a sulky grunt and said: "I not know nothing about no keys. I was in my bed. You not see me here naked?"

Bomba, beside her, shifted about his feet uncomfortably.

Hendrickje pointed at them. "You two know of this! Bomba! Speak up! Where are the keys for the tanks? Produce them this instant!"

"Not know, Missy," said Bomba. He changed the candle to his other hand, glancing about shiftily.

"Grandma, let's break open the locks," said Pedro. "We have no time. That trash roof will fall in any moment."

"Dissak, break open the locks. Hurry!"

Dissak and Hoobak and Marrak rushed off. Pedro

squeezed past Bomba and his mother and dashed after them. Hendrickje took two paces up to Bomba and grasped him by the throat. Her eyes, in the candlelight, were bestial.

"Where are those keys? Tell me! Or, by God, I'll have you branded and tarred and feathered this very night!"

Bomba could have hurled her off with ease, but the fear she struck into him made his knees weak; his knees literally knocked together. He quavered: "I not know, Missy." The candle sagged forward and dripped grease on to the floor. Jacques reached out and took it from him. They heard Lumea call from the dining room: "Grandma! The roof has fallen in!" And David: "The one wall is caving in!"

Hendrickje snatched the candle from Jacques and jabbed it under Bomba's chin. "Tell me! Tell me! Who did that out there, Bomba? Who did it? Was it you and Missy Rosaria?"

Bomba yelled with pain and sprang back. The candle had gone out, but the glare of those in the dining room struck into the pantry. Rosaria was turning to go when Hendrickje, like a puma, flew after her and grabbed her arm. "Come! Come! Don't go. We're going to settle this now. You two know about this fiendish act. Confess it, confess it! Jacques, light the candle again. Bring in two from the dining room. Let me watch the faces of these two devils."

Jacques obeyed. He placed two candlesticks on a dresser. The fire did not interest him; only this scene in the pantry. He kept sucking in his lip and massaging his wrist, his green eyes wide.

"I'll crack every bone in your body, you dirty harlot, if you don't confess. It was you and this black brute who set fire to that logie!"

Rosarie jerked her arm free and stepped back. "Go to hell! What right you got ask me questions?"

Bomba was edging toward the outer door. Hendrickje turned upon him. "Stay where you are, Bomba! Not one inch further!"

"Grandma, come and see! The whole thing is collapsing!"

"Look at the sparks!"

Pedro came in, breathless. "Grandma, it's no use. He's finished. He's burnt up. They can't get at him."

His nightshirt was wet and soiled, for he had been helping to throw water on the fire. He was about to rush away again when his grandmother stayed him. "Pedro, call Dissak and Dooley and Raffy. Let Marrak remain and direct the others in putting out the fire. Quick! Call them."

"Very well, Grandma." He hurried off.

Jacques was huddled in the space between the dresser and the cupboard in which the kitchen pots and pans were kept.

Rosaria was muttering to herself in a surly voice, her way into the dining room barred by her mother-in-law. Outside, the crackling of the flames and the shouts of the men made an awesome confusion in the night. In the dining room, Lumea and David and Juliana and Laurens kept calling out news about the fire in an intermittent running commentary.

"They're beating out the flames now!" David called just as footsteps pattered on the three steps at the pantry door and Dissak and Dooley and Raffy came in. They were sweaty and blowing hard.

"Dissak! Raffy! Dooley! Seize Bomba and this woman and take them upstairs. It was they who set the fire!"

Bomba uttered a whimper and darted into the dining room. Dissak ran in after him. David, on the point of shouting another comment on the fire, felt a rough push and saw Bomba jump through the window and land on the ground four or five feet below. Then Dissak came up and jumped after him and began to chase him across the compound.

In the pantry Jacques kept his lip sucked in hard as he watched his grandmother and Dooley and Raffy struggling with his mother. Rosaria squirmed and kicked and used her head as a butting ram. She bit Dooley on his wrist and drew blood. David and Lumea came scampering in from the dining room, but Juliana and Laurens watched Dissak chasing Bomba.

Bomba tripped against the roots of a sapodilla tree and fell, and Dissak sprang upon him and the two men began to roll about on the ground, barely visible in the glow of the dying fire. Other slaves came up to assist Dissak.

In the pantry Rosaria struggled with savagery. Dooley tried to grab her legs, but she kicked out and sent him staggering. He rushed in again and wrapped his arms about her thighs, gorillalike. That put her off balance, and Raffy who was holding her one arm and Hendrickje the other went down with her in a confused pile, Dooley's head pinned between Rosaria's body and Raffy's chest. Dooley had to relax his gorilla hold, and Rosaria squirmed free and began to kick out and bite. She caught Hendrickje a blow on the cheekbone, then Raffy hit her a hefty blow in the face and Dooley tumbled her backward and kneeled on her chest, Raffy quickly pinning down her arms. She spat out obscenities in Spanish and Dutch, struggling all the while, her full loose breasts waggling around like two separate living things shiny and sweaty in the candlelight.

Jacques cried out and cringed back as his grandmother crouched down and began to hammer her fists down on Rosaria's face.

David and Lumea were fascinated by the sight.

"What has Mother done?" David muttered, for the fourth time.

Jacques cried out from his corner: "Grandma, you'll kill her! You'll kill her! Please don't hit her any more!"

"She's a murderer!" his grandmother shouted, staggering erect. "A fiend of hell! It was she who set the fire! That poor man burnt to death! Put her in the stocks, men! Take her outside! Where is Bomba? Has Dissak caught him yet?"

Dissak and two others were bringing Bomba who wailed and begged for mercy. "Missy Rosaria tell me to do it! Missy send me. I not want to do it, but Missy order. I must obey if Missy order me."

"Put him in the stocks, Dissak. Take him off!" Hendrickje kicked Rosaria savagely as the men bore her outside. "Take her out! Leave them both in the stocks until tomorrow. I'm going to tear them limb from limb, I swear it!"

Jacques, meanwhile, had taken a candle and gone upstairs to his father's room. He pushed the door in cautiously and peered inside.

Adrian was awake. He sat in a chair, his chin resting in a cupped hand. He turned his head and stared blankly at Jacques. There was no recognition in his sunken eyes. His unkempt beard was clogged with bits of dried food. The whole room smelt frowsy and fetid. The bedsheet looked soiled and gray as though it had not been changed for weeks. Jacques heard his father muttering to himself, but he could not make out the words. He withdrew the candle, shut the door softly and returned downstairs to the others. He told them: "Father is all right. The noise didn't upset him. He's sitting in a chair talking to himself as he does during the day."

David wanted to know whether they had found any bones among the ruins. Pedro said they wouldn't be able to search for anything until daylight. "The embers are still glowing. They can't do anything until they are out. But why should Mother and Bomba have done a thing like this? That's what I can't understand. Why kill off Bangara because she and Grandma had a row over Juliana? And those keys—what happened to them?"

"Mother must have taken them off the nail and hidden them so as to delay the men getting water from the tanks."

"Yes, I believe Lumea is right," David nodded. "It's that. The keys are upstairs in Mother's room. Jacques, go up and see if you find them."

Jacques was off at once. He came down presently jingling the keys. "I found them on the dressing table."

"You see that!" David exclaimed. "Mother did it. Grandma was right to beat her face. Mother is a murderer."

"And Bomba confessed," Lumea said. "They're both dirty murderers."

"What do you think Grandma is going to do with

them tomorrow?" There was a pained, nervous look on Jacques' face as he asked the question.

"She's going to brand Bomba, of course. Bomba is only a slave, so it won't be necessary to have him sent to Fort Nassau for trial before the Council of Justice. I don't know what she'll do with Mother. Perhaps she'll put her to sit on broken bottles," Pedro added in an offhand voice.

"By law they should be tried," said Lumea. "They should both be taken to Fort Nassau to appear before the Council of Justice."

"We all know that," shrugged Pedro, "but whoever bothers to go to all that trouble over a mere slave! The matter can be settled by us here."

David chortled and danced about. "Think of the fun! I like brandings. The last time it was Bukky. Remember when Bukky stole those plantains and yams! He fainted after the first iron."

Dissak came in and hung the keys for the stocks on the nail over the sideboard where they were always kept, and David asked him: "You've locked them in securely, Dissak? They won't escape?"

"No, Massa. I lock them in good. They can't get away," smiled Dissak.

Hendrickje was calling from upstairs. "Come up! All of you down there! Get back to your beds!"

They went racing up the stairs—all of them save Jacques who lingered to say to Dissak: "Dissak, tomorrow you must attend to Father. His beard is dirty with food. And give his room a cleaning out."

"Very well, Massa. I do dat tomorrow."

Jacques went upstairs slowly. In bed, he did not join in the talking, and after the others were asleep he was still awake.

The noise of voices outside gradually died away. A beetle buzzed in the darkness above the tester. He could hear it hitting itself about in the rafters. Suddenly he got out of bed and left the room silently. He went downstairs, tiptoed his way across the sitting room and dining room. He stopped at the sideboard, pulled out a drawer in careful silence, and using it as a ledge, hauled himself up until he could reach the bunch of keys on the nail. He secured them, got down and crept into the pantry, then let himself out, hesitated near the steps, looking slowly round. He then crossed quickly to where the stocks were under the sapodilla trees.

He heard a gasp from his mother. "Who that?"

Nearby, Bomba stirred and lifted his head.

"Don't make noise, Mother. Please. I've come to set you free."

"Massa Jacques?"

"Yes, Bomba. Quiet. Please."

"You got the keys, Jacques?"

"Yes, Mother, I've got them. I can't bear to know they're treating you like this. That's why I want to set you free. You think you can get away somewhere where they can't find you?"

"Yes. Yes, we get away. Turn the keys quick. Good boy! Good boy!"

"If Grandma knew she'd kill me."

When they were both free he said: "What about some food? You want me to get you something from the pantry before you go?"

"No, no. Not bother about that. We find somehow."

"You may be hungry later. And you're naked. Let me get you some clothes and food."

"Yes, Missy, he right. We might have to walk around for days before we come to somebody who can help us."

"Hurry, then, Jacques. Good boy."

He returned to the house, hung the keys over the sideboard again, then crept upstairs to his mother's room. In passing his grandmother's room he trembled. But he was still undiscovered as he let himself out through the pantry door with the bundle of his mother's clothes he had wrapped together hurriedly. He took them to her, then hurried back into the pantry and got food for them. He was nearly whimpering with excitement as he handed to her the parcel with the foodstuffs.

"You must take care of yourself, Mother. Don't let snakes bite you. I'm so sorry Grandma beat you like that. Did she hurt you badly?"

"No, that nothing. Only little blood come. I make her pay for that soon, yes. Don't worry, boy." She patted his head briefly. "You good boy, Jacques. I not think you so good. Go upstairs quick before they find you."

He hurried away, but paused halfway across the compound to glance back. Like ghostly shapes he could make them out in the starlight. They were still under the sapodilla trees. They seemed to be discussing which way to go. He began to massage his wrist nervously. Then he saw them move off and vanish into the darkness.

V

"There is a traitor in this house," said Hendrickje, "and I mean to discover who it is. I locked that pantry door myself after you had all gone to bed. Whoever it was took down those keys and went outside and set the prisoners free is in this room. I didn't do it, and your father, in his condition, could not have done it. Therefore it is one of you children who is guilty. Which one of you was it? Pedro! Was it you?"

"No, Grandma. I swear it wasn't."

"You're so seasoned a liar you'd swear by the thing you hold most sacred and still be telling a falsehood."

"I mean it, Grandma. It wasn't I. I went to bed with the others. We all went to bed together."

"Yes," David nodded. "We all went to bed together."

"Yes," said Lumea. "We all went to bed together."

Jacques had a suggestion to make. "Grandma, the two dining room windows were open. David and Lumea and Juliana and Laurens were standing at them looking out at the fire. Isn't it possible that one of the slaves could have climbed in and got the keys? Mother might have promised him a bribe to do it."

Pedro snapped his fingers. "Hell! I never thought of that."

"It must be that," said Lumea. "Mother bribed one of the slaves."

Hendrickje frowned. "Those two windows remained open, did they?"

"Yes, Grandma. I'm sure it was through there the person who got the keys must have come in," said Jacques. He spoke calmly, his manner languid and casual.

"It didn't occur to me that those two windows had remained open," Hendrickje said. She looked thoughtful for a moment, then said: "Very well. You may all go." She went into the pantry, and they heard her calling Dissak. Pedro said: "I think I know who it is. It's that fellow in Number Seven Gang—Pajaro. He always liked Mother. I've heard him say he wished he were in Bomba's place."

"That's right," Lumea agreed, clenching her hands. "It's he, Pedro. It's he. I've caught him more than once spying on Mother from his logie when she went to feed the rabbits."

"That's no evidence," said Pedro. "They all spied on Mother. What do you expect when she walked around the place with only a thin bodice on and nothing underneath?"

"Last night she didn't even have that on," David chortled.

"I'm sure it's Pajaro," said Pedro, nodding. "I'm going to tell Grandma. He ought to get the branding instead."

"But didn't you just say there was no definite evidence against him?" said Jacques. "Why jump on him and say he did it?"

"Oh, well, one of them did it, so what does it matter? The point is to mete out a good branding and teach them a lesson. Even if Pajaro didn't do it, the one who did will see what happens to him and take warning."

"That doesn't sound fair to me," murmured Jacques.

"You don't have to be fair to slaves," said Pedro. "Oh, Grandma!"

Hendrickje had just come in. "Yes? What is it?"

"I believe we have our man. It's Pajaro who did it."

"Pajaro? Well, I did mention his name to Dissak as a suspect. What gives you reason to think it might be he?"

"He was hanging around the house before Dissak locked Mother and Bomba in the stocks. I saw him myself from the window here."

Jacques opened his mouth to say something, then shut it.

Hendrickje grunted. "Is that so?" She gave Pedro a shrewd look. "I hope you're not lying."

"No, Grandma. That's the truth. Dave, don't you remember last night we looked out there and saw Pajaro? The light from the candles was shining down through the window and I saw him. I even told Dave that Pajaro must be waiting around there because Mother was in the house here naked. He likes Mother, Grandma. I heard him say already he wished he were in Bomba's place."

"Weren't you outside helping to put out the fire? How is it you were able to tell David this?"

Pedro, however, never lost his head when lying. He said: "Don't you remember I came in for a few minutes when you and Rosaria and the men were fighting in the pantry? It's then I saw him. Dave, you remember, don't you?"

"That's right, Grandma. We both saw him."

"I saw him, too," Lumea nodded. "I didn't think anything of it at the time. He was moving about under the window."

Hendrickje looked slowly from one to the other of them and smiled slightly. "Are you prepared to say this before Pajaro's face?"

"Yes, Grandma!" Pedro said.

"Yes, Grandma!" David said.

Lumea, too, without hesitation, said: "Yes, Grandma!"

Hendrickje looked at Jacques. "What of you, Jacques?"

"No, Grandma. I was in the pantry with you and Mother all the time. Don't you remember I was standing near the dresser?"

"Yes, I do recall having seen you in there. Laurens! Juliana! Come here! Did you see Pajaro outside the dining room windows at any time last night?"

Laurens glanced at Pedro, hesitated, then nodded. "Yes, Grandma."

Juliana shook her head. "I don't remember seeing him, Grandma."

An hour or so later Pajaro said: "Massa Pedro, you say you see me outside the window there last night, Massa?"

"I did. You were hanging about under the window in a very queer way."

"Yes, I saw you, too," David said. "You were prowling about."

"Yes, prowling about," Laurens nodded. "Prowling all about."

"That's right," Lumea confirmed. "Prowling everywhere."

"Missy Hendrickje! I swear it true, Missy. I never come nowhere near the house. All the time I help throw water on the fire. True, Missy."

His mistress smiled stonily, her arms folded across her breast. "It is most peculiar, Pajaro, that four of my grandchildren should state so emphatically that they saw you out there. No, I'm afraid the evidence is against you."

"Missy, I can call Dakky and Mebbara and let them tell you. I was wid them all the time. I not come nowhere near this house."

Hendrickje stiffened. "Who are Dakky and Mebbara? Am I to take the word of two slaves against the word of four van Groenwegels? Dissak! Take him away! Put him in the stocks and prepare the branding irons!"

Pajaro did not go easily. He fought. With hate-filled eyes, he shouted: "Missy Hendrickje, one day you must sorry for this! You do wrong plenty time. You punish me and I not do nothing. I same human like

you, Missy. Your grandchildren tell lies, and you believe them. Your day coming soon, Missy!"

Dissak clouted him. "Shut your mouth! Shut up!"
And Dooley gave him a chuck and kicked his ankles.

"Grandma, may we watch the branding?" Pedro
asked.

"Certainly, Pedro. Certainly."

Jacques turned off and went upstairs, a strained
look on his face. Later, David came up into the room
and found him sitting on the table by the bed looking
through a Greek lexicon.

"Aren't you coming down to see the branding,
Jacques? The irons are nearly ready."

"Yes, I'm coming—presently. I was looking up a
word."

"It's a long time we haven't had a really good
branding," David said. "Bukky spoiled the fun the last
time by fainting after the first iron. They're giving
Pajaro three irons. The surgeon has just had a look at
him. He says Pajaro can stand three irons."

VI

Three days later Hendrickje was taking the children
with their lessons in the dining room when Dooley
came in and told them: "They catch Bomba, Missy.
Massa Laplace catch him up-creek and send him. He
outside now, Missy. His hands and feet tie up."

The children exclaimed excitedly, but their
grandmother merely nodded and said to Dooley:
"Take down the keys, Dooley, and have him put in the
stocks. I'll be out in an hour's time to deal with him."

"You not coming out now, Missy?" Dooley was
evidently disappointed. He must have been hoping that
he would have created a first-class sensation.

His mistress shook her head. "No. In about an
hour's time. And I think I have told you before,
Dooley, not to disturb me during lesson time unless it
is a matter of extraordinary importance."

Dooley took down the keys and left with a crest-
fallen air.

Hendrickje silenced the children sternly. "You have morbid dispositions." She glanced at Jacques who alone was silent. "You seem rather pale, Jacques—as well as silent. I hope nothing is on your mind."

"No, Grandma. Nothing. Nothing at all."

His grandmother smiled enigmatically, and the lesson went on. When, after about half an hour, it came to an end, Hendrickje made her way upstairs. Pedro called after her: "Grandma! Aren't you going outside to punish Bomba?"

Hendrickje did not even turn her head in response.

"She can be so queer when she wants," Lumea remarked as they hurried out into the compound. Bomba was a miserable, dejected figure in the stocks. He kept groaning softly.

"What's happened to Mother, Bomba?" Lumea asked him.

"Did a snake bite her, Bomba?" Laurens asked.

"Why didn't she come back, too?" Juliana wanted to know.

"Come on, speak up, you murderer!" Pedro prodded him with his foot.

Bomba made no reply. He groaned, his head bowed. There was blood on his forehead and on his wrists and ankles.

"They must have had him in the stocks at the Laplace plantation," said David. "There's blood on his wrists and ankles."

"Speak up, speak up!" Pedro urged, kicking the slave. "What happened?"

Bomba kept his silence.

"You won't speak, eh? Very well. The red-hot tongs will make you. Wait until Grandma comes downstairs."

Dusk, however, began to gather, and Hendrickje had made no move in the matter. Dissak went up to her room and knocked on the door.

"Who is that?"

"Me, Dissak, Missy!"

"Get downstairs! I must not be disturbed for the rest of the evening. When I'm pleased to come down and see after Bomba I shall do so."

When the children were going to bed Pedro said: "You can be certain she has a good reason for delaying. Perhaps she wants to torture him in mind. Remember we read in a book about the old Inquisitors —how they used to torture their victims by leaving them in suspense for days and weeks before inflicting any torture."

"Grandma is clever," David said. "She's good at torturing."

Jacques did not fall asleep. He stared into the darkness long after the others were breathing heavily and regularly. At about ten o'clock he got out of bed and left the room, crept silently downstairs and let himself out of the house by the pantry door. Looking cautiously around the dark compound, he made his way toward Bomba. The wretched fellow seemed to be dozing, his head slumped forward. When Jacques hissed: "Quiet! Don't make a sound, Bomba. It's Massa Jacques," Bomba started.

"Massa Jacques?"

"Yes."

"You got the keys, Massa? You loose me out again?"

"No, I'm sorry, Bomba. I haven't got them. Since what happened some nights ago Dissak has kept the keys on his person."

"Ow, Massa Jacques, I suffer too bad, Massa."

"I'm sorry. I wish I could help you. I hate to see people suffer. I hate cruelty. But what I came to ask you about was Mother. What happened to her? I'm so anxious. Is she safe?"

"Yes, Massa. She safe. Massa Laplace take her to live with him. He like her, and as soon as she arrive at his house he take her in. But he say he have to send me back here. I try to get away, but he make his men hold me and put me in the stocks, and Missy Rosaria, she not even beg for me, Massa. She just left me so— after all I do for her. I take her through the bush safe,

I give her my share food, I stay awake while she sleep at night to watch over her—all that I do for her and she not even beg Massa Laplace to help me."

"That's terrible, Bomba. I'm sorry about that, too. If I could get the keys I'd try to get you away again before they brand you, but Dissak will never leave them where I can get at them, I'm certain."

"Ow, Massa, I suffer too bad. They not give me nothing to eat since I come here. I hungry and thirsty bad."

"I'll get you something." Jacques patted his head. "Poor fellow. I miss you a lot. If you weren't suffering so much I'd ask you to tell me a jumbie story. You were really good at those tales, Bomba."

Bomba gave a deep moan.

"Wait a bit and I'll go and get you something to eat and drink."

"Thank you, Massa. Thank you."

Jacques was getting to his feet when the soft footsteps came and the tall figure appeared dimly from around the trunk of the sapodilla tree. The voice was controlled and almost motherly and benevolent. "Please don't be alarmed, Jacques. Don't make a noise, my boy. Simply come with me."

Jacques trembled. No words would come.

She urged him gently forward, her hand on his shoulder as though to guide him in the dark. Near the pantry door he said: "Grandma, I only went out to ask him about Mother. I meant no harm."

"Sssh! We mustn't disturb the rest of them, Jacques. Not a word until I tell you you may speak. Mind. Not a word!"

She made him tiptoe up the stairs, and she tiptoed, too. She took him into her room, closed and locked the door after her, lit two candles and told him: "Now we can speak—but quietly."

He stared at her with a frightened, puzzled dismay. She was in her nightgown, her silver hair, as always, in two loose plaits down her back. There was a mysterious smile on her face, and she was calm: not in any way angry or upset. She pulled a chair up to the bed and told him to sit down, and she seated herself on the edge of the bed. He stared past her at the image on the shelf over the dressing table: the image of a bush-god carved out of purple-heart wood by Bangara. It had stood on that self over ten years, before Jacques was born.

"You're a strange little boy," Hendrickje said. "You puzzle me in many ways. The questions you ask sometimes and your little vices—spying on the slave girls and ogling them on the sly in your casual, droll fashion. A mere boy of eight. And your compassion and consideration for other people. And your cowardice. Standing by and letting that innocent man be branded. Your secrecy and slyness—and your peculiar sense of humor. Yes, you're a strange little boy."

He trembled all the time.

"I suppose you're in dread of the punishment to come?"

"Grandma, I meant no harm. It was Mother I wanted to ask after."

"Yet, you should be punished. Don't you think you ought to be?"

He swallowed.

"You opened the stocks and let your mother and Bomba escape. Don't you think you deserve to be severely punished?"

He said nothing.

"Most certainly you do, Jacques—but I'm going to pardon you." She stretched out and caressed him under the chin. "I'm not through and through a monster, my boy. I have my soft side, and, somehow, I admire you for what you have done."

She was silent for an interval, a musing look on her face. Then she grunted faintly. "We're a terrible family. The brutality dates far back. Kaywana was a murderer. She killed one of Wakkatai's daughters—in cold blood. And Adriansen was a sly, cunning fellow. It was even rumored that he had secret dealings with our enemies at the time: the Spaniards in Trinidad and the Orinoco. The brutal and cunning streaks have come down all the way. What happened when the slaves panicked in the bedrooms in 1666? Tell me."

"Great-grantfather Laurens went mad for a moment and shot one of the slaves at point-blank range."

"That's it. Soft and humane a man as he was, the brutal sreak was always there underneath. He attacked me that day when I informed him that I intended to marry your grandfather Ignatius. Struck me. I saw the beast in his eyes. I couldn't believe it was he. It seemed so unlike him."

She was silent again, her freckled face at repose, her gray-green eyes reminiscent. In the soft candle-light her wrinkles were not so pronounced. She looked much younger than her age.

She suddenly glanced at him, an appraising gleam in her eyes. "I wonder what sort of man you're going to grow into."

He smiled weakly and said in a timid voice: "I don't think you'll die in a hurry, Grandma. You'll live to see for yourself."

"You think so? I believe you're right. I'll live to see you all men. I'm made of tough material. Like your Great-grand-aunt Susannah. I'll go on to ninety. I feel I can do it."

After a moment she rose. "It's time for bed now." She beckoned him up, patted his head and said: "Go downstairs and take something for Bomba to eat and drink as you had intended doing."

"You don't mind me doing that, Grandma!"

"No. Go on. And you can relieve his mind by telling him that he won't be branded. Tell him I've decided to pardon him."

"Very well, Grandma."

VII

From that day Jacques became her favorite, though her partiality never manifested itself in open demon-strations; it took a subtle form: a sly, seemingly absent-minded pat in passing him on the stairs, a teasing jocularity at lessons when he was guilty of neglect, a blind eye when she happened to catch him near the slave girls' quarters.

Besides pardoning Bomba, she made him one of

her lieutenants, and sent Juliana to the Teuffers in his care. He was on mule back with her in the fields the day of the next sensational occurrence.

They were moving along the dam on the extreme outskirts of the plantation, the canes of her own fields lisping softly in the noonday breeze, on the one hand, and, on the other, the dense foliage of the coffee trees of the adjoining plantation a mass of glittering green in the hot sunshine and casting a deep gloom beneath.

In the distance the horns were cooing their summons to the field slaves to gather for the midday meal, and, far away, a bell clanged harshly, for some planters used a bell.

They had just turned on to the lateral dam which would take them toward the house when the report split the silence.

Bomba heard his mistress gasp and saw her whip fall. She was clutching at her bosom. She sagged and dropped with a crouching thud to the dam.

Bomba cried out and dismounted. When he saw the blood and noticed how still his mistress lay he looked around wildly, irresolute. He heard a rustling amongst the coffee trees on the neighboring plantation and a scurry of footsteps. Had a glimpse of a skirt.

He saw two figures on mule back approaching at at gallop along the dam. It was Hoobak and Dissak.

The surgeon said to Pedro: "The ball has lodged a little above her right lung. It would be dangerous to attempt to take it out—and I haven't the instruments with which to perform such an operation."

"Then what's going to happen? Is she going to die?"

The surgeon looked doubtful. "She may recover —and she may not. Only God can decide that."

"To hell with God! There's no God. What you mean is that you can't do anything more for her. Isn't that what you mean?"

"I'm afraid that is just what I mean," said the surgeon stiffly.

After he had gone back to the little cottage which

he shared with the Chief Carpenter, Pedro said: "We have to avenge this. It's Mother who did it."

"Of course it's Mother," David nodded. "She's a beast. We must get her, Pedro. And Raoul Laplace, too. He never liked Grandma. It's he who abetted Mother in this. We must get them both."

"How are you going to get them?" Jacques asked.

"By watching out for them," said Pedro. "Jacques, you and I can do it. We're the best shots. We must go over to the Laplace plantation tomorrow at dusk and lie in waiting. I know a good spot outside the house where we can train a musket on anyone in the dining room or the southern bedrooms."

"Supposed we're discovered."

"Then we'll shoot our way out. But we won't be discovered."

Jacques looked troubled. "I don't like killing people, Pedro—especially Mother."

"She's a murderer. She murdered Bangara, and now it looks as if she's murdered Grandma, too."

"I'd like to come, too," said David. "Pedro, let me come."

"Very well, we'll see."

"I'm coming, too, Pedro," said Lumea. "I can shoot as well as you and Jacques."

"We don't want a crowd," David frowned. "And you're a girl."

"No, she must come with us," Pedro ruled. "She's a good shot, and we may have to fire several rounds. We'll need loaders."

Jacques seemed dismayed. "Pedro, are you serious about this?"

"Certainly I am. We must avenge what has happened. We're van Groenwegels. We must fight for each other. Remember what Grandma has always told us? A van Groenwegel for a van Groenwegel. We must stick together and defend each other." His eyes glittered. He looked like a full man.

"Good talk," said David, flushing. "I agree with that."

"I agree, too," said Laurens. "Pedro, couldn't I come, too?"

"No, you're too young, Laurens, and your foot would be a hindrance."

Laurens moved his foot along the floor, suddenly conscious of his deformity. His six-year-old eyes grew tearful. He did not ask again.

Jacques, trembling, went upstairs to see his grandmother. He entered the room without knocking, and found Teekaila, Hendrickje's female household slave, squatting on the floor near the bed.

Hendrickje was conscious. She turned her head—she lay flat on her back—and when she saw him she smiled.

"Is it all right for me to come in, Grandma?"

"Yes, my boy." She touched the bed with a hand which had rested on her stomach a moment before. "Sit here."

He sat beside her and asked her how she was. "Are you in pain?"

"Yes, a slight burning in my chest—up here. But it's not unbearable. Not more than I can stand. I'm a van Groenwegel."

"I was worried. The surgeon says your condition is doubtful. The ball is still in you and he can't take it out."

"The surgeon is an incompetent jackass. He's no different from any of the rest of them in this colony. I only keep him here because I can't get a better than he." She locked her teeth together hard, and after a moment said: "Don't be worried about me, my boy. I'll get better. A ball in my chest isn't enough to kill me."

"I'm so glad." Relief came to his face. He smiled and touched her cheek. Then suddenly the troubled look returned to his face. "Grandma, there's something terrible I want to talk to you about." He glanced at Teekaila. "Could Teekaila go outside? I prefer to talk to you alone."

"Teekaila! Outside! Massa Jacques will call you back presently."

The woman went out, and Jacques said: "Grandma, Pedro says we must avenge this deed. He says it was Mother and Raoul Laplace who did this to you."

He told her of the plan for tomorrow evening. "I don't like shooting people. Do you think it's my duty as a van Groenwegel to do it?"

She said nothing for a moment, then, after another spasm of pain had passed, moved her head in the affirmative. "Yes, Jacques, do it. You're a good shot—both you and Pedro. I've seen you at practice. It's a good plan. Kill them. I know it seems a terrible thing for me, your grandmother, to advise you to do. You aren't even nine yet. But Pedro is right. Go with them and wait for those two brutes. It was Laplace who fired the shot, I'm certain. Your mother is a bad shot. I've proved it often in the fields when I had her with me at practice. Nevertheless, it was she who urged Laplace to do it. They took advantage of the fact that no one would be in the coffee fields on the Toulouse plantation. Reaping time isn't for another six weeks. It was a cowardly act, Jacques. Go and avenge it. It will be good experience for you, my boy. This is a country and an age in which we have to live desperately if we're to survive. Only violence can suffice. We'll let dogs like Raoul Laplace know that we are their betters. Rascally Huguenot! Get him, Jacques, my boy! Get him!"

"And—and kill Mother, too?"

"Yes, kill her, too. She'll be a menace to us always if we let her live." She squeezed his knee. "Don't be soft, Jacques. Show me you have the guts of a true van Groenwegel. Think of me when you're shooting."

"Very well, Grandma. I'll do it."

Though he was not one of the shooting party, Laurens helped them to clean and prepare the muskets. All the following morning they were engaged in getting ready for the exploit. After the midday meal Pedro told them his plan of strategy. "It's no use going all the way overland," he said. "It's nearly fifteen miles by the tracks. We'd be dead tired by the time we got there. So we'll go up-creek by boat as far as the Siki Creek, and then do the rest of the way by the old Indian trail. The weather is dry now, so the trail will be hard."

"Pedro, remember that's where we trapped that

big tapir last month! And Jacques got a ball in its left eye and brought it down!"

"Yes, I remember. That trail will take us as far as the cane fields on Laplace's plantation, but we'll move round to the south and take to the coffee fields and then crawl through the provision patches until we come out near the two big vats. You know those wooden vats?"

"Yes. There's a big jamoon tree near them. Remember we raided it when it was bearing last year? The time when I got my knee gashed." Lumea pulled up her skirt to show them the scar.

"That's the tree we're going to use as our firing position," Pedro nodded. "It's got three branches that run horizontal, and three of us can perch ourselves on them with ease without being seen when it's darkish."

"But there'll be four of us!"

"One of us will have to remain below. David, I think it will have to be you. Lumea is a better shot. You'll have to be a loader."

David's face fell. "I can shoot as well as Lumea, Pedro."

"You know very well you can't. You can throw a knife better than any of us, but with a musket you're second-rate."

"Perhaps I can take some knives to throw, then, in case we're attacked. What do you say, Pedro? Let me take some knives."

"No harm. Take some. We'll need you to scout around as well as load, so don't think your job isn't an important one." His voice quavered excitedly. "By God! This is going to be the best adventure we've ever had! You heard what Grandma told Jacques yesterday! We must live desperately. We must let those other people know that we're van Groenwegels—their betters. We don't let anybody fire upon us and get away with it!"

"Good talk!" David agreed.

"Good talk!" Laurens confirmed.

"Yes, that's the way to do it," said Lumea.

Jacques nodded faintly. "Of course," he said.

They set out at four that afternoon and entered the Siki Creek by a quarter to five. The jungle met overhead, and the sunlight penetrated only in slim odd shafts slanting in through the bamboos and tall *mucca-mucca* shrubs with their arrow-shaped leaves that watched them in dark-green solemnity from the banks in unending rows. They could hear the low croaking of an alligator, and David was eager to search for it, but Pedro said they had no time to spare. Floating clumps of *missouri* grass hindered their progress now and then, but they had anticipated this and had brought cutlasses. This was familiar territory. Since they had known themselves they had been roaming over the countryside; their grandmother encouraged them in outdoor activities. "Roam everywhere," she had told them, "and learn the country well. Get wet in the rain. Let insects bite you. Learn to be good swimmers and boatmen. Let these things be secondary only to one thing—your shooting."

It must have been nearly half-past five before they reached the opening in the bush where the old Indian trail started. The sunshine came redly through the bush, and tree-frogs had begun their nighttime fluting amid the undergrowth. The air was chilly and rank with the scent of leaves and wild flowers. Overhead, they heard the churlish screech of a hawk and a fluttering amongst the foliage of a tall *courida* tree.

"There's a bird's nest up there," Lumea said. "I believe that hawk has young ones. Either that or it's after the young ones of another bird."

"Couldn't we take a shot at it, Pedro?"

"No, Dave, no. We can't do any shooting until we get to that jamoon tree—and then it's Mother we're going to bring down—or Laplace."

"Both of them, you mean," said Lumea, and Pedro nodded and agreed. "Yes, both of them, the murderers!"

They set out along the track, Pedro, Jacques and Lumea each carrying a musket, David the ammunition sack and five knives in sheaths, the latter strung around his waist, handles up, in readiness for drawing.

His small boyish waist could barely accommodate them.

When they reached the cane fields the sun had not yet disappeared, but by the time they had begun to creep through the coffee fields dusk had set in in earnest. Fireflies flashed in the gloom under the trees, and insects made a high-pitched cheeping. Pedro called a halt once to listen. He thought he had heard the hiss of a *labaria*.

"It came from that way."

After a moment they moved on. A few minutes later there was a swift rustling amongst the dry leaves on the ground, but it turned out to be a salampenter. David hurled a knife after it but it had grown too dark and he only succeeded in snipping off its tail. He recovered his knife. "If it had been brighter I'd have got him dead in the back," he said.

Darkness had come down when they were crawling through the provision patches, but a four-day-old moon crescent in the west threw a soft, pale radiance over everything, making the cassava leaves glimmer dully atop the slim, knotted stalks. The eddoe leaves, too, glimmered.

Ahead of them they could hear the flat dum-dum-dum of a tom-tom and a wailing chant of voices. The plantation house was in sight, the reddish glow of candlelight in one or two windows.

They saw the jamoon tree, slim and tall and twisted, its trunk ascending in three main columns that branched outward horizontally and then became lost amid the thick foliage higher up.

Jacques was trembling when they got to the base of the tree.

Pedro whispered: "Each of us will take a separate branch, and, Dave, you'll pass up the muskets when we're up. Boots off now!"

Because of snakes, they had worn long, thick-leathered boots. These would have hindered them in climbing, hence Pedro's order to take them off.

"Dave, you're in charge of everything on the ground—boots and ammunition. Keep each pair by itself and ready so we won't have to fumble to find them when we come down. It won't do if we have to go sorting out each other's boots when we come down. We've got to move fast."

"You leave it to me," David said, his voice shaking with excitement. They heard voices in the logies about a hundred yards to their left: the slaves talking. The beating of the tom-tom and the wailing chant continued. A salempenter darted with a rustle from a clump of shrubs near by and made for the bigger of the two water vats, also on their left. Lumea said: "If one of us could get on top one of those vats we'd have a good view of the bedroom over that way."

Pedro, however, disagreed with this suggestion. "We'd be too exposed up there. Don't forget the moonlight."

"Pedro, suppose we don't happen to see Mother appear at any of the windows," Jacques posed. "Isn't it a long chance we're taking?"

"She must appear," Pedro said. "It is a chance, I admit, but not such a big one. She always goes upstairs to bed at about seven. You know how hot she is, and especially as this fellow Laplace and herself have just got together. They're going to be like two demons to be in bed early. That's his room there, unless he's changed it recently. The old father and aunt have the end room there. We've got to be careful not to injure either of them. The old man once gave me a lift in his *corial* that time when I went fishing with Dooley and our own *corial* went adrift."

"The old aunt is good, too," Lumea nodded. "She caught me raiding their guavas one day, and instead of shouting at me she smiled and called me into the house and gave me some of her preserves. She can make lovely fruit preserves."

"Raoul hasn't taken after them at all. He's a beast to the slaves—especially the women. I hear he can't enjoy them unless he beats them until they scream."

David chortled. "I hope he's been doing that to Mother. It would have served her right. Murdering poor Bangara and shooting Grandma."

"Up we go! I see light in the dining room. Perhaps we can get them when they're at table."

They went up with the ease of long practice, and David passed up the muskets, after loading them. Pedro, from his position, could see into the southern bedrooms without trouble. All the windows were open, but at the moment the rooms were in darkness. Jacques, from his position at the other end, commanded the northwestern room through its western windows. Lumea, in the middle, had much the same advantage as Pedro, though the windows of the southwestern room came more directly within her range of fire. Jacques could command the southwestern room, too, through its three western windows. The northeastern room was the only one that did not come within their line of fire at all, but Pedro was certain that it had not been occupied since the death of the widow Marie Leblanc, the grandmother of Raoul Laplace.

Nearly a quarter of an hour must have gone by without any sign of activity in the house, then they saw a slave go past a window in the dining room. David, below, hissed up: "That looks like Zimbally—the girl with the extra finger on her right hand."

"Yes, I think it was," hissed back Lumea. "She's a kitchen slave."

About ten minutes later they heard a deep cough. Then someone came to one of the dining room windows and spat outside. It was the old aunt.

"If only it had been Raoul!" Lumea hissed.

"Or Mother!"

Pedro called hoarsely: "Don't whisper too much. Sounds carry!"

Jacques watched the house. A shifty patch of moonlight kept moving on his left temple—sometimes going as low as his cheekbone and revealing the tiny freckles. And the twitching of his facial muscles.

Suddenly they heard a shrill laugh, prolonged, vulgar and voluptuous. It was their mother. Male laughter came, too, in deep hacking guffaws.

There was a smell of food in the air.

Pedro and Lumea kept their gazes concentrated on the dining room windows, their muskets trained and ready.

They heard footsteps. Their mother's laughter

streaked out into the night again. David, despite Pedro's warning, hissed up: "I'm sure they're coming into the dining room now!"

Lumea and Pedro were too rigid and alert to reply.

The tom-tom thumped unconcernedly on the cool air. The wailing voices went on monotonously. Once or twice David caused a crack-crack of dry leaves when he shifted about his feet in his excitement.

Jacques was cold-fingered.

Abruptly light glowed in the southwestern room. Someone was lighting a candle. "Look! Look up there!" hissed David. Pedro snapped across hoarsely at Lumea: "Get ready!"

Jacques felt his heart beating as though it were contained in the core of the tree. Within his own body there was only the echo of it.

As the candle brightened in the room they made out the furniture: a big wardrobe, the four-poster, a dressing table, a chest of drawers. . . . A section of each was visible from one or other of the windows. . . . A figure was standing near the chest of drawers. A man. It was Raoul Laplace. Lumea commanded the best position to get him, but of a sudden he moved out of view. Jacques had him now. Lumea was just about to call to Jacques when Jacques fired.

They heard a yell, and Lumea saw the Frenchman stagger off toward the bed. Almost at once came another cry—then a shriek. Their mother. Pedro saw her flash past a window in the southwestern room. Then Lumea saw her appear and bend out of view. She was screaming. Shouts and voices began to disrupt the peace of the evening. They heard footsteps hurrying about in the dining room.

Lumea saw the figure of her mother rise into view. She fired. Pedro fired half a second later. Their mother collapsed out of view with a shriek. Pedro snapped: "Down! Down!" They all went scrambling down. Lumea's musket clattered down, falling from her grasp before David could take it. She landed on top of it and cut her foot. She hopped about, wringing her hands and making lisping sounds of pain.

"Hell! Oh, hell! I've cut my foot, Pedro!"

"Get your boots on! Quick!"

She sat down and hauled on her boots, groaning the while. Pedro, who had hauled on his already, assisted her up and urged her toward the provision patches. They made no attempt at stealth now, but dashed through the cassava shrubs as fast as they could go, trampled down the eddoes that came in their path, Lumea uttering shrill sounds of pain. They got to the shelter of the coffee trees without signs of pursuit, and Pedro panted: "Not so fast now! Jacques, slow up there! Lumea's foot is cut. We must keep together and help her."

The moonlight made pale mysterious patterns on the ground, and now and then a salempenter or a lizard scuttled away with a crackling of alarm. They heard the dulcet "hoo-yoo!" of a goatsucker. Goatsuckers always lay flat on their breasts on the ground and uttered their "hoo-yoo!" call just before flying off.

Lumea limped on with them. Pedro held her arm, but she told him: "I can bear it," and shook off his hand.

Once they heard a lashing, hissing noise and knew without doubt that it was a snake—probably a brown, whiplike *labaria* that one of them had trodden upon.

Soon they saw the canes waving in the soft moonlight, and within a few minutes had skirted them and were on the Indian trail. They were blowing hard but triumphant. "We got them! We got them!" David kept saying. "By hell, we got them!"

David was carrying Lumea's musket for her, and Pedro asked her: "You wouldn't like Dave and me to lift you, Lumea?"

"No," she said through her teeth. "What's a little pain?"

David crowed and said: "See that! She's a true van Groenwegel. Blood! Blood, by God!" He tapped his knives. "I wish any of the devils can come after us. I'd send a few knives into their hides before they knew what was happening. Eh, Pedro?"

"Of course. But they can't get us now. We've put too much ground between us and them. Hell! That was exciting. I wonder if we killed them. Tomorrow we'll hear. I'll get Dissak to talk to some of their slaves and find out what happened."

"Anyway, so long as we winged them, that's what matters. We've got our revenge."

When they were in the boat and had emerged into the main stream Pedro examined Lumea's foot. The cut was about two inches long on the tender hollow part of her foot, but it was not very deep.

"It will soon heal," said Lumea. "It was worth it. I'm sure my ball got Mother as well as yours, Pedro."

"You're a good shot, Lumea. You did well. You're a great sister to have. They haven't got another like you along this whole creek."

"Not in the whole colony," said David. "It's the blood in her. Van Groenwegel blood."

Laurens and Dissak and Marrak and Raffy were at the landing place awaiting them. . . . "You get them, Massa Pedro? . . . "What happen, Massa?" . . . "Lumea, what's wrong with your foot? They fired at you?" . . .

It was Jacques who detached himself from them to run up to the house to tell his grandmother what had happened.

She had a slight temperature, she told him, and he could see the feverish light in her eyes, but she asked eagerly: "What happened, my boy? Did you all come back safely?"

When he told her what had happened she touched his hand and uttered a sound of triumph. "I'm proud of you. Proud of you, by God! I'm not going to be a disappointed old woman. Tell the others to come up and let me congratulate them. Go and call them, Jacques."

Jacques went, and a few minutes later they all went in to her, talking and gesticulating, Laurens dancing about, forgetful of his deformed foot and behaving as though he had been one of the shooting party. At the door Dissak and Marrak stood smiling with admiration.

Hendrickje gripped their hands, one after the other, including Laurens. She said to Laurens: "I know you were with them in spirit, my boy. When you get older you'll be just as daring. Just as much a van Groenwegel." She patted his head.

Jacques, who had caught some of the spirit of triumph, suddenly frowned in concern. "Grandma, you said you have a temperature. You're exciting yourself too much. It may be bad for the wound. The surgeon said that you shouldn't excite yourself."

"He's right," said Pedro, subdued. "The surgeon said you should be as quiet as possible, Grandma."

"A little excitement won't kill me off," said Hendrickje. Her cheeks, however, were flushed, and Pedro insisted that she must be left alone. Jacques went across to call the surgeon, and when the surgeon came he said: "I don't like her condition at all. Her temperature has risen. You children should never have gone near to her this evening."

"Do you think one of us should sit up with her, Mynheer?"

"Teekaila is with her."

"Yes, but Teekaila," said Jacques, "will fall asleep and forget all about her. I wouldn't mind sitting up with her."

"No, my boy. She will want to talk to you. That won't do. She must be quiet. You go to bed. I've done what I could."

The next two days were anxious ones. The temperature kept on, and once it became so high that Hendrickje was delirious. Jacques stood outside her door and heard her talking to herself. She talked about the Essequibo and about Ignatius. Jacques heard her cry: "Don't dare to console me! I haven't given up! I'll never give up! Never! Nothing will defeat me!" At another time he heard her sobbing. "I want some affection, Ignatius. I'm a woman. Please give me some affection."

Meanwhile, Dissak brought them news from the Laplace plantation where he had been talking with some of the field slaves in the absence of the overseers. "Missy Rosaria dead," he told them. "They say she get a ball through her chest and one through her neck. But Massa Laplace only get hurt in de shoulder.

They bury Missy Rosaria yesterday. They say young Massa Laplace swearing all day he mean to report the matter to Fort Nassau. As soon as he get well he say he going to bring the murderers to justice. That's what he say."

David laughed. "Bring the murderers to justice! Wasn't Mother a murderer! And hasn't he attempted to murder Grandma!"

"He can be ignored," sneered Pedro. "He doesn't dare to report it to the fort authorities, because he knows he'll have to explain who shot Grandma. And, in any case, nobody saw us. They have no evidence against us."

"I'm sure it was my ball that got Mother in the neck," Lumea gloated. "I aimed right there. It must have ripped open her windpipe."

"We should go up and tell Grandma," said David. "This is great news."

"We can't do that," Jacques objected. "Her fever is getting worse."

"You think she's going to die Jacques?"

"I don't know. Haggeman is anxious. He says he doesn't like the turn she has taken this past day or so."

Dissak nodded. "I ask the Massa Doctor this morning and he say she very bad. Better not go up and tell her nothing, Massa."

"What's going to happen if she dies?" said Lumea in dismay.

"I'll have to take charge, of course," Pedro said.

"You're only a boy. How could you take charge?"

"I'm eleven next month, and I know about the place. I can manage."

"Grandma won't die," said Laurens. "She's too tall and strong."

"If she dies we'll have to go back and kill Raoul Laplace," said Pedro. "That would be the first thing to do after burying her."

Suddenly footsteps sounded in the sitting room. Bare feet running.

"Who's that?"

It was one of the kitchen slaves. One of the girls Jacques was fond of spying at. She had been gathering greens in the kitchen garden, for her hands were filled with bunches of leaves.

"Massa Pedro! Massa David! Come quick!" she cried.

"What's happened, Cyana?"

She dropped the greens on the dining table. "Massa Pedro, come and see. Outside under Massa Adrian's window. Massa Adrian fall out the window from upstairs."

They went rushing after her.

Adrian lay in a crumpled heap under one of the windows of his room.

"I just hear a bup!" Cyana told them, "and when I look I see Massa down there lying still. Massa Pedro, he dead?"

Jacques dashed off for the surgeon.

A few minutes later Mynheer Haggeman shook his head. "He's dead. His neck is broken."

"Everybody seems to be getting dead or dying nowadays," said Laurens. "It's so funny. Bangara, and then Grandma gets shot and then Mother is dead—and now Father."

"That window should have been barred up," said Pedro.

Jacques murmured: "It's better for him like this. He was so unhappy."

"Grandma says people who are mad are never really unhappy," said Laurens. "You think he did it on purpose, Jacques?"

Jacques made no reply.

"If Grandma dies today, that will be four dead for the month."

"Shut up, Laurens! Shut up!"

Three days later, however the surgeon pronounced that Hendrickje was out of danger. The temperature had dropped and she was healing well. She was not told of Adrian's death, though, until a week later when she was definitely better.

Sitting up in bed, a pile of pillows at her back, she told her grandchildren: "We have seen some desperate events these past few weeks, my children, but Fate was on our side. The way is now clear for you all. Your mother served her purpose in bringing you into the world, but she would have been a hindrance to you in the future. She was an ignorant, dissolute person, and we are well rid of her. Your father, too, had become useless, but he, happily, has also been struck off. The path is now without obstacles." She smiled round at them. "I'm so proud of you. You've brought my early dreams true. You're the kind of children I had hoped to have myself. You have blood. Fire-blood!"

They shifted about self-consciously, but there was pleasure on their faces. Even Jacques seemed pleased; he was moved.

"From now on there's nothing to stop us, children. We're going to advance to power. We're going to spread. We'll make ourselves known throughout the country as the most feared family. We'll be feared because of our reputation of aggressiveness. Always bear in mind. This is a brutal world. Life is cold and heartless. Among the plants, among the beasts, among men—yes, among men, too—it is the strongest that survive. The weak go under. There are people who will tell you that we are human and superior to the beasts and plants, and that, therefore, we ought to be kindly and soft. These people are, in their way, right, but, unfortunately, they cannot tell us how we are to eradicate the basic brute in us all, how we are to prevent some men from behaving like beasts even though they are human. If all men could be saintly and good and kind, there would be no necessity to adopt cruel methods in order to survive, but this is not so. The saints are few, the demons are many, and unless we can outwit the demons we shall perish. Life is struggle, struggle—all the time struggle. You can only get what you want by fighting for it. Be meek and surrendering and you're lost. The demons will conquer—and laugh you to scorn! Never surrender! Never retreat! Remember our blood and traditions as a family."

Jacques interrupted. "But, Grandma, didn't old Adriansen say that peaceful methods were always better than warlike ones? The speech he made at Cartabo the night of the uprising in 1628——"

"Adriansen was a bluffer, my boy. He was a wily old man. And as a young man he was no less wily. Great-grandfather Laurens always told me that. He said Adriansen was a cunning schemer. He lived by his wits, and if he saw an opportunity of getting something without resorting to bloodshed then he took the peaceful line of argument. But that was a mere ruse. Underneath, he was a fighter—like Kaywana. Make no mistake about it, Jacques. Adriansen was a hard man. He got what he wanted. No one could take advantage of him." She smiled and looked round at them again. "You and I, my children, have the old blood in us. Your Grandfather Ignatius was a bad link. So was your father. But these are gone. We the strong ones remain, and it is our business to carry on the name from strength to strength." She looked at Pedro. "Pedro, are you with me? Do you pledge to be a true van Groenwegel and to live up always to our fighting traditions?"

"I should think so, Grandma! They won't ever get me down. I'll fight to the end. The van Groenwegels never run!"

"I, too, Grandma!" exclaimed David. "The van Groenwegels never run!"

"You can depend upon me, Grandma," Lumea vowed. "No surrender!"

"I shall be the best musketeer, Grandma," said Laurens. "And I'll throw knives like Dave!"

Jacques was looking at Bangara's image and biting his nails. His grandmother did not press him for an expression of loyalty. She gave him a sly smile of affection.

IX   The Twenty-First February, 1763

I

From Aert to Hendrickje:

22nd May 1738

    . . . the new Secretary, Laurens Storm van's Gravesande, his wife, sister and five children have arrived. They arrived on the 14th, and Commander Gelskerke invited us over to the Huis Naby to meet them. They are people of culture and refinement, and Essequibo will be the better off for their society. . . . This fellow Gravesande has impressed me very favorably. He is a military man and possesses much fire, imagination and initiative. Indeed, as I have remarked to him, I often feel that he must be very similar to what Adriansen was like. Already he has inspected the new wooden fort Gelskerke had so much trouble in getting the Directors to agree to erect on Flag Island downriver, and his criticisms were most blunt and scathing. He has condemned the whole structure. He states—and I agree with him—that a wooden fort is worthless, for palisades are hardly erected on one side when those on the other side are falling down. He is forwarding a report to the Directors, with Gelskerke's hearty approval, and recommending that a brick fort be erected instead—and that without delay. . . . Now that it has been definitely decided to abandon the Cartabo-Kyk-over-al area as the seat of Government, most planters are planning to vacate the old worn-out estates up here and move nearer to the mouth of the river in keeping with de Heere's policy of coastal cultivation and also to be within easy reach of Flag Island (in future to be called Fort Island). The change is rather upsetting, but I can see no help for it, and, accordingly, have begun to make preparations to go. . . .

Jacques to Hubertus:

9th July 1738

. . . I'm glad to hear that you have a talent for sketching, but Grandma is alarmed. She's writing to tell Great-uncle Aert that you must on no account be encouraged to paint or draw, but that you must be sent away to Amsterdam to study land-surveying and to put your talent to some practical use, as there will be great need for land-surveyors in this country in the future, what with new concessions being granted and more people coming in. As for myself, I have no talents at all, but I'm a good shot, and I can beat Pedro and Lumea to swim across the Creek. Dave, though younger, can beat any of us at swimming. . . . Give my regrets to Faustina, and tell her that I hope to meet her one day, and that many times I find myself wondering what she is like and whom she resembles. I hope she won't think me forward in giving you this message for her. . . .

Aert to Hendrickje:

27th November 1739

. . . after much difficulty, we are now securely settled in our new house on our new plantation, some miles north of Fort Island which was formally opened on the 5th of October when the Council of Justice met there for the first time. We miss Cartabo very much, especially as we have left one or two good friends behind, and, naturally, from a point of sentiment, we regret having had to abandon a place which has been in the possession of the family for so many decades and on which stands the grave of our esteemed ancestor Kaywana. . . .

Jacques to Hubertus:

20th May 1740

. . . like yourselves in Essequibo, our Governor[1] Lossner is contemplating a new fort on the

[1] The title "Commandeur" had now been abolished in Berbice.

mouth of the Berbice. I think we need it, too. We could do with several more. These slaves are showing a great deal of spirit nowadays, and I feel that one day soon something terrible will happen—a great rebellion, perhaps. Grandma and the others, of course, ridicule such an idea, saying that the slaves are too ignorant and cowed to attempt such a move. I never contradict them, but I do smile to myself and wonder sometimes. We treat them so cruelly—apart from branding them and beating them, some planters have introduced such tortures as making them lie naked on broken bottles and tying them down over a nest of stinging ants. Pedro has invented one of his own. He told Grandma and Grandma thought it so good an idea that she adopted it. A smooth, flattish stone is put over a fire to get hot, and the slave to be punished is made to stand and *watch* it getting hot, knowing that he is going to be made to sit on it with his trousers off. I hate seeing acts of cruelty like this, but the others glory in them. I suppose I must be made differently, though I always do my best to seem one of the group, and, naturally, I shall always stand by the family. . . .

Aert to Hendrickje:

11*th April* 1741

. . . however, before I tell you of family matters, let me acquaint you of the sensational news which has just been made known to us. As you know, since the revocation of the Edict of Nantes in 1685, French Huguenots have been permitted to settle in our colonies in these parts, but these have always been considered naturalized Dutch subjects. Now, to the dismay of the whole colony, Gelskerke and this over-zealous Secretary of his, van's Gravesande, have between them inveigled the Directors into permitting settlers of all nationalities to come and stake concessions in Essequibo. Moreover, in order to encourage them to come, it has been announced that these new settlers will be considered exempt from taxes for a period of ten years. We are all very much disturbed over this new move, Hendrickje, though

Gelskerke and van's Gravesande want to assure us that it is in the interests of progress. . . . Already I have heard that Englishmen in the West Indies are preparing to come over in swarms. . . .

I received a letter a week or two ago from Gert Naar stating that Aunt Susannah died in Para-maraibo early in January at the age of ninety-two. He says that apart from her own children and grands and great-grands, over a hundred people attended the funeral which was an elaborate affair. Do you think you will live to the age of ninety-two? . . .

Jacques to Faustina:

9th August 1742

. . . since I have begun to correspond with you I feel a very good person, though I know I have no right to feel so. You're perfectly right. We have a bad name all over the colony. Ever since that shooting affray, three or four years ago, when we avenged what Mother did to Bangara and Grandma, our name has been looked upon as a black one, and we have hardly any friends. The few we have are the cruel ones who go in for the most brutal tortures imaginable. Yesterday, the Fouries, up-creek, hacked off the hand of an old slave and plunged the bleeding stump into a pot of boiling tar. Can you credit such barbarity? I tell you, one day these slaves are going to get to-gether and rise up against us whites. I never say that aloud, but within myself I do a lot of think-ing. . . . However, let me go on talking of your-self. From the description you have given me about what you look like I was able to dream about you last night, and I'm sure the person I saw was none other than you, Faustina. One day when we meet I shall see if you were the same person I saw in this dream. . . .

Aert to Hendrickje:

20th July 1742

. . . Gelskerke died on the 16th, and, it goes without saying, that van's Gravesande will fall into his place automatically. . . . Just as we had expected, Englishmen and their families are swarming all over the colony. Soon Essequibo will be more English than Dutch. . . . Your fears, I am glad to report, are not being realized. Hubertus, despite his talent for sketching, is most enthusiastic on becoming a good overseer. Indeed, he has made a suggestion which I consider very promising for a boy of his age. There is much talk in the air at present of opening up the Demerary River to settlers, and Hubertus expressed the wish that the moment official sanction has been received from the Directors I should apply for a concession and send him with a few slaves to start cultivation. He is his father over again, not only in appearance but also in disposition, and we are very proud of him. I understand that your boy Jacques has been corresponding for some time with Faustina, Mathilde's illegitimate daughter. This is very satisfactory, and I think you are wise in encouraging these children to keep in touch with each other. Faustina is developing into a most charming young lady, but, unfortunately, her mother continues to grow embittered and soured with the passage of the years, and often makes herself extremely disagreeable to the poor girl and to every one around her. . . .

Faustina to Jacques:

28th September 1744

. . . something happened last week that brought to my mind the fears you are always expressing in your letters over the slaves. An Englishman called Simpson,[1] who came over here recently with his wife and three slaves from Barbados and settled a little way downriver, was murdered in a most disgusting manner by two of his own slaves. Their names are Cudjoe[2] and Quacco. They chopped him to pieces because he reproved them for idling, and later, when they returned to the cottage where the wife was anxiously awaiting her husband's return, they would have murdered

[1], [2]Actual names.

her, too, if she had not got suspicious and called upon a neighboring planter for assistance in searching for her husband whom she assumed must have been lost in the bush—at least, she assumed that until these two slaves came home and behaved in a queer manner. Later they confessed to the murder after the body had been found, and were sentenced to death by the Council of Justice. Grandfather was present at the execution, and from his description, it was a terrible affair. One of the men was pinched with red-hot tongs seven times and then burnt alive. And to make his agony worse, a shower of rain came down and put out the fire, so that it had to be lit afresh. It was nearly an hour and a half before he died. And would you believe it, he never even flinched, Grandfather said, nor showed any signs of penitence. He just turned to Mrs. Simpson, who had come to see him done to death, and said: "Missy, is this what you bring me here for? To suffer like this?" Because of the delay in the first execution, Grandfather says that the second man was strangled before being burnt. . . . Yes, I believe you are right, Jacques. One day these negroes will get out of hand and something dreadful will happen. Like yourself, I hate cruelty. . . .

Aert to Hendrickje:

17th October 1746

. . . yes, we are certainly advancing, Hendrickje. Tomorrow the official notice granting permission to settle the Demerary will be published, and I am taking immediate steps to apply for a good concession. . . . Everything is moving ahead rapidly. Apart from the fact that the Burgher Militia has been considerably improved—a Burgher Officer, apart from his military duties, can also act as a Justice of the Peace—the College of Kiesheers[1] is proving very successful, and it is most gratifying to know that at long last we free planters have been given a voice in the affairs of government. . . .

---

[1]Kiesheers—electors or choosers.

Jacques to Faustina:

8th February 1748

. . . we celebrated Grandma's seventy-fifth birthday and Pedro's twentieth in one, as the two birthdays fall within a few days of each other. We held a grand banquet, and invited the de Groots and the Vernsobres and André Fourie (the cruel manager of Plantation Magdalenenburg I have told you of so often) and two or three others. I'm afraid it was rather riotous an affair and did not end until midnight. The guests were too drunk to think of returning home that night, and, in fact, did not wake until nine the next morning. You would be surprised to know how much Grandma entered into the spirit of things despite her age. Her hair is white, it is true, and her wrinkles are deeper, but the spiritual part of her remains as youthful as ever. I wouldn't dream of telling you this if we hadn't agreed to confide in each other as we do, but I do believe that she is as sensual as she was at forty or fifty. Not that I blame her, of course, for as I have told you, I am no saint myself. On the contrary, this weakness of mine for women seems fatal. I squirm as I write it, for I hate to think that I'm shocking you—however, I know that you will understand. I may as well confess, while I am about it, that two of the slave girls are already pregnant by me. At eighteen, that is bad, isn't it? However, you must realize that we were brought up to feel that there is nothing terrifying in sexual relations. Our moral values are entirely different from yours, for you have been bred in sheltered refinement; we here, Faustina, are animals—educated, it is true, but lawless and without scruples. If I myself am a little more humane, if I happen to possess more compassion, than the others it is by sheer chance of heredity, so to speak, coupled with the good influence your letters have had on me. . . .

Faustina to Jacques:

27th February 1748

. . . you are entirely mistaken in thinking that what you said shocked me. If you imagine you are singular you are wrong. Here in Essequibo moral values are by no means high, and you would be astounded if I were to relate what goes on among people who are supposed to be respectable and God-fearing Christians. At least, you on the Canje admit that you have no belief in God, but these here actually attend services at Fort Zeelandia on Sunday and pretend they are good and pious folk. I can't stand hypocrisy, Jacques. I admire and respect a person far more if he or she is frank and admits their faults openly, but the person who pretends to be perfect and, in reality, is foul at heart earns only my contempt. . . .

Hubertus is doing very well in Demerary. You can see that he was born with planting in his blood. He has written telling us that he is in love with an English girl, one Rosalind Maybury, and that we must not be surprised if we hear that there has been a wedding. He is very popular with the English, and is learning to speak the language (no doubt, ably assisted by Miss Rosalind Maybury). . . .

As for myself, I am afraid I cannot say I am always happy here. Mother can be so annoying at times. She gets more and more discontented with life as she gets older, and simply will not accustom herself to the fact that my illegitimacy is a circumstance that cannot be helped. It doesn't bother me at all, and that is quite honest, so I don't see why it should trouble her so much. . . .

No, I didn't like the last sentence in your letter. Why should you think yourself not good enough to touch the hem of my skirt? You must never depreciate yourself, Jacques. Always believe in yourself, no matter what other people may think. That is my policy, and it works. If you feel you are degenerate and worthless you will in time become really so. . . .

Jacques to Faustina:

17th April 1758

. . . I have some exciting news. Grandma has applied for and secured a concession on the Berbice River, some miles above the fort and not far from the Teuffers, and she has decided that I shall run this new plantation. As I have often mentioned, since that incident years ago when she caught me talking to Bomba and took me up to her room, she has looked on me as a favorite, and she realizes that I am not of the same stamp as the others. I must say, she has treated me with much sympathy and understanding, and she has never rated me for being soft. She knows I don't like taking part in the cruel punishments that are meted out to the slaves and she never insists that I do. . . . This is going to be a revolution in my life. I have always wanted to get away from this sordid atmosphere and start on my own somewhere else. On this new plantation I shall be near to Juliana and Cousin Flora and her family, and, naturally, I shall be *persona grata* in the homes of the "people who matter," as Grandma terms them. As you can well guess, of course, this is her chief reason in wanting me to get settled on this new plantation. It's in keeping with her policy that the family must spread. . . .

There is something else I want to talk of, but I'm too excited now to broach the subject, and it's nothing I can discuss lightly or hastily. In my next letter, perhaps. . . .

When next you hear from me it will be from the Berbice. . . .

Faustina to Jacques:

2nd June 1758

. . . yes, even Grandfather appears to be obsessed with this idea that our family must be the most influential one along the whole Wild Coast, though from what I can gather, your grandmother seems to take the idea far more seriously. However, I'm glad for your sake that you have been given the opportunity to go off on your own and prove your worth. . . .

Jacques to Faustina:

30th July 1758

. . . Juliana is growing into a fine girl. I'm glad she left the Canje at an early age. The influence of Cousin Flora's household upon her has been most beneficial, and from what I can see of her, she is as sweet a person as you are—which brings me to what I wanted to discuss in my last letter but could not find the courage to. . . .

Faustina to Jacques:

4th September 1758

. . . I fear it is a rather startling proposal, Jacques. I admit I am a little taken off my feet. It seems so obvious a thing to say, yet I think it must be said. We have known each other only through our letters, and I am two years your senior. How do you know that you will like me as I am in physical appearance—especially as a wife? I do consider that it would be rash of me to say yes unconditionally. . . . No, you may put your heart at rest. There is no other to whom I have ever given any thought. I confess I am in a great turmoil with myself, and don't know what to say. . . .

Jacques to Faustina:

12th November 1758

. . . I have a good suggestion to make. Why couldn't you and Cousin Mathilde come and spend time with Cousin Flora and her family? In this way we should be able to see a great deal of each other, and then we should find no difficulty in arriving at a decision. . . .

Faustina to Jacques:

2nd January 1759

. . . Grandfather thinks it a splendid idea, but, as you can well imagine, Mother is putting a thousand obstacles in the way. However I believe we shall soon break down her objections, especially now that Aunt Flora's letter has arrived to back up yours. . . .

Jacques to Faustina:

3rd February 1759

. . . much as it is going to be a disappointment
to me, and, I hope, to you, because I flatter myself you are as eager to meet me as I am to meet
you, I must tell you that it will be unwise for
you to come now. You will have to postpone
your visit, Faustina my dear. An epidemic has
broken out in the colony, and I should not like
you to come here and fall a victim to it. We are
puzzled as to how it could have started. It is a
cross between enteric fever and dysentery, and
started on the Company plantations. We call it
the Sickness for want of a more specific name.
Some think it has started as a result of the poor
food the Company plantations serve to their
slaves, because up to now it's the Company
slaves who have suffered most. Personally, I
doubt this theory, for the disease is becoming general, and both private and Company planters are
falling victim to it. White and black are going
down, and everybody is in dread of being attacked. When writing my last letter it had already
started, but we had thought nothing of it and that
it would have died out, but there can be no doubt
now that it's really serious, and medical aid is
so poor in these parts that I think all who have no
urgent business in the colony should keep far. . . .

Faustina to Jacques:

13th March 1759

. . . it certainly has been a great disappointment, for we had almost been on the point of arranging for our passages. I do hope none of you
will be attacked, Jacques. You say you don't believe in God, but I do and I shall pray fervently
to Him and ask Him to protect you. It would
break my heart if anything should happen to you.
Yes, I mean that, silly as it may seem. . . .

Jacques to Faustina:

29th March 1759

. . . it doesn't seem silly in any way. . . . Instead of getting better, it seems to be getting worse. The General Superintendent of the Company plantations has succumbed to it, and so has his son. So have several other people we knew well about here. . . .

Faustina to Jacques:

6th April 1759

. . . I'm so excited I can hardly hold the quill. The Sickness has broken out here, too, and I've spoken to Mother and convinced her that as the danger has come into our own colony now I can see no reason why we should not go to Berbice. And, Jacques, she has agreed! And we are coming! Mother is writing to Aunt Flora by this same post to tell her to expect us. . . .

II

They came early in June when the long rain season was in full swing. When the slave brought the message to Jacques that the ship had arrived, Jacques rode four miles through pouring rain to get to the Teuffers. The rain held up after the first mile, but he was already soaked to the skin. By the time he got to the house his clothes had partly dried, but his hair lay pasted to his head, two unruly locks drooping over his temple. This was how Faustina first set eyes on him.

He did not apologize for his appearance. He took her hand and said: "It's good seeing you after all those letters," twinkling at her with his droll green eyes.

"You look almost as I'd expected you to look," she said, "even in your present soaked condition." She had deep blue eyes, and her hair was a tint between copper and gold. He told her later, when they were alone together: "Everything about you is precisely as I had pictured it. Except the mischievous light that comes into your eyes sometimes. I hadn't foreseen that. I think it's the most exciting thing about you."

She told him: "I don't feel half as shy with you as I had thought I would." She added: "I seem younger than you, though—I mean I feel I look younger."

"You do look younger."

"I didn't mean it that way. What I want to say is that you have a dangerous, experienced look that I didn't think you would have, judging from your letters. It makes me feel I'm a child beside you."

"It's the Indian in me, I suppose. We all have that look. The dangerous look. By the way, I've written to them on the Canje to tell them you've come, and I was going to suggest that you took a trip with me there to meet them. You can ride, can't you?"

"Yes. I should be glad to come. I'd love to meet Aunt Hendrickje."

They were on the veranda to greet Jacques and Faustina. Pedro, tallish and broad shouldered, was a virile ox of a fellow, his black eyes and black hair alive with a crackling masculine force. Lumea was almost as tall, a handsome, well-built creature with a sensual mouth like Rosaria's. David, short and tough, had his arms akimbo and his feet apart like some aggressive colossus, though he had a cheerful smile when he put out his hand.

Laurens, with his deformed foot and uneven shoulders, gave her such an openly lascivious look that she colored.

Hendrickje brushed her hand aside and gave her a hug. "I couldn't dream of shaking your hand, my child. I know you too intimately already—through this infatuated grandson of mine." She laughed, and the multitude of wrinkles around her eyes put out new branches to link up with the deeper ones down her cheeks.

"You're still quite straight, Aunt Hendrickje. I thought Jacques was exaggerating when he used to tell me how erect you were."

Hendrickje nodded. "It will take more than

eighty-six years to bend my back, Faustina. There's tough material in me, child."

"The old blood!" barked Pedro.

"The old blood!" barked David.

"Grandma will never die," Laurens said. He uttered a whinnying noise and scraped his deformed foot along the floor. "She'll just melt away into the morning mists."

"Laurens is our poet," Lumea laughed—a husky laugh. Jacques gave her a swift glance, a memory of his mother tingling in his consciousness. His eyes narrowed sensitively.

"We'll have something to eat first, then we'll show you over the house," said Hendrickje. She spoke in a voice of finality, and made beckoning gestures toward the dining room. Jacques, however, very quietly, intervened with: "Grandma, I think Faustina would prefer to have a wash first. Remember she wasn't brought up on the Canje."

Hendrickje chuckled. "Thanks, Jacques, for the reminder. My child, you must pardon my thoughtlessness. After all, it would seem as if age is beginning to tell. Let me show you to your room, and I'll have a tub brought up."

"I'll take care of the tub," said Lumea. "You take her up, Grandma."

"You see what willing grandchildren I have, Faustina, my dear! Ready to fall over themselves to be of some use."

Later, when they were at table, Pedro insisted that Faustina should sample some of his red wine. "Brewed it myself," he said.

"If you prefer gin, just drop me a hint," said David. "I have a flagon up in my room I reserve for special occasions."

"The last time he brought it out," Laurens said, "was on the occasion of the birth of Pedro's last brat."

Hendrickje glanced reprovingly at Laurens. "Now, Laurens! Reserve your indiscretions for another time."

"Face the truth, Grandma, however indelicate!" Laurens whinnied.

"By God! He's got you there, old lady!" grinned Pedro. "Your own maxim."

"Floored in her own pen!" David thumped his chest and made a stamping noise under the table.

"See what I have to put up with, my child!" sighed Hendrickje. But there was a simpering look of pleasure and satisfaction on her face. "Only animals, that's what they are. Untamed wild beasts. But I like them so. It's the old blood."

"The old blood!" Pedro echoed.

"The old blood!" David echoed, stamping.

"Christ! What's happening out there!" Lumea sprang up and dashed to a window, and her brothers with loud scraping of chairs rose and followed.

Except Jacques. Jacques glanced at Faustina and wagged his head as much as to say: "I think I warned you what they were like." And Faustina smiled, and he knew that she was saying in reply: "Don't worry. I'm interested. It doesn't trouble me."

"What's the matter, children?" asked Hendrickje. "Another fight?"

"Atta again!" snapped Pedro. He hurried out of the room at a run, with muttered oaths. David followed him.

Laurens frowned: "That fellow Atta is going to cause serious trouble before long. I think we ought to get rid of him. Grandma, the Vernsobres want two good males. Fourie was speaking to me yesterday."

Hendrickje shrugged. "I leave it to your discretion, my boy. If Fourie can tame Atta then by all means hand him over and get something less subversive in exchange."

"He's a nuisance," flared Lumea. "Always spouting trouble. He's doing his best to stir up the others. Like that other bad man at Magdalenenburg. Cuffy, or whatever his name is."

"Quacco is another one," Laurens nodded. "I'm going to get rid of both of them. Fourie will know how to handle them."

He watched Pedro rush up and break the two men apart. Pedro clouted both of them hard on the head. "You again, Atta! You again, damn you! This is your quarrel. You started this. Don't say a word. I know it's you!"

"You judging bad, Massa Pedro. Atta don't do everything wrong on this plantation. And I always telling you not to hit me in me head. Flog me if you got to flog me, because I'm a slave. But don't hit me head!"

"Massa Pedro, he call me a coward," the other fellow panted. His name was Magouri. "He talking against you all, Massa. He say we must do you harm whenever we get de chance, and because I tell him I grow up on this plantation since I was a boy and can't do you all no harm he tell me I am a coward—and he hit me in my face."

"Very well, Magouri. Thanks." Pedro clapped his hands, and after a moment three slaves came running up from the direction of the storehouse. Bakkara, Memphis and Dak. Big hard-muscled fellows. They belonged to Pedro's special faithful bodyguard. There were five of them in all.

"Bakkara, take charge. Have Atta put in the stocks—and keep him there until we can attend to him. Off with him!"

"Very good, Massa."

They seized Atta, but he made no attempt to resist. As they were taking him away he looked back and said: "One day you got to remember all you doing now, Massa Pedro. You going to remember Atta, Massa Pedro."

When the meal was resumed Faustina asked: "Is there much of this kind of trouble up here?"

There was a chorus of assent. Pedro told her: "Every day there's some disturbance, but we have them well in hand, never fear!"

"They won't bring any nonsense to the van Groenwegels and get off," Laurens rumbled, shifting his foot along the floor. "We know how to treat troublemakers."

"We sell or exchange them," said Lumea with heavy sarcasm.

Laurens whinnied. "That's it! That's our system. When torture and lashes prove ineffectual, we simply get rid of them quietly."

'You take a look out of your window at the compound at five this afternoon," Pedro told her, "and you'll see how we punish them. I sentenced three of them this morning to the hot stone."

"That's Pedro's own little invention, my child," Hendrickje tittered. "Pedro is extremely ingenious at inventing new tortures."

Faustina smiled. "Jacques has told me about the hot stone."

"Is there anything he hasn't told you of in his letters?"

"I can guess a few things he hasn't," said Laurens.

Jacques shook his head solemnly. "Wrong. I confessed everything, Laurens—even some of your sins, too."

The room exploded with laughter. David stamped, and Laurens' thin, finicky laughter rose and fell grotesquely amid the raucous riot of sound. Hendrickje's face crinkled into fresh wrinkles as her imposing person shook with mirth.

When the meal was over they took Faustina on a tour around the house and the compound. Pedro remarked when they were upstairs: "As Jacques has told you everything in his letters, we don't need to conceal the fact that this is the room where Mother and Bomba used to 'make sweet.' Did Jacques tell you of some of her expressions?"

Later, in the compound, Lumea said: "This was where Bangara's logie stood before Mother and Bomba locked him in and set it on fire."

"Bangara was the mulatto who used to be my lover, Faustina," said Hendrickje. "He knew his job, too, I can assure you, my child. Irritatingly superstitious in his ignorant way, but when it came to bedtime affairs I certainly had nothing to complain of."

Faustina's face was very pink, though she did her best to pretend that she was not shocked. She changed the subject adroitly by asking after Hoobak the *obeah* man. "He was the one who used to boil death-broths, wasn't he? I think you mentioned something about that, Jacques."

"He's still alive," Hendrickje nodded. "He used

to be one of my lieutenants, but, poor fellow, he's too old now to engage in active work, so I let him do light tasks about the logies—sweeping and mopping up. Dooley and Dissak have both died of the Sickness."

"Is it very rampant up here?"

"Not as bad as on the Berbice," David told her. "We've lost one or two of the older slaves. If you're strong you're seldom attacked."

"We aren't afraid of it," said Hendrickje. "We're hard here. Steel and stone. We laugh at man, beast and disease."

"Not to mention God," murmured Jacques.

"Grandma is the hardest of us all!" thundered Pedro.

"The hardest of us all!" echoed David. He thumped his chest.

"Hard as a *sawari* nut," said Laurens.

They spoke fervently. Faustina could see from the glances they threw at their grandmother how deep were their love and respect for her, how they venerated her, yet regarded her as one of themselves: a good companion to be gently lampooned and criticized.

Later that day, when Faustina was reading on the back veranda, Hendrickje came out and stood beside her chair and said: "Before you go we must have a quiet chat, my girl. So that we may get to know each other."

"It will be a pleasure, Aunt Hendrickje."

"For me, too. You're a splendid girl. I'm fond of you already." She spoke quietly, with a note of tenderness. Her old eyes had a pensive, faraway gleam and her thin lips were set in a slight fixed smile that, somehow, gave her an air of doting. She nodded as though enveloped in a web of musings, and when she grunted Faustina could detect the quaver of senility in the sound. Despite this, however, she was an impressive figure. Her height and carriage could not be overlooked. She had unmistakable dignity and a positiveness of mien that precluded any sentiments of kindly patronage, or compassion for her age, on the part of the spectator. Even when she rested her hand on the back of the chair to steady herself one did not feel inclined to regard her as a fellow human in a state of physical decline. The aura of vitality that surrounded her was too strong. The power of her will could be felt as though it were a palpable emanation moving like a deep, quiet wind about her.

The following morning she took Faustina into her room, and in the course of their conversation paced in a restless, fevered manner about the room, nodding and grunting.

"Nothing much has happened during the past twenty years or so, my child," she said, her gaze out on the gray, drizzly morning. "Life has been fairly even and uneventful, but they have been my best years. Since Adrian and Rosaria were wiped off the scene I have had everything my way. I have realized many little dreams. I've seen these boys grow up as I would have wanted my own children to grow up. They're tough, knotty daredevils. Except Jacques, of course— my pet boy. He was always the soft one, though I've never taken him to task about it. I have too tender a spot for him. He's such an odd mixture—lovable despite his fleshly weaknesses—and I say that merely in a conventional sense, for I don't consider them real weaknesses. The urges of the flesh are natural and therefore legitimate. Jacques has a strong sense of family loyalty. That, at least, can be said of him. I love Jacques." She turned suddenly and said: "You love him, too, Faustina, don't you?"

"Yes."

"I'm glad. Funny boy, Jacques. Courtship by post. It's just the sort of thing he would go in for. He was always different. He used to be so concerned over his father. The only one of the children who remembered Adrian's existence in that room over there. You're going to marry him, I hope?"

"Yes, I think so, Aunt Hendrickje."

"Good. I'm satisfied. I'd foreseen it, that's why I sent him off to the Berbice to get settled on a place of his own. We must spread, Faustina. Our goal is power, power. The pinnacles." She began to pace again, hands behind her back clasping and unclasping. "We have to justify the blood in us. It's grand blood. Fire-blood.

We must always be on top. Masters! The Wild Coast must tremble at our name." She paused and looked at Faustina, and the girl could not meet her gaze. "Didn't your grandfather tell you the tales of old?"

"You mean about Kaywana and Adriansen and the raid of 1666? Oh, yes. Since we were little things. He's very family-conscious, and I think your letters have helped to make him more so, Aunt Hendrickje."

Hendrickje uttered a sound of satisfaction, and after a pensive silence said: "I'm a contented woman, Faustina. I've had a hard struggle to get what I want, but I've got it. The rest is mere trimming. Pedro has already agreed to go to Suriname—in about five or six years' time. I want him to find a wife first. It's so difficult finding wives for these boys. They aren't popular. Too loud and fiery for the poor mediocrities about here, though women like them on the sly. Oh, yes, the women like them, and before long there'll be a few elopements. David has his eye on a robust young French creature downstream, and she's off her head over him, but her parents and uncle guard her like a lump of gold. They've threatened to shoot her if they catch her fiddling around with David. Two weeks ago they thrashed her within an inch of her life because she waved at him when he was passing in a *corial*. And Laurens is weak on a girl on the Berbice River—one Amelia George. But she won't look at him, poor fellow. She's soft on Jacques, though Jacques treats her with smiling aloofness. All the women are wild about Jacques, my dear. He has a way with them. Since he was eight. You should have seen him ogling the slave girls and spying on them undressing. Poor Jacques. Your letters have done a lot to steady him. He might have been keeping a harem now if it hadn't been for you."

Later, when she was alone with Jacques, Faustina said: "She's a strange woman. She has an air of greatness —and yet I find that I'm more inclined to regard her with awe than with admiration."

"I know what you mean. She's a colossus, but a hollow colossus. I love and respect her because of long and close association, but I'm not fooled. She has a warped mind, Faustina. She's an evil genius."

"Yet you love and respect her?"

"Why shouldn't I? I have no claims to a halo myself."

She was silent for a moment, thoughtful, then said: "She asked me whether I intend to marry you."

"And you replied?"

"I told her yes."

He gripped her arm. "You're generous. It makes me afraid."

"Why afraid?"

"The weak vein I've always told you about. At depth, I'm no better than any of them. Perhaps I'm even worse—because, at least, they have stern guts." He laughed softly. "In a minute you'll be scolding me for depreciating myself."

"You haven't found yourself, Jacques, but there's nothing the matter with you. I think you're a fine man, and I don't form hasty opinions."

III

The wedding was planned for October, but it did not take place until February of the following year, because in the meantime Mathilde, Faustina's mother, took ill with the Sickness and died. She died on October 2nd, not two weeks after Governor van Ryswijck, who succumbed to the Sickness on September 21st. In January, old Mynheer Teuffer also fell victim to the epidemic. As a result, the wedding was a quiet affair, confined to members of the family. Lumea and David came to represent the Canje house. Pedro and Laurens remained behind to see that nothing went wrong, and Hendrickje was compelled to admit that she was too old to do the journey.

"She sends her heartiest wishes for your future happiness," David told Jacques, "and she says you must see they're all sons."

"Tell her I prefer girls," Jacques murmured solemnly.

"She knows that already," Lumea said, with equal solemnity.

David said to Faustina: "You're going to have to watch him with the eyes of a tiger cat, Sister Faustina. He takes them at all ages—from fourteen to forty."

Faustina replied with a smile: "I have too much confidence in myself to have to watch him."

About two months after they were married, Jacques encountered Amelia George on the track that ran parallel with the river, the track that linked one plantation with another. Like himself, she was on muleback and picking her way cautiously, for a few fitful showers had turned the track muddy and treacherous. She was a girl of about twenty, decidedly attractive in figure, though she did not have a remarkably pretty face.

She greeted him in her usual shyish way, her gray eyes squinting a trifle—a mannerism of hers—as she smiled.

They would have passed each other and gone their separate ways as they had done so many times before, but on this occasion a *marabunta*—a species of wasp —intervened. It darted down from the hanging nest on the branch of a wild cacao tree, startled by the fluttering wings of a hawk that swooped past suddenly. It jerked its sting into the girl's cheek, and she cried out and brushed frantically at her face, dismounting hurriedly.

Jacques turned and rode up. "What's wrong?" Then he saw her cheek with the tiny red spot on it. "Phew! A black one, was it?"

She nodded, biting her lip in pain.

"Only one remedy when a black *marabunta* stings you, Amelia—unless you want a dose of fever." Without asking her permission, he leant toward her, pinched the punctured part of her cheek between his fingers, and putting his mouth to it, sucked out the poison. She made no attempt to push him off, though she was obviously surprised. He felt her hand tremulous on his arm. When he turned aside and spat she said in an uncertain voice: "Thank you."

"Permit me to say thanks instead," he smiled. "It

was a pleasant task. I must see and cultivate these black *marabuntas*."

She gave him a swift smile and murmured: "You speak as if you forget you're married," and there was no shyness in her manner now. Only a breathlessness.

He shrugged. "I have never claimed strength of character." He put out his hand. "Shall I help you to mount?"

Before she went off he told her: "See and put some salve on that cheek of yours."

"Wouldn't you like to come home and do it for me?"

He laughed and waved her on. "Tempt me not, Amelia."

On his arrival home he related the incident in detail to Faustina, and she laughed and said: "It doesn't make me jealous. I don't reckon infidelity in mere physical contact—even if it had been closer contact I wouldn't have minded."

"I wish I could say the same. I'm so painfully earthy."

"That's a delusion of yours, Jacques. Much of the time you live in the clouds without knowing it. I can tell you quite honestly that it wouldn't trouble me if you were physically intimate with a dozen women—so long as I was certain that your heart was with me."

He gave her a long, solemn look. "My stars tell me, dear beloved, that one day I shall have cause to remind you of that."

Shortly after Christmas Hendrickje wrote asking after her great-grandson. "By now there should, at least, have been some news of his coming," she wrote. "Please don't disappoint me, children. Hurry up."

Jacques wrote back: "My *daughter* will come when it suits her. We are not worrying. Did you hear that Governor van Hoogenheim's wife died last week of the Sickness? And they only arrived in November. Which illustrates how sudden life and death can be. It may be you next week—and you talk of our not disappointing you. Faustina sends her love. How are Pedro's two mulatto boys? Are you still doting on them? Keep well. The van Groenwegels never run—they merely drift into wickedness. Jacques."

Faustina did not become pregnant until May the following year. She was about four months advanced when she and Jacques attended Juliana's wedding. Juliana got married to Vincent Teuffer, Flora's eldest son.

The banquet was a grand affair, and people from all the neighboring plantations were invited, for the Teuffers had many friends.

Among the guests was Predicant Ramring, with his wife and daughter, of the church at Peereboom, down-river. Mynheer Charbon and his son, Jan, were there, too; they were from Plantation Oosterbeck. Also Mynheer and Mevrouw Schriender from Plantation Hollandia. The Georges and the Zublis. And Mynheer Abbensetts of Plantation Solitude, who was a member of the Council of Goverment. The widow Johansen and Herr Mittelholzer, the Swiss-German manager of Plantation de Vreede, a little below the Company plantation, Peereboom.

It was purely accidental that Jacques happened to find himself next to Amelia George at table. He told her: "I wish I could arrange for a *marabunta* nest in the ceiling."

"I'm beginning to wonder," she said, "if there could be one under the table."

"Never mind my knee. It was always sensitive to the touch of soft things."

"Who is doing the tempting now?"

He made a gesture of insouciance. "Shall I pass you the salt?"

Despite the festive spirit that possessed everyone today, the big subject of conversation was the Sickness.

Mynheer Schriender told them that two of his slaves had died the day before. He shook his head gravely. "I don't know what's going to be the fate of this colony before long if this epidemic continues as it's doing. The doctors seem quite helpless."

"Don't call them doctors for God's sake!" Mynheer George exclaimed. "It's an insult to the medical profession to term the men we have here doctors. They know as much about medicine as my old mule."

"My dear George, is there anything in this colony that isn't rotten to the core!" Mynheer Abbensetts snorted and made a sweeping gesture of contempt with his hands. "I'm tired of talking. Tired. How many times haven't I stood up in that Council Chamber and slated the Directors! But what useful purpose has it served! They never heed. They're too confoundedly mean, that's what it boils down to."

"Quite right," agreed Mynheer Charbon. "All they're interested in are their dividends. They don't care what happens to us here."

"Look at Fort Nassau!" thundered on Mynheer Abbensetts. "Half the soldiers are down with the Sickness. The palisades are falling to pieces, and no attempt is ever made to repair them. If an attack came from anywhere tomorrow we'd be at the mercy of the enemy. That fort couldn't stand up to a platoon of beetles!"

"Agreed! Agreed!"

"Hoogenheim, mind you, does his best. We couldn't find a better man to govern the colony. But Hoogenheim alone in the midst of a pack of incapable officials can't settle everything—especially as the Directors won't give him a free hand to spend what ought to be spent on the place."

"Exactly. And look at the Secretary he has under him!"

Abbensetts snorted again. "Secretary! If I wasn't in polite company I'd tell you what's my name for him. Harkenroth! He's a stinking farce! The personification of slackness and carelessness. And there's Wijs, the Orphan-master—another slack good-for-nothing! Always in some slave woman's logie," he added in a murmur. "And Hattinga, the land surveyor, is a hopeless drunkard, as everybody knows. Even our friend Predicant Ramring there"—a twinkle came into his eyes—"even he is a disturbing element: an element that conduces to lack of progress. Always meddling in the affairs of Government. Isn't it the truth, Predicant? Can you deny it?"

The Predicant chuckled and wagged a finger at him. "Very well, Abbensetts. Very well. Another time we'll have it out. This chicken is too good. I never mix politics with chicken."

There was general laughter, though everyone knew that there lay a great deal of seriousness behind what Abbensetts had said. Predicant Ramring did interfere in Government matters—especially matters affecting the slaves and the amount of land that the Church ought to be allowed to cultivate, both matters that only the Directors could give a ruling on but which the Predicant expected the Governor and his Council to settle, and settle in his favor.

Abbensetts had not finished. "The Burgher Militia are a pack of cowards!" he shouted. The gin had begun to have its effect, and Mynheer Abbensetts was naturally of a fiery temperament. "They aren't fit to be called men. If a half-baked musket went off within a mile of them they'd take to their heels. What we want is a regular force of military men—men properly equipped and clothed and fed, and, above all, properly trained. Look what happened in '51! In '56! In '59— just a year or two ago! Those riots and murders at Fort Nassau among the soldiers. The men are undisciplined. They're badly fed, badly clothed, so what can you expect! I've talked about it until I'm sick. I've talked about it in private, I've talked about it in the Council Chamber. I can't do more."

"What you can do now is to eat, Abbensetts," chuckled the Predicant.

"Oh, you! You can eat comfortably! You parsons are better off than anybody else in this colony. You sit back in your cottages and live off the cream of the land. You have the slaves at your feet. You fool them to your heart's content with your patter about God and Jesus Christ and Heaven and Hell, and get them so scared of you they feel you're a little Almighty. You get a free lodging, free meals at the Governor's table, and, on top of that, a salary of nine hundred guilders per annum. Isn't that good living? Do you want anything better?"

"Yes, the wine you sent me last month could have been of a much better quality."

"Why don't you write home and complain to the Directors? Like Frauendorff before you! He was so dissatisfied with the *fat* living that he had to keep a private journal to record complaints! Complaints! Think of it! Oh, yes, I know all about it, Ramring. Frauendorff used to send in bits of scandal and complaints to the Directors. It's just luck that the Directors didn't pay any attention. In fact, they replied telling him that he was a faultfinder and lacked Christian charity! Ho, ho, ho! How do you like that! Eh? How do you like that, Ramring!"

Jacques murmured to Amelia: "Are you keen on politics?"

"Not at all," she said.

"Then I think perhaps we can follow the example of one or two of the others and make our exit."

They went out on the veranda, and when he saw the moonlight he suggested that they should take a stroll along the track.

She glanced at him in surprise. "Now?"

"Now."

"Do you think that would be discreet?"

"Not very. Are you coming?"

She went with him, but kept glancing back so frequently that he had to tell her about Lot's wife. She said: "I'm wondering about yours."

"She's upstairs with Paula Teuffer. Paula has a cold." He offered her his arm. "If you're not afraid."

"To take your arm? Why should I be?"

"Exactly."

"You're very odd, Jacques," she smiled.

"My grandmother has always thought so. You aren't the first."

Light fell palely upon the plantation from a three-day-old crescent, and tree frogs were fluting around them as they made their way along the track. She asked him if he liked the moonlight, and he said: "Not particularly. Moonlight like this always reminds me of a certain rather grim occasion twenty-odd years ago."

"What occasion was that?"

"I never talk about it."

She squeezed his arm. "I've heard terrible tales about you, Jacques."

"They are all true."

"Have you and your brothers really such a bad name up the Canje?"

"We're an atrocious family, Amelia."

"I don't agree. Juliana is a dear—and so is Faustina and your Cousin Flora." She pressed his arm again. "And you yourself."

"My mother was the very Devil himself in female form. If you had met her you would have known. I liked her, all the same."

"I hear you and Pedro and Lumea went out after her one night and shot her down."

"There was moonlight like this that night."

She glanced about her with a simulation of nervousness, pressing herself against him as though in fear. "The moonlight is not very bright. I hope none of the slaves are about tonight. They seem so aggressive and self-assertive nowadays. Do those on the Canje give much trouble?"

"A great deal. We have to keep a strict eye on them all the time, but Pedro and the others know how to handle them. Higher up, I understand, there's a fellow called Cuffy who is inciting them to make themselves as annoying as they possibly can. He's the most dangerous of the lot, though Fourie and his overseers don't seem to think so. I believe they're underestimating that fellow."

"What's his name, did you say?"

"Cuffy. He belongs to the Vernsobres of Magdalenenburg."

"That's the place with the very cruel manager, André Fourie?"

"André Fourie Niffens den Timmerman, to give him his full name. Perfectly correct. He's an archbrute."

"Do you agree that the private planters treat their slaves far worse than the Company people?"

"There's no doubt about that. A definite fact. You won't find many troublemakers on the Company plantations. It's the private planters with their savage methods of torture who drive these fellows to be aggressive."

"Are there other troublemakers up the Canje besides Cuffy?"

"Several. There's a fellow called Atta whom we sold not too long ago. And higher up, I've heard, there are one or two more. Akkara and Accabre and Quacco and Baube. Yes, and Goussari—all sedition-mongers."

They had reached a spot where the bush opened out on their left. They could see the sluggish black water glimmering in the pale moonlight. Over on the other bank, fireflies flashed amid the hanging foliage of the wild cacao and the fine, feathery fronds of *aeta* and manicole palms. They paused here automatically, and kept looking, and inhaling the wet, leafy air.

"That's lovely."

"Yes." He nodded with a slightly detached air.

They could hear the water sucking at the bank near their feet—a soft, hypnotic sound. Sillip-sillip, it went. Sillip-sillip. Lulling. A tinkly bubbling came suddenly, and a ripple began to circle outward. In the background was the fluting of the tree frogs.

"It's very lonely here, isn't it?"

He nodded.

She glanced up at him. "You seem so thoughtful."

He smiled, and, tilting his head, returned her look. The shadow of his shoulder was upon her chin. He turned her toward him, pulled her against him and kissed her. She did not withdraw or protest. Even when his hands moved down her arms and over her breasts—very lightly at first, then with purpose and intensity—she still remained quiescent. A limpness seemed to have come over her: a limpness of mind and body.

Fortunately, it was September, the middle of the long dry season, and the earth was dry, though some of the shrubs they brushed against were wet with a heavy dew. Once his head touched a clump of dragon's blood, and for nearly the whole of the half an hour that they were there she could see the tiny blebs of moisture glistening on his temple in the moonlight.

Neither of them uttered a word.

It was not until she was putting her clothes right and they were on the point of resuming their walk that she broke the silence. She said with a quiet, excited breathlessness: "Do you think badly of me for this?"

He shook his head. "I'm the bad one. I was married last year."

She hung her head. "I liked you since that first day I saw you when you came to live in these parts, some years ago. Do you remember the morning you came to see Juliana?"

"I hardly noticed you then. You've grown up amazingly since."

"Jacques, you won't say anything of this, will you?"

"That's so naïve. Don't lose your composure. It will remain with us. Sometimes I do hate myself."

"Why?"

"This."

"How do you mean?"

He shrugged. "I'm in love with my wife."

"Oh."

"After this I'll have to watch myself."

"It won't happen again. It was an accident. I'm going to avoid you as much as I can in future."

After a silence she asked: "What excuse are you going to make when you get back?"

"None at all. We went for a walk because we weren't in the mood to listen to Councillor Abbensetts ranting the Government to pieces. That's the truth." He gave her a sly look and added: "The truth need not be elaborated."

"Will Faustina believe that?"

"I trust so." A sensitive, pained look passed over his face. "Faustina is good. Big and generous. If she did discover about this it wouldn't make any difference to our relations."

"I can hardly believe that, Jacques."

The glance he gave her was almost contemptuous. His casual air of drollery had vanished. "You may not believe it but it's true. She's big and noble. You don't find her kind often." He fell silent, but after a moment said abruptly: "And you. You have such a splendid body. You've never known a man before. Why did you let me?"

"That's simple to answer. Because I wanted you to be the first."

He shrugged.

"I feel weak all over whenever I see you."

He made no comment.

"I wonder how I shall be able to face you in day-light, Jacques."

"That will be easy. Simply smile politely and say good day, as you have always done, and I shall do the same. Amelia, this isn't as dreadful as people like to make out it is. Only these Predicants with their God and Jesus Christ and their convenient moral doctrines make events like this seem terrifying. We won't go to hell because of tonight." He laughed. "You should have grown up with us on the Canje to see how casual we were about such matters."

"Isn't your sister virtuous?"

"Lumea?" He laughed again. "She had a stillborn child at sixteen."

"What! Who was the father?"

"Pedro."

"Jacques! I don't believe it!"

He patted her arm. "Not so pretty, is it?"

Later, when they got back, Faustina believed him.

"I knew it must have been some such reason that drove you two out," she said. When she reached up to kiss him, however—they were alone in the guest room —he turned away his face. His hands were clenched.

"Is something wrong, Jacques?"

"No. Nothing."

She stared at him, and a look of slow enlighten-ment came alive on her face. "Did anything happen between you?"

He nodded.

They undressed in silence.

"It was a rotten thing to do," he said, "looked at

in the light of accepted conventions. I ought to have restrained myself. I have no excuse to make for myself."

She said nothing, but she was very white and tense. There was agitation in her movements.

During the night he heard her sobbing beside him. Sobbing softly into her pillow.

The next morning, before they set out for their home, she told him: "I forgive you, but please don't remind me of what I said once. I'll get used to it—I mean to the idea of what you've done. Not to your always doing it, though. I'm human, Jacques. I can feel jealous like anybody else. I could tear her to bits for—for letting you."

IV

In February of the following year, 1762, she gave birth to a son, and they called him Raphael, because Faustina hoped that he would become a great painter like Raphael Sanzio. Jacques twinkled: "Don't let Grandma hear you expressing such a wish. She detests painters."

Hendrickje wrote in triumph: "I am a happy woman today. I have not struggled in vain. We have beaten Destiny. Nothing can keep us now from reaching the pinnacles. I can see the shade of Grandfather Willem strutting proudly before me in this room, and I can see his face beaming with satisfaction. Let them all be sons, my boy, and tell them the tales of old, Jacques. Hammer into them the consciousness of the grand blood that runs in their veins. The old blood, Jacques! The fire-blood. . . ."

Gifts deluged down upon young Raphael from his uncles and aunt on the Canje. Pedro sent a large cask of wine, with instructions that it was not to be drawn from until Raphael was twenty-one. David's gift was a set of six daggers—"teach him to throw these like his uncle"—but Laurens and Lumea, more conventional, sent sugar and coffee. Hendrickje decided, practically, on a money gift; a jar containing a hundred florins.

Not satisfied with these demonstrations of their delight, there was a spree "in honor of the coming into the world of a legitimate van Groenwegel," as Laurens put it. They invited all their cronies, and the old house flamed with wild laughter and drunken catcalls. Upstairs, in her room, Hendrickje slept through it soundly.

It lasted all night. By morning everyone was dazed and prostrate from an excess of wine. Hosts and guests lay strewn around the sitting room and dining room asleep. On the dining table Lumea sprawled on her back—completely nude.

At six o'clock something happened.

The slaves who had come with the guests the evening before had slept under the trees in the compound. In the usual course of things, two of them strolled into the house to see whether their masters were ready to leave. They saw the drunken figures. They saw Lumea on the dining table. They hurried outside and talked about it to the others.

"This our chance," one of them said. "Let's go inside the house and give them a beating. The missy naked on the table. We can take her in a corner and give her what the massas give her last night."

"The old lady might come down and cry out."

"We can deal with her if she make noise. She nearly ninety."

"They'll shoot us if we trouble her. They bad massas here."

"But how they going to stop us? They drunk. They not able to move."

"Fourteen of us here—and only ten of them in there. Let's do it. We can tie up their hands and feet first."

"Yes, Bagga right. Let's go and do it. Beat them good. Remember what Cuffy tell us? Don't miss a chance to hit them. Every time we get the chance we must beat them up. Break up their property."

Bagga chortled. "That missy got good legs. She naked on the table, all ready for us. Come, let's go."

They hesitated under the trees, talking. Mumbling. Glancing toward the house. At length they decided.

They would do it. Beat up the massas and rape the missy. Get revenge on them.

They should not, however, have hesitated so long. It was this pause that told against them—and the fact that they had failed to consider the possible attitude of the Bodyguard.

From the very outset their intentions had been divined by Memphis. Memphis, from a pantry window, had overheard a remark and had seen them gathering and talking and glancing toward the house. He hurried into the sitting room and shook Pedro awake, dashed water into his face and slapped his cheeks and forehead. He told Pedro of his fears and they woke David. Then Memphis hurried off to the kitchen to rouse the four other members of the Bodyguard.

Bagga and his companions, unaware of these developments, entered the house—some by the front door, some by the kitchen door. They moved across the sitting room. They moved through the pantry. No one stopped them. In the kitchen the Bodyguard pretended to be sound asleep on their rude mattresses on the floor.

The intruders in the sitting room stooped to yank up Gert de Groot and Hendrik de Fruizt. "Pull them up! Come on! Lash them! Treat them same as they treat us!"

"Oh, so!"

That was Pedro. Bleary-eyed, tousled; the black locks were damp on his forehead. Pedro had a musket presented at them.

"God! Look! Massa, wake up!"

Pedro uttered a deep hacking sound. Like the bark of a racoon.

"Get out! Quick!"

Bagga decided to be defiant. "He can't shoot on us! Slave cost money. He can't kill us."

The others stood still, irresolute.

"Remember what Akkara tell us! They value us. They know we cost money. They can't kill us, because we do their work. If they shoot us they won't got nobody to work for them, and they'll punish and turn poor."

Bang!

The room hazed and vibrated. Bagga yelled and crumpled up, a ball in his thigh.

In the dining room—just before the musket exploded—David's hand make a flicking motion across his face, and a knife gashed deeply into the upper arm of the slave who had bent over the dining table to fondle Lumea's prostrate body. David was standing on the stairway. His hand flicked again, and another knife found its mark—this time in the buttocks of another man who was attempting to yank up Fernand Brauer. David worked in silence.

The unwounded intruders scampered back into the pantry, but Stragga and Dak and Bakkara intercepted them.

Hendrickje appeared at the top of the stairs and asked what was the matter. David turned his head and told her: "Just a little trouble."

Lumea slept through everything. Like Laurens upstairs in bed with one of his mistresses, a girl called Yemba. Lumea and Laurens did not wake until after nine o'clock. By then the fires were blazing fiercely in the compound and operations were in full swing. The air was filled with the groans of humans in pain. The air stank with the odor of scorched human flesh.

Hendrickje entered the dining room and slapped Lumea on the buttocks. "Get some clothes on, you vile bitch. There has been trouble."

"I see that—and smell it. Hell! I've got a headache, Grandma!"

Hendrickje tittered, shepherding Pedro's two mulatto sons, Ziddy and Janny, into the sitting room for their lessons. Their kinky hair did not upset her; old age had altered her views on the subject of hair. "You're fortunate you have nothing worse," she said to Lumea over her shoulder. "Dave said you were the center of attraction."

"Was I? The sons of hogs! Did they put their black paws on me?"

Ziddy, who was nine, wanted to go outside to

watch the brandings, but his great-grandmother told him: "No, it's time for lessons, my boy. Afterwards Uncle Dave will take you into the fields for musket practice. Now, Janny! Come back! Come back from that window or you'll be whipped!"

Janny came back. He was eight, and gave promise of growing into a huge specimen like his father. He had his Grandfather Adrian's forehead. Hendrickje patted his shoulder and smiled down affectionately upon him. "So much spirit, eh? So much spirit. The old blood. It must come out. Never mind the black taint. Ziddy, still, please! Sit still!"

On the morning of July 6th, that same year, at about six o'clock, there came a loud knocking on the front door of the van Groenwegel residence on the Berbice River.

Jacques called down from a window; he was puzzled. "Who's that?"

It was a soldier from the fort.

"What's the trouble, my man?"

"An order from Captain Lentzeng to muster, Mynheer!"

"To muster? What for? What's happened?"

"There's some trouble upriver, Mynheer! Will you please come down and sign the circular?"

Jacques went down and signed the circular. Like every other planter, he was a member of the Burgher Militia.

On his return upstairs he told Faustina: "It's on Laurens Kunckler's plantations—Goedland and Goed Fortuin. When he was at the Council meeting yesterday, the slaves took advantage of his absence to plunder his house. They took all the muskets and ammunition they could lay their hands on, and after burning the house flat, made off into the bush. They frightened off the Accaway Postholder who arrived at the fort last night with the news."

"Jacques! That's serious."

"Of course it is." He was dressing.

"You're not afraid to go?"

"Not particularly—but I don't say I'm pleased at

the prospect of potting at ambushed negroes and being potted at in return." He stretched out and tweaked her chin. "I think you'd better spend the day at the Teuffers. I may not be back until tomorrow."

"Most certainly not. Suppose the trouble spreads to this part of the river."

He gave her a surprised look. "All the more reason why you should not remain in this house alone."

"Have you forgotten our family motto? We never run."

He stared at her—with genuine incredulity—then laughed. "Well! I wouldn't have dreamt you were given that way, too."

"What do you mean? Weren't we all brought up that way?"

"That's so," he nodded, his face solemn. "We never run."

"Your grandmother would be shocked if she were here to observe your attitude," she smiled.

"I have no doubt. Kiss me good-bye."

"Aren't you going to eat something first?"

"They'll provide some sort of meal at the fort, I suppose."

"Take care of yourself, Jacques."

"You insist on staying here, then?"

"Yes, I'll stay. I'll keep a few muskets upstairs here."

At about nine o'clock a slave arrived from the Teuffers with a message. Juliana wanted to know whether Faustina was not coming. "She say not safe remain alone in house here, Missy," the man said. "Better to go home with them until the Massa come back home here."

"Tell her I prefer to remain here in case anything should happen. Tell her it's my duty to be here. Any more news, Gratta?"

"I hear the Governor take boat up the river, Missy —boat with plenty sandbags in case the bad men fire on them. That's all I hear, Missy."

During the next two or three days only scrappy news drifted in. One report went that the Burgher

Militia and the soldiers from the fort had failed to suppress the rebel slaves and that other slaves had joined them. "I hear they moving fast toward the Canje, Missy. Plenty trouble coming soon. Plenty trouble."

Not an hour later, however, an Indian from up-river told Faustina: "They not gone toward the Canje. They still in the bush. I hear they kill two white men and wound plenty more."

Faustina was in the dining room when Juliana and Paula Teuffer, her sister-in-law, arrived. They wanted to know if Faustina had heard anything they had not heard. Juliana had something of Hendrickje's build; she was not as tall, but she had a very dignified carriage and the same full-bosomed, erect figure.

"I heard two white men have been killed. Do you know who they were?"

"No," said Faustina.

"There's a rumor that the Burgher Militia took to its heels."

"I don't believe that," Faustina flashed. "I think the best thing will be to close our ears to rumors."

"Let's go for a ride," Paul suggested. "It will get our minds off the subject."

"No, thank you."

"A swim, then."

"I'm a poor swimmer," said Juliana. "I wasn't brought up on the Canje, Paula, remember—and I've always been scared of *perai*."

"Faustina, how have your slaves been behaving?"

"No trouble at all. Jacques treats them well. They're fond of us. We only flog them when we can't avoid it."

"I'm afraid we can't say the same for our place. There are quite a few subversive spirits there—and, of course, Vincent and Marcus and Hart aren't particularly soft in their methods."

"There's going to be serious trouble one of these days, Juliana. Most people seem to regard this slave question as a minor one, but I don't agree. The negroes are beginning to realize how hopelessly outnumbered we whites are. Think of it! Three-hundred-odd whites against three thousand slaves!¹ Do you know what that would mean if there were to be a general uprising!"

"Let's hope there won't be any such thing, my dear."

"We wouldn't stand a chance. It would be whole-sale massacre."

At about four o'clock that afternoon they heard a confusion of shouts on the river, and Juliana and Paula hurried to the landing place to see what it was about. When they came back to the house they told Faustina: "It was a boatload of militiamen. Vincent and Jacques are coming in one of the other boats. They're safe."

"Everything is over, they said. They've captured some of the rebels."

"These slaves could never hope to bring off any really serious rebellion," said Paula. "We have them too cowed."

When Jacques arrived an hour or so later, however, and gave them an account of what had happened, Paula did not speak so confidently.

In his muddy boots and disheveled clothes, his musket butt resting on the floor, he stood on the veranda and told them the story of the past three days. He was disgusted. "You mustn't always disregard rumors," he said. "There was plenty of running away. Those niggers went off into the bush, cut down a few trees and erected a rough sort or stockade, and it didn't take more than that to send the brave Burgher Militia scampering. Vincent, incidentally, was among those who ran."

"Vincent ran!"

"I'm afraid he did. And so did Hart and Marcus and seventy-five per cent of the valiant force. There were about fourteen or fifteen of us left behind the earthworks with Lieutenant Theilen after the niggers opened fire from their improvised defense works. Lent-zeng himself ran—and he's the Burgher captain, mind you." He laughed. "You can see for yourself now what

¹Official figures: 346 whites, 3833 slaves, in 1762.

will happen if a general uprising materialized. Don't think these niggers are fools. They know well how weak we are—and how much guts we've got."

"But how were they defeated eventually?" Paula asked.

Jacques shrugged. "There were only thirty-six of them. They couldn't hold out indefinitely. Theilen managed, at last, to entice them out of their stockade. He staged a mock attack from one side, and when the niggers thought he was on the run they couldn't resist the temptation; they dashed out in a sortie and ran right into the ambush that had been set for them."

Juliana was dismayed. "I can hardly believe it. Vincent running away. And his mother a van Groenwegel. I'm ashamed of him."

Jacques chuckled. "So much for the old blood."

Up the Canje, Hendrickje sniffed and growled: "Weak blood, damn them! Weak blood! Thank heaven he doesn't bear our name!"

"Those Teuffers are poor stuff," Pedro agreed. "I always knew it."

Laurens pawed the floor with his deformed foot and scowled. "That's why," he said, "we've got to be careful whom we pick for wives. I'd shoot a son of mine if he behaved like that."

"Black hogs," growled Lumea. "They should attempt making trouble up here. They'd soon realize what they were up against. They wouldn't bring that kind of thing to the van Groenwegels."

"Not to the van Groenwegels," echoed David, strutting about and tapping his chest with his clenched hand.

His grandmother regarded him with doting eyes. "Grandfather Willem over again. That strutting about. That's it, my children!" she said in a louder voice. She shook her fist at an invisible enemy. "Keep up the fighting spirit. Don't let anything depress you. Ziddy! Come here! It's time for your porridge, my boy. Come!" She hurried fussily after Ziddy who, unheeding, made for the back veranda where he and Janny were engaged in knife-throwing practice. One of the knives had strayed into the sitting room and Ziddy had come in to retrieve it.

"This incident should be a lesson to us planters," Pedro was saying. "It's a warning, and if we don't heed it the consequences are going to be disastrous. There's too much complacency around."

"Anyway, we're well armed," said David, still strutting. "We've got enough ammunition for a three-year siege. And there's one thing with me: I'm never averse to a good rousing battle. My knife stock is heavy."

Lumea laughed. "You're a bloodthirsty rascal, Dave. But things won't happen the way you want them. There will never be any slave uprising in this colony. We've got them too much under our heels. They can rave and spout sedition among themselves, but when it comes to taking action they haven't got the guts—nor the intelligence—to marshal themselves into a fighting force. This Berbice River incident is a mere flare-up—and that only came about because Kunckler happened to turn his back for a moment. Had he been present on those plantations, they would never have run amok. It was the same with that Poelwyk affair in 1731. The manager went to church one Sunday and in his absence the hogs ran wild."

"I disagree," frowned Laurens. "That's how most of the planters feel—that so long as they show their faces about their plantations and raise the big stick they'll avoid trouble. It's a smug attitude. They're blind to the signs. Trouble is brewing, there's no doubt about it. There's a definitely aggressive spirit smouldering in these negroes, and the temperature is rising every day. Those fellows higher up are being underrated. Cuffy and Akkara and Atta and that lot. Those niggers mean business. They should be got rid of. They're originating a dangerous movement against the whites in this colony, and you hear my word, the day isn't far off when the magazine is going to explode."

V

In September they received news of the death of Aert at the age of eighty-seven. "This means the end of the Essequibo plantation," wrote Hubertus, "unless I can secure a good manager. Grandfather Aert was active to the day of his death, and the slaves loved him, but the overseers are hated and I am fearing trouble soon. I was wondering if it wouldn't be possible for David or Laurens to come out and run the place. I think it would be a pity to abandon our Essequibo plantation, in view of our family connections with that part of the country. The Demerary plantation here keeps me fully occupied, and a wife and four daughters don't lighten my responsibilities. Please give me an early reply and let me know what David and Laurens feel on the matter. I know Pedro has been ear-marked for Suriname, that's why I haven't suggested him. . . ."

David and Laurens shook their heads.

"I have no inclination to go to the Essequibo," Laurens frowned. "That colony is on the decline. I hear Kyk-over-al and Cartabo are in jungle again. The best thing Hubertus can do is to sell the place and enlarge the Demerary concern. Demerary is far ahead of Essequibo now. That's where we should concentrate our energies."

"Laurens is right," David agreed. "If it had been Demerary I would have gone, but I'm not going to any backward place like Essequibo."

"It's erroneous to describe Essequibo as backward," Lumea said. "The prospects are still good there. The only trouble is that the planters won't move down the river fast enough and leave the worn-out lands upstream. In Demerary they've already established two plantations on the seacoast, and the English, of course, have done a lot since they came. Hubertus did the right thing in marrying that Maybury girl. It will give our family prestige with both the Dutch and the English in Demerary."

"All the same," said their grandmother, "we have

to consider our old policy of spreading, my children. We must have our foothold everywhere. Essequibo may have taken second place to Demerary in recent years, but it's not yet a dead colony—and it's the birthplace of Kaywana——"

"Grandma!"

"Grandma!"

"What is it?"

"Are you forgetting your family history?"

"What did I say? Wasn't Kaywana born in Essequibo? Good heavens! But how foolish of me! She was born on the Corentyne, of course. Ah, well! I'm getting old, my children." She tittered and said to David: "Dave, I believe it's nothing but that French jade who's stopping you from wanting to go to the Essequibo."

"Who? Marlisse? Nonsense. She couldn't hold me back if I wanted to go. I'm looking at the proposition in a rational light, Grandma. Family sentiment is one thing, but we can't let it dominate our reason."

Pedro, silent until now, took his pipe from his mouth and nodded. "Dave is right, Grandma. We're prepared to go far where the traditions of the family are involved, but there's a limit we mustn't go beyond."

Hendrickje looked deliberately from one to the other of them. There was in her manner a vague panic, a vague alarm. Her hand trembled slightly as she rested it on the sideboard. A nerve in her cheek twitched.

The eyes of the others grew shifty; wandered about the room. David stroked his eyebrows. Pedro fiddled with his pipe. Laurens adjusted his cravat; he was never without a cravat. Lumea glanced from the dining table to the window, seemed to become interested in something in the compound.

"This is not a very vital issue," Hendrickje said; her voice was the voice of the former Hendrickje, hard and clipped. All in a flash she had ceased to be senile. "In many respects I agree with your arguments concerning the decline of Essequibo as a colony, and I shall leave it to Hubertus to decide whether to dispose of the plantation there or hire a capable manager to carry it on. What disturbs me, however, is that remark of yours, David—and that remark of yours, Pedro. I can only hope that you don't speak from your heart of hearts when you attempt to belittle our family sentiments—our family traditions——"

David and Pedro interrupted her in chorus. And Laurens.

"Most certainly not, Grandma!"

"You don't imagine we'd want to let down the old blood!"

"You've misunderstood me, Grandma," said David.

"We value our traditions," said Pedro. "We'll stand by the family to the end."

"The bitter end," vowed Lumea.

Hendrickje nodded. "Very well, my children. Thank you for reassuring me. For an instant, though, I was certainly inclined to think that a little rot had set in. Remember, everything depends upon you. Time and myself will soon have closed our accounts. It may be this year—even tomorrow—it may be next year. If you soften up, all is lost."

"To me," Jacques was saying to Amelia on the Berbice, "you're extremely human. You have no need to be ashamed."

"I still feel like a beast, Jacques."

"You didn't cause the thunderstorm, nor are you responsible for the circumstance that Faustina happens to be spending the day at the Teuffers. Stop crying, my dear." He dried her eyes.

She kept her head bent.

He said, smiling: "My grandmother believes that whatever is destined to happen must happen. But, she will add, not knowing what has been destined for the morrow, you make your own plans for the future and dream of power and renown. You have a beautiful body, Amelia. Go home now and dream of lovely things for the future."

VI

On February the 4th of the following year, 1763, Bakkara said to Pedro: "Massa, watch Peddy and Jemmara. They talking against you."

Pedro grunted. "Talking, eh? But nothing else of a definite nature? What I mean is, have you at any time seen them storing sticks or stones or knives or any sort of weapon?"

"No, Massa, I not see that, but I watching them good. Jemmara hate you bad because you brand him last month."

"That's not news." Pedro, however, looked reflective, flicking his whip against his leg. Suddenly he nodded. "Very well, Bakkara. Keep a sharp watch on the bad men. By the way, what of Bemba? He was inclined to be fractious yesterday. Have you heard him saying anything, too?"

"No, Massa, but I watching him."

"Excellent."

Later, Hendrickje said: "I think you're making too much of this whispering among them, Pedro. Slaves always whisper and grumble."

"It's got beyond the stage of whispering and grumbling, Grandma. Something is going on that we don't know about."

"Pedro, I do hope you aren't developing into a coward in your old age."

"I see more than you see, old lady. You're ninety tomorrow."

On February the 6th, when David was in Field Number Four, a stone flew past his head, and when he turned, another came at him and grazed his shoulder. He said nothing. He urged his mule toward the clump of shrubs on the lateral dam where he suspected the trouble lay.

Two figures got up and ran.

David's hand went to his waist—then came up. There was a glint in the sun and a faint singing lisp.

One of the running figures stumbled to a halt and clapped a hand to his hip. The other figure disappeared amid the canes before David's hand could come into play again.

David rode up and grasped the wounded man by the collar. "What's the other fellow's name, Jemmara?"

"Ow, Massa! Me bleeding. Me bleeding bad!"

"What's the name of the other fellow, Jemmara?"

"Ow, Massa! I not throw the stones. Me bleeding. Don't punish me more, Massa David."

David was twisting the man's arm slowly—powerfully.

"The name of the fellow who was with you, Jemmara?"

"Bakky, Massa. Bakky. Ow, Massa! Me arm! Me sick man, Massa."

"Get back to your quarters, you filthy raccoon! Get off! Wait! Give me that knife." David wiped the blade clean on Jemmara's overall before tucking it back into the sheath at his waist.

"Massa, I sick. I bleeding. Please don't brand me."

"Stop whining. Ah, here's Stragga. Take charge here, Stragga. Get this lump of filth off to his quarters, and after his wound has been attended to dump him in the stocks until this afternoon."

"Good, Massa David. Leave him to me."

On February the 12th Marraka threatened Lumea with a cutlass, so Pedro had twelve lashes administered as well as an application of the red-hot tongs, followed by ten minutes on broken bottles.

That same night a fire occurred in the Carpenter's shed. But Dankje, one of the Bodyguard, saw the flames in time, and, with Dak, another member of the faithful five, put them out before much damage had been done.

Nobody knew how the fire had started, but there were brambles and old rags in piles in the shed. Pedro said to Marraka: "Let's hear about this, Marraka. Did you set that fire last night?"

"No, Massa Pedro."

"Are you quite sure?"

Marraka writhed and shrieked, and Pedro raised the branding iron. The smell of burnt flesh fumed in the air.

"Still not sure about it, Marraka?"

Marraka confessed. It was he who had set the fire.

On the seventeenth David and Laurens visited André Fourie at Plantation Magdalenenburg. Fourie was thin and thin-lipped; when he smiled his lips vanished completely. He told David: "Yes, there is a bit of trouble about here, David, my boy, but nothing that we can't handle—and handle very easily." He made soft grunting sounds of mirth, his pale-green eyes alight with evil. He kept tapping the nails of his fingers together lightly. "You know us? We have our little methods. Very effective."

Laurens, meanwhile, was talking with the Chief Carpenter, Cassian Corbeau, who was also assistant manager.

"We're not blind to it, Laurens. We have our eyes on the bad men. That fellow Atta you sold to us is a terror. But I do touch him up—well, not exactly affectionately, if you grasp my meaning. It's possible you may find many little traces of our encounters on the soles of his feet and in the palms of his hands. Hee, hee!"

"We have another one we want to dispose of. Fellow called Marraka. A good worker, but subversive. We bought him higher up, and at first it seemed as if he might have made a good leader or driver, but we know better now. He's been spurring the others on to violence. He tried to burn down the Carpenter's shed the other night."

"That's the sort of animal, eh? Good. Send him along. Fourie and I can shape him up. We know how to get them tamed. Fire and iron does it, Laurens. Fire and iron—and sometimes a little acid. Hee, hee!"

David was saying to Fourie: "Things are looking queer, all the same. Have you many you can depend on if anything happened?"

Fourie shrugged. "One or two. Just one or two.

I never trouble very much, though. No chance of them getting out of hand in a big way. Here and there we'll continue to have trouble, no doubt. Like that affair on Kunckler's two plantations on the Berbice. But they can't mount anything on a large scale. They're too ignorant. They'll never be able to marshal themselves into an organized rebel force."

On the eighteenth Marraka had vanished. A search failed, and David said: "He must have heard, somehow, of the pending sale. He knows what to expect from Fourie and Corbeau. Damned fool! He must be rounded up. Where does he think he's going to hide? Unless he keeps in the bush and starves!"

On the nineteenth Pedro was in Field Number Two when a musket banged among the coffee trees on the neighboring plantation and a ball sang past his head. Pedro saw a wisp of smoke curling upward amidst the coffee trees. He raised his musket and fired. There was a scamper of feet and a crackling of dry leaves.

The twentieth, Sunday, was uneventful.

VII

Monday the twenty-first.

It was a fine, cool morning; this was the short dry season. In the east the sky was flecked with ranks of pink clouds, and the air was pleasant with an invigorating chilliness. Black-and-yellow plantain birds and some kiskadees were disporting themselves on top the water tanks and fluttering up into the air to catch insects —flying ants and tiny snow-white creatures, like ghostly mosquitoes, that hovered and drifted in happy unconcern on the faint breeze.

Hendrickje, at a window, saw the distant cane fields pale green and unreal in the soft morning mist. The sun had not yet come up. Beyond the cane fields the mist lurked amid the shaded spaces in the foliage of the jungle that bordered the Canje Creek, and here it

had a pinkish look, for it reflected the light of the
clouds. A fresh, leafy scent rose from the earth, and
dew glistened in the trees in the compound.

There were two small beds in Hendrickje's room,
one on either side of the big four-poster; Ziddy slept
in one, Janny in the other.

Hendrickje turned and looked at them; they were
still asleep.

A smile of affection passed over her face.

Two rooms away David and Laurens, who slept
in one big bed, had just got up. Laurens stood at an
eastern window stretching himself. David sat in the big
armchair smoking his early morning pipe.

"The air smells good this morning," Laurens commented. He yawned and arched his back and scratched
his head, shook his fists at the rafters.

David made a mumbling sound in acknowledgment.

Laurens leant out of the window and grunted.
"Guess who is leaving the house, Dave."

David did not guess.

"Rassiki," said Laurens.

David made a gesture of insouciance.

"I can't see what Pedro finds in her."

"Just what you find in Yuani."

Laurens was on the point of retorting when he
stiffened and assumed a listening attitude.

"I heard a rumor last week," said David, "that
Jacques is having an affair with your heart's desire on
the Berbice."

Laurens put up his hand for silence.

"What's the trouble?"

Out in the morning, coming from the east, Laurens thought he could hear a sound—a vague squalling
sigh. A low wavering sough of noise. It might have been
a jumbie yawning before sleep after a night's wandering in the Canje jungle.

"What's it, Laurens?"

"Come, Dave."

David rose and joined his brother at the window.

"Listen," said Laurens.

His thin, two-foot-long pipe poised before him, David assumed a listening attitude.

For a while only the fluttering and twittering of the kiskadees and plantain birds could be heard. Then suddenly through these sounds came the other. Far away. Vague. It seemed to waver as the wind veered.

David looked at Laurens. "Most unearthly."

They stood listening.

"I don't like it, Dave."

David kept his head cocked, frowning.

"Something has happened. Up-creek."

"What sort of something?"

David laid his pipe down carefully on top of the chest of drawers. "That sound is coming from the direction of Magdalenenburg."

Laurens looked uneasy. Shifted his foot along the floor.

"We'd better get dressed," said David.

"But Fourie and Corbeau both said there was no chance of anything serious."

"Fourie and Corbeau are not God."

Laurens called out to Pedro, and Pedro answered in a sleepy voice.

"Get out of bed and go to the window, Pedro. Listen and tell us what you think."

Pedro clicked his tongue and did not move. They heard the thump of bare feet in the corridor, and Lumea, in her nightgown, came in.

"Dave, what's that sound yonder? Have you heard it?"

"Can't enlighten you, but it bodes no good."

"It seems to be coming from the Vernsobres' place."

When he was dressed David went down into the kitchen where the Bodyguard always slept. They were awake and smoking. They squatted on the rough mattresses which Pedro had had made for them, but on seeing David, they rose at once with exclamations of surprise.

"Massa David! You down already?"

David grinned. "Given you a surprise, eh? Look here, I believe there has been some trouble up-creek. I want one of you to go and do a little scouting around. Who's the man?"

They all volunteered.

"Dak, I think you're the best horseman. You go. Take my horse, and go by the tracks—the regular tracks. Don't cut across anybody's fields."

"Very good, Massa David."

"Have something to eat first. All of you eat. I have a special job for each man. Memphis, you and Bakkara must take a ride around the outer dams and keep an eye out. Stragga, you go into the fields and report on what's happening. Talk to the drivers and hear how things are going. Dankje, you remain here and watch the situation with the household slaves. You must all carry whips—hide whips. Or cutlasses."

By nine o'clock the noise in the distance was definite. A wailing of human voices, it grew louder and sometimes faded, but it never died away completely.

Hendrickje was of the opinion that it was a ration riot on Horstenburg. "Those Horstenburg people have been giving short rations of late. Don't you remember what de Fruizt told us last week?"

"Anyway, we're taking no chances," Pedro said. "I'm determined not to be caught off guard."

"Itching for an opportunity to do battle, eh, my boy? The old blood. The old blood." Hendrickje went upstairs to her room, making doting sounds of mirth. A few minutes later she called Ziddy and Janny up from the compound. "Come and have your bath, Ziddy! Janny! You dirty boys!"

At about ten o'clock Stragga came in a hurry to Laurens who was in Field Number Three. "Massa Laurens! Bauri and Yukka and Tamba left the gang. They gone off on to the next plantation."

"Very well, Stragga. Let them go."

Almost at the same time Memphis was reporting to David in Field Number Seven: "Massa David, trouble happen in Number Four. Baccabre and Majak fighting with three others."

David rode fast to Number Four. When he got

there he slashed right and left with his hide whip. That broke them up. They cowered back and glared at him. Baccabre shouted: "Me not afraid of white man!" And Majak took courage and flashed: "All Christians cruel! Wait and see what coming for them soon! They got to punish as how they make us punish!"

David slashed him across his face, and he howled and cringed away, his hands up in defense. David slashed Baccabre across the back. Baccabre did not cringe. He caught the whip and tugged it from his master's grasp. In silence David reached down to his waist. His hand came up and there was a glint. The knife buried itself into Baccabre's left hip. But even that did not cow the fellow. He slashed with all his strength at David. David evaded the lashes and brought his hand into play again. This time Baccabre staggered off coughing and clutching his throat. He crumpled up and lay still amid a pool of blood.

"Get me the knives, Stragga, and remove the corpse," said David. "And my whip. If there's any more trouble let me know. I'll be somewhere in the vicinity of Number Two or Number Three."

"Very well, Massa."

At about half-past eleven Dak arrived back from his scouting expedition. He was in a state of great excitement. There were gashes on his cheek and on the back of his hand. His right sleeve was ripped down.

"Massa Pedro! Massa David! Big, big trouble break out yonder, Massa! Big, big trouble! All slaves on Magdalenenburg, Stevensburg, Horstenburg, all of them open riot!"

"On Magdalenenburg!"

"Yes, Massa Pedro. That's where it begin. They kill off Massa Fourie and Massa Corbeau and four other white people."

"Fourie and Corbeau! Killed off! Nonsense! Dak, is this true? Are you sure?"

"Sure, Massa. Sure, sure. I talk with plenty slaves who run off in the bush because they not want to join in, and they tell me so. They say Massa Fourie and Massa Corbeau first to get kill off. Cuffy and Atta and

Akkara at the head of the riot, Massa, and the men joining in from all over the place. One-two who not bad men run off into the bush and hide, but all the others joining in and they burning and killing white people. Massa, big, big trouble open this morning, I tell you. Big trouble."

Pedro rubbed his chin hard. "About how many of them would you say there are, Dak? Can you give us any idea?"

"Plenty, plenty, Massa. Nearly a thousand, I sure. Slaves from other plantations joining in with them all the time."

"Very well, Dak. You've done well. Rest and have a good long smoke. Get something into your stomach, too. Call Stragga."

"Yes, Massa." Dak went off, very pleased with himself.

When Stragga came Pedro told him: "Go back to the fields and tell Massa Laurens to let the drivers blow the horns for meals immediately. Tell him everybody must come in at once. Stress that. At once."

"Yes, Massa."

"And, Stragga?"

"Yes, Massa Pedro?"

"Tell the others—except Dak—to stand by for orders. Be waiting in the kitchen in about half an hour's time."

"Very good, Massa."

Fifteen minutes later the horns were cooing in the fields, and on the back veranda Hendrickje, hearing Ziddy and Janny read, frowned and murmured: "I shouldn't have thought it was as late as that." She lowered the book and rose. "Now, don't run off, my boys. I'll be back in a moment. Read over the last paragraph to yourselves."

She went into the pantry and looked out into the compound. She saw David and called: "David! Is it half-past twelve already?"

"No. Only a quarter to."

"Then why are the horns blowing in the fields?"

He approached and told her: "We've decided to

call them in at once. There's serious trouble up-creek, Grandma. Fourie and Corbeau have been murdered. Horstenburg and Stevensburg are in a mess."

"Where did you hear such a tale?"

"Dak went off scouting."

"Where is Pedro?"

"Somewhere by the tanks. Do you want him?"

"No, no, my boy. I'll see him later. Let me go back to those two rascals. David!"

"Yes, Grandma?"

"How is your courage?"

"Excellent, Grandma." He struck his chest, grinning. "The old blood."

Later, when the slaves were gathered in the compound, their black faces sullen and wondering, Pedro told them: "After eating, you will every one of you go to his quarters—and remain there. There will be no work this afternoon. I must see no one wandering about the compound or anywhere on this plantation beyond the logie yard. Is that clear?"

A low rumble of assent came from the crowd. There were no smiles.

Pedro stood, musket at the slope. With his free hand he toyed with his hide whip. Flicked it about in the air.

Behind him stood David and Laurens, both with muskets, too. Laurens had a pistol in a holster at his hip, and the handles of David's knives jutted up in a menacing fence around his waist.

At about two o'clock Pedro and David were patrolling the lateral track that led to the Creek when they heard a mumble of voices in the bush to their right, accompanied by the sound of horses' hoofs. Ahead, where the main track opened into the one they were on, a party came into view. Four slaves with pack mules and three white people on horseback. One seemed to be a woman.

"Pedro, it's Gert de Groot and his father and sister!"

They advanced to meet them. Gert, who had been

one of the carousers at the spree in celebration of the birth of Jacques' son, seemed on the point of fainting. His head was bandaged, and the bandage was soaked with blood. Blood had run down on to his tunic. On the horse with Gert's father sat Lucia. Her hair hung loosely about her neck and shoulders, and her lip was bleeding. She seemed to have only a blanket about her. Her legs hung bare and white, the white smeared near a knee with blood from a gash on her thigh. Her eyes looked distracted. She hung her head at the approach of Pedro and David.

The older man told Pedro: "We barely got away in time. They burnt our house." His voice was husky. "This is the end, van Groenwegel. This is the end of Berbice."

"Where is your wife, Mynheer?"

"They got her. She tried to escape by the front door, but they intercepted her in the portico and took her away."

Gert was telling David: "We couldn't do anything against them. I had to fight my way through the bush to get to Father. They went into Lucia's room and I heard her yelling for help. I simply had to hide behind the toolshed and wait. I couldn't go upstairs to help her. They were all over the house. Father had already gone, and they'd killed our carpenter and the overseer and about five of our loyal slaves."

"When did this happen?"

"About five this morning. They came from Magdalenenburg and Horstenburg. Cuffy is leading them. They slaughtered Fourie and Corbeau, I've heard. I tell you, we hadn't a chance, David. Not a chance. They took us by complete surprise. Hell! The damned monsters! When I think of what they did to Lucia! He began to sob. "I must pay them back for this, Dave. I know the fellows who went into Lucia's room. Atta was one. And Goussari."

"Atta, eh?"

Mynheer de Groot told Pedro: "I've heard they have veered off toward the Corentyne, but they'll soon move back this way. We're trying to get to Fort Nassau as quickly as we can. Aren't you getting out, too, van Groenwegel? Why are you still around here?"

"We're fighting it out. We never run Mynheer. Why not stay and join forces with us?"

"That would be madness. Do you know how many of them there are? They were only two or three hundred up to seven o'clock this morning, but they must number nearly a thousand by now. Every plantation they overrun they absorb a hundred or more into their ranks."

"All the same, we're staying, Mynheer. We're quite agreed on that."

Later that day Lumea said: "Let them go. They're a set of weaklivered cowards, these planters. Running. Running from a clump of black hogs! I'm not so sorry for Lucia." She laughed. "Atta and his boys must certainly have enjoyed themselves."

"You're a depraved bitch, Lumea," David growled.

"It may be your turn before long," Laurens said. "And they won't be soft, either. They don't love you, Lumea."

"They'll never get that opportunity. I'd shoot myself first. They'd have to do it on my dead body, by God! And mine wouldn't be the only dead body lying around before I went down, I swear!"

Laurens pawed the floor with his deformed foot. "That's the talk, Lumea! Fighting talk! Remember you're a van Groenwegel. The van Groenwegels never run. They fight to the death!"

"Spoken!" cried their grandmother dramatically from the stairway. "That's the spirit! That's the talk I like to hear!" She came down and approached them, Ziddy and Janny trailing after her. "Let the others run off to Fort Nassau, children. We won't beg them to stay and help us defend. We'll stand together alone."

Pedro laughed ironically. "It's looking that way every minute," he said. "The surgeon and the Chief Carpenter took their departure a few minutes ago."

"Dashan and van Goos have gone, have they?" Hendrickje sniffed. "Very well. We want no cowards in our midst, white or black." She looked around at them. "How are you feeling, my sons? Lumea?"

"Full of blood," said Pedro.

"The old blood!" David raised his arm.

"The old blood!" said Laurens.

"We'll have a drop on that!" Lumea mooted.

"A toast to Kaywana, by God!" barked Pedro.

"That's it," nodded Hendrickje. "A toast to Kaywana!"

"And old Willem!"

"Great-aunt Rosa!"

"The van Groenwegels never run!"

All that afternoon the three brothers patrolled the plantation, muskets at the ready. At home Lumea had armed herself, too. She went from window to window, staring across the fields in the distance toward the dark-green jungle that bordered the Creek.

Hendrickje, too, moved around, tense-faced, Ziddy and Janny following her everywhere and asking innumerable questions.

Dankje kept indoors to keep an eye on the household slaves.

The field slaves were in or around their logies. Memphis and Dak and Stragga watched them, listening, prying here, there; flicking their whips about with an air of authority.

Bakkara had gone off on horseback up-creek on a scouting expedition.

In the distance the wailing sough of voices had ceased. All was silence now. But, on the horizon, in the east and south, Lumea and Hendrickje saw ominous columns of black smoke. And very faintly now and then, on the breeze, would come the pop-pop-pop of musket fire.

The day was fine. Cloudless overhead. Only in the south and west could one or two thin strips of cirrus be observed. The heat, however, was not intense. February was always a cool month.

Later in the afternoon more planters came through with tales of violence. Mynheer van Rueff said: "They shot my little girl before my eyes. Just held her like that, the fiends, and riddled her with shots from a pistol. Wait till this rising is put down! I shall slaughter

five of the brutes in the worst way possible for every
hair on that poor little creature's head. I swear that.
It's a solemn oath!"

His wife had been captured. And his brother. He
and his son and two loyal slaves had escaped into the
bush. They had hidden until the horde had passed on,
then had wandered about until they regained the track.

When Pedro suggested that they should remain and
put up a fight in the house with them they shook their
heads.

"We couldn't do anything against that band of hoo-
ligans, van Groenwegel. It's utterly foolhardy to think
of remaining here. At any instant they'll be heading
this way. We are making for Fort Nassau. It's the only
haven we can seek at a time like this."

Lumea sniffed. "I don't think much of that as a
haven."

"If we all got together we could give them something to think about," Hendrickje told him, her tone
hard and contemptuous. "It's because you planters are
running away that these sons of swine can muster the
courage to carry on this insurrection. Don't you realize
that, Mynheer van Rueff? Why don't you stand up and
fight and show them you're a white man?"

Mynheer van Rueff sighed. "It's all well and good
to talk in that heroic vein, Mevrouw, but wait until
they reach here, then you'll see for yourself. They know
no mercy, those butchers! No mercy whatever!"

Laurens laughed harshly. "No fear! We're not asking for any. We might die, but we mean to go down
fighting, by God!"

Soon after came Monsieur Boissière and his two
girls and little boy. The boy was about eight and was
badly wounded in the foot. He seemed to have been
chopped across the instep. The two girls, one about
fourteen, one about sixteen, were in rags that hardly
covered their bruised bodies. The younger one had a
blood-soaked bandage wrapped around her head like a
low turban; when Lumea tried to take off the bandage
to attend to the wounds the girl demurred, moaning.
"My ears," she said. "Please don't."

"Is something the matter with your ears?"

The girl nodded, her eyes tightly shut.

Then Lumea realized what the trouble was. She edged away the bandage gently, and saw. The girl's ears had been cut off.

The other one was in a far worse plight. She was weak and could hardly lift her feet to walk. She had to be taken upstairs. She kept groaning, her arms hugged across her body as though trying to conceal her nakedness. Blood had soaked the few dirty rags that covered her hips. Then it came upon Lumea that the girl's arms were not hugged across her body because of modesty. On closer examination Lumea saw that her breasts had been sliced off. She died while her father and brother were downstairs eating.

Like the others before him, Monsieur Boissière went. He did not even wait to see his daughter buried. He had no sooner finished eating when he was up and calling to his eight faithful slaves to get ready to resume the journey to Fort Nassau. They had no horses; they were travelling on foot.

Laurens cursed, but his grandmother patted his arm and told him to control himself. She was calm— even self-satisfied and quietly elated. "Don't get heated, my dear Laurens," she smiled. "We have greater reason now to be proud of the stuff of which we're made. Didn't I always drum it into you, my children? It's blood that counts. Blood! We have different blood in us. Fire-blood! Fighter-blood! I can hear Grandfather Willem saying it. I can see him shaking his fist and strutting around. He is with us now. His shade is watching us— and he is proud! Proud of you, my children!" Her voice shook, and her eyes flashed with the old light. Her hands clenched and unclenched, and she walked up and down with a feverish air, tall, lean and vulturine, almost trembling in the obsession that gripped her.

Soon after the Boissières had departed Bakkara returned from his scouting expedition. He was suffering from superficial wounds in the arm and buttocks. He told them: "They nearly killed me, Massa. But I get away safe—and I know their plans. They coming this way soon as dark fall. All of them didn't go toward the

Corentyne. Only a hundred or so gone that way with Atta. They had a big quarrel. Atta quarrel with Cuffy and Akkara, but Cuffy and Akkara got more men with them. Atta wanted to get away with everybody and cross over to Suriname, but Cuffy and Akkara say no, they must conquer Berbice first. Cuffy say he is governor of Berbice, and he say he going to kill out all Christians and make Berbice black-man colony. They got plenty white people prisoners, Massa. They killing some and keeping some to bargain with."

"What time do you think they should get here?" David asked.

"Soon, Massa. Sundown time or little after. They moving fast coming. You going to stay and fight, Massa?"

"That goes without saying, Bakkara. Are you with us?"

"Wherever you there I there, Massa David."

VIII

The wailing could be heard again in the distance. A ghost-noise that grew louder as the sun sank in the west and the day faded. Soon they could hear it coming like a rhythmical chant out of the twilight that was settling over the fields and the mysterious jungle beyond the fields.

The barricades went up.

Hendrickje did not attempt to interfere, but she moved upstairs and downstairs, clasping her hands together, avidly interested in everything going on about her. That bird-like predatory glint was always in her gray-green eyes. Occasionally a senile purring of satisfaction would come from her.

At about a quarter to six Memphis came in with the report for which they had been waiting. He said: "Massa Pedro, nineteen of them I sure about—but the rest. . . ." He shook his head. "No, Massa, we can't trust the others in the house here with muskets. They might turn against us."

Pedro glanced at his grandmother who stood by

listening eagerly. "I think nineteen is a lot. What do you say, Grandma?"

Hendrickje nodded. "Yes, I hadn't expected so many," she said.

"And we've got the muskets to supply them with," said David. "We certainly aren't short of arms and ammunition."

"What about the tools from the Carpenter's shed?" Hendrickje asked. "Have you had them brought into the house, Memphis?"

"Yes, Missy. They in the kitchen and the pantry."

"And the food is all right," said David. "I saw after that myself a short while ago. Mabella and Yuani and Katrina will see after the cooking. I thought of Yemba, too, but she might be hysterical. Can't trust her."

"What of the other women and the children? Are there none we can trust in the house here? They would be useful as loaders."

"I might be able to get three or four, Missy. I hear plenty of them talking against us."

At about seven o'clock, when night had descended in black earnest, the rebels arrived. They came chanting through the gloom—over the fields; the coffee fields and the cane fields; the provision patches. Along the dams.

Pedro and David stood at a barricaded window upstairs and smoked and talked as they looked out into the dark.

Dankje called out from the other side of the room: "Massa Pedro, Demba and some of our men and women going along there now to join the bad men."

"Let them go, Dankje. One day they'll regret it, you may be sure."

David added: "One day they'll be sorry they took such a drastic step—every one of them out there."

Downstairs, Lumea and Laurens were trying to persuade their grandmother to go up to her room.

"You can't stay down here, Grandma," Lumea told her. "It will be dangerous. And you know that if you remain down here Ziddy and Janny will want to be with you."

Hendrickje tittered. "Very well, my children. I'll obey. I suppose I must resign myself to taking orders from you. Ziddy! Come here! Janny! Stop peering outside. There's not a single thing for you to see. Come!"

"Let one of the men upstairs put your armchair in the corridor," Laurens advised. "Don't stay in your room."

"Very well, Laurens. Very well. I may be ninety, but I still have my wits about me." She tittered again, and patted Ziddy's head. "This is '66 again, Ziddy. This is '66. You remember what happened in 1666?"

"That was when Grandfather Willem and the others stayed and fought Major Scott and the Caribs. They opened the door of the big barn and put the packing cases before it and fired upon the enemy."

"And they fired from the house, too," said Janny. "Grandfather Laurens and Grandmother Susannah. Grandfather Laurens smashed in the head of an Indian with the butt of his musket."

"That's it! Hee, hee! That's it!"

Downstairs, Lumea snapped out orders like the men. She was in charge of the party of men in the pantry and kitchen. She wore overalls like a field slave.

Bakkara came in from the pantry and told Laurens and his sister: "They reach the water tanks, Massa. Missy Lumea, you better come now."

"Very well, Bakkara. I'm coming at once."

"Upstairs, Pedro was saying: "They're having a conference with the deserters by the logies, it would appear."

David grunted in agreement, and knocked out his pipe against the leg of a barricading table.

Outside, the noise of voices ringed the house. Figures could be made out dimly under the trees and near the logies and the water tanks.

David glanced around at the lighted candles on the floor and said doubtfully: "Do you think it wise to have light in the house?"

Pedro nodded. "It's necessary. We don't want any fumbling about in the dark—and we have to keep our eyes on these men Memphis brought in. We can't afford to take chances, David."

A voice outside hailed out to them. "Van Groen-wegels! We talking to you! Listen to what we have to say!"

Some of the noise died down.

"Hear us good what we have to say, van Groen-wegels! Your men here say you want to fight us! We not want to fight you! We got to go to Fort Nassau quick to take over Berbice! If you surrender we treat you good, but if you make us stop here to fight we going to kill you bad!"

Pedro chuckled. "Ignore them."

"The impertinent jackals."

"What you say, van Groenwegels? You agree to surrender?"

From downstairs they heard Laurens bawl: "Get to hell, you swine! You're talking to people now—not to cowards!"

An uproar of yells went up, but above the din the spokesman managed to make himself heard again. "Very well, van Groenwegels! Since you want to meet bad death we'll fight you and get you out of the house! This is Cuffy speaking. I is Governor of Berbice now. Hoogenheim not Governor no more!"

Pedro guffawed.

"Dave, get to your position on the other side and make preparations to welcome the Governor and his entourage."

David left the room. He was in charge of the men on the other side of the house—the southern bedrooms. He patted his grandmother as he passed her in the corridor. She was seated in her favorite armchair. Ziddy and Janny, squatting at her feet on the floor, each had a candle and kept trying to drop grease on each other's toes.

"The fun is about to begin, Grandma," David said. "Cuffy says he's Governor of Berbice. He shouted up and asked us to surrender like good boys. Laurens replied appropriately."

His grandmother tittered. "Have you sent off a messenger to the fort to condole with Hoogenheim?"

At that instant the muskets began to explode outside first on the northern side, then on the southern.

Ziddy and Janny sprang up with excited exclamations. David hurried off.

A volley banged out downstairs from the sitting room windows. Then Pedro's men opened fire upstairs. In the pantry Lumea gave the order to fire; Dak was with her. Above her, David opened fire, too, from the southern windows; Stragga was with David. Memphis and Bakkara were with Laurens in the dining room and sitting room.

The noise was tremendous, and the fumes of gunpowder drifted into the corridors. Hendrickje rose and began to pace the corridor, Ziddy and Janny marching after her, step for step, like torchbearers in a church procession, the candles flickering and dimming down as odd draughts caught the yellow flames.

In Lumea's room a stone crashed in and bumped and somersaulted along the floor. A shot made a chipping spatter in the rafters above David.

In the sitting room a stone smashed a hole through a picture. Another hit Laurens a glancing blow on the right side of his neck but did not draw blood. Laurens muttered obscenities and reached back for the musket Yuani had loaded for him. Memphis had managed to get as many as nine trustworthy women to help them load. Upstairs, Rassiki, Pedro's favorite mistress, was in attendance on her master. David's Mabella was with him. They had all been well coached in the business of loading.

In the pantry a ball had snicked Lumea's right shoulder, and long trickles of blood streaked the whole arm. But Lumea went on firing. Her hair had come loose and hung down her back. Hair like Hendrickje's in the old days. Long and brown.

A ball knocked over a candlestick in one of the northern rooms, and Pedro sprang away from the window to put it right and relight it. As he went back to his post he bawled: "Concentrate on the sapodilla trees! Don't fire blind! Aim wherever you see flashes!"

Outside, the night boomed and flashed—and yelled. The rebels did not lack muskets and ammunition. They were all around the house. Under the sapodilla trees, under the mango trees. Near the water tanks.

Near the toolshed. Near and inside the quarters of the slaves.

Pedro and David sweated; they had divested themselves of their upper garments. In the sitting room, however, Laurens was dressed as though for a ball—with cravat and shoes with silver buckles. Though he sweated like any of the others he refused to take off anything.

They were having it hottest at the back of the house. One of Lumea's slaves had been hit and was out of the fight; the ball had got him in the stomach, and he lay curled up in a corner of the kitchen, moaning.

Abruptly, from around the larger water tank, a thick clump of figures appeared and came toward the kitchen and pantry, defiant of the shots. Lumea saw one stumble and crumple up; she could see him writhing about dimly in the starlight. Two others staggered off. The rest came on.

Lumea put down her musket and snapped: "Dak! Rukky! Jakarri! Put down your guns! Get those hatchets and hammers and stand by at the windows! Strike them down as they try to climb in! Quick!"

The tools and implements from the Carpenter's shed lay stacked together in a corner. The men dashed for them. Lumea snatched up her musket again and told the women loaders to keep back from the windows. "Back! Back! Keep clear! Give the men room!"

Upstairs, David saw what was happening and called to his men to stop firing. He dashed in to Stragga. "Downstairs! They're trying to break into the pantry. Come on, men! Stragga, bring them down! Everybody! Get out of my way, Mabella, damn you!"

Hendrickje stopped in her pacing as David and his men hurried out of the rooms. "What's the matter, Dave?"

"They're trying to break in at the pantry!"

In the pantry, Dak said: "Missy Lumea, stand back and let me get into your place. Quick, Missy!"

Lumea obeyed at once, her loaded musket at the ready. Her eyes were defiant and fearless. Her lip was cut where her musket butt had accidentally collided with it.

At the windows the attackers were clambering in. Their breath could be heard panting fiercely amidst the confused thud and tumble of their struggling bodies. Rukky got the first one; his hammer came down with a crunch on the invader's head, and the man collapsed, his skull in a mess.

Jakarri was not so successful. He hit his adversary a glancing blow on the shoulder, the man recovered and dived at Jakarri. Lumea discharged her musket at him, but it was Jakarri who received the shot. Jakarri went down, wounded in the groin. At this moment David and his men arrived, David brought down a hammer with a cracking thud on the rebel's temple, and the man pitched sideways and collapsed on his face, his head making a puddle on the floor.

At the windows, hatchets and chisels and hammers did gruesome work. Attacker after attacker fell back into the yard with a split skull or a chopped neck. Groans and yells mingled with a coughing and spitting and the scrambling and tumbling of bodies.

More attackers came from around the water tanks and hurled themselves at the house. Lumea had thrown down her musket and snatched up a hatchet. She saved Dak from a stab in the throat when one of the rebels flung himself forward and sent Dak staggering back toward David who was hacking at another invader just entered. Lumea brought down her hatchet with such force that she severed the invader's head clean from his body. She gasped and recoiled in horror, and Dak went sprawling over the thumping, headless body, but recovered in time to rush to Rukky's assistance at a window. An invader had slipped in and slashed Rukky across the chest with a cutlass, ripping his overalls but merely bruising Rukky's chest. Before Dak could strike, Stragga had brought down the troublesome one with a single blow dealt with a heavy mallet.

The attack failed. The survivors ran off back toward the water tanks.

The pantry floor was slippery with thick smears and clots of blood.

Lumea rapped: "Your muskets again! Start loading and be ready!"

"Upstairs, my men!" David shouted. "Stragga, up with our men! Don't get in Missy Lumea's way!"

David's party went upstairs again. On his way across the dining room, however, David saw something. The rebels were staging a rush at the sitting room windows similar to the one at the back. David halted.

"Stragga! Come back down! Bring them down again!"

Hendrickje, who had come down the stairs in her eagerness to discover what had been happening in the pantry, called up: "Stragga! Come back down! Massa David is calling you and your men!"

Upstairs, Ziddy and Janny hung perilously over the banisters in an effort to see downstairs. Their great-grandmother had forbidden them to move even one step down the stairs.

Stragga and his men came clattering down again.

"What happen, Massa David?"

"Get hammers and hatchets from the pantry and fly into the sitting room. They're attacking Massa Laurens."

David hurried toward the sitting room. Paused just inside the doorway. Three of the rebels were in already. Bakkara and Memphis were each grappling with one, and the third was just recovering after his leap into the room. He was rising to rush at one of Laurens' men when David's hand went to his waist and came up. . . .

The invader crashed forward on his face, a knife in his left eye. The cutlass he had had in his hand made a clatter on the floor, and Bakkara stepped back on to the blade almost at the same instant as Laurens' pistol banged and Bakkara's adversary crumpled up.

Then Stragga and his men came in from the pantry, and Pedro and his squad could be heard thundering down the stairs.

David posted himself in a corner of the room.

Five or six of the rebels were in now. One of them was rushing at Stragga with a cutlass while Stragga was attacking another with a hammer. David's hand went down and came up. Stragga's attacker toppled over, coughing and spitting blood, a knife in his throat.

An invader managed to wrest a hatchet from one

of Laurens' men and was aiming a blow when a knife got him in the side of the neck.

David never even muttered an obscenity.

Pedro hacked right and left with a hatchet. He brought down three of the enemy within less than ten seconds. He sprang around and lashed out with a powerful intensity. He was like a tiger. Once, one of Cuffy's men who had just come in rushed at him with cutlass waving. Pedro charged to meet him, and with one sweeping blow sent the cutlass clattering out of the man's hand and severed the fellow's head all in the same movement. He did not pause to survey his fallen adversary but pivoted around in a sharp motion and sprang off to help Bakkara who was tackling two newcomers. Before he could get to them a knife whizzed past his head and sank into the neck of one of Bakkara's opponents. Pedro chopped the other one down before Bakkara could bring his own hatchet into play. Bakkara gasped: "Look behind you, Massa Pedro!" And Pedro turned in time to see the rebel leaping at him. He stepped aside, and his arm swept around and down. The man grunted and crashed in a heap, his face an unrecognizable mess.

In the pantry Lumea had difficulty restraining Dak. Dak said: "Let me go and help them in the sitting room, Missy," but Lumea snapped: "You remain where you are, Dak. Don't be a fool. If we leave here unprotected they'll make another rush and take us from the rear. Massa Pedro and the others can handle them, have no fear!"

At the foot of the stairway Hendrickje stood, a tense, erect figure, staring into the sitting room. Her eyes had a fixed, glassy intensity. At the balustrade above, Ziddy and Janny kept pleading to be allowed to come down, but Hendrickje ignored them. She might have been in a trance.

David was retrieving knives. He made dashes from corpse to corpse. Once, three bloody knives in hand, he saw two rebels converging on Laurens who was shouting to get his men into position at the windows. In perhaps one and the fraction of another second two knives whizzed across the spacious room, and both the black men staggered and dived head foremost for the floor, one of them with a saber dropping the weapon to tug at the knife protruding from the back of his neck. The other one made hiccuping sounds and lay still.

It was Laurens who saved the situation eventually. Laurens hobbled around with incredible activity. His cravat had been torn loose and dangled raggedly down his chest. Pistol in hand, he bawled and directed the men. While Pedro leapt about hacking in blind abandon and David played his deadly silent knife game, Laurens kept shouting: "Stand by the windows! Post yourselves at the windows! Strike them down as they enter!" It was this insistent command that prevented the battle from becoming hopelessly confused and out of hand, for the rebels kept swarming up on to the veranda and pushing past the door and window defenses.

Stragga and Dankje guarded the two door positions effectively; hardly a man got in but was hacked down with a single blow from Stragga's or Dankje's hatchet; Stragga sometimes dropped his hatchet and snatched up a hammer. But the windows had been left unprotected here and there, the defenders either having left their posts to tackle rebels who had managed to get in or having been forcibly thrown back by the attackers. Cuffy's men were at a great disadvantage in attempting to hoist themselves through the windows, and now that Laurens succeeded in getting a man to every window again the situation suddenly blackened for the rebels.

About eight of the invaders were in the room struggling with Pedro and his men when the windows became squares of death for newcomers. Every man who tried to hoist himself up and scramble through now crashed back with a split skull or a slashed neck. It was gruesome at the windows.

Once a stone caught one of the defenders on the chin and the man staggered back. Two rebels at once jostled to clamber over the sill into the room. One received a knife in his right eye, another collapsed backwards when Laurens fired point-blank into his face and called up another man to take the place of the stunned slave.

Meantime, the eight other rebels had been reduced to three. Pedro had got four of them, and had been about to chop down another when David flicked a knife that caught the man in the hollow part of his temple.

Pedro was bleeding in about five or six different places on his chest, face and arms from gashes and bruises received from cutlasses and hangers. David was untouched, though his hands were red and sticky with blood from retrieved knives. David's eyes were like shifty points of polished steel. They missed nothing. At one window two attackers tried to force past at the same time, one of them aiming a cutlass-stroke at the defending slave. David's hand flicked twice, and even before the defending slave could bring down his hammer both attackers had crumpled forward into the room spluttering, with blood gushing from their throats.

Within seconds there were no more live rebels in the room, and the doors and windows continued to be sites of cruel executions. The floor was piled with dead rebels, and blood made patchy whorls everywhere. More defenders now manned the window positions, and Cuffy must have realized that to continue hurling men blindly against the house would not prove profitable, for suddenly the attacks ceased, and the defending slaves became petrified figures with hammers or hatchets raised in readiness for intruders who never appeared.

Laurens shouted orders to get the barricades back into place, and Pedro, blowing hard, his eyes and hair wild and black, bawled to Dankje: "Clear these corpses out of the way! Heave them through the doors!"

David snapped: "Wait there! Get that knife first! Pull out the knives before you throw them outside!"

There were seventeen of Cuffy's men on the floor with smashed skulls or slit throats. Five others were headless. One of the heads had rolled, or been kicked, into the dining room, and a wall candle had guttered down grease upon the blank, gaping face.

Laurens had a gashed chin, and three of the defending slaves had been killed and two injured, one with a smashed knee, the other with a gash down his back and a lopped-off thumb. Dankje had an ugly wrist wound.

The corpses were hurled out of the doors across the veranda and down the stairs, for Laurens was so eager that the barricades should be put up into place again that he refused to let any corpse be shoved out of the window.

At the back of the house firing had broken out again, and David, having collected all his knives but one, shouted: "Upstairs again, men! All my men! Stragga! Upstairs to your positions!"

The firing from outside, however, was spasmodic, and when David and Stragga went upstairs and opened hostilities again with their muskets the rebels gave up their efforts. They could be heard yelling and talking confusedly by the water tanks and the logies.

Uncertain firing started up in front, but that, too, petered out. Laurens was still shouting to the men and the loaders to get into their places. The women loaders had retreated into the dining room when the attackers had broken into the sitting room.

Hendrickje had returned upstairs and was pacing the corridor again, chuckling to herself and muttering, an obsessed being. Ziddy and Janny did not march after her; they were still peering down the well of the staircase at the candle-lit scene. They had seen the severed head on which the candle grease had dripped. Ziddy was certain he could make out a lifeless hand on the floor near the biggest of the water jars.

"Father must have cut it off, I'm sure," said Ziddy.

"That's a pool of blood near that big toe. Look!" Janny pointed.

Their father and his men came hurrying up the stairs, bloody and blowing after their exertions. Hendrickje stopped and called: "Bravo, Pedro! Bravo!" and Pedro uttered a barking sound of acknowledgment before charging into the room where he had left his musket and Rassiki.

Rassiki was hiding under the bed, and crawled out when she heard the footsteps. "Massa Pedro, you safe? Oh, look at the blood on you!"

"Get up! Where is Banja?"

"She in the next room, Massa Pedro. I have the guns loaded for you here. Massa Pedro, you bleeding!"

Pedro and his men had hardly got into their places at the windows when out of the confusion of yells outside came a voice—the voice that had spoken before the battle.

"Van Groenwegels! Listen to me! This is Cuffy speaking!"

Pedro snapped at his men: "Quiet! Let's hear what he is saying!"

"Van Groenwegels! You listening to me?"

Pedro bellowed: "Speak, you raccoon! Say what you want to say!"

"Van Groenwegels! Listen good to what I say! I is Governor of Berbice! You understand that? My captain is Akkara. You fight good, van Groenwegels! You kill plenty of my men! We going to make you pay for this, Christians! You can't beat black man now, because we are the masters in Berbice now! If you want to surrender now we'll let you surrender and we'll give you a fair trial. We not got time to go on fighting because we got other places to go and attend to, and I have to reach Fort Nassau soon to take over the government. But I warn you, van Groenwegels! When I come back it going to be worse for you. We going to have more men with us then—over three thousand! And we going to kill you in the worse way you can think! So if you surrender now it will be better for you. What you say, van Groenwegels? You agree to surrender now?"

Pedro bellowed back in reply: "Go to hell, Cuffy! You blasted impertinent nigger! You may be Governor for the other white men who have fled, but not for us! Not for the van Groenwegels! You'll have to pull this house down beam by beam and board by board to get us out! Furthermore, here's a more tangible answer!" Pedro's musket roared.

After a cackling welter of voices had died down into silence, they heard Cuffy again. "Very well, van Groenwegels! Since you want to fight me then we going to fight! But not now! You can't get away from this colony, so I can wait until later to come back for you.

And don't blame us for what happen then! We going to cut you up piece by piece. We going to murder you in the worse way you never think about!"

"Fire on them," barked Pedro.

His men opened fire, but there was no return fire.

During the next hour or so they had to stand at the windows and watch their out buildings consumed by flames.

Hendrickje, like a trapped monster, moved upstairs and down. "Let them do their worst out there. Let them burn and pillage. It won't break our spirit." She stopped in the dining room and watched Lumea and Pedro attending to a wounded slave. "I haven't lived and struggled in vain," she murmured. "This day is a day that must be marked. The 21st of February 1763. Even 1666 cannot compare with this. Grandfather Willem should have been here to see this day. I have kept my word to him. I promised him that we should go down the decades with honor and glory. Here is our glory! By God! Here is our glory, I say!"

Laurens, hobbling past at that moment, paused and raised his arm, his teeth flashing in a grin. "The old blood, Grandma!"

"Yes, Laurens, the old blood. Tonight I can die in peace. We have touched the pinnacles tonight, my boy. The pinnacles!" She wagged her head and uttered a groaning, senile sound. She began to pace again, her eyes harrowed-looking with emotion. "The pinnacles," she kept muttering.

Laurens regarded her with indulgence, but under his indulgence could be detected the admiration and deep devotion.

Ziddy and Janny were asleep on the floor near the foot of the stairway.

"The pinnacles," muttered Hendrickje, moving past them and beginning to ascend the stairs.

X   The Soft Streak

I

THIS day, the 21st of February 1763, had been simply another day much like yesterday—at Fort Nassau. The business of government had gone on as usual. Two slave ships had arrived some days ago, the *Adriana Petronella,* under Captain Kock, and the *Standvastigheid,* under Captain Laurensen. In port, too, were the *Berbice Welfare* and another vessel. This, however, was nothing strange; ships were always coming and going. No one thought that the presence of four ships at Fort Nassau at this particular time would prove a circumstance of tremendous importance.

Life on the Berbice River went on as before. Governor Wolfert Simon van Hoogenheim and his officials dined at Fort Nassau, and now and then the conversation would touch on the Sickness and its ravages; now and then the Governor would make reference to the state of Secretary Harkenroth's books, ignoring the unwritten laws of table conviviality to chide the Secretary for his careless, slipshod methods. At times, in disgust, he would drop a remark or two concerning the drunkenness of Land-surveyor Hattinga and the debauchery of Orphan-master Wijs.

On the plantations, too, life went on as before. The managers rode round their cane fields, inspecting, and listening to the reports of their overseers and negro drivers, giving orders or reproving the overseers or drivers if there had been signs of negligence. At midday the overseer or the assistant manager blew the horn or clanged the bell to call the slaves in from the fields for meals. In the late afternoon the overseer and the manager decided what punishments were to be meted out —and saw them meted out.

When the Governor and his officials and the planters and their families went to bed on this night nobody had the slightest knowledge of what had happened on the Canje.

The Canje Postholder, like the planters and their families high up the Creek, had fled and was hiding in the bush—too terrified to make an attempt to get word through to Fort Nassau. And even those planters—like the Boissières and the de Groots—who had attempted to get to the fort never got there; they died of their wounds or from the hardships of the journey, or were overtaken, made prisoner, tortured and hacked to death. One or two were kept as hostages.

So Fort Nassau passed the nights of the twenty-first and the twenty-second and the twenty-third hearing only the buzz and churr of insects and the bubbling of fallen palm berries in the black river—the sucking sound of the water on the banks. Those who happened to be awake heard these sounds—like the sentries who kept reluctant guard: the sentries who were weak and debilitated from recent bouts of the Sickness. The others, like Governor van Hoogenheim and Secretary Harkenroth and Land-surveyor Hattinga and the Colonel and Captain and two lieutenants and the Surgeon-Major, probably heard nothing at all, for these slept soundly—with a soundness none of them deserved, save Hoogenheim—the one man among them who must have done a thoroughly honest day's work.

The planters, too, slept soundly. The Teuffers. The van Groenwegels. The Charbons at Plantation Oosterbeck. The Schrienders at Hollandia. Mynheer Abbensetts at Solitude. Herr Mittelholzer at de Vreede. And the Georges and the Zublis and the widow Johansen. At the church-house at Peereboom, Predicant Ramring and his family.

All slept peacefully. Only one leisurely parrot snake, twining its way amid the fronds of a tall *paraipee* palm which had pushed its plume above the other jungle trees, watched the reddish glow in the distance over the jungle—far in the east and in the south where houses and sheds, sugar mills and storehouses were on fire. But that was a long way off, and the parrot snake was too indifferent over the fate of men to sound an alarm.

II

On the twenty-fourth, on the twenty-fifth, on the twenty-sixth, life went on as before at Fort Nassau and on the Berbice plantations.

Late on the night of the twenty-seventh, however, the Charbons of Oosterbeck heard a hammering on their kitchen door.[1]

Jan, a light sleeper, awoke and went to a window that looked down upon the kitchen stairs. "Who is that? What's wrong?" he shouted. His father woke and joined him at the window.

"Massa Charbon! Massa Mittelholzer send me to you! He say dress quick and come over to his house! He say plenty trouble down-river! Slaves murdered Christians and burning the houses!"

"What!"

"Yes, Massa! He say hurry come over with your family and bring your guns and shot. He say no time for lost! You must hurry!"

"Good heavens! What could have happened to these niggers all of a sudden! Very well, my man! Go back and tell Massa Mittelholzer we'll be over in a short while!"

In a moment all was bustle in the Charbon household. Within an hour they were at Herr Mittelholzer's house at de Vreede.

From down-river came a wailing of shouts and confused noises, and over the jungle and the cultivated fields they could make out a glow where houses were on fire.

"Mittelholzer! What's happened? What's got into the heads of these black fools!" Mynheer Charbon was excited and pale. "Have you heard the rights of the affair? Where did the trouble start?"

"We'll discuss that later, Charbon. Let's get the doors barricaded first," said Mittelholzer. "Things are looking serious tonight. This is no chance uprising. It's been planned."

[1]This incident is based on a story related by Jan Charbon and quoted in Rodway's *History of British Guiana*, Vol. I, pp. 193-4.

While Charbon and some slaves assisted him to barricade the doors Mittelholzer said: "It seems to have started on the Canje. A whole horde of them broke through the bush and came out at Huis Dageraat in New Amsterdam.[1] They haven't attacked the fort, but they're plundering everything they come upon. They're murdering right and left."

"But how so suddenly! I could have fainted when your slave brought the message. We never had the slightest hint that the negroes on the Canje had run amok. Where was the Canje Postholder? Why didn't he send word through and warn the Governor so that the proper measures could be taken?"

"You ask why! Have you heard of a colony more slackly run that this! I knew it would happen some day. Look at the condition of the fort. It's no fort at all. The men are all sick. Of the twenty there I hear eight are down in bed and the others feeble and hardly recovered from the last bout of the Sickness. Captain Lentzeng is a coward and drunkard—like Hattinga and Harkenroth and the rest of them—so what do you expect?"

There was a shout from outside the house. Mittelholzer rushed to a window. "What's happened out there? Who is that?"

It was a slave. He said he was from the Georges' plantation. He told them: "Massa George send to say trouble down-river. He say you must come and bring your gun, Massa. He say you must go to Predicant Ramring's house at Peereboom. All other Christians gathering there."

"Very well. Tell Massa George thanks. Tell him Massa Charbon and his family and myself will be there first thing in the morning, but we're holding out here for the night." He clapped suddenly to attract the man's attention; he was moving off. "What's the news? Have you heard what plantations have been overrun?"

"Yes, Massa. Plantation Hollandia and Lilienburg

[1]Township about a mile from Fort Nassau, down-river. Not to be confused with present-day town.

in riot. The slaves there gone bad and burning the houses and killing the massas."

"Great heavens!"

"I hear Massa Abbensetts at Solitude send message to the Governor for help to hold out at Solitude, Massa!"

At about this same time Jacques, a little way downriver, heard a drumming sound in his sleep. He was alone in the house, for Faustina was spending a week at the Teuffers. Juliana's baby was suffering from diarrhea and Juliana needed Faustina's assistance in nursing the infant back to health.

Jacques awoke to realize that the drumming sound was not a dream figment; someone was knocking at the front door.

He sprang up and hauled on his trousers and coat and made his way downstairs. He had no doubt about the caller; it was Graat the overseer. Yesterday Graat had told him he would drop in tonight for the bottle of kill-devil rum Jacques had promised him. It was always good policy to humor an overseer like Graat, Jacques felt, especially as he was new to the plantation. Graat had come to work with Jacques only a fortnight ago. He was a down-and-out whom Jacques had met at Fort Nassau and taken pity on.

When he was at the sideboard Jacques heard the knocking again—very loud and insistent. He called out: "Very well, Graat! I'm awake! Don't be impatient. I'm coming!"

"Jacques! It's I! Hurry, please!"

Jacques straightened up, his hand arrested on the door of the sideboard. "I must be dreaming, surely," he muttered. He rose and hurried to the door. "Amelia! Good God! At this time of the night!"

"I had to come, Jacques. I had to come."

"What's the matter? Come in."

"Jacques, something terrible has happened. I'm almost afraid to tell you."

"I think I can guess. You're going to have a child by me, and your parents have put you out. You had a quarrel."

"Oh, they'd never do that. No, it isn't that, Jacques. It's the slaves. They've run amok. They're at Lilienburg and Hollandia, burning and looting. Father was sending a slave to tell you, but I dashed off before anyone could ask a question. You've got to leave here now, Jacques. Get your musket and some things ready and let's leave for Peereboom. We're going to Predicant Ramring's house."

"Come, come! What's this, Amelia? Surely you don't expect me to accede to such a request without a good reason. Why should we run off to Peereboom because of a slight riot at Lilenburg and Hollandia!"

"It's not slight. It's serious. The slaves are in rebellion on other plantations. I hear they've come from the Canje and urged these here to join them. It's a big rising, Jacques. There are hundreds of them."

"But when did all this happen?"

"Only this evening. Look at the sky there. Don't you see the glow?"

"Phew! It never occurred to me to look at the sky."

"Come and let's go."

"How can I go with you? What of Faustina and our child! Don't you expect me to see after their safety first!"

She was silent an instant, then said: "That is what I've been dreading to have to tell you. You can't get to Faustina, Jacques."

"What do you mean?"

"Just that. I tell you, it isn't a local uprising. Dozens of plantations have been overrun. There's a rumor that the Lutheran Predicant didn't succeed in escaping. He barricaded his house and tried to make them see reason by talking to them from a window, but they wouldn't listen and set fire to the house, and when he was coming down the stairs they pounced on him and murdered[1] him."

[1]This rumour did circulate on the night of the 27th, but was later proved to be false. The Lutheran church and the Predicant's house, as it happened, were the only buildings not burnt in New Amsterdam.

Jacques had a hypnotized look. He muttered to himself.

She grasped his arm. "Don't stare like that and talk to yourself. Time is going. I ran a big risk in coming here to you. Some of the rebels may be about here already. We must go back quickly to our place. There's a boat waiting to take us to Peereboom, but I'm not waiting for that. The two of us can ride. The track is still open, I've heard. But if we delay it may be overrun. Get your musket and some things and let's go. Please."

"I'm not going with you. I must go to the Teuffers. By the way, how did you hear this? How do you know they have been overrun?"

"Slaves came and told us. All that way—from Lilienburg to the Teuffers—has been overrun. I hear the Schrienders have been captured. They were taken by surprise and didn't have a chance."

"Thanks for coming. Now go back, Amelia. Leave me and go back—quickly."

"What are you going to do? The rebels will be here at any moment."

"I don't care. I've got to go to the Teuffers. Good God! I must go and see what's happened to my wife and child. Faustina is pregnant. I can't run off with you to Peereboom and forget the rest of them."

"But there's nothing you can do. Nothing. Don't you understand?"

"There must be something I can do. I'm going to make an attempt to get to the Teuffers' place."

"You can't get there, Jacques. They'll take you prisoner and torture you to death. They're murdering every white person they can lay their hands on. It's foolish to talk of going to the Teuffers' place now. You can't help Faustina by doing that. It would be like purposely giving yourself up to the rebels."

Without a word he left her and went upstairs.

She waited, and when he returned he was carrying his musket and ammunition pouch.

"Jacques, I'm going with you wherever you go. Understand that."

"No heroics, Amelia. Get off. Back to your people. I'm going into danger. Let me go alone."

"You couldn't stop me if you tried. I'm coming."

He shrugged. "I don't think we have much time for debating. Come on, then."

They took the track that led toward the Teuffers' plantation. About them the fireflies flashed tranquilly among the low shrubs and ferns, and the air was wet but invigorating with the smell of leaves and wild flowers. A goatsucker cried "Hoo-yoo!" somewhere on their right amidst a clump of swizzlestick trees. It might have been any other peaceful night.

They had gone hardly a quarter of a mile along the track when dark figures appeared ahead, and they heard voices. It was a party of slaves.

Jacques drew rein, and Amelia followed suit.

The negroes came on, jabbering excitedly.

Jacques leveled his musket and called: "Stop there! One yard further and some of you will be on the way to hell!"

The party came to a stumbling halt. Frightened mumblings broke out, then a voice called: "Massa Jacques! Don't fire upon us. Me Rabby here. Nobody here make trouble, Massa. We walk peaceful, Massa Jacques."

"Rabby! What are you doing here?"

"I hear trouble up that way, Massa Jacques, so I go to hear, and I meet these others coming, so we all walk along."

"Who are the others? Where are they from?"

"Some from Lilienburg and Hollandia. Not everybody turn bad tonight, Massa. Some behave good."

"Is there anybody from the Teuffers' place?"

"Yes, Massa. One here from Massa Teuffer. Bad news for you, Massa Jacques. We just talking about it."

"What bad news? Have you heard what's happened to Missy?"

"Missy Faustina and the baby safe, Massa. They get away. But Missy Juliana get captured. I too sorry, Massa Jacques. Missy Juliana such a nice lady. She treat us good when we go there."

"How was she captured, Rabby? Are you sure of this?"

Another slave answered. "She was in the *corial* with some Indians—she and her baby, Massa," he said. He seemed to be the Teuffer slave, for he spoke as though divulging first-hand information. "They move off good from the bank, Massa, but the bad men begin to fire at them, and somehow one of the Indians get hit and the *corial* overturn and Missy Juliana not able to swim good. Instead of swimming out to the other boat with Missy Flora and Missy Faustina she swim back to the bank and the bad men pull her out the water. Her baby get drowned, Massa."

Jacques rubbed his cheek hard. "Where have the others gone? Missy Faustina and Missy Flora and the rest? Did you hear?"

"They safe, Massa. They gone down the river to the fort. Missy Juliana could have go with them, too, Massa, if she did swim out to them. They call out to her to swim and come, but she not able to swim good. She get frightened and confused and swim ashore."

"Don't venture that way, Massa," said Rabby. "Turn back. Bad trouble up that way. They firing upon everybody."

Jacques glanced at Amelia. "I'm afraid it will have to be Peereboom for us, after all." He told Rabby: "Rabby, tell the others to keep things going the best way they can for me. I know you won't let me down. I have to go to Peereboom."

"Yes, Massa Jacques. We keep things good for you. You always treat us good, Massa. We not turn against you. I going to try and get news from Fort Nassau about Missy Faustina and come and tell you. Stay good, Massa!"

III

When the Charbons and Mittelholzer arrived at the church house at Peereboom the following morning they found there a group of other people—nearly thirty whites. Jacques and Amelia were there—and Amelia's people. Also the Zublis. Everything was in a turmoil of preparation for the expected attack. Predicant Ramring told them: "The rebels have reached the neighboring plantation. You're not by any means too early."

"What is Hoogenheim doing?" asked Charbon excitedly. "Why doesn't he dispatch help for us? Are we going to be left here to defend this house by ourselves?"

The Predicant shrugged. "I'm afraid I can't supply the answer to that, Charbon. You know yourself what a mess this government is in. I tried to get a message through, but I don't know whether it was delivered. And the good God alone knows if the fort itself hasn't been captured by this time. We can only trust in Him above and defend ourselves with the arms at our disposal. That is all we can do, I fear."

"I understand Captain Lentzeng sent around a circular last night to a few of the Burgher Militia," Zubli said. "Those he could get in contact with, at any rate. He ordered them to gather at Mon Repos and Rozenburg, just next to Schriender's place at Hollandia."

"I heard that, too," Predicant Ramring said. "And they did turn out. But just as you could have expected, judging from what happened at Kunckler's place last July, they hadn't the courage to attack. I hear not one of them has lifted a finger to move against the rebels. They're still at Mon Repos whining like a pack of frightened puppies. Sometimes one is really ashamed of one's white blood."

An hour later, when a mulatto called Jan Broer arrived, they learnt more about the cowardice of the Burgher Militia. Jan Broer told them: "They gone from Mon Repos and Rozenburg, Massas. Captain Lentzeng and all of them. They run back when they see the bad men. They at Solitude now with Massa Abbensetts. Massa Abbensetts brave man, yes. The rebels afraid to attack him there. He shout and tell them he not moving from his house. He staying and fighting to the last. He send to the Governor for help early this morning, and the Governor order Captain Kock to take the slave ship, *Adriana Petronella,* and go up the river to help Massa Abbensetts."

"If Kock reinforces Abbensetts and his men they'll probably be able to come on here and relieve us," said the Predicant.

George uttered a grunt of doubt. "Personally, from what little I've seen of Kock during the past week, I haven't much faith in him."

"Well, gentlemen, we can only hope for the best and trust in the Lord," said the Predicant. "In the meantime we have two or three days' supply of food and water, and we shall hold out to the best of our ability, praying earnestly to Him above for succor."

Jacques, leaning casually against a table barricade at a window, gave Amelia a cynical glance. "Heard that? Pray earnestly to Him above."

She smiled. "You don't believe in God, I've heard."

"I don't."

"You look very grim and quiet, Jacques. Are you afraid?"

"My spirit isn't here," he murmured, staring out at the river. The house stood about fifty yards from the water's edge.

"I wish I didn't feel this way about you," she said. "It's humiliating."

He smiled and patted her arm. "No strong feeling should ever be humiliating. Only a few people are capable of feeling strongly."

They heard musket fire down-river.

He muttered something about the Canje, but when she asked him what he had said he shook his head and moved off to go and speak to one of the other men.

A *corial* with two Indians hurried past on the river.

In the dining room somebody was saying that the best thing might be to go off into the bush and hide, that they could not hold out here against hundreds of negroes.

At about nine o'clock they saw two boatloads of rebels on the river. They were shouting and gesticulating, and for a moment it seemed they were about to go past, but suddenly the boats headed for the bank.

Within a few minutes the attack was on. The negroes fired from the boats. Some had approached at the back of the house and were firing, too.

The women shrieked and hid themselves under the tables in the dining room and sitting room and under the beds upstairs.

In the dining room a ball hit the chain from which the chandelier for three candles was suspended. Amelia left her corner near the sideboard and took the chandelier off its hook. She looked about irresolutely, then decided to take it into the pantry.

Jacques, who was firing at a pantry window, glanced round and smiled, winking. "Brought something for me?"

She put the chandelier in a corner and said: "Don't let them hit you. I'm praying for you."

"You do pray, do you! Well, I shouldn't be surprised. You're not a heathen like me."

"Don't say that, Jacques. You're not a heathen."

"The truth, my dear."

"Not at heart. I'm sure you're not."

His musket exploded. "By God! I got him, the stinking rascal!" He chortled. "The old blood, Amelia! The old blood!"

All that day, until seven in the evening, the battle went on.

"They're preparing for a long siege, by the look of things," Zubli remarked, and Jacques replied: "I like sieges—while the food and ammunition last."

The night was quiet. The women and children arranged themselves for sleep upstairs in the rooms and on improvised beds on the floor of the dining room. The men roughed it in the sitting room, taking turns to watch. One kept watch in the gallery, one at a sitting room window, one in the pantry.

Shortly before midnight, when Jacques was in the pantry doing a four-hour spell that would expire at one o'clock, a figure in white appeared silently out of the darkness.

He chuckled. "You? Even here and at this hour?"

She said that she was restless and could not sleep.

"In view of the situation, a plausible excuse."

"Don't mock me, Jacques."

"It's a compliment to you when I mock you. I only mock people whom I credit with a sense of humor."

"When is your watch up?"

"One o'clock—since you insist on my confirming it."

"I guessed it was one, but I wasn't sure."

"You lie delightfully, Amelia."

"Let me stay with you until one o'clock."

"As you wish."

"Jacques, I believe I'm really in love with you."

"Not merely in lust?"

"You needn't put it so brutally."

"Life is brutal. Grandma always harped that at us. She was right. She says life is a blind, brutal scheme, and to be a success you must face up to ugly as well as pleasant truths."

"Don't you believe in being humane?"

"Certainly. I'm always on the side of humaneness —but I'm also on the side of truth. And it's the truth that force gets things done. Weakness doesn't. Weakness ends in defeat and death."

"And so what do you conclude from that? That we should always be hurting each other?"

"No. I merely conclude that life is an insoluble problem and that as such we must be prepared to make the best of a bad business. Pity the weak, but don't respect them, don't coddle them. Be humane to the weak, but be ruthless when threatened by either weak or strong."

"But if the weak are weak, how can they threaten you?"

"There is no terror, Amelia, like the terror of the frustrated weak." He jerked his chin out at the night. "Why do you think they're murdering and looting without restraint? That's the way of the weak when they gain a sudden and temporary advantage over the strong."

She uttered an indulgent, affectionate sound.

After a silence he said: "I wonder how they fared up the Canje." He spoke into the night, as though addressing some spectral presence. "I would have given anything to have been with them. They must have fought like demons."

"Fought like demons! How could they have resisted a horde like this!"

He stiffened. "Because they're van Groenwegels."

"I've heard about your family traditions. You never run from an enemy, isn't that it?"

He grunted assent.

"I think you're the least clannish of them."

He made no comment.

"Your spirit seems far away, Jacques. I'm beginning to be lonely."

"My spirit is here. There are desperate niggers out there."

"I'm in my nightgown. You knew, didn't you?"

"Yes."

She waited, and after a moment he stretched out and touched her.

Upstairs, somebody had begun to snore spasmodically. Snorting and stopping. Fireflies flashed near the water tank and over the maize fields. A raucous laugh came ribboning through the dark. The insects churred tirelessly. They could smell the jungle and the river—a wet, vegetable scent, dank and heavy in the night air, but refreshing.

"You sense the wetness in the air?" he said. "I can smell wild flowers. I'm on the Canje, Amelia. The Siki Creek. We're hunting alligators, and it's getting on for seven o'clock, though there's moonlight and we can hear a goatsucker hoo-yoo-ing in the bamboo thicket. The *mucca-mucca* shrubs are watching us from the edge of the water like thin men nodding in the dark." He kissed her and began to fondle her.

A few minutes later she helped him to take off his boots, for his boots would have made a noise on the floor.

On the following night she came to him again, this time when he was on the one-to-five watch. She came on

Wednesday night, too. For the situation remained quiet. No attacks came, though the negroes had left a force to keep an eye on them and to make sure that they did not attempt to leave the house.

Water and food were getting low, and the women were losing spirit and weeping. The men cursed the government for not doing anything about relieving them.

On Wednesday night Jacques was on watch in the gallery when Amelia came. He said: "It will be risky out here."

"I don't think so," she whispered back. "Not if we go right up in the corner over there."

"You're overheated, Amelia."

"Don't say things like that, please!"

"What's it I told you my grandmother said?"

"Sometimes it isn't humane to speak the truth. She should have drilled that into you, too."

"It is better to seem inhumane than to live in a soap bubble."

"You appear to want to hurt me on purpose. Don't you like me even a little bit?"

"A foolish question. I should be very insensitive if I didn't like you more than a little bit." He smiled. "You have much in you that anyone can respect. Bigness. Even your family, smug and planter-complacent, haven't been able to smother your bigness of spirit."

"What makes you think I have bigness of spirit?"

"Your courage in being friendly with me. Your courage in taking risks. Your honesty in being yourself at all costs—in not being ashamed to show your feelings and revel in the delights of your senses."

When he was kissing her they heard a gasp and started apart.

In the starlight that flooded in at the window they recognized Jannetje Zubli. She exclaimed: "Oh!" and turned and hurried away.

Jacques laughed softly. "Your name will be afire tomorrow in the house. I'm sure she knew it was you."

"I know she does. She's been eyeing me oddly since yesterday."

In the morning, however, nobody had time to

think of scandals, for the rebels appeared in force and attacked. It was a fierce attack, and lasted until noon, then slackened. Water was almost gone. Food was severely rationed. The attack was renewed at about one o'clock and continued until well after six, when suddenly the firing ceased outside and they heard a voice hail out:

"Christians! You had enough now? When you think you're ready to surrender, tell us!"

Amelia's father replied: "But why must you people behave in such a shocking manner?"[1]

"Why? Because you Christians cruel! You flog and brand us and torture us! We don't want any more white people in this colony!"[2]

"We can be gentlemen ourselves!" another voice bawled. "All the plantations are ours now, and you have to be prepared to give them up!"[3]

"Oh, have we?" growled Charbon. "You devils! You'll see whether we have to be prepared to give them up!"

The Predicant called out: "My people, this is your old friend the Predicant speaking! You know I have always tried my utmost to be kind to you. Won't you listen to me and, for my sake, leave us in peace so that we may go to the fort?"

Jeering shouts went up, but the spokesman replied: "We know you're a good man, Predicant! You're a man of God. We'll talk to you. From now we call a truce until tomorrow morning. When tomorrow morning come we going to talk again and tell you what we decide!"

"Very well, my man! We shall abide by your suggestions. I'm sure when the morrow breaks we shall find a solution to our difficulties!"

That night there was little sleep. Most of them remained awake discussing the new development.

"I don't like the idea of palavering with these niggers," said Zubli. "They've forgotten themselves

[1], [2], [3]According to Predicant Ramring's account, these were the actual words used.

enough as it is. It's bad policy to let them feel we are prepared to talk to them on an equal basis."

The Predicant smiled shrewdly. "That's not the attitude to adopt at a time like this, Zubli. Remember our position. Water is practically gone, and we can't get more from the tanks. Food, too, is another problem. And we must consider our womenfolk and the children. No, I think we shall have to humble ourselves and talk peace with them. I have an idea they will let us go unmolested. They are not a bad lot at heart. It all depends upon how you handle them."

"Oh, you've always championed them," growled Charbon. "A pack of dirty monkeys, that's what they are! The plantations are theirs! The damned impudence!"

"It's galling," said George. "And I don't trust them one inch. They're a treacherous lot. It would be just like them to agree to our going down to the fort and then opening fire upon us."

"No, no!" frowned the Predicant. "They won't do that, I'm positive. Be charitable, George! Be charitable! I know these people. They may have black skins, but I can tell you, they have a sense of honor that is most remarkable. I'm sure they won't harm us if they agree to let us go."

"Anyway, they haven't agreed yet. Let's wait and hear what they'll have to say in the morning."

In the pantry Amelia said to Jacques. "Whatever happens, I want you to promise me never to feel guilty, Jacques. We couldn't help this happening. You mustn't let it trouble your conscience."

Jacques smiled in the dark. "Your conclusion," he said, "concerning my attitude to our relationship is entirely astray. My conscience is unaffected. But if you want to know the truth, Amelia, I'm rather disgusted with myself. I've always been aware of a certain weakness in my spiritual structure, and it is this that depresses me. At the moment my self-respect is not at a very high level."

After a silence she said. "It's going to be hellish for me when we get to Fort Nassau."

"Oh, you're taking it for granted we'll get there?"

"Well, isn't it likely? I don't suppose these niggers will molest us any more. They seem willing now to listen to reason."

He made no comment.

"Faustina is expecting a baby, isn't she?"

"Yes."

"Jacques, I feel I can kill for you. Do anything."

He nodded slightly.

In the candlelit sitting room and dining room the others kept murmuring on and pacing and glancing anxiously toward the river. The women whispered and wept, and occasionally the children were fretful.

The smell of gunpowder was everywhere. The woodwork was chipped and frayed from the musket balls. Pictures were smashed and torn. The floor was dusty and strewn with paper and bits of dried food, and there was all the time the smell of sweat and grime of human bodies.

"I'm even beginning to be jealous of Faustina. I know it's wrong and foolish of me, but I can't help it. It's so humiliating for me to be aware that it's she whom you care about, and in spite of this to know that I can't keep away from you."

When daylight broke the rebels resumed the talks. The spokesman, a tall fellow from Plantation Oosterlyk— Zubli said he was from there—called out: "Christians! We're all men together. You have guns and powder! But not as much as we got! We got fourteen barrels! And we sure you can't leave this plantation! So we going to talk peace as your parson ask!"[1]

"We respect your word, my man!" called the Predicant. "Speak on and we'll listen to your terms! We have nothing against you, remember! We don't like firing upon you, and we have children here—women and children. And they are hungry. I'm sure you won't like to see any harm come to them. No, my people, let

---

[1] Actual words, according to Rodway: "We are men, and have fourteen barrels of powder yet, and you shall not leave this estate."

us discuss this situation in a friendly spirit and come to a happy decision. As you say, we're all men together. Let us talk and show the rest of the colony that we here, at least, can be civilized!"

One of the rebels called: "You white people didn't show us no good feeling when we was slaves under you last week! You beat us. You brand us. You put us in the stocks. You shame us in every way. Black man got feelings same as white man, parson!"

"Yes, my man, you're quite right. I agree with you. I know you are human like any of us here, and I know you have feelings—and big hearts. Yes, big hearts! That is why I am appealing to you to be generous to us in our plight. Show us that you are big—even bigger than we have been toward you in the past. Show us that you can be even better Christians in your conduct than we have been. We are in your hands, and we know you will be kind and let us go in peace!"

"How white man come to speak so small now?"

"Since when you get so humble, parson!"

"You know you in trouble so you begging us!"

The tall fellow called for silence and began to confer with the others. After a while he shouted: "What you want us to let you do? Just go up to the fort?"

"Yes, that is all!" the Predicant called back. "Let us get into our boats and go to the fort! Nothing more we ask, my man!"

"And what we going to get in return for letting you go?"

The Predicant hesitated, then smiled and replied: "I'm afraid we have little that can be of use to you, my friends, but if you wish us to leave our arms and ammunition with you as a token of goodwill, then we will do so!"

After a murmured conference with his companions, the tall fellow from Oosterlyk called: "All right! We agree to let you go. We don't want no guns or powder from you. We got plenty. Take everything you got and go. But we want you to tell the Governor that the plantations belong to us and that we are our own masters from now!"

"Thank you, my man! We'll take your message. You're generous and we respect you for it. I knew that your hearts were big! You're Christians!"

"You didn't think so a few days ago. I don't mean you, Predicant. You always talk to us kind. But the others with you treat us like animals. We wasn't Christians to them!"

The Predicant thought it discreet not to reply to this.

"Get going!" the tall fellow bawled. "We promise not to trouble you. Get into the punt and these two boats on the right here!"

"Thank you, my man! We thank you deeply. I shall remember your face and shall do whatever I can for you if it is humanly possible. Thank you!"

The Predicant turned from the window with a sigh of relief and triumph. "See, my people! Nothing like soft, kind words! The Christian spirit. The Christian way of doing things. It must triumph in the long run!"

Jacques gave a sickly smile and winked at Amelia.

Zubli frowned and mumbled: "All well and good, but we aren't out of the house yet. Wait until we're at the fort before we crow."

"Personally, I don't trust them at all," Mittelholzer growled.

"Nor do I," said George. "Damned black brutes! Big hearts! What big hearts can they have! Wait until this rising is put down. See how we'll tar and feather their hides again!"

"George! George! That's unworthy of you. Remember you're a white man and a Christian. They are black, but they are human. It is up to you to prove your Christianity by being charitable and generous of heart."

"Pah! None of that soft talk impresses me! They're baboons! Human, indeed! Baboons! That's where they've sprung from!"

As they prepared to leave, Jacques squeezed Amelia's arm. "Afraid?"

"A little," she smiled. "And you?"

"More than a little. I don't trust niggers."

"Don't speak that way, Jacques. I think they've been good to let us go in this peaceful manner."

He shrugged.

"They're whispering about us—the women. Have you noticed?"

He nodded.

The Predicant told them before they left: "I'll meet you later at the fort. My wife and sister and I will come on today some time as it's necessary for us to see after the house and restore some order." He shook hands with them and smiled. "Good-bye, my friends. Good-bye! Trust in God always, my dear people. God is our only anchor in times such as these."

Jacques chuckled as they went down the stairs. "Trust in God. Trust in our wiles, he means. All that hocus-pocus. I can't tolerate hocus-pocus, Amelia. Our grandmother doesn't care two hoots about God—nor do I. Absurd delusion! Why do men have to delude themselves with such ideas!"

"You mustn't say that, Jacques. How can you call God a delusion!"

"Because I think. I think, Amelia. Another nasty habit I inherited from my grandmother, the old harridan!"

She laughed.

"That's what's hindering us, Amelia. Religion. God. Jesus Christ. All that empty, unrealistic nonsense! That's what's keeping back our civilization. That's why we can have insurrections like this. People are being kept too ignorant and superstitious—and the Church is responsible for more than half the ignorance and superstition."

"Jacques!"

"I mean it. It's the truth. I hate the Church! I hate religion! It maddens me to think that we can call ourselves intelligent creatures of the eighteenth century and still retain such piffling conceptions! We're not living in the Middle Ages. We're supposed to be advanced in thought."

They were about to get into the boat. "We're supposed to be progressing—not going back to the days of savages. Even here in this colony, remote as it is from the center of culture, we try to tell ourselves that we are moving with the times—and yet we can still talk of fictitious places like heaven and hell and believe in an old man up in the sky who watches us day and night and punishes us for our misdeeds. God! What is God? Up there is infinite space. Stardust! God! Look! Watch! See for yourself! Trust in God! Ha, ha! Trust in God, our only anchor in times such as these! Quick! Down! This is how the good God helps his Christian devotees, Amelia!"

He pulled her down with him into some low shrubs that grew near the water, the craft rocking perilously and sheering off. . . .

"Charbon! My God! Quick!" . . . "The beasts!" . . .

"Down! Down there!" . . . "Jump overboard!" . . . "Zubli!"

"The children, Hendrik!"

The air exploded. The air thundered. One boat overturned, and the women shrieked scrambling and tumbling about and grasping at the shrubs that grew on the bank.

Zubli fell forward against the side of the punt, his coat stained red. . . . "George! Help me here! Help me!" But George was among the others struggling in the water; he was a poor swimmer. The best swimmers seemed to be young Jan Charbon and Mittelholzer. Jan and Mittelholzer struck out strongly and in a moment had vanished around a clump of wild cacao trees.

"Can you swim?" Jacques asked Amelia.

"Very feebly," she said.

"Too bad."

"Go and leave me, Jacques. Go. Swim and save yourself. Quick!"

He laughed. "Don't trust me, Amelia. I'm a coward—but I'm not quite that rotten."

Shots whistled over their heads, clipping bits off the tops of the shrubs. A grasshopper alighted on Jacques' cheek. Darted off.

"White swine!"

"White bitches!"

"Make us suffer, remember! Take some back now!"

"Pepper them good!"

"Black man got feelings, too!"

"Kill them! Kill all of them!"

"They beat us! They brand us! They put our foot in boiling water!"

"Jacques! There's Jannetje Zubli!"

"I see her. I'm no hero, I tell you."

Jannetje was hauling one of the younger children toward the punt. Suddenly she screamed. Her brother fell away from her with a scraping thud; the back of his coat began to turn red. Jannetje left him and stumbled off toward the punt. She tripped up against a log and fell; she seemed to have hurt her ankle, for when she made an attempt to get up she groaned and collapsed again, clutching her foot.

The rebels were rushing up from the fields.

"Get them! Get them!"

"Don't let them get away! Hold all of them!"

The tall fellow from Oosterlyk bawled from the boat: "Keep the women! Don't kill the women. We want the women!"

"Keep some of the men prisoners, too. We can torture them like how they torture us. Brand them and put them in the stocks!"

Jacques and Amelia watched them coming. Jacques rose leisurely. He had lost his musket; it had fallen into the water over the side of the boat. He helped Amelia up, and called out: "Go on! Fire! Fire on us and get it over!"

"Who that?"

"That van Groenwegel!"

"Don't shoot him. He got to get torture. He can't get kill off easy. He got to burn in a slow fire."

They swarmed around.

"Remember your days on the Canje, van Groenwegel! Remember what your brothers do to black man! You got to get brand on the chest, too. Same as your brothers brand black man on the Canje."

"Look at his missy. She got good meat."

"Cuffy and Akkara will attend to her."

They seized Jannetje, and Jannetje shrieked and struggled, trying to beat them off with her fists. She looked frantically about and saw Jacques and called: "Mynheer van Groenwegel! Save me! Kill me! Don't let them touch me. Please! Please!"

Jacques gave a slight smile. He stood passive, like Amelia, while the rebels emptied his pockets. They were pawing Amelia's body all over and making lewd comments. She put up no resistance.

Some of the rebels were running up the stairs of the Predicant's house, but the tall fellow from Oosterlyk shouted: "No! No! Don't trouble the Predicant and his ladies! He's a man of God! He speak with God! Don't touch him!"[1]

Jacques felt a jab in the small of his back. A voice bawled in his ear: "Walk! Go on, van Groenwegel! Walk toward the fields!" As Jacques moved off a foot landed in the seat of his trousers.

They told Amelia to walk, too, and she, too, got a kick.

Behind them, the water was alive with cries and arms and legs threshing about and bodies writhing to resist capture, and black men yelling and excited and gloating.

They slapped Amelia's behind and tore down her bodice, and kept darting their hands at her bared bosom. Like Jacques, however, she took it without protest and walked on toward the fields.

IV

Jannetje Zubli sobbed all the way. She kept looking at Jacques and Amelia and imploring them to kill her. That was a mistake. Had she not sobbed and struggled they might not have stripped her naked as they had done. They might not have taken such wanton delight in clipping off clumps of her hair and scattering the locks into the bushes. Once they stuffed a few locks into

[1]Dalton, Vol. I, p. 198.

her mouth and she spluttered and coughed and shrieked.

There were others like her. A golden-haired girl of about eighteen and a woman of about thirty. They stripped them, too, because they sobbed and struggled and called their captors dirty, impertinent niggers. The woman of thirty even tried to threaten the rebels in a haughty voice, forgetting that they were masters now. They laughed and slapped her behind. The golden-haired girl had an ugly birthmark on the small of her back. The rebels held her by the ankles and made her walk a little distance on her hands, joking about the birthmark. They tickled her and prodded her.

One of the men prisoners, infuriated, hit out at her persecutors, and because of this they stripped him and cut off his private parts, hacked him to bits and pelted the bits into the bush. They daubed the faces of some of the other prisoners with his blood.

They daubed Jacques' face. And Amelia's. Amelia stopped and groaned and retched, and when she bent forward to retch they laughed and slapped her behind.

Jacques breathed deeply. His manner was one of pained aloofness.

Many of the men sobbed openly and without shame. Some got kicks—in the behind. Those who got them in front generally collapsed and doubled up, groaning. But they were soon yanked up violently. Once, one of them bled so badly that the rebels decided to call a halt. They castrated the injured man, flinging the parts cut off into the bush.

Plantation Hollandia was the rebel headquarters. When they arrived there, Jacques looked about the compound at the other white prisoners. He recognized Mevrouw Schriender. She was in the stocks, naked; her back was sore and wealed, her head bowed; she moaned softly, her hair in a tangled mass over her shoulders and arms. The widow Johansen was there, too; she, too, was in the stocks, but she seemed unconscious. Two other prisoners, men, were bound hand and foot and lay naked on broken bottles; they were twisted in unnatural postures, their white skins streaked with blood.

The Schrienders' house was Cuffy's headquarters, it appeared.

After much talking and shouting, Cuffy and Akkara came out to have a look at the new batch of prisoners. Jacques recognized them at once.

Cuffy was a medium-sized fellow, very tough-looking. He walked with a slight limp. When he smiled he showed perfect teeth.

Akkara was tall and burly, but his teeth were not so good, and when he talked into the faces of the prisoners his breath was unpleasant. He put his face up to Jacques' and said chucklingly: "So we got you, too, van Groenwegel! You remember the days on the Canje? Your brothers used to brand us bad, eh? Not you. You wasn't so bad. I always hear that you never treat your men so bad. But you still got to pay for what they do. Yes, van Groenwegel. You got to pay for what your brothers do. They fight us good up yonder. They hold out against us and kill plenty of our men. But we going to go back and drive them out as soon as we capture Fort Nassau." He laughed. "Cuffy! Cuffy, look who here with us!"

Cuffy strolled over. "Van Groenwegel, eh? So they catch you, too. I didn't expect to see you. Your brothers fight us up the Canje. They kill plenty of our men. They bar up the house and fire upon us and they refuse to surrender. You van Groenwegels is big fighter-people, eh? I always hear so. All right. But we going to go back and get them. Soon. Just wait till I capture Hoogenheim." He looked at Amelia. "So this is your wife?"

Jacques murmured a negative.

"That's his wife! He lying!" one of the other men called. "He was with her when we hold him in the water."

Cuffy grunted. "So you want to protect her by saying she not your wife, eh, van Groenwegel? She nice." He stretched out and pinched Amelia's cheek, and Amelia glanced quickly at Jacques, as though fearful lest he lost his temper and did something to endanger his life. But Jacques did not even blink. His face remained passive and abstracted. He was looking about him slowly, almost as though he might not have been in his right senses. Even when Cuffy fondled Amelia's breasts, Jacques seemed not to be aware of any slight done to her.

One of the men came up and said: "She not his wife, Governor. She Missy George. She belong to this part of the river."

Cuffy's eyes glittered. "Stop that! Stop that! No missy here! No missy and massa! We the massas now! Our own women is the missies! These white dogs is our slaves!" The tenseness abruptly left him. He turned to Amelia again, smiled and patted her cheek. "George, I like you. You is for me, Georgie. I got to treat you good. You got good meat." He turned and clapped his hands. "Hey over there! Rebby! Rebby! Come!"

Rebby, a short, thin fellow with a squint, came up at a run.

"Yes, Governor? You want something, Governor?"

"Rebby, take this girl upstairs and put her in my room. Give her water to wash her face—and get some clothes for her."

"Yes, Governor."

"And see and keep your hands off her."

Rebby grinned. "All right, Governor."

Cuffy slapped her behind and told her to go with Rebby, and again she gave Jacques a swift, anxious glance. But he made no move. As she walked off with Rebby toward the house the realization seemed to come upon her what was the matter with Jacques. He was afraid. Even the blood the rebels had daubed on his face could not hide his pallor. It was fear that kept him looking aloof and quiet.

Cuffy began to realize this, too. Cuffy said: "Why you looking so quiet, van Groenwegel? You proud? Or you frighten?" His mouth twisted in a sneer. "Yes, I believe you frighten of us. And you say you is a van Groenwegel? Big fighter-people!"

Akkara and two others came up with ropes. "We ready for him, Cuffy," Akkara said. But Cuffy put up his hand. "Wait a little, Akkara. He and me got to talk. He not so bad like his brothers. I always hear how he never used to treat the men so cruel."

"But he got to pay for what they do," said Akkara. "His brothers."

"Yes, he got to pay!" shouted one of the others. "He can't get off!"

Cuffy nodded. "He must pay. No fear, all of them got to pay. You see how he frighten where he stand now? He soft. Wait, Akkara. Don't trouble him yet. I got to test him out. I think I might be able to use him. Van Groenwegel, I want a secretary. I got to have letters write to send to Hoogenheim. How you say about turning my secretary?"

Jacques nodded.

Cuffy looked surprised. "You agree? You turn my secretary?"

Jacques nodded again.

Cuffy stared at him, then looked at Akkara and the others. "Yes, he frighten bad. You see? He frighten. Very well, van Groenwegel. Shake my hand, since you agree."

Jacques put out his hand and gripped Cuffy's. Cuffy held his hand tight and looked round. "Boys! Look! Van Groenwegel shaking my hand! He agree to turn my secretary! He so frighten he have to agree!"

Some of the prisoners stared.

The rebels began to crowd around.

Jacques bowed his head. A choked sound came from him.

Cuffy grinned and withdrew his hand. "Well, van Groenwegel, since you is my secretary I got to treat you good. Shake hands with Akkara. Akkara is my captain. When you speak to him you got to call him Captain Akkara. Remember that. And I is Governor. You got to call me Governor. Go on. Shake hands with Captain Akkara. The Captain waiting."

Jacques pressed his hands to his face.

Cuffy laughed. "You see that! He soft, boys! He not like those other brothers on the Canje. He coward. All right, don't trouble him, boys. Take him to the house and leave him alone. I want him to write letters for me to Hoogenheim. He got his uses, so we must treat him good."

"He got to pay, Cuffy!" Akkara insisted. "He got to pay!"

"We should brand him like how his brothers brand black man!"

"Put him on broken bottles!"

"Sssh! Sssh!" Cuffy raised his hand. "Don't worry. He going to pay. I got my own way to make him pay. He and that woman Rebby take upstairs been having times together. I can see from the way she look at him. I going to make him pay through her." He turned and gave instructions to one of the men, beckoning toward the house, and the man went off.

A few minutes later, after he had had a wash, Jacques found himself being led upstairs. "Where are you taking me to?" he asked the man, and the man replied: "Wait and you will see."

They went along the corridor, and Rebby, standing as though on guard outside the door of one of the bedrooms, squinted at them as they halted. "Where you taking him, Banwak?" Rebby wanted to know.

Banwak said: "He got to go in here with the woman. Governor say I must put him in with her until he come upstairs."

Rebby looked doubtful. "You sure Governor say so?"

"Yes. Governor say so."

After they had let him into the room Rebby pulled the door closed again and resumed his guard.

Jacques saw Amelia sitting by a window, pale but tearless. She had washed and put on a dress which seemed too big for her; it probably belonged to Mevrouw Schriender. A dark-blue silk dress.

She did not rise. She looked at him and smiled and said: "I hear you're the new secretary, Jacques."

Without meeting her gaze, he nodded.

"Why have they put you in here? Did they say?"

He shook his head and moved over to a window.

She rose and joined him and pressed herself against him. "You're afraid," she said.

He nodded.

"I don't blame you. Look what they've done to the others!"

He said nothing, staring outside.

"They're beasts. Beasts."

"Not more so," he said, "than the beasts we have been toward them."

"I know. We have been cruel to them. Jacques, what's going to happen to us eventually?"

"I refuse to think of the future, Amelia."

They stood in silence watching the rebels in the compound.

"I can't stand pain," said Jacques, after a long interval. "I'm a physical coward. It's no use my pretending to be what I'm not, Amelia." He clutched the windowsill fiercely. "It's the soft streak in me. Grandma always told us about the soft streak. They knew I was the one it had come out in. Hell! The old blood! The old blood! I feel desperate."

She touched his arm. "I understand how you feel."

He was about to say something, but the door opened and Cuffy came in.

"I know so. I know you and she was good friends, van Groenwegel. I could see from the way she look at you when you was outside. That's why I tell Banwak to put you in here with her."

Jacques and Amelia said nothing.

Cuffy put his hands into his pockets and stood with his feet apart, watching them. "So you is his woman, Georgie. You and he sleep with each other. I always hear he like his women."

Cuffy began to strut up and down. He had a slightly contemplative air. Suddenly he paused and said to them: "I is Governor now. What I say is law for we all."

He watched them, as though trying to discern what effect his words had had on them. Their faces remained impassive. He frowned, licked his lips in a baffled way and began to strut again.

After a moment he stopped and said: "He's my secretary now, Georgie. He frighten of me bad. He not like his brothers. He can't take pain. The big one Pedro fight like a wild animal. He kill plenty of my men. My men say they never see anybody fight like how his brother Pedro fight. But your man here soft. He going to write letters for me to Hoogenheim. I sending Mevrouw Schriender to Fort Nassau with a letter to the old Governor, and I want van Groenwegel to write it for me. You white filth never teach us black men to read and write, so I got to get you to write for me."

They stood by the window watching him. Jacques very pale. Amelia biting her lower lip.

Cuffy put his arms akimbo. His eyes had a self-satisfied glint. Yet there was a shyness about him, as though behind all his bravado he was still in awe of them. Still knew that they were his superiors. He said: "Van Groenwegel, you see me here? I'm a cruel man. I'm black. You white people say I'm not human like you. I'm just an animal who got to work for you like your horses and your mules and your oxen. You got your God in the sky. God not for me. So you say." He rubbed his cheek. He lowered his gaze. Took a limping pace or two about and halted again.

"I know I am dirt to you. You is white. I got black skin." He turned off and seemed to ponder something. He glanced at them suddenly and said: "I got to make you white people pay for what you do to us black men. I got to make you suffer same as you make us suffer. You see how I limp when I walk? A white man like you make that so. André Fourie do that to me. He make my foot lame." He seemed to be egging himself into a rage of bitterness. "That what you all do to me. You do it to plenty of us. But now we the massas, and you white people got to get back some of what you do to us. We not going to spare you—none of you. Black men got the plantations now. Black man is Governor." He struck his chest. "I is Governor of Berbice, you understand? Me Cuffy who used to work for you. Me Cuffy who you brand with hot iron." He ripped open his shirt. "Look! Look and see! See the marks! That's what you Christians do to me! You never think I got feelings like you. Well, now my turn come. Georgie, stand up where you is and take off your clothes. Go on!"

Amelia made no move to obey. Beside her,

Jacques turned slightly and began to stare out of the window.

"You know you have to do it, Georgie. Nobody not here to rescue you. Not even van Groenwegel here can't do nothing to help you. He too soft. He not got no guts. He can't dare hit me."

Amelia still made no move.

"I can take them off for you. And you going to get hurt, because I'm a cruel man. You white people make me cruel. You can't expect me to treat you soft. Go on, Georgie. I orders you to take off your clothes. I waiting for you to obey me."

Amelia took a few paces away from the window, turned her back and began to undress.

"Face me while you undress. Don't turn your back on me. I is the Governor of Berbice. You got to treat me with respect. Van Groenwegel! Look inside the room. Look at her and watch her undressing!"

Jacques turned at once.

"Don't look down on the floor. Look up at her. Look up! The Governor order you to do it!" His face twitched. "I going to shame you Christians! I going to make you see if you better than me because I black!"

When Amelia was naked, Cuffy grunted. He licked his lips, his gaze shifty. His head trembled. He paced about and then stopped and glared at Jacques. "Van Groenwegel, you see your woman! Look at her! She standing with all her clothes off! Naked! You see how she hanging her head. She shame. Yes, she shame!"

His breath came in a strangled manner. He thrust his hands into his pockets and withdrew them again; they were trembling. "Last week—before the twenty-first of this month—if I try to touch her skirt you white people give me twenty lashes and brand me on my chest. But now I is Governor! Your woman got to stand before me naked and do what I tell her to do. Georgie, get into bed! Go on! I orders you!"

Amelia stood where she was.

"Yes, that hard for you to do. You never think one day come when you got to lie in bed with black man, eh, Georgie? But that what you got to do now." He moved toward her and halted. "I got no mercy on

you. I is Governor now. Yes, me Cuffy standing here.
I is Governor, and you is my woman. You hear that,
van Groenwegel? From now she is my woman. And not
just for lust I want her. I want her so I can shame her
—and shame her! Every day I going to shame her like
now you white people shame our black women." He
put out his hand and fondled her breasts. His head
trembled. He gulped. "Yes, Georgie, I got to shame
you. I got to make you so shame you never want to
look black man in the face again and think yourself
better than him. Night and morning I going to shame
you. You going to turn sick with shame!" He slapped
her face. She was crying softly. "Just for shaming you
I going to shame you! Get into bed! Get in!" He spat in
her face. "Get in!"

She turned off and got into the big four-poster.
Sat awkwardly, her arms hugged loosely about her
knees.

"May I leave the room now if you don't mind?"
said Jacques. He was blinking rapidly, and little nerves
twitched in his cheeks and at the corners of his mouth.

Cuffy turned on him. "You staying in here! What
you think I had you put in here for, van Groenwegel?
It's for this! So you can stay and watch me and her in
bed. Sit down there! Sit down in that chair and watch
her and me what we going to do in bed now!"

Jacques made no move to obey.

"You hear me! Sit down—or I call in a man to
take you out and put you in the stocks so that they
can brand your back like how the others going to get
brand in a little while. You prefer that?"

Jacques still made no move.

"You prefer that? Talk up!"

Jacques said quietly: "I suppose there's no point
in appealing to your sense of decency?"

"Decency! *My* sense of decency!" Cuffy laughed.
He backed away a pace or two and looked at Jacques.
"You expect me to have decency! You look on me a
black man, van Groenwegel, and talk about decency!
Where I could get decency from?"

Jacques began to glance about the room in a distracted manner. He looked at the tester of the bed, at

the rafters, at the dressing table. He glanced out of the window. The leaves of the sandbox tree glittered in the bright sunshine, and he could hear the subdued swashing rustle of the vast billowing foliage. A child was crying near the logies—a very piteous sound; there might be hunger in it as well as pain.

"You make me laugh, van Groenwegel. I always think you was more sensible than to ask me a thing like that."

"Perhaps I should have known better," Jacques murmured.

"I know it going to be hard for you to watch me and her in bed. But I glad it going to hurt you. I want to hurt you, van Groenwegel. I been waiting years and years for this time when I can punish you Christians for the misery what you bring on us black men. I glad it going to give you pain. Sit down there in that chair and keep your eyes on the bed. Go on. Sit down—or else outside you go to the stocks!"

Jacques crossed over to a chair by the dressing table and sat down.

Cuffy grunted and glanced at Amelia. "Georgie! Look at him! Look at your man! You see how he frighten! You see how he coward! He can't take a branding, so he got to stay in the room here and watch you and me enjoy ourselves in bed. That the man they call van Groenwegel. Man who come from big fighter-family!"

Cuffy laughed and got into bed with her.

V

Three days later, when Jacques told her that her spirit was magnificent, she replied that it was only because of the thought of him that she could hold out. "But for you, I think I should have taken my life already," she said. "It's only the awareness of what has gone before between us that prevents my spirit from breaking. And I keep remembering the things you say your grandmother has told you—how life is brutal and about facing ugly truths. All those things keep running through my head when I'm undergoing the nightmare in the room up there. They help to steady me—and—and help me to drown some of the abhorrence."

It was on the morning of March the 7th when she told him this—every morning since her ordeal had begun she had been able to exchange a few words with him.

At night he slept on the dining room floor, and every morning at six it was his duty to sweep the dining room and pantry and kitchen. Amelia's duty, at the same hour, consisted in bringing down the slop pail and taking it out to the latrine. He always hung about in the dining room and waited for her to appear. She wore a smock—a soiled pink calico smock that once had clothed the body of a slave woman. It had one or two rents in front.

Jacques was in the garb of a field slave. Overalls.

"You don't look so bad in that smock, Amelia."

She touched his hair and uttered an affectionate sound. "It would be like you to say that. Ironical even in adversity."

"It's in times of adversity that irony is most necessary," he said. "That's something else you should remember."

She remembered it later that day when he was upstairs in Cuffy's room. Cuffy, hands in his pockets, strutted about the room dictating a letter. Jacques, sitting at the dressing table, cleared temporarily for secretarial work, turned once and smiled at her, his eyes saying: "Remember what I said this morning?" And she smiled back: "Yes, I can recognize the irony in this, no fear!" She squatted in a corner on the floor, for, in accordance with Cuffy's policy of shame, she was not allowed to sit in chairs.

Cuffy suddenly paused in his strutting, and said: "Scratch out what I just talk. Begin again. Start it off like this. Say: 'Cuffy, Governor of Berbice and his Captain, Akkara, send their greetings to your late Honorable.' " He strutted.

Jacques wrote.

"You got that down?"

"Every word of it."

"Write again. Say: 'The cause of this war is because our allowances have been stopped—especially by certain of our masters—Barkey, de Graaf, Isaac Hermans and Lentzeng.' Write that down."

Jacques wrote it down.

"Write again. Tell him: 'You must go away to Holland, Hoogenheim—at once. If you agree to do this and you fire four guns as a signal, the fort will remain good—we won't trouble it.' Put that down."

Jacques put it down.

"You got it down? Say again: 'But if you refuse to do this, then fire three guns as a signal that you don't agree to my orders, and I will come down with my men at once and fight it out with you.' "

When Jacques had finished writing this, Cuffy told him to read over what he had written, and when Jacques had complied Cuffy grunted and said: "Yes, that good. Tomorrow morning that got to be sent to Hoogenheim. I going to give it to Mevrouw Schriender to take to the fort. I sending her and her child back as messengers. All right, van Groenwegel, get up and go downstairs. Go and help in the kitchen."

That night it was not so difficult for Jacques to creep out into the darkness and whisper a messaeg into Mevrouw Schriender's ear. He told her: "Tell my wife for me that I'm safe and that she must not be worried. Tell her to take care of herself, and that my feelings toward her are the same as they have ever been. Tell her that nothing between us can ever change."

It was on Thursday morning, the tenth, that he told Amelia: "I hold you very high in my esteem, but what is between Faustina and me could never be wiped out. While it's possible I could find myself in love with you, the fact will always remain that Faustina has possession of my imagination. She is too strongly welded to the dreams in my past for me to forget her or put her aside. I could no more dismiss her from my life than I could dismiss from my memory the jamoon tree and the Siki Creek, the *mucca-muccas* and the goatsuckers in the moonlight. The roots of my intimacy with her go too far back in the past. Too many of my fancies and too many of hers are tangled among those letters of ours."

She nodded, staring before her in silence.

He touched her wrist. "Even as you are now, you have dignity." He wagged his head, contemplating the broom, tapping it against his ankle. "Dignity and guts. You have both."

"My love for you is so real that nothing can defeat me. The thought of you is my securest defense against the loathing that often threatens to overwhelm me."

"You're becoming lyrical."

She smiled and touched his unkempt hair, and it was during the silence that followed his remark that they heard the voice in the corridor, at the top of the stairs.

"So this is how the two lovebirds does their talking."

Cuffy came down. He did not hurry.

"I suspect that you was taking too long to carry out the slops in the morning, Georgie."

"I'm afraid it was my fault," Jacques murmured. "I stopped her to ask her something."

Cuffy walked up to him and slapped his face.

Amelia said in an unflustered voice: "You needn't make any excuse for me, Jacques." She looked at Cuffy. "Please understand that it is equally my fault."

"My fault what? What you supposed to address me as?"

"Governor. It's equally my fault, Governor."

Cuffy slapped her face. "I going to humble you, Georgie. You still too proud." He moistened his lips. A nerve under his right eye twitched, giving his face, for an instant, a grotesque look; it was as though the whole side of his face were about to shrivel up from sheer emotional tension. When he spoke again his voice was breathless and jerky. "You still speak to me cold. You still sneer at me. You still think I'm dirt."

He stopped and swallowed, his hands clenching spasmodically.

"Dirt, Georgie. You think me dirt. Because I black."

They could hear the breath wheezing in him. His eyes were half shut. He had the look as though he were about to pounce.

He mumbled something inaudible. Rage made it inaudible.

"I going to break you," he said, at length, and with what seemed an effort. "Break you, Georgie. Me Cuffy. Dis black man! You proud bitch!"

He spat on her. Spat in her face.

She stood erect, looking through him, the spittle running down her cheek.

"Put down that pail!"

She put down the pail and wiped her cheek with her arm.

"You got to get shame and shame and shame. I got to shame you till you respect me, till you know, till you feel inside you that I is your equal. Your better! Yes, your better!" There was saliva at the corners of his mouth. He kept looking at the floor in swift, agitated glances. His gaze jerked up suddenly. "Georgie, pull off your smock."

She made no move. She seemed about to break—about to turn off and sob.

Jacques uttered a growl. "You damned brute," he said. "You despicable, filthy black fiend."

Cuffy turned. He brought his hand up slowly and scratched his chin. He said in a mutter: "Very well, van Groenwegel. You curse me. You get courage sudden."

Jacques stood with trembling head, his hands clenched hard.

"She giving you courage." He turned again to Amelia. "Pull off your smock, Georgie. I gives you ten seconds to obey me."

She obeyed, and stood nude, waiting.

"Take up the pail."

She took it up.

"That's right. You is my slave. You is my woman. I is as good as you. No! I is better than you! You hear me? You understand? Better. Answer me! Say: 'Yes, Governor. I understands you.'"

"Yes, Governor. I understand you."

"You proud. But I Cuffy going to get you humble.

Walk toward the front door. Van Groenwegel, walk after her."

She walked, and Jacques moved after her.

When they were about to pass through the front door the guard grinned and stared.

Cuffy said: "Stop, Georgie."

They all came to a stop.

Cuffy looked at the guard. "Peddy, this is my woman. You see her here? This is my slave—my white slave. See her here naked? Look at her good. Look at her all over and shame her. Go on. Put your eyes on her. All over her! All over! She not your missy no more! Look at her and shame her till she can't shame!"

"Yes, Governor, I looking." Peddy grinned self-consciously.

"Slap her behind."

Peddy shuffled his feet about.

Cuffy scowled. "I gives you an order, Peddy. What you frighten of? She is my slave. You black but you as good as her. Do what I say!"

Peddy did it—halfheartedly, showing his teeth all the while.

Jacques kept a stolid face. Amelia winced, but nothing more.

"Peddy," said Cuffy, "you still a slave."

Peddy giggled.

"Yes, Peddy, you still feel she too good for you to touch because she white and you black." Cuffy blinked, breathing as though with labor. "Peddy, you taking orders from me. Me Cuffy. Finger up her belly. Stoop down and do it."

Peddy sniggered, hesitated, then obeyed. He rose in a hurry.

Cuffy ordered him to stoop down again. "Go on. Do as I say. Shame her. The proud bitch! Shame her, Peddy. Yes, do that again. And again."

Cuffy watched Amelia's face. Watched and waited.

"She won't break. Go on, Peddy. Don't stop. She feel that last one. Do more. Do more. Don't stop shaming her."

Peddy did more.

But Amelia did not break.

Cuffy looked from side to side in a spasm of frustration.

Peddy went on. His shyness was gone. He reveled in his task now.

Amelia, however, held out. She stood like a breathing statue.

The tension in Cuffy's manner suddenly went. "All right, Peddy. Stop. We got to try something else. This day I mean to break her. Georgie, walk. Walk outside. Take your pail to the cesspit. Walk after her, van Groenwegel. I want you to watch everything that going to happen."

They walked.

After she had emptied the contents of the pail into the cesspit, Cuffy said: "Put down the pail and go to the middle of the yard there. You, too, van Groenwegel."

From the other side of the house came the sound of voices, and a man appeared at the run and approached Cuffy and said: "Governor, guess who here! Atta and his men and some more white prisoners."

"Atta come back, eh? Why he didn't go over to Suriname as he say he was going? He see now he made a mistake?"

Atta and his men came crowding into the compound. Atta exclaimed: "What! Can't be true! Van Groenwegel! You here!"

"Yes, we catch him, Atta," said Cuffy. "And what about you? You catch the Governor of Suriname yet?"

Atta laughed. "I change me mind about going over there, Cuffy. I decide to come this way. They got strong forces in Suriname, so I say to myself I better go back and make friends again with Cuffy."

"All black man is my friend," said Cuffy carelessly. He tilted his head and regarded Atta. "But you got to understand, Atta, that I is Governor and my orders is got to be obeyed."

Atta laughed again. "We understand that, Governor Cuffy. Don't get frighten. Atta know who is Governor and who not." He turned again to Jacques. "Van Groenwegel, I surprised to see you here. How you manage to get captured? I always think your family never surrender."

Jacques retained a stolid face.

Atta grunted amiably. "I got your sister there with the prisoners. We pick her up with some others down the river. The boys say they have plenty good times with her last night. Look at her coming there now!" He beckoned and called: "Hey! Bring the van Groenwegel woman over here, Jappa! Mevrouw Teuffer! Bring her here!"

They brought her. She was in rags that hardly covered her white, bruised body. Her hair was in a straggly mass about her neck and shoulders. Her blue eyes gleamed with a weary but determined light.

Amelia muttered: "My God. My God." And Jacques uttered a quick, dry sound, his hands clenching.

Atta guffawed. "See her here, van Groenwegel! Early this morning she and me was in bed. I told your brothers up the Canje that one day I must get pay back for how they treat me. I glad you here. You and your sister going to suffer bad. Cuffy, you must leave these two to me. I going to take care of them."

Cuffy grunted. "Van Groenwegel is my secretary, but from this morning I having him put in the stocks. He curse me. I got to make him pay."

Atta looked Jacques over. He kicked him casually on the shin. "Yes, van Groenwegel, you and your sister got to get good torture. This is my day. Up yonder on the Canje your brothers still holding out in the house. They can fight good. I surround them for two days and nights, but they won't give in. They bar up the windows and doors and fire on my men. We rush the house, and they cut down plenty of my men at the windows. That Pedro one! He fight like a wild beast, but the day must come when he and me will meet. I going to get him. In the meantime, you and your sister got to pay for your brothers' sins. Don't hope for rescue. We is masters in Berbice now. Fort Nassau done with and over. On Tuesday Hoogenheim had the guns spiked, and he set the fort on fire, and he and all the refugees gone down the river in the ships what been in port. They gone to Plantation Dageraad. Hoogenheim's days is done, van Groenwegel. Black man master now." He slapped his thigh. "All you white people is our slaves." He stretched out and fondled Juliana's chin. "Tonight you and me again, Mevrouw. I must send and tell Pedro how you and me sleep together. When he and me meet we going got plenty little things to talk over."

Cuffy said: "I have a job to do now, Atta. This white bitch here is my woman. Her name is George. I call her Georgie. She too proud, and I got to tame her. Tell your boys to sit around and watch and see how I going to shame her. I determined to break her spirit this day."

Atta grunted approval. "Good. She is your woman, eh? Yes, she got a proud look. You must break her, Governor. Break them all."

The men were made to sit around the compound in a circle, and Cuffy gave muttered instructions to Rebby who went off to the house. Cuffy and Atta conferred, and Atta, too, sent a man to the house.

Presently, Rebby and Atta's man returned, each with a bowl of food. Rebby handed his bowl to Amelia, and Atta's man handed his to Juliana.

Cuffy ordered Amelia to eat, and Atta ordered Juliana.

The two women began to eat, using their fingers; no implements had been provided. Juliana ate hungrily.

Suddenly Cuffy and Atta acted. Cuffy snatched the bowl from Amelia and spat into it—a thick blob of spittle. Atta did the same with Juliana's bowl. The bowls were handed back, and the women were told to go on eating.

Shouts of approval went up round the compound.

"That's right, Governor! Shame her!"

"Make them eat black man's spit!"

"Force it down their throats!"

Neither Juliana nor Amelia would eat. Juliana glared at Atta and muttered: "You stinking cur!" Atta clouted her and snarled: "Eat! Eat, you white bitch!"

Cuffy did not clout. He kicked. "Eat! Eat!" The words left his mouth like shots.

For answer Amelia hurled the bowl from her. It smashed at Rebby's feet. Juliana, a second later, hurled her bowl straight at Atta's chest.

Cuffy snarled and kicked. And kicked.

Atta laughed and said: "Woman got spirit. I like your spirit, Mevrouw. Jappa, go and get her another bowl of food. She deserve it." Atta also added some muttered instructions, and when Jappa returned he brought not only another bowl of food for Juliana but also a bottle of rum. Juliana took the second bowl and ate hungrily.

Atta took a gulp of rum from the bottle and offered the bottle to Jappa who took a swig, too. Cuffy glared at them and shook a finger at Atta. "What I always tell you about that kill-devil, Atta! I not tell you that first morning on the Canje that we have to keep off rum until we conquer these white dogs? Suppose we get attacked one day and everybody drunk and can't fight! Send that bottle back to the house. At once!"

"Why I can't drink some kill-devil if I want to, Cuffy? I not man for myself?"

"You man for yourself, but I is Governor here, and what I say is law for everybody. I say to send that rum back to the house."

Atta looked dangerous for a moment. Then he shrugged and grinned. He glanced at Goussari and Accabre who squatted near by eating, and winked. "Goussari! Accabre! You hearing what Cuffy saying. He Governor. He ordering me what to do. Me Atta!"

Accabre gave a sly smile but said nothing. He was an *obeah* man.

Goussari waved casually and smiled: "Don't lose your temper, Atta."

Atta laughed. "You right, Goussari. All right, Governor Cuffy. Atta going to obey you. Balkana, take this kill-devil back to the house. Governor Cuffy say no rum drinking this morning. Atta got to obey."

After the rum had been taken back to the house Cuffy beckoned to a man, and when he came up told him: "Burra, you and Dakky and Mabbara go and bring the coal pots and the branding irons. And two hide whips."

Jacques struggled and howled when they stripped him. "Don't touch me! Don't touch me! I'll do anything you want! Don't brand me! I beseech you, Cuffy! I beseech you!"

"Georgie, you see how your man behaving! You see how soft he is! You not shame for him?"

Atta laughed: "Big fighter-family he come from. Van Groenwegel, you disgrace your family. When the other boys up the Canje hear how you behave they must feel shame."

Amelia and Juliana kept their faces averted. Juliana sat hugging her knees; she had finished eating. Amelia kept her legs close together, stretched out straight, her hands in her lap.

When the whip slashed down on his bare back, Jacques panted and gasped and blubbered and begged for mercy, and the rebels laughed and reminded him of the days on the Canje.

"Remember your brothers, van Groenwegel! Remember how they used to brand us and put us to lie on broken bottles!"

They branded him on his thigh and on his chest, and he fainted.

Atta said: "His sister must get some lashes now. I got a big debt to settle with these van Groenwegels."

Atta gave Juliana six lashes on her bare back. Juliana shut her eyes and bit her lip, but not a sound came from her. Atta nodded and said: "Cuffy, she can take it. The woman got more guts than her brother. Take her up into the house, Jappa."

Amelia behaved the same. She uttered not a sound. But Cuffy lacked Atta's sense of humor. He raved. He kicked her and snarled: "You won't scream, eh, Georgie? You won't scream. I don't know what more to do to break you. You got a hard spirit." He clouted her, stamped on her legs, slashed her again and again—across her back, across her breast. She shut her eyes and screwed up her face and panted, but not even a whimper passed her lips.

Cuffy, at length, threw down the whip in a rage of

frustration. He told Rebby to take her to the house, and strutted off, low gibbering sounds issuing from him. He paused and looked back at her, opened his mouth to say something. His head trembled, and he gulped. He turned again and moved on toward the house.

Late that night, when Jacques was dozing near the trunk of the sandbox tree, secure in the stocks, a voice whispered: "Massa Jacques!"

Jacques started into consciousness and saw someone crouching beside him in the dark; the starlight was not bright enough for him to make out who it was.

"Massa Jacques, it's Rabby, Massa."

"Rabby! My God! Have you come in with them, too?"

"Sssh! Not talk so loud. No, Massa, I not join in with them. I only fool them I join in so I can come and help you. I come this morning with Atta and his men. Four others come with me—Passy, Debarra, Cobby and Tengo. We all faithful, Massa, but we got to fool the others that we on their side because we want to help you and Missy Juliana."

"Thank you, Rabby, but please be careful. Did you go to the fort as you promised? Have you seen the Missy?"

"Yes, Massa. I go to the fort. I talk with the Missy. She and the baby safe. She get your message when Mevrouw Schriender come on Thursday with the letter for the Governor, and she say I must tell you she feel same way for you. Things too confused, Massa, or she would have write."

"Is it true that the fort has been abandoned?"

"Yes, Massa Jacques. Since Tuesday night. The Governor had all the guns spiked and the buildings burned down, and they all gone down the river to Plantation Dageraad. Massa, the people so coward! They not want to fight. The white men make noise and say they must go aboard the ships. They send in protest to the Governor and the Council and say they can't fight and that the Governor must let them go aboard the ships and move down the river. They all afraid to fight. Massa Abbensetts hold out at his house at Plantation

Solitude, but nobody would help him. The Governor
order Captain Kock to take his ship, the *Adriana Petronella,* up the river to help Massa Abbensetts and the
people at Peereboom, but Captain Kock himself coward
like the other white men, and he go up about a mile
and cast anchor opposite Plantation Fortuyn. He won't
go on no further. Massa Abbensetts had to come down
to the fort and give up his plantation, and now they all
gone down the river to Dageraad. The Governor and
Massa Abbensetts only brave men at the fort. They
wanted to stay, but the other white men say no, so they
had to burn the fort and leave."

"And Missy Faustina has gone with then?"

"Yes, Massa. She on the *Standvastigheid.* She
brave lady. She not cry and behave like the other ladies."

"She's a van Groenwegel, Rabby. The old blood.
It's only I who got the soft streak."

"Never mind, Massa. You treat us good. We going to help you. Soon as we get the chance we will try
to get you and Missy Juliana away."

"They'll kill you if they discover you're a traitor.
Tell the others to be careful. There's another lady I'd
like you to help if possible. Missy George. She's a good
friend, Rabby."

"Whoever you want us help we help, Massa."

"What about the other men on my place? What
has happened to them?"

"Some still there on the plantation, Massa. Some
gone in the bush hiding, and one or two gone down to
Fort St. Andries with the missy. All slaves not bad,
Massa. Plenty at Dageraad fighting on the Governor's
side—and even plenty here now with Cuffy only join
because Cuffy threaten to kill them if they not come in
with him."

"Very well, Rabby. I think I see a guard by the
stable. Hurry off before you're discovered."

"Stay good, Massa Jacques. We help you to escape
soon."

VI

Week after week went by, however, and Rabby and the four faithful others were unable to effect an escape. Jacques was taken out of the stocks and put into the Carpenter's shed with nine other prisoners, and the shed was kept under close guard day and night. Juliana and Amelia, as mistresses of Atta and Cuffy, respectively, never left the house except under escort.

On Friday the eighteenth Jan Charbon was brought to headquarters. After wandering about the bush for nearly fourteen days, he had been captured at Plantation Oosterlyk where the rebels had stripped him of all his clothes and threatened to give him two hundred lashes and cut off his head. He was put in the stocks, and Cuffy told him: "So we still catch you, after all, Charbon. I hear you and Mittelholzer get away from Peereboom. The two of you swim off and hide in the bush. Where Mittelholzer?"

"I don't know. I lost touch with him at Oosterlyk over a week ago. We were trying to get some food there and we were attacked. We had to run off and hide in the bush again. From then I became separated from him. We'd wandered round in the bush for nearly a week before that. We managed to get some food once from Doornboom."

"Very well. Tomorrow we going to deal with you, Charbon. You look hungry and thirsty. Recover first. Tomorrow we'll decide how many lashes you must get."

On the morning of the twenty-ninth a rumor came up the river that set the whole camp mumbling with alarm.

"Soldiers from Suriname arrived yesterday," Jacques heard one man saying. The man was talking to the guard outside the Carpenter's shed. "Hoogenheim and the Christians all went to Fort St. Andries, but I hear they coming back to Dageraad to make an attack on us from there."

"Cuffy say nothing like Hoogenheim can stop him."

"Let's see if Cuffy can keep his word."

Near the stable, Atta and his cronies, Accabre and Goussari, were discussing the situation and working *obeah*. Accabre smiled slyly and rolled palm seeds along the ground. A black candle was burning in the shade of a calabash with a vent at the top. Accabre muttered a few words in an African dialect, and sprinkled a little greenish powder from the bill of a toucan on each of the palm seeds.

"Watch how the powder settle," said Accabre, lifting the seeds with care. "I read plenty in this powder, Atta."

"What it say, Accabre?" asked Atta.

"It say a big man among us going to dead soon."

"A big man going to dead?"

Accabre nodded. "A big man. An important man. And the powder say that when this big man dead we all got to go to the Canje again, and Atta got to take lead of black men and conquer the Christians in Berbice."

Under the sandbox tree, Cuffy was talking to Jan Charbon. Jan had been taken out of the stocks a few days ago, and was allowed to sleep in the house and walk around the compound.[1] They had given him good clothes. Cuffy said to him: "Well, Charbon, you can't say we not treat you good these past few days. Now it got to be your turn to treat us good. I want a new secretary, Charbon. Van Groenwegel no use to me no more. He try to interfere with my woman, so he got to stay in prison and punish. What you say? You agree to write letters for me?"

Jan nodded. "Very well, I'll do it." He was physically exhausted and his spirit was broken.

"Good man. I got an urgent letter I want you to write. Hoogenheim and his men have returned to Dag-

---

[1] He received fifty lashes and was kept in the stocks six days where he witnessed horse-whippings and the murder of two prisoners as well as atrocities to women and children. (Rodway, Vol. I, pp. 193-4).

eraad. They left there and went to Fort St. Andries, but now they come back to Dageraad, so I got to send out to tell him what my terms is."

When they were in Cuffy's room a few minutes later, Cuffy rapped his chest and said: "I got to let Hoogenheim know who is the real Governor of Berbice. You yourself got to take this letter and deliver it to Hoogenheim, Charbon." He continued to rap his chest. "Hoogenheim got to know that black man on top now —and black man got to stay on top. Hoogenheim must turn humble. I going to shame him—like I shame her there." He jerked his thumb toward where Amelia squatted on the floor in her smock.

Cuffy moved over to her and put his foot in her lap.

She took no notice.

"I got to make Hoogenheim crawl and kiss my foot. Kiss my foot, Georgie."

Amelia ignored him.

He grunted, gave her a prod in the stomach with his toes and moved away. "You see how stubborn she is, Charbon! I can't tame her yet. The only way I get her to obey me is if I threaten to injure van Groenwegel. That the only way. She stubborn, Charbon. She stubborn. But I going to break down her pride. I must break her."

A few minutes later, when Jan was seated at the dressing table with quill and paper, Cuffy strutted about the room and said: "I want you to begin it this way: 'Cuffy, Governor of Berbice to Hoogenheim.'" He halted. "No, change that. We got to make it sound important." He was thoughtful a moment, then nodded. "Say: 'Cuffy, Governor of the negroes of Berbice and Captain Akkara sends their greetings to your late Honorable.' Yes, that's it. Put that down."

Jan put it down and waited.

Amelia began to smile. She could not restrain herself. She sniggered.

Cuffy stopped strutting and glared at her. "So you laugh at me, Georgie. Very good. Cuffy never forget an insult." He resumed his strutting. And his dictation.

It was nearly an hour before he was satisfied that he had done a good job. "Read over the whole thing now and let me hear how it go," he said.

Jan sighed wearily and complied.

" 'Cuffy, Governor of the negroes of Berbice and Captain Akkara send their greetings to your late Honorable. We don't want war; we see clearly that you do want war.

" 'Barkey and his servant, de Graaf, Schoock, Dell, van Lentzeng and Frederik Betgen, but more especially Mynheer Barkey and his servant, and de Graaf, are the principal originators of the riot which has occurred in Berbice. The Governor, Cuffy, was present when it commenced, and was very angry at it. The Governor of Berbice asks Your Honor that Your Honor will come and speak with him; don't be afraid! But if you won't come, we will fight as long as one Christian remains in Berbice. The Governor will give Your Honor half of Berbice, and all the negroes will go high up the river, but don't think they will remain slaves. Those negroes that Your Honor has on the ships, they can remain slaves. The Governor greets Your Honor.' "[1]

"Very good. That very good, Charbon. You shape it out nice for me. I going to send you with it to Dageraad in a few days' time. But perhaps I mightn't have to send you after all, so don't raise your hopes too high. Today is Tuesday. On Saturday coming, the second of April, we attacking Hoogenheim. We going to test him out to see how strong he is. I attacking him with seven hundred men, and we going to see how he stand up to me. If we don't capture him, then I'll send you with this letter to him."

He stopped at a window and looked down into the compound where Akkara was drilling the men. They were marching with muskets at the slope, in four lines.

Near the stable, Atta and Accabre and Goussari squatted, talking and working their *obeah*. Accabre seemed to be boiling something in a small pot suspended over the black candle in the calabash. Goussari

[1] Actual wording—as translated from the Dutch by Rodway.

glanced toward the house and said something confidentially to Atta. Then Accabre, too, bent his head in a conspiratorial manner and said something.

Cuffy turned off from the window with an ominous grunt.

VII

At nine o'clock on Friday night Cuffy came to his room and said to Amelia: "Georgie, I'm going into battle. At eleven o'clock we leaving for Dageraad. We attacking Hoogenheim at dawn. But you staying in this room, and you needn't try to escape. I'm leaving guards for the prisoners—and special guards for you and the other women in this house."

Amelia ignored him.

"Get up from there and come here to me."

She rose from the floor and came.

"Hold my face and kiss me."

She made no move to obey.

"That is always the hardest thing for you to bring yourself to do, but you got to do it. You got to kiss me good-bye in white-man fashion. You got to know I is Governor. Your boss. You is my woman. Hold my face and kiss me, Georgie. On my lips."

No response from Amelia.

"I waiting, Georgie. The Governor waiting."

She stared through him.

"You being disrespectful to the Governor, Georgie."

Outside, the voices of the men sounded in a confused, excited jabbering. Now and then Akkara could be heard bawling at them to get into line and be orderly. Once Atta's mocking laugh came clearly through the din.

"I going to count, Georgie. For every second you delay, ten lashes for van Groenwegel." He began to clap his hands and count.

She took a pace forward, shut her eyes, held his face, kissed his lips briefly, then turned off and began to return to her corner.

"Come back!"

She came back.

"Always got to threaten you with hurting van Groenwegel before you can obey me. I don't know what to do to break you, woman. I don't know what to do. Kiss me again. Do it!"

She did it again.

"Say: 'I love you, Governor.' "

She would not say it.

"Say it! Or lashes and hot iron for van Groenwegel!"

She said it—tonelessly, like a recitation.

"Say: 'I hope you come back safely, Governor.' "

"I hope you come back safely, Governor."

"Yes, you hard to break. But I must do it. I going to shame you and shame you till you fall down and cry at my feet and beg me to have mercy on you."

"That day will never, never come."

He stood and watched her, tremblingly incoherent. Then turned off and left the room.

At about ten o'clock the following morning, when complete silence enveloped the rebel camp, the crunch-crunch of the guard's footsteps outside the Carpenter's shed suddenly ceased. The ten prisoners in the shed thought nothing of this until the door opened and the guard called in a loud voice: "You ask for water, van Groenwegel! Here the water! Take it!"

Jacques gasped, but had the presence of mind not to express his amazement in words. The guard near the stable might have heard. He got up and went to the door and murmured: "Jankarra! When did you arrive?"

Jankarra, one of his field drivers, murmured back: "Only yesterday, Massa Jacques. Take the water quick —and a letter here from Missy."

"You know that Rabby and some others are here, too?"

"Yes, Massa, I talk with them yesterday."

When Jankarra had shut the door and secured it, Jacques went back into his nook near the workbench and read the letter.

The "Standvastigheid",
Fort St. Andries.
23rd March 1763.

My dearest,

I never dreamt that the day would come again when I would have to write a letter to you—and under conditions like these! But it's no use my trying to express what I feel at this moment, Jacques, I leave that to your imagination, and it is such a good imagination that I know it won't require any words from me on paper to help it to picture all the things that have been going on within me these past few troublous weeks.

I'm writing this in my bunk, and can you guess why? Jacques, *they* have arrived! How I wish I could see your dear, quaint face when you read this! Yes, Jacques—*they!* Two of them. I'm the mother of twins, and both boys. In the middle of this dreadful confusion and these horrible happenings, Jacques, twins! Can't you imagine how Grandma Hendrickje would have rejoiced if we could have got word to her! Poor dear, I wonder how they fared up yonder on the Creek. But that's a solemn note, and I feel so happy, Jacques, in spite of everything—just at this moment. Everyone is so kind to me; Aunt Flora and Mother Teuffer and Paula and Marcus and Vincent and the other people on board here. And that message you sent to me by Mevrouw Schriender when we were at Fort Nassau meant so much to me. I do wish I could say all I want to. I keep telling myself that everything will be well in the long run and that if it is the will of Destiny not all the most horrible rebels in the world could keep you from coming back safely to me. Yes, I am worried, Jacques, dear. I know it would be silly to try to pretend to you of all people that I am not. You are so quick to see through pretences. But then you know how brave I am; you know how well I can stand up to the rough knocks of life. That is what I am doing now. Standing up bravely to everything and willing myself not to let morbid thoughts take possession of me. You are doing the same, too, I am

confident. I can just see you twinkling impassively through all your tribulations and showing them
what stuff a van Groenwegel is made of. Jacques,
the cowardice at Fort Nassau was terrible, terrible! I feel ashamed of my complexion. To think
that white men could have been guilty of such
behavior! The men simply refused to fight. They
crowded aboard the ships with the women and
children, and the Governor had to order them
ashore again, but even when very reluctantly they
returned they still clamored to be allowed to go
back aboard. They sent in two petitions to the
Governor. And the captains of the vessels were
hardly any better. Captain Kock could easily
have relieved you people at Peereboom and
helped Mynheer Abbensetts at Plantation Solitude, but when the Governor ordered him to go
up-river he simply proceeded for about a mile and
cast anchor opposite Plantations Fortuyn and
Zublies Lust. Oh, it was terrible, Jacques. The
Governor and Mynheer Abbensetts were the only
men who showed any courage. But perhaps we
should not be surprised. Remember how the
Burgher Militia behaved in July last on Kunckler's plantations? You were there yourself, so you
know. One day, if even I don't ever see you
again, someone will come and tell me how brave
you were and how grandly you faced everything
like a true van Groenwegel. . . .

He read it over and over. At about four o'clock, when
the first shouts of the returning warriors began to filter
into the shed, he was still reading it.

A stout gentleman came across and touched him
on the shoulder. "Van Groenwegel, have you heard?
Cuffy was repulsed." His voice was excited. "Hoogenheim and the Government forces drove them off."

Jacques looked up. "Excellent. Very good news,"
he said, and bent his attention on the letter again.

Outside, the sound of voices grew louder and more
distinct.

"We lost the war. . . ."

"Hoogenheim strong at Dageraad. . . ."

"Plenty of our men get killed. . . ."

". . . I can just see you twinkling impassively through all your tribulations and showing them what stuff a van Groenwegel is made of. . . ."

"We never able to beat Hoogenheim. . . ."

"I always know Cuffy was leading us into trouble. . . ."

"How we can hope to beat Christians with all their guns and soldiermen! Cuffy foolish to start this rebellion. . . ."

". . . One day, if even I don't ever see you again, someone will come and tell me how brave you were and how grandly you faced everything like a true van Groenwegel. . . ."

Under the sandbox tree Atta said to Cuffy: "Governor, what happen you let Hoogenheim remain at Dageraad? We think you was going to capture him and bring him here this evening."

"You not fight with us? Why you jeering? Why you not capture him?"

Atta shrugged. "When I plan my battle, Cuffy, Hoogenheim or no white man can't stand up to me. But you is Governor. I only do what you say. I know before we leave here last night that Hoogenheim would beat us."

Cuffy rapped his chest. "You can mock me, Atta, but my day not done yet. Hoogenheim will hear from me again. This is only a test. Wait till I bring my full strength against him. This very month I going to attack him again."

Goussari sniggered, and Accabre smiled mysteriously and rattled the pebbles and palm seeds in his pocket.

Cuffy sniffed. "I not afraid of *obeah,* Atta. The men on my side. That what matter. *Obeah* can't trouble me." He moved away, then paused. "Tomorrow morning Charbon will take a letter I make him write to Hoogenheim. That will show Hoogenheim I'm not yet beat. That will make him see I still got plenty fight in me." He struck his chest. "Don't crow yet, Atta. I is still Governor of Berbice."

VIII

When the end of the month came, Cuffy's big offensive had not yet materialized, though Akkara drilled the men every day, and more and more men kept arriving. Huts and *benabs* had been erected, and some of the rebels slept in hammocks slung between the branches of trees.

Atta and Goussari and Accabre continued to jeer, but Cuffy ignored them and went ahead with his preparations.

Early in May news came from Dageraad. Hoogenheim had issued a list of premiums and rewards. For every rebel shot—twenty florins. For every rebel taken alive—fifty florins. For the capture of Akkara—four hundred florins. And for Cuffy—five hundred.

When Cuffy heard this he did not laugh. He said: "Let him try to capture me. Hoogenheim don't know that his day coming fast. Next week this same time Hoogenheim either dead or in the stocks under that tree."

"Somebody's day who I know well coming soon, too," Atta muttered. He and his cronies squatted near the stable. Accabre was burning chicken feathers over the flame of a black candle.

Cuffy overheard the remark. "You not talk wrong, Atta. I can see the day of reckoning between you and me. It not far off."

Atta ignored him. He glanced at Accabre. "What the feathers tell you, Accabre? Tell me the future."

Cuffy went upstairs to his room.

"Georgie, you hear the news? Hoogenheim think he can scare me. He offer reward for my capture. Five hundred florins. He don't know that in a few days I bringing my whole force against him. I have over fifteen hundred men who going to fight with me. On the thirteenth of this month of May I going to strike at Hoogenheim. The final blow. Come over here and sit in my lap, Georgie."

She came and sat in his lap. Her face was drawn and pale. She had aged during the past few weeks, but her eyes remained cold and defiant.

He explored her person casually—without passion. "Hoogenheim won't send no replies to my letters, Georgie, but I going to humble him—like I going to humble Atta out there. Let Atta and Accabre work *obeah* against me. On the thirteenth—four days from now—the big reckoning will come and I will be master of all Berbice colony. Say something, Georgie. Say something to me. Talk to me. I'm a human being like you!"

He might not have spoken, she did not turn her head even.

"Get off my lap!" He hurled her off.

She rose and returned to her corner.

"Come here to me! Come, you bitch! You proud bitch!"

She came.

"You determined I mustn't break you, eh?"

She stared through him.

He slapped her face.

Her eyes grew moist, but she still stared through him.

"I human like you, Georgie! I human! No matter my skin black. I can fight. I can fire musket. Just like your fellow Christian. Van Groenwegel no better than me. I can do everything he can do. I would have know how to read and write if I had been taught. You and he not better than me, Georgie. None of you is better than me." He looked about him feverishly. "I don't know what more to do to make you respect me. I don't know what more to do to shame you and make you know I is your equal. Your better! Yes, your better!" He gulped. "Kiss me! Hold my face and kiss me! Go on! Otherwise lashes for van Groenwegel!"

She held his face and kissed him.

"You see! You kiss me as if you is a stone rubbing a stone. I human, Georgie! I human like you! Don't treat me like this." There was a sob in his voice. He was trembling. He held his head between his hands and paced about distractedly. "If only I could get you to see I human. If only you can smile at me *once* as if you recognize me as a *man!*"

He came to a halt and regarded her. Like a baffled puppy. After a moment he groaned and rapped his chest once or twice, then turned slowly and left the room.

IX

The long rainy season was setting in. Heavy May showers sometimes turned the compound into a morass. But preparations for the attack continued. On Thursday, the twelfth, the whole rebel camp was transferred to Plantation Herstelling, the plantation adjoining Dageraad.

Jacques, with fourteen other white prisoners, was imprisoned in an old toolshed. The floor of the shed was damp, and among the spades and shovels stacked away in corners the lisp and crackle of insects could be heard. There were three women prisoners with them, and one of them moaned and shivered; she was going down with the Sickness. Within the past three weeks four prisoners had died of the Sickness.

The bustle and confusion of the first night gave Rabby his opportunity. The door was unlocked and Jacques heard an urgent hiss.

"Massa Jacques! Massa Jacques!"

Jacques was at the door in a second. "What's it, Rabby?"

"Tomorrow morning, Massa. Look out for me and Tengo and Cobby at five. Be sure you not asleep at five o'clock, Massa."

"What are you going to do? Attempt a getaway?"

Rabby did not reply. He shut the door and locked it. Jacques heard voices and footsteps approaching. "What you doing here, Rabby? You come to keep guard?" Jacques heard Rabby reply: "Yes, I keeping guard now. Akkara put me here. He say I must stay here till eight o'clock. Then I coming again at five in the morning."

"I want somebody for the other prisoners in the cottage over there. We have some prisoners we got to guard."

"Ask Jankarra," Rabby said. "He not doing nothing now, Peddy."

"No, it got to be a more reliable person. Cuffy's woman among these prisoners. We got to get a man I know personally. All right, don't worry. I will find somebody."

Peddy's footsteps receded.

One of the prisoners whispered: "Perhaps we can all get away if this fellow will help us."

Jacques mumbled: "Yes, of course," in an absent-minded voice.

Water dripped monotonously on the roof of the shed. The smell of humanity and damp boards filled the air.

"I believe there's going to be trouble among these fellows," one of the prisoners murmured. "Atta seems to be disagreeing with Cuffy, and he has quite a following of his own."

"Oh, they'll soon be smashed up. They'll never stand up to the Government forces."

"Tomorrow will be the deciding battle."

"I heard one of them saying that Hoogenheim has received fresh soldiers from St. Eustatius. Two ships arrived last week."

The ill woman moaned throughout the night.

For Jacques, the night was a fantasy of murmurings and fleeting nightmares, for he dozed in spite of his resolve to remain awake. He dreamt of fire and thunderstorms. Lightning flashed brassily, and rain came down in coarse drops. He saw Juliana stumbling through the bush in rags. She called his name, looking desperately about. Atta was after her, but Amelia was after Atta with a cutlass. There was spittle on her face, but her eyes were bright and defiant. . . . Cuffy appeared from behind a clump of shrubs and hurled a knife at her, but the knife fell to the ground and began to jump about like a living thing. It made a rattling sound like chains. Like chains being shaken. . . .

He awoke. It was the door. He stumbled up and moved across.

Rabby hissed: "Come, Massa Jacques!"

There was a stirring among the other prisoners.

"Can't we take some of these others with us, Rabby?"

"No, Massa. Only you can come. It not work good with more. They will catch us if more come. Quick! Come!" Rabby tugged at his arm with urgency, and Jacques slipped out into the dark. A voice in the shed murmured: "Who is that? That you, van Groenwegel? Have they come for us?"

Rabby shut the door quickly and secured it.

Jacques became aware of the presence of another man. "Is that Tengo there?" he hissed, and heard Tengo reply: "Sssh, Massa! Not talk!"

A hand grasped Jacques' arm and urged him forward. In the starlight he could barely make out Tengo and another man who, he decided, must be Cobby. They were dressed in dark clothes and seemed to be armed.

Suddenly leaves crackled under their feet, and Rabby hissed: "Go slow, Massa."

They went slowly. They were passing through tall shrubs. They could hear the murmur of voices far to their right.

After a moment they found themselves in a provision patch. Jacques could feel eddoe leaves brushing his bare knees. They emerged on to a track after a while. Jacques heard the sucking of water.

"Are we approaching the river, Rabby?"

"Yes, Massa. We got to hide by the bank. I got a spot where they can't find us. We got to wait there till the battle on, and then Passy and Debarra and Jankarra going to come with a boat. Plenty of the men going to desert later, Massa, when the fight on. I hear them saying so. They not want to fight. They know Hoogenheim going to beat them. He got new soldier-men from the West Indies. Cuffy can't beat him. And ships in the river with guns to bomb the bad men."

"What about Missy Juliana and Missy George?

Can't we do something about them, too? Where are they? I heard something about a cottage."

"We can't go that way, Massa. Strong guards round that cottage. That is the cottage where the Carpenter used to live. When the fight going on we can try and go that way."

"Sssh!" cautioned Tengo. "Some of them coming up the track."

They heard voices approaching.

Rabby urged Jacques into a clump of ferns and creepers, and the voices went past within a few feet of them.

When all had grown quiet again, Rabby led the way into a track that wound between swizzlestick trees. The ground became sandy and rose steeply. The darkness had lightened somewhat, and they could make out a dense canopy of vines and palm fronds above. Jacques nearly stumbled into the long, jutting thorns of a fallen palm trunk. The swizzlestick trees gave place to wild pines and wild cacao, with a clump of manicole palms here and there like slim black ghosts looming up before them.

"We safe now, Massa," said Rabby. "Nobody ever come this way. I spy out this part of the bush myself yesterday. This track is an old Indian track. Nobody ever use it."

"What time has the attack been planned for?" Jacques asked him.

"As soon as daylight break, I hear, Massa. The men already gone up to where they going to fight near Dageraad. Cuffy and Akkara and Atta, all of them gone already. We not got long to wait before the battle start."

They were descending now. Through the trees ahead they could see the sky. It was streaked with carmine and purple. Jacques listened to the soft, sensual sucking of water amid vegetation.

They came to a tiny clearing on the bank of the river, and Rabby said that this was their destination for the time being. Long ago this clearing must have been a regular landing place for *corials,* but the jungle now hung well out over the water, and ferns and dragon's blood fringed the bank. The ground was not so sandy here—it was a crumbly loam—and in the gray light of dawn they could see innumerable *aeta* palm seeds strewn about amid the short grass and low herbs and ferns. Frogs were fluting, and the nighttime churr of insects had not yet ceased. The dank, wet odor of the black water came up to their senses, and Jacques found himself smiling reminiscently.

Tengo had brought a sack with food—bread and dried meat and *sawari* nuts already rid of their hard shells—and Rabby suggested that they should eat something. "We might have to get on the move any time, Massa. Better to eat now."

When they were eating they heard musket fire downriver, but it was only spasmodic and soon faded off. It did not come again.

"I believe the Governor sending out scouts to see what Cuffy and his men doing. Yesterday Lieutenant Theilen and another officer-massa was out with some men in the bush looking around."

At six o'clock—by Rabby's reckoning—all was still quiet, and Jacques began to get restless. "What's keeping them back? Didn't you say they were going to open the attack at daybreak?"

"Yes, Massa, so I hear them talk."

From where they were they could look downriver and see the two vessels at anchor—the *Seven Provinces* and the *St. Eustatius*. Rabby told Jacques that these were the two ships which had brought the reinforcements from St. Eustatius in the West Indies. Jacques said: "If it hadn't been for the two missies we could have swum out to them, Rabby. They aren't more than a quarter of a mile off."

Rabby shook his head. "Bad men would see us and fire upon us from the bank, Massa. Too big risk."

The sun topped the ragged line of the jungle on the opposite bank, but still there were no signs of hostility downriver. At about eight o'clock—again by Rabby's reckoning—they heard more spasmodic musket fire, but, like earlier, that too died away.

Jacques sat in silence, listening to the sucking of the water. Suddenly he asked Rabby: "Where are we going to flee to when the others arrive with this boat?"

"We got to try to get the path that lead to the Canje, Massa. If we can get to that and reach the Canje, we can trust to luck to get a boat to take us to Fort St. Andries."

"Sounds a long chance to me." Jacques gave a start and said: "Why couldn't we take the regular trail for the upper Canje, Rabby? My people are still holding out up there."

"Massa, you not want to go to your wife at Fort St. Andries?"

Jacques looked troubled. He murmured: "That's so. But there are other considerations, Rabby. I have to think of Missy George and my sister—Missy Juliana. It doesn't seem right that I should take them on a wild adventure on a track we hardly know anything about —that is, of course, assuming that we succeed in effecting their escape this morning." He was silent again. Abruptly he looked at Rabby and said: "If you want to know the truth, Rabby, I'm itching to get back to the old house on the Canje. I want to be with my brothers and grandmother. I'd have given anything to have been there with them when they were attacked. I want to get to them, Rabby." He rose and clenched his hands. "Yes, that's my one aim now. To get into the old house and help them defend it if the necessity arises again."

"I hear they fight good, Massa. Massa Pedro especially. I hear he kill plenty of the bad men when they try to rush the house."

Jacques nodded, a pained, sensitive look on his face. "The old blood, Rabby. The old blood." He moved toward the water's edge.

The men gave him curious glances. He stood staring at fallen *mora* blossoms, a yellowish dust on the surface of the water. He had a vacant, haunted air.

"The strong and the weak," muttered Jacques.

The men said nothing. Only watching him.

After a long silence he turned and looked at them. "I've decided. It's the old house. We're going to take the regular trail and get to the upper Canje somehow. Somehow, Rabby, I must get back to my old home.

I'm a sentimentalist." He gave a brief, awkward laugh.

"Whatever you want to do, Massa, we will do," said Rabby.

"I've got to do something to redeem my cowardice," said Jacques. "I couldn't go through the rest of my life a guilty man."

The sun was high above the horizon.

"What would you say the time is now, Rabby?"

Rabby shaded his eyes, tilted his head and said: "Nearly half-past nine, Massa Jacques."

"Something seems to have gone wrong with the new Governor's plan of battle."

Not half an hour later, however, musket fire broke out again, and this time it had a concentrated note. They heard the wailing of voices, and Cobby said: "Massa Jacques, the fight start. Let me go up on the hill and watch so I can tell you how things going."

"Can you see what's happening from the top of the rise?"

"Yes, Massa—if I climb on a tree I can see."

"Better stay here, Cobby," said Rabby. "Any time the other men might come with the boat."

"By the way, where is this boat, Rabby?"

"Plenty boats by the landing place higher up, Massa."

The firing increased in volume. Suddenly they heard a boom out on the river. Jacques ran down to the water's edge and looked downriver. He saw a downy cloud of smoke. Almost at once another cloud appeared, and the air vibrated to the sound of another boom. On land they heard the crash of the exploding bomb.

"They're using mortars."

A flock of parrots passed low overhead, chattering animatedly.

"Cobby, let's go up and try to get a glimpse of the battle. Rabby, you remain here with Tengo in case the boat comes."

"Very good, Massa."

At the top of the rise Jacques and Cobby climbed into the branches of a *courida* tree. The musket firing had risen to a fierce pitch in the depression to the north and east where Plantation Dageraad lay. They could see the panorama of cane fields and provision patches stretching into the distance, and, about a mile away, the residence and outhouses on Dageraad.

"They have earthworks round the house," Cobby told Jacques. "I can make them out, Massa."

"So can I," nodded his master.

Black ants were giving Jacques trouble. He had to keep brushing at his legs. The ships in the river kept lobbing over bombs. Only the masts of the vessels were visible from their tree; the fringe of the jungle along the bank acted as a screen so that the river was out of their range of view. They could see the smoke rising above the jungle, however, and the boom-boom added an impressive note to the general din of wailing voices and musket fire. A haze of smoke swirled continuously over the pale-green canes, and now and then they would see the canes wave frantically as the concealed attackers rushed forward. The bombs from the ships seemed ineffectual; most of them landed in the jungle fringe or on the outskirts of the cane fields. They sent up jagged sprays of leaves and earth and white puffs of smoke.

The black ants kept crawling up Jacques' legs.

Suddenly they heard a soaring wail of shouts, and the musket fire began to fizzle out. Then it started up again. The cane fields hazed, and among the cassava stalks and eddoes of the provision patches a few black figures could be seen moving swiftly in the direction of Dageraad. The next instant, however, the figures were moving in the opposite direction. Jacques saw the glint of steel in the bright sunshine. The musket fire died down, rose again, died down. A bomb exploded on a patch of yam vines, and they heards yells and saw vegetation flying. The white smoke billowed up and spread out and made a thinning haze over the greens of the provision patches. Figures seemed to be moving in both directions now. The wailing of voices criss-crossed. Suddenly musket fire broke out in determined, angry bursts, and they saw the cane fields hazing again.

Something whined past Jacques' ear, and a crackling amid the branches of some swizzlestick trees sounded beneath them.

Jacques began to descend. "Come down, Cobby. We've seen enough. Let's get back to the others and see if the boat has arrived yet."

Some minutes later, when they rejoined Rabby and Tengo, they found that there still was no sign of the boat. Rabby said: "It must take them a little time to get away and run back, Massa. They got to do it quiet or else the other men will fire upon them. Cuffy say all deserters will be shot."

Jacques paced impatiently. "I can't stand delay and suspense."

Tengo said: "Massa Jacques, perhaps we can go back to Herstelling now and see if we can get the missies away. Most of the men must be fighting. Cobby and Rabby and I can knock the guards on the head and you can take the musket and smash down the door meanwhile."

Jacques looked at Rabby. "Rabby, what do you say to that?"

Rabby nodded. "It might work, Massa."

Cobby, too, thought it might work.

Jacques looked contemplative. "What of the boat, though? Suppose it comes while we're away."

The men were silent, shifting about their feet.

"No, we must wait here," ruled Jacques finally. "It would be pointless to rescue the missies only to come here and find that we had no means of conveying them across the river."

When the sun was overhead the noise of battle was still loud, and the boat had not yet arrived. Cobby wanted to go back to the top of the rise to watch the progress of the battle. Jacques said irritably: "What's the use, Cobby? What could you see from up there!" He rose abruptly and beckoned. "Very well, come on. Let's go. Better than remaining here to grow old watching our fingers and toes."

Rabby accompanied them, but there was nothing new to see. The battle seemed to have shifted more to the east—nearer the river. Bombs still exploded haphazard amid the provision patches and the fringes of the jungle.

Rabby said the time must be about half-past one. The sun beat down upon them fiercely.

They were on the point of descending from the tree when Rabby cried: "Massa, look! The ships firing different way now, you notice! The bombs going over that way near the middle cane fields."

Jacques nodded, shading his eyes. "You're right. They've discovered their error at last."

They heard a confused wailing. The musket fire began to die down. Cobby pointed. "Look, Massa! They running. The bombs too much for them in the fields!"

An intent expression settled on Jacques' face. "I believe this is the turning point. They're in retreat."

The bombs continued to raise white plumes of smoke amid the canes. The ships had got the right range in earnest now.

"Down we go," said Jacques. "We must get back to Tengo."

"Look, Massa! Look! Soldier men chasing them!"

"Hoogenheim has made a sortie. That's the end of Cuffy. Come, let's get back to the landing place."

The distant wail of voices grew in intensity. They could see the rebels in flight. The sun flashed on the steel of sabers and knives. The swish-swish of the violently agitated canes came clearly on the air.

Arrived back at the landing place, Rabby said: "Perhaps this is the best time to go and rescue the missies."

"We can't venture back in that direction now," said Jacques. "We've got to concentrate our energies on getting across to the other bank. Cuffy is sure to make for the Canje now. We can follow him and see what we can do about getting the missies safely out of his hands."

The shouting was getting nearer and more confused. Jacques kept gazing anxiously up and down the river, but there was no sign of any small craft like the one they were expecting.

Suddenly they heard a crashing, crackling sound

at the top of the rise. Rabby snatched up his musket and stood ready. Jacques armed himself with Tengo's hanger, his face white.

It turned out to be Jankarra. He was blowing, and shiny with sweat. Slung over his back was a bulging sack. His clothes were torn and blood-spattered. He told them: "I nearly didn't come. I couldn't slip away before. They had their eyes on us. Not till the ships change their fire and the bombs begin to fall all round us that Debarra and me manage to run off. Everybody begin to run. Massa, I never run so fast in all my life."

"But where's the boat, Jankarra? And the others? What's happened?"

"Debarra gone round for the boat. He coming soon with it. Passy get killed, Massa. A bomb explode just near him and four others. Massa, plenty men get killed. And plenty gone over to the Governor's side. I could have gone, too, but I had to come back to see about you. Soldiers run out and chasing Cuffy and his men. Lieutenant Theilen leading them. I hear the Governor had a close escape. A ball cut through his coat, but it didn't pass into his body."[1]

"What you bring in your sack?" asked Cobby.

"Food and trousers for Massa. I had it ready since last night. I rush in the house when I come back from the fighting and pick it up and come straight here. Massa, they have strong guards around the cottage, but if we make a quick rush we can beat them in the confusion and rescue the missies. The guards only got cutlasses—no muskets. Cuffy had to take all the muskets to fight with."

"We can't attempt that now, Jankarra," said Jacques, avoiding the man's gaze. "What I'm going to suggest is that you remain with Cuffy and his lot and keep in contact with us. We'll take the trail for the Canje and keep in hiding so that we can follow Cuffy's movements and await our chance to rescue the two missies——"

"Massa! The boat coming!" Tengo called from the water's edge.

[1]Dalton, Vol. I, p. 205.

"Is it? Fine. Jankarra, you'll do that for me, won't you?"

"Yes, Massa. Good plan. They not suspect me. Peddy not like me too much, but Cuffy and Akkara talk to me good."

The boat was pulling in. Debarra's left sleeve was soaked with blood. He told them: "I first man to get to the landing place. Come in quick and let's get off. Jankarra, you bring the food and the trousers for Massa?"

"Yes, they in the sack here."

They heard shouts and crackling sounds not far off. Jacques and Rabby and Cobby got into the boat. Tengo was in already. Jacques smiled at Jankarra and said: "You're a good fellow, Jankarra. You're all good fellows. I won't forget this."

When they were in midstream Cobby said: "Massa, suppose Cuffy not take the Canje trail. Suppose he go higher up the river here, how we will rescue the missies?"

Jacques said: "I've thought of that, but we'll have to hope for the best. I'm fairly certain Cuffy will flee straight back to the Canje."

X

Jacques proved right. Cuffy did take the trail for the Canje. A mere straggling, disorganized rabble now, the rebels quarreled most of the time, and frequently there were fights between the disciples of Cuffy and Atta.

Jacques and his men kept track of them continuously. Cuffy camped in the open air every night, and every night Jacques was able to get in touch with Jankarra. Jankarra kept Jacques and his men supplied with food—sometimes at great risk of discovery.

When they were crossing the stretch of savannah country midway between the Berbice and Canje watershed the risk became tenfold, for there were only isolated clumps of black sage to act as cover. Now and then a lone *courida* tree.

Amelia and Juliana, with three or four other women prisoners, were kept under heavy guard and never allowed to stray near the fringe of the camp. Jankarra told Jacques: "We got to wait our chance, Massa. One night if a big fight take place and everything confused we can try to get them away, but we can't do nothing while things quiet."

One night, after the long trek had entered its third week, a serious quarrel developed and seemed to give promise of a free fight. Jacques and his men waited behind a clump of black sage and watched the situation. It was on the fourth day of Cuffy's new camp; often he would camp on one spot for four or five days.

The quarrel started when Cuffy began to strut around rapping his chest and reiterating: "I not beat yet. I not beat yet. If Hoogenheim think I beat, he wrong. He going to see I not beat yet."

A few guffaws and catcalls came from Atta and his group near the fringe of the camp. Atta called: "But Hoogenheim got hundreds of your men on his side now, Cuffy! And plenty more deserting all the time!"

"Yes, Governor! How about the three hundred men who desert at Dageraad! Next time you try to fight Hoogenheim a thousand might desert!"

Loud laughter spiraled round the camp.

Cuffy stopped strutting and folded his arms across his chest. The light from the crackling brambles and palm logs augmented the ominousness of his pose as he stood there glowering at Atta and his men.

Near an isolated clump of *aeta* palms on the hard savannah land Accabre squatted, a sinister ghoul in the shadows. Accabre was boiling a concoction of beetles and bones in a pot suspended over four black candles.

"Let all who mock go on mocking," said Cuffy. "The day will come when the mockers going to regret the words they use."

"Don't worry with them, Cuffy," Akkara growled. "Some people can only talk and make a lot of noise, but they can't do nothing."

Amelia turned her face aside to avoid Akkara's breath. Akkara sat next to her. She and another woman prisoner, Akkara's mistress, were eating out of bowls. Amelia's face looked drawn, and her eyes had a tired, resigned appearance, but her general bearing was one of defiance still. She kept her head erect.

Abruptly, Cuffy looked around and called out: "We going to see who is big man and who not big man, Atta! Everybody who on my side stand up! Everybody who not on my side keep sit down. Stand up, all who for me! Go on! Stand up, let me see!"

About three-quarters of the men stood up at once.

"We all for you, Cuffy! Not worry with Atta!"

"Atta stupid man!"

"Who say Atta stupid more than Cuffy?"

"Since when Cuffy turn Governor! Cuffy is a slave like me. He never can rule Berbice!"

"Shut your mouth! Shut your mouth!"

One of Atta's men, more in playfulness than anything else, put out his hand and grabbed an ankle of one of the men standing. The man toppled over, and there was a loud clamor of angry snarls. Within a minute a free fight was in progress. Cuffy and Atta bawled and gesticulated in an effort to restore order.

Jankarra took opportunity of this diversion to slink off and look for Jacques. By an agreement between Jacques and Jankarra, Jacques and his men always kept to the west of Cuffy's camp at night, so Jankarra did not have much difficulty in finding them. He dumped down a sack of food and told Jacques: "Massa, things looking serious. Keep ready in case we can manage to get the missies away. Don't move from this spot."

"Where is Missy Juliana? I haven't seen her."

"She with Atta and his men, near the *aeta* palms, Massa."

To their disappointment, however, the fight did not last long, nor become general. Cuffy and Atta soon brought it under control. Before he sat down near Amelia, Cuffy shouted across at Atta: "One day all this trouble must stop, Atta. One day I going to break your spirit!"

Atta called back: "You can't even break Georgie's spirit you looking to break mine! Shut your mouth, Cuffy!"

"I going to break both you and her. I going to

tame both you and Georgie." He glanced at Amelia. "You hear what he saying, Georgie? He defying me to break you." He rapped his chest. "But I going to do it." He knocked the bowl of food out of her hand.

She smiled and folded her hands in her lap.

"Why you don't leave her alone now, Cuffy? You not ill-treat her enough?"

"No, Akkara. I not leaving her alone. She and Atta got to go down before me and beg for mercy. I'm a determined man. Once I set out to do something nobody can stop me. I going to break both of them. Yes, you, Georgie. If you don't break under me, then it's a sign that Hoogenheim stronger than me. If you beat me, then Hoogenheim beat me." He took up her bowl, scraped up some of the scattered food and put it into the bowl again, handed the bowl to her and snapped: "Stand up and eat that!"

She took it from him, and flung the contents into his face.

"Nowadays that van Groenwegel not here for me to threaten with a beating you got plenty of courage, Georgie. But I still going to break you."

He rose and kicked her. Went on kicking her until Akkara restrained him. From the other side of the camp came jeers and mocking laughter.

Three nights later, when they were in the vicinity of Plantation Magdalenenburg, an alarm went up. They were in cultivated territory now, and Jacques and his men were in a coffee field when Jankarra came and told them the reason for the signs of activity in the rebel camp. Cuffy had occupied the outhouses of a plundered plantation—the residence itself was a burnt-out ruin—and some stragglers had arrived from across the Canje Creek and brought the news that soldiers were approaching along the Indian trail from the Corentyne.

"The bad men preparing to run off and leave all the goods they dig up near the vat yesterday, Massa," said Jankarra. "I hear the soldiers not more than half a mile off. Perhaps they crossing the creek this minute."

"What goods they dig up near the vat?" asked Cobby.

"Plenty goods in jars. Silk and jewelery and money and other things. Atta and his men dig them up, but Accabre say they must seal up the jars again and leave them buried for a week before opening them again, because the jars was buried with two dead men, and the dead men's spirits must be driven away first before they can touch any of the valuables."

"I know who buried those jars," said Jacques. "It was Raoul Laplace—before he got away. He always kept his valuables in jars. I know that vat very well, Jankarra. There used to be a jamoon tree near it." He grunted reminiscently. "Which way is Cuffy going now, Jankarra? Do you know?"

"He going south into the bush, and then he say they will take the trail and come round back to the creek at Magdalenenburg."

"Ah, I see. My brothers and I once had to adopt a similar strategy when the overseers on the Toulouse plantation were after us for shooting one of their sheep. I'll meet you by the bamboos behind the outer dam on Magdalenenburg, Jankarra."

"Good, Massa. I meet you there night after next."

Two nights later Jacques thought Jankarra would fail them. Jankarra was not familiar with the countryside, and rain poured and the night was dark. Cobby and Tengo expressed doubt as to their direction, but Jacques told them: "Don't trouble. I can find my way blindfold, Cobby." But for Jacques they might have lost their way hopelessly. They found the bamboos near the dam, but after a wait of nearly two hours there was no sign of Jankarra. The rain held off, but water made a swift gurgling on every hand. The dam was muddy and treacherous. Over the canes, toward the north, there was a glow, and Rabby said: "Cuffy's camp must be over that way, Massa." And Jacques nodded. "Yes, they're in the pasture land beyond the coffee fields. I know the spot."

They heard a squelching, and saw a dark figure approaching from the west along the dam. It seemed hesitant and not sure of itself. Tengo took a chance and called: "Jankara! That you?"

It was Jankarra. He told them: "We might get a chance tonight. Plenty happen. The soldiers who come after Cuffy from the Corentyne find the jars what Atta's men left behind. Atta's men didn't bury them good, and the soldiers dig them up easy and take out the valuables. They had a big quarrel over sharing out the jewelry and silk and the other things. Cuffy send men to spy on them, and the men come back and say they witness the quarrel. The soldiers had Indians with them who the Governor get to help fight the bad men, and the soldier-officers wanted to give the best things to the Indians as a reward for fighting, but the ordinary soldiers say no, and they all had this big quarrel, and plenty of the soldiers desert and heading now for Magdalenenburg to join with Cuffy and his men. Over forty of them on their way to join up with Cuffy. But Cuffy suspicious of them, and he send out a party to take them by surprise and capture them. Best thing now is for us to move up near so we can rescue the missies if confusion take place when they bring in the soldiers."

Jankarra wanted to go the way he had come, but Jacques showed them a short cut through the cane fields. "This is familiar territory, Jankara. The territory of my youth. I feel I have the advantage over any enemy in this part of the colony." His voice quavered with excitement. He might have been eight again and engaged on a daring escapade with Pedro and David and Lumea.

A few minutes later, crouching among the coffee trees, they looked out upon the rebel camp in the pasture. Fires, as usual, were burning, but the wood seemed wet from the rain and smoked profusely.

They could see Cuffy and Akkara sitting around one of the fires. Amelia and Akkara's white mistress were nearby but were not visible to Jacques and his party.

On the other side, toward the west, Atta and his men were grouped around another fire. They had a glum look.

The rebels kept glancing frequently toward the northeast where a track opened into the pasture from the bush. It was that way the ambush party had gone. It was there it would appear when the white soldiers were captured.

"Trouble coming, Akkara," said Cuffy. "I feel it. Atta making serious trouble now."

Akkara nodded, and threw a glance toward the track opening. Goatsuckers hoo-yoo-ed to each other among the coffee trees. One of the men got up and poked the fire and it sent up sparks and crackled. The smoke wavered around, blue and woody-smelling, making the eyes smart.

Overhead it was starry, but the stars had a watery look, and there would be more rain before dawn. Perhaps before midnight. They could hear the sound of water gurgling in trenches about the plantation. Tree frogs fluted cheerfully, reveling in the wet.

A commotion of voices suddenly became evident in the bush in the northeast, and Jankarra muttered to Jacques: "They coming back, Massa. They must be capture the soldier men."

One or two of the rebels began to move toward the track opening. Atta and Goussari had risen. Akkara began to move away, but Cuffy stayed him. "You wait here till they come, Akkara. They must bring them to us here. We send them to do the job. They all my men."

The commotion swelled, and the ambush party appeared. They had carried out their mission successfully. The white soldiers were firm captives, some grasped by their tunics, some by their arms, some by the seats of their trousers, some by their hair. They jabbered wildly, one or two of them struggling and protesting.

Quacco and Baube, who had been given charge of the ambush party, brought the prisoners before Cuffy and Akkara. Cuffy rose with an air of ceremony, his chest thrown out importantly. Akkara, unassuming and awkward, stumbled to his feet, the saber which he always wore at his waist clink-clanking.

Amelia continued to sit where she was.

"Who the leader?" snapped Cuffy. "I only talking to the leader."

After a minor scuffle a blue-eyed fellow was pushed forward. Baube said: "He the leader, Governor."

"You the leader, white man?" Cuffy asked the man.

"Yes, I'm the leader. We're trying to explain the position to your men. We have come to join forces——"

"What your name?" Cuffy interrupted.

"Jean Renaud. I'm French, but I came with the expedition from the Corentyne. This is our Surgeon."

"You know what is my name? I'm Cuffy, Governor Cuffy of Berbice."

"Yes, I concluded so. Well, we've come to join you, Cuffy. We're on your side. We don't want to fight you. We have plans to go on to the Orinoco, and we want you and your men to help us and come with us. We can start our own community in the bush. We can look for gold and get rich. I was trying to explain this to your men, but they wouldn't listen. We've deserted our officers and we want to fight with you."

"You think Cuffy is a fool, Christian?"

"But no, my friend. I speak the truth. Surgeon, do I not speak the truth when I say we want to fight with Cuffy?"

"Yes, yes," said the Surgeon, a tall, slim, gray-eyed man. His tunic was in rags, and he had been badly mauled about the face.

The other white men joined in in a chorus of assent.

"We have come to fight with you, Cuffy! We are loyal to you!"

"You must believe us!"

Cuffy uttered sneering sounds. He waved his hand and said: "Peddy, make a count and tell me how many of them here!"

"I count them already, Governor," Peddy grinned. "Forty-two."

"Forty-two, eh? All right." Cuffy strutted about, looking contemplative. He cast a swift glance at Atta and his men who hung around in the background, watching the proceedings. Abruptly he halted and asked the Frenchman: "Who is this surgeon you talk about?"

"I am the Surgeon," said the gray-eyed man.

"You? Very well." Cuffy waved his hand. "Surgeon, you stand aside. Let him go, men. Let the Surgeon stand aside."

The Surgeon stepped aside with an air of wonder and apprehension.

Cuffy beckoned to Peddy, and when Peddy came muttered something to him in an undertone. Peddy nodded, looked a trifle blank, but hurried off at once.

Cuffy stood with arms folded and head at an angle while the Frenchman, in halting Dutch, tried to plead with him and assure him that his men had come to join the insurrection. "I speak the truth, Cuffy. That is our intention, my friend——"

"To you I is Governor Cuffy, Frenchman. And I is no friend to you."

Peddy returned. He had in his hand a canvas bag. Cuffy took this bag from him and shook it, and there was a rattling sound.

Atta and his men looked on with wondering frowns.

Among the coffee trees Jankarra muttered to Jacques: "I believe he going to work *obeah* on them, Massa."

Cuffy called for silence. "Listen to me! White men, you say you come to join in with us. Perhaps you talking the truth—and perhaps you telling lies. We black men can't trust you. But what we can do is to make you serve us. I need about twelve or fourteen men to help me. I want some of you white men to drill my men and clean guns, and I want a surgeon. The surgeon here is all right. He safe. So what I decide to do is to keep fourteen of you, white men. The rest of you got to get kill off now before you make trouble."

A gasp went up from some of the prisoners. Evidently all of them did not understand Dutch.

Cuffy's men shouted in approval.

"That's right, Governor! Kill them off!"

"White spies! They come to betray us!"

Cuffy raised his hand for silence. "I got in this bag here," he shouted, "forty-two palm seeds. Twenty-eight of them is small seeds. But the other fourteen seeds is large ones. These seeds is going to decide who must live and who must die." He put his hand into the bag, fumbled and took out a large seed. "Surgeon, this is your seed. I choose it for you because you got to live. The Governor decide that. We not taking no chance for you. The thirteen other large seeds in the bag here mean that thirteen of your white men friends will live. Every man who draw a small seed will got to die."

Cuffy began to strut. He told the prisoners: "That's what I decide, Christians. I Cuffy, Governor of Berbice, makes that decision. This black man who all you Christians treat like dirt. I going to say if you live and if you not live." He struck his chest rapping blows with his knuckles. "I is Governor—not Hoogenheim! I is the big master in Berbice. This nigger! And what this nigger say is that he pass sentence upon you this night!"

"Good talk, Governor! Good talk!" called Atta.

Cuffy ignored him. He shook the bag with the seeds, then turned and beckoned to Amelia. "Georgie! Come! Get up. Don't sit there as if you gone to sleep. You got work to do. You is the Governor's woman. I call upon you to draw the lots!"

"To do what?"

"I say I call upon you to draw the lots. You got to put your hand in the bag and pull out the seeds so as to let us see who must live and who got to get kill off. That's what I ordering you to do, Georgie."

She looked about her a little distractedly, silent.

"Yes, that hurt you, Georgie. I can see it. I know it hurt you. You don't like helping to send your fellow Christians to their death. But you got to do it. I the Governor orders you to do it."

She smiled. "And suppose I refuse?"

"I was waiting to hear you say that. Since we not got van Groenwegel here to threaten with lashes and hot iron you get more stubborn and more stubborn every day. Very good, Georgie. If you refuse to draw the lots I will order my men to lay out all these white dogs and cut their throats—every one! The surgeon, too! All! I won't spare one. What you say now?"

"It's certainly an effective way of gaining your point. Very well. Hold out the bag."

Cuffy beckoned to one of the prisoners, a short, thickly-built fellow with sandy hair and blue-green eyes. He was wounded in the arm.

"You step forward. Push him forward!"

They pushed him forward. Kicked him. He stood gulping and wild-eyed, glancing from Cuffy to Amelia.

Cuffy held out the bag to Amelia, shaking it continuously. "Go on. Pull one, Georgie. Let us see if your God going to save this one here."

Amelia's face was impassive. When she withdrew her hand from the bag, the man's eyes bulged. He uttered a dry sob. It was a small seed.

They took him aside.

So it went on. Once there was a tall, slim fellow whose gray eyes looked straight at Amelia, calm and unafraid, even a trifle contemptuous. He seemed perfectly resigned. But his was a large seed, and Cuffy laughed and said: "No, long man! Death not for you. Your God with you tonight."

The twenty-eight were stripped and bound and piled together in the mud. One or two struggled and broke free, trying to make a dash for the coffee trees. These were hacked to pieces. Then Cuffy and Akkara and Peddy set to work with horse pistols on the rest. One by one they were shot—some in the head, some in the heart.

It was when the last three were writhing and pleading that a sudden commotion broke out among Atta's men on the other side of the clearing. Jankarra said to Jacques: "I must go and see what wrong, Massa. Wait a little bit and I will come back." They heard reports. Muskets and pistols. And shrieks. The shrieks of women.

Jankarra hurried off, and Jacques and the others watched him mingling with the crowd that was moving toward the bush in the northeast.

Cuffy and Akkara, meantime, had completed their work. Cuffy waved his pistol at the fourteen survivors and told them: "From this minute you is my slaves, Christians. And if any of you try to escape, same what happen to your friends tonight will happen to you, so take warning. I'm a cruel man. I have no mercy on none of you white Christians."

It was nearly half an hour before Jankarra returned to Jacques. He was agitated. "Massa Jacques! Trouble, Massa! Big trouble!"

"What's it, Jankarra?"

"Massa, they kill Missy Juliana. They shoot her down when she run."

"What!"

"Yes, Massa. Goussari shoot her down. She and two other missies run off. They was trying to escape in the bush. One missy get shot in her leg, but Missy Juliana and the other missy get killed."

Jacques nodded. "Another grim instance of the futility of human endeavor. After all our pains—the rain and the mud and the discomforts we've been through —this! Grandma is right. Life is a brutal, haphazard game."

After a silence, Jankarra asked: "What we going to do now, Massa?"

Jacques said: "We'll go on, Jankarra. Missy George is a good friend. She means a great deal to me."

XI

Through the rains of June and the thunderstorms of July the hide-and-seek game went on. It was not so difficult now, for Cuffy established his camp definitely at Magdalenenburg.

The knowledge that he was so near to his old home was a great temptation to Jacques, and more than once he almost decided to give up the chase and go home. One morning, when Tengo and Rabby had gone off to forage for food and Jacques and Debarra were sitting on the veranda of a silent, deserted plantation house, Jacques said to Debarra: "Missy Faustina has told me, and rightly, that I'm not a practical man. She said I'm a giant of goodness whose head is lost in the clouds. It's only within the past few weeks that I've begun to look down at the earth, and what I behold is so gruesome I could lift my face to the stars again and retire to my dreams as of yore. But that would be shirking my earthly responsibilities, so we must go on, Debarra. Missy George is a noble woman. A woman of the earth—and strong like the earth. In many respects she reminds me of my grandmother." He got up and began to pace. "I keep talking so much nonsense. I believe before long I'll become like that great-granduncle of mine we've always heard about. Reinald, I think he was called. The fellow who lost his nerve in 1666 during the Scott raid: Debarra, how do I impress you? I should appreciate it if you would be frank."

Debarra only grinned.

One day, toward the end of August, when the rains had begun to thin off, Jacques, against the advice of Rabby and the others, went off on a ramble alone, and climbed to the top of a star-apple tree where, for over an hour, he remained swaying gently in the wind and watching the old house in the distance. He could see the upper storey only; the lower part of the house was obscured by trees.

In early September they had an encounter with two rebels who surprised them on a dam aback of Magdalenenburg. Rabby snatched up his musket and rapped: "Stand just where you is!"

The two men were unarmed. They halted.

"Where you come from?" Rabby asked them. "You Cuffy's men?"

"We from the camp," one of them replied. "Where you from? Who that Christian with you?"

Jacques and the others came up. "What are we going to do with them, Rabby? We'll have to keep them with us, or they'll go back and inform on us and we'll have scouts on our track."

Rabby said: "Massa, leave them to me." He snapped at the two men: "Turn round and walk. Go on!"

"Where are you taking them to, Rabby?"

"Leave them to me, Massa. Don't follow me." Rabby turned his head. "Tengo! Come with me!"

Tengo followed them, and Jacques watched them disappear into a clump of bamboos. Jacques kept pulling slowly at his stubble of beard.

After a moment there was a report amid the bamboos. A moan. A thud and a threshing about. Then silence. Rabby and Tengo returned. Tengo was wiping the blade of a cutlass in the grass as he approached.

"Only way, Massa Jacques," said Rabby.

"Quite so, Rabby. Shouldn't we have them buried, lest their bodies are found and investigations made?"

"You right, Massa. Tengo, come with me. We must bury them."

It was not until the middle of October that Jankarra told them one night: "Massa Jacques, they going to hold a meeting in the pasture tomorrow night to decide whether to go back to the Berbice River. I believe trouble going to happen. Atta and Goussari had a quarrel, and Accabre not talking to anybody now—not even to Atta and Goussari. I sure they going to have a big quarrel tomorrow night. Make sure you come."

The following night Jacques and his party stationed themselves in the coffee field. Jacques was not very hopeful. He told Cobby: "This will probably just be another night of vigilance that will end in failure."

There was a moon in the east, and the sky was cloudless. A true October night. The ground was parched and cracked, and the air sweet with the scent of dry twigs and dry-weather earth.

In the pasture the rebels had lit only one fire. Some of them sat talking in murmurs, but there was a group beating a tom-tom and chanting. From the direction of the logies and the toolshed—the only buildings which had not been burnt down in February—came the sound of loud voices.

Jankarra came and told them: "I sure something going to happen tonight, Massa Jacques. I hear Cuffy challenge Atta to a fight. Atta say Cuffy take a barrel of powder what belong to him."

A little later events seemed to bear out the truth of this rumor. Cuffy appeared with his cronies—Amelia and Akkara's mistress were with him—carrying a small barrel under his arm, a barrel that had every look of being a powder barrel. He placed it beside him when he squatted down, and from his gestures Jacques and his party could see that the barrel was the subject under discussion. The tom-toms and the general uproar made it impossible for Jacques to make out what Cuffy was saying.

Suddenly Akkara rose and clapped his hands, calling in his powerful drillmaster voice for silence. The mumbling and shouting and the tom-tom beating gradually died down.

Cuffy rose. He looked round and called: "Give me silence to talk!" He bent and took up the barrel. "I want you all to talk fair and honest! If any man among you see this barrel in Atta's logie, stand up and tell me! I talking to my men now! My men! Stand up and tell me. Don't be afraid to talk. Tell me if you see it in Atta's logie."

Two men stood up.

"Governor, I see the barrel in Atta's logie."

"You see it, Demba?"

"Yes, Governor. You ask me to talk true. Well, I talk true. I see that same barrel in Atta's logie up to yesterday."

"Good. Cudjoe, what about you? You see it, too?"

"Yes, Governor. I see it. Yesterday morning I see it there."

"In Atta's logie?"

"Yes, Governor. In Atta's logie."

"Very good, Cudjoe. Sit down." There was a note of menace in Cuffy's tone. He put down the barrel. Atta's men broke into an uproar of heated discussion. Atta rose and shouted: "I hope everybody hear what Demba and Cudjoe say! That barrel of powder belong to me—and I got to get it back before this night out!"

Jacques whispered to Jankarra: "Where are the white soldiers they captured? The ones that survived?"

"They got them locked up in the toolshed and under guard, Massa. They don't let them out at night."

Cuffy was calling for silence again. The noise began to die down. Cuffy shouted: "Nobody need make no trouble over this matter! I know how to settle it. Atta challenge me to a fight if we can't agree, and I ready to fight him! Let him come! I not afraid of Atta!"

Atta jostled his way through the crowd toward Cuffy, shouting: "I ready, Cuffy! I not afraid of you!"

Jacques whispered: "Jankarra, get back among them. This situation is looking very propitious. There's nobody paying attention to Missy George at the moment."

Jankarra was off at once, moving with such stealth and silence that he might have been one of the shadows thrown by the fire against the trees. They saw him, a few minutes later, jostling his way unhurriedly through the crowd and shouting and waving his arms like any of the others.

Meanwhile, Cuffy and Atta had come to grips and were struggling on the ground. The crowd stood around them and shouted encouragement. Jacques and his party could only conjecture what was happening.

Suddenly there was a roar, and Jacques heard shouts of "Cuffy done! Atta beat him!"

"Get up, Cuffy! Get up quick!" It was Akkara's desperate cry. There was a sob in it.

Another roar.

"Atta win! Atta win!"

The roar spread like a rushing, enveloping flame over the crowd. There was a milling and stirring and a jostling. Free fights broke out everywhere.

"Get Akkara! He's a dog! He betray us!"

"Hold Goussari! Goussari mustn't get away!"

Like shadows intermingling and then magically taking substance, Jankarra and Amelia came into view and then dodged in amidst the coffee trees. Jacques gripped Amelia's arm and said: "Come, Amelia. This way—quick!" She hurried off with him, Jankarra and the others following.

Behind them, in the pasture, the sound of conflict rose. Suddenly Jacques hissed: "Stop!" They heard footsteps amid the dry leaves, and the sound of someone panting. A dim shape darted past where they were crouched at the base of a coffee tree. Something was clutched in its grasp. Jacques breathed: "It's Cuffy." He rose, and urged Amelia toward the right. "This way! We must get after him!"

"No, Jacques. Let him go. Don't think of revenge now. We must escape—that's the main thing."

"You keep by me. I'm giving orders. He's a fugitive like us, and by Christ, if I can get face to face with him alone there's going to be hell coming to life this night!" There was a rasp in his voice.

At odd seconds, as they advanced, they would get a glimpse of the shape moving ahead of them. Cuffy was in a hurry, it was obvious, and it was no easy business keeping pace with him.

Suddenly Jacques made them halt again. "He's stopped. No, there he is! This way!" They went on.

Jankarra gasped: "Atta beat him good, Massa. Smash up his face with blows. But he managed to get away with the barrel of powder in the mix-up. I believe he trying to hide it before they can catch him."

Jankarra proved right, for not long after they saw Cuffy streaking across a small clearing, and the barrel of powder was no longer in his grasp. In the moonlight they had a glimpse of something like a horse pistol in his hand. He glanced back in their direction as though suddenly conscious of being pursued.

They were among sugarcanes now. Jacques gasped: "This way!" and led them out on to a dam. "He's cutting across the fields. If we move up this dam we'll be able to head him off when he comes out."

"Massa, careful! He got pistol. He might fire on you."

"And I've got a cutlass. I might chop off his head."

They hurried along the dam, Jacques well ahead of them. The canes waved gently, pale-green and fairy-like in the bright moonlight. Insects churred in a high-pitched chorus, and one could smell the dry-weather aroma of grass and starved herbs and shrubs, strong and spicy in the fresh, dew-laden air.

Amidst the canes they could hear a steady threshing noise. Abruptly, it stopped, and Jacques halted and dropped flat, hissing: "Down! I believe he's seen us!"

They lay flat on the hard, grassy dam. Jacques began to crawl forward toward the drain that separated the dam from the cane field, silently and with the stealth of a salampenter. He signaled to the others to remain where they were.

The canes made a faint lisping in the cool, soft drive of breeze that came from the southeast—a land breeze, heavy with the scent of the jungle. A cricket hopped away from near Amelia's cheek.

Jacques was entering the canes now. They saw a flash amid the canes ahead of them, heard a report. There was a thud, a groan and a threshing about. They saw Jacques rise and rush forward. Heard him call to them.

He was chuckling when they caught up with him among the canes. "I don't think," he said, "there's much we can do for His Excellency, except hope he will writhe in torture in Hades."

"Is he dead, Jacques?"

"He's shot himself through the heart," said Jacques. "With the horse pistol. Come, let's be off. No time for elegiac reflections." He glanced at the slaves. "Jankarra! You know what you have to do. Rabby! Tengo! Get started, all of you. You know your jobs."

"Yes, Massa. Don't trouble," Rabby assured him.

"What's the plan, Jacques? Where are they going?"

"They're making for the Laplace plantation to get two *corials,* and you're coming with me to the Siki Creek where they'll meet us."

"But why can't we go with them?"

"For two reasons. It will mean our having to go too far out of our way and in territory where we'd run the risk of being recaptured. And the second reason is that I want to have you to myself for a while."

He led her along the dam and then into a track that wound between clumps of bamboos.

"Jacques, wouldn't it be possible for us to get a word of warning to your people? Atta is planning to attack the house and wipe them out."

"Is that a fact? Did you hear that?"

"Yes. I heard them discussing it. Atta and his

men are going there to attack them before the night is out. Atta wants to head back to the Berbice River, but he's short of powder and shot. He knows your people are well stocked, and he's determined to get what they have."

"Thanks for the information, Amelia. I had intended going there in any event. As soon as I see you off at the Siki Creek I'll be on my way to the old house."

"See me off? Aren't you coming with me?"

"I'm afraid not. I'm joining my people. I could have been with them months ago, but I made a pact with myself that until I saw you safely out of the hands of those black brutes I'd never approach within a stone's throw of the old place."

"Jankarra told me about your resolve. But why go and join them? Couldn't you get them away and let's all go to Fort St. Andries? Aren't you anxious to see Faustina?"

"Faustina is safe. My duty is to stand by the family and defend our home. I'm going to fight with them. The van Groenwegels never run, Amelia."

"That grandmother of yours. I always knew she had a strong hold on you. My dear! I do hope you'll succeed in beating them off. Atta has got so desperate of late. Accabre has fallen out with him. They're divided into various little factions now."

"Yes, I've heard. Goussari, too, has a little clique of his own, I understand."

They were moving through what had once been a well-kept provision patch. Now there were vines and weeds. They heard a goatsucker hoo-yoo-ing amid the bamboos they had left behind, and Jacques turned his head.

"Do you hear that? A goatsucker. Amelia, you won't ever know how much that bird means to me. This is my terrain. The bird sounds and the smells of the shrubs and the grass and the earth."

There was an odd excitability in his manner. He kept looking round at the wild, moonlit scene, moving across the provision beds with a sureness that came of long familiarity with everything about him.

"It's the soft streak in me, I suppose," he said. "Great-great-grandmother Griselda. Great-grandfather Reinald. And Grandfather Ignatius, the artist. Uncle Cornelis. They were the soft ones." He laughed. "Don't take me too seriously, Amelia. I'm in a spiritual decline."

"You haven't changed one bit, Jacques."

"Which reminds me to tell you how much I've admired you all these months. You have been magnificent. Sometimes I feel breathless and incredulous. I never thought that any human could have been capable of such endurance. Even at this minute I can't quite convince myself that you are beside me here alive and talking."

Musket fire broke out in the distance behind them.

"Are you sure we're on the right track for this creeklet you spoke of?" She uttered a sound of uncertainty. "I'm trembling with fear, despite your compliments and your high opinion of me."

"You needn't entertain the slightest fear of our losing our way," he told her. "I could tell you every tree you'll find in this bush we're approaching—every tree and shrub. A thunderstorm caught Pedro and me just about here one afternoon, and a *cookerit* palm fell right before our path. The lightning hacked it down as though a giant had used a giant cutlass on it. I was about seventeen then, and Pedro and I were on the track of a *labba*-tiger that was worrying our goats."

"You're so sentimental, Jacques."

"Down!"

She dropped quickly, and lying in the stunted, itchy grass and ferns, they saw three shapes moving toward a track opening on the left. One of them was armed with what looked like an arquebus.

"Three stragglers. I believe they're Atta's men, Jacques. He sent some men to scout around your people's house."

"I wish I had a musket with me. I'd have given them something to take back to Atta. Come on, let's hurry. We mustn't waste more time than is absolutely necessary. I hope those men get the *corials*."

"You seem to have planned everything to the last detail."

"We had several months in which to do our planning."

When they were on the old Indian trail that led out to the Siki Creek he told her: "When you get to Fort St. Andries tell Faustina I've done my duty to the family. Tell her that's why I couldn't turn up along with you."

Amelia made no comment.

"Have you a good memory for messages?"

"Fairly good. I'll tell her anything you want me to."

"Fine. Well, tell her the soft streak came out in me. Tell her I was a shameful coward when the test came, but that, in the long run, the old blood came to the fore. Tell her I mean to fight to the death defending our home and that if she never sees me again she can be certain that I went down in battle and had no regrets. By the way, did you know that I'm the father of twins—both boys?"

"I didn't. Congratulations."

"Thank you." He said it with such droll solemnity that she asked him to stop and kiss her, so he stopped and kissed her.

"Tell her, too," he said as they went on, "that it is a matter of indifference to me whether she tells our sons the tales of old or not, for I'm convinced now that heredity decides all family histories. If our sons have it in them to be brutes nothing will stop them from being brutes; if they have it in them to be humane, then all the elements of heaven and earth could not change them. Tell her that events like this insurrection should make us realize that we humans are not as noble as we would like to think ourselves. We overrate ourselves immensely. Under their layer of culture and refinement civilized men are animals, and it doesn't need much urging to have them flying at each other's throats. Therefore while the Christian philosophy is an excellent one—a civilized philosophy—we must live up to its ideals only in so far as it enables us to be humane one to another; it must not be allowed to convert us into sentimental weaklings: we must always remember the animal and we must always be prepared for outbreaks of savagery. And in order that savagery might be kept in check we must be strong—physically strong. Physical strength results in moral strength. Strength respects strength, and peace follows. Strength despises weakness and strife follows. Tell her I've come to learn these past months, after much reflection, that it is instinctive for all creatures to despise weakness; weak people secretly despise themselves for their weakness. Even those who may say they abhor a show of force in their deep selves admire strength and are contemptuous of weakness. Strength, I have discovered, to be effective, should be employed in a reasoned and unemotional manner; my grandmother employed it in a fanatical manner, that is why she brought suffering to so many. Strength sometimes falls into the wrong hands; this is in the nature of the haphazardness of things: there is no cure for it. So long as men are men—that is to say, self-tamed animals—there will be physical violence to the end of time. A sad and depressing conclusion to come to, but the truth. Tell her, Amelia, that she must always face the truth, no matter how sad, depressing or forbidding the truth may seem; the fool who attempts to evade the truth or escape from reality is doomed from the beginning. Tell her it is much more fruitful and satisfying to keep grappling with the difficulties of human thought and human conduct than to surrender oneself to the rigid grooves of a pattern of thought and conduct devised by people who went before us. That, tell her, is the easy way, and in the easy way lies complacency—and weakness. And weakness is always bad. Strength is always good."

They were nearing the Siki Creek. The jungle met overhead, and the moonlight filtered through in slim shafts. They could hear the tree frogs in the bamboos, and now and then a rustle would sound in the gloom beyond the *awara* and *cookerit* palms on their right. The smell of creek water was in the air, a wet, vegetable scent that permeated everything around them—the trees and the carpet of dry leaves as well as the air. Even the chirrup of the tree frogs seemed drenched with it. The silent bamboos might have been breathing it in through the ends of their thin, feathery leaves. They heard the low croaking of an alligator, and abruptly they were at the water's edge, gazing at the cool, still blackness of the Siki Creek with coins and flakes of moonlight serene on its surface.

"Same old Siki Creek," smiled Jacques. "See it. No different from what it was when we used to come here as boys. Same as it was that evening when we were on our way to shoot Mother and Raoul Laplace." He glanced at her. "Can you imagine yourself setting out on an expedition to kill your mother, Amelia?"

She said nothing. They listened to the alligator croaking.

Suddenly they heard the splash of paddles, and two *corials* came into view around the bend.

"I won't forget the messages for Faustina."

"I know you won't, Amelia."

When she was getting into one of the small craft, Jacques said to Jankarra: "Take good care of her." He stretched out his hand. "Give me your hand, Jankarra. Debarra. Cobby. Tengo. Rabby. My good friends."

He watched them moving off, the moonlight on them in flakes. Coins.

"Amelia!"

"Yes, Jacques!"

"Keep an eye out for *marabuntas!*"

For several minutes after the two *corials* had vanished round the bend he stood gazing around him. At the bamboos. And the *mucca-muccas*. The long, slim, bare stems of the *mucca-muccas* were in dense shadow, but here and there the moonlight glimmered on the shiny, arrow-shaped leaves. Secretive and intelligent the leaves looked. And old. As though these might have been the very same shrubs his boy's eyes had gazed upon that afternoon when he and Pedro and David and Lumea had landed here on their way to the Laplace plantation. The *missouri* grass looked the same, too, as though these might have been the very clumps that he had seen floating in the black water that afternoon. The alligator might be no sentimental conjecture, for alligators lived for centuries. It could be the identical one croaking there now.

In the distance, musket fire.

He stood with his head cocked. Listening to a goatsucker. "Hoo-yoo! Hoo-yoo!" . . . Like cool blebs of creek water drifting through the jungle spirit-like. . . . "Hoo-yoo!"

With a soft grunt he plunged into the water and in four swift strokes was across. He clambered out, and the next instant was on the trail that would take him to the coffee fields on the Toulouse plantation. It was amid the coffee trees on the Toulouse plantation that Raoul Laplace and Rosaria had lain in waiting for his grandmother. You simply had to cross the lateral dam and you were on van Groenwegel territory. You took the longitudinal dam and moved straight toward Field Seven, then you turned left past the provision patches and went on between the old storehouse and the logies of the field slaves, and before you, within hailing distance, loomed the old house.

XII

On the 2nd of January 1764 Governor van Hoogenheim was in a good mood, for the day before a letter had reached him from one Colonel de Salve saying that the Colonel had arrived at Fort St. Andries with a force of six hundred and sixty men, troops of the Netherlands.

On this same day a haggard young lady in rags, accompanied by five slaves, presented herself before the Governor. The young lady said her name was Amelia George and that she had been in the hands of the rebels since the disaster of Peereboom on March the 4th and that she had only succeeded in escaping from them with these five faithful slaves when Cuffy had shot himself after being defeated in a fight with Atta over a barrel of powder. She did not hesitate to mention that Cuffy had forced her to become his mistress. Her gaze was steady, and she seemed indifferent to such a petty consideration as feminine modesty.

The first person she asked after was Mevrouw van Groenwegel, and when she was informed that most of the civilian refugees had left the colony for Demerary or Suriname her face grew blank with dismay. Then Mynheer Abbensetts told her: "I think Mevrouw van Groenwegel is among the few still at Fort St. Andries. She is the lady who had twins on the *Standvastigheid,* don't you remember, Hoogenheim?"

"Would it be possible for me to go to Fort St. Andries to take a message to her?" Amelia asked.

It might have been because the Governor was in such a good mood, or it might have been the steady, undefeated light in her eyes that moved him to a deep respect and compassion. However, without delay he set about to make arrangements for her to be conveyed to Fort St. Andries, and two days later she stepped ashore near the fort at the mouth of the river and was conducted to one of several *benabs* which had been erected to accommodate refugees.

Faustina listened to Amelia without interrupting, then nodded and said quietly: "Thank you. I think you have been incredibly brave." She was as pale and haggard as Amelia, and as undefeated.

"I should have gone to Demerary," she said, after a silence. "My cousin, Hubertus, has written twice trying to persuade me to come. But I can't leave until I hear something definite about Jacques."

She told Amelia her own tale of the past months.

"What of the others?" asked Amelia. "Your Aunt Flora and the Teuffers?"

"Paula and Sarah and Mother Teuffer have gone to Suriname. Aunt Flora and Vincent and Marcus are dead. They went down with the Sickness."

"The Sickness?"

"Yes. It's been terrible, Amelia. The whole crew of the *Standvastigheid,* including the Captain and the Mate, died of it. All the soldiers who fought at Dageraad in May are dead, too. Mynheer Abbensetts is the only member of the Governing Council alive."

After a long silence Amelia asked: "What have you named them? The twins?"

"Edward and Storm," Faustina told her.

A drizzle was falling, and the sky was overcast. It was the short rainy season. *Vicissi* duck were passing overhead, on their way to the swamps of the Corentyne, squeaking in little remote bleak flakes of sound.

"Amelia."

"Yes?"

"You never heard what happened when Atta and his men attacked them?"

"No."

About a week later they heard that Akkara and Goussari had surrendered themselves and had offered their services to the Government on condition that they were pardoned. Hoogenheim accepted the offer, so Akkara and Goussari had gone off again to set traps for the other rebels. They were after Atta's blood. Every other week they arrived at Dageraad with a party of rebels whom they had persuaded to come over to the Government's side. Others who proved more difficult to persuade were led into ambushes and taken prisoner. By the middle of February there were nearly eight hundred prisoners under guard at New Amsterdam, near Fort Nassau. On March the 2nd a hundred prisoners were selected for trial as ringleaders. Fifty-three were sentenced to death and forty-seven allowed to go free. Fifteen were tied to stakes and burnt to death, sixteen were broken on the wheel, and twenty-two hanged.

But Atta and Accabre were still at large. Each had his own body of men and were deadly enemies. Atta was reported to be somewhere near the Wikki Creek on the Berbice, and Accabre was behind Plantation Markey where he had fortified himself and his men within a stockade of sharp bamboos. The heavy rains had begun, however, and Colonel de Salve and his men were active. On March the 23rd Accabre was defeated and taken prisoner. He smiled his mysterious *obeah*-man smile, unruffled and in no way fearful.

Atta put up a better fight. It was not until April the 15th that Atta was caught, and then it was only through the strategy of Akkara and Goussari that they succeeded in getting him. Unlike Accabre, Atta broke down, and when they brought him before the Governor, he whimpered and fell down before Hoogenheim, trying to kiss the Governor's feet. Accabre, who was present, uttered a mocking laugh and cried: "You not ashamed, Atta? That's all the courage you got, after all your big talk!"

In dying, both Atta and Accabre were brave. When Atta was being broken on the wheel, he called out: "The Governor right! I'm suffering what I deserve!"[1]

On the morning after the execution Faustina and Amelia arrived at Dageraad. With the permission of the Governor, they were allowed to question some of the prisoners.

During the first few minutes every man Faustina spoke to said he was one of Accabre's men. Amelia was more fortunate. After the fourth attempt she came upon one who said he had fought with Atta, so Amelia beckoned to Faustina to come.

He was a short, rather surly fellow, and when Faustina asked him whether he knew what had happened to the van Groenwegels he looked up and uttered a deep growl. He said yes, he knew. He was in no way penitent. Later they discovered that he was under sentence of death.

They asked him to tell them what had happened, and he growled again, and, after some hesitation, told them.

[1] Actual words.

XI Finale: Like Kaywana

"STOP there! Give the password!"

A soft laugh came from the shadows near the large water tank. "Has it come to that now, Dave? What's tonight's password? The van Groenwegels never run?"

"Jacques!"

"I fear it is."

"What the devil are you doing in this part of the country?"

"I am a sentimentalist, Dave."

Jacques emerged into the moonlight, and David exclaimed: "Look at your condition! I can hardly recognize you!"

"I can well believe that."

As they were entering the house, through the pantry door, they heard Pedro call from the window upstairs: "Is that Bakkara, Dave?"

"No, it's Jacques!"

"Jacques?"

"The soft streak, Pedro!" Jacques called.

Entering the dining room, they heard Pedro upstairs shouting to the others to wake up, and a few minutes later the house was alive with footsteps and voices.

Only Hendrickje and Janny and Ziddy were in nightclothes. Lumea was in overalls, and Laurens and Pedro in shirt and trousers. Like David.

"Look at him!" Lumea exclaimed. "My God! He's like a wild man of the bush! It's only his eyes I recognize."

"I could have made him out by his brow," said Hendrickje. "He has Grandfather Willem's brow." She spoke with an air of subdued fire. Her manner was slightly forced. Jacques knew at once that something was wrong. Her eyes held the old inhuman glitter. The glitter that Ignatius had known. And Adrian after the

610

surrender of Fort Nassau. The glitter that Jacques had seen on the night of Bangara's death by fire.

Her hair hung down her back in two loose plaits. Like pewter snakes, thought Jacques. He had a swift picture of her smashing her fists down on to his mother's face.

"What has brought you back to us, Jacques?" There was nothing soft or affectionate in her voice. The doting Hendrickje of a year ago had vanished. This version seemed to exude a subtle malevolence.

"Grandma, what has happened to you in my absence? You don't seem exactly pleased to see me. Me your pet grandson, besides."

His grandmother grunted. There was a silence. Jacques heard the others stirring. Heard the lisp of feet on the floor. Jacques glanced round and saw that David and Pedro were frowning heavily. Lumea stared blankly in the direction of the pantry, and Laurens kept scraping his deformed foot along the floor. Even Ziddy and Janny, in their long white nightshirts behind their great-grandmother, had a tense, uncomfortable air.

"I confess," said Jacques, "that I'm a trifle puzzled. After having heard such effulgent accounts of your successful battles up here, I should have expected to find a more robust spirit among you. What has happened?"

Hendrickje answered. "The rot," she said, "has set in, Jacques. That is what has happened."

"The rot?"

"Yes, Jacques. The rot. Your brothers and sister want to leave the house. They want to run. They want to let down our traditions."

Jacques looked from one to the other of them. "They want to run?"

Pedro uttered what sounded like a sigh. "Jacques," he said, "we've discussed this so often I'm tired of it. Anyway, I'll tell you. We've told Grandma again and again that it isn't that we want to let down the traditions of the family. We're not disloyal. It's merely that there comes a time when we must put reason before sentiment——"

"Reason before sentiment! You hear him,

Jacques!" Hendrickje advanced a pace, a clenched hand poised before her. "Reason before sentiment! Note the excuse! I tell you, the rot has set in. Since September last year I suspected that something was a little wrong in the hearts of David and Pedro. They turned down a project put by Hubertus to go and manage the Demerary plantation—or the Essequibo, whichever it was. Pedro dropped a remark on that occasion that bothered me. Now I know for certain that my instinct was right. The rot was there."

Pedro sighed again. "Jacques, hear me out, please. Let me relate to you what's happened during the past few months. You'll better be able to judge. In February we stood up to an attack from Cuffy. We won—but we lost four of the nineteen men whom Memphis brought in to fight with us. Not a week later we were attacked again by Atta and his men on their return from the Corentyne. In that attack we lost Stragga as well as seven of the remaining fourteen men we had with us. By the end of May those who had survived had deserted us. One by one they went, and we never saw them again. Some time in June, Dak came in with the news that soldiers had come up the creek and were about to attack Cuffy. Then it appeared there was some dispute among the soldiers and a party of them deserted and were captured by the rebels. Memphis brought us this news, but in the process of obtaining it he had been shot at, and he was so seriously wounded that he died two days later. Two weeks ago Bakkara went off on another scouting expedition, and up to now he hasn't returned. That means that besides ourselves, we have only Dak and Dankje and two women loaders. We had three, but Mabella died of the Sickness. And added to this, we're living on corn and yams and an occasional fish when we can succeed in catching one, for the country about here simply swarms with straggling bands of rebels.

"Under conditions like these, Jacques, do you think it unreasonable for us to suggest that we should make some attempt to get to Fort St. Andries, or somewhere, at least, where we would be able to put up a decent fight? We have four *corials,* and, with luck, we might be able to make the trip to Fort St. Andries in a fortnight. Perhaps much longer, but that's not the point. The great question is which is the wiser course? To remain here and be butchered hopelessly if we're attacked again, or to make a getaway while the creek is open and there's a chance of our winning through to Fort St. Andries? That is the proposition we've put to Grandma. We haven't run. We haven't let down the family traditions. We stayed and withstood two terrible attacks. No one could accuse us of cowardice."

David grunted and said: "We've had the four corials packed and ready at the landing place for the past three or four weeks, but Grandma resists every effort of ours to persuade her to come with us. She just gets into a rage every time we broach the subject."

Jacques smiled. He took a deep breath and said: "To be honest, I'm too taken aback to say what I think."

"What do you mean, taken aback?" said Pedro. "Don't you agree with us that our proposal is reasonable?"

"Oh, certainly. Very reasonable. But—well, it's like this, Pedro. You see, my sole object in coming home here was to help you defend. I came prepared to fight—and to go down fighting."

They looked at him.

Hendrickje had been pacing up and down. She stopped. In the uncertain light of a stump of candle on the dining table, she might have been a specter materialized out of the gloom near the stairway.

"What did you say, Jacques? Repeat that!"

Jacques shrugged. "Oh, please don't think I'm trying to sound heroic. I was merely stating a fact. I said I came here to fight—to stand by the family and go down in battle if we have to go down. I'd always understood that that was the keynote of our philosophy as a family—to die rather than surrender or flee—but, as I've said already, I'm a sentimentalist."

Hendrickje uttered a crowing sound of triumph. "Thank you, Jacques! Thank you! My God! And you are the soft one! Did you hear that, Pedro! David! Lumea! Laurens! Your brother whom we have always looked upon as the weak link—the soft streak! My God! This is what I've lived to see. Pedro and David and Laurens in a funk. Lumea. And Jacques ready to stand by the family and go down fighting." Her voice broke.

Jacques cleared his throat affectedly and said: "Perhaps it won't be amiss if I mentioned that at the moment we are in danger, so whatever decisions you want to make it would be advisable to make them without a minute's delay."

"What do you mean, in danger?" David asked.

"Atta and his men are advancing upon us. At any moment they will be here—and I mean that literally. At any moment."

"Why didn't you warn us right away, then?"

"My dear fellow, if there's one thing I can't resist it's a strong dramatic situation. It's my weakness. I simply *had* to hear you say your parts before delivering my warning."

Once again Hendrickje paused in her pacing. Her eyes flashed from one to the other of them. Hawklike, eager, desperately hopeful. So great was the fanaticism that gripped her that she seemed unawed by Jacques' revelation that they were in danger. Only the moral issue seemed to concern her—not their physical situation.

"Decide, decide!" she shouted. "What are you going to do? Didn't you hear what Jacques said! Atta and his men are coming. Are you running, or are you going to stay?"

They were all silent.

Janny was biting his thumb.

"Jacques!"

"Yes, Grandma?"

"What are you doing? Are you staying?"

"Yes. Yes, you can count on me for staying."

Pedro barked: "Jacques, what damned absurdity is this! Do you mean to tell me you want to remain in this house to be butchered by those black lumps of filth! Don't you realize that we're in a hopeless position? How could we do anything against that horde?"

Jacques shrugged. "If you'll remember, when we were boys I was reluctant to shoot Mother, but when Grandma convinced me that it was the right thing to do I forgot reason and my personal feelings and joined the expedition. Remember that, Pedro?"

"What has that got to do with our position here tonight?"

"Much. In the same manner that I considered it my duty when I was a boy to hunt down and shoot our mother I consider it my duty now to stay and fight. In both instances the issue at stake is loyalty to the group—and the traditions of the group. The question of whether to do the right thing by the family, irrespective of reason or personal feelings, or not. Don't blame me, Pedro. In a manner of speaking, it's a matter outside of me. It was the way I was brought up. It comes all the way down from old Willem. To act otherwise I should feel a cur."

Pedro snorted. "You always had cobweb on the brain, Jacques. Very well, if you want to stay you can stay. I'm off. And by Christ! I know I'm no coward. I've proved a dozen times I've got as much guts as all the white men in this colony put together. But I'm no blind, heroic imbecile. If there were the slimmest chance of holding out here I'd be the first to suggest we stay and give the black hounds what they deserve. But I can't fight two or three hundred savages and expect to come off the victor. Dave, are you coming with me?"

"Most certainly. I'm going up now to wake Dak and Dankje."

"Lumea? What of you?"

Lumea hesitated, then said: "Yes, I'm coming, too."

"Laurens?"

Laurens shifted about his foot and said: "I can't go and leave Grandma here, Pedro. I'll stay."

Pedro and David stood staring at him. Lumea

was squeezing her fingers, a troubled look on her face.

Hendrickje uttered a cracked sound. "Look at them! Look at them, Jacques! Wavering! My God! Is it possible! After all their bluster and histrionics in February! The old blood! The old blood, they swore! I heard them myself calling the Boissières and the van Rueffs poltroons for not putting up a defense, for not staying and helping us to fight—and that was before Memphis had announced that we would be able to use nineteen of our slaves. In February they were ready to stand up to a thousand black men. Now their courage has rotted away and they're talking like the Boissières and the van Rueffs! My God! Think of it! Why did I live to behold this! It is better I had died in February. I've lived too long. Yes, I've lived too long."

She began to pace again.

In silence, Pedro and David went upstairs. When they were halfway up, Lumea began to ascend after them.

Laurens stood by a window peering past the table barricade at the compound, Ziddy and Janny were seated on the dining table, Ziddy yawning sleepily.

Abruptly Hendrickje said: "Laurens, why don't you go with them? Go! I don't want you to remain against your will."

Laurens made no reply. Made no move.

Jacques murmured: "Well, well. Look what I've come home to find. And after all these months of dreaming. Heroic dreaming." He approached Ziddy and Janny and patted their heads. "You boys have grown. You have your great-grandmother's chin, Ziddy."

Ziddy smiled shyly.

"I wonder what my three boys will look like in ten years' time. By the way, Grandma! Would you be interested to learn that I'm the father of twins?"

"What's that, Jacques?"

"I said I'm the father of twins—twin boys. Faustina gave birth to them in March at Fort St.

Andries. She was aboard the *Standvastigheid*. You are now the possessor of three legitimate male great-grandsons."

"Twin boys, eh?" Some of the tenseness left her manner. "That's splendid, my boy. Splendid." A low groaning sound came from her. "We've only had twins once before in the family. Uncle Reinald's two girls —Octavia and Luise."

They heard Laurens exclaim.

"What is it, Laurens?"

"I have an idea I saw something move under the mango trees."

"Atta's scouts are everywhere," Jacques nodded.

"What names has she given to them, Jacques?"

"She evidently hadn't named them yet, when I heard from her. I was a prisoner in Cuffy's hands when the letter was smuggled to me."

Laurens turned. "You were a prisoner in Cuffy's hands?"

"I was his secretary at first."

"Are you joking?"

"I'm serious. I wrote a letter for him to Hoogenheim. You see, I was too frightened of the lashes and of the branding iron. Though, in the long run, I got them anyway. You should have heard me yell for mercy, Laurens. Then you would have known how really soft I am."

Laurens and Hendrickje stared at him in silence.

"Juliana took her lashes without a grunt. A brave van Groenwegel. I wept with pride when I remembered it afterwards."

"What's happened to her?"

"She was shot dead a few months ago on Magdalenenburg. Atta had forced her to become his mistress, and she was trying to escape."

"Good God!"

They were silent for a while, hearing the footsteps of Pedro and the others upstairs.

"The weak and the strong," murmured Jacques.

"What's that?"

"Nothing, Laurens. Just being philosophic."

Hendrickje said: "Jacques, I'm beginning to feel that despite your softness, you are the hero among us."

Jacques laughed. "Wrong, old lady. I wasn't born to be a hero. Heroes are strong. I'm one of the weak who have discovered the depressing truth that it takes strength to make a secure world. Physical as well as moral strength. Weakness of any sort results in disaster—the disaster we see all around us today in this colony. The truth. Let's face the truth. It's your own teaching, Grandma."

His grandmother stood looking pensive and baffled.

"The stronger always survive," murmured Jacques.

David and Pedro and Lumea were coming downstairs, accompanied by Dak and Dankje who had been asleep at the far end of the corridor. They were armed with muskets and had sacks slung over their shoulders. Lumea looked shifty-eyed and half-ashamed, but Pedro and David held their heads erect.

"We're going," said Pedro.

Hendrickje made no response, did not even glance at them.

Jacques said: "Good luck to you. Wish I could come with you."

Laurens waved his hand with a simulation of casualness and said: "Take care of yourselves. Jacques says Atta has scouts prowling about."

"We'll take care of them," nodded David, tapping the knives at his waist.

When they were moving toward the pantry Lumea paused and looked back and said: "Jacques, there are loaded muskets upstairs—and two pistols. If . . . you'll know what to do if the need arises."

"Thank you, Lumea."

"Laurens, you'd better come and barricade the door after us."

"Very well. I'll do that." Laurens moved after her into the pantry.

Jacques crossed to a window and watched them pass out through the pantry door. A smile came to his face. He was remembering the night when he had crept out to go and release his mother and Bomba from the stocks. The moonlight was very bright. That night there had been no moonlight. . . . He watched his brothers and sister crossing the compound. Only Lumea looked back. He was certain he heard a sob. . . .

The three of them, with the two faithful black men, entered the shadows under the mango trees, then he saw them emerge on to the open space between the mango trees and the ruins of the Carpenter's shed. Shrubs had grown up amid the charred beams. Black sage and wild foxglove and some of the tall, slim plants with long, pointed leaves that bore the sweet-smelling white flowers which he and the others, as children, had known as jumbie-flowers. One or two fireflies were flashing among them. . . . A soft, cool breeze was blowing. He breathed in the fragrance of dry-weather grass and dry-weather shrubs. If only, he thought, life could be just a soft, cool breeze at night-time and the fragrance of dry-weather plants; moonlight and the memory of one's childhood escapades; black sage and wild foxglove . . . jumbie-flowers and the cry of a goatsucker far away near the creek . . . Instead of which . . . there were other flashes beside the blue-white flashes of the fireflies. Red, ugly flashes. The night became a roar of noise. . . . Jacques saw David's hand go to his waist, but in the same instant David crumpled up. Dak tried to dash back toward the mango trees, but he, too, went down. Pedro crashed over on to his face, his arms silhouetted for a half-second against the flashes amid the shrubs. Lumea succeeded in reaching the compound, then stumbled, clutched at her throat and sagged and fell.

Jacques did not wait to see what happened to Dankje. He shouted to his grandmother to get upstairs. Laurens gasped: "Bring the muskets from upstairs, Ziddy! Janny! Hurry, boys!"

Outside, the moonlight was alive with shouting figures.

"Come, Ziddy! Janny!" Hendrickje beckoned to

the two boys. "Upstairs with you! You're taking orders from me!"

Laurens adjusted the barricades at the windows, his uneven, hobbling footsteps weird in the moonlit dusk of the sitting room. He called to Jacques to come and help him. "We have some muskets in here, Jacques."

Jacques saw Yuani and Rassiki coming down the stairs. They were wringing their hands and whimpering, "Where Massa Pedro?"

Jacques ran into the sitting room. "Where are the muskets, Laurens?"

"They're here. They're loaded already." He exclaimed: "Quick! they're rushing the windows, Jacques!"

Upstairs, Hendrickje took the two boys into the room Laurens and David used to occupy. The door faced the stairway directly.

"Ziddy, go into the next room and bring the muskets. There are four of them in there. Janny, come and help me with this table."

"What are we going to do, Grandma?" asked Janny. Ziddy had run off into the next room to get the muskets.

"Don't ask questions. Simply obey," his great-grandmother told him. So he helped her to lift the table from the window and place it before the open door. Ziddy entered from the next room with the four muskets. He stumbled under the burden. Hendrickje helped him to lift them over to the table.

"Grandma, what are we going to do?" insisted Janny. His voice sounded frightened.

"We are going to defend ourselves, Janny," his great-grandmother answered. "We are going to fight to the death as Kaywana did. Get behind those muskets. Both of you! Now is your chance to prove how well you can handle a musket."

"Must we fire on them when they come up the stairs, Grandma?" Ziddy spoke with excitement and enthusiasm.

"Yes, you must fire upon them as they come up the stairs, my boy."

"But, Grandma, we can't keep them all off," said Janny, trembling.

"No, Janny, but we shall kill a few before we go down. Come! Ziddy has more guts than you. Hurry! Get ready to fire when I give the word."

"I'm going to riddle them through and through," said Ziddy. "Just let them come upstairs!"

"That's the spirit, my boy," said Hendrickje. "Fight. Never surrender. Even in the face of certain death—resist. Resist!"

The two boys had got into position at the table. They held the muskets ready.

"I'll give the word to fire," said Hendrickje.

Downstairs the rebels had broken in. Jacques and Laurens could be heard shouting at each other. A musket exploded, and there were yells and groans. And the din of scampering footsteps in the dining room and sitting room. Sounds of scuffling. The house thundered again as a musket went off. A defiant curse from Laurens. Laurens began to shout to his grandmother in warning—but his voice stopped abruptly. Yuani shrieked.

There was a quick stammer of foot-treads on the lower stairs, and they heard Jacques cry: "Grandma! The pistols! Get it over quickly!"

A musket banged. They heard Jacques laugh and snarl almost in the same breath. There was a confusion of yells and a thump-thump and panting. A musket banged again. Footsteps began to drum on the stairs.

"Ready, boys! Wait for the word to fire!"

They heard Jacques snarl downstairs. A pistol went off.

"Fire, boys! Let them have it!"

The muskets thundered on the table, and the table shook. The air hazed with the fumes of gunpowder.

The footsteps on the stairs became jumbled and uncertain and yells flared along the corridor and wavered up and down the well of the stairs.

"The old lady firing on us!"

"We going to brand her in the worse way!"

Hendrickje was reloading the two muskets just discharged. There was nothing flurried in her actions. In the candlelight she was smiling slightly. Her plaits had unraveled, and her hair hung loose down her back.

Ziddy and Janny fired again. Janny seemed less afraid now.

There were shrieks on the stairs, and a thud-thud as of a body rolling down. Ziddy chortled and said: "I got one of them! I got one!"

Hendrickje moved across with the two muskets she had reloaded. She took away the two discharged and mechanically began to load them. She stood by the big four-poster. The shot and powder were on the bed.

Footsteps still scampered remotely downstairs, and suddenly they heard Jacques' voice again. Shrill and defiant. Desperate. A pistol went off and a yell and thump followed. . . . "Massa Jacques!" shrieked Rassiki. There was a moaning. It sounded like Yuani.

"Ready, Janny? They're coming up again!"

Jacques' voice again. A musket went off. Foottreads. Still scampering. As though a hide-and-seek game in the dark was in progress.

Ziddy and Janny fired.

Hendrickje had already placed the other pair of muskets on the table, loaded and ready. She took away the ones discharged. Loaded them.

There was a moaning. Hendrickje and the boys waited.

"We must get the old lady!"

"Massa Jacques!" shrieked Rassiki. "Ow, Massa Jacques!"

Two reports in quick succession. Two shrieks from Rassiki. A desperate scuffling in the sitting room. Yells. Thuds. And the moaning of somebody dying on the stairway. Somebody in pain.

"We got him! We got him!"

"Ow, Massa Jacques!"

A wailing from Rassiki. The wailing ceased suddenly. With a hiccup.

A frenzied drumming sounded on the stairs. And shouts.

"Fire, Janny!"

The muskets exploded. Simultaneously came a bang and flash on the stairs.

Ziddy yelled and staggered off. Janny wailed in fear and ran toward the door that gave into the next room.

"Get back to your places, boys!"

But Ziddy was gasping and coughing in a corner of the room, blood pouring from his mouth. In the next room, Janny dived under the bed.

Hendrickje rushed to the table and grasped one of the muskets. But even as she was steadying it to fire the table heaved as though the floor under it had billowed up.

List of Persons and Events
of
Historical Existence

Corentyne settlement wiped out by Spaniards in 1611.

Aert Adriansen van Groenwegel, trader and sea captain. His arrival in Guiana from Zeeland with three ships in 1616. His secret dealings with the Spaniards; his intrigues with the Indians. His negotiations with the English in Barbados. Dispatch of thirty Indians to that island in 1627. Return of a fugitive Indian from Barbados in 1628. Uprising and quelling of uprising. Adriansen's appointment as Commandeur in 1657. His death in 1664.

The Commandeur of Kyk-over-al at the time of Adriansen's arrival.

Jacob Canijn appointed Commandeur in 1623.

The building of forts to resist Spaniards.

Spanish raids.

Abraham van Peere, trader from Vlissingen. His visit to Guiana in 1627. His colonizing expedition up the Berbice River.

Major John Scott. His raid in 1666. Plundering and devastation of plantations. Pomeroon Fort wiped out. Kyk-over-al captured. Recaptured by *Commandeur Mathys Bergenaar* of Fort Nassau in Berbice.

Gradual resuscitation of plantations.

Hendrik Rol, new Commandeur. His trading activities. *Van Berkel,* Factor of Berbice, invited by Rol to visit Kyk-over-al to discuss trade and settle disputes in respect to the boundary between the Essequibo and Berbice colonies, 1672. Rol's formal and lavish reception of Van Berkel. Death of Rol, 31st March 1676.

Jacob Harz takes temporary command of colony. Dismissed in 1678.

Abraham Beekman appointed Commandeur, 1678. In

same year, establishment of first Court of Policy and Justice.

Friction between *De Jonge* of Pomeroon and Beekman.

Pomeroon Fort raided in 1689 by French, and plundered. De Jonge in flight. Arrives at Kyk-over-al.

Predicant Heynans sent out from Holland in 1688.

Berbice attacked and plundered by *Du Casse* in 1689. *Commandeur de Feer* calls truce.

Beekman dismissed in 1690. *Samuel Beekman* appointed.

Samuel Beekman died 1707. *Pieter van der Heyden Resen* appointed.

Raid by French privateer headed by *Antoine Ferry* in 1708.

Another raid in 1709 by two French privateers. Essequibo again devastated.

Commandeur de Heere succeeds van der Heyden Resen as Commandeur.

De Waterman, Commandeur of Berbice.

Bombardment of Fort Nassau by *Baron de Mouans,* henchman of *Jacques Cassard,* in 1712. Treachery of *François Tirol,* French soldier. Surrender of fort. Harsh terms of surrender.

Secretary Gelskerke of Essequibo. Later Commandeur. His disputes with Commandeur van der Heyden Resen.

The building of the Huis Naby by van der Heyden Resen at Cartabo. Epidemic in Essequibo, 1716. Difficulties of coffee-growing. Revision of constitution in 1718; new Court of Policy and Justice. De Heere advocates coastal cultivation.

Governor Lossner of Berbice.

Laurens Storm van's Gravesande, Secretary, and family, arrive in 1738. Later Gravesande appointed Commandeur. Then Directeur-General of Essequibo-Demerary.

Fort Island displaces Kyk-over-al as seat of Government, 1739. Essequibo declared open to settlers of any nationality, 1741. Demerary River declared open to settlers, 1746.

Simpson and wife, English settlers in Essequibo.

Murder of Simpson by his slaves, Cudjoe and Quacco. Execution of Cudjoe and Quacco. Mrs. Simpson present at execution.

Berbice a flourishing colony.

Van Ryswijck, governor. Died of Sickness, 21st September 1759.

Wolfert Simon van Hoogenheim, Governor, arrived in 1760.

The *Vernsobres,* proprietors of Plantation Magdalenenburg, upper Canje Creek. *André Fourie Niffins den Timmerman,* manager, noted for his cruelty to slaves.

Predicant Ramring and family of Plantation Peereboom.

Mynheer Charbon and son *Jan* of Plantation Oosterbeck.

Mevrouw Schriender of Plantation Hollandia.

The *George* and *Zubli* families. *"Amelia" George.*

Mynheer Abbensetts of Plantation Solitude. Councillor.

Mevrouw Johansen.

Herr C. Mittelholzer, Swiss-German manager of Plantation de Vreede.

Harkenroth, Secretary to Governor. *Wijs,* Orphanmaster; *Hattinga* Land-surveyor.

Lieutenant Theilen, of Fort Nassau.

Riots by soldiers at Fort Nassau in 1751, 1756, 1759.

Outbreak of epidemic called the Sickness in 1759.

Governor's wife dies of Sickness three weeks after arrival, 1760.

Trouble on *Laurens Kunckler's* plantations in 1762. Burgher Militia called out by *Captain Lentzeng.* Rising put down.

Insurrection starts on Plantation Magdalenenburg 21st February 1763. *Cuffy,* leader of rebels. *Akkara,* his Captain. Other leaders: *Atta, Goussari, Accabre, Quacco, Baube.* Rebels reach Berbice River, 27th. Cowardice of settlers. Mynheer Abbensetts stands firm for a time at Plantation Solitude. Hoogenheim compelled to spike guns of fort and retreat to Plantation Dageraad. Shortly after to Fort St. Andries, then back to

Dageraad. Siege of Peereboom. Conditional surrender of beleaguered whites. Treachery of rebels. Massacre. "Amelia" George captured among others. Atrocities. Murder, mutilation.

Jan Broer, a mulatto.

Captain *Kock.*

"Amelia" George forced to become Cuffy's mistress.

Cuffy's correspondence. Jan Charbon captured. Turns Secretary to Cuffy, then sent as messenger to Hoogenheim with letter. Mevrouw Schriender also used as messenger. Rewards offered for rebel leaders.

Battles of Dageraad. Government forces augmented by troops from St. Eustatius. Toll of Sickness. Defeat of rebels at Dageraad. They flee back to Canje.

Jean Renaud, renegade soldier, and other deserters. Capture and massacre of deserters by Cuffy, after drawing of lots. Cuffy and Atta quarrel over a barrel of powder. Fight. Cuffy defeated. Commits suicide with horse pistol. Eventual capture of rebel leaders. Mass executions. Meanwhile, "Amelia" George has escaped with five loyal slaves. Reaches Dageraad on 2nd January 1764.

Colonel de Salve and soldiers.